THREE MAJOR FIGURES IN SCIENCE FICTION TODAY PICK THE STORIES WHICH CHANGED THEIR LIVES!

ERIC FLINT:
Author of *1632* and many other novels.
Co-Founder and Librarian of the Baen Free Library.

DAVID DRAKE:
Author of *Hammer's Slammers* and many other novels.

JAMES PATRICK BAEN:
SF editor of Ace Books.
SF editor of Tor Books.
Publisher of Baen Books.

Poul Anderson: *Turning Point*
Christopher Anvil: *The Gentle Earth*
Isaac Asimov: *The Last Question*
Fredric Brown: *Answer*
L. Sprague de Camp: *A Gun for Dinosaur*
John W. Campbell: *Who Goes There?*
Arthur C. Clarke: *Rescue Party*
Gordon R. Dickson: *St. Dragon and the George*
Chester S. Geier: *Environment*
Robert Ernest Gilbert: *Thy Rocks and Rills*
Tom Godwin: *The Cold Equations*
Lee Gregor: *Heavy Planet*
Wyman Guin: *Trigger Tide*
Robert A. Heinlein: *The Menace from Earth*
C.M. Kornbluth: *The Only Thing We Learn*
Fritz Leiber: *A Pail of Air*
Keith Laumer: *The Last Command*
Murray Leinster: *The Aliens*
P. Schuyler Miller: *Spawn*
C. L. Moore: *Shambleau*
H. Beam Piper: *Omnilingual*
Rick Raphael: *Code Three*
Ross Rocklynne: *Quietus*
James H. Schmitz: *Goblin Night*
Robert Sheckley: *Hunting Problem*
Michael Shaara: *All the Way Back*
Theodore Sturgeon: *Thunder and Roses*
Jack Vance: *Liane the Wayfarer*
A. E. van Vogt: *Black Destroyer*

THERE HASN'T BEEN A SCIENCE FICTION ANTHOLOGY TO COMPARE WITH THIS ONE IN MORE THAN FIFTY YEARS!

BAEN BOOKS
by DAVID DRAKE & ERIC FLINT
The Tyrant

The Belisarius Series
An Oblique Approach
In the Heart of Darkness
Destiny's Shield
Fortune's Stroke
The Tide of Victory
The Dance of Time

**For a complete list of Baen Books by these authors,
please go to www.baen.com**

THE WORLD TURNED
UPSIDE DOWN

edited by

DAVID DRAKE
ERIC FLINT
JIM BAEN

THE WORLD TURNED UPSIDE DOWN

This is a work of fiction. All the characters and events portrayed in this book are fictional, and any resemblance to real people or incidents is purely coincidental.

A Baen Book

Baen Publishing Enterprises
P.O. Box 1403
Riverdale, NY 10471
www.baen.com

ISBN 10: 1-4165-2068-6
ISBN 13: 978-1-4165-2068-9

Cover art by Tom Kidd

First Baen paperback printing, June 2006

Distributed by Simon & Schuster
1230 Avenue of the Americas
New York, NY 10020

Library of Congress Cataloging-in-Publication Data: 2004021812

Printed in the United States of America

10 9 8 7 6 5 4 3 2 1

TABLE OF CONTENTS

DEDICATION:

To Dr. Olga Vasileyeva

From Jim, with love.
From Dave, with affection.
From Eric, with respect.

Preface

This anthology started in the course of a conversation I had with Jim Baen regarding possible future prospects for reissuing old science fiction authors. In the course of advancing this or that idea, Jim interrupted me and said what he'd like to see immediately would be for Dave Drake and myself to select those stories which had the most impact on us as teenagers and got us interested in science fiction in the first place. "Call it *The World Turned Upside Down*," he said.

I liked the idea, and so did Dave when Jim and I raised it with him. The one change Dave proposed, however, was that Jim serve as one of the editors of the volume, not simply as the publisher. That seemed eminently rational, given that by then Jim had already advanced half a dozen stories he wanted included in it because of the effect they'd had on him as a teenager.

So. This does not purport to be an anthology that contains "the best stories of science fiction"—although all of us think this volume contains a superb collection of stories. But that was not the fundamental criterion by which we made our selection. The stories were selected because of the impact they had on us several decades ago, as we were growing up in the '50s and '60s.

Some authors are missing, unfortunately. In some cases—Andre Norton being the major example, here—because the stories the author wrote which had such an effect on us were novels, and there just wasn't room in such an anthology for novel-length works. In other cases, because we were unable to obtain the rights for the stories we wanted from the agencies representing some of the estates.

We got most of what we wanted, though. And . . . here it is. *The World Turned Upside Down.*

—Eric Flint
March 2004

Rescue Party

by Arthur C. Clarke

PREFACE BY ERIC FLINT

I'm certain this wasn't the first science fiction story I ever read, because I still remember those vividly. Three novels, all read when I was twelve years old and living in the small town of Shaver Lake (pop. 500) in the Sierra Nevada mountains in California: Robert Heinlein's *Citizen of the Galaxy*, Tom Godwin's *The Survivors* and Andre Norton's *Star Rangers*.

I must have started reading Arthur C. Clarke soon thereafter, though. The two stories that introduced me to him—as I remember, anyway—were this one and "Jupiter V," and those two stories fixed Clarke permanently as one of the central triad in my own personal pantheon of SF's great writers. (The other two being Robert Heinlein and Andre Norton.)

We chose this one, rather than "Jupiter V," at my request. I wanted this one because, of all the stories ever written in science fiction, this is the one which first demonstrated to me that science fiction could be inspirational as well as fascinating. So I thought at the age of twelve or possibly thirteen. More than four decades have now gone by, and I haven't changed my mind at all.

Who was to blame? For three days Alveron's thoughts had come back to that question, and still he had found no answer. A creature of a less civilized or a less sensitive race would never have

3

let it torture his mind, and would have satisfied himself with the assurance that no one could be responsible for the working of fate. But Alveron and his kind had been lords of the Universe since the dawn of history, since that far distant age when the Time Barrier had been folded round the cosmos by the unknown powers that lay beyond the Beginning. To them had been given all knowledge—and with infinite knowledge went infinite responsibility. If there were mistakes and errors in the administration of the galaxy, the fault lay on the heads of Alveron and his people. And this was no mere mistake: it was one of the greatest tragedies in history.

The crew still knew nothing. Even Rugon, his closest friend and the ship's deputy captain, had been told only part of the truth. But now the doomed worlds lay less than a billion miles ahead. In a few hours, they would be landing on the third planet.

Once again Alveron read the message from Base; then, with a flick of a tentacle that no human eye could have followed, he pressed the "General Attention" button. Throughout the mile-long cylinder that was the Galactic Survey Ship S9000, creatures of many races laid down their work to listen to the words of their captain.

"I know you have all been wondering," began Alveron, "why we were ordered to abandon our survey and to proceed at such an acceleration to this region of space. Some of you may realize what this acceleration means. Our ship is on its last voyage: the generators have already been running for sixty hours at Ultimate Overload. We will be very lucky if we return to Base under our own power.

"We are approaching a sun which is about to become a Nova. Detonation will occur in seven hours, with an uncertainty of one hour, leaving us a maximum of only four hours for exploration. There are ten planets in the system about to be destroyed—and there is a civilization on the third. That fact was discovered only a few days ago. It is our tragic mission to contact that doomed race and if possible to save some of its members. I know that there is little we can do in so short a time with this single ship. No other machine can possibly reach the system before detonation occurs."

There was a long pause during which there could have been no sound or movement in the whole of the mighty ship as it sped silently toward the worlds ahead. Alveron knew what his companions were thinking and he tried to answer their unspoken question.

"You will wonder how such a disaster, the greatest of which we have any record, has been allowed to occur. On one point I can reassure you. The fault does not lie with the Survey.

"As you know, with our present fleet of under twelve thousand ships, it is possible to re-examine each of the eight thousand million solar systems in the Galaxy at intervals of about a million years. Most worlds change very little in so short a time as that.

"Less than four hundred thousand years ago, the survey ship S5060 examined the planets of the system we are approaching. It found intelligence on none of them, though the third planet was teeming with animal life and two other worlds had once been inhabited. The usual report was submitted and the system is due for its next examination in six hundred thousand years.

"It now appears that in the incredibly short period since the last survey, intelligent life has appeared in the system. The first intimation of this occurred when unknown radio signals were detected on the planet Kulath in the system X29.35, Y34.76, Z27.93. Bearings were taken on them; they were coming from the system ahead.

"Kulath is two hundred light-years from here, so those radio waves had been on their way for two centuries. Thus for at least that period of time a civilization has existed on one of these worlds—a civilization that can generate electromagnetic waves and all that that implies.

"An immediate telescopic examination of the system was made and it was then found that the sun was in the unstable pre-nova stage. Detonation might occur at any moment, and indeed might have done so while the light waves were on their way to Kulath.

"There was a slight delay while the supervelocity scanners on Kulath II were focused on to the system. They showed that the explosion had not yet occurred but was only a few hours away. If Kulath had been a fraction of a light-year further from this sun, we should never have known of its civilization until it had ceased to exist.

"The Administrator of Kulath contacted the Sector Base immediately, and I was ordered to proceed to the system at once. Our object is to save what members we can of the doomed race, if indeed there are any left. But we have assumed that a civilization possessing radio could have protected itself against any rise of temperature that may have already occurred.

"This ship and the two tenders will each explore a section of the planet. Commander Torkalee will take Number One, Commander Orostron Number Two. They will have just under four hours in which to explore this world. At the end of that time, they must be back in the ship. It will be leaving then, with or without them. I will give the two commanders detailed instructions in the control room immediately.

"That is all. We enter atmosphere in two hours."

On the world once known as Earth the fires were dying out: there was nothing left to burn. The great forests that had swept across the planet like a tidal wave with the passing of the cities were now no more than glowing charcoal and the smoke of their funeral pyres still stained the sky. But the last hours were still to come, for the surface rocks had not yet begun to flow. The continents were dimly visible through the haze, but their outlines meant nothing to the watchers in the approaching ship. The charts they possessed were out of date by a dozen Ice Ages and more deluges than one.

The S9000 had driven past Jupiter and seen at once that no life could exist in those half-gaseous oceans of compressed hydrocarbons, now erupting furiously under the sun's abnormal heat. Mars and the outer planets they had missed, and Alveron realized that the worlds nearer the sun than Earth would be already melting. It was more than likely, he thought sadly, that the tragedy of this unknown race was already finished. Deep in his heart, he thought it might be better so. The ship could only have carried a few hundred survivors, and the problem of selection had been haunting his mind.

Rugon, Chief of Communications and Deputy Captain, came into the control room. For the last hour he had been striving to detect radiation from Earth, but in vain.

"We're too late," he announced gloomily. "I've monitored the whole spectrum and the ether's dead except for our own stations and some two-hundred-year-old programs from Kulath. Nothing in this system is radiating any more."

He moved toward the giant vision screen with a graceful flowing motion that no mere biped could ever hope to imitate. Alveron said nothing; he had been expecting this news.

One entire wall of the control room was taken up by the screen, a great black rectangle that gave an impression of almost infinite depth. Three of Rugon's slender control tentacles, useless for heavy work but incredibly swift at all manipulation, flickered over the selector dials and the screen lit up with a thousand points of light. The star field flowed swiftly past as Rugon adjusted the controls, bringing the projector to bear upon the sun itself.

No man of Earth would have recognized the monstrous shape that filled the screen. The sun's light was white no longer: great violet-blue clouds covered half its surface and from them long streamers of flame were erupting into space. At one point an enormous prominence had reared itself out of the photosphere, far out even into the flickering veils of the corona. It was as though a tree of fire had taken root in the surface of the sun—a tree that stood half a million miles high and whose branches were rivers of flame sweeping through space at hundreds of miles a second.

"I suppose," said Rugon presently, "that you are quite satisfied about the astronomers' calculations. After all—"

"Oh, we're perfectly safe," said Alveron confidently. "I've spoken to Kulath Observatory and they have been making some additional checks through our own instruments. That uncertainty of an hour includes a private safety margin which they won't tell me in case I feel tempted to stay any longer."

He glanced at the instrument board.

"The pilot should have brought us to the atmosphere now. Switch the screen back to the planet, please. Ah, there they go!"

There was a sudden tremor underfoot and a raucous clanging of alarms, instantly stilled. Across the vision screen two slim projectiles dived toward the looming mass of Earth. For a few miles they traveled together, then they separated, one vanishing abruptly as it entered the shadow of the planet.

Slowly the huge mother ship, with its thousand times greater mass, descended after them into the raging storms that already were tearing down the deserted cities of Man.

It was night in the hemisphere over which Orostron drove his tiny command. Like Torkalee, his mission was to photograph and record, and to report progress to the mother ship. The little scout had no room for specimens or passengers. If contact was made with the inhabitants of this world, the S9000 would come at once. There would be no time for parleying. If there was any trouble the rescue would be by force and the explanations could come later.

The ruined land beneath was bathed with an eerie, flickering light, for a great auroral display was raging over half the world. But the image on the vision screen was independent of external light, and it showed clearly a waste of barren rock that seemed never to have known any form of life. Presumably this desert land must come to an end somewhere. Orostron increased his speed to the highest value he dared risk in so dense an atmosphere.

The machine fled on through the storm, and presently the desert of rock began to climb toward the sky. A great mountain range lay ahead, its peaks lost in the smoke-laden clouds. Orostron directed the scanners toward the horizon, and on the vision screen the line of mountains seemed suddenly very close and menacing. He started to climb rapidly. It was difficult to imagine a more unpromising land in which to find civilization and he wondered if it would be wise to change course. He decided against it. Five minutes later, he had his reward.

Miles below lay a decapitated mountain, the whole of its summit sheared away by some tremendous feat of engineering. Rising out of the rock and straddling the artificial plateau was an intricate structure of metal girders, supporting masses of machinery. Orostron brought his ship to a halt and spiraled down toward the mountain.

The slight Doppler blur had now vanished, and the picture on the screen was clear-cut. The latticework was supporting some scores of great metal mirrors, pointing skyward at an angle of forty-five degrees to the horizontal. They were slightly concave, and each had some complicated mechanism at its focus. There seemed something impressive and purposeful about the great array; every mirror was aimed at precisely the same spot in the sky—or beyond.

Orostron turned to his colleagues.

"It looks like some kind of observatory to me," he said. "Have you ever seen anything like it before?"

Klarten, a multitentacled, tripedal creature from a globular cluster at the edge of the Milky Way, had a different theory.

"That's communication equipment. Those reflectors are for focusing electromagnetic beams. I've seen the same kind of installation on a hundred worlds before. It may even be the station that Kulath picked up—though that's rather unlikely, for the beams would be very narrow from mirrors that size."

"That would explain why Rugon could detect no radiation before we landed," added Hansur II, one of the twin beings from the planet Thargon.

Orostron did not agree at all.

"If that is a radio station, it must be built for interplanetary communication. Look at the way the mirrors are pointed. I don't believe that a race which has only had radio for two centuries can have crossed space. It took my people six thousand years to do it."

"We managed it in three," said Hansur II mildly, speaking a few seconds ahead of his twin. Before the inevitable argument could develop, Klarten began to wave his tentacles with excitement. While the others had been talking, he had started the automatic monitor.

"Here it is! Listen!"

He threw a switch, and the little room was filled with a raucous whining sound, continually changing in pitch but nevertheless retaining certain characteristics that were difficult to define.

The four explorers listened intently for a minute; then Orostron said, "Surely that can't be any form of speech! No creature could produce sounds as quickly as that!"

Hansur I had come to the same conclusion. "That's a television program. Don't you think so, Klarten?"

The other agreed.

"Yes, and each of those mirrors seems to be radiating a different program. I wonder where they're going? If I'm correct, one of the other planets in the system must lie along those beams. We can soon check that."

Orostron called the S9000 and reported the discovery. Both Rugon and Alveron were greatly excited, and made a quick check of the astronomical records.

The result was surprising—and disappointing. None of the other nine planets lay anywhere near the line of transmission. The great mirrors appeared to be pointing blindly into space.

There seemed only one conclusion to be drawn, and Klarten was the first to voice it.

"They had interplanetary communication," he said. "But the station must be deserted now, and the transmitters no longer controlled. They haven't been switched off, and are just pointing where they were left."

"Well, we'll soon find out," said Orostron. "I'm going to land."

He brought the machine slowly down to the level of the great metal mirrors, and past them until it came to rest on the mountain rock. A hundred yards away, a white stone building crouched beneath the maze of steel girders. It was windowless, but there were several doors in the wall facing them.

Orostron watched his companions climb into their protective suits and wished he could follow. But someone had to stay in the machine to keep in touch with the mother ship. Those were Alveron's instructions, and they were very wise. One never knew what would happen on a world that was being explored for the first time, especially under conditions such as these.

Very cautiously, the three explorers stepped out of the airlock and adjusted the antigravity field of their suits. Then, each with the mode of locomotion peculiar to his race, the little party went toward the building, the Hansur twins leading and Klarten following close behind. His gravity control was apparently giving trouble, for he suddenly fell to the ground, rather to the amusement of his colleagues. Orostron saw them pause for a moment at the nearest door—then it opened slowly and they disappeared from sight.

So Orostron waited, with what patience he could, while the storm rose around him and the light of the aurora grew even brighter in the sky. At the agreed times he called the mother ship and received brief acknowledgments from Rugon. He wondered how Torkalee was faring, halfway round the planet, but he could not contact him through the crash and thunder of solar interference.

It did not take Klarten and the Hansurs long to discover that their theories were largely correct. The building was a radio station, and it was utterly deserted. It consisted of one tremendous room with a few small offices leading from it. In the main chamber, row after row of electrical equipment stretched into the distance; lights flickered and winked on hundreds of control panels, and a dull glow came from the elements in a great avenue of vacuum tubes.

But Klarten was not impressed. The first radio sets his race had built were now fossilized in strata a thousand million years old. Man, who had possessed electrical machines for only a few centuries, could not compete with those who had known them for half the lifetime of the Earth.

Nevertheless, the party kept their recorders running as they explored the building. There was still one problem to be solved. The deserted station was broadcasting programs, but where were they coming from? The central switchboard had been quickly located. It was designed to handle scores of programs simultaneously, but the source of those programs was lost in a maze of cables that vanished underground. Back in the S9000, Rugon was trying to analyze the broadcasts and perhaps his researches would reveal their origin. It was impossible to trace cables that might lead across continents.

The party wasted little time at the deserted station. There was nothing they could learn from it, and they were seeking life rather than scientific information. A few minutes later the little ship rose swiftly from the plateau and headed toward the plains that must lie beyond the mountains. Less than three hours were still left to them.

As the array of enigmatic mirrors dropped out of sight, Orostron was struck by a sudden thought. Was it imagination, or had they all moved through a small angle while he had been waiting, as if they were still compensating for the rotation of the Earth? He could not be sure, and he dismissed the matter as unimportant. It would only mean that the directing mechanism was still working, after a fashion.

They discovered the city fifteen minutes later. It was a great, sprawling metropolis, built around a river that had disappeared leaving an ugly scar winding its way among the great buildings and beneath bridges that looked very incongruous now.

Even from the air, the city looked deserted. But only two and a half hours were left—there was no time for further exploration. Orostron made his decision, and landed near the largest structure he could see. It seemed reasonable to suppose that some creatures would have sought shelter in the strongest buildings, where they would be safe until the very end.

The deepest caves—the heart of the planet itself—would give no protection when the final cataclysm came. Even if this race had reached the outer planets, its doom would only be delayed by the few hours it would take for the ravening wavefronts to cross the Solar System.

Orostron could not know that the city had been deserted not for a few days or weeks, but for over a century. For the culture of cities, which had outlasted so many civilizations had been doomed at last when the helicopter brought universal transportation. Within a few generations the great masses of mankind, knowing that they could reach any part of the globe in a matter of hours, had gone back to the fields and forests for which they had always longed. The new civilization had machines and resources of which earlier ages had never dreamed, but it was essentially rural and no longer bound to the steel and concrete warrens that had dominated the centuries before. Such cities as still remained were specialized centers of research, administration or entertainment; the others had been allowed to decay, where it was too much trouble to destroy them. The dozen or so greatest of all cities, and the ancient university towns, had scarcely changed and would have lasted for many generations to come. But the cities that had been founded on steam and iron and surface transportation had passed with the industries that had nourished them.

And so while Orostron waited in the tender, his colleagues

raced through endless empty corridors and deserted halls, taking innumerable photographs but learning nothing of the creatures who had used these buildings. There were libraries, meeting places, council rooms, thousands of offices—all were empty and deep with dust. If they had not seen the radio station on its mountain eyrie, the explorers could well have believed that this world had known no life for centuries.

Through the long minutes of waiting, Orostron tried to imagine where this race could have vanished. Perhaps they had killed themselves knowing that escape was impossible; perhaps they had built great shelters in the bowels of the planet, and even now were cowering in their millions beneath his feet, waiting for the end. He began to fear that he would never know.

It was almost a relief when at last he had to give the order for the return. Soon he would know if Torkalee's party had been more fortunate. And he was anxious to get back to the mother ship, for as the minutes passed the suspense had become more and more acute. There had always been the thought in his mind: What if the astronomers of Kulath have made a mistake? He would begin to feel happy when the walls of the S9000 were around him. He would be happier still when they were out in space and this ominous sun was shrinking far astern.

As soon as his colleagues had entered the airlock, Orostron hurled his tiny machine into the sky and set the controls to home on the S9000. Then he turned to his friends.

"Well, what have you found?" he asked.

Klarten produced a large roll of canvas and spread it out on the floor.

"This is what they were like," he said quietly. "Bipeds, with only two arms. They seem to have managed well, in spite of that handicap. Only two eyes as well, unless there are others in the back. We were lucky to find this; it's about the only thing they left behind."

The ancient oil painting stared stonily back at the three creatures regarding it so intently. By the irony of fate, its complete worthlessness had saved it from oblivion. When the city had been evacuated, no one had bothered to move Alderman John Richards, 1909-1974. For a century and a half he had been gathering dust while far away from the old cities the new civilization had been rising to heights no earlier culture had ever known.

"That was almost all we found," said Klarten. "The city must have been deserted for years. I'm afraid our expedition has been a failure. If there are any living beings on this world, they've hidden themselves too well for us to find them."

His commander was forced to agree.

"It was an almost impossible task," he said. "If we'd had weeks instead of hours we might have succeeded. For all we know, they may even have built shelters under the sea. No one seems to have thought of that."

He glanced quickly at the indicators and corrected the course.

"We'll be there in five minutes. Alveron seems to be moving rather quickly. I wonder if Torkalee has found anything."

The S9000 was hanging a few miles above the seaboard of a blazing continent when Orostron homed upon it. The danger line was thirty minutes away and there was no time to lose. Skillfully, he maneuvered the little ship into its launching tube and the party stepped out of the airlock.

There was a small crowd waiting for them. That was to be expected, but Orostron could see at once that something more than curiosity had brought his friends here. Even before a word was spoken, he knew that something was wrong.

"Torkalee hasn't returned. He's lost his party and we're going to the rescue. Come along to the control room at once."

From the beginning, Torkalee had been luckier than Orostron. He had followed the zone of twilight, keeping away from the intolerable glare of the sun, until he came to the shores of an inland sea. It was a very recent sea, one of the latest of Man's works, for the land it covered had been desert less than a century before. In a few hours it would be desert again, for the water was boiling and clouds of steam were rising to the skies. But they could not veil the loveliness of the great white city that overlooked the tideless sea.

Flying machines were still parked neatly round the square in which Torkalee landed. They were disappointingly primitive, though beautifully finished, and depended on rotating airfoils for support. Nowhere was there any sign of life, but the place gave the impression that its inhabitants were not very far away. Lights were still shining from some of the windows.

Torkalee's three companions lost no time in leaving the machine. Leader of the party, by seniority of rank and race was T'sinadree, who like Alveron himself had been born on one of the ancient planets of the Central Suns. Next came Alarkane, from a race which was one of the youngest in the Universe and took a perverse pride in the fact. Last came one of the strange beings from the system of Palador. It was nameless, like all its kind, for it possessed no identity of its own, being merely a mobile but still dependent cell in the consciousness of its race. Though it and its fellows had long been scattered over the galaxy in the exploration of countless worlds, some unknown link still bound them together as inexorably as the living cells in a human body.

When a creature of Palador spoke, the pronoun it used was always "We." There was not, nor could there ever be, any first person singular in the language of Palador.

The great doors of the splendid building baffled the explorers, though any human child would have known their secret. T'sinadree wasted no time on them but called Torkalee on his personal transmitter. Then the three hurried aside while their commander maneuvered his machine into the best position. There was a brief burst of intolerable flame; the massive steelwork flickered once at the edge of the visible spectrum and was gone. The stones were still glowing when the eager party hurried into the building, the beams of their light projectors fanning before them.

The torches were not needed. Before them lay a great hall, glowing with light from lines of tubes along the ceiling. On either side, the hall opened out into long corridors, while straight ahead a massive stairway swept majestically toward the upper floors.

For a moment T'sinadree hesitated. Then, since one way was as good as another, he led his companions down the first corridor.

The feeling that life was near had now become very strong. At any moment, it seemed, they might be confronted by the creatures of this world. If they showed hostility—and they could scarcely be blamed if they did—the paralyzers would be used at once.

The tension was very great as the party entered the first room, and only relaxed when they saw that it held nothing but machines—row after row of them, now stilled and silent. Lining the enormous room were thousands of metal filing cabinets, forming a continuous wall as far as the eye could reach. And that was all; there was no furniture, nothing but the cabinets and the mysterious machines.

Alarkane, always the quickest of the three, was already examining the cabinets. Each held many thousand sheets of tough, thin material, perforated with innumerable holes and slots. The Paladorian appropriated one of the cards and Alarkane recorded the scene together with some close-ups of the machines. Then they left. The great room, which had been one of the marvels of the world, meant nothing to them. No living eye would ever again see that wonderful battery of almost human Hollerith analyzers and the five thousand million punched cards holding all that could be recorded on each man, woman and child on the planet.

It was clear that this building had been used very recently. With growing excitement, the explorers hurried on to the next room. This they found to be an enormous library, for millions of books lay all around them on miles and miles of shelving. Here, though the explorers could not know it, were the records of all the laws that Man had ever passed, and all the speeches that had ever been made in his council chambers.

T'sinadree was deciding his plan of action, when Alarkane drew his attention to one of the racks a hundred yards away. It was half empty, unlike all the others. Around it books lay in a tumbled heap on the floor, as if knocked down by someone in frantic haste. The signs were unmistakable. Not long ago, other creatures had been this way. Faint wheel marks were clearly visible on the floor to the acute sense of Alarkane, though the others could see nothing. Alarkane could even detect footprints, but knowing nothing of the creatures that had formed them he could not say which way they led.

The sense of nearness was stronger than ever now, but it was nearness in time, not in space. Alarkane voiced the thoughts of the party.

"Those books must have been valuable, and someone has come to rescue them—rather as an afterthought, I should say. That means there must be a place of refuge, possibly not very far away. Perhaps we may be able to find some other clues that will lead us to it."

T'sinadree agreed; the Paladorian wasn't enthusiastic.

"That may be so," it said, "but the refuge may be anywhere on the planet, and we have just two hours left. Let us waste no more time if we hope to rescue these people."

The party hurried forward once more, pausing only to collect a few books that might be useful to the scientists at Base—though it was doubtful if they could ever be translated. They soon found that the great building was composed largely of small rooms, all showing signs of recent occupation. Most of them were in a neat and tidy condition, but one or two were very much the reverse. The explorers were particularly puzzled by one room—clearly an office of some kind—that appeared to have been completely wrecked. The floor was littered with papers, the furniture had been smashed, and smoke was pouring through the broken windows from the fires outside.

T'sinadree was rather alarmed.

"Surely no dangerous animal could have got into a place like this!" he exclaimed, fingering his paralyzer nervously.

Alarkane did not answer. He began to make that annoying sound which his race called "laughter." It was several minutes before he would explain what had amused him.

"I don't think any animal has done it," he said. "In fact, the explanation is very simple. Suppose *you* had been working all your life in this room, dealing with endless papers, year after year. And suddenly, you are told that you will never see it again, that your work is finished, and that you can leave it forever. More than that—no one will come after you. Everything is finished. How would you make your exit, T'sinadree?"

The other thought for a moment.

"Well, I suppose I'd just tidy things up and leave. That's what seems to have happened in all the other rooms."

Alarkane laughed again.

"I'm quite sure you would. But some individuals have a different psychology. I think I should have liked the creature that used this room."

He did not explain himself further, and his two colleagues puzzled over his words for quite a while before they gave it up.

It came as something of a shock when Torkalee gave the order to return. They had gathered a great deal of information, but had found no clue that might lead them to the missing inhabitants of this world. That problem was as baffling as ever, and now it seemed that it would never be solved. There were only forty minutes left before the S9000 would be departing.

They were halfway back to the tender when they saw the semicircular passage leading down into the depths of the building. Its architectural style was quite different from that used elsewhere, and the gently sloping floor was an irresistible attraction to creatures whose many legs had grown weary of the marble staircases which only bipeds could have built in such profusion. T'sinadree had been the worst sufferer, for he normally employed twelve legs and could use twenty when he was in a hurry, though no one had ever seen him perform this feat.

The party stopped dead and looked down the passageway with a single thought. A tunnel, leading down into the depths of Earth! At its end, they might yet find the people of this world and rescue some of them from their fate. For there was still time to call the mother ship if the need arose.

T'sinadree signaled to his commander and Torkalee brought the little machine immediately overhead. There might not be time for the party to retrace its footsteps through the maze of passages, so meticulously recorded in the Paladorian mind that there was no possibility of going astray. If speed was necessary, Torkalee could blast his way through the dozen floors above their head. In any case, it should not take long to find what lay at the end of the passage.

It took only thirty seconds. The tunnel ended quite abruptly in a very curious cylindrical room with magnificently padded seats along the walls. There was no way out save that by which they had come and it was several seconds before the purpose of the chamber dawned on Alarkane's mind. It was a pity, he thought, that they would never have time to use this. The thought was suddenly interrupted by a cry from T'sinadree. Alarkane wheeled around, and saw that the entrance had closed silently behind them.

Even in that first moment of panic, Alarkane found himself thinking with some admiration: Whoever they were, they knew how to build automatic machinery!

The Paladorian was the first to speak. It waved one of its tentacles toward the seats.

"We think it would be best to be seated," it said. The multiplex mind of Palador had already analyzed the situation and knew what was coming.

They did not have long to wait before a low-pitched hum came from a grill overhead, and for the very last time in history a human, even if lifeless, voice was heard on Earth. The words were meaningless, though the trapped explorers could guess their message clearly enough.

"Choose your stations, please, and be seated."

Simultaneously, a wall panel at one end of the compartment glowed with light. On it was a simple map, consisting of a series of a dozen circles connected by a line. Each of the circles had writing alongside it, and beside the writing were two buttons of different colors.

Alarkane looked questioningly at his leader.

"Don't touch them," said T'sinadree. "If we leave the controls alone, the doors may open again."

He was wrong. The engineers who had designed the automatic subway had assumed that anyone who entered it would naturally wish to go somewhere. If they selected no intermediate station, their destination could only be the end of the line.

There was another pause while the relays and thyratrons waited for their orders. In those thirty seconds, if they had known what to do, the party could have opened the doors and left the subway. But they did not know, and the machines geared to a human psychology acted for them.

The surge of acceleration was not very great; the lavish upholstery was a luxury, not a necessity. Only an almost imperceptible vibration told of the speed at which they were traveling through the bowels of the earth, on a journey the duration of which they could not even guess. And in thirty minutes, the S9000 would be leaving the Solar System.

There was a long silence in the speeding machine. T'sinadree and Alarkane were thinking rapidly. So was the Paladorian, though in a different fashion. The conception of personal death was meaningless to it, for the destruction of a single unit meant no more to the group mind than the loss of a nail-paring to a man. But it could, though with great difficulty, appreciate the plight of individual intelligences such as Alarkane and T'sinadree, and it was anxious to help them if it could.

Alarkane had managed to contact Torkalee with his personal transmitter, though the signal was very weak and seemed to be fading quickly. Rapidly he explained the situation, and almost at once the signals became clearer. Torkalee was following the path of the machine, flying above the ground under which they were speeding to their unknown destination. That was the first indication they had of the fact that they were traveling at nearly a thousand miles an hour, and very soon after that Torkalee was able to give the still more disturbing news that they were rapidly approaching the sea. While they were beneath the land, there was a hope, though a slender one, that they might stop the machine and escape. But under the ocean—not all the brains and the machinery in the great mother ship could save them. No one could have devised a more perfect trap.

T'sinadree had been examining the wall map with great attention. Its meaning was obvious, and along the line connecting the circles a tiny spot of light was crawling. It was already halfway to the first of the stations marked.

"I'm going to press one of those buttons," said T'sinadree at last. "It won't do any harm, and we may learn something."

"I agree. Which will you try first?"

"There are only two kinds, and it won't matter if we try the wrong one first. I suppose one is to start the machine and the other is to stop it."

Alarkane was not very hopeful.

"It started without any button pressing," he said. "I think it's completely automatic and we can't control it from here at all."

T'sinadree could not agree.

"These buttons are clearly associated with the stations, and there's no point in having them unless you can use them to stop yourself. The only question is, which is the right one?"

His analysis was perfectly correct. The machine could be stopped at any intermediate station. They had only been on their way ten minutes, and if they could leave now, no harm would have been done. It was just bad luck that T'sinadree's first choice was the wrong button.

The little light on the map crawled slowly through the illuminated circle without checking its speed. And at the same time Torkalee called from the ship overhead.

"You have just passed underneath a city and are heading out to sea. There cannot be another stop for nearly a thousand miles."

Alveron had given up all hope of finding life on this world. The S9000 had roamed over half the planet, never staying long in one place, descending ever and again in an effort to attract attention. There had been no response; Earth seemed utterly dead. If any of its inhabitants were still alive, thought Alveron, they must have hidden themselves in its depths where no help could reach them, though their doom would be nonetheless certain.

Rugon brought news of the disaster. The great ship ceased its fruitless searching and fled back through the storm to the ocean above which Torkalee's little tender was still following the track of the buried machine.

The scene was truly terrifying. Not since the days when Earth was born had there been such seas as this. Mountains of water were racing before the storm which had now reached velocities of many hundred miles an hour. Even at this distance from the mainland the air was full of flying debris—trees, fragments of houses, sheets of metal, anything that had not been anchored to the ground. No airborne machine could have lived for a moment in such a gale. And ever and again even the roar of the wind was drowned as the vast water-mountains met head-on with a crash that seemed to shake the sky.

Fortunately, there had been no serious earthquakes yet. Far beneath the bed of the ocean, the wonderful piece of engineering which had been the World President's private vacuum-subway was still working perfectly, unaffected by the tumult and destruction above. It would continue to work until the last minute of the Earth's existence, which, if the astronomers were right, was not much more than fifteen minutes away—though precisely how much more Alveron would have given a great deal to know. It would be nearly an hour before the trapped party could reach land and even the slightest hope of rescue.

Alveron's instructions had been precise, though even without them he would never have dreamed of taking any risks with the great machine that had been entrusted to his care. Had he been human, the decision to abandon the trapped members of his crew would have been desperately hard to make. But he came of a race far more sensitive than Man, a race that so loved the things of the spirit that long ago, and with infinite reluctance, it had taken over control of the Universe since only thus could it be sure that justice was being done. Alveron would need all his superhuman gifts to carry him through the next few hours.

Meanwhile, a mile below the bed of the ocean Alarkane and T'sinadree were very busy indeed with their private communicators. Fifteen minutes is not a long time in which to wind up the affairs of a lifetime. It is indeed, scarcely long enough to dictate more than a few of those farewell messages which at such moments are so much more important than all other matters.

All the while the Paladorian had remained silent and motionless, saying not a word. The other two, resigned to their fate and engrossed in their personal affairs, had given it no thought. They were startled when suddenly it began to address them in its peculiarly passionless voice.

"We perceive that you are making certain arrangements concerning your anticipated destruction. That will probably be unnecessary. Captain Alveron hopes to rescue us if we can stop this machine when we reach land again."

Both T'sinadree and Alarkane were too surprised to say anything for a moment. Then the latter gasped, "How do you know?"

It was a foolish question, for he remembered at once that there were several Paladorians—if one could use the phrase—in the S9000, and consequently their companion knew everything that was happening in the mother ship. So he did not wait for an answer but continued, "Alveron can't do that! He daren't take such a risk!"

"There will be no risk," said the Paladorian. "We have told him what to do. It is really very simple."

Alarkane and T'sinadree looked at their companion with something approaching awe, realizing now what must have happened. In moments of crisis, the single units comprising the Paladorian mind could link together in an organization no less close than that of any physical brain. At such moments they formed an intellect more powerful than any other in the Universe. All ordinary problems could be solved by a few hundred or thousand units. Very rarely, millions would be needed, and on two historic occasions the billions of cells of the entire Paladorian consciousness had been welded together to deal with emergencies that threatened the race. The mind of Palador was one of the greatest mental resources of the Universe; its full force was seldom required, but the knowledge that it was available was supremely comforting to other races. Alarkane wondered how many cells had coordinated to deal with this particular emergency. He also wondered how so trivial an incident had ever come to its attention.

To that question he was never to know the answer, though he might have guessed it had he known that the chillingly remote Paladorian mind possessed an almost human streak of vanity. Long ago, Alarkane had written a book trying to prove that eventually all intelligent races would sacrifice individual consciousness and that one day only group-minds would remain in the Universe. Palador, he had said, was the first of those ultimate intellects, and the vast, dispersed mind had not been displeased.

They had no time to ask any further questions before Alveron himself began to speak through their communicators.

"Alveron calling! We're staying on this planet until the detonation waves reach it, so we may be able to rescue you. You're heading toward a city on the coast which you'll reach in forty minutes at your present speed. If you cannot stop yourselves then, we're going to blast the tunnel behind and ahead of you to cut off your power. Then we'll sink a shaft to get you out—the chief engineer says he can do it in five minutes with the main projectors. So you should be safe within an hour, unless the sun blows up before."

"And if that happens, you'll be destroyed as well! You mustn't take such a risk!"

"Don't let that worry you; we're perfectly safe. When the sun detonates, the explosion wave will take several minutes to rise to its maximum. But apart from that, we're on the night side of the planet, behind an eight-thousand-mile screen of rock. When the first warning of the explosion comes, we will accelerate out of the Solar System, keeping in the shadow of the planet. Under our maximum drive, we will reach the velocity of light before leaving the cone of shadow, and the sun cannot harm us then."

T'sinadree was still afraid to hope. Another objection came at once into his mind.

"Yes, but how will you get any warning, here on the night side of the planet?"

"Very easily," replied Alveron. "This world has a moon which is now visible from this hemisphere. We have telescopes trained on it. If it shows any sudden increase in brilliance, our main drive goes on automatically and we'll be thrown out of the system."

The logic was flawless. Alveron, cautious as ever, was taking no chances. It would be many minutes before the eight-thousand-mile shield of rock and metal could be destroyed by the fires of the exploding sun. In that time, the S9000 could have reached the safety of the velocity of light.

Alarkane pressed the second button when they were still several miles from the coast. He did not expect anything to happen then, assuming that the machine could not stop between stations. It seemed too good to be true when, a few minutes later, the machine's slight vibration died away and they came to a halt.

The doors slid silently apart. Even before they were fully open, the three had left the compartment. They were taking no more chances. Before them a long tunnel stretched into the distance, rising slowly out of sight. They were starting along it when suddenly Alveron's voice called from the communicators.

"Stay where you are! We're going to blast!"

The ground shuddered once, and far ahead there came the rumble of falling rock. Again the earth shook—and a hundred yards ahead the passageway vanished abruptly. A tremendous vertical shaft had been cut clean through it.

The party hurried forward again until they came to the end of the corridor and stood waiting on its lip. The shaft in which it ended was a full thousand feet across and descended into the earth as far as the torches could throw their beams. Overhead, the storm clouds fled beneath a moon that no man would have recognized, so luridly brilliant was its disk. And, most glorious of all sights, the S9000 floated high above, the great projectors that had drilled this enormous pit still glowing cherry red.

A dark shape detached itself from the mother ship and dropped swiftly toward the ground. Torkalee was returning to collect his friends. A little later, Alveron greeted them in the control room. He waved to the great vision screen and said quietly, "See, we were barely in time."

The continent below them was slowly settling beneath the mile-high waves that were attacking its coasts. The last that anyone was ever to see of Earth was a great plain, bathed with the silver light of the abnormally brilliant moon. Across its face the waters were pouring in a glittering flood toward a distant range of mountains. The sea had won its final victory, but its triumph would be short-lived for soon sea and land would be no more. Even as the silent party in the control room watched the destruction below, the infinitely greater catastrophe to which this was only the prelude came swiftly upon them.

It was as though dawn had broken suddenly over this moonlit landscape. But it was not dawn: it was only the moon, shining with the brilliance of a second sun. For perhaps thirty seconds that awesome, unnatural light burnt fiercely on the doomed land beneath. Then there came a sudden flashing of indicator lights across the control board. The main drive was on. For a second Alveron glanced at the indicators and checked their information. When he looked again at the screen, Earth was gone.

The magnificent, desperately overstrained generators quietly died when the S9000 was passing the orbit of Persephone. It did not matter, the sun could never harm them now, and although the ship was speeding helplessly out into the lonely night of interstellar space, it would only be a matter of days before rescue came.

There was irony in that. A day ago, they had been the rescuers, going to the aid of a race that now no longer existed. Not for the first time Alveron wondered about the world that had just per-ished. He tried, in vain, to picture it as it had been in its glory, the streets of its cities thronged with life. Primitive though its people had been, they might have offered much to the Universe. If only they could have made contact! Regret was useless; long before their coming, the people of this world must have buried themselves in its iron heart. And now they and their civilization would remain a mystery for the rest of time.

Alveron was glad when his thoughts were interrupted by Rugon's entrance. The chief of communications had been very busy ever since the take-off, trying to analyze the programs radiated by the transmitter Orostron had discovered. The problem was not a dif-ficult one, but it demanded the construction of special equipment, and that had taken time.

"Well, what have you found?" asked Alveron.

"Quite a lot," replied his friend. "There's something mysterious here, and I don't understand it.

"It didn't take long to find how the vision transmissions were built up, and we've been able to convert them to suit our own equipment. It seems that there were cameras all over the planet, surveying points of interest. Some of them were apparently in cities, on the tops of very high buildings. The cameras were rotating continuously to give panoramic views. In the programs we've recorded there are about twenty different scenes.

"In addition, there are a number of transmissions of a different kind, neither sound nor vision. They seem to be purely scientific—possibly instrument readings or something of that sort. All these programs were going out simultaneously on different frequency bands.

"Now there must be a reason for all this. Orostron still thinks that the station simply wasn't switched off when it was deserted. But these aren't the sort of programs such a station would normally radiate at all. It was certainly used for interplanetary relaying— Klarten was quite right there. So these people must have crossed space, since none of the other planets had any life at the time of the last survey. Don't you agree?"

Alveron was following intently.

"Yes, that seems reasonable enough. But it's also certain that the beam was pointing to none of the other planets. I checked that myself."

"I know," said Rugon. "What I want to discover is why a giant interplanetary relay station is busily transmitting pictures of a world about to be destroyed—pictures that would be of immense interest to scientists and astronomers. Someone had gone to a lot of trouble to arrange all those panoramic cameras. I am convinced that those beams were going somewhere."

Alveron started up.

"Do you imagine that there might be an outer planet that hasn't been reported?" he asked. "If so, your theory's certainly wrong. The beam wasn't even pointing in the plane of the Solar System. And even if it were—just look at this."

He switched on the vision screen and adjusted the controls. Against the velvet curtain of space was hanging a blue-white sphere, apparently composed of many concentric shells of incandescent gas. Even though its immense distance made all movement invisible, it was clearly expanding at an enormous rate. At its center was a blinding point of light—the white dwarf star that the sun had now become.

"You probably don't realize just how big that sphere is," said Alveron. "Look at this."

He increased the magnification until only the center portion of the nova was visible. Close to its heart were two minute condensations, one on either side of the nucleus.

"Those are the two giant planets of the system. They have still managed to retain their existence—after a fashion. And they were several hundred million miles from the sun. The nova is still expanding—but it's already twice the size of the Solar System."

Rugon was silent for a moment.

"Perhaps you're right," he said, rather grudgingly. "You've disposed of my first theory. But you still haven't satisfied me."

He made several swift circuits of the room before speaking again. Alveron waited patiently. He knew the almost intuitive powers of his friend, who could often solve a problem when mere logic seemed insufficient.

Then, rather slowly, Rugon began to speak again.

"What do you think of this?" he said. "Suppose we've completely underestimated this people? Orostron did it once—he thought they could never have crossed space, since they'd only known radio for two centuries. Hansur II told me that. Well, Orostron was quite wrong. Perhaps we're all wrong. I've had a look at the material that Klarten brought back from the transmitter. He wasn't impressed by what he found, but it's a marvelous achievement for so short a time. There were devices in that station that belonged to civilizations thousands of years older. Alveron, can we follow that beam to see where it leads?"

Alveron said nothing for a full minute. He had been more than half expecting the question, but it was not an easy one to answer. The main generators had gone completely. There was no point in trying to repair them. But there was still power available, and while there was power, anything could be done in time. It would mean a lot of improvisation, and some difficult maneuvers, for the ship still had its enormous initial velocity. Yes, it could be done, and the activity would keep the crew from becoming further depressed, now that the reaction caused by the mission's failure had started to set in. The news that the nearest heavy repair ship could not reach them for three weeks had also caused a slump in morale.

The engineers, as usual, made a tremendous fuss. Again as usual, they did the job in half the time they had dismissed as being absolutely impossible. Very slowly, over many hours, the great ship began to discard the speed its main drive had given it in as many minutes. In a tremendous curve, millions of miles in radius, the S9000 changed its course and the star fields shifted round it.

The maneuver took three days, but at the end of that time the ship was limping along a course parallel to the beam that had once come from Earth. They were heading out into emptiness, the blazing sphere that had been the sun dwindling slowly behind them. By the standards of interstellar flight, they were almost stationary.

For hours Rugon strained over his instruments, driving his detector beams far ahead into space. There were certainly no planets within many light-years; there was no doubt of that. From time to time Alveron came to see him and always he had to give the same reply: "Nothing to report." About a fifth of the time Rugon's intuition let him down badly; he began to wonder if this was such an occasion.

Not until a week later did the needles of the mass-detectors quiver feebly at the ends of their scales. But Rugon said nothing, not even to his captain. He waited until he was sure, and he went on waiting until even the short-range scanners began to react, and to build up the first faint pictures on the vision screen. Still he waited patiently until he could interpret the images. Then, when he knew that his wildest fancy was even less than the truth, he called his colleagues into the control room.

The picture on the vision screen was the familiar one of endless star fields, sun beyond sun to the very limits of the Universe. Near the center of the screen a distant nebula made a patch of haze that was difficult for the eye to grasp.

Rugon increased the magnification. The stars flowed out of the field; the little nebula expanded until it filled the screen and then—it was a nebula no longer. A simultaneous gasp of amazement came from all the company at the sight that lay before them.

Lying across league after league of space, ranged in a vast three-dimensional array of rows and columns with the precision of a marching army, were thousands of tiny pencils of light. They were moving swiftly; the whole immense lattice holding its shape as a single unit. Even as Alveron and his comrades watched, the formation began to drift off the screen and Rugon had to recenter the controls.

After a long pause, Rugon started to speak.

"This is the race," he said softly, "that has known radio for only two centuries—the race that we believed had crept to die in the heart of its planet. I have examined those images under the highest possible magnification.

"That is the greatest fleet of which there has ever been a record. Each of those points of light represents a ship larger than our own. Of course, they are very primitive—what you see on the screen are the jets of their rockets. Yes, they dared to use rockets to bridge interstellar space! You realize what that means. It would take them centuries to reach the nearest star. The whole race must have embarked on this journey in the hope that its descendants would complete it, generations later.

"To measure the extent of their accomplishment, think of the ages it took us to conquer space, and the longer ages still before we attempted to reach the stars. Even if we were threatened with annihilation, could we have done so much in so short a time? Remember, this is the youngest civilization in the Universe. Four hundred thousand years ago it did not even exist. What will it be a million years from now?"

An hour later, Orostron left the crippled mother ship to make contact with the great fleet ahead. As the little torpedo disappeared among the stars, Alveron turned to his friend and made a remark that Rugon was often to remember in the years ahead.

"I wonder what they'll be like?" he mused. "Will they be nothing but wonderful engineers, with no art or philosophy? They're going to have such a surprise when Orostron reaches them—I expect it will be rather a blow to their pride. It's funny how all isolated races think they're the only people in the Universe. But they should be grateful to us; we're going to save them a good many hundred years of travel."

Alveron glanced at the Milky Way, lying like a veil of silver mist across the vision screen. He waved toward it with a sweep of a tentacle that embraced the whole circle of the galaxy, from the Central Planets to the lonely suns of the Rim.

"You know," he said to Rugon, "I feel rather afraid of these people. Suppose they don't like our little Federation?" He waved once more toward the star-clouds that lay massed across the screen, glowing with the light of their countless suns.

"Something tells me they'll be very determined people," he added. "We had better be polite to them. After all, we only outnumber them about a thousand million to one."

Rugon laughed at his captain's little joke.

Twenty years afterward, the remark didn't seem funny.

The Menace from Earth

by Robert Heinlein

My name is Holly Jones and I'm fifteen. I'm very intelligent but it doesn't show, because I look like an underdone angel. Insipid.

I was born right here in Luna City, which seems to surprise Earthside types. Actually, I'm third generation; my grandparents pioneered in Site One, where the Memorial is. I live with my parents in Artemis Apartments, the new co-op in Pressure Five, eight hundred feet down near City Hall. But I'm not there much; I'm too busy.

Mornings I attend Tech High and afternoons I study or go flying with Jeff Hardesty—he's my partner—or whenever a tourist ship is in I guide groundhogs. This day the *Gripsholm* grounded at noon so I went straight from school to American Express.

The first gaggle of tourists was trickling in from Quarantine but I didn't push forward as Mr. Dorcas, the manager, knows I'm the best. Guiding is just temporary (I'm really a spaceship designer), but if you're doing a job you ought to do it well.

Mr. Dorcas spotted me. "Holly! Here, please. Miss Brentwood, Holly Jones will be your guide."

"'Holly,'" she repeated. "What a quaint name. Are you really a guide, dear?"

I'm tolerant of groundhogs—some of my best friends are from Earth. As Daddy says, being born on Luna is luck, not judgment, and most people Earthside are stuck there. After all, Jesus and Guatama Buddha and Dr. Einstein were all groundhogs.

But they can be irritating. If high school kids weren't guides, whom could they hire? "My license says so," I said briskly and looked her over the way she was looking me over.

Her face was sort of familiar and I thought perhaps I had seen her picture in those society things you see in Earthside magazines—one of the rich playgirls we get too many of. She was almost loathsomely lovely . . . nylon skin, soft, wavy, silver-blond hair, basic specs about 35-24-34 and enough this and that to make me feel like a matchstick drawing, a low, intimate voice and everything necessary to make plainer females think about pacts with the Devil. But I did not feel apprehensive; she was a groundhog and groundhogs don't count.

"All city guides are girls," Mr. Dorcas explained. "Holly is very competent."

"Oh, I'm sure," she answered quickly and went into tourist routine number one: surprise that a guide was needed just to find her hotel, amazement at no taxicabs, same for no porters, and raised eyebrows at the prospect of two girls walking alone through "an underground city."

Mr. Dorcas was patient, ending with: "Miss Brentwood, Luna City is the only metropolis in the Solar System where a woman is really safe—no dark alleys, no deserted neighborhoods, no criminal element."

I didn't listen; I just held out my tariff card for Mr. Dorcas to stamp and picked up her bags. Guides shouldn't carry bags and most tourists are delighted to experience the fact that their thirty-pound allowance weighs only five pounds. But I wanted to get her moving.

We were in the tunnel outside and me with a foot on the slide-belt when she stopped. "I forgot! I want a city map."

"None available."

"Really?"

"There's only one. That's why you need a guide."

"But why don't they supply them? Or would that throw you guides out of work?"

See? "You think guiding is makework? Miss Brentwood, labor is so scarce they'd hire monkeys if they could."

"Then why not print maps?"

"Because Luna City isn't flat like—" I almost said, "—groundhog cities," but I caught myself.

"—like Earthside cities," I went on. "All you saw from space was the meteor shield. Underneath it spreads out and goes down for miles in a dozen pressure zones."

"Yes, I know, but why not a map for each level?"

Groundhogs always say, "Yes, I know, but——"

"I can show you the one city map. It's a stereo tank twenty feet high and even so all you see clearly are big things like the Hall of the Mountain King and hydroponics farms and the Bats' Cave."

"'The Bat's Cave,'" she repeated. "That's where they fly, isn't it?"

"Yes, that's where we fly."

"Oh, I want to see it!"

"OK. It first . . . or the city map?"

She decided to go to her hotel first. The regular route to the Zurich is to slide up and west through Gray's Tunnel past the Martian Embassy, get off at the Mormon Temple, and take a pressure lock down to Diana Boulevard. But I know all the shortcuts; we got off at Macy-Gimbel Upper to go down their personnel hoist. I thought she would enjoy it.

But when I told her to grab a hand grip as it dropped past her, she peered down the shaft and edged back. "You're joking."

I was about to take her back the regular way when a neighbor of ours came down the hoist. I said, "Hello, Mrs. Greenberg," and she called back, "Hi, Holly. How are your folks?"

Susie Greenberg is more than plump. She was hanging by one hand with young David tucked in her other arm and holding the *Daily Lunatic*, reading as she dropped. Miss Brentwood stared, bit her lip, and said, "How do I do it?"

I said, "Oh, use both hands; I'll take the bags." I tied the handles together with my hanky and went first.

She was shaking when we got to the bottom. "Goodness, Holly, how do you stand it? Don't you get homesick?"

Tourist question number six . . . I said, "I've been to Earth," and let it drop. Two years ago Mother made me visit my aunt in Omaha and I was *miserable*—hot and cold and dirty and beset by creepy-crawlies. I weighed a ton and I ached and my aunt was always chivvying me to go outdoors and exercise when all I wanted was to crawl into a tub and be quietly wretched. And I had hay fever. Probably you've never heard of hay fever—you don't die but you wish you could.

I was supposed to go to a girls' boarding school but I phoned Daddy and told him I was desperate and he let me come home. What groundhogs can't understand is that *they* live in savagery. But groundhogs are groundhogs and loonies are loonies and never the twain shall meet.

Like all the best hotels the Zurich is in Pressure One on the west side so that it can have a view of Earth. I helped Miss Brentwood register with the roboclerk and found her room; it had its own port. She went straight to it, began staring at Earth and going *ooh!* and *ahh!*

I glanced past her and saw that it was a few minutes past thirteen; sunset sliced straight down the tip of India—early enough to snag another client. "Will that be all, Miss Brentwood?"

Instead of answering she said in an awed voice, "Holly, isn't that the most beautiful sight you ever saw?"

"It's nice," I agreed. The view on that side is monotonous except for Earth hanging in the sky—but Earth is what tourists always look at even though they've just left it. Still, Earth is pretty. The changing weather is interesting if you don't have to be in it. Did you ever endure a summer in Omaha?

"It's gorgeous," she whispered.

"Sure," I agreed. "Do you want to go somewhere? Or will you sign my card?"

"What? Excuse me, I was daydreaming. No, not right now—yes, I do! Holly, I want to go out *there!* I must! Is there time? How much longer will it be light?"

"Huh? It's two days to sunset."

She looked startled. "How quaint. Holly, can you get us space suits? I've got to go outside."

I didn't wince—I'm used to tourist talk. I suppose a pressure suit looked like a space suit to them. I simply said, "We girls aren't licensed outside. But I can phone a friend."

Jeff Hardesty is my partner in spaceship designing, so I throw business his way. Jeff is eighteen and already in Goddard Institute, but I'm pushing hard to catch up so that we can set up offices for our firm: "Jones & Hardesty, Spaceship Engineers." I'm very bright in mathematics, which is everything in space engineering, so I'll get my degree pretty fast. Meanwhile we design ships anyhow.

I didn't tell Miss Brentwood this, as tourists think a girl my age can't possibly be a spaceship designer.

Jeff has arranged his classes to let him guide on Tuesdays and Thursdays; he waits at West City Lock and studies between clients. I reached him on the lockmaster's phone. Jeff grinned and said, "Hi, Scale Model."

"Hi, Penalty Weight. Free to take a client?"

"Well, I was supposed to guide a family party, but they're late."

"Cancel them. Miss Brentwood . . . step into pickup, please. This is Mr. Hardesty."

Jeff's eyes widened and I felt uneasy. But it did not occur to me that Jeff could be attracted by a *groundhog* . . . even though it is conceded that men are robot slaves of their body chemistry in such matters. I knew she was exceptionally decorative, but it was unthinkable that Jeff could be captivated by any groundhog, no matter how well designed. They don't speak our language!

I am not romantic about Jeff; we are simply partners. But anything that affects Jones & Hardesty affects me.

When we joined him at West Lock he almost stepped on his tongue in a disgusting display of adolescent rut. I was ashamed of him and, for the first time, apprehensive. Why are males so childish?

Miss Brentwood didn't seem to mind his behavior. Jeff is a big hulk; suited up for outside he looks like a Frost giant from *Das Rheingold*; she smiled up at him and thanked him for changing his schedule. He looked even sillier and told her it was a pleasure.

I keep my pressure suit at West Lock so that when I switch a client to Jeff he can invite me to come along for the walk. This time he hardly spoke to me after that platinum menace was in sight. But I helped her pick out a suit and took her into the dressing room and fitted it. Those rental suits take careful adjusting or they will pinch you in tender places once out in vacuum . . . besides those things about them that one girl ought to explain to another.

When I came out with her, not wearing my own, Jeff didn't even ask why I hadn't suited up—he took her arm and started toward the lock. I had to butt in to get her to sign my tariff card.

The days that followed were the longest in my life. I saw Jeff only once . . . on the slidebelt in Diana boulevard, going the other way. She was with him.

Though I saw him but once, I knew what was going on. He was cutting classes and three nights running he took her to the Earthview Room of the Duncan Hines. None of my business!—I hope she had more luck teaching him to dance than I had. Jeff is a free citizen and if he wanted to make an utter fool of himself neglecting school and losing sleep over an upholstered groundhog that was his business.

But he should not have neglected the firm's business!

Jones & Hardesty had a tremendous backlog because we were designing Starship *Prometheus*. This project we had been slaving over for a year, flying not more than twice a week in order to devote time to it—and that's a sacrifice.

Of course you can't build a starship today, because of the power plant. But Daddy thinks that there will soon be a technological break-through and mass-conversion power plants will be built—which means starships. Daddy ought to know—he's Luna Chief Engineer for Space Lanes and Fermi Lecturer at Goddard Institute. So Jeff and I are designing a self-supporting interstellar ship on that assumption: quarters, auxiliaries, surgery, labs—everything.

Daddy thinks it's just practice but Mother knows better—Mother is a mathematical chemist for General Synthetics of Luna and is nearly as smart as I am. She realizes that Jones & Hardesty plans to be ready with a finished proposal while other designers are still floundering.

Which was why I was furious with Jeff for wasting time over this creature. We had been working every possible chance. Jeff would show up after dinner, we would finish our homework, then get down to real work, the *Prometheus* . . . checking each other's computations, fighting bitterly over details, and having a wonderful time. But the very day I introduced him to Ariel Brentwood, he failed to appear. I had finished my lessons and was wondering whether to start or wait for him—we were making a radical change in power plant shielding—when his mother phoned me. "Jeff asked me to call you, dear. He's having dinner with a tourist client and can't come over."

Mrs. Hardesty was watching me so I looked puzzled and said, "Jeff thought I was expecting him? He has his dates mixed." I don't think she believed me; she agreed too quickly.

All that week I was slowly convinced against my will that Jones & Hardesty was being liquidated. Jeff didn't break any more dates—how can you break a date that hasn't been made?—but we always went flying Thursday afternoons unless one of us was guiding. He didn't call. Oh, I know where he was; he took her iceskating in Fingal's Cave.

I stayed home and worked on the *Prometheus*, recalculating masses and moment arms for hydroponics and stores on the basis of the shielding change. But I made mistakes and twice I had to look up logarithms instead of remembering . . . I was so used to wrangling with Jeff over everything that I just couldn't function.

Presently I looked at the name plate of the sheet I was revising. "Jones & Hardesty" it read, like all the rest. I said to myself,

"Holly Jones, quit bluffing; this may be The End. You knew that someday Jeff would fall for somebody."

"Of course . . . but not a *groundhog*."

"But he *did*. What kind of an engineer are you if you can't face facts? She's beautiful and rich—she'll get her father to give him a job Earthside. You hear me? *Earthside!* So you look for another partner . . . or go into business on your own."

I erased "Jones & Hardesty" and lettered "Jones & Company" and stared at it. Then I started to erase that, too—but it smeared; I had dripped a tear on it. Which was ridiculous!

The following Tuesday both Daddy and Mother were home for lunch which was unusual as Daddy lunches at the spaceport. Now Daddy can't even see you unless you're a spaceship but that day he picked to notice that I had dialed only a salad and hadn't finished it. "That plate is about eight hundred calories short," he said, peering at it. "You can't boost without fuel—aren't you well?"

"Quite well, thank you," I answered with dignity.

"Mmm . . . now that I think back, you've been moping for several days. Maybe you need a checkup." He looked at Mother.

"I do not either need a checkup!" I had *not* been moping—doesn't a woman have a right not to chatter?

But I hate to have doctors poking at me so I added, "It happens I'm eating lightly because I'm going flying this afternoon. But if you insist, I'll order pot roast and potatoes and sleep instead!"

"Easy, punkin'," he answered gently. "I didn't mean to intrude. Get yourself a snack when you're through . . . and say hello to Jeff for me."

I simply answered, "OK," and asked to be excused; I was humiliated by the assumption that I couldn't fly without Mr. Jefferson Hardesty but did not wish to discuss it.

Daddy called after me, "Don't be late for dinner," and Mother said, "Now, Jacob—" and to me, "Fly until you're tired, dear; you haven't been getting much exercise. I'll leave your dinner in the warmer. Anything you'd like?"

"No, whatever you dial for yourself." I just wasn't interested in food, which isn't like me. As I headed for Bats' Cave I wondered if I had caught something. But my cheeks didn't feel warm and my stomach wasn't upset even if I wasn't hungry.

Then I had a horrible thought. Could it be that I was jealous? *Me?*

It was unthinkable. I am not romantic; I am a career woman. Jeff had been my partner and pal, and under my guidance he could have become a great spaceship designer, but our relationship was straightforward . . . a mutual respect for each other's abilities, with never any of that lovey-dovey stuff. A career woman can't afford such things—why look at all the professional time Mother had lost over having me!

No, I couldn't be jealous; I was simply worried sick because my partner had become involved with a groundhog. Jeff isn't bright about women and, besides, he's never been to Earth and has illusions about it. If she lured him Earthside, Jones & Hardesty was finished.

And somehow "Jones & Company" wasn't a substitute: the *Prometheus* might never be built.

I was at Bats' Cave when I reached this dismal conclusion. I didn't feel like flying but I went to the locker room and got my wings anyhow.

Most of the stuff written about Bats' Cave gives a wrong impression. It's the air storage tank for the city, just like all the colonies have—the place where the scavenger pumps, deep down, deliver the air until it's needed. We just happen to be lucky enough to have one big enough to fly in. But it never was built, or anything like that; it's just a big volcanic bubble, two miles across, and if it had broken through, way back when, it would have been a crater.

Tourists sometimes pity us loonies because we have no chance to swim. Well, I tried it in Omaha and got water up my nose and scared myself silly. Water is for drinking, not playing in; I'll take flying. I've heard groundhogs say, oh yes, they had "flown" many times. But that's not *flying*. I did what they talk about, between White Sands and Omaha. I felt awful and got sick. Those things aren't safe.

I left my shoes and skirt in the locker room and slipped my tail surfaces on my feet, then zipped into my wings and got someone to tighten the shoulder straps. My wings aren't ready-made condors; they are Storer-Gulls, custom-made for my weight distribution and dimensions. I've cost Daddy a pretty penny in wings, outgrowing them so often, but these latest I bought myself with guide fees.

They're lovely!—titanalloy struts as light and strong as bird bones, tension-compensated wrist-pinion and shoulder joints, natural action in the alula slots, and automatic flap action in stalling. The wing skeleton is dressed in styrene feather-foils with individual quilling of scapulars and primaries. They almost fly themselves.

I folded my wings and went into the lock. While it was cycling I opened my left wing and thumbed the alula control—I had noticed a tendency to sideslip the last time I was airborne. But the alula opened properly and I decided I must have been overcontrolling, easy to do with Storer-Gulls; they're extremely maneuverable. Then the door showed green and I folded the wing and hurried out, while glancing at the barometer. Seventeen pounds—two more than Earth sea-level and nearly twice what we use in the city; even an ostrich could fly in that. I perked up and felt sorry for all groundhogs, tied down by six times proper weight, who never, never, *never* could fly.

Not even I could, on Earth. My wing loading is less than a pound per square foot, as wings and all I weigh less than twenty pounds. Earthside that would be over a hundred pounds and I could flap forever and never get off the ground.

I felt so good that I forgot about Jeff and his weakness. I spread my wings, ran a few steps, warped for lift and grabbed air—lifted my feet and was airborne.

I sculled gently and let myself glide toward the air intake at the middle of the floor—the Baby's Ladder, we call it, because you can ride the updraft clear to the roof, half a mile above, and never move a wing. When I felt it I leaned right, spoiling with right primaries, corrected, and settled in a counterclockwise soaring glide and let it carry me toward the roof.

A couple of hundred feet up, I looked around. The cave was almost empty, not more than two hundred in the air and half that number perched or on the ground—room enough for didoes. So as soon as I was up five hundred feet I leaned out of the updraft and began to beat. Gliding is no effort but flying is as hard work as you care to make it. In gliding I support a mere ten pounds on each arm—shucks, on Earth you work harder than that lying in bed. The lift that keeps you in the air doesn't take any work; you get it free from the shape of your wings just as long as there is air pouring past them.

Even without an updraft all a level glide takes is gentle sculling with your finger tips to maintain air speed; a feeble old lady could do it. The lift comes from differential air pressures but you don't have to understand it; you just scull a little and the air supports you, as if you were lying in an utterly perfect bed. Sculling keeps you moving forward just like sculling a rowboat ... or so I'm told; I've never been in a rowboat. I had a chance to in Nebraska but I'm not that foolhardy.

But when you're really flying, you scull with forearms as well as hands and add power with your shoulder muscles. Instead of only the outer quills of your primaries changing pitch (as in gliding), now your primaries and secondaries clear back to the joint warp sharply on each downbeat and recovery; they no longer lift, they force you forward—while your weight is carried by your scapulars, up under your armpits.

So you fly faster, or climb, or both, through controlling the angle of attack with your feet—with the tail surfaces you wear on your feet, I mean.

Oh dear, this sounds complicated and isn't—you just *do* it. You fly exactly as a bird flies. Baby birds can learn it and they aren't very bright. Anyhow, it's easy as breathing after you learn . . . and more fun than you can imagine!

I climbed to the roof with powerful beats, increasing my angle of attack and slotting my alulae for lift without burble—climbing at an angle that would stall most fliers. I'm little but it's all muscle and I've been flying since I was six. Once up there I glided and looked around. Down at the floor near the south wall tourists were trying glide wings—if you call those things "wings." Along the west wall the visitors' gallery was loaded with goggling tourists. I wondered if Jeff and his Circe character were there and decided to go down and find out.

So I went into a steep dive and swooped toward the gallery, leveled off and flew very fast along it. I didn't spot Jeff and his groundhog-gess but I wasn't watching where I was going and overtook another flier, almost collided. I glimpsed him just in time to stall and drop under, and fell fifty feet before I got control. Neither of us was in danger as the gallery is two hundred feet up, but I looked silly and it was my own fault; I had violated a safety rule.

There aren't many rules but they are necessary; the first is that orange wings always have the right of way—they're beginners. This flier did not have orange wings but I was overtaking. The flier underneath—or being overtaken—or nearer the wall—or turning counterclockwise, in that order, has the right of way.

I felt foolish and wondered who had seen me, so I went all the way back up, made sure I had clear air, then stooped like a hawk toward the gallery, spilling wings, lifting tail, and letting myself fall like a rock.

I completed my stoop in front of the gallery, lowering and spreading my tail so hard I could feel leg muscles knot and grabbing air with both wings, alulae slotted. I pulled level in an extremely fast glide along the gallery. I could see their eyes pop and thought smugly, "There! That'll show 'em!"

When darn if somebody didn't stoop on *me!* The blast from a flier braking right over me almost knocked me out of control. I grabbed air and stopped a sideslip, used some shipyard words and looked around to see who had blitzed me. I knew the black-and-gold wing pattern—Mary Muhlenburg, my best girl friend. She swung toward me, pivoting on a wing tip. "Hi, Holly! Scared you, didn't I?"

"You did not! You better be careful; the flightmaster'll ground you for a month!"

"Slim chance! He's down for coffee."

I flew away, still annoyed, and started to climb. Mary called after me, but I ignored her, thinking, "Mary my girl, I'm going to get over you and fly you right out of the air."

This was a foolish thought as Mary flies every day and has shoulders and pectoral muscles like Mrs. Hercules. By the time she caught up with me I had cooled off and we flew side by side, still climbing. "Perch?" she called out.

"Perch," I agreed. Mary has lovely gossip and I could use a breather. We turned toward our usual perch, a ceiling brace for flood lamps—it isn't supposed to be a perch but the flightmaster hardly ever comes up there.

Mary flew in ahead of me, braked and stalled dead to a perfect landing. I skidded a little but Mary stuck out a wing and steadied me. It isn't easy to come into a perch, especially when you have to approach level. Two years ago a boy who had just graduated from orange wings tried it . . . knocked off his left alula and primaries on a strut—went fluttering and spinning down two thousand feet and crashed. He could have saved himself—you can come in safely with a badly damaged wing if you spill air with the other and accept the steeper glide, then stall as you land. But this poor kid didn't know how; he broke his neck, dead as Icarus. I haven't used that perch since.

We folded our wings and Mary sidled over. "Jeff is looking for you," she said with a sly grin.

My insides jumped but I answered coolly, "So? I didn't know he was here."

"Sure. Down there," she added, pointing with her left wing. "Spot him?"

Jeff wears striped red and silver, but she was pointing at the tourist glide slope, a mile away. "No."

"He's there all right." She looked at me sidewise. "But I wouldn't look him up if I were you."

"Why not? Or for that matter, why should I?" Mary can be exasperating.

"Huh? You always run when he whistles. But he has that Earthside siren in tow again today; you might find it embarrassing."

"Mary, whatever are you talking about?"

"Huh? Don't kid me, Holly Jones; you know what I mean."

"I'm sure I don't," I answered with cold dignity.

"Humph! Then you're the only person in Luna City who doesn't. Everybody knows you're crazy about Jeff; everybody knows she's cut you out . . . and that you are simply simmering with jealousy."

Mary is my dearest friend but someday I'm going to skin her for a rug. "Mary, that's preposterously ridiculous! How can you even think such a thing?"

"Look, darling, you don't have to pretend. I'm for you." She patted my shoulders with her secondaries.

So I pushed her over backwards. She fell a hundred feet, straightened out, circled and climbed, and came in beside me, still grinning. It gave me time to decide what to say.

"Mary Muhlenburg, in the first place I am not crazy about anyone, least of all Jeff Hardesty. He and I are simply friends. So it's utterly nonsensical to talk about me being 'jealous.' In the second place Miss Brentwood is a lady and doesn't go around 'cutting out' anyone, least of all me. In the third place she is simply a tourist Jeff is guiding—business, nothing more."

"Sure, sure," Mary agreed placidly. "I was wrong. Still—" She shrugged her wings and shut up.

"'Still' what? Mary, don't be mealy-mouthed."

"Mmm . . . I was wondering how you knew I was talking about Ariel Brentwood—since there isn't anything to it."

"Why, you mentioned her name."

"I did not."

I thought frantically. "Uh, maybe not. But it's perfectly simple. Miss Brentwood is a client I turned over to Jeff myself, so I assumed that she must be the tourist you meant."

"So? I don't recall even saying she was a tourist. But since she is just a tourist you two are splitting, why aren't you doing the inside guiding while Jeff sticks to outside work? I thought you guides had an agreement?"

"Huh? If he has been guiding her inside the city, I'm not aware of it—"

"You're the only one who isn't."

"—and I'm not interested; that's up to the grievance committee. But Jeff wouldn't take a fee for inside guiding in any case."

"Oh, sure!—not one he could *bank*. Well, Holly, seeing I was wrong, why don't you give him a hand with her? She wants to learn to glide."

Butting in on that pair was farthest from my mind. "If Mr. Hardesty wants my help, he will ask me. In the meantime I shall mind my own business . . . a practice I recommend to you!"

"Relax, shipmate," she answered, unruffled. "I was doing you a favor."

"Thank you, I don't need one."

"So I'll be on my way—got to practice for the gymkhana." She leaned forward and dropped off. But she didn't practice aerobatics; she dived straight for the tourist slope.

I watched her out of sight, then snaked my left hand out the hand slit and got at my hanky—awkward when you are wearing wings but the floodlights had made my eyes water. I wiped them and blew my nose and put my hanky away and wiggled my hand back into place, then checked everything, thumbs, toes, and fingers, preparatory to dropping off.

But I didn't. I just sat there, wings drooping, and thought. I had to admit that Mary was partly right; Jeff's head was turned completely . . . over a *groundhog*. So sooner or later he would go Earthside and Jones & Hardesty was finished.

Then I reminded myself that I had been planning to be a spaceship designer like Daddy long before Jeff and I teamed up. I wasn't dependent on anyone; I could stand alone, like Joan of Arc, or Lise Meitner.

I felt better . . . a cold, stern pride, like Lucifer in *Paradise Lost*.

I recognized the red and silver of Jeff's wings while he was far off and I thought about slipping quietly away. But Jeff can overtake me if he tries, so I decided, "Holly, don't be a fool! You have no reason to run . . . just be coolly polite."

He landed by me but didn't sidle up. "Hi, Decimal Point."

"Hi, Zero. Uh, stolen much lately?"

"Just the City Bank but they made me put it back." He frowned and added, "Holly, are you mad at me?"

"Why, Jeff, whatever gave you such a silly notion?"

"Uh . . . something Mary the Mouth said."

"Her? Don't pay any attention to what *she* says. Half of it's always wrong and she doesn't mean the rest."

"Yeah, a short circuit between her ears. Then you aren't mad?"

"Of *course* not. Why should I be?"

"No reason I know of. I haven't been around to work on the ship for a few days ... but I've been awfully busy."

"Think nothing of it. I've been terribly busy myself."

"Uh, that's fine. Look, Test Sample, do me a favor. Help me out with a friend—a client, that is—well, she's a friend, too. She wants to learn to use glide wings."

I pretended to consider it. "Anyone I know?"

"Oh, yes. Fact is, you introduced us. Ariel Brentwood."

"'Brentwood'? Jeff, there are so many tourists. Let me think. Tall girl? Blonde? Extremely pretty?"

He grinned like a goof and I almost pushed him off. "That's Ariel!"

"I recall her ... she expected me to carry her bags. But you don't need help, Jeff. She seemed very clever. Good sense of balance."

"Oh, yes, sure, all of that. Well, the fact is, I want you two to know each other. She's ... well, she's just wonderful, Holly. A real person all the way through. You'll love her when you know her better. Uh ... this seemed like a good chance."

I felt dizzy. "Why, that's very thoughtful, Jeff, but I doubt if she wants to know me better. I'm just a servant she hired—you know groundhogs."

"But she's not at all like the ordinary groundhog. And she does want to know you better—she *told* me so!"

After you told her to think so! I muttered. But I had talked myself into a corner. If I had not been hampered by polite upbringing I would have said, "On your way, vacuum skull! I'm not interested in your groundhog girl friends"—but what I did say was, "OK, Jeff," then gathered the fox to my bosom and dropped off into a glide.

So I taught Ariel Brentwood to "fly." Look, those so-called wings they let tourists wear have fifty square feet of lift surface, no controls except warp in the primaries, a built-in dihedral to make them stable as a table, and a few meaningless degrees of hinging to let the wearer think that he is "flying" by waving his arms. The tail is rigid, and canted so that if you stall (almost impossible) you land on your feet. All a tourist does is run a few yards, lift up his feet (he can't avoid it) and slide down a blanket of air. Then he can tell his grandchildren how he flew, really *flew*, "just like a bird."

An ape could learn to "fly" that much.

I put myself to the humiliation of strapping on a set of the silly things and had Ariel watch while I swung into the Baby's Ladder and let it carry me up a hundred feet to show her that you really and truly could "fly" with them. Then I thankfully got rid of them, strapped her into a larger set, and put on my beautiful Storer-Gulls. I had chased Jeff away (two instructors is too many), but when he saw her wing up, he swooped down and landed by us.

I looked up. "You again."

"Hello, Ariel. Hi, Blip. Say, you've got her shoulder straps too tight."

"Tut, tut," I said. "One coach at a time, remember? If you want to help, shuck those gaudy fins and put on some gliders ... then I'll use you to show how not to. Otherwise get above two hundred feet and stay there; we don't need any dining-lounge pilots."

Jeff pouted like a brat but Ariel backed me up. "Do what teacher says, Jeff. That's a good boy."

He wouldn't put on gliders but he didn't stay clear either. He circled around us, watching, and got bawled out by the flightmaster for cluttering the tourist area.

I admit Ariel was a good pupil. She didn't even get sore when I suggested that she was rather mature across the hips to balance well; she just said that she had noticed that I had the slimmest behind around there and she envied me. So I quit trying to get her goat, and found myself almost liking her as long as I kept my mind firmly on teaching. She tried hard and learned fast—good reflexes and (despite my dirty crack) good balance. I remarked on it and she admitted diffidently that she had had ballet training.

About mid-afternoon she said, "Could I possibly try real wings?"

"Huh? Gee, Ariel, I don't think so."

"Why not?"

There she had me. She had already done all that could be done with those atrocious gliders. If she was to learn more, she had to have real wings. "Ariel, it's dangerous. It's not what you've been doing, believe me. You might get hurt, even killed."

"Would you be held responsible?"

"No. You signed a release when you came in."

"Then I'd like to try it."

I bit my lip. If she had cracked up without my help, I wouldn't have shed a tear—but to let her do something too dangerous while she was my pupil ... well, it smacked of David and Uriah. "Ariel,

I can't stop you . . . but I should put my wings away and not have anything to do with it."

It was her turn to bite her lip. "If you feel that way, I can't ask you to coach me. But I still want to. Perhaps Jeff will help me."

"He probably will," I blurted out, "if he is as big a fool as I think he is!"

Her company face slipped but she didn't say anything because just then Jeff stalled in beside us. "What's the discussion?"

We both tried to tell him and confused him for he got the idea I had suggested it, and started bawling me out. Was I crazy? Was I trying to get Ariel hurt? Didn't I have any sense?

"*Shut up!*" I yelled, then added quietly but firmly, "Jefferson Hardesty, you wanted me to teach your girl friend, so I agreed. But don't butt in and don't think you can get away with talking to me like that. Now beat it! Take wing. Grab air!"

He swelled up and said slowly, "I absolutely forbid it."

Silence for five long counts. Then Ariel said quietly, "Come, Holly. Let's get me some wings."

"Right, Ariel."

But they don't rent real wings. Fliers have their own; they have to. However, there are second-hand ones for sale because kids outgrow them, or people shift to custom-made ones, or something. I found Mr. Schultz who keeps the key, and said that Ariel was thinking of buying but I wouldn't let her without a tryout. After picking over forty-odd pairs I found a set which Johnny Queveras had outgrown but which I knew were all right. Nevertheless I inspected them carefully. I could hardly reach the finger controls but they fitted Ariel.

While I was helping her into the tail surfaces I said, "Ariel? This is still a bad idea."

"I know. But we can't let men think they own us."

"I suppose not."

"They do own us, of course. But we shouldn't let them know it." She was feeling out the tail controls. "The big toes spread them?"

"Yes. But don't do it. Just keep your feet together and toes pointed. Look, Ariel, you really aren't ready. Today all you will do is glide, just as you've been doing. Promise?"

She looked me in the eye. "I'll do exactly what you say . . . not even take wing unless you OK it."

"OK. Ready?"

"I'm ready."

"All right. Wups! I goofed. They aren't orange."

"Does it matter?"

"It sure does." There followed a weary argument because Mr. Schultz didn't want to spray them orange for a tryout. Ariel settled it by buying them, then we had to wait a bit while the solvent dried.

We went back to the tourist slope and I let her glide, cautioning her to hold both alulae open with her thumbs for more lift at slow speeds, while barely sculling with her fingers. She did fine, and stumbled in landing only once. Jeff stuck around, cutting figure eights above us, but we ignored him. Presently I taught her to turn in a wide, gentle bank—you can turn those awful glider things but it takes skill; they're only meant for straight glide.

Finally I landed by her and said, "Had enough?"

"I'll never have enough! But I'll unwing if you say."

"Tired?"

"No." She glanced over her wing at the Baby's Ladder; a dozen fliers were going up it, wings motionless, soaring lazily. "I wish I could do that just once. It must be heaven."

I chewed it over. "Actually, the higher you are, the safer you are."

"Then why not?"

"Mmm . . . safer *provided* you know what you're doing. Going up that draft is just gliding like you've been doing. You lie still and let it lift you half a mile high. Then you come down the same way, circling the wall in a gentle glide. But you're going to be tempted to do something you don't understand yet—flap your wings, or cut some caper."

She shook her head solemnly. "I won't do anything you haven't taught me."

I was still worried. "Look, it's only half a mile up but you cover five miles getting there and more getting down. Half an hour at least. Will your arms take it?"

"I'm sure they will."

"Well . . . you can start down anytime; you don't have to go all the way. Flex your arms a little now and then, so they won't cramp. Just don't flap your wings."

"I won't."

"OK." I spread my wings. "Follow me."

I led her into the updraft, leaned gently right, then back left to start the counterclockwise climb, all the while sculling very slowly so that she could keep up. Once we were in the groove I called out, "Steady as you are!" and cut out suddenly, climbed and took station thirty feet over and behind her. "Ariel?"

"Yes, Holly?"

"I'll stay over you. Don't crane your neck; you don't have to watch me, I have to watch you. You're doing fine."

"I feel fine!"

"Wiggle a little. Don't stiffen up. It's a long way to the roof. You can scull harder if you want to."

"Aye aye, Cap'n!"

"Not tired?"

"Heavens, no! Girl, I'm living!" She giggled. "And mama said I'd never be an angel!"

I didn't answer because red-and-silver wings came charging at me, braked suddenly and settled into a circle between me and Ariel. Jeff's face was almost as red as his wings. "What the devil do you think you are doing?"

"Orange wings!" I yelled. "Keep clear!"

"Get down out of here! Both of you!"

"Get out from between me and my pupil. You know the rules."

"Ariel!" Jeff shouted. "Lean out of the circle and glide down. I'll stay with you."

"Jeff Hardesty," I said savagely, "I give you three seconds to get out from between us—then I'm going to report you for violation of Rule One. For the third time—*Orange Wings!*"

Jeff growled something, dipped his right wing and dropped out of formation. The idiot sideslipped within five feet of Ariel's wing tip. I should have reported him for that; all the room you can give a beginner is none too much.

I said, "OK, Ariel?"

"OK, Holly. I'm sorry Jeff is angry."

"He'll get over it. Tell me if you feel tired."

"I'm not. I want to go all the way up. How high are we?"

"Four hundred feet, maybe."

Jeff flew below us a while, then climbed and flew over us . . . probably for the same reason I did: to see better. It suited me to have two of us watching her as long as he didn't interfere; I was beginning to fret that Ariel might not realize that the way down was going to be as long and tiring as the way up. I was hoping she would cry uncle. I knew I could glide until forced down by starvation. But a beginner gets tense.

Jeff stayed generally over us, sweeping back and forth—he's too active to glide very long—while Ariel and I continued to soar, winding slowly up toward the roof. It finally occurred to me when we were about halfway up that I could cry uncle myself; I didn't have to wait for Ariel to weaken. So I called out, "Ariel? Tired now?"

"No."

"Well, I am. Could we go down, please?"

She didn't argue, she just said, "All right. What am I to do?"

"Lean right and get out of the circle." I intended to have her move out five or six hundred feet, get into the return down draft, and circle the cave down instead of up. I glanced up, looking for Jeff. I finally spotted him some distance away and much higher but coming toward us. I called out, "Jeff! See you on the ground." He might not have heard me but he would see if he didn't hear; I glanced back at Ariel.

I couldn't find her.

Then I saw her, a hundred feet below—flailing her wings and falling, out of control.

I didn't know how it happened. Maybe she leaned too far, went into a sideslip and started to struggle. But I didn't try to figure it out; I was simply filled with horror. I seemed to hang there frozen for an hour while I watched her.

But the fact appears to be that I screamed "*Jeff!*" and broke into a stoop.

But I didn't seem to fall, couldn't overtake her. I spilled my wings completely—but couldn't manage to fall; she was as far away as ever.

You do start slowly, of course; our low gravity is the only thing that makes human flying possible. Even a stone falls a scant three feet in the first second. But that first second seemed endless.

Then I knew I was falling. I could feel rushing air—but I still didn't seem to close on her. Her struggles must have slowed her somewhat, while I was in an intentional stoop, wings spilled and raised over my head, falling as fast as possible. I had a wild notion that if I could pull even with her, I could shout sense into her head, get her to dive, then straighten out in a glide. But I couldn't *reach* her.

This nightmare dragged on for hours.

Actually we didn't have room to fall for more than twenty seconds; that's all it takes to stoop a thousand feet. But twenty seconds can be horribly long . . . long enough to regret every foolish thing I had ever done or said, long enough to say a prayer for us both . . . and to say good-by to Jeff in my heart. Long enough to see the floor rushing toward us and know that we were both going to crash if I didn't overtake her mighty quick.

I glanced up and Jeff was stooping right over us but a long way up. I looked down at once ... and I was overtaking her ... I was passing her—*I was under her!*

Then I was braking with everything I had, almost pulling my wings off. I grabbed air, held it, and started to beat without ever going to level flight. I beat once, twice, three times ... and hit her from below, jarring us both.

Then the floor hit us.

I felt feeble and dreamily contented. I was on my back in a dim room. I think Mother was with me and I know Daddy was. My nose itched and I tried to scratch it, but my arms wouldn't work. I fell asleep again.

I woke up hungry and wide awake. I was in a hospital bed and my arms still wouldn't work, which wasn't surprising as they were both in casts. A nurse came in with a tray. "Hungry?" she asked.

"Starved," I admitted.

"We'll fix that." She started feeding me like a baby.

I dodged the third spoonful and demanded. "What happened to my arms?"

"Hush," she said and gagged me with a spoon.

But a nice doctor came in later and answered my question. "Nothing much. Three simple fractures. At your age you'll heal in no time. But we like your company so I'm holding you for observation of possible internal injury."

"I'm not hurt inside," I told him. "At least, I don't hurt."

"I told you it was just an excuse."

"Uh, Doctor?"

"Well?"

"Will I be able to fly again?" I waited, scared.

"Certainly. I've seen men hurt worse get up and go three rounds."

"Oh. Well, thanks. Doctor? What happened to the other girl? Is she ... did she ...?"

"Brentwood? She's here."

"She's right here," Ariel agreed from the door. "May I come in?"

My jaw dropped, then I said, "Yeah. Sure. Come in."

The doctor said, "Don't stay long," and left. I said, "Well, sit down."

"Thanks." She hopped instead of walked and I saw that one foot was bandaged. She got on the end of the bed.

"You hurt your foot."

She shrugged. "Nothing. A sprain and a torn ligament. Two cracked ribs. But I would have been dead. You know why I'm not?"

I didn't answer. She touched one of my casts. "That's why. You broke my fall and I landed on top of you. You saved my life and I broke both your arms."

"You don't have to thank me. I would have done it for any-body."

"I believe you and I wasn't thanking you. You can't thank a person for saving your life. I just wanted to make sure you knew that I knew it."

I didn't have an answer so I said, "Where's Jeff? Is he all right?"

"He'll be along soon. Jeff's not hurt . . . though I'm surprised he didn't break both ankles. He stalled in beside us so hard that he should have. But Holly . . . Holly my very dear . . . I slipped in so that you and I could talk about him before he got here."

I changed the subject quickly. Whatever they had given me made me feel dreamy and good, but not beyond being embar-rassed. "Ariel, what happened? You were getting along fine—then suddenly you were in trouble."

She looked sheepish. "My own fault. You said we were going down, so I looked down. Really looked, I mean. Before that, all my thoughts had been about climbing clear to the roof; I hadn't thought about how far down the floor was. Then I looked down . . . and got dizzy and panicky and went all to pieces." She shrugged. "You were right. I wasn't ready."

I thought about it and nodded. "I see. But don't worry—when my arms are well, I'll take you up again."

She touched my foot. "Dear Holly. But I won' be flying again; I'm going back where I belong."

"Earthside?"

"Yes. I'm taking the *Billy Mitchell* on Wednesday."

"Oh. I'm sorry."

She frowned slightly. "Are you? Holly, you don't like me, do you?"

I was startled silly. What can you say? Especially when it's true? "Well," I said slowly, "I don't dislike you. I just don't know you very well."

She nodded. "And I don't know you very well . . . even though I got to know you a lot better in a very few seconds. But Holly . . . listen please and don't get angry. It's about Jeff. He hasn't treated you very well the last few days—while I've been here, I mean. But don't be angry with him. I'm leaving and everything will be the same."

That ripped it open and I couldn't ignore it, because if I did, she would assume all sorts of things that weren't so. So I had to explain . . . about me being a career woman . . . how, if I had seemed upset, it was simply distress at breaking up the firm of Jones & Hardesty before it even finished its first starship . . . how I was *not* in love with Jeff but simply valued him as a friend and associate . . . but if Jones & Hardesty couldn't carry on, then Jones & Company would. "So you see, Ariel, it isn't necessary for you to give up Jeff. If you feel you owe me something, just forget it. It isn't necessary."

She blinked and I saw with amazement that she was holding back tears. "Holly, Holly . . . you don't understand at all."

"I understand all right. I'm not a child."

"No, you're a grown woman . . . but you haven't found it out." She held up a finger. "One—Jeff doesn't love me."

"I don't believe it."

"Two . . . I don't love him."

"I don't believe that, either."

"Three . . . you say you don't love him—but we'll take that up when we come to it. Holly, am I beautiful?"

Changing the subject is a female trait but I'll never learn to do it that fast. "Huh?"

"I said, 'Am I beautiful?'"

"You know darn well you are!"

"Yes. I can sing a bit and dance, but I would get few parts if I were not, because I'm no better than a third-rate actress. So I have to be beautiful. How old am I?"

I managed not to boggle. "Huh? Older than Jeff thinks you are. Twenty-one, at least. Maybe twenty-two."

She sighed. "Holly, I'm old enough to be your mother."

"Huh? I don't believe that either."

"I'm glad it doesn't show. But that's why, though Jeff is a dear, there never was a chance that I could fall in love with him. But how I feel about him doesn't matter; the important thing is that *he* loves *you*."

"*What?* That's the silliest thing you've said yet! Oh, he *likes* me—or did. But that's all." I gulped. "And it's all I want. Why, you should hear the way he talks to me."

"I have. But boys that age can't say what they mean; they get embarrassed."

"But—"

"Wait, Holly. I saw something you didn't because you were knocked cold. When you and I bumped, do you know what happened?"

"Uh, no."

"Jeff arrived like an avenging angel, a split second behind us. He was ripping his wings off as he hit, getting his arms free. He didn't even look at me. He just stepped across me and picked you up and cradled you in his arms, all the while bawling his eyes out."

"He *did?*"

"He did."

I mulled it over. Maybe the big lunk did kind of like me, after all.

Ariel went on, "So you see, Holly, even if you don't love him, you must be very gentle with him, because he loves you and you can hurt him terribly."

I tried to think. Romance was still something that a career woman should shun ... but if Jeff really did feel that way—well ... would it be compromising my ideals to marry him just to keep him happy? To keep the firm together? Eventually, that is?

But if I did, it wouldn't be Jones & Hardesty; it would be Hardesty & Hardesty.

Ariel was still talking: "—you might even fall in love with him. It does happen, hon, and if it did, you'd be sorry if you had chased him away. Some other girl would grab him; he's awfully nice."

"But—" I shut up for I heard Jeff's step—I can always tell it. He stopped in the door and looked at us, frowning.

"Hi, Ariel."

"Hi, Jeff."

"Hi, Fraction." He looked me over. "My, but you're a mess."

"You aren't pretty yourself. I hear you have flat feet."

"Permanently. How do you brush your teeth with those things on your arms?"

"I don't."

Ariel slid off the bed, balanced on one foot. "Must run. See you later, kids."

"So long, Ariel."

"Good-by, Ariel. Uh ... thanks."

Jeff closed the door after she hopped away, came to the bed and said gruffly, "Hold still."

Then he put his arms around me and kissed me.

Well, I couldn't stop him, could I? With both arms broken? Besides, it was consonant with the new policy for the firm. I was startled speechless because Jeff never kisses me, except birthday kisses, which don't count. But I tried to kiss back and show that I appreciated it.

I don't know what the stuff was they had been giving me but my ears began to ring and I felt dizzy again.

Then he was leaning over me. "Runt," he said mournfully, "you sure give me a lot of grief."

"You're no bargain yourself, flathead," I answered with dignity.

"I suppose not." He looked me over sadly. "What are you crying for?"

I didn't know that I had been. Then I remembered why. "Oh, Jeff—I busted my pretty wings!"

"We'll get you more. Uh, brace yourself. I'm going to do it again."

"All right." He did.

I suppose Hardesty & Hardesty has more rhythm than Jones & Hardesty.

It really sounds better.

AFTERWORD BY ERIC FLINT

Once we settled on Clarke's *Rescue Party* as the opening story for the anthology, the choice for the second story was practically automatic: This one.

Well . . . not quite. The part that was more or less automatic was that it would be *some* story by Robert Heinlein. The question of which story in particular, however, was something we had to kick back and forth for a while.

We faced a bit of a problem. For all of us as teenagers, *the* Heinlein was not really the Heinlein who wrote short stories. It was the Heinlein who wrote that seemingly inexhaustible fountain of young adult novels: *Rocket Ship Galileo, Citizen of the Galaxy, Have Spacesuit—Will Travel, Tunnel in the Sky, Time for the Stars, The Star Beast, Farmer in the Sky, Space Cadet, The Rolling Stones, Starman Jones . . .* the list seemed to go on and on.

If books had infinite pages—or book buyers had infinitely deep pockets—we would have selected one of those short YA novels for the anthology. Alas, pages are finite and the pockets of customers more finite still, so we had to find another alternative.

We chose this story, because of all Heinlein's short fiction it probably best captures the spirit of his great young adult novels. Most of Heinlein's short fiction is quite different, often much grimmer, and—speaking for me, at least, if not necessarily Jim or Dave—not something which had much of an impact on me in my so-called formative years.

Plus, there was another bonus. Again, for me at least. I'm sure I first read this story when I was thirteen. I think that because I remember being absolutely fascinated by the fact that: a) the protagonist from whose viewpoint the story is told is a *girl;* b) she was really bright; c) she was often confused by her own motives and uncertain of herself, for all that she pretended otherwise.

Leaving factor "a" aside, factors "b" and "c" described me at that age to a T. That bizarre age in a boy's life when girls had gone from being a very familiar, well-understood and mostly boring phenomenon to something that had suddenly become incredibly mysterious, even more fascinating—and completely confusing.

After reading the story, I remember thinking that I really, really hoped Heinlein knew what he was talking about—and that the depiction of women and girls you generally ran across in science fiction of the time was baloney. With few exceptions, in SF of the time, a female character was doing well if she achieved one-dimensionality. And that dimension was invariably good looks. This was no help at all. I already knew girls were good-looking. What I needed to know was everything else—everything that Heinlein had put at the center of *his* story.

A year later I was fourteen and I had my first girlfriend, who remained so throughout my high school years. And whatever doubts I might have had that Robert A. Heinlein was *the* Heinlein were dispelled forever.

Code Three

by Rick Raphael

PREFACE BY ERIC FLINT

This story made its way into the anthology by accident. We had never planned to include it at the beginning. In fact, none of us had even remembered the story, or the author—whose career in science fiction only lasted a few years and ended long ago. Instead, we'd wanted to include a story by Eric Frank Russell, a writer whom we'd all enjoyed for years and who had been especially significant for me as a youngster.

Alas, the decision on which stories get included in an anthology like this aren't simply made by the editors. The estates (or, in some cases, still-living authors) obviously have a say in the matter also. And, in the case of Eric Frank Russell, the agency representing the estate proved too difficult for us to deal with. (Never mind the details. Expletives would have to be deleted. Many many many expletives.)

I was the one who handled the negotiations with that estate, and after they finally fell through, I was in a foul mood. I'd *really* wanted a Russell story. So I decided to work off my frustration with some long-postponed manual labor: unpacking several big boxes of old science fiction magazines I'd purchased for my editing work and filing them away.

Halfway through the first box, which was full of old *Analog* magazines, a cover illustration caught my eye. Jumped out at me, to be more precise. In a split second, I not only recognized that cover but I remembered the story it illustrated and the name of the author—Rick Raphael's novella *Code Three,* which I hadn't read in something like forty years but now recalled very vividly.

This was . . . a very good sign. So I immediately sat down and read the story, wondering if I'd still like it as much as I could remember liking it as a teenager.

As it happened, if anything, I liked it even more. As an experienced writer now well into middle age—being charitable to myself—I could spot little subtleties and nuances which I'm sure I missed as a sixteen-year-old.

I then called Dave on the phone and I began describing the story to him. Before I'd gotten out more than three sentences, *he* remembered it also—even though, like me, he hadn't read it in many years.

Oh, a *very* good sign.

So, here it is. The third story of the anthology, to serve all of us as a reminder that science fiction was constructed by many people, not simply a small number of famous writers. Rick Raphael came and went, but he had his moment in the sun.

———

The late afternoon sun hid behind gray banks of snow clouds and a cold wind whipped loose leaves across the drill field in front of the Philadelphia Barracks of the North American Continental Thruway Patrol. There was the feel of snow in the air but the thermometer hovered just at the freezing mark and the clouds could turn either into icy rain or snow.

Patrol Sergeant Ben Martin stepped out of the door of the barracks and shivered as a blast of wind hit him. He pulled up the zipper on his loose blue uniform coveralls and paused to gauge the storm clouds building up to the west.

The broad planes of his sunburned face turned into the driving cold wind for a moment and then he looked back down at the weather report secured to the top of a stack of papers on his clipboard.

Behind him, the door of the barracks was shouldered open by his junior partner, Patrol Trooper Clay Ferguson. The young, tall Canadian officer's arms were loaded with paper sacks and his patrol work helmet dangled by its strap from the crook of his arm.

Clay turned and moved from the doorway into the wind. A sudden gust swept around the corner of the building and a small sack perched atop one of the larger bags in his arms blew to the ground and began tumbling towards the drill field.

"Ben," he yelled, "grab the bag."

The sergeant lunged as the sack bounded by and made the retrieve. He walked back to Ferguson and eyed the load of bags in the blond-haired officer's arms.

"Just what is all this?" he inquired.

"Groceries," the youngster grinned. "Or to be more exact, little gourmet items for our moments of gracious living."

Ferguson turned into the walk leading to the motor pool and Martin swung into step beside him. "Want me to carry some of that junk?"

"Junk," Clay cried indignantly. "You keep your grimy paws off these delicacies, peasant. You'll get yours in due time and perhaps it will help Kelly and me to make a more polished product of you instead of the clodlike cop you are today."

Martin chuckled. This patrol would mark the start of the second year that he, Clay Ferguson and Medical-Surgical Officer Kelly Lightfoot had been teamed together. After twenty-two patrols, cooped up in a semiarmored vehicle with a man for ten days at a time, you got to know him pretty well. And you either liked him or you hated his guts.

As senior officer, Martin had the right to reject or keep his partner after their first eleven-month duty tour. Martin had elected to retain the lanky Canadian. As soon as they had pulled into New York Barracks at the end of their last patrol, he had made his decisions. After eleven months and twenty-two patrols on the Continental Thruways, each team had a thirty-day furlough coming.

Martin and Ferguson had headed for the city the minute they put their signatures on the last of the stack of reports needed at the end of a tour. Then, for five days and nights, they tied one on. MSO Kelly Lightfoot had made a beeline for a Columbia Medical School seminar on tissue regeneration. On the sixth day, Clay staggered out of bed, swigged down a handful of antireaction pills, showered, shaved and dressed and then waved good-by. Twenty minutes later he was aboard a jet, heading for his parents' home in Edmonton, Alberta. Martin soloed around the city for another week, then rented a car and raced up to his sister's home in Burlington, Vermont, to play Uncle Bountiful to Carol's three kids and to lap up as much as possible of his sister's real cooking.

While the troopers and their med officer relaxed, a service crew moved their car down to the Philadelphia motor pool for a full overhaul and refitting for the next torturous eleven-month tour of duty.

The two patrol troopers had reported into the Philadelphia Barracks five days ago—Martin several pounds heavier courtesy of his sister's cooking; Ferguson several pounds lighter courtesy of three assorted, starry-eyed, uniform-struck Alberta maidens.

They turned into the gate of the motor pool and nodded to the sentry at the gate. To their left, the vast shop buildings echoed to the sound of body-banging equipment and roaring jet engines. The darkening sky made the brilliant lights of the shop seem even brighter and the hulls of a dozen patrol cars cast deep shadows around the work crews.

The troopers turned into the dispatcher's office and Clay carefully placed the bags on a table beside the counter. Martin peered into one of the bags. "Seriously, kid, what do you have in that grab bag?"

"Oh, just a few essentials," Clay replied. "*Pate de foie gras,* sharp cheese, a smidgen of cooking wine, a handful of spices. You know, stuff like that. Like I said—essentials."

"Essentials," Martin snorted, "you give your brains to one of those Alberta chicks of yours for a souvenir?"

"Look, Ben," Ferguson said earnestly, "I suffered for eleven months in that tin mausoleum on tracks because of what you fondly like to think is edible food. You've got as much culinary imagination as Beulah. I take that back. Even Beulah turns out some better smells when she's riding on high jet than you'll ever get out of her galley in the next one hundred years. This tour, I intend to eat like a human being once again. And I'll teach you how to boil water without burning it."

"Why you ungrateful young—" Martin yelped.

The patrol dispatcher, who had been listening with amused tolerance, leaned across the counter.

"If Oscar Waldorf is through with his culinary lecture, gentlemen," he said, "perhaps you two could be persuaded to take a little pleasure ride. It's a lovely night for a drive and it's just twenty-six hundred miles to the next service station. If you two aren't cooking anything at the moment, I know that NorCon would simply adore having the services of two such distinguished Continental Commandos."

Ferguson flushed and Martin scowled at the dispatcher. "Very funny, clown. I'll recommend you for trooper status one of these days."

"Not me," the dispatcher protested. "I'm a married man. You'll never get me out on the road in one of those blood-and-gut factories."

"So quit sounding off to us heroes," Martin said, "and give us the clearances."

The dispatcher opened a loose-leaf reference book on the counter and then punched the first of a series of buttons on a panel. Behind him, the wall lighted with a map of the eastern United States to the Mississippi River. Ferguson and Martin had pencils out and poised over their clipboards.

The dispatcher glanced at the order board across the room where patrol car numbers and team names were displayed on an illuminated board. "Car 56—Martin-Ferguson-Lightfoot," glowed with an amber light. In the column to the right was the number "26-W." The dispatcher punched another button. A broad belt of multi-colored lines representing the eastern segment of North America Thruway 26 flashed onto the map in a band extending from Philadelphia to St. Louis. The thruway went on to Los Angeles on its western segment, not shown on the map. Ten bands of color—each five separated by a narrow clear strip, detailed the thruway. Martin and Ferguson were concerned with the northern five bands; NAT 26-westbound. Other unlighted lines radiated out in tangential spokes to the north and south along the length of the multi-colored belt of NAT 26.

This was just one small segment of the Continental Thruway system that spanned North America from coast to coast and criss-crossed north and sound under the Three Nation Road Compact from the southern tip of Mexico into Canada and Alaska.

Each arterial cut a five-mile-wide path across the continent and from one end to the other, the only structures along the roadways were the turretlike NorCon Patrol check and relay stations—looming up at one-hundred-mile intervals like the fire control islands of earlier-day aircraft carries.

Car 56 with Trooper Sergeant Ben Martin, Trooper Clay Ferguson and Medical-Surgical Officer Kelly Lightfoot, would take their first ten-day patrol on NAT 26-west. Barring major disaster, they would eat, sleep and work the entire time from their car; out of sight of any but distant cities until they had reached Los Angeles at the end of the patrol. Then a five-day resupply and briefing period and back onto another thruway.

During the coming patrol they would cross ten state lines as if they didn't exist. And as far as thruway traffic control and authority was concerned, state and national boundaries actually didn't exist. With the growth of the old interstate highway system and the Alcan Highway it became increasingly evident that variation in motor vehicle laws from state to state and country to country were creating impossible situations for any uniform safety control.

With the establishment of the Continental Thruway System two decades later, came the birth of the supra-cop—The North American Thruway Patrol—known as NorCon. Within the five-mile bands of the thruways—all federally-owned land by each of the three nations—the blue-coveralled "Continental Commandos" of NorCon were the sole law enforcement agency and authority. Violators of thruway law were cited into NorCon district traffic courts located in the nearest city to each access port along every thruway.

There was no challenge to the authority of NorCon. Public demand for faster and more powerful vehicles had forced the automotive industry to put more and more power under the touch of the ever-growing millions of drivers crowding the continent's roads. Piston drive gave way to turbojet; turbojet was boosted by a modification of ram jet and air-cushion drive was added. In the last two years, the first of the nuclear reaction mass engines had hit the roads. Even as the hot Ferraris and Jags of the mid-'60s would have been suicide vehicles on the T-model roads of the '20s so would today's vehicles be on the interstates of the '60s. But building roads capable of handling three hundred to four hundred miles an hour speeds was beyond the financial and engineering capabilities of individual states and nations. Thus grew the continental thruways with their four speed lanes in each direction, each a half-mile wide separated east and west and north and south by a half-mile-wide landscaped divider. Under the Three Nation Compact, the thruways now wove a net across the entire North American continent.

On the big wall map, NAT 26-west showed as four colored lines; blue and yellow as the two high and ultra-high speed lanes; green and white for the intermediate and slow lanes. Between the blue and yellow and the white and green was a red band. This was the police emergency lane, never used by other than official vehicles and crossed by the traveling public shifting from one speed lane to another only at sweeping crossovers.

The dispatcher picked up an electric pointer and aimed the light beam at the map. Referring to his notes, he began to recite.

"Resurfacing crews working on 26-W blue at milestone Marker 185 to Marker 187, estimated clearance 0300 hours Tuesday—Let's see, that's tomorrow morning."

The two officers were writing the information down on their trip-analysis sheets.

"Ohio State is playing Cal under the lights at Columbus tonight so you can expect a traffic surge sometime shortly after 2300 hours but most of it will stay in the green and white. Watch out for the drunks though. They might filter out onto the blue or yellow.

"The crossover for NAT 163 has painting crews working. Might watch out for any crud on the roadway. And they've got the entrance blocked there so that all 163 exchange traffic is being re-routed to 164 west of Chillicothe."

The dispatcher thumbed through his reference sheets. "That seems to be about all. No, wait a minute. This is on your trick. The Army's got a priority missile convoy moving out of the Aberdeen Proving Grounds bound for the west coast tonight at 1800 hours. It will be moving at green lane speeds so you might watch out for it. They'll have thirty-four units in the convoy. And that is all. Oh, yes. Kelly's already aboard. I guess you know about the weather."

Martin nodded. "Yup. We should be hitting light snows by 2300 hours tonight in this area and it could be anything from snow to ice-rain after that." He grinned at his younger partner. "The vacation is over, sonny. Tonight we make a man out of you."

Ferguson grinned back. "Nuts to you, pop. I've got character witnesses back in Edmonton who'll give you glowing testimonials about my manhood."

"Testimonials aren't legal unless they're given by adults," Martin retorted. "Come on, lover boy. Duty calls."

Clay carefully embraced his armload of bundles and the two officers turned to leave. The dispatcher leaned across the counter.

"Oh, Ferguson, one thing I forgot. There's some light corrugations in red lane just east of St. Louis. You might be careful with your soufflés in that area. Wouldn't want them to fall, you know."

Clay paused and started to turn back. The grinning dispatcher ducked into the back office and slammed the door.

The wind had died down by the time the troopers entered the brilliantly lighted parking area. The temperature seemed warmer with the lessening winds but in actuality, the mercury was dropping. The snow clouds to the west were much nearer and the overcast was getting darker.

But under the great overhead light tubes, the parking area was brighter than day. A dozen huge patrol vehicles were parked on the front "hot" line. Scores more were lined out in ranks to the back of the parking zone. Martin and Ferguson walked down the line of military blue cars. Number 56 was fifth on the line. Service mechs were just re-housing fueling lines into a ground panel as the troopers walked up. The technician corporal was the first to speak. "All set, Sarge," he said. "We had to change an induction jet at the last minute and I had the port engine running up to reline the flow. Thought I'd better top 'er off for you, though, before you pull out. She sounds like a purring kitten."

He tossed the pair a waving salute and then moved out to his service dolly where three other mechs were waiting.

"Beulah looks like she's been to the beauty shop and had the works," Martin said. He reached out and slapped the maglurium plates. "Welcome home, sweetheart. I see you've kept a candle in the window for your wandering son." Ferguson looked up at the lighted cab, sixteen feet above the pavement.

Car 56—Beulah to her team—was a standard NorCon Patrol vehicle. She was sixty feet long, twelve feet wide and twelve feet high; topped by a four-foot-high bubble canopy over her cab. All the way across her nose was a three-foot-wide luminescent strip. This was the variable beam headlight that could cut a day-bright swath of light through night, fog, rain or snow and could be varied in intensity, width and elevation. Immediately above the headlight strip were two red-black plastic panels which when lighted, sent out a flashing red emergency signal that could be seen for miles. Similar emergency lights and back-up white light strips adorned Beulah's stern. Her bow rounded down like an old-time tank and blended into the track assembly of her dual propulsion system. With the exception of the cabin bubble and a two-foot stepdown on the last fifteen feet of her hull, Beulah was free of external protrusions. Racked into a flush-decked recess on one side of the hull was a crane arm with a two-hundred-ton lift capacity. Several round hatches covered other extensible gear and periscopes used in the scores of multiple operations the Nor Con cars were called upon to accomplish on routine road patrols.

Beulah resembled a gigantic offspring of a military tank, sans heavy armament. But even a small stinger was part of the patrol car equipment. As for armament, Beulah had weapons to meet every conceivable skirmish in the deadly battle to keep Continental Thruways fast-moving and safe. Her own two-hundred-fifty-ton bulk could reach speeds of close to six hundred miles an hour utilizing one or both of her two independent propulsion systems.

At ultra-high speeds, Beulah never touched the ground—floating on an impeller air cushion and driven forward by a pair of one hundred fifty thousand pound thrust jets and ram jets. At intermediate high speeds, both her air cushion and the four-foot-wide tracks on each side of the car pushed her along at two hundred-mile-an-hour-plus speeds. Synchro mechanisms reduced the air cushion as the speeds dropped to afford more surface traction for the tracks. For slow speeds and heavy duty, the tracks carried the burden.

Martin thumbed open the portside ground-level cabin door.

"I'll start the outside check," he told Clay. "You stow that garbage of yours in the galley and start on the dispensary. I'll help you after I finish out here."

As the younger officer entered the car and headed up the short flight of steps to the working deck, the sergeant unclipped a check list from the inside of the door and turned towards the stern of the big vehicle.

Clay mounted to the work deck and turned back to the little galley just aft of the cab. As compact as a spaceship kitchen—as a matter of fact, designed almost identically from models on the Moon run—the galley had but three feet of open counter space. Everything else, sink, range, oven and freezer, were built-ins with pull-downs for use as needed. He set his bags on the small counter to put away after the pre-start check. Aft of the galley and on the same side of the passageway were the double-decked bunks for the patrol troopers. Across the passageway was a tiny latrine and shower. Clay tossed his helmet on the lower bunk as he went down the passageway. At the bulkhead to the rear, he pressed a wall panel and a thick, insulated door slid back to admit him to the engine compartment. The service crews had shut down the big power plants and turned off the air exchangers and already the heat from the massive engines made the compartment uncomfortably warm.

He hurried through into a small machine shop. In an emergency, the troopers could turn out small parts for disabled vehicles or for other uses. It also stocked a good supply of the most common failure parts. Racked against the ceiling were banks of cutting torches, a grim reminder that death and injury still rode the thruways with increasing frequency.

In the tank storage space between the ceiling and top of the hull were the chemical fire-fighting liquids and foam that could be applied by nozzles, hoses and towers now telescoped into recesses in the hull. Along both sides and beneath the galley, bunks, engine and machine-shop compartments between the walls, deck and hull, were Beulah's fuel storage tanks.

The last after compartment was a complete dispensary, one that would have made the emergency room or even the light surgery rooms of earlier-day hospitals proud.

Clay tapped on the door and went through. Medical-Surgical Officer Kelly Lightfoot was sitting on the deck, stowing sterile bandage packs into a lower locker. She looked up at Clay and smiled. "Well, well, you DID manage to tear yourself away from your adoring bevies," she said. She flicked back a wisp of golden-red hair from her forehead and stood up. The patrol-blue uniform coverall with its belted waist didn't do much to hide a lovely, properly curved figure. She walked over to the tall Canadian trooper and reached up and grabbed his ear. She pulled his head down, examined one side critically and then quickly snatched at his other ear and repeated the scrutiny. She let go of his ear and stepped back. "Damned if you didn't get all the lipstick marks off, too."

Clay flushed. "Cut it out, Kelly," he said. "Sometimes you act just like my mother."

The olive-complexioned redhead grinned at him and turned back to her stack of boxes on the deck. She bent over and lifted one of the boxes to the operating table. Clay eyed her trim figure. "You might act like ma sometimes," he said, "but you sure don't look like her."

It was the Irish-Cherokee Indian girl's turn to flush. She became very busy with the contents of the box. "Where's Ben?" she asked over her shoulder.

"Making outside check. You about finished in here?"

Kelly turned and slowly scanned the confines of the dispensary. With the exception of the boxes on the table and floor, everything was behind secured locker doors. In one corner, the compact diagnostician—capable of analyzing many known human bodily ailments and every possible violent injury to the body—was locked in its riding clamps. Surgical trays and instrument racks were all hidden behind locker doors along with medical and surgical supplies. On either side of the emergency ramp door at the stern of the vehicle, three collapsible auto-litters hung from clamps. Six hospital bunks in two tiers of three each, lined another wall. On patrol, Kelly utilized one of the hospital bunks for her own use except when they might all be occupied with accident or other kind of patients. And this would never be for more than a short period, just long enough to transfer them to a regular ambulance or hospital vehicle. Her meager supply of personal items needed for the ten-day patrol were stowed in a small locker and she shared the latrine with the male members of the team.

Kelly completed her scan, glanced down at the check list in her hand. "I'll have these boxes stowed in five minutes. Everything else is secure." She raised her hand to her forehead in mock salute. "Medical-Surgical Officer Lightfoot reports dispensary ready for patrol, sir."

Clay smiled and made a check-mark on his clipboard. "How was the seminar, Kelly?" he asked.

Kelly hiked herself onto the edge of the operating table. "Wonderful, Clay, just wonderful. I never saw so many good-looking, young, rich and eligible doctors together in one place in all my life."

She sighed and smiled vacantly into space.

Clay snorted. "I thought you were supposed to be learning something new about tissue regeneration," he said.

"Generation, regeneration, who cares," Kelly grinned.

Clay started to say something, got flustered and wheeled around to leave—and bounded right off Ben Martin's chest. Ferguson mumbled something and pushed past the older officer.

Ben looked after him and then turned back to Car 56's combination doctor, surgeon and nurse. "Glad to see the hostess aboard for this cruise. I hope you make the passengers more comfortable than you've just made the first mate. What did you do to Clay, Kelly?"

"Hi, Ben," Kelly said. "Oh, don't worry about junior. He just gets all fluttery when a girl takes away his masculine prerogative to make cleverly lewd witticisms. He'll be all right. Have a happy holiday, Ben? You look positively fat."

Ben patted his stomach. "Carol's good cooking. Had a nice restful time. And how about you. That couldn't have been all work. You've got a marvelous tan."

"Don't worry," Kelly laughed, "I had no intention of letting it be all study. I spent just about as much time under the sun dome at the pool as I did in class. I learned a lot, though."

Ben grinned and headed back to the front of the car. "Tell me more after we're on the road," he said from the doorway. "We'll be rolling in ten minutes."

When he reached the cab, Clay was already in the right-hand control seat and was running down the instrument panel check. The sergeant lifted the hatch door between the two control seats and punched on a light to illuminate the stark compartment at the lower front end of the car. A steel grill with a dogged handle on the upper side covered the opening under the hatch cover. Two swing-down bunks were racked up against the walls on either side and the front hull door was without an inside handle. This was the patrol car brig, used for bringing in unwilling violators or other violent or criminal subjects who might crop up in the course of a patrol tour. Satisfied with the appearance of the brig, Ben closed the hatch cover and slid into his own control seat on the left of the cab. Both control seats were molded and plastiformed padded to the contours of the troopers and the armrests on both were studded with buttons and a series of small, finger-operated knobs. All drive, communication and fire fighting controls for the massive vehicle were centered in the knobs and buttons on the seat arms, while acceleration and braking controls were duplicated in two footrest pedals beneath their feet.

Ben settled into his seat and glanced down to make sure his work-helmet was racked beside him. He reached over and flipped a bank of switches on the instrument panel. "All communications to 'on,'" he said. Clay made a checkmark on his list. "All pre-engine start check complete," Clay replied.

"In that case, the senior trooper said, "let's give Beulah some exercise. Start engines."

Clay's fingers danced across the array of buttons on his seat arms and flicked lightly at the throttle knobs. From deep within the engine compartment came the muted, shrill whine of the starter engines, followed a split-second later by the full-throated roar of the jets as they caught fire. Clay eased the throttles back and the engine noise softened to a muffled roar.

Martin fingered a press-panel on the right arm of his seat.

"Car 56 to Philly Control," Ben called.

The speakers mounted around the cab came to life. "Go ahead Five Six."

"Five Six fired up and ready to roll," Martin said.

"Affirmative Five Six," came the reply. "You're clear to roll. Philly Check estimates white density 300; green, 840; blue, 400; yellow, 75."

Both troopers made mental note of the traffic densities in their first one-hundred-mile patrol segment; an estimated three hundred vehicles for each ten miles of thruway in the white or fifty to one hundred miles an hour lane; eight hundred forty vehicles in the one hundred to one hundred fifty miles an hour green, and so on. More than sixteen thousand westbound vehicles on the thruway in the first one hundred miles; nearly five thousand of them traveling at speeds between one hundred fifty and three hundred miles an hour.

Over the always-hot intercom throughout the big car Ben called out. "All set, Kelly?"

"I'm making coffee," Kelly answered from the galley. "Let 'er roll."

Martin started to kick off the brakes, then stopped. "Ooops," he exclaimed, "almost forgot." His finger touched another button and a blaring horn reverberated through the vehicle.

In the galley, Kelly hurled herself into a corner. Her body activated a pressure plant and a pair of mummy-like plastifoam plates slid curvingly out the wall and locked her in a soft cocoon. A dozen similar safety clamps were located throughout the car at every working and relaxation station.

In the same instance, both Ben and Clay touched another plate on their control seats. From kiosk-type columns behind each seat, pairs of body-molded crash pads snapped into place to encase both troopers in their seats, their bodies cushioned and locked into place. Only their fingers were loose beneath the spongy substance to work arm controls. The half-molds included headforms with a padded band that locked across their foreheads to hold their heads rigidly against the backs of their reinforced seats. The instant all three crew members were locked into their safety gear, the bull horn ceased.

"All tight," Ben called out as he wiggled and tried to free himself from the cocoon. Kelly and Clay tested their harnesses.

Satisfied that the safety cocoons were operating properly, Ben released them and the molds slid back into their recesses. The cocoons were triggered automatically in any emergency run or chase at speeds in excess of two hundred miles an hour.

Again he kicked off the brakes, pressed down on the foot feed and Car 56—Beulah—rolled out of the Philadelphia motor pool on the start of its ten-day patrol.

The motor pool exit opened into a quarter-mile wide tunnel sloping gently down into the bowels of the great city. Car 56 glided down the slight incline at a steady fifty miles an hour. A mile from the mouth of the tunnel the roadway leveled off and Ben kicked Beulah up another twenty-five miles an hour. Ahead, the main tunnel ended in a series of smaller portal ways, each emblazoned with a huge illuminated number designating a continental thruway.

Ben throttled back and began edging to the left lanes. Other patrol cars were heading down the main passageway, bound for their assigned thruways. As Ben eased down to a slow thirty, another patrol vehicle slid alongside. The two troopers in the cab waved. Clay flicked on the "car-to-car" transmit.

The senior trooper in Car 104 looked over at Martin and Ferguson. "If it isn't the gruesome twosome," he called. "Where have you been? We thought the front office had finally caught up with you and found out that neither one of you could read or write and that they had canned you."

"We can't read," Ben quipped back. "That's why we're still on the job. The front office would never hire anyone who would embarrass you two by being smarter than either of you. Where're you headed, Eddie?"

"Got 154-north," the other officer said.

"Hey," Clay called out, "I've got a real hot doll in Toronto and I'll gladly sell her phone number for a proper price."

"Wouldn't want to hurt you, Clay," the other officer replied. "If I called her up and took her out, she'd throw rocks at you the next time you drew the run. It's all for your own good."

"Oh, go get lost in a cloverleaf," Clay retorted.

The other car broke the connection and with a wave, veered off to the right. The thruway entrances were just ahead. Martin aimed Beulah at the lighted orifice topped by the number 26-W. The patrol car slid into the narrower tunnel, glided along for another mile, and then turned its bow upwards. Three minutes later, they emerged from the tunnel into the red patrol lane of Continental Thruway 26-West. The late afternoon sky was a covering of gray wool and a drop or two of moisture struck the front face of the cab canopy. For a mile on either side of the police lane, streams of cars sped westward. Ben eyed the sky, the traffic and then peered at the outer hull thermometer. It read thirty-two degrees. He made a mental bet with himself that the weather bureau was off on its snow estimates by six hours. His Vermont upbringing told him it would be flurrying within the hour.

He increased speed to a steady one hundred and the car sped silently and easily along the police lane. Across the cab, Clay peered pensively at the steady stream of cars and cargo carriers racing by in the green and blue lanes—all of them moving faster than the patrol car.

The young officer turned in his seat and looked at his partner.

"You know, Ben," he said gravely, "I sometimes wonder if those oldtime cowboys got as tired looking at the south end of northbound cows as I get looking at the vanishing tail pipes of cars."

The radio came to life.

"Philly Control to Car 56."

Clay touched his transmit plate. "This is Five Six. Go ahead."

"You've got a bad one at Marker 82," Control said. "A sideswipe in the white."

"Couldn't be too bad in the white," Ben broke in, thinking of the one-hundred mile-an-hour limit in the slow lane.

"That's not the problem," Control came back. "One of the sideswiped vehicles was flipped around and bounded into the green, and that's where the real mess is. Make it code three."

"Five Six acknowledge," Ben said. "On the way."

He slammed forward on the throttles. The bull horn blared and a second later, with MSO Kelly Lightfoot snugged in her dispensary cocoon and both troopers in body cushions, Car 56 lifted a foot from the roadway, and leaped forward on a turbulent pad of air. It accelerated from one hundred to two hundred fifty miles an hour.

The great red emergency lights on the bow and stern began to blink and from the special transmitter in the hull a radio siren wail raced ahead of the car to be picked up by the emergency receptor antennas required on all vehicles.

The working part of the patrol had begun.

Conversation died in the speeding car, partly because of the concentration required by the troopers, secondly because all transmissions whether intercom or radio, on a code two or three run, were taped and monitored by Control. In the center of the instrument panel, an oversized radiodometer was clicking off the mileage marks as the car passed each milestone. The milestone posts beamed a coded signal across all five lanes and as each vehicle passed the marker, the radiodometer clicked up another number.

Car 56 had been at MM 23 when the call came. Now, at better than four miles a minute, Beulah whipped past MM 45 with ten minutes yet to go to reach the scene of the accident. Light flurries of wet snow bounced off the canopy, leaving thin, fast-drying trails of moisture. Although it was still a few minutes short of 1700 hours, the last of the winter afternoon light was being lost behind the heavy snow clouds overhead. Ben turned on the patrol car's dazzling headlight and to the left and right, Clay could see streaks of white lights from the traffic on the green and blue lanes on either side of the quarter-mile wide emergency lane.

The radio filled them in on the movement of other patrol emergency vehicles being routed to the accident site. Car 82, also assigned to NAT 26-West, was more than one hundred fifty miles ahead of Beulah. Pittsburgh Control ordered Eight Two to hold fast to cover anything else that might come up while Five Six was handling the current crisis. Eastbound Car 119 was ordered to cut across to the scene to assist Beulah's crew, and another eastbound patrol vehicle was held in place to cover for One One Nine.

At mile marker 80, yellow caution lights were flashing on all westbound lanes, triggered by Philadelphia Control the instant the word of the crash had been received. Traffic was slowing down and piling up despite the half-mile wide lanes.

"Philly Control this is Car 56."

"Go ahead Five Six."

"It's piling up in the green and white," Ben said. "Let's divert to blue on slowdown and seal the yellow."

"Philly Control acknowledged," came the reply.

The flashing amber caution lights on all lanes switched to red. As Ben began de-acceleration, diagonal red flashing barriers rose out of the roadway on the green and white lanes at the 85 mile marker and lane crossing. This channeled all traffic from both lanes to the left and into the blue lane where the flashing reds now prohibited speeds in excess of fifty miles an hour around the emergency situation. At the same time, all crossovers on the ultra high yellow lane were sealed by barriers to prevent changing of lanes into the over-congested area.

As Car 56's speed dropped back below the two hundred mile an hour mark the cocoon automatically slid open. Freed from her safety restraints, Kelly jumped for the rear entrance of the dispensary and cleared the racking clamps from the six auto-litters. That done, she opened another locker and reached for the mobile first-aid kit. She slid it to the door entrance on its retractable casters. She slipped on her work helmet with the built-in transmitter and then sat down on the seat by the rear door to wait until the car stopped.

Car 56 was now less than two miles from the scene of the crash and traffic in the green lane to the left was at a standstill. A half mile farther westward, lights were still moving slowly along the white lane. Ahead, the troopers could see a faint wisp of smoke rising from the heaviest congregation of headlights. Both officers had their work helmets on and Clay had left his seat and descended to the side door, ready to jump out the minute the car stopped.

Martin saw a clear area in the green lane and swung the car over the dividing curbing. The big tracks floated the patrol car over the two-foot high, rounded abutment that divided each speed lane. Snow was falling faster as the headlight picked out a tangled mass of wreckage smoldering a hundred feet inside the median separating the green and white lanes. A crumpled body lay on the pavement twenty feet from the biggest clump of smashed metal, and other fragments of vehicles were strung out down the roadway for fifty feet. There was no movement.

NorCon thruway laws were strict and none were more rigidly enforced than the regulation that no one other than a member of the patrol set foot outside of their vehicle while on any thruway traffic lane. This meant not giving any assistance whatsoever to accident victims. The ruling had been called inhuman, monstrous, unthinkable, and lawmakers in the three nations of the compact had forced NorCon to revoke the rule in the early days of the thruways. After speeding cars and cargo carriers had cut down twice as many do-gooders on foot at accident scenes than the accidents themselves caused, the law was reinstated. The lives of the many were more vital than the lives of a few.

Martin halted the patrol vehicle a few feet from the wreckage and Beulah was still rocking gently on her tracks by the time both Patrol Trooper Clay Ferguson and MSO Kelly Lightfoot hit the pavement on the run.

In the cab, Martin called in on the radio. "Car 56 is on scene. Release blue at Marker 95 and resume speeds all lanes at Marker 95 in—" he paused and looked back at the halted traffic piled up before the lane had been closed "—seven minutes." He jumped for the steps and sprinted out of the patrol car in the wake of Ferguson and Kelly.

The team's surgeon was kneeling beside the inert body on the road. After an ear to the chest, Kelly opened her field kit bag and slapped an electrode to the victim's temple. The needle on the encephalic meter in the lid of the kit never flickered. Kelly shut the bag and hurried with it over to the mass of wreckage. A thin column of black, oily smoke rose from somewhere near the bottom of the heap. It was almost impossible to identify at a glance whether the mangled metal was the remains of one or more cars. Only the absence of track equipment made it certain that they even had been passenger vehicles.

Clay was carefully climbing up the side of the piled up wrecks to a window that gaped near the top.

"Work fast, kid," Martin called up. "Something's burning down there and this whole thing may go up. I'll get this traffic moving."

He turned to face the halted mass of cars and cargo carriers east of the wreck. He flipped a switch that cut his helmet transmitter into the remote standard vehicular radio circuit aboard the patrol car.

"Attention, please, all cars in green lane. All cars in the left line move out now, the next line fall in behind. You are directed to clear the area immediately. Maintain fifty miles an hour for the next mile. You may resume desired speeds and change lanes at mile Marker 95. I repeat, all cars in green lane . . ." he went over the instructions once more, relayed through Beulah's transmitter to the standard receivers on all cars. He was still talking as the traffic began to move.

By the time he turned back to help his teammates, cars were moving in a steady stream past the huge, red-flashing bulk of the patrol car.

Both Clay and Kelly were lying flat across the smashed, upturned side of the uppermost car in the pile. Kelly had her field bag open on the ground and she was reaching down through the smashed window.

"What is it, Clay?" Martin called.

The younger officer looked down over his shoulder. "We've got a woman alive down here but she's wedged in tight. She's hurt pretty badly and Kelly's trying to slip a hypo into her now. Get the arm out, Ben."

Martin ran back to the patrol car and flipped up a panel on the hull. He pulled back on one of the several levers recessed into the hull and the big wrecking crane swung smoothly out of its cradle and over the wreckage. The end of the crane arm was directly over Ferguson. "Lemme have the spreaders," Clay called. The arm dipped and from either side of the tip, a pair of flanges shot out like tusks on an elephant. "Put 'er in neutral," Clay directed. Martin pressed another lever and the crane now could be moved in any direction by fingertip pulls at its extremity. Ferguson carefully guided the crane with its projecting tusks into the smashed orifice of the car window. "O.K., Ben, spread it."

The crane locked into position and the entire arm split open in a "V" from its base. Martin pressed steadily on the two levers controlling each side of the divided arm and the tusks dug into the sides of the smashed window. There was a steady screeching of tearing and ripping metal as the crane tore window and frame apart. "Hold it," Ferguson yelled and then eased himself into the widened hole.

"Ben," Kelly called from her perch atop the wreckage, "litter."

Martin raced to the rear of the patrol car where the sloping ramp stood open to the lighted dispensary. He snatched at one of the autolitters and triggered its tiny drive motor. A homing beacon in his helmet guided the litter as it rolled down the ramp, turned by itself and rolled across the pavement a foot behind him. It stopped when he stopped and Ben touched another switch, cutting the homing beacon.

Clay's head appeared out of the hole. "Get it up here, Ben. I can get her out. And I think there's another one alive still further down."

Martin raised the crane and its ripper bars retracted. The split arms spewed a pair of cables terminating in magnalocks. The cables dangled over the ends of the autolitter, caught the lift plates on the litter and a second later, the cart was swinging beside the smashed window as Clay and Kelly eased the torn body of a woman out of the wreckage and onto the litter. As Ben brought the litter back to the pavement, the column of smoke had thickened. He disconnected the cables and homed the stretcher back to the patrol car. The hospital cart with its unconscious victim rolled smoothly back to the car, up the ramp and into the dispensary to the surgical table.

Martin climbed up the wreckage beside Kelly. Inside the twisted interior of the car, the thick smoke all but obscured the bent back of the younger trooper and his powerful handlight barely penetrated the gloom. Blood was smeared over almost every surface and the stink of leaking jet fuel was virtually overpowering. From the depths of the nightmarish scene came a tortured scream. Kelly reached into a coverall pocket and produced another sedation hypo. She squirmed around and started to slip down into the wreckage with Ferguson. Martin grabbed her arm. "No, Kelly, this thing's ready to blow. Come on, Clay, get out of there. Now!"

Ferguson continued to pry at the twisted plates below him.

"I said 'get out of there' Ferguson," the senior officer roared. "And that's an order."

Clay straightened up and put his hands on the edge of the window to boost himself out. "Ben, there's a guy alive down there. We just can't leave him."

"Get down from there, Kelly," Martin ordered. "I know that man's down there just as well as you do, Clay. But we won't be helping him one damn bit if we get blown to hell and gone right along with him. Now get outta there and maybe we can pull this thing apart and get to him before it does blow."

The lanky Canadian eased out of the window and the two troopers moved back to the patrol car. Kelly was already in her dispensary, working on the injured woman.

Martin slid into his control seat. "Shut your ramp, Kelly," he called over the intercom. "I'm going to move around to the other side."

The radio broke in. "Car 119 to Car 56, we're just turning into the divider. Be there in a minute."

"Snap it up," Ben replied. "We need you in a hurry."

As he maneuvered Beulah around the wreckage he snapped orders to Ferguson.

"Get the foam nozzles up, just in case, and then stand by on the crane."

A mile away, they saw the flashing emergency lights of Car 119 as it raced diagonally across the yellow and blue lanes, whipping with ponderous ease through the moving traffic.

"Take the south side, 119," Martin called out. "We'll try and pull this mess apart."

"Affirmative," came the reply. Even before the other patrol vehicle came to a halt, its crane was swinging out from the side, and the ganged magnalocks were dangling from their cables.

"O.K., kid," Ben ordered, "hook it."

At the interior crane controls, Clay swung Beulah's crane and cable mags towards the wreckage. The magnalocks slammed into the metallic mess with a bang almost at the same instant the locks hit the other side from Car 119.

Clay eased up the cable slack. "Good," Ben called to both Clay and the operating trooper in the other car, "now let's pull it . . . LOOK OUT! FOAM . . . FOAM . . . FOAM," he yelled.

The ugly, deep red fireball from the exploding wreckage was still growing as Clay slammed down on the fire-control panel.

A curtain of thick chemical foam burst from the poised nozzles atop Beulah's hull and a split-second later, another stream of foam erupted from the other patrol car. The dense, oxygen-absorbing retardant blanket snuffed the fire out in three seconds. The cranes were still secured to the foam-covered heap of metal. "Never mind the caution," Ben called out, "get it apart. Fast."

Both crane operators slammed their controls into reverse and with an ear-splitting screech, the twisted frames of the two vehicles ripped apart into tumbled heaps of broken metal and plastics. Martin and Ferguson jumped down the hatch steps and into ankle-deep foam and oil. They waded and slipped around the front of the car to join the troopers from the other car.

Ferguson was pawing at the scum-covered foam near the mangled section of one of the cars. "He should be right about," Clay paused and bent over, "here." He straightened up as the others gathered around the scorched and ripped body of a man, half-submerged in the thick foam. "Kelly," he called over the helmet transmitter, "open your door. We'll need a couple of sacks."

He trudged to the rear of the patrol car and met the girl standing in the door with a pair of folded plastic morgue bags in her hands. Behind her, Clay could see the body of the woman on the surgical table, an array of tubes and probes leading to plasma drip bottles and other equipment racked out over the table.

"How is she?"

"Not good," Kelly replied. "Skull fracture, ruptured spleen, broken ribs and double leg fractures. I've already called for an ambulance."

Ferguson nodded, took the bags from her and waded back through the foam.

The four troopers worked in the silence of the deserted traffic lane. A hundred yards away, traffic was moving steadily in the slow white lane. Three-quarters of a mile to the south, fast and ultra high traffic sped at its normal pace in the blue and yellow lanes. Westbound green was still being rerouted into the slower white lane, around the scene of the accident. It was now twenty-six minutes since Car 56 had received the accident call. The light snow flurries had turned to a steady fall of thick wet flakes, melting as they hit on the warm pavement but beginning to coat the pitiful flotsam of the accident.

The troopers finished the gruesome task of getting the bodies into the morgue sacks and laid beside the dispensary ramp for the ambulance to pick up with the surviving victim. Car 119's

MSO had joined Kelly in Beulah's dispensary to give what help she might. The four patrol troopers began the grim task of probing the scattered wreckage for other possible victims, personal possessions and identification. They were stacking a small pile of hand luggage when the long, low bulk of the ambulance swung out of the police lane and rolled to a stop. Longer than the patrol cars but without the non-medical emergency facilities, the ambulance was in reality a mobile hospital. A full, scrubbed-up surgical team was waiting in the main operating room even as the ramps opened and the techs headed for Car 56. The team had been briefed by radio on the condition of the patient; had read the full recordings of the diagnostician; and were watching transmitted pulse and respiration graphs on their own screens while the transfer was being made.

The two women MSOs had unlocked the surgical table in Beulah's dispensary and a plastic tent covered not only the table and the patient, but also the plasma and Regen racks overhead. The entire table and rig slid down the ramp onto a motor-driven dolly from the ambulance. Without delay, it wheeled across the open few feet of pavement into the ambulance and to the surgery room. The techs locked the table into place in the other vehicle and left the surgery. From a storage compartment, they wheeled out a fresh patrol dispensary table and rack and placed it in Kelly's miniature surgery. The dead went into the morgue aboard the ambulance, the ramp closed and the ambulance swung around and headed across the traffic lanes to eastbound NAT-26 and Philadelphia.

Outside, the four troopers had completed the task of collecting what little information they could from the smashed vehicles.

They returned to their cars and One One Nine's medical-surgical officer headed back to her own cubbyhole.

The other patrol car swung into position almost touching Beulah's left flank. With Ben at the control seat, on command, both cars extended broad bulldozer blades from their bows. "Let's go," Ben ordered. The two patrol vehicles moved slowly down the roadway, pushing all of the scattered scraps and parts onto a single great heap. They backed off, shifted direction towards the center police lane and began shoving the debris, foam and snow out of the green lane. At the edge of the police lane, both cars unshipped cranes and magnalifted the junk over the divider barrier onto the one-hundred-foot-wide service strip bordering the police lane. A slow cargo wrecker was already on the way from Pittsburgh barracks to pick up the wreckage and haul it away. When the last of the metallic debris had been deposited off the traffic lane, Martin called Control.

"Car 56 is clear. NAT 26-west green is clear."

Philly Control acknowledged. Seven miles to the east, the amber warning lights went dark and the detour barrier at Crossover 85 sank back into the roadway. Three minutes later, traffic was again flashing by on green lane past the two halted patrol cars.

"Pitt Control, this is Car 119 clear of accident," the other car reported.

"Car 119 resume eastbound patrol," came the reply.

The other patrol car pulled away. The two troopers waved at Martin and Ferguson in Beulah. "See you later and thanks," Ben called out. He switched to intercom. "Kelly. Any ID on that woman?"

"Not a thing, Ben," she replied. "About forty years old, and she had a wedding band. She never was conscious, so I can't help you."

Ben nodded and looked over at his partner. "Go get into some dry clothes, kid," he said, "while I finish the report. Then you can take it for a while."

Clay nodded and headed back to the crew quarters.

Ben racked his helmet beside his seat and fished out a cigarette. He reached for an accident report form from the work rack behind his seat and began writing, glancing up from time to time to gaze thoughtfully at the scene of the accident. When he had finished, he thumbed the radio transmitter and called Philly Control. Somewhere in the bloody, oil and foam covered pile of wreckage were the registration plates for the two vehicles involved. When the wrecker collected the debris, it would be machine sifted in Pittsburgh and the plates fed to records and then relayed to Philadelphia where the identifications could be added to Ben's report. When he had finished reading his report he asked, "How's the woman?"

"Still alive, but just barely," Philly Control answered. "Ben, did you say there were just two vehicles involved?"

"That's all we found," Martin replied.

"And were they both in the green?"

"Yes, why?"

"That's funny," Philly controller replied, "we got the calls as a sideswipe in white that put one of the cars over into the green. There should have been a third vehicle."

"That's right," Ben exclaimed. "We were so busy trying to get that gal out and then making the try for the other man I never even thought to look for another car. You suppose that guy took off?"

"It's possible," the controller said. "I'm calling a gate filter until we know for sure. I've got the car number on the driver that reported the accident. I'll get hold of him and see if he can give us a lead on the third car. You go ahead with your patrol and I'll let you know what I find out."

"Affirmative," Ben replied. He eased the patrol car onto the police lane and turned west once again. Clay reappeared in the cab, dressed in fresh coveralls. "I'll take it, Ben. You go and clean up now. Kelly's got a pot of fresh coffee in the galley." Ferguson slid into his control seat.

A light skiff of snow covered the service strip and the dividers as Car 56 swung back westward in the red lane. Snow was falling steadily but melting as it touched the warm ferrophalt pavement in all lanes. The wet roadways glistened with the lights of hundreds of vehicles. The chronometer read 1840 hours. Clay pushed the car up to a steady 75, just about apace with the slowest traffic in the white lane. To the south, densities were much lighter in the blue and yellow lanes and even the green had thinned out. It would stay moderately light now for another hour until the dinner stops were over and the night travelers again rolled onto the thruways.

Kelly was putting frozen steaks into the infra-oven as Ben walked through to crew quarters. Her coverall sleeves were rolled to the elbows as she worked and a vagrant strand of copper hair curled over her forehead. As Martin passed by, he caught a faint whisper of perfume and he smiled appreciatively.

In the tiny crew quarters, he shut the door to the galley and stripped out of his wet coveralls and boots. He eyed the shower stall across the passageway.

"Hey, mother," he yelled to Kelly, "have I got time for a shower before dinner?"

"Yes, but make it a quickie," she called back.

Five minutes later he stepped into the galley, his dark, crew-cut hair still damp. Kelly was setting plastic, disposable dishes on the little swing-down table that doubled as a food bar and work desk. Ben peered into a simmering pot and sniffed. "Smells good. What's for dinner, Hiawatha?"

"Nothing fancy. Steak, potatoes, green beans, apple pie and coffee."

Ben's mouth watered. "You know, sometimes I wonder whether one of your ancestors didn't come out of New England. Your menus always seem to coincide with my ideas of a perfect meal." He noted the two places set at the table. Ben glanced out the galley port into the headlight-striped darkness. Traffic was still light. In the distance, the night sky glowed with the lights of Chambersburg, north of the thruway.

"We might as well pull up for dinner," he said. "It's pretty slow out there."

Kelly shoved dishes over and began laying out a third setting. About half the time on patrol, the crew ate in shifts on the go, with one of the patrol troopers in the cab at all times. When traffic permitted, they pulled off to the service strip and ate together. With the communications system always in service, control stations could reach them anywhere in the big vehicle.

The sergeant stepped into the cab and tapped Ferguson on the shoulder. "Dinnertime, Clay. Pull her over and we'll try some of your gracious living."

"Light the candles and pour the wine," Clay quipped, "I'll be with you in a second."

Car 56 swung out to the edge of the police lane and slowed down. Clay eased the car onto the strip and stopped. He checked the radiodometer and called in. "Pitt Control, this is Car 56 at Marker 158. Dinner is being served in the dining car to the rear. Please do not disturb."

"Affirmative, Car 56," Pittsburgh Control responded. "Eat heartily, it may be going out of style." Clay grinned and flipped the radio to remote and headed for the galley.

Seated around the little table, the trio cut into their steaks. Parked at the north edge of the police lane, the patrol car was just a few feet from the green lane divider strip and cars and cargo carriers flashed by as they ate.

Clay chewed on a sliver of steak and looked at Kelly. "I'd marry you, Pocahontas, if you'd ever learn to cook steaks like beef instead of curing them like your ancestral buffalo robes. When are you going to learn that good beef has to be bloody to be edible?"

The girl glared at him. "If that's what it takes to make it edible, you're going to be an epicurean delight in just about one second if I hear another word about my cooking. And that's also the second crack about my noble ancestors in the past five minutes. I've always wondered about the surgical techniques my great-great-great grandpop used when he lifted a paleface's hair. One more word, Clay Ferguson, and I'll have your scalp flying from Beulah's antenna like a coontail on a kid's scooter."

Ben bellowed and nearly choked. "Hey, kid," he spluttered at Clay, "ever notice how the wrong one of her ancestors keeps coming to the surface? That was the Irish."

Clay polished off the last of his steak and reached for the individual frozen pies Kelly had put in the oven with the steak. "Now that's another point," he said, waving his fork at Kelly. "The Irish lived so long on potatoes and prayers that when they get a piece of meat on their menu, they don't know how to do anything but boil it."

"That tears it," the girl exploded. She pushed back from the table and stood up. "I've cooked the last meal this big, dumb Canuck will ever get from me. I hope you get chronic indigestion and then come crawling to me for help. I've got something back there I've been wanting to dose you with for a long time."

She stormed out of the galley and slammed the door behind her. Ben grinned at the stunned look on Clay's face. "Now what got her on the warpath?" Clay asked. Before Ben could answer the radio speaker in the ceiling came to life.

"Car 56 this is Pitt Control."

Martin reached for the transmit switch beside the galley table. "This is Five Six, go ahead."

"Relay from Philly Control," the speaker blared. "Reference the accident at Marker 92 at 1648 hours this date; Philly Control reports a third vehicle definitely involved."

Ben pulled out a pencil and Clay shoved a message pad across the table.

"James J. Newhall, address 3409 Glen Cove Drive, New York City, license number BHT 4591 dash 747 dash 1609, was witness to the initial impact. He reports that a white over green, late model Travelaire, with two men in it, sideswiped one of the two vehicles involved in the fatal accident. The Travelaire did not stop but accelerated after the impact. Newhall was unable to get the full license number but the first six units were QABR dash 46 ... rest of numerals unknown."

Ben cut in. "Have we got identification on our fatalities yet?"

"Affirmative, Five Six," the radio replied. "The driver of the car struck by the hit-and-run was a Herman Lawrence Hanover, age forty-two, of 13460 One Hundred Eighty-First Street South, Camden, New Jersey, license number LFM 4151 dash 603 dash 2738. With him was his wife, Clara, age forty-one, same address. Driver of the green lane car was George R. Hamilton, age thirty-five, address Box 493, Route 12, Tucumcari, New Mexico."

Ben broke in once more. "You indicate all three are fatalities.

Is this correct, Pitt Control? The woman was alive when she was transferred to the ambulance."

"Stand by, Five Six, and I'll check."

A moment later Pitt Control was back. "That is affirmative, Five Six. The woman died at 1745 hours. Here is additional information. A vehicle answering to the general description of the hit-and-run vehicle is believed to have been involved in an armed robbery and multiple murder earlier this date at Wilmington, Delaware. Philly Control is now checking for additional details. Gate filters have been established on NAT 26-West from Marker-Exit 100 to Marker-Exit 700. Also, filters on all interchanges. Pitt Control out."

Kelly Lightfoot, her not-too-serious peeve forgotten, had come back into the galley to listen to the radio exchange. The men got up from the table and Clay gathered the disposable dishware and tossed them into the waste receiver.

"We'd better get rolling," Ben said, "those clowns could still be on the thruway, although they could have got off before the filters went up."

They moved to the cab and took their places. The big engines roared into action as Ben rolled Car 56 back onto the policeway. Kelly finished straightening up in the galley and then came forward to sit on the jump seat between the two troopers. The snow had stopped again but the roadways were still slick and glistening under the headlights. Beulah rolled steadily along on her broad tracks, now cruising at one hundred miles an hour. The steady whine of the cold night wind penetrated faintly into the sound-proofed and insulated cabin canopy. Clay cut out the cabin lights, leaving only the instrument panel glowing faintly along with the phosphorescent buttons and knobs on the arms of the control seats.

A heavy express cargo carrier flashed by a quarter of a mile away in the blue lane, its big bulk lit up like a Christmas tree with running and warning lights. To their right, Clay caught the first glimpse of a set of flashing amber warning lights coming up from behind in the green lane. A minute later, a huge cargo carrier came abreast of the patrol car and then pulled ahead. On its side was a glowing star of the United States Army. A minute later, another Army carrier rolled by.

"That's the missile convoy out of Aberdeen," Clay told Kelly. "I wish our hit-runner had tackled one of those babies. We'd have scraped him up instead of those other people."

The convoy rolled on past at a steady one hundred twenty-five miles an hour. Car 56 flashed under a crossover and into a long, gentle curve. The chronometer clicked up to 2100 hours and the radio sang out. "Cars 207, 56 and 82, this is Pitt Control. 2100 hours density report follows ..."

Pittsburgh Control read off the figures for the three cars. Car 82 was one hundred fifty miles ahead of Beulah, Car 207 about the same distance to the rear. The density report ended and a new voice came on the air.

"Attention all cars and all stations, this is Washington Criminal Control." The new voice paused, and across the continent, troopers on every thruway, control station, checkpoint and relay block, reached for clipboard and pen.

"Washington Criminal Control continuing, all cars and all stations, special attention to all units east of the Mississippi. At 1510 hours this date, two men held up the First National Bank of Wilmington, Delaware, and escaped with an estimated one hundred seventy-five thousand dollars. A bank guard and two tellers, together with five bank customers were killed by these subjects using automatic weapon fire to make good their escape. They were observed leaving the scene in a late model, white-over-green Travelaire sedan, license unknown. A car of the same make, model and color was stolen from Annapolis, Maryland, a short time prior to the holdup. The stolen vehicle, now believed to be the getaway car, bears USN license number QABR dash 468 dash 1113 ..."

"That's our baby," Ben murmured as he and Clay scribbled on their message forms.

" ... Motor number ZB 1069432," Washington Criminal Control continued. "This car is also now believed to have been involved in a hit-and-run fatal accident on NAT 26-West at Marker 92 at approximately 1648 hours this date.

"Subject Number One is described as WMA, twenty to twenty-five years, five feet, eleven inches tall, medium complexion, dark hair and eyes, wearing a dark-gray sports jacket and dark pants, and wearing a gray sports cap. He was wearing a ring with a large red stone on his left hand.

"Subject Number Two is described as WMA, twenty to twenty-five years, six feet, light, ruddy complexion and reddish brown hair, light colored eyes. Has scar on back left side of neck. Wearing light-brown suit, green shirt and dark tie, no hat.

"These subjects are believed to be armed and psychotically dangerous. If observed, approach with extreme caution and inform nearest control of contact. Both subjects now under multiple federal warrants charging bank robbery, murder and hit-and-run murder. All cars and stations acknowledge. Washington Criminal Control out."

The air chattered as the cars checked into their nearest controls with "acknowledged."

"This looks like it could be a long night," Kelly said, rising to her feet. "I'm going to sack out. Call me if you need me."

"Good night, princess," Ben called.

"Hey, Hiawatha," Clay called out as Kelly paused in the galley door. "I didn't mean what I said about your steaks. Your great-great-great grandpop would have gone around with his bare scalp hanging out if he had had to use a buffalo hide cured like that steak was cooked."

He reached back at the same instant and slammed the cabin door just as Kelly came charging back. She slammed into the door, screamed and then went storming back to the dispensary while Clay doubled over in laugher.

Ben smiled at his junior partner. "Boy, you're gonna regret that. Don't say I didn't warn you."

Martin turned control over to the younger trooper and relaxed in his seat to go over the APB from Washington. Car 56 bored steadily through the night. The thruway climbed easily up the slight grade cut through the hills north of Wheeling, West Virginia, and once more snow began falling.

Clay reached over and flipped on the video scanners. Four small screens, one for each of the westbound lanes, glowed with a soft red light. The monitors were synchronized with the radiodometer and changed view at every ten-mile marker. Viewing cameras mounted on towers between each lane, lined the thruway, aimed eastward at the on-coming traffic back to the next bank of cameras ten miles away. Infra-red circuits took over from standard scan at dark. A selector system in the cars gave the troopers the option of viewing either the block they were currently patrolling; the one ahead of the next ten-mile block; or, the one they had just passed. As a rule, the selection was based on the speed of the car. Beamed signals from each block automatically switched the view as the patrol car went past the towers. Clay put the slower lane screens on the block they were in, turned the blue and yellow lanes to the block ahead.

They rolled past the interchange with NAT 114-South out of Cleveland and the traffic densities picked up in all lanes as many of the southbound vehicles turned west on to NAT 26. The screens flicked and Clay came alert. Some fifteen miles ahead in the one-hundred-fifty-to-two-hundred-mile an hour blue lane, a glowing dot remained motionless in the middle of the lane and the other racing lights of the blue lane traffic were sheering around it like a racing river current parting around a boulder.

"Trouble," he said to Martin, as he shoved forward on the throttle.

A stalled car in the middle of the highspeed lane was an invitation to disaster. The bull horn blared as Beulah leaped past the two hundred mile an hour mark and safety cocoons slid into place. Aft in the dispensary, Kelly was sealed into her bunk by a cocoon rolling out of the wall and encasing the hospital bed.

Car 56 slanted across the police lane with red lights flashing and edged into the traffic flow in the blue lane. The great, red winking lights and the emergency radio siren signal began clearing a path for the troopers. Vehicles began edging to both sides of the lane to shift to crossovers to the yellow or green lanes. Clay aimed Beulah at the motionless dot on the screen and eased back from the four-mile-a-minute speed. The patrol car slowed and the headlight picked up the stalled vehicle a mile ahead. The cocoons opened and Ben slipped on his work helmet and dropped down the steps to the side hatch. Clay brought Beulah to a halt a dozen yards directly to the rear of the stalled car, the great bulk of the patrol vehicle with its warning lights serving as a shield against any possible fuzzy-headed speeders that might not be observing the road.

As Martin reached for the door, the Wanted bulletin flashed through his head. "What make of car is that, Clay?"

"Old jalopy Tritan with some souped-up rigs. Probably kids," the junior officer replied. "It looks O.K."

Ben nodded and swung down out of the patrol car. He walked quickly to the other car, flashing his handlight on the side of the vehicle as he went up to the driver. The interior lights were on and inside, two obviously frightened young couples smiled with relief at the sight of the uniform coveralls. A freckled-faced teen-ager in a dinner jacket was in the driver's seat and had the blister window open. He grinned up at Martin. "Boy, am I glad to see you, officer," he said.

"What's the problem?" Ben asked.

"I guess she blew an impeller," the youth answered. "We were heading for a school dance at Cincinnati and she was boiling along like she was in orbit when blooey she just quit."

Ben surveyed the old jet sedan. "What year is this clunker?" he asked. The kid told him. "You kids have been told not to use this lane for any vehicle that old." He waved his hand in protest as the youngster started to tell him how many modifications he had made on the car. "It doesn't make one bit of difference whether you've put a first-stage Moon booster on this wreck. It's not supposed to be in the blue or yellow. And this thing probably shouldn't have been allowed out of the white—or even on the thruway."

The youngster flushed and bit his lip in embarrassment at the giggles from the two evening-frocked girls in the car.

"Well, let's get you out of here." Ben touched his throat mike. "Drop a light, Clay and then let's haul this junk pile away."

In the patrol car, Ferguson reached down beside his seat and tugged at a lever. From a recess in Beulah's stern, a big portable red warning light dropped to the pavement. As it touched the surface, it automatically flashed to life, sending out a bright, flashing red warning signal into the face of any approaching traffic. Clay eased the patrol car around the stalled vehicle and then backed slow into position, guided by Martin's radioed instructions. A tow-bar extruded from the back of the police vehicle and a magnaclamp locked onto the front end of the teenager's car. The older officer walked back to the portable warning light and rolled it on its four wheels to the rear plate of the jalopy where another magnalock secured it to the car. Beulah's two big rear warning lights still shone above the low silhouette of the passenger car, along with the mobile lamp on the jalopy. Martin walked back to the patrol car and climbed in.

He slid into his seat and nodded at Clay. The patrol car, with the disabled vehicle in tow moved forward and slanted left towards the police lane. Martin noted the mileage marker on the radiodometer and fingered the transmitter. "Chillicothe Control this is Car 56."

"This Chillicothe. Go ahead Five Six."

"We picked up some kids in a stalled heap on the blue at Marker 382 and we've got them in tow now," Ben said. "Have a wrecker meet us and take them off our hands."

"Affirmative, Five Six. Wrecker will pick you up at Marker 412."

Clay headed the patrol car and its trailed load into an emergency entrance to the middle police lane and slowly rolled westward. The senior trooper reached into his records rack and pulled out a citation book.

"You going to nail these kids?" Clay asked.

"You're damned right I am," Martin replied, beginning to fill in the violation report. "I'd rather have this kid hurting in the pocketbook than dead. If we turn him loose, he'll think he got away with it this time and try it again. The next time he might not be so lucky."

"I suppose you're right," Clay said, "but it does seem a little rough."

Ben swung around in his seat and surveyed his junior officer. "Sometimes I think you spent four years in the patrol academy with your head up your jet pipes," he said. He fished out another cigarette and took a deep drag.

"You've had four solid years of law; three years of electronics and jet and air-drive engine mechanics and engineering; pre-med, psychology, math, English, Spanish and a smattering of Portuguese, to say nothing of dozens of other subjects. You graduated in the upper tenth of your class with a B.S. in both Transportation and Criminology which is why you're riding patrol and not punching a computer or tinkering with an engine. You'd think with all that education that somewhere along the line you'd have learned to think with your head instead of your emotions."

Clay kept a studied watch on the roadway. The minute Ben had turned and swung his legs over the side of the seat and pulled out a cigarette, Clay knew that it was school time in Car 56. Instructor Sergeant Ben Martin was in a lecturing mood. It was time for all good pupils to keep their big, fat mouths shut.

"Remember San Francisco de Borja?" Ben queried. Clay nodded. "And you still think I'm too rough on them?" Ben pressed.

Ferguson's memory went back to last year's fifth patrol. He and Ben with Kelly riding hospital, had been assigned to NAT 200-North, running out of Villahermosa on the Guatamalan border of Mexico to Edmonton Barracks in Canada. It was the second night of the patrol. Some seven hundred fifty miles north of Mexico City, near the town of San Francisco de Borja, a gang of teenage Mexican youngsters had gone roaring up the yellow at speeds touching on four hundred miles an hour. Their car, a beat-up, fifteen-year-old veteran of less speedy and much rockier local mountain roads, had been gimmicked by the kids so that it bore no resemblance to its original manufacture.

From a junkyard they had obtained a battered air lift, smashed almost beyond use in the crackup of a ten-thousand dollar sports cruiser. The kids pried, pounded and bent the twisted impeller lift blades back into some semblance of alignment. From another wreck of a cargo carrier came a pair of 4000-pound thrust engines. They had jury-rigged the entire mess so that it stuck together on the old heap. Then they hit the thruway—nine of them packed into the jalopy—the oldest one just seventeen years old. They were doing three hundred fifty when they flashed past the patrol car and Ben had roared off in pursuit. The senior officer whipped the big patrol car across the crowded high speed blue lane, jockeyed into the ultra-high yellow and then turned on the power.

By this time the kids realized they had been spotted and they cranked their makeshift power plant up to the last notch. The most they could get out of it was four hundred and it was doing just that as Car 56, clocking better than five hundred, pulled in behind them. The patrol car was still three hundred yards astern when one of the bent and re-bent impeller blades let go. The out-of-balance fan, turning at close to 35,000 rpm's, flew to pieces and the air cushion vanished. At four hundred miles an hour, the body of the old jalopy fell the twelve inches to the pavement and both front wheels caved under. There was a momentary shower of sparks, then the entire vehicle snapped cart-wheeling more than eighty feet into the air and exploded. Pieces of car and bodies were scattered for a mile down the thruway and the only whole, identifiable human bodies were those of the three youngsters thrown out and sent hurtling to their deaths more than two hundred feet away.

Clay's mind snapped back to the present.

"Write 'em up," he said quietly to Martin. The senior officer gave a satisfied nod and turned back to his citation pad.

At marker 412, which was also the Columbus turnoff, a big patrol wrecker was parked on the side strip, engines idling, service and warning lights blinking. Clay pulled the patrol car alongside and stopped. He disconnected the tow bar and the two officers climbed out into the cold night air. They walked back to the teenager's car. Clay went to the rear of the disabled car and unhooked the warning light while Martin went to the driver's window. He had his citation book in hand. The youngster in the driver's seat went white at the sight of the violation pad. "May I see your license, please," Ben asked. The boy fumbled in a back pocket and then produced a thin, metallic tab with his name, age, address and license number etched into the indestructible and unalterable metal.

"Also your car registration," Ben added. The youth unclipped a similar metal strip from the dashboard.

The trooper took the two tabs and walked to the rear of the patrol car. He slid back to a panel to reveal two thin slots in the hull. Martin slid the driver's license into one of the slots, the registration tab into the other. He pressed a button below each slot. Inside the car, a magnetic reader and auto-transmitter "scanned" the magnetic symbols implanted in the tags. The information was fed instantly to Continental Headquarters Records division at Colorado Springs. In fractions of a second, the great computers at Records were comparing the information on the tags with all previous traffic citations issued anywhere in the North American continent in the past forty-five years since the birth of the Patrol. The information from the driver's license and registration tab had been relayed from Beulah via the nearest patrol relay point. The answer came back the same way.

Above the license recording slot were two small lights. The first flashed green, "license is in order and valid." The second flashed green as well, "no previous citations." Ben withdrew the tag from the slot. Had the first light come on red, he would have placed the driver under arrest immediately. Had the second light turned amber, it would have indicated a previous minor violation. This, Ben would have noted on the new citation. If the second light had been red, this would have meant either a major previous violation or more than one minor citation. Again, the driver would have been under immediate arrest. The law was mandatory. One big strike and you're out—two foul tips and the same story. And "out" meant just that. Fines, possibly jail or prison sentence and lifetime revocation of driving privileges.

Ben flipped the car registration slot to "stand-by" and went back to the teenager's car. Even though they were parked on the service strip of the police emergency lane, out of all traffic, the youngsters stayed in the car. This one point of the law they knew and knew well. Survival chances were dim anytime something went wrong on the highspeed thruways. That little margin of luck vanished once outside the not-too-much-better security of the vehicle body.

Martin finished writing and then slipped the driver's license into a pocket worked into the back of the metallic paper foil of the citation blank. He handed the pad into the window to the driver together with a carbon stylus.

The boy's lip trembled and he signed the citation with a shaky hand.

Ben ripped off the citation blank and license, fed them into the slot on the patrol car and pressed both the car registration and license "record" buttons. Ten seconds later the permanent record of the citation was on file in Colorado Springs and a duplicate recording of the action was in the Continental traffic court docket recorder nearest to the driver's hometown. Now, no power in three nations could "fix" that ticket. Ben withdrew the citation and registration tag and walked back to the car. He handed the boy the license and registration tab, together with a copy of the citation. Ben bent down to peer into the car.

"I made it as light on you as I could," he told the young diver. "You're charged with improper use of the thruway. That's a minor violation. By rights, I should have cited you for illegal usage." He looked around slowly at each of the young people. "You look like nice kids," he said. "I think you'll grow up to be nice people. I want you around long enough to be able to vote in a few years. Who knows, maybe I'll be running for president then and I'll need your votes. It's a cinch that falling apart in the middle of two-hundred-mile an hour traffic is no way to treat future voters.

"Good night, Kids." He smiled and walked away from the car. The three young passengers smiled back at Ben. The young driver just stared unhappily at the citation.

Clay stood talking with the wrecker crewmen. Ben nodded to him and mounted into the patrol car. The young Canadian crushed out his cigarette and swung up behind the sergeant. Clay went to the control seat when he saw Martin pause in the door to the galley.

"I'm going to get a cup of coffee," the older officer said, "and then take the first shift. You keep Beulah 'til I get back."

Clay nodded and pushed the throttles forward. Car 56 rolled back into the police lane while behind it, the wrecker hooked onto the disabled car and swung north into the crossover. Clay checked both the chronometer and the radiodometer and then reported in. "Cinncy Control this is Car 56 back in service." Cincinnati Control acknowledged.

Ten minute later, Ben reappeared in the cab, slid into the left-hand seat. "Hit the sack, kid," he told Ferguson. The chronometer read 2204. "I'll wake you at midnight—or sooner, if anything breaks."

Ferguson stood up and stretched, then went into the galley. He poured himself a cup of coffee and carrying it with him, went back to the crew quarters. He closed the door to the galley and sat down on the lower bunk to sip his coffee. When he had finished, he tossed the cup into the basket, reached and dimmed the cubby lights and kicked off his boots. Still in his coveralls, Clay stretched out on the bunk and sighed luxuriously. He reached up and pressed a switch on the bulkhead above his pillow and the muted sounds of music from a standard broadcast commercial station drifted into the bunk area. Clay closed his eyes and let the sounds of the music and the muted rumble of the engines lull him to sleep. It took almost fifteen seconds for him to be in deep slumber.

Ben pushed Beulah up to her steady seventy-five-mile-an-hour cruising speed, moved to the center of the quarter-mile-wide police lane and locked her tracks into autodrive. He relaxed back in his seat and divided his gaze between the video monitors and the actual scene on either side of him in the night. Once again the sky was lighted, this time much brighter on the horizon as the roadways swept to the south of Cincinnati.

Traffic was once again heavy and fast with the blue and green carrying almost equal loads while white was really crowded and even the yellow "zoom" lane was beginning to fill. The 2200 hour density reports from Cinncy had been given before the Ohio State-Cal football game traffic had hit the thruways and densities now were peaking near twenty thousand vehicles for the one-hundred-mile block of westbound NAT 26 out of Cincinnati.

Back to the east, near the eastern Ohio state line, Martin could hear Car 207 calling for a wrecker and meat wagon. Beulah rumbled on through the night. The video monitors flicked to the next ten-mile stretch as the patrol car rolled past another interchange. More vehicles streamed onto the westbound thruways, crossing over and dropping down into the same lanes they held coming out of the north-south road. Seven years on patrols had created automatic reflexes in the trooper sergeant. Out of the mass of cars and cargoes streaming along the rushing tide of traffic, his eye picked out the track of one vehicle slanting across the white lane just a shade faster than the flow of traffic. The vehicle was still four or five miles ahead. It wasn't enough out of the ordinary to cause more than a second, almost unconscious glance, on the part of the veteran officer. He kept his view shifting from screen to screen and out to the sides of the car.

But the reflexes took hold again as his eye caught the track of the same vehicle as it hit the crossover from white to green, squeezed into the faster lane and continued its sloping run towards the next faster crossover. Now Martin followed the movement of the car almost constantly. The moving blip had made the cutover across the half-mile wide green lane in the span of one crossover and was now whipping into the merger lane that would take it over the top of the police lane and drop down into the one hundred fifty to two hundred mile an hour blue. If the object of his scrutiny straightened out in the blue, he'd let it go. The driver had been bordered on violation in his fast crossover in the face of heavy traffic. If he kept it up in the now-crowded high-speed lane, he was asking for sudden death. The monitors flicked to the next block and Ben waited just long enough to see the speeding car make a move to the left, cutting in front of a speeding cargo carrier. Ben slammed Beulah into high. Once again the bull horn blared as the cocoons slammed shut, this time locking both Clay and Kelly into their bunks, sealing Ben into the control seat.

Beulah lifted on her air cushion and the twin jets roared as she accelerated down the police lane at three hundred miles an hour. Ben closed the gap on the speeder in less than a minute and then edged over to the south side of the police lane to make the jump into the blue lane. The red emergency lights and the radio siren had already cleared a hole for him in the traffic pattern and he eased back on the finger throttles as the patrol car sailed over the divider and into the blue traffic lane. Now he had eyeball contact with the speeding car, still edging over towards the ultra-high lane. On either side of the patrol car traffic gave way, falling back or moving to the left and right. Car 56 was now directly behind the speeding passenger vehicle. Ben fingered the cut-in switch that put his voice signal onto the standard vehicular emergency frequency—the band that carried the automatic siren-warning to all vehicles.

The patrol car was still hitting above the two-hundred-mile-an-hour mark and was five hundred feet behind the speeder. The headlamp bathed the other car in a white glare, punctuated with angry red flashes from the emergency lights.

"You are directed to halt or be fired upon," Ben's voice roared out over the emergency frequency. Almost without warning, the speeding car began braking down with such deceleration that the gargantuan patrol car with its greater mass came close to smashing over it and crushing the small passenger vehicle like an insect. Ben cut all forward power, punched up full retrojet and at the instant he felt Beulah's tracks touch the pavement as the air cushion blew, he slammed on the brakes. Only the safety cocoon kept Martin from being hurled against the instrument panel and in their bunks, Kelly Lightfoot and Clay Ferguson felt their insides dragging down into their legs.

The safety cocoons snapped open and Clay jumped into his boots and leaped for the cab. "Speeder," Ben snapped as he jumped down the steps to the side hatch. Ferguson snatched up his helmet from the rack beside his seat and leaped down to join his partner. Ben ran up to the stopped car through a thick haze of smoke from the retrojets of the patrol car and the friction-burning braking of both vehicles. Ferguson circled to the other side of the car. As they flashed their handlights into the car, they saw the driver of the car kneeling on the floor beside the reclined passenger seat. A woman lay stretched out on the seat, twisting in pain. The man raised an agonized face to the officers. "My wife's going to have her baby right here!"

"Kelly," Ben yelled into his helmet transmitter. "Maternity!"

The dispensary ramp was halfway down before Ben had finished calling. Kelly jumped to the ground and sprinted around the corner of the patrol car, medical bag in hand.

She shoved Clay out of the way and opened the door on the passenger side. On the seat, the woman moaned and then muffled a scream. The patrol doctor laid her palm on the distended belly. "How fast are your pains coming?" she asked. Clay and Ben had moved away from the car a few feet.

"Litter," Kelly snapped over her shoulder. Clay raced for the patrol car while Ben unshipped a portable warning light and rolled it down the lane behind the patrol car. He flipped it to amber "caution" and "pass." Blinking amber arrows pointed to the left and right of the halted passenger vehicle and traffic in the blue lane began picking up speed and parting around the obstructions.

By the time he returned to the patrol car, Kelly had the expectant mother in the dispensary. She slammed the door in the faces of the three men and then she went to work.

The woman's husband slumped against the side of the patrol vehicle.

Ben dug out his pack of cigarettes and handed one to the shaking driver.

He waited until the man had taken a few drags before speaking.

"Mister, I don't know if you realize it or not but you came close to killing your wife, your baby and yourself," Ben said softly, "to say nothing of the possibility of killing several other families. Just what did you think you were doing?"

The driver's shoulders sagged and his hand shook as he took the cigarette from his mouth. "Honestly, officer, I don't know. I just got frightened to death," he said. He peered up at Martin. "This is our first baby, you see, and Ellen wasn't due for another week. We thought it would be all right to visit my folks in Cleveland and Ellen was feeling just fine. Well, anyway, we started home tonight—we live in Jefferson City—and just about the time I got on the thruway, Ellen started having pains. I was never so scared in my life. She screamed once and then tried to muffle them but I knew what was happening and all I could think of was to get her to a hospital. I guess I went out of my head, what with her moaning and the traffic and everything. The only place I could think of that had a hospital was Evansville, and I was going to get her there come hell or high water." The young man tossed away the half-smoked cigarette and looked up at the closed dispensary door. "Do you think she's all right?"

Ben sighed resignedly and put his hand on the man's shoulder. "Don't you worry a bit. She's got one of the best doctors in the continent in there with her. Come on." He took the husband by the arm and led him around to the patrol car cab hatch. "You climb up there and sit down. I'll be with you in a second."

The senior officer signaled to Ferguson. "Let's get his car out of the traffic, Clay," he directed. "You drive it."

Ben went back and retrieved the caution blinker and re-racked it in the side of the patrol car, then climbed up into the cab. He took his seat at the controls and indicated the jump seat next to him. "Sit down, son. We're going to get us and your car out of this mess before we all get clobbered."

He flicked the headlamp at Ferguson in the control seat of the passenger car and the two vehicles moved out. Ben kept the emergency lights on while they eased carefully cross-stream to the north and the safety of the police lane. Clay picked up speed at the outer edge of the blue lane and rolled along until he reached the first "patrol only" entrance through the divider to the service strip. Ben followed him in and then turned off the red blinkers and brought the patrol car to a halt behind the other vehicle.

The worried husband stood up and looked to the rear of the car. "What's making it so long?" he asked anxiously. "They've been in there a long time."

Ben smiled. "Sit down, son. These things take time. Don't you worry. If there were anything wrong, Kelly would let us know. She can talk to us on the intercom anytime she wants anything."

The man sat back down. "What's your name?" Ben inquired.

"Haverstraw," the husband replied distractedly, "George Haverstraw. I'm an accountant. That's my wife back there," he cried, pointing to the closed galley door. "That's Ellen."

"I know," Ben said gently. "You told us that."

Clay had come back to the patrol car and dropped into his seat across from the young husband. "Got a name picked out for the baby?" he asked.

Haverstraw's face lighted. "Oh, yes," he exclaimed. "If it's a boy, we're going to call him Harmon Pierce Haverstraw. That was my grandfather's name. And if she's a girl, it's going to be Caroline May after Ellen's mother and grandmother."

The intercom came to life. "Anyone up there?" Kelly's voice asked. Before they could answer, the wail of a baby sounded over the system. Haverstraw yelled.

"Congratulations, Mr. Haverstraw," Kelly said, "you've got a fine-looking son."

"Hey," the happy young father yelped, "hey, how about that? I've got a son." He pounded the two grinning troopers on the back. Suddenly he froze. "What about Ellen? How's Ellen?" he called out.

"She's just fine," Kelly replied. "We'll let you in here in a couple of minutes but we've got to get us gals and your new son looking pretty for papa. Just relax."

Haverstraw sank down onto the jump seat with a happy dazed look on his face.

Ben smiled and reached for the radio. "I guess our newest citizen deserves a ride in style," he said. "We're going to have to transfer Mrs. Haverstraw and er, oh yes, Master Harmon Pierce to an ambulance and then to a hospital now, George. You have any preference on where they go?"

"Gosh, no," the man replied. "I guess the closest one to wherever we are." He paused thoughtfully. "Just where are we? I've lost all sense of distance or time or anything else."

Ben looked at the radiodometer. "We're just about due south of Indianapolis. How would that be?"

"Oh, that's fine," Haverstraw replied.

"You can come back now, Mr. Haverstraw," Kelly called out. Haverstraw jumped up. Clay got up with him. "Come on, papa," he grinned, "I'll show you the way."

Ben smiled and then called into Indianapolis Control for an ambulance.

"Ambulance on the way," Control replied. "Don't you need a wrecker, too, Five Six?"

Ben grinned. "Not this time. We didn't lose one. We gained one."

He got up and went back to have a look at Harmon Pierce Haverstraw, age five minutes, temporary address, North American Continental Thruway 26-West, Mile Marker 632.

Five minutes later, mother and baby were in the ambulance heading north to the hospital. Haverstraw, calmed down with a sedative administered by Kelly, had nearly wrung their hands off in gratitude as he said good-by.

"I'll mail you all cigars when I get home," he shouted as he waved and climbed into his car.

Beulah's trio watched the new father ease carefully into the traffic as the ambulance headed down the police-way. Haverstraw would have to cut over to the next exchange and then go north to Indianapolis. He'd arrive later than his family. This time, he was the very picture of careful driving and caution as he threaded his way across the green.

"I wonder if he knows what brand of cigars I smoke?" Kelly mused.

The chrono clicked up to 2335 as Car 56 resumed patrol. Kelly plumped down onto the jump seat beside Ben. Clay was fiddling in the galley. "Why don't you go back to the sack?" Ben called.

"What, for a lousy twenty-five minutes," Clay replied. "I had a good nap before you turned the burners up to high. Besides, I'm hungry. Anyone else want a snack?"

Ben shook his head. "No, thanks," Kelly said. Ferguson finished slapping together a sandwich. Munching on it, he headed into the engine room to make the midnight check. Car 56 had now been on patrol eight hours. Only two hundred thirty-two hours and two thousand miles to go.

Kelly looked around at the departing back of the younger trooper. "I'll bet this is the only car in NorCon that has to stock twenty days of groceries for a ten-day patrol," she said.

Ben chuckled. "He's still a growing boy."

"Well, if he is, it's all between the ears," the girl replied. "You'd think that after a year I would have realized that nothing could penetrate that thick Canuck's skull. He gets me so mad sometimes that I want to forget I'm a lady." She paused thoughtfully. "Come to think of it. No one ever accused me of being a lady in the first place."

"Sounds like love," Ben smiled.

Hunched over on the jump seat with her elbows on her knees and her chin cupped in both hands, Kelly gave the senior officer a quizzical sideways look.

Ben was watching his monitors and missed the glance. Kelly sighed and stared out into the light streaked night of the thruway. The heavy surge of football traffic had distributed itself into the general flow on the road and while all lanes were busy, there were no indications of any overcrowding or jam-ups. Much of the pattern was shifting from passenger to cargo vehicle as it neared midnight. The football crowds were filtering off at each exchange and exit and the California fans had worked into the blue and yellow—mostly the yellow—for the long trip home. The fewer passenger cars on the thruway and the increase in cargo carriers gave the troopers a breathing spell. The men in the control buckets of the three hundred and four hundred-ton cargo vehicles were the real pros of the thruways; careful, courteous and fast. The NorCon patrol cars could settle down to watch out for the occasional nuts and drunks that might bring disaster.

Once again, Martin had the patrol car on auto drive in the center of the police lane and he steeled back in his seat. Beside him, Kelly stared moodily into the night.

"How come you've never married, Ben?" she asked. The senior trooper gave her a startled look. "Why, I guess for the same reason you're still a maiden," he answered. "This just doesn't seem to be the right kind of a job for a married man."

Kelly shook her head. "No, it's not the same thing with me," she said. "At least, not entirely the same thing. If I got married, I'd have to quit the Patrol and you wouldn't. And secondly, if you must know the truth, I've never been asked."

Ben looked thoughtfully at the copper-haired Irish-Indian girl. All of a sudden she seemed to have changed in his eyes. He shook his head and turned back to the road monitors.

"I just don't think that a patrol trooper has any business getting married and trying to keep a marriage happy and make a home for a family thirty days out of every three hundred sixty, with an occasional weekend home if you're lucky enough to draw your hometown for a terminal point. This might help the population rate but it sure doesn't do anything for the institution of matrimony."

"I know some troopers that are married," Kelly said.

"But there aren't very many," Ben countered. "Comes the time they pull me off the cars and stick me behind a desk somewhere, then I'll think about it."

"You might be too old by then," Kelly murmured.

Ben grinned. "You sound as though you're worried about it," he said.

"No," Kelly replied softly, "no, I'm not worried about it. Just thinking." She averted her eyes and looked out into the night again. "I wonder what NorCon would do with a husband-wife team?" she murmured, almost to herself.

Ben looked sharply at her and frowned. "Why, they'd probably split them up," he said.

"Split what up?" Clay inquired, standing in the door of the cab.

"Split up all troopers named Clay Ferguson," Kelly said disgustedly, "and use them for firewood—especially the heads. They say that hardwood burns long and leaves a fine ash. And that's what you've been for years."

She sat erect in the jump seat and looked sourly at the young trooper.

Clay shuddered at the pun and squeezed by the girl to get to his seat. "I'll take it now, pop," he said. "Go get your geriatrics treatment."

Ben got out of his seat with a snort. "I'll 'pop' you, skinhead," he snapped. "You may be eight years younger than I am but you only have one third the virility and one tenth the brains. And eight years from now you'll still be in deficit spending on both counts."

"Careful, venerable lord of my destiny," Clay admonished with a grin, "remember how I spent my vacation and remember how you spent yours before you go making unsubstantiated statements about my virility."

Kelly stood up. "If you two will excuse me, I'll go back to the dispensary and take a good jolt of male hormones and then we can come back and finish this man-to-man talk in good locker room company."

"Don't you dare," Ben cried. "I wouldn't let you tamper with one single, tiny one of your feminine traits, princess. I like you just the way you are."

Kelly looked at him with a wide-eyed, cherubic smile. "You really mean that, Ben?"

The older trooper flushed briefly and then turned quickly into the galley. "I'm going to try for some shut-eye. Wake me at two, Clay, if nothing else breaks." He turned to Kelly who was still smiling at him. "And watch out for that lascivious young goat."

"It's all just talk, talk, talk," she said scornfully. "You go to bed, Ben. I'm going to try something new in psychiatric annals. I'm going to try and psychoanalyze a dummy." She sat back down on the jump seat.

At 2400 hours it was Vincennes Check with the density reports, all down in the past hour. The patrol was settling into what looked like a quiet night routine. Kelly chatted with Ferguson for another half hour and then rose again. "I think I'll try to get some sleep," she said. "I'll put on a fresh pot of coffee for you two before I turn in."

She rattled around in the galley for some time. "Whatcha cooking?" Clay called out. "Making coffee," Kelly replied.

"It take all that time to make coffee?" Clay queried.

"No," she said. "I'm also getting a few things ready so we can have a fast breakfast in case we have to eat on the run. I'm just about through now."

A couple of minutes later she stuck her head into the cab. "Coffee's done. Want some?"

Clay nodded. "Please, princess."

She poured him a cup and set it in the rack beside his seat.

"Thanks," Clay said. "Good night, Hiawatha."

"Good night, Babe," she replied.

"You mean 'Paul Bunyon,' don't you?" Clay asked. "'Babe' was his blue ox."

"I know what I said," Kelly retorted and strolled back to the dispensary. As she passed through the crew cubby, she glanced at Ben sleeping on the bunk recently vacated by Ferguson. She paused and carefully and gently pulled a blanket up over his sleeping form. She smiled down at the trooper and then went softly to her compartment.

In the cab, Clay sipped at his coffee and kept watchful eyes on the video monitors. Beulah was back on auto drive and Clay had dropped her speed to a slow fifty as the traffic thinned.

At 0200 hours he left the cab long enough to go back and shake Ben awake and was himself re-awakened at 0400 to take back control. He let Ben sleep an extra hour before routing him out of the bunk again at 0700. The thin, gray light of the winter morning was just taking hold when Ben came back into the cab.

Clay had pulled Beulah off to the service strip and was stopped while he finished transcribing his scribbled notes from the 0700 Washington Criminal Control broadcast.

Ben ran his hand sleepily over his close-cropped head. "Anything exciting?" he asked with a yawn. Clay shook his head. "Same old thing. 'All cars exercise special vigilance over illegal crossovers. Keep all lanes within legal speed limits.' Same old noise."

"Anything new on our hit-runner?"

"Nope."

"Good morning, knights of the open road," Kelly said from the galley door. "Obviously you both went to sleep after I left and allowed our helpless citizens to slaughter each other."

"How do you figure that one?" Ben laughed.

"Oh, it's very simple," she replied. "I managed to get in a full seven hours of sleep. When you sleep, I sleep. I slept. Ergo, you did likewise."

"Nope," Clay said, "for once we had a really quiet night. Let's hope the day is of like disposition."

Kelly began laying out the breakfast things. "You guys want eggs this morning?"

"You gonna cook again today?" Clay inquired.

"Only breakfast," Kelly said. "You have the honors for the rest of the day. The diner is now open and we're taking orders."

"I'll have mine over easy," Ben said. "Make mine sunny-up," Clay called.

Kelly began breaking eggs into the pan, muttering to herself. "Over easy, sunny-up, I like 'em scrambled. Next tour I take I'm going to get on a team where everyone likes scrambled eggs."

A few minutes later, Beulah's crew sat down to breakfast. Ben had just dipped into his egg yolk when the radio blared. "Attention all cars. Special attention Cars 207, 56 and 82."

"Just once," Ben said, "just once, I want to sit down to a meal and get it all down my gullet before that radio gives me indigestion." He laid down his fork and reached for the message pad.

The radio broadcast continued. "A late model, white over green Travelaire, containing two men and believed to be the subjects wanted in earlier broadcast on murder, robbery and hit-run murder, was involved in a service station robbery and murder at Vandalia, Illinois, at approximately 0710 this date. NorCon Criminal Division believes this subject car escaped filter check and left NAT 26-West sometime during the night.

"Owner of this stolen vehicle states it had only half tanks of fuel at the time it was taken. This would indicate wanted subjects stopped for fuel. It is further believed they were recognized by the station attendant from video bulletins sent out by this department last date and that he was shot and killed to prevent giving alarm.

"The shots alerted residents of the area and the subject car was last seen headed south. This vehicle may attempt to regain access to NAT 26-West or it may take another thruway. All units are warned once again to approach this vehicle with extreme caution and only with the assistance of another unit where possible. Acknowledge. Washington Criminal Control out."

Ben looked at the chrono. "They hit Vandalia at 0710, eh. Even in the yellow they couldn't get this far for another half hour. Let's finish breakfast. It may be a long time until lunch."

The crew returned to their meal. While Kelly was cleaning up after breakfast, Clay ran the quick morning engine room check. In the cab, Ben opened the arms rack and brought out two machine pistols and belts. He checked them for loads and laid one on Clay's control seat. He strapped the other around his waist. Then he flipped up a cover in the front panel of the cab. It exposed the breech mechanisms of a pair of twin-mounted 25 mm autocannon. The ammunition loads were full. Satisfied, Ben shut the inspection port and climbed into his seat. Clay came forward, saw the machine pistol on his seat and strapped it on without a word. He settled himself in his seat. "Engine room check is all green. Let's go rabbit hunting."

Car 56 moved slowly out into the police lane. Both troopers had their individual sets of video monitors on in front of their seats and were watching them intently. In the growing light of day, a white-topped car was going to be easy to spot.

It had all the earmarks of being another wintry, overcast day. The outside temperature at 0800 was right on the twenty-nine-degree mark and the threat of more snow remained in the air. The 0800 density reports from St. Louis Control were below the 14,000 mark in all lanes in the one-hundred-mile block west of the city. That was to be expected. They listened to the eastbound densities peaking at twenty-six thousand vehicles in the same block, all heading into the metropolis and their jobs. The 0800, 1200 and 1600 hours density reports also carried the weather forecasts for a five-hundred-mile radius from the broadcasting control point. Decreasing temperatures with light to moderate snow was in the works for Car 56 for the first couple of hundred miles west of St. Louis, turning to almost blizzard conditions in central Kansas. Extra units had already been put into service on all thruways through the Midwest and snow-burners were waging a losing battle from Wichita west to the Rockies around Alamosa, Colorado.

Outside the temperature was below freezing; inside the patrol car it was a comfortable sixty-eight degrees. Kelly had cleaned the galley and taken her place on the jump seat between the two troopers. With all three of them in the cab, Ben cut from the intercom to commercial broadcast to catch the early morning newscasts and some pleasant music. The patrol vehicle glided along at a leisurely sixty miles an hour. An hour out of St. Louis, a big liquid cargo carrier was stopped on the inner edge of the green lane against the divider to the police lane. The trucker had dropped both warning barriers and lights a half mile back. Ben brought Beulah to a halt across the divider from the stopped carrier. "Dropped a track pin," the driver called out to the officers.

Ben backed Beulah across the divider behind the stalled carrier to give them protection while they tried to assist the stalled vehicle.

Donning work helmets to maintain contact with the patrol car, and its remote radio system, the two troopers dismounted and went to see what needed fixing. Kelly drifted back to the dispensary and stretched out on one of the hospital bunks and picked up a new novel.

Beulah's well-equipped machine shop stock room produced a matching pin and it was merely a matter of lifting the stalled carrier and driving it into place in the track assembly. Ben brought the patrol car alongside the carrier and unshipped the crane. Twenty minutes later, Clay and the carrier driver had the new part installed and the tanker was on his way once again.

Clay climbed into the cab and surveyed his grease-stained uniform coveralls and filthy hands. "Your nose is smudged, too, dearie," Martin observed.

Clay grinned, "I'm going to shower and change clothes. Try and see if you can drive this thing until I get back without increasing the pedestrian fatality rate." He ducked back into the crew cubby and stripped his coveralls.

Bored with her book, Kelly wandered back to the cab and took Clay's vacant control seat. The snow had started falling again and in the mid-morning light it tended to soften the harsh, utilitarian landscape of the broad thruway stretching ahead to infinity and spreading out in a mile of speeding traffic on either hand.

"Attention all cars on NAT 26-West and East," Washington Criminal Control radio blared. "Special attention Cars 56 and 82. Suspect vehicle, white over green Travelaire reported re-entered NAT 26-West on St. Louis interchange 179. St. Louis Control reports communications difficulty in delayed report. Vehicle now believed . . ."

"Car 56, Car 56," St. Louis Control broke in. "Our pigeon is in your zone. Commercial carrier reports near miss sideswipe three minutes ago in blue lane approximately three miles west of mile Marker 957.

"Repeating. Car 56, suspect car—"

Ben glanced at the radiodometer. It read 969, then clicked to 970.

"This is Five Six, St. Louis," he broke in, "acknowledged. Our position is mile marker 970 . . ."

Kelly had been glued to the video monitors since the first of the bulletin. Suddenly she screamed and banged Ben on the shoulder. "There they are. There they are," she cried, pointing at the blue lane monitor.

Martin took one look at the white-topped car cutting through traffic in the blue lane and slammed Beulah into high. The safety cocoons slammed shut almost on the first notes of the bull horn. Trapped in the shower, Clay was locked into the stall dripping wet as the water automatically shut off with the movement of the cocoon.

"I have them in sight," Ben reported, as the patrol car lifted on its air pad and leaped forward. "They're in the blue five miles ahead of me and cutting over to the yellow. I estimate their speed at two twenty-five. I am in pursuit."

Traffic gave way as Car 56 hurtled the divider into the blue.

The radio continued to snap orders.

"Cars 112, 206, 76 and 93 establish roadblocks at mile marker crossover 1032. Car 82 divert all blue and yellow to green and white."

Eight Two was one hundred fifty miles ahead but at three-hundred-mile-an-hour speeds, 82's team was very much a part of the operation. This would clear the two high-speed lanes if the suspect car hadn't been caught sooner.

"Cars 414, 227 and 290 in NAT-26-East, move into the yellow to cover in case our pigeon decides to fly the median." The controller continued to move cars into covering positions in the area on all crossovers and turnoffs. The sweating dispatcher looked at his lighted map board and mentally cursed the lack of enough units to cover every exit. State and local authorities already had been notified in the event the fugitives left the thruways and tried to escape on a state freeway.

In Car 56, Ben kept the patrol car roaring down the blue lane through the speeding westbound traffic. The standard emergency signal was doing a partial job of clearing the path, but at those speeds, driver reaction times weren't always fast enough. Ahead, the fleeing suspect car brushed against a light sedan, sending it careening and rocking across the lane. The driver fought for control as it swerved and screeched on its tilting frame. He brought it to a halt amid a haze of blue smoke from burning brakes and bent metal. The white over green Travelaire never slowed, fighting its way out of the blue into the ultra-high yellow and lighter traffic. Ben kept Beulah in bulldog pursuit.

The sideswipe ahead had sent other cars veering in panic and a cluster inadvertently bunched up in the path of the roaring patrol car. Like a flock of hawk-frightened chickens, they tried to scatter as they saw and heard the massive police vehicle bearing down on them. But like chickens, they couldn't decide which way to run. It was a matter of five or six seconds before they parted enough to let the patrol car through. Ben had no choice but to cut the throttle and punch once on the retrojets to brake the hurtling patrol car. The momentary drops in speed unlocked the safety cocoons and in an instant, Clay had leaped from the shower stall and sped to the cab. Hearing, rather than seeing his partner, Martin snapped over his shoulder, "Unrack the rifles. That's the car." Clay reached for the gun rack at the rear of the cab.

Kelly took one look at the young trooper and jumped for the doorway to the galley. A second later she was back. Without a word, she handed the nude Ferguson a dangling pair of uniform coveralls. Clay gasped, dropped the rifles and grabbed the coveralls from her hand and clutched them to his figure. His face was beet-red. Still without speaking, Kelly turned and ran back to her dispensary to be ready for the next acceleration.

Clay was into the coveralls and in his seat almost at the instant Martin whipped the patrol car through the hole in the blue traffic and shoved her into high once more.

There was no question about the fact that the occupants of the fugitive car knew they were being pursued. They shot through the crossover into the yellow lane and now were hurtling down the thruway close to the four-hundred-mile-an-hour mark.

Martin had Beulah riding just under three hundred to make the crossover, still ten miles behind the suspect car and following on video monitor. The air still crackled with commands as St. Louis and Washington Control maneuvered other cars into position as the pursuit went westward past other units blocking exit routes.

Clay read aloud the radiodometer numerals as they clicked off a mile every nine seconds. Car 56 roared into the yellow and the instant Ben had it straightened out, he slammed all finger throttles to full power. Beulah snapped forward and even at three hundred miles an hour, the sudden acceleration pasted the car's crew against the backs of their cushioned seats. The patrol car shot forward at more than five hundred miles an hour.

The image of the Travelaire grew on the video monitor and then the two troopers had it in actual sight, a white, racing dot on the broad avenue of the thruway six miles ahead.

Clay triggered the controls for the forward bow cannon and a panel box flashed to "ready fire" signal.

"Negative," Martin ordered. "We're coming up on the roadblock. You might miss and hit one of our cars."

"Car 56 to Control," the senior trooper called. "Watch out at the roadblock. He's doing at least five hundred in the yellow and he'll never be able to stop."

Two hundred miles east, the St. Louis controller made a snap decision. "Abandon roadblock. Roadblock cars start west. Maintain two hundred until subject comes into monitor view. Car 56, continue speed estimates of subject car. Maybe we can box him in."

At the roadblock forty-five miles ahead of the speeding fugitives and their relentless pursuer, the four patrol cars pivoted and spread out across the roadway some five hundred feet apart. They lunged forward and lifted up to air-cushion jet drive at just over two hundred miles an hour. Eight pairs of eyes were fixed on video monitors set for the ten-mile block to the rear of the four vehicles.

Beulah's indicated ground speed now edged towards the five hundred fifty mark, close to the maximum speeds the vehicles could attain.

The gap continued to close, but more slowly. "He's firing hotter," Ben called out. "Estimating five thirty on subject vehicle."

Now Car 56 was about three miles astern and still the gap

closed. The fugitive car flashed past the site of the abandoned roadblock and fifteen seconds later all four patrol cars racing ahead of the Travelaire broke into almost simultaneous reports of "Here he comes."

A second later, Clay Ferguson yelled out, "There he goes. He's boondocking, he's boondocking."

"He has you spotted," Martin broke in. "He's heading for the median. Cut, cut, cut. Get out in there ahead of him."

The driver of the fugitive car had seen the bulk of the four big patrol cruisers outlined against the slight rise in the thruway almost at the instant he flashed onto their screens ten miles behind them. He broke speed, rocked wildly from side to side, fighting for control and then cut diagonally to the left, heading for the outer edge of the thruway and the unpaved, half-mile-wide strip of landscaped earth that separated the east and westbound segments of NAT-26.

The white and green car was still riding on its airpad when it hit the low, rounded curbing at the edge of the thruway. It hurtled into the air and sailed for a hundred feet across the gently-sloping snow-covered grass, came smashing down in a thick hedgerow of bushes—and kept going.

Car 56 slowed and headed for the curbing. "Watch it, kids," Ben snapped over the intercom, "we may be buying a plot in a second."

Still traveling more than five hundred miles an hour, the huge patrol car hit the curbing and bounced into the air like a rocket boosted elephant. It tilted and smashed its nose in a slanting blow into the snow-covered ground. The sound of smashing and breaking equipment mingled with the roar of the thundering jets, tracks and air drives as the car fought its way back to level travel. It surged forward and smashed through the hedgerow and plunged down the sloping snowbank after the fleeing car.

"Clay," Ben called in a strained voice, "take 'er."

Ferguson's fingers were already in position. "You all right, Ben?" he asked anxiously.

"Think I dislocated a neck vertebra," Ben replied. "I can't move my head. Go get 'em, kid."

"Try not to move your head at all, Ben," Kelly called from her cocoon in the dispensary. "I'll be there the minute we slow down."

A half mile ahead, the fugitive car plowed along the bottom of the gentle draw in a cloud of snow, trying to fight its way up the opposite slope and onto the eastbound thruway.

But the Travelaire was never designed for driving on anything but a modern superhighway. Car 56 slammed through the snow and down to the bottom of the draw. A quarter of a mile ahead of the fugitives, the first of the four roadblock units came plowing over the rise.

The car's speed dropped quickly to under a hundred and the cocoons were again retracted. Ben slumped forward in his seat and caught himself. He eased back with a gasp of pain, his head held rigidly straight. Almost the instant he started to straighten up, Kelly flung herself through the cab door. She clasped his forehead and held his head against the back of the control seat.

Suddenly, the fugitive car spun sideways, bogged in the wet snow and muddy ground beneath and stopped. Clay bore down on it and was about two hundred yards away when the canopy of the other vehicle popped open and a sheet of automatic weapons fire raked the patrol car. Only the low angle of the sedan and the nearness of the bulky patrol car saved the troopers. Explosive bullets smashed into the patrol car canopy and sent shards of plastiglass showering down on the trio.

An instant later, the bow cannon of the first of the cut-off patrol units opened fire. An ugly, yellow-red blossom of smoke and fire erupted from the front of the Travelaire and it burst into flames. A second later, the figure of a man staggered out of the burning car, clothes and hair aflame. He took four plunging steps and then fell face down in the snow. The car burned and crackled and a thick funereal pyre of oily, black smoke billowed into the gray sky. It was snowing heavily now, and before the troopers could dismount and plow to the fallen man, a thin layer of snow covered his burned body.

An hour later, Car 56 was again on NAT 26-West, this time heading for Wichita barracks and needed repairs. In the dispensary, Ben Martin was stretched out on a hospital bunk with a traction brace around his neck and a copper-haired medical-surgical patrolwoman fussing over him.

In the cab, Clay peered through the now almost-blinding blizzard that whirled and skirled thick snow across the thruway. Traffic densities were virtually zero despite the efforts of the dragonlike snow-burners trying to keep the roadways clear. The young trooper shivered despite the heavy jacket over his coveralls. Wind whistled through the shell holes in Beulah's canopy and snow sifted and drifted against the back bulkhead.

The cab communications system had been smashed by the gunfire and Clay wore his work helmet both for communications and warmth.

The door to the galley cracked open and Kelly stuck her head in. "How much farther, Clay?" she asked.

"We should be in the barracks in about twenty minutes," the shivering trooper replied.

"I'll fix you a cup of hot coffee," Kelly said. "You look like you need it."

Over the helmet intercom Clay heard her shoving things around in the galley. "My heavens, but this place is a mess," she exclaimed. "I can't even find the coffee bin. That steeplechase driving has got to stop." She paused.

"Clay," she called out, "Have you been drinking in here? It smells like a brewery."

Clay raised mournful eyes to the shattered canopy above him. "My cooking wine," he sighed.

Hunting Problem

by Robert Sheckley

PREFACE BY DAVID DRAKE

In the 1950s, Robert Sheckley's short stories appeared frequently in the top range of SF magazines. They were always funny: sometimes cynically funny, sometimes bitterly funny, sometimes horrifically funny... but often enough warmly funny. This is a warmly funny story.

One other thing, though: a Sheckley story was never *merely* funny.

It was the last troop meeting before the big Scouter Jamboree, and all the patrols had turned out. Patrol 22—the Soaring Falcon Patrol—was camped in a shady hollow, holding a tentacle pull. The Brave Bison Patrol, number 31, was moving around a little stream. The Bisons were practicing their skill at drinking liquids, and laughing excitedly at the odd sensation.

And the Charging Mirash Patrol, number 19, was waiting for Scouter Drog, who was late as usual.

Drog hurtled down from the ten-thousand-foot level, went solid, and hastily crawled into the circle of scouters. "Gee," he said, "I'm sorry. I didn't realize what time—"

The Patrol Leader glared at him. "You're out of uniform, Drog."

"Sorry, sir," Drog said, hastily extruding a tentacle he had forgotten.

The others giggled. Drog blushed a dim orange. He wished he were invisible.

But it wouldn't be proper right now.

"I will open our meeting with the Scouter Creed," the Patrol Leader said. He cleared his throat. "We, the Young Scouters of the planet Elbonai, pledge to perpetuate the skills and virtues of our pioneering ancestors. For that purpose, we Scouters adopt the shape our forebears were born to when they conquered the virgin wilderness of Elbonai. We hereby resolve—"

Scouter Drog adjusted his hearing receptors to amplify the Leader's soft voice. The Creed always thrilled him. It was hard to believe that his ancestors had once been earthbound. Today the Elbonai were aerial beings, maintaining only the minimum of body, fueling by cosmic radiation at the twenty-thousand-foot level, sensing by direct perception, coming down only for sentimental or sacramental purposes. They had come a long way since the Age of Pioneering. The modern world had begun with the Age of Submolecular Control, which was followed by the present age of Direct Control.

" . . . honesty and fair play," the Leader was saying. "And we further resolve to drink liquids, as they did, and to eat solid food, and to increase our skill in their tools and methods."

The invocation completed, the youngsters scattered around the plain. The Patrol Leader came up to Drog.

"This is the last meeting before the Jamboree," the Leader said.

"I know," Drog said.

"And you are the only second-class scouter in the Charging Mirash Patrol. All the others are first-class, or at least Junior Pioneers. What will people think about our patrol?"

Drog squirmed uncomfortably. "It isn't entirely my fault," he said. "I know I failed the tests in swimming and bomb making, but those just aren't my skills. It isn't fair to expect me to know everything. Even among the pioneers there were specialists. No one was expected to know all—"

"And just what are your skills?" the Leader interrupted.

"Forest and Mountain Lore," Drog answered eagerly. "Tracking and hunting."

The Leader studied him for a moment. Then he said slowly,

"Drog, how would you like one last chance to make first class, and win an achievement badge as well?"

"I'd do anything!" Drog cried.

"Very well," the Patrol Leader said. "What is the name of our patrol?"

"The Charging Mirash Patrol."

"And what is a Mirash?"

"A large and ferocious animal," Drog answered promptly. "Once they inhabited large parts of Elbonai, and our ancestors fought many savage battles with them. Now they are extinct."

"Not quite," the Leader said. "A scouter was exploring the woods five hundred miles north of here, coordinates S-233 by 482-W, and he came upon a pride of three Mirash, all bulls, and therefore huntable. I want you, Drog, to track them down, to stalk them, using Forest and Mountain Lore. Then, utilizing only pioneering tools and methods, I want you to bring back the pelt of one Mirash. Do you think you can do it?"

"I know I can, sir!"

"Go at once," the Leader said. "We will fasten the pelt to our flagstaff. We will undoubtedly be commended at the Jamboree."

"Yes, *sir*!" Drog hastily gathered up his equipment, filled his canteen with liquid, packed a lunch of solid food, and set out.

A few minutes later, he had levitated himself to the general area of S-233 by 482-W. It was a wild and romantic country of jagged rocks and scrubby trees, thick underbrush in the valleys, snow on the peaks. Drog looked around, somewhat troubled.

He had told the Patrol Leader a slight untruth.

The fact of the matter was, he wasn't particularly skilled in Forest and Mountain Lore, hunting or tracking. He wasn't particularly skilled in anything except dreaming away long hours among the clouds at the five-thousand-foot level. What if he failed to find a Mirash? What if the Mirash found him first?

But that couldn't happen, he assured himself. In a pinch, he could always gestibulize. Who would ever know?

In another moment he picked up a faint trace of Mirash scent. And then he saw a slight movement about twenty yards away, near a curious T-shaped formation of rock.

Was it really going to be this easy? How nice! Quietly he adopted an appropriate camouflage and edged forward.

∽   ∽   ∽

The mountain trail became steeper, and the sun beat harshly down. Paxton was sweating, even in his air-conditioned coverall. And he was heartily sick of being a good sport.

"Just when are we leaving this place?" he asked.

Herrera slapped him genially on the shoulder. "Don't you wanna get rich?"

"We're rich already," Paxton said.

"But not rich enough," Herrera told him, his long brown face creasing into a brilliant grin.

Stellman came up, puffing under the weight of his testing equipment. He set it carefully on the path and sat down. "You gentlemen interested in a short breather?" he asked.

"Why not?" Herrera said. "All the time in the world." He sat down with his back against a T-shaped formation of rock.

Stellman lighted a pipe and Herrera found a cigar in the zippered pocket of his coverall. Paxton watched them for a while. Then he asked, "Well, when *are* we getting off this planet? Or do we set up permanent residence?"

Herrera just grinned and scratched a light for his cigar.

"Well, how about it?" Paxton shouted.

"Relax, you're outvoted," Stellman said. "We formed this company as three equal partners."

"All using *my* money," Paxton said.

"Of course. That's why we took you in. Herrera had the practical mining experience. I had the theoretical knowledge and a pilot's license. You had the money."

"But we've got plenty of stuff on board now," Paxton said. "The storage compartments are completely filled. Why can't we go to some civilized place now and start spending?"

"Herrera and I don't have your aristocratic attitude toward wealth," Stellman said with exaggerated patience. "Herrera and I have the childish desire to fill every nook and cranny with treasure. Gold nuggets in the fuel tanks, emeralds in the flour cans, diamonds a foot deep on deck. And this is just the place for it. All manner of costly baubles are lying around just begging to be picked up. We want to be disgustingly, abysmally rich, Paxton."

Paxton hadn't been listening. He was staring intently at a point near the edge of the trail. In a low voice, he said, "That tree just moved."

Herrera burst into laughter. "Monsters, I suppose," he sneered.

"Be calm," Stellman said mournfully. "My boy, I am a middle-aged man, overweight and easily frightened. Do you think I'd stay here if there were the slightest danger?"

"There! It moved again!"

"We surveyed this planet three months ago," Stellman said. "We found no intelligent beings, no dangerous animals, no poisonous plants, remember? All we found were woods and mountains and gold and lakes and emeralds and rivers and diamonds. If there were something here, wouldn't it have attacked us long before?"

"I'm telling you I saw it move," Paxton insisted.

Herrera stood up. "This tree?" he asked Paxton.

"Yes. See, it doesn't even look like the others. Different texture—"

In a single synchronized movement, Herrera pulled a Mark II blaster from a side holster and fired three charges into the tree. The tree and all underbrush for ten yards around burst into flame and crumpled.

"All gone now," Herrera said.

Paxton rubbed his jaw. "I heard it scream when you shot it."

"Sure. But it's dead now," Herrera said soothingly. "If anything else moves, you just tell me, I shoot it. Now we find some more little emeralds, huh?"

Paxton and Stellman lifted their packs and followed Herrera up the trail. Stellman said in a low, amused voice, "Direct sort of fellow, isn't he?"

Slowly Drog returned to consciousness. The Mirash's flaming weapon had caught him in camouflage, almost completely unshielded. He still couldn't understand how it had happened. There had been no premonitory fear-scent, no snorting, no snarling, no warning whatsoever. The Mirash had attacked with blind suddenness, without waiting to see whether he was friend or foe.

At last Drog understood the nature of the beast he was up against.

He waited until the hoofbeats of the three bull Mirash had faded into the distance. Then, painfully, he tried to extrude a visual receptor. Nothing happened. He had a moment of utter panic. If his central nervous system was damaged, this was the end.

He tried again. This time, a piece of rock slid off him, and he was able to reconstruct.

Quickly he performed an internal scansion. He sighed with relief. It had been a close thing. Instinctively he had quondicated at the flash moment and it had saved his life.

He tried to think of another course of action, but the shock of that sudden, vicious, unpremeditated assault had driven all Hunting Lore out of his mind. He found that he had absolutely no desire to encounter the savage Mirash again.

Suppose he returned without the stupid hide? He could tell the Patrol Leader that the Mirash were all females, and therefore unhuntable. A Young Scouter's word was honored, so no one would question him, or even check up.

But that would never do. How could he even consider it?

Well, he told himself gloomily, he could resign from the Scouters, put an end to the whole ridiculous business; the campfires, the singing, the games, the comradeship . . .

This would never do, Drog decided, taking himself firmly in hand. He was acting as though the Mirash were antagonists capable of planning against him. But the Mirash were not even intelligent beings. No creature without tentacles had ever developed true intelligence. That was Etlib's Law, and it had never been disputed.

In a battle between intelligence and instinctive cunning, intelligence always won. It had to. All he had to do was figure out how.

Drog began to track the Mirash again, following their odor. What colonial weapon should he use? A small atomic bomb? No, that would more than likely ruin the hide.

He stopped suddenly and laughed. It was really very simple, when one applied oneself. Why should he come into direct and dangerous contact with the Mirash? The time had come to use his brain, his understanding of animal psychology, his knowledge of Lures and Snares.

Instead of tracking the Mirash, he would go to their den.

And there he would set a trap.

Their temporary camp was in a cave, and by the time they arrived there it was sunset. Every crag and pinnacle of rock threw a precise and sharp-edged shadow. The ship lay five miles below them on the valley floor, its metallic hide glistening red and silver. In their packs were a dozen emeralds, small, but of an excellent color.

At an hour like this, Paxton thought of a small Ohio town, a soda fountain, a girl with bright hair. Herrera smiled to himself, contemplating certain gaudy ways of spending a million dollars before settling down to the serious business of ranching. And Stellman was already phrasing his Ph.D. thesis on extraterrestrial mineral deposits.

They were all in a pleasant, relaxed mood. Paxton had recovered completely from his earlier attack of nerves. Now he wished an alien monster *would* show up—a green one, by preference—chasing a lovely, scantily clad woman.

"Home again," Stellman said as they approached the entrance of the cave. "Want beef stew tonight?" It was his turn to cook.

"With onions," Paxton said, starting into the cave. He jumped back abruptly. "What's that?"

A few feet from the mouth of the cave was a small roast beef, still steaming hot, four large diamonds, and a bottle of whiskey.

"That's odd," Stellman said. "And a trifle unnerving."

Paxton bent down to examine a diamond. Herrera pulled him back.

"Might be booby-trapped."

"There aren't any wires," Paxton said.

Herrera stared at the roast beef, the diamonds, the bottle of whiskey. He looked very unhappy.

"I don't trust this," he said.

"Maybe there *are* natives here," Stellman said. "Very timid ones. This might be their goodwill offering."

"Sure," Herrera said. "They sent to Terra for a bottle of Old Space Ranger just for us."

"What are we going to do?" Paxton asked.

"Stand clear," Herrera said. "Move 'way back." He broke off a long branch from a nearby tree and poked gingerly at the diamonds.

"Nothing's happening," Paxton said.

The long grass Herrera was standing on whipped tightly around his ankles. The ground beneath him surged, broke into a neat disk fifteen feet in diameter and, trailing root-ends, began to lift itself into the air. Herrera tried to jump free, but the grass held him like a thousand green tentacles.

"Hang on!" Paxton yelled idiotically, rushed forward and grabbed a corner of the rising disk of earth. It dipped steeply, stopped for a moment, and began to rise again. By then Herrera had his knife out, and was slashing the grass around his ankles. Stellman came unfrozen when he saw Paxton rising past his head.

Stellman seized him by the ankles, arresting the flight of the disk once more. Herrera wrenched one foot free and threw himself over the edge. The other ankle was held for a moment, then the tough grass parted under his weight. He dropped headfirst to the ground, at the last moment ducking his head and landing on his shoulders. Paxton let go of the disk and fell, landing on Stellman's stomach.

The disk of earth, with its cargo of roast beef, whiskey and diamonds, continued to rise until it was out of sight.

The sun had set. Without speaking, the three men entered their cave, blasters drawn. They built a roaring fire at the mouth and moved back into the cave's interior.

"We'll guard in shifts tonight," Herrera said.

Paxton and Stellman nodded.

Herrera said, "I think you're right, Paxton. We've stayed here long enough."

"Too long," Paxton said.

Herrera shrugged his shoulders. "As soon as it's light, we return to the ship and get out of here."

"If," Stellman said, "we are able to reach the ship."

Drog was quite discouraged. With a sinking heart he had watched the premature springing of his trap, the struggle, and the escape of the Mirash. It had been such a splendid Mirash, too. The biggest of the three!

He knew now what he had done wrong. In his eagerness, he had overbaited his trap. Just the minerals would have been sufficient, for Mirash were notoriously mineral-tropic. But no, he had to improve on pioneer methods, he had to use food stimuli as well. No wonder they had reacted suspiciously, with their senses so overburdened.

Now they were enraged, alert, and decidedly dangerous.

And a thoroughly aroused Mirash was one of the most fearsome sights in the Galaxy.

Drog felt very much alone as Elbonai's twin moons rose in the western sky. He could see the Mirash campfire blazing in the mouth of their cave. And by direct perception he could see the Mirash crouched within, every sense alert, weapons ready.

Was a Mirash hide really worth all this trouble?

Drog decided that he would much rather be floating at the five-thousand-foot level, sculpturing cloud formations and dreaming. He wanted to sop up radiation instead of eating nasty old solid food. And what use was all this hunting and trapping, anyhow? Worthless skills that his people had outgrown.

For a moment he almost had himself convinced. And then, in a flash of pure perception, he understood what it was all about.

True, the Elbonaians had outgrown their competition, developed past all danger of competition. But the Universe was wide, and capable of many surprises. Who could foresee what would come, what new dangers the race might have to face? And how could they meet them if the hunting instinct was lost?

No, the old ways had to be preserved, to serve as patterns; as reminders that peaceable, intelligent life was an unstable entity in an unfriendly Universe.

He was going to get that Mirash hide, or die trying!

The most important thing was to get them out of that cave. Now his hunting knowledge had returned to him.

Quickly, skillfully, he shaped a Mirash horn.

"Did you hear that?" Paxton asked.

"I thought I heard something," Stellman said, and they all listened intently.

The sound came again. It was a voice crying, "Oh, help, help me!"

"It's a girl!" Paxton jumped to his feet.

"It *sounds* like a girl," Stellman said.

"Please, help me," the girl's voice wailed. "I can't hold out much longer. Is there anyone who can help me?"

Blood rushed to Paxton's face. In a flash he saw her, small, exquisite, standing beside her wrecked sports-spacer (what a foolhardy trip it had been!) with monsters, green and slimy, closing in on her. And then *he* arrived, a foul alien beast.

Paxton picked up a spare blaster. "I'm going out there," he said coolly.

"Sit down, you moron!" Herrera ordered.

"But you heard her, didn't you?"

"That can't be a girl," Herrera said. "What would a girl be doing on this planet?"

"I'm going to find out," Paxton said, brandishing two blasters. "Maybe a spaceliner crashed, or she could have been out joyriding, and—"

"Siddown!" Herrera yelled.

"He's right," Stellman tried to reason with Paxton. "Even if a girl *is* out there, which I doubt, there's nothing we can do."

"Oh, help, help, it's coming after me!" the girl's voice screamed.

"Get out of my way," Paxton said, his voice low and dangerous.

"You're really going?" Herrera asked incredulously.

"Yes! Are you going to stop me?"

"Go ahead." Herrera gestured at the entrance of the cave.

"We can't let him!" Stellman gasped.

"Why not? His funeral," Herrera said lazily.

"Don't worry about me," Paxton said. "I'll be back in fifteen minutes—with her!" He turned on his heel and started toward the entrance. Herrera leaned forward and, with considerable precision, clubbed Paxton behind the ear with a stick of firewood. Stellman caught him as he fell.

They stretched Paxton out in the rear of the cave and returned to their vigil. The lady in distress moaned and pleaded for the next five hours. Much too long, as Paxton had to agree, even for a movie serial.

A gloomy, rain-splattered daybreak found Drog still camped a hundred yards from the cave. He saw the Mirash emerge in a tight group, weapons ready, eyes watching warily for any movement.

Why had the Mirash horn failed? The Scouter Manual said it was an infallible means of attracting the bull Mirash. But perhaps this wasn't mating season.

They were moving in the direction of a metallic ovoid which Drog recognized as a primitive spatial conveyance. It was crude, but once inside it the Mirash were safe from him.

He could simply trevest them, and that would end it. But it wouldn't be very humane. Above all, the ancient Elbonaians had been gentle and merciful, and a Young Scouter tried to be like them. Besides, trevestment wasn't a true pioneering method.

That left ilitrocy. It was the oldest trick in the book, and he'd have to get close to work it. But he had nothing to lose.

And luckily, climatic conditions were perfect for it.

It started as a thin ground-mist. But, as the watery sun climbed the gray sky, fog began forming.

Herrera cursed angrily as it grew more dense. "Keep close together now. Of all the luck!"

Soon they were walking with their hands on each others' shoulders, blasters ready, peering into the impenetrable fog.

"Herrera?"

"Yeah?"

"Are you sure we're going in the right direction?"

"Sure. I took a compass course before the fog closed in."

"Suppose your compass is off?"

"Don't even think about it."

They walked on, picking their way carefully over the rock-strewn ground.

"I think I see the ship," Paxton said.

"No, not yet," Herrera said.

Stellman stumbled over a rock, dropped his blaster, picked it up again and fumbled around for Herrera's shoulder. He found it and walked on.

"I think we're almost there," Herrera said.

"I sure hope so," Paxton said. "I've had enough."

"Think your girl friend's waiting for you at the ship?"

"Don't rub it in."

"Okay," Herrera said. "Hey, Stellman, you better grab hold of my shoulder again. No sense getting separated."

"I am holding your shoulder," Stellman said.

"You're not."

"I am, I tell you!"

"Look I guess I know if someone's holding my shoulder or not."

"Am I holding your shoulder, Paxton?"

"No," Paxton said.

"That's bad," Stellman said, very slowly. "That's bad, indeed."

"Why?"

"Because I'm definitely holding *someone's* shoulder."

Herrera yelled, "Get down, get down quick, give me room to shoot!" But it was too late. A sweet-sour odor was in the air. Stellman and Paxton smelled it and collapsed. Herrera ran forward blindly, trying to hold his breath. He stumbled and fell over a rock, tried to get back on his feet—

And everything went black.

The fog lifted suddenly and Drog was standing alone, smiling triumphantly. He pulled out a long-bladed skinning knife and bent over the nearest Mirash.

The spaceship hurtled toward Terra at a velocity which threatened momentarily to burn out the overdrive. Herrera, hunched over the controls, finally regained his self-control and cut the speed down to normal. His usual tan face was still ashen, and his hands shook on the instruments.

Stellman came in from the bunkroom and flopped wearily in the co-pilot's seat.

"How's Paxton?" Herrera asked.

"I dosed him with Drona-3," Stellman said. "He's going to be all right."

"He's a good kid," Herrera said.

"It's just shock, for the most part," Stellman said. "When he comes to, I'm going to put him to work counting diamonds. Counting diamonds is the best of therapies, I understand."

Herrera grinned, and his face began to regain its normal color. "I feel like doing a little diamond-cutting myself, now that it's all turned out okay." Then his long face became serious. "But I ask you, Stellman, who could figure it? I still don't understand!"

The Scouter Jamboree was a glorious spectacle. The Soaring Falcon Patrol, number 22, gave a short pantomime showing the clearing of the land on Elbonai. The Brave Bisons, number 31, were in full pioneer dress.

And at the head of patrol 19, the Charging Mirash Patrol, was Drog, a first-class Scouter now, wearing a glittering achievement badge. He was carrying the Patrol flag—the position of honor—and everyone cheered to see it.

Because waving proudly from the flagpole was the firm, fine-textured, characteristic skin of an adult Mirash, its zippers, tubes, gauges, buttons and holsters flashing merrily in the sunshine.

AFTERWORD BY JIM BAEN
When I read this story in my early teens, I laughed my head off. When I thought back on it, though, I realized that "Hunting Problem" might have been the first time a writer showed me that people who didn't look anything like me might be, well...people.

Black Destroyer

by A. E. Van Vogt

PREFACE BY DAVID DRAKE

You can get an argument as to when the Golden Age of Science Fiction ended. (Well, you can get an argument if you're talking with the right people.) Almost everybody agrees that the Golden Age started with the July, 1939, issue of *Astounding*, however. That's because its cover story was "Black Destroyer," the first published SF by A. E. Van Vogt.

I didn't know that when I first read the story in *Tales of Space and Time*, edited by Healy and McComas, when I was thirteen. Back then I didn't know much of anything, about authors or writing or SF. But I knew "Black Destroyer" was amazing, not only for what was in the story (and considered as either adventure or horror, it's a very taut, suspenseful piece) but even more for the implicit background, the sciences and technologies that didn't exist in my adolescent world—or anywhere else outside the story, as I now know.

When I was thirteen, everything was possible. "Black Destroyer" is one of the few stories that gave—and give—form to those infinite possibilities.

O̲n and on Coeurl prowled! The black, moonless, almost starless night yielded reluctantly before a grim reddish dawn that crept

121

up from his left. A vague, dull light it was, that gave no sense of approaching warmth, no comfort, nothing but a cold, diffuse lightness, slowly revealing a nightmare landscape.

Black, jagged rock and black, unliving plain took form around him, as a pale-red sun peered at last above the grotesque horizon. It was then Coeurl recognized suddenly that he was on familiar ground.

He stopped short. Tenseness flamed along his nerves. His muscles pressed with sudden, unrelenting strength against his bones. His great forelegs—twice as long as his hindlegs—twitched with a shuddering movement that arched every razor-sharp claw. The thick tentacles that sprouted from his shoulders ceased their weaving undulation, and grew taut with anxious alertness.

Utterly appalled, he twisted his great cat head from side to side, while the little hairlike tendrils that formed each ear vibrated frantically, testing every vagrant breeze, every throb in the ether.

But there was no response, no swift tingling along his intricate nervous system, not the faintest suggestion anywhere of the presence of the all-necessary id. Hopelessly, Coeurl crouched, an enormous catlike figure silhouetted against the dim reddish skyline, like a distorted etching of a black tiger resting on a black rock in a shadow world.

He had known this day would come. Through all the centuries of restless search, this day had loomed ever nearer, blacker, more frightening—this inevitable hour when he must return to the point where he began his systematic hunt in a world almost depleted of id-creatures.

The truth struck in waves like an endless, rhythmic ache at the seat of his ego. When he had started, there had been a few id-creatures in every hundred square miles, to be mercilessly rooted out. Only too well Coeurl knew in this ultimate hour that he had missed none. There were no id-creatures left to eat. In all the hundreds of thousands of square miles that he had made his own by right of ruthless conquest—until no neighboring coeurl dared to question his sovereignty—there was no id to feed the otherwise immortal engine that was his body.

Square foot by square foot he had gone over it. And now—he recognized the knoll of rock just ahead, and the black rock bridge that formed a queer, curling tunnel to his right. It was in that tunnel he had lain for days, waiting for the simple-minded, snakelike id-creature to come forth from its hole in the rock to bask in the sun—his first kill after he had realized the absolute necessity of organized extermination.

He licked his lips in brief gloating memory of the moment his slavering jaws tore the victim into precious toothsome bits. But the dark fear of an idless universe swept the sweet remembrance from his consciousness, leaving only certainty of death.

He snarled audibly, a defiant, devilish sound that quavered on the air, echoed and re-echoed among the rocks, and shuddered back along his nerves—instinctive and hellish expression of his will to live.

And then—abruptly—it came.

He saw it emerge out of the distance on a long downward slant, a tiny glowing spot that grew enormously into a metal ball. The great shining globe hissed by above Coeurl, slowing visibly in quick deceleration. It sped over a black line of hills to the right, hovered almost motionless for a second, then sank down out of sight.

Coeurl exploded from his startled immobility. With tiger speed, he flowed down among the rocks. His round, black eyes burned with the horrible desire that was an agony within him. His ear tendrils vibrated a message of id in such tremendous quantities that his body felt sick with the pangs of his abnormal hunger.

The little red sun was a crimson ball in the purple-black heavens when he crept up from behind a mass of rock and gazed from its shadows at the crumbling, gigantic ruins of the city that sprawled below him. The silvery globe, in spite of its great size, looked strangely inconspicuous against that vast, fairylike reach of ruins. Yet about it was a leashed aliveness, a dynamic quiescence that, after a moment, made it stand out, dominating the foreground. A massive, rock-crushing thing of metal, it rested on a cradle made by its own weight in the harsh, resisting plain which began abruptly at the outskirts of the dead metropolis.

Coeurl gazed at the strange, two-legged creatures who stood in little groups near the brilliantly lighted opening that yawned at the base of the ship. His throat thickened with the immediacy of his need; and his brain grew dark with the first wild impulse to burst forth in furious charge and smash these flimsy, helpless-looking creatures whose bodies emitted the id-vibrations.

Mists of memory stopped that mad rush when it was still only electricity surging through his muscles. Memory that brought fear in an acid stream of weakness, pouring along his nerves, poisoning the reservoirs of his strength. He had time to see that the creatures wore things over their real bodies, shimmering transparent material that glittered in strange, burning flashes in the rays of the sun.

Other memories came suddenly. Of dim days when the city that spread below was the living, breathing heart of an age of glory that dissolved in a single century before flaming guns whose wielders knew only that for the survivors there would be an ever-narrowing supply of id.

It was the remembrance of those guns that held him there, cringing in a wave of terror that blurred his reason. He saw himself smashed by balls of metal and burned by searing flame.

Came cunning—understanding of the presence of these creatures. This, Coeurl reasoned for the first time, was a scientific expedition from another star. In the olden days, the coeurls had thought of space travel, but disaster came too swiftly for it ever to be more than a thought.

Scientists meant investigation, not destruction. Scientists in their way were fools. Bold with his knowledge, he emerged into the open. He saw the creatures become aware of him. They turned and stared. One, the smallest of the group, detached a shining metal rod from a sheath, and held it casually in one hand. Coeurl loped on, shaken to his core by the action; but it was too late to turn back.

Commander Hal Morton heard little Gregory Kent, the chemist, laugh with the embarrassed half gurgle with which he invariably announced inner uncertainty. He saw Kent fingering the spindly metalite weapon.

Kent said: "I'll take no chances with anything as big as that."

Commander Morton allowed his own deep chuckle to echo along the communicators. "That," he grunted finally, "is one of the reasons why you're on this expedition, Kent—because you never leave anything to chance."

His chuckle trailed off into silence. Instinctively, as he watched the monster approach them across that black rock plain, he moved forward until he stood a little in advance of the others, his huge form bulking the transparent metalite suit. The comments of the men pattered through the radio communicator into his ears:

"I'd hate to meet that baby on a dark night in an alley."

"Don't be silly. This is obviously an intelligent creature. Probably a member of the ruling race."

"It looks like nothing else than a big cat, if you forget those tentacles sticking out from its shoulders, and make allowances for those monster forelegs."

"Its physical development," said a voice, which Morton recognized as that of Siedel, the psychologist, "presupposes an animal-like adaptation to surroundings, not an intellectual one. On the other hand, its coming to us like this is not the act of an animal but of a creature possessing a mental awareness of our possible identity. You will notice that its movements are stiff, denoting caution, which suggests fear and consciousness of our weapons. I'd like to get a good look at the end of its tentacles. If they taper into handlike appendages that can really grip objects, then the conclusion would be inescapable that it is a descendant of the inhabitants of this city. It would be a great help if we could establish communication with it, even though appearances indicate that it has degenerated into a historyless primitive."

Coeurl stopped when he was still ten feet from the foremost creature. The sense of id was so overwhelming that his brain drifted to the ultimate verge of chaos. He felt as if his limbs were bathed in molten liquid; his very vision was not quite clear, as the sheer sensuality of his desire thundered through his being.

The men—all except the little one with the shining metal rod in his fingers—came closer. Coeurl saw that they were frankly and curiously examining him. Their lips were moving, and their voices beat in a monotonous, meaningless rhythm on his ear tendrils. At the same time he had the sense of waves of a much higher frequency—his own communication level—only it was a machine-like clicking that jarred his brain. With a distinct effort to appear friendly, he broadcast his name from his ear tendrils, at the same time pointing at himself with one curving tentacle.

Gourlay, chief of communications, drawled: "I got a sort of static in my radio when he wiggled those hairs, Morton. Do you think—"

"Looks very much like it," the leader answered the unfinished question. "That means a job for you, Gourlay. If it speaks by means of radio waves, it might not be altogether impossible that you can create some sort of television picture of its vibrations, or teach him the Morse code."

"Ah," said Siedel. "I was right. The tentacles each develop into seven strong fingers. Provided the nervous system is complicated enough, those fingers could, with training, operate any machine."

Morton said: "I think we'd better go in and have some lunch. Afterward, we've got to get busy. The material men can set up their machines and start gathering data on the planet's metal possibilities, and so on. The others can do a little careful exploring. I'd like some notes on architecture and on the scientific development of this race, and particularly what happened to wreck the civilization. On earth civilization after civilization crumbled, but always a new one sprang up in its dust. Why didn't that happen here? Any questions?"

"Yes. What about pussy? Look, he wants to come in with us."

Commander Morton frowned, an action that emphasized the deep-space pallor of his face. "I wish there was some way we could take it in with us, without forcibly capturing it. Kent, what do you think?"

"I think we should first decide whether it's an it or a him, and call it one or the other. I'm in favor of him. As for taking him in with us—" The little chemist shook his head decisively. "Impossible. This atmosphere is twenty-eight per cent chlorine. Our oxygen would be pure dynamite to his lungs."

The commander chuckled. "He doesn't believe that, apparently." He watched the catlike monster follow the first two men through the great door. The men kept an anxious distance from him, then glanced at Morton questioningly. Morton waved his hand. "O.K. Open the second lock and let him get a whiff of the oxygen. That'll cure him."

A moment later, he cursed his amazement. "By Heaven, he doesn't even notice the difference! That means he hasn't any lungs, or else the chlorine is not what his lungs use. Let him in! You bet he can go in! Smith, here's a treasure house for a biologist—harmless enough if we're careful. We can always handle him. But what a metabolism!"

Smith, a tall, thin, bony chap with a long, mournful face, said in an oddly forceful voice: "In all our travels, we've found only two higher forms of life. Those dependent on chlorine, and those who need oxygen—the two elements that support combustion. I'm prepared to stake my reputation that no complicated organism could ever adapt itself to both gases in a natural way. At first thought I should say here is an extremely advanced form of life. This race long ago discovered truths of biology that we are just beginning to suspect. Morton, we mustn't let this creature get away if we can help it."

"If his anxiety to get inside is any criterion," Commander Morton laughed, "then our difficulty will be to get rid of him."

He moved into the lock with Coeurl and the two men. The

automatic machinery hummed; and in a few minutes they were standing at the bottom of a series of elevators that led up to the living quarters.

"Does that go up?" One of the men flicked a thumb in the direction of the monster.

"Better send him up alone, if he'll go in."

Coeurl offered no objection, until he heard the door slam behind him; and the closed cage shot upward. He whirled with a savage snarl, his reason swirling into chaos. With one leap, he pounced at the door. The metal bent under his plunge, and the desperate pain maddened him. Now, he was all trapped animal. He smashed at the metal with his paws, bending it like so much tin. He tore great bars loose with his thick tentacles. The machinery screeched; there were horrible jerks as the limitless power pulled the cage along in spite of projecting pieces of metal that scraped the outside walls. And then the cage stopped, and he snatched off the rest of the door and hurtled into the corridor.

He waited there until Morton and the men came up with drawn weapons. "We're fools," Morton said. "We should have shown him how it works. He thought we'd double-crossed him."

He motioned to the monster, and saw the savage glow fade from the coal-black eyes as he opened and closed the door with elaborate gestures to show the operation.

Coeurl ended the lesson by trotting into the large room to his right. He lay down on the rugged floor, and fought down the electric tautness of his nerves and muscles. A very fury of rage against himself for his fright consumed him. It seemed to his burning brain that he had lost the advantage of appearing a mild and harmless creature. His strength must have startled and dismayed them.

It meant greater danger in the task which he now knew he must accomplish: To kill everything in the ship, and take the machine back to their world in search of unlimited id.

With unwinking eyes, Coeurl lay and watched the two men clearing away the loose rubble from the metal doorway of the huge old building. His whole body ached with the hunger of his cells for id. The craving tore through his palpitant muscles, and throbbed like a living thing in his brain. His every nerve quivered to be off after the men who had wandered into the city. One of them, he knew, had gone—alone.

The dragging minutes fled; and still he restrained himself, still he lay there watching, aware that the men knew he watched. They floated a metal machine from the ship to the rock mass that blocked the great half-open door, under the direction of a third man. No flicker of their fingers escaped his fierce stare, and slowly, as the simplicity of the machinery became apparent to him, contempt grew upon him.

He knew what to expect finally, when the flame flared in incandescent violence and ate ravenously at the hard rock beneath. But in spite of his preknowledge, he deliberately jumped and snarled as if in fear, as that white heat burst forth. His ear tendrils caught the laughter of the men, their curious pleasure at his simulated dismay.

The door was released, and Morton came over and went inside with the third man. The latter shook his head.

"It's a shambles. You can catch the drift of the stuff. Obviously, they used atomic energy, but . . . but it's in wheel form. That's a peculiar development. In our science, atomic energy brought in the nonwheel machine. It's possible that here they've progressed *further* to a new type of wheel mechanics. I hope their libraries are better preserved than this, or we'll never know. What could have happened to a civilization to make it vanish like this?"

A third voice broke through the communicators: "This is Siedel. I heard your question, Pennons. Psychologically and sociologically speaking, the only reason why a territory becomes uninhabited is lack of food."

"But they're so advanced scientifically, why didn't they develop space flying and go elsewhere for their food?"

"Ask Gunlie Lester," interjected Morton. "I heard him expounding some theory even before we landed."

The astronomer answered the first call. "I've still got to verify all my facts, but this desolate world is the only planet revolving around that miserable red sun. There's nothing else. No moon, not even a planetoid. And the nearest star system is *nine hundred light-years* away.

"So tremendous would have been the problem of the ruling race of this world, that in one jump they would not only have had to solve interplanetary but interstellar space traveling. When you consider how slow our own development was—first the moon, then Venus—each success leading to the next, and after centuries to the nearest stars; and last of all to the anti-accelerators that permitted galactic travel—considering all this, I maintain it would be impossible for any race to create such machines without practical experience. And, with the nearest star so far away, they had no incentive for the space adventuring that makes for experience."

Coeurl was trotting briskly over to another group. But now, in the driving appetite that consumed him, and in the frenzy of his high scorn, he paid no attention to what they were doing. Memories of past knowledge, jarred into activity by what he had seen, flowed into his consciousness in an ever-developing and more vivid stream.

From group to group he sped, a nervous dynamo—jumpy, sick with his awful hunger. A little car rolled up, stopping in front of him, and a formidable camera whirred as it took a picture of him. Over on a mound of rock, a gigantic telescope was rearing up toward the sky. Nearby, a disintegrating machine drilled its searing fire into an ever-deepening hole, down and down, straight down.

Coeurl's mind became a blur of things he watched with half attention. And ever more imminent grew the moment when he knew he could no longer carry on the torture of acting. His brain strained with an irresistible impatience; his body burned with the fury of his eagerness to be off after the man who had gone alone into the city.

He could stand it no longer. A green foam misted his mouth, maddening him. He saw that, for the bare moment, nobody was looking.

Like a shot from a gun, he was off. He floated along in great, gliding leaps, a shadow among the shadows of the rocks. In a minute, the harsh terrain hid the spaceship and the two-legged beings.

Coeurl forgot the ship, forgot everything but his purpose, as if his brain had been wiped clear by a magic, memory-erasing brush. He circled widely, then raced into the city, along deserted streets, taking short cuts with the ease of familiarity, through gaping holes in time-weakened walls, through long corridors of moldering buildings. He slowed to a crouching lope as his ear tendrils caught the id vibrations.

Suddenly, he stopped and peered from a scatter of fallen rock. The man was standing at what must once have been a window, sending the glaring rays of his flashlight into the gloomy interior. The flashlight clicked off. The man, a heavy-set, powerful fellow, walked off with quick, alert steps. Coeurl didn't like that alertness. It presaged trouble; it meant lightning reaction to danger.

Coeurl waited till the human being vanished around a corner, then he padded into the open. He was running now, tremendously faster than a man could walk, because his plan was clear in his brain. Like a wraith, he slipped down the next street, past a long block of buildings. He turned the first corner at top speed; and then, with dragging belly, crept into the half-darkness between the building and a huge chunk of debris. The street ahead was barred by a solid line of loose rubble that made it like a valley, ending in a narrow, bottlelike neck. The neck had its outlet just below Coeurl.

His ear tendrils caught the low-frequency waves of whistling. The sound throbbed through his being; and suddenly terror caught with icy fingers at his brain. The man would have a gun. Suppose he leveled one burst of atomic energy—*one burst*—before his own muscles could whip out in murder fury.

A little shower of rocks streamed past. And then the man was beneath him. Coeurl reached out and struck a single crushing blow at the shimmering transparent headpiece of the spacesuit. There was a tearing sound of metal and a gushing of blood. The man doubled up as if part of him had been telescoped. For a moment, his bones and legs and muscles combined miraculously to keep him standing. Then he crumpled with a metallic clank of his space armor.

Fear completely evaporated, Coeurl leaped out of hiding. With ravenous speed, he smashed the metal and the body within it to bits. Great chunks of metal, torn piecemeal from the suit, sprayed the ground. Bones cracked. Flesh crunched.

It was simple to tune in on the vibrations of the id, and to create the violent chemical disorganization that freed it from the crushed bone. The id was, Coeurl discovered, mostly in the bone.

He felt revived, almost reborn. Here was more food than he had had in the whole past year.

Three minutes, and it was over, and Coeurl was off like a thing fleeing dire danger. Cautiously, he approached the glistening globe from the opposite side to that by which he had left. The men were all busy at their tasks. Gliding noiselessly, Coeurl slipped unnoticed up to a group of men.

Morton stared down at the horror of tattered flesh, metal and blood on the rock at his feet, and felt a tightening in his throat that prevented speech. He heard Kent say:

"He *would* go alone, damn him!" The little chemist's voice held a sob imprisoned; and Morton remembered that Kent and Jarvey had chummed together for years in the way only two men can.

"The worst part of it is," shuddered one of the men, "it looks like a senseless murder. His body is spread out like little lumps of flattened jelly, but it seems to be all there. I'd almost wager that if we weighed everything here, there'd still be one hundred and seventy-five pounds by earth gravity. That'd be about one hundred and seventy pounds here."

Smith broke in, his mournful face lined with gloom: "The killer attacked Jarvey, and then discovered his flesh was alien—uneatable. Just like our big cat. Wouldn't eat anything we set before him—" His words died out in sudden, queer silence. Then he said slowly: "Say, what about that creature? He's big enough and strong enough to have done this with his own little paws."

Morton frowned. "It's a thought. After all, he's the only living thing we've seen. We can't just execute him on suspicion, of course—"

"Besides," said one of the men, "he was never out of my sight."

Before Morton could speak, Siedel, the psychologist, snapped, "Positive about that?"

The man hesitated. "Maybe he was for a few minutes. He was wandering around so much, looking at everything."

"Exactly," said Siedel with satisfaction. He turned to Morton. "You see, commander, I, too, had the impression that he was always around; and yet, thinking back over it, I find gaps. There were moments—probably long minutes—when he was completely out of sight."

Morton's face was dark with thought, as Kent broke in fiercely: "I say, take no chances. Kill the brute on suspicion before he does any more damage."

Morton said slowly: "Korita, you've been wandering around with Cranessy and Van Horne. Do you think pussy is a descendant of the ruling class of this planet?"

The tall Japanese archeologist stared at the sky as if collecting his mind. "Commander Morton," he said finally, respectfully, "there is a mystery here. Take a look, all of you, at that majestic skyline. Notice the almost Gothic outline of the architecture. In spite of the megalopolis which they created, these people were close to the soil. The buildings are not simply ornamented. They are ornamental in themselves. Here is the equivalent of the Doric column, the Egyptian pyramid, the Gothic cathedral, growing out of the ground, earnest, big with destiny. If this lonely, desolate world can be regarded as a mother earth, then the land had a warm, a spiritual place in the hearts of the race.

"The effect is emphasized by the winding streets. Their machines prove they were mathematicians, but they were artists first; and so they did not create the geometrically designed cities of the ultra-sophisticated world metropolis. There is a genuine artistic abandon, a deep joyous emotion written in the curving and unmathematical arrangements of houses, buildings and avenues; a sense of inten-sity, of divine belief in an inner certainty. This is not a decadent, hoary-with-age civilization, but a young and vigorous culture, confident, strong with purpose.

"There it ended. Abruptly, as if at this point culture had its Battle of Tours, and began to collapse like the ancient Mohammedan civi-lization. Or as if in one leap it spanned the centuries and entered the period of contending states. In the Chinese civilization that period occupied 480-230 B.C., at the end of which the State of Tsin saw the beginning of the Chinese Empire. This phase Egypt experienced between 1780-1580 B.C., of which the last century was the 'Hyksos'—unmentionable—time. The classical experienced it from Chæronea—338—and, at the pitch of horror, from the Gracchi—133—to Actium—31 B.C. The West European Americans were devastated by it in the nineteenth and twentieth centuries, and modern historians agree that, nominally, we entered the same phase fifty years ago; though, of course, we have solved the problem.

"You may ask, commander, what has all this to do with your question? My answer is: there is no record of a culture entering abruptly into the period of contending states. It is always a slow development; and the first step is a merciless questioning of all that was once held sacred. Inner certainties cease to exist, are dissolved before the ruthless probings of scientific and analytic minds. The skeptic becomes the highest type of being.

"I say that this culture ended abruptly in its most flourishing age. The sociological effects of such a catastrophe would be a sud-den vanishing of morals, a reversion to almost bestial criminality, unleavened by any sense of ideal, a callous indifference to death. If this . . . this pussy is a descendant of such a race, then he will be a cunning creature, a thief in the night, a cold-blooded murderer, who would cut his own brother's throat for gain."

"That's enough!" It was Kent's clipped voice. "Commander, I'm willing to act the role of executioner."

Smith interrupted sharply: "Listen, Morton, you're not going to kill that cat yet, even if he is guilty. He's a biological treasure house."

Kent and Smith were glaring angrily at each other. Morton frowned at them thoughtfully, then said: "Korita, I'm inclined to accept your theory as a working basis. But one question: Pussy comes from a period earlier than our own? That is, we are entering the highly civilized era of our culture, while he became suddenly historyless in the most vigorous period of his. *But* it is possible that his culture is a later one on this planet than ours is in the galactic-wide system we have civilized?"

"Exactly. His may be the middle of the tenth civilization of his world; while ours is the end of the eighth sprung from earth, each of the ten, of course, having been builded on the ruins of the one before it."

"In that case, pussy would not know anything about the skepticism that made it possible for us to find him out so positively as a criminal and murderer?"

"No; it would be literally magic to him."

Morton was smiling grimly. "Then I think you'll get your wish, Smith. We'll let pussy live; and if there are any fatalities, now that we know him, it will be due to rank carelessness. There's just the chance, of course, that we're wrong. Like Siedel, I also have the impression that he was always around. But now—we can't leave poor Jarvey here like this. We'll put him in a coffin and bury him."

"No, we won't!" Kent barked. He flushed. "I beg your pardon, commander. I didn't mean it that way. I maintain pussy wanted something from that body. It looks to be all there, but something must be missing. I'm going to find out what, and pin this murder on him so that you'll have to believe it beyond the shadow of a doubt."

It was late night when Morton looked up from a book and saw Kent emerge through the door that led from the laboratories below.

Kent carried a large, flat bowl in his hands; his tired eyes flashed across at Morton, and he said in a weary, yet harsh, voice: "Now watch!"

He started toward Coeurl, who lay sprawled on the great rug, pretending to be asleep.

Morton stopped him. "Wait a minute, Kent. Any other time, I

wouldn't question your actions, but you look ill; you're overwrought. What have you got there?"

Kent turned, and Morton saw that his first impression had been but a flashing glimpse of the truth. There were dark pouches under the little chemist's gray eyes—eyes that gazed feverishly from sunken cheeks in an ascetic face.

"I've found the missing element," Kent said. "It's phosphorus. There wasn't so much as a square millimeter of phosphorus left in Jarvey's bones. Every bit of it had been drained out—by what super-chemistry I don't know. There are ways of getting phosphorus out of the human body. For instance, a quick way was what happened to the workman who helped build this ship. Remember, he fell into fifteen tons of molten metalite—at least, so his relatives claimed—but the company wouldn't pay compensation until the metalite, on analysis, was found to contain a high percentage of phosphorus—"

"What about the bowl of food?" somebody interrupted. Men were putting away magazines and books, looking up with interest.

"It's got organic phosphorus in it. He'll get the scent, or whatever it is that he uses instead of scent—"

"I think he gets the vibrations of things," Gourlay interjected lazily. "Sometimes, when he wiggles those tendrils, I get a distinct static on the radio. And then, again, there's no reaction, as if he's moved higher or lower on the wave scale. He seems to control the vibrations at will."

Kent waited with obvious impatience until Gourlay's last word, then abruptly went on: "All right, then, when he gets the vibration of the phosphorus and reacts to it like an animal, then—well, we can decide what we've proved by his reaction. May I go ahead, Morton?"

"There are three things wrong with your plan," Morton said. "In the first place, you seem to assume that he is only animal; you seem to have forgotten he may not be hungry after Jarvey; you seem to think that he will not be suspicious. But set the bowl down. His reaction may tell us something."

Coeurl stared with unblinking black eyes as the man set the bowl before him. His ear tendrils instantly caught the id-vibrations from the contents of the bowl—and he gave it not even a second glance.

He recognized this two-legged being as the one who had held the weapon that morning. Danger! With a snarl, he floated to his feet. He caught the bowl with the fingerlike appendages at the end of one looping tentacle, and emptied its contents into the face of Kent, who shrank back with a yell.

Explosively, Coeurl flung the bowl aside and snapped a hawser-thick tentacle around the cursing man's waist. He didn't bother with the gun that hung from Kent's belt. It was only a vibration gun, he sensed—atomic powered, but not an atomic disintegrator. He tossed the kicking Kent onto the nearest couch—and realized with a hiss of dismay that he should have disarmed the man.

Not that the gun was dangerous—but, as the man furiously wiped the gruel from his face with one hand, he reached with the other for his weapon. Coeurl crouched back as the gun was raised slowly and a white beam of flame was discharged at his massive head.

His ear tendrils hummed as they canceled the efforts of the vibration gun. His round, black eyes narrowed as he caught the movement of men reaching for their metalite guns. Morton's voice lashed across the silence.

"Stop!"

Kent clicked off his weapon; and Coeurl crouched down, quivering with fury at this man who had forced him to reveal something of his power.

"Kent," said Morton coldly, "you're not the type to lose your head. You deliberately tried to kill pussy, knowing that the majority of us are in favor of keeping him alive. You know what our rule is: If anyone objects to my decisions, he must say so *at the time*. If the majority object, my decisions are overruled. In this case, no one but you objected, and, therefore, your action in taking the law into your own hands is most reprehensible, and automatically debars you from voting for a year."

Kent stared grimly at the circle of faces. "Korita was right when he said ours was a highly civilized age. It's decadent." Passion flamed harshly in his voice. "My God, isn't there a man here who can see the horror of the situation? Jarvey dead only a few hours, and this creature, whom we all know to be guilty, lying there unchained, planning his next murder; and the victim is right here in this room. What kind of men are we—fools, cynics, ghouls—or is it that our civilization is so steeped in reason that we can contemplate a murderer sympathetically?"

He fixed brooding eyes on Coeurl. "You were right, Morton, that's no animal. That's a devil from the deepest hell of this forgotten planet, whirling its solitary way around a dying sun."

"Don't go melodramatic on us," Morton said. "Your analysis is all wrong, so far as I'm concerned. We're not ghouls or cynics; we're simply scientists, and pussy here is going to be studied. Now that we suspect him, we doubt his ability to trap any of us. One against a hundred hasn't a chance." He glanced around. "Do I speak for all of us?"

"Not for me, commander!" It was Smith who spoke, and, as Morton stared in amazement, he continued: "In the excitement and momentary confusion, no one seems to have noticed that when Kent fired his vibration gun, the beam hit this creature squarely on his cat head—and didn't hurt him."

Morton's amazed glance went from Smith to Coeurl, and back to Smith again. "Are you certain it hit him? As you say, it all happened so swiftly—when pussy wasn't hurt I simply assumed that Kent had missed him."

"He hit him in the face," Smith said positively. "A vibration gun, of course, can't even kill a man right away—but it can injure him. There's no sign of injury on pussy, though, not even a singed hair."

"Perhaps his skin is a good insulation against heat of any kind."

"Perhaps. But in view of our uncertainty, I think we should lock him up in the cage."

While Morton frowned darkly in thought, Kent spoke up. "Now you're talking sense, Smith."

Morton asked: "Then you would be satisfied, Kent, if we put him in the cage?"

Kent considered, finally: "Yes. If four inches of micro-steel can't hold him, we'd better give him the ship."

Coeurl followed the men as they went out into the corridor. He trotted docilely along as Morton unmistakably motioned him through a door he had not hitherto seen. He found himself in a square, solid metal room. The door clanged metallically behind him; he felt the flow of power as the electric lock clicked home.

His lips parted in a grimace of hate, as he realized the trap, but he gave no other outward reaction. It occurred to him that he had progressed a long way from the sunk-into-primitiveness creature who, a few hours before, had gone incoherent with fear in an elevator cage. Now, a thousand memories of his powers were reawakened in his brain; ten thousand cunnings were, after ages of disuse, once again part of his very being.

He sat quite still for a moment on the short, heavy haunches

into which his body tapered, his ear tendrils examining his surroundings. Finally, he lay down, his eyes glowing with contemptuous fire. The fools! The poor fools!

It was about an hour later when he heard the man—Smith—
fumbling overhead. Vibrations poured upon him, and for just an
instant he was startled. He leaped to his feet in pure terror—and
then realized that the vibrations *were* vibrations, not atomic explosions. Somebody was taking pictures of the inside of his body.

He crouched down again, but his ear tendrils vibrated, and he
thought contemptuously: the silly fool would be surprised when
he tried to develop those pictures.

After a while the man went away, and for a long time there
were noises of men doing things far away. That, too, died away
slowly.

Coeurl lay waiting, as he felt the silence creep over the ship.
In the long ago, before the dawn of immortality, the coeurls, too,
had slept at night; and the memory of it had been revived the day
before when he saw some of the men dozing. At last, the vibration of two pairs of feet, pacing, pacing endlessly, was the only
human-made frequency that throbbed on his ear tendrils.

Tensely, he listened to the two watchmen. The first one walked
slowly past the cage door. Then about thirty feet behind him
came the second. Coeurl sensed the alertness of these men; knew
that he could never surprise either while they walked separately.
It meant—he must be doubly careful!

Fifteen minutes, and they came again. The moment they were
past, he switched his sense from their vibrations to a vastly higher
range. The pulsating violence of the atomic engines stammered its
soft story to his brain. The electric dynamos hummed their muffled
song of pure power. He felt the whisper of that flow through the
wires in the walls of his cage, and through the electric lock of his
door. He forced his quivering body into straining immobility, his
senses seeking, searching, to tune in on that sibilant tempest of
energy. Suddenly, his ear tendrils vibrated in harmony—he caught
the surging charge into shrillness of that rippling force wave.

There was a sharp click of metal on metal. With a gentle touch
of one tentacle, Coeurl pushed open the door, and glided out into
the dully gleaming corridor. For just a moment he felt contempt,
a glow of superiority, as he thought of the stupid creatures who
dared to match their wit against a coeurl. And in that moment,
he suddenly thought of other coeurls. A queer, exultant sense of
race pounded through his being; the driving hate of centuries of

ruthless competition yielded reluctantly before pride of kinship with the future rulers of all space.

Suddenly, he felt weighed down by his limitations, his need for other coeurls, his aloneness—one against a hundred, with the stake all eternity; the starry universe itself beckoned his rapacious, vaulting ambition. If he failed, there would never be a second chance—no time to revive long-rotted machinery, and attempt to solve the secret of space travel.

He padded along on tensed paws—through the salon—into the next corridor—and came to the first bedroom door. It stood half open. One swift flow of synchronized muscles, one swiftly lashing tentacle that caught the unresisting throat of the sleeping man, crushing it; and the lifeless head rolled crazily, the body twitched once.

Seven bedrooms; seven dead men. It was the seventh taste of murder that brought a sudden return of lust, a pure, unbounded desire to kill, return of a millennium-old habit of destroying everything containing the precious id.

As the twelfth man slipped convulsively into death, Coeurl emerged abruptly from the sensuous joy of the kill to the sound of footsteps.

They were not near—that was what brought wave after wave of fright swirling into the chaos that suddenly became his brain.

The watchmen were coming slowly along the corridor toward the door of the cage where he had been imprisoned. In a moment, the first man would see the open door—and sound the alarm.

Coeurl caught at the vanishing remnants of his reason. With frantic speed, careless now of accidental sounds, he raced—along the corridor with its bedroom doors—through the salon. He emerged into the next corridor, cringing in awful anticipation of the atomic flame he expected would stab into his face.

The two men were together, standing side by side. For one single instant, Coeurl could scarcely believe his tremendous good luck. Like a fool the second had come running when he saw the other stop before the open door. They looked up, paralyzed, before the nightmare of claws and tentacles, the ferocious cat head and hate-filled eyes.

The first man went for his gun, but the second, physically frozen before the doom he saw, uttered a shriek, a shrill cry of horror that floated along the corridors—and ended in a curious gargle, as Coeurl flung the two corpses with one irresistible motion the full length of the corridor. He didn't want the dead bodies found near the cage. That was his one hope.

Shaking in every nerve and muscle, conscious of the terrible error he had made, unable to think coherently, he plunged into the cage. The door clicked softly shut behind him. Power flowed once more through the electric lock.

He crouched tensely, simulating sleep, as he heard the rush of many feet, caught the vibration of excited voices. He knew when somebody actuated the cage audioscope and looked in. A few moments now, and the other bodies would be discovered.

"Siedel gone!" Morton said numbly. "What are we going to do without Siedel? And Breckenridge! And Coulter and— Horrible!"

He covered his face with his hands, but only for an instant. He looked up grimly, his heavy chin outthrust as he stared into the stern faces that surrounded him. "If anybody's got so much as a germ of an idea, bring it out."

"Space madness!"

"I've thought of that. But there hasn't been a case of a man going mad for fifty years. Dr. Eggert will test everybody, of course, and right now he's looking at the bodies with that possibility in mind."

As he finished, he saw the doctor coming through the door. Men crowded aside to make way for him.

"I heard you, commander," Dr. Eggert said, "and I think I can say right now that the space-madness theory is out. The throats of these men have been squeezed to a jelly. No human being could have exerted such enormous strength without using a machine."

Morton saw that the doctor's eyes kept looking down the corridor, and he shook his head and groaned:

"It's no use suspecting pussy, doctor. He's in his cage, pacing up and down. Obviously heard the racket and— Man alive! You can't suspect him. That cage was built to hold literally *anything*—four inches of micro-steel—and there's not a scratch on the door. Kent, even you won't say, 'Kill him on suspicion,' because there can't be any suspicion, unless there's a new science here, beyond anything we can imagine—"

"On the contrary," said Smith flatly, "we have all the evidence we need. I used the telefluor on him—you know the arrangement we have on top of the cage—and tried to take some pictures. They just blurred. Pussy jumped when the telefluor was turned on, as if he felt the vibrations.

"You all know what Gourlay said before? This beast can apparently receive and send vibrations of any lengths. The way he dominated the power of Kent's gun is final proof of his special ability to interfere with energy."

"What in the name of all hells have we got here?" one of the men groaned. "Why, if he can control that power, and send it out in any vibrations, there's nothing to stop him killing all of us."

"Which proves," snapped Morton, "that he isn't invincible, or he would have done it long ago."

Very deliberately, he walked over to the mechanism that controlled the prison cage.

"You're not going to open the door!" Kent gasped, reaching for his gun.

"No, but if I pull this switch, electricity will flow through the floor, and electrocute whatever's inside. We've never had to use this before, so you had probably forgotten about it."

He jerked the switch hard over. Blue fire flashed from the metal, and a bank of fuses above his head exploded with a single bang.

Morton frowned. "That's funny. Those fuses shouldn't have blown! Well, we can't even look in, now. That wrecked the audios, too."

Smith said: "If he could interfere with the electric lock, enough to open the door, then he probably probed every possible danger and was ready to interfere when you threw that switch."

"At least, it proves he's vulnerable to our energies!" Morton smiled grimly. "Because he rendered them harmless. The important thing is, we've got him behind four inches of the toughest of metal. At the worst we can open the door and ray him to death. But first, I think we'll try to use the telefluor power cable—"

A commotion from inside the cage interrupted his words. A heavy body crashed against a wall, followed by a dull thump.

"He knows what we were trying to do!" Smith grunted to Morton. "And I'll bet it's a very sick pussy in there. What a fool he was to go back into that cage and does he realize it!"

The tension was relaxing; men were smiling nervously, and there was even a ripple of humorless laughter at the picture Smith drew of the monster's discomfiture.

"What I'd like to know," said Pennons, the engineer, "is, why did the telefluor meter dial jump and waver at full power when pussy made that noise? It's right under my nose here, and the dial jumped like a house afire!"

There was silence both without and within the cage, then Morton said: "It may mean he's coming out. Back, everybody, and keep your guns ready. Pussy was a fool to think he could conquer a hundred men, but he's by far the most formidable creature in the galactic system. He may come out of that door, rather than die like a rat in a trap. And he's just tough enough to take some of us with him—if we're not careful."

The men back slowly in a solid body; and somebody said: "That's funny. I thought I heard the elevator."

"Elevator!" Morton echoed. "Are you sure, man?"

"Just for a moment I was!" The man, a member of the crew, hesitated. "We were all shuffling our feet—"

"Take somebody with you, and go look. Bring whoever dared to run off back here—"

There was a jar, a horrible jerk, as the whole gigantic body of the ship careened under them. Morton was flung to the floor with a violence that stunned him. He fought back to consciousness, aware of the other men lying all around him. He shouted: "Who the devil started those engines!"

The agonizing acceleration continued; his feet dragged with awful exertion, as he fumbled with the nearest audioscope, and punched the engine-room number. The picture that flooded onto the screen brought a deep bellow to his lips:

"It's pussy! He's in the engine room—and we're heading straight out into space."

The screen went black even as he spoke, and he could see no more.

It was Morton who first staggered across the salon floor to the supply room where the spacesuits were kept. After fumbling almost blindly into his own suit, he cut the effects of the body-torturing acceleration, and brought suits to the semiconscious men on the floor. In a few moments, other men were assisting him; and then it was only a matter of minutes before everybody was clad in metalite, with anti-acceleration motors running at half power.

It was Morton then who, after first looking into the cage, opened the door and stood, silent as the others who crowded about him, to stare at the gaping hole in the rear wall. The hole was a frightful thing of jagged edges and horribly bent metal, and it opened upon another corridor.

"I'll swear," whispered Pennons, "that it's impossible. The ten-ton hammer in the machine shops couldn't more than dent four inches of micro with one blow—and we only heard one. It would take at least a minute for an atomic disintegrator to do the job. Morton, this is a super-being."

Morton saw that Smith was examining the break in the wall. The biologist looked up. "If only Breckinridge weren't dead! We need a metallurgist to explain this. Look!"

He touched the broken edge of the metal. A piece crumbled in his finger and slithered away in a fine shower of dust to the floor. Morton noticed for the first time that there was a little pile of metallic debris and dust.

"You've hit it." Morton nodded. "No miracle of strength here. The monster merely used his special powers to interfere with the electronic tensions holding the metal together. That would account, too, for the drain on the telefluor power cable that Pennons noticed. The thing used the power with his body as a transforming medium, smashed through the wall, ran down the corridor to the elevator shaft, and so down to the engine room."

"In the meantime, commander," Kent said quietly, "we are faced with a super-being in control of the ship, completely dominating the engine room and its almost unlimited power, and in possession of the best part of the machine shops."

Morton felt the silence, while the men pondered the chemist's words. Their anxiety was a tangible thing that lay heavily upon their faces; in every expression was the growing realization that here was the ultimate situation in their lives; their very existence was at stake and perhaps much more. Morton voiced the thought in everybody's mind:

"Suppose he wins. He's utterly ruthless, and he probably sees galactic power within his grasp."

"Kent is wrong," barked the chief navigator. "The thing doesn't dominate the engine room. We've still got the control room, and that gives us *first* control of all the machines. You fellows may not know the mechanical set-up we have; but, though he can eventually disconnect us, we can cut off all the switches in the engine room *now*. Commander, why didn't you just shut off the power instead of putting us into spacesuits? At the very least you could have adjusted the ship to the acceleration."

"For two reasons," Morton answered. "Individually, we're safer within the force fields of our spacesuits. And we can't afford to give up our advantages in panicky moves."

"Advantages! What other advantages have we got?"

"We know things about him," Morton replied. "And right now, we're going to make a test. Pennons, detail five men to each of the four approaches to the engine room. Take atomic disintegrators to blast through the big doors. They're all shut, I noticed. He's locked himself in.

"Selenski, you go up to the control room and shut off everything except the drive engines. Gear them to the master switch, and shut them off all at once. One thing, though—leave the acceleration on full blast. No anti-acceleration must be applied to the ship. Understand?"

"Aye, sir!" The pilot saluted.

"And report to me through the communicators if any of the machines start to run again." He faced the men. "I'm going to lead the main approach. Kent, you take No. 2; Smith, No. 3, and Pennons, No. 4. We're going to find out right now if we're dealing with unlimited science, or a creature limited like the rest of us. I'll bet on the second possibility."

Morton had an empty sense of walking endlessly, as he moved, a giant of a man in his transparent space armor, along the glistening metal tube that was the main corridor of the engine-room floor. Reason told him the creature had already shown feet of clay, yet the feeling that here was an invincible being persisted.

He spoke into the communicator: "It's not use trying to sneak up on him. He can probably hear a pin drop. So just wheel up your units. He hasn't been in that engine room long enough to do anything.

"As I've said, this is largely a test attack. In the first place, we could never forgive ourselves if we didn't try to conquer him now, before he's had time to prepare against us. But, aside from the possibility that we can destroy him immediately, I have a theory.

"The idea goes something like this: Those doors are built to withstand accidental atomic explosions, and it will take fifteen minutes for the atomic disintegrators to smash them. During that period the monster will have no power. True, the drive will be on, but that's straight atomic explosion. My theory is, he can't touch stuff like that; and in a few minutes you'll see what I mean—I hope."

His voice was suddenly crisp: "Ready, Selenski?"

"Aye, ready."

"Then cut the master switch."

The corridor—the whole ship, Morton knew—was abruptly plunged into darkness. Morton clicked on the dazzling light of his spacesuit; the other men did the same, their faces pale and drawn.

"Blast!" Morton barked into his communicator.

The mobile units throbbed; and then pure atomic flame ravened out and poured upon the hard metal of the door. The first molten droplet rolled reluctantly, not down, but up the door. The second was more normal. It followed a shaky downward course. The third rolled sideways—for this was pure force, not subject to gravitation. Other drops followed until a dozen streams trickled sedately yet unevenly in every direction—streams of hellish, sparkling fire, bright as fairy gems, alive with the coruscating fury of atoms suddenly tortured, and running blindly, crazy with pain.

The minutes ate at time like a slow acid. At last Morton asked huskily:

"Selenski?"

"Nothing yet, commander."

Morton half whispered: "But he must be doing something. He can't be just waiting in there like a cornered rat. Selenski?"

"Nothing, commander."

Seven minutes, eight minutes, then twelve.

"Commander!" It was Selenski's voice, taut. "He's got the electric dynamo running."

Morton drew a deep breath, and heard one of his men say:

"That's funny. We can't get any deeper. Boss, take a look at this."

Morton looked. The little scintillating streams had frozen rigid. The ferocity of the disintegrators vented in vain against metal grown suddenly invulnerable.

Morton sighed. "Our test is over. Leave two men guarding every corridor. The others come up to the control room."

He seated himself a few minutes later before the massive control keyboard. "So far as I'm concerned the test was a success. We know that of all the machines in the engine room, the most important to the monster was the electric dynamo. He must have worked in a frenzy of terror while we were at the doors."

"Of course, it's easy to see what he did," Pennons said. "Once he had the power he increased the electronic tensions of the door to their ultimate."

"The main thing is this," Smith chimed in. "He works with vibrations only so far as his special powers are concerned, and the energy must come from outside himself. Atomic energy in its pure form, not being vibration, he can't handle any differently than we can."

Kent said glumly: "The main point in my opinion is that he stopped us cold. What's the good of knowing that his control over vibrations did it? If we can't break through those doors with our atomic disintegrators, we're finished."

Morton shook his head. "Not finished—but we'll have to do some planning. First, though, I'll start these engines. It'll be harder for him to get control of them when they're running."

He pulled the master switch back into place with a jerk. There was a hum, as scores of machines leaped into violent life in the engine room a hundred feet below. The noises sank to a steady vibration of throbbing power.

Three hours later, Morton paced up and down before the men gathered in the salon. His dark hair was uncombed; the space pallor of his strong face emphasized rather than detracted from the outthrust aggressiveness of his jaw. When he spoke, his deep voice was crisp to the point of sharpness:

"To make sure that our plans are fully coordinated, I'm going to ask each expert in turn to outline his part in the overpowering of this creature. Pennons first!"

Pennons stood up briskly. He was not a big man, Morton thought, yet he looked big, perhaps because of his air of authority. This man knew engines, and the history of engines. Morton had heard him trace a machine through its evolution from a simple toy to the highly complicated modern instrument. He had studied machine development on a hundred planets; and there was literally nothing fundamental that he didn't know about mechanics. It was almost weird to hear Pennons, who could have spoken for a thousand hours and still only have touched upon his subject, say with absurd brevity:

"We've set up a relay in the control room to start and stop every engine rhythmically. The trip lever will work a hundred times a second, and the effect will be to create vibrations of every description. There is just a possibility that one or more of the machines will burst, on the principle of soldiers crossing a bridge in step—you've heard that old story, no doubt—but in my opinion there is no real danger of a break of that tough metal. The main purpose is simply to interfere with the interference of the creature, and smash through the doors."

"Gourlay next!" barked Morton.

Gourlay climbed lazily to his feet. He looked sleepy, as if he was somewhat bored by the whole proceedings, yet Morton knew he loved people to think him lazy, a good-for-nothing slouch, who spent his days in slumber and his nights catching forty winks. His title was chief communication engineer, but his knowledge extended to every vibration field; and he was probably, with the possible exception of Kent, the fastest thinker on the ship. His voice drawled out, and—Morton noted—the very deliberate assurance of it had a soothing effect on the men—anxious faces relaxed, bodies leaned back more restfully:

"Once inside," Gourlay said, "we've rigged up vibration screens of pure force that should stop nearly everything he's got on the ball. They work on the principle of reflection, so that everything he sends will be reflected back to him. In addition, we've got plenty of spare electric energy that we'll just feed him from mobile copper cups. There must be a limit to his capacity for handling power with those insulated nerves of his."

"Selenski!" called Morton.

The chief pilot was already standing, as if he had anticipated Morton's call. And that, Morton reflected, was the man. His nerves had that rocklike steadiness which is the first requirement of the master controller of a great ship's movements; yet that very steadiness seemed to rest on dynamite ready to explode at its owner's volition. He was not a man of great learning, but he "reacted" to stimuli so fast that he always seemed to be anticipating.

"The impression I've received of the plan is that it must be cumulative. Just when the creature thinks that he can't stand any more, another thing happens to add to his trouble and confusion. When the uproar's at its height, I'm supposed to cut in the anti-accelerators. The commander thinks with Gunlie Lester that these creatures will know nothing about anti-acceleration. It's a development, pure and simple, of the science of interstellar flight, and couldn't have been developed in any other way. We think when the creature feels the first effects of the anti-acceleration—you all remember the caved-in feeling you had the first month—it won't know what to think or do."

"Korita next."

"I can only offer you encouragement," said the archeologist, "on the basis of my theory that the monster has all the characteristics of a criminal of the early ages of any civilization, complicated by an apparent reversion to primitiveness. The suggestion has been made by Smith that his knowledge of science is puzzling, and could only mean that we are dealing with an actual inhabitant, not a descendant of the inhabitants of the dead city we visited. This would ascribe virtual immortality to our enemy, a possibility which is borne out by his ability to breathe both oxygen and chlorine—or neither—but even that makes no difference. He comes from a certain age in his civilization; and he has sunk so low that his ideas are mostly memories of that age.

"In spite of all the powers of his body, he lost his head in the elevator the first morning, until he remembered. He placed himself in such a position that he was forced to reveal his special powers against vibrations. He bungled the mass murders a few hours ago. In fact, his whole record is one of the low cunning of the primitive, egotistical mind which has little or no conception of the vast organization with which it is confronted.

"He is like the ancient German soldier who felt superior to the elderly Roman scholar, yet the latter was part of a mighty civilization of which the Germans of that day stood in awe.

"You may suggest that the sack of Rome by the Germans in later years defeats my argument; however, modern historians agree that the 'sack' was an historical accident, and not history in the true sense of the word. The movement of the 'Sea-peoples' which set in against the Egyptian civilization from 1400 B.C. succeeded only as regards the Cretan island-realm—their mighty expeditions against the Libyan and Phoenician coasts, with the accompaniment of Viking fleets, failed as those of the Huns failed against the Chinese Empire. Rome would have been abandoned in any event. Ancient, glorious Samarra was desolate by the tenth century; Pataliputra, Asoka's great capital, was an immense and completely uninhabited waste of houses when the Chinese traveler Hsinantang visited it about A.D. 635.

"We have, then, a primitive, and that primitive is now far out in space, completely outside of his natural habitat. I say, let's go in and win."

One of the men grumbled, as Korita finished: "You can talk about the sack of Rome being an accident, and about this fellow being a primitive, but the facts are facts. It looks to me as if Rome is about to fall again; and it won't be no primitive that did it, either. This guy's got plenty of what it takes."

Morton smiled grimly at the man, a member of the crew. "We'll see about that—right now!"

In the blazing brilliance of the gigantic machine shop, Coeurl slaved. The forty-foot, cigar-shaped spaceship was nearly finished.

With a grunt of effort, he completed the laborious installation of the drive engines, and paused to survey his craft.

Its interior, visible through the one aperture in the outer wall, was pitifully small. There was literally room for nothing but the engines—and a narrow space for himself.

He plunged frantically back to work as he heard the approach of the men, and the sudden change in the tempest-like thunder of the engines—a rhythmical off-and-on hum, shriller in tone, sharper, more nerve-racking than the deep-throated, steady throb that had preceded it. Suddenly, there were the atomic disintegrators again at the massive outer doors.

He fought them off, but never wavered from his task. Every mighty muscle of his powerful body strained as he carried great loads of tools, machines and instruments, and dumped them into the bottom of his makeshift ship. There was no time to fit anything into place, no time for anything—no time—no time.

The thought pounded at his reason. He felt strangely weary for the first time in his long and vigorous existence. With a last, tortured heave, he jerked the gigantic sheet of metal into the gaping aperture of the ship—and stood there for a terrible minute, balancing it precariously.

He knew the doors were going down. Half a dozen disintegrators concentrating on one point were irresistibly, though slowly, eating away the remaining inches. With a gasp, he released his mind from the doors and concentrated every ounce of his mind on the yard-thick outer wall, toward which the blunt nose of his ship was pointing.

His body cringed from the surging power that flowed from the electric dynamo through his ear tendrils into that resisting wall. The whole inside of him felt on fire, and he knew that he was dangerously close to carrying his ultimate load.

And still he stood there, shuddering with the awful pain, holding the unfastened metal plate with hard-clenched tentacles. His massive head pointed as in dread fascination at that bitterly hard wall.

He heard one of the engine-room doors crash inward. Men shouted; disintegrators rolled forward, their raging power unchecked. Coeurl heard the floor of the engine room hiss in protest, as those beams of atomic energy tore everything in their path to bits. The machines rolled closer; cautious footsteps sounded behind them. In a minute they would be at the flimsy doors separating the engine room from the machine shop.

Suddenly, Coeurl was satisfied. With a snarl of hate, a vindictive glow of feral eyes, he ducked into his little craft, and pulled the metal plate down into place as if it was a hatchway.

His ear tendrils hummed, as he softened the edges of the surrounding metal. In an instant, the plate was more than welded—it was part of his ship, a seamless, rivetless part of a whole that was solid opaque metal except for two transparent areas, one in the front, one in the rear.

His tentacle embraced the power drive with almost sensuous tenderness. There was a forward surge of his fragile machine, straight at the great outer wall of the machine shops. The nose of the forty-foot craft touched—and the wall dissolved in a glittering shower of dust.

Coeurl felt the barest retarding movement; and then he kicked the nose of the machine out into the cold of space, twisted it about, and headed back in the direction from which the big ship had been coming all these hours.

Men in space armor stood in the jagged hole that yawned in the lower reaches of the gigantic globe. The men and the great ship grew smaller. Then the men were gone; and there was only the ship with its blaze of a thousand blurring portholes. The ball shrank incredibly, too small now for individual portholes to be visible.

Almost straight ahead, Coeurl saw a tiny, dim, reddish ball—his own sun, he realized. He headed toward it at full speed. There were caves where he could hide and with other coeurls build secretly a spaceship in which they could reach other planets safety—now that he knew how.

His body ached from the agony of acceleration, yet he dared not let up for a single instant. He glanced back, half in terror. The globe was still there, a tiny dot of light in the immense blackness of space. Suddenly it twinkled and was gone.

For a brief moment, he had the empty, frightened impression that just before it disappeared, it moved. But he could see nothing. He could not escape the belief that they had shut off all their lights, and were sneaking up on him in the darkness. Worried and uncertain, he looked through the forward transparent plate.

A tremor of dismay shot through him. The dim red sun toward which he was heading was not growing larger. *It was becoming smaller* by the instant, and it grew visibly tinier during the next five minutes, became a pale-red dot in the sky—and vanished like the ship.

Fear came then, a blinding surge of it, that swept through his being and left him chilled with the sense of the unknown. For minutes, he stared frantically into the space ahead, searching for some landmark. But only the remote stars glimmered there, unwinking points against a velvet background of unfathomable distance.

Wait! One of the points was growing larger. With every muscle and nerve tensed, Coeurl watched the point becoming a dot, a round ball of light—red light. Bigger, bigger, it grew. Suddenly, the red light shimmered and turned white—and there, before him, was the great globe of the spaceship, lights glaring from every porthole, the very ship which a few minutes before he had watched vanish behind him.

Something happened to Coeurl in that moment. His brain was spinning like a flywheel, faster, faster, more incoherently. Suddenly, the wheel flew apart into a million aching fragments. His eyes almost started from their sockets as, like a maddened animal, he raged in his small quarters.

His tentacles clutched at precious instruments and flung them insensately; his paws smashed in fury at the very walls of his ship. Finally, in a brief flash of sanity, he knew that he couldn't face the inevitable fire of atomic disintegrators.

It was a simple thing to create the violent disorganization that freed every drop of id from his vital organs.

They found him lying dead in a little pool of phosphorus.

"Poor pussy," said Morton. "I wonder what he thought when he saw us appear ahead of him, after his own sun disappeared. Knowing nothing of anti-accelerators, he couldn't know that we could stop short in space, whereas it would take him more than three hours to decelerate; and in the meantime he'd be drawing farther and farther away from where he wanted to go. He couldn't know that by stopping, we flashed past him at millions of miles a second. Of course, he didn't have a chance once he left our ship. The whole world must have seemed topsy-turvy."

"Never mind the sympathy," he heard Kent say behind him. "We've got a job—to kill every cat in that miserable world."

Korita murmured softly: "That should be simple. They are but primitives; and we have merely to sit down, and they will come to us, cunningly expecting to delude us."

Smith snapped: "You fellows make me sick! Pussy was the toughest nut we ever had to crack. He had everything he needed to defeat us—"

Morton smiled as Korita interrupted blandly: "Exactly, my dear Smith, except that he reacted according to the biological impulses of his type. His defeat was already foreshadowed when we unerringly analyzed him as a criminal from a certain era of his civilization.

"It was history, honorable Mr. Smith, our knowledge of history that defeated him," said the Japanese archeologist, reverting to the ancient politeness of his race.

<hr/>

AFTERWORD BY ERIC FLINT

I first read "Black Destroyer" at about the same age David did—thirteen, the age which Terry Carr once quipped was the age that defined everybody's "Golden Age"—although I read it in the version which Van Vogt rewrote as the first episode in his quasi-novel *The Voyage of the Space Beagle*. It really doesn't matter. I was devouring anything by Van Vogt I could get my hands on, then. Many years later, looking back from the vantage point of an adult, I find aspects of Van Vogt's writing which I dislike—especially his tendency to lean heavily on the theme of the superman who manipulates the human race for its own good. But I was oblivious to all that as a teenager. All that struck me—as it still does, whatever my reservations in other respects—is Van Vogt's superb ability to depict a future with a truly galactic sweep and scope to it. I found that inspiring then, and I still do.

A Pail of Air

by Fritz Leiber

PREFACE BY ERIC FLINT

My reaction when I first read this story, somewhere around the age of fifteen, was perhaps bizarre. "A Pail of Air" is a story about survival in the face of desperate circumstances, and there are no ifs, ands or buts about it.

There is no atmosphere . . . bitter cold . . . only way you can breathe is to dig up a pail of liquid oxygen and heat it . . .

Yup, that's *desperate.*

Still, I had pretty much the same reaction I had to L. Sprague de Camp's "A Gun for Dinosaur," a story which appears later in this anthology and about which I make some remarks in an afterword. Desperate circumstances . . . impossible odds . . . almost alone . . .

Oh, how *cool.*

Like I said, a bizarre reaction. I didn't even have the excuse of being a stupid adolescent. I wasn't stupid. Already by the age of fourteen I could rip off the great suave mantras regarding adventure, with a curled lip I'd learned from studying David Niven in the movies.

Adventure. Ah, yes. That's someone else having a very rough go of it very far away.

Adventure. Yes. My idea of adventure is carrying a pint of bitters from one smoked-filled room to the next.

Granted, I didn't really have any idea what "bitters" were. (A few years later I found out, and the decline of the British empire

153

was no longer a mystery to me.) But I understood the gist of the wisecrack well enough—and fully subscribed to the sentiment.

I still do. And now, from the vantage point of my mid-fifties wisdom and sagacity, I can look back on the reaction of that callow youngster and realize that he was . . . well, completely correct.

This is just one hell of a cool story. If you look at it the right way, as much fun as one of Leiber's famous Fahfrd and the Grey Mouser tales.

Okay. You have to squint.

———————

Pa had sent me out to get an extra pail of air. I'd just about scooped it full and most of the warmth had leaked from my fingers when I saw the thing.

You know, at first I thought it was a young lady. Yes, a beautiful young lady's face all glowing in the dark and looking at me from the fifth floor of the opposite apartment, which hereabouts is the floor just above the white blanket of frozen air. I'd never seen a live young lady before, except in the old magazines—Sis is just a kid and Ma is pretty sick and miserable—and it gave me such a start that I dropped the pail. Who wouldn't, knowing everyone on Earth was dead except Pa and Ma and Sis and you?

Even at that, I don't suppose I should have been surprised. We all see things now and then. Ma has some pretty bad ones, to judge from the way she bugs her eyes at nothing and just screams and screams and huddles back against the blankets hanging around the Nest. Pa says it is natural we should react like that sometimes.

When I'd recovered the pail and could look again at the opposite apartment, I got an idea of what Ma might be feeling at those times, for I saw it wasn't a young lady at all but simply a light—a tiny light that moved stealthily from window to window, just as if one of the cruel little stars had come down out of the airless sky to investigate why the Earth had gone away from the Sun, and maybe to hunt down something to torment or terrify, now that the Earth didn't have the Sun's protection.

I tell you, the thought of it gave me the creeps. I just stood there shaking, and almost froze my feet and did frost my helmet so solid on the inside that I couldn't have seen the light even if it had come out of one of the windows to get me. Then I had the wit to go back inside.

Pretty soon I was feeling my familiar way through the thirty or so blankets and rugs Pa has got hung around to slow down the escape of air from the Nest, and I wasn't quite so scared. I began to hear the tick-ticking of the clocks in the Nest and knew I was getting back into air, because there's no sound outside in the vacuum, of course. But my mind was still crawly and uneasy as I pushed through the last blankets—Pa's got them faced with aluminum foil to hold in the heat—and came into the Nest.

Let me tell you about the Nest. It's low and snug, just room for the four of us and our things. The floor is covered with thick woolly rugs. Three of the sides are blankets, and the blankets roofing it touch Pa's head. He tells me it's inside a much bigger room, but I've never seen the real walls or ceiling.

Against one of the blankets is a big set of shelves, with tools and books and other stuff, and on top of it a whole row of clocks. Pa's very fussy about keeping them wound. He says we must never forget time, and without a sun or moon, that would be easy to do.

The fourth wall has blankets all over except around the fireplace, in which there is a fire that must never go out. It keeps us from freezing and does a lot more besides. One of us must always watch it. Some of the clocks are alarm and we can use them to remind us. In the early days there was only Ma to take turns with Pa—I think of that when she gets difficult—but now there's me to help, and Sis too.

It's Pa who is the chief guardian of the fire, though. I always think of him that way: a tall man sitting cross-legged, frowning anxiously at the fire, his lined face golden in its light, and every so often carefully placing on it a piece of coal from the big heap beside it. Pa tells me there used to be guardians of the fire sometimes in the very old days—vestal virgins, he calls them—although there was unfrozen air all around then and you didn't really need one.

He was sitting just that way now, though he got up quick to take the pail from me and bawl me out for loitering—he'd spotted my frozen helmet right off. That roused Ma and she joined in picking on me. She's always trying to get the load off her feelings, Pa explains. Sis let off a couple of silly squeals too.

Pa handled the pail of air in a twist of cloth. Now that it was inside the Nest, you could really feel its coldness. It just seemed to suck the heat out of everything. Even the flames cringed away from it as Pa put it down close by the fire.

Yet it's that glimmery white stuff in the pail that keeps us alive. It slowly melts and vanishes and refreshes the Nest and feeds the fire. The blankets keep it from escaping too fast. Pa'd like to seal the whole place, but he can't—building's too earthquake-twisted, and besides he has to leave the chimney open for smoke.

Pa says air is tiny molecules that fly away like a flash if there isn't something to stop them. We have to watch sharp not to let the air run low. Pa always keeps a big reserve supply of it in buckets behind the first blankets, along with extra coal and cans of food and other things, such as pails of snow to melt for water. We have to go way down to the bottom floor for that stuff, which is a mean trip, and get it through a door to outside.

You see, when the Earth got cold, all the water in the air froze first and made a blanket ten feet thick or so everywhere, and then down on top of that dropped the crystals of frozen air, making another white blanket sixty or seventy feet thick maybe.

Of course, all the parts of the air didn't freeze and snow down at the same time.

First to drop out was the carbon dioxide—when you're shoveling for water, you have to make sure you don't go too high and get any of that stuff mixed in, for it would put you to sleep, maybe for good, and make the fire go out. Next there's the nitrogen, which doesn't count one way or the other, though it's the biggest part of the blanket. On top of that and easy to get at, which is lucky for us, there's the oxygen that keeps us alive. Pa says we live better than kings ever did, breathing pure oxygen, but we're used to it and don't notice. Finally, at the very top, there's a slick of liquid helium, which is funny stuff. All of these gases in neat separate layers. Like a pussy caffay, Pa laughingly says, whatever that is.

I was busting to tell them all about what I'd seen, and so as soon as I'd ducked out of my helmet and while I was still climbing out of my suit, I cut loose. Right away Ma got nervous and began making eyes at the entry-slit in the blankets and wringing her hands together—the hand where she'd lost three fingers from frostbite inside the good one, as usual. I could tell that Pa was annoyed at me scaring her and wanted to explain it all away quickly, yet could see I wasn't fooling.

"And you watched this light for some time, son?" he asked when I finished.

I hadn't said anything about first thinking it was a young lady's face. Somehow that part embarrassed me.

"Long enough for it to pass five windows and go to the next floor."

"And it didn't look like stray electricity or crawling liquid or starlight focused by a growing crystal, or anything like that?"

He wasn't just making up those ideas. Odd things happen in a world that's about as cold as can be, and just when you think matter would be frozen dead, it takes on a strange new life. A slimy stuff comes crawling toward the Nest, just like an animal snuffing for heat—that's the liquid helium. And once, when I was little, a bolt of lightning—not even Pa could figure where it came from—hit the nearby steeple and crawled up and down it for weeks, until the glow finally died.

"Not like anything I ever saw," I told him.

He stood for a moment frowning. Then, "I'll go out with you, and you show it to me," he said.

Ma raised a howl at the idea of being left alone, and Sis joined in, too, but Pa quieted them. We started climbing into our outside clothes—mine had been warming by the fire. Pa made them. They have plastic headpieces that were once big double-duty transparent food cans, but they keep heat and air in and can replace the air for a little while, long enough for our trips for water and coal and food and so on.

Ma started moaning again, "I've always known there was something outside there, waiting to get us. I've felt it for years—something that's part of the cold and hates all warmth and wants to destroy the Nest. It's been watching us all this time, and now it's coming after us. It'll get you and then come for me. Don't go, Harry!"

Pa had everything on but his helmet. He knelt by the fireplace and reached in and shook the long metal rod that goes up the chimney and knocks off the ice that keeps trying to clog it. Once a week he goes up on the roof to check if it's working all right. That's our worst trip and Pa won't let me make it alone.

"Sis," Pa said quietly, "come watch the fire. Keep an eye on the air, too. If it gets low or doesn't seem to be boiling fast enough, fetch another bucket from behind the blanket. But mind your hands. Use the cloth to pick up the bucket."

Sis quit helping Ma be frightened and came over and did as she was told. Ma quieted down pretty suddenly, though her eyes were still kind of wild as she watched Pa fix on his helmet tight and pick up a pail and the two of us go out.

ᖇ   ᖇ   ᖇ

Pa led the way and I took hold of his belt. It's a funny thing, I'm not afraid to go by myself, but when Pa's along I always want to hold on to him. Habit, I guess, and then there's no denying that this time I was a bit scared.

You see, it's this way. We know that everything is dead out there. Pa heard the last radio voices fade away years ago, and had seen some of the last folks die who weren't as lucky or well-protected as us. So we knew that if there was something groping around out there, it couldn't be anything human or friendly.

Besides that, there's a feeling that comes with it always being night, *cold* night. Pa says there used to be some of that feeling even in the old days, but then every morning the Sun would come and chase it away. I have to take his word for that, not ever remembering the Sun as being anything more than a big star. You see, I hadn't been born when the dark star snatched us away from the Sun, and by now it's dragged us out beyond the orbit of the planet Pluto, Pa says, and taking us farther out all the time.

I found myself wondering whether there mightn't be something on the dark star that wanted us, and if that was why it had captured the Earth. Just then we came to the end of the corridor and I followed Pa out on the balcony.

I don't know what the city looked like in the old days, but now it's beautiful. The starlight lets you see pretty well—there's quite a bit of light in those steady points speckling the blackness above. (Pa says the stars used to twinkle once, but that was because there was air.) We are on a hill and the shimmery plain drops away from us and then flattens out, cut up into neat squares by the troughs that used to be streets. I sometimes make my mashed potatoes look like it, before I pour on the gravy.

Some taller buildings push up out of the feathery plain, topped by rounded caps of air crystals, like the fur hood Ma wears, only whiter. On those buildings you can see the darker squares of windows, underlined by white dashes of air crystals. Some of them are on a slant, for many of the buildings are pretty badly twisted by the quakes and all the rest that happened when the dark star captured the Earth.

Here and there a few icicles hang, water icicles from the first days of the cold, other icicles of frozen air that melted on the roofs and dripped and froze again. Sometimes one of those icicles will catch the light of a star and send it to you so brightly you think the star has swooped into the city. That was one of the things Pa had been thinking of when I told him about the light, but I had thought of it myself first and known it wasn't so.

He touched his helmet to mine so we could talk easier and he asked me to point out the windows to him. But there wasn't any light moving around inside them now, or anywhere else. To my surprise, Pa didn't bawl me out and tell me I'd been seeing things. He looked all around quite a while after filling his pail, and just as we were going inside he whipped around without warning, as if to take some peeping thing off guard.

I could feel it, too. The old peace was gone. There was something lurking out there, watching, waiting, getting ready.

Inside, he said to me, touching helmets, "If you see something like that again, son, don't tell the others. Your Ma's sort of nervous these days and we owe her all the feeling of safety we can give her. Once—it was when your sister was born—I was ready to give up and die, but your Mother kept me trying. Another time she kept the fire going a whole week all by herself when I was sick. Nursed me and took care of the two of you, too.

"You know that game we sometimes play, sitting in a square in the Nest, tossing a ball around? Courage is like a ball, son. A person can hold it only so long, and then he's got to toss it to someone else. When it's tossed your way, you've got to catch it and hold it tight—and hope there'll be someone else to toss it to when you get tired of being brave."

His talking to me that way made me feel grown-up and good. But it didn't wipe away the thing outside from the back of my mind—or the fact that Pa took it seriously.

It's hard to hide your feelings about such a thing. When we got back in the Nest and took off our outside clothes, Pa laughed about it all and told them it was nothing and kidded me for having such an imagination, but his words fell flat. He didn't convince Ma and Sis any more than he did me. It looked for a minute like we were all fumbling the courage-ball. Something had to be done, and almost before I knew what I was going to say, I heard myself asking Pa to tell us about the old days, and how it all happened.

He sometimes doesn't mind telling that story, and Sis and I sure like to listen to it, and he got my idea. So we were all settled around the fire in a wink, and Ma pushed up some cans to thaw for supper, and Pa began. Before he did, though, I noticed him casually get a hammer from the shelf and lay it down beside him.

It was the same old story as always—I think I could recite the main thread of it in my sleep—though Pa always puts in a new detail or two and keeps improving it in spots.

He told us how the Earth had been swinging around the Sun ever so steady and warm, and the people on it fixing to make money and wars and have a good time and get power and treat each other right or wrong, when without warning there comes charging out of space this dead star, this burned out sun, and upsets everything.

You know, I find it hard to believe in the way those people felt, any more than I can believe in the swarming number of them. Imagine people getting ready for the horrible sort of war they were cooking up. Wanting it even, or at least wishing it were over so as to end their nervousness. As if all folks didn't have to hang together and pool every bit of warmth just to keep alive. And how can they have hoped to end danger, any more than we can hope to end the cold?

Sometimes I think Pa exaggerates and makes things out too black. He's cross with us once in a while and was probably cross with all those folks. Still, some of the things I read in the old magazines sound pretty wild. He may be right.

The dark star, as Pa went on telling it, rushed in pretty fast and there wasn't much time to get ready. At the beginning they tried to keep it a secret from most people, but then the truth came out, what with the earthquakes and floods—imagine, oceans of *unfrozen* water!—and people seeing stars blotted out by something on a clear night. First off they thought it would hit the Sun, and then they thought it would hit the Earth. There was even the start of a rush to get to a place called China, because people thought the star would hit on the other side. But then they found it wasn't going to hit either side, but was going to come very close to the Earth.

Most of the other planets were on the other side of the Sun and didn't get involved. The Sun and the newcomer fought over the Earth for a little while—pulling it this way and that, like two dogs growling over a bone, Pa described it this time—and then the newcomer won and carried us off. The Sun got a consolation prize, though. At the last minute he managed to hold on to the Moon.

That was the time of the monster earthquakes and floods, twenty times worse than anything before. It was also the time of the Big Jerk, as Pa calls it, when all Earth got yanked suddenly, just as Pa has done to me once or twice, grabbing me by the collar to do it, when I've been sitting too far from the fire.

You see, the dark star was going through space faster than the Sun, and in the opposite direction, and it had to wrench the world considerably in order to take it away.

The Big Jerk didn't last long. It was over as soon as the Earth was settled down in its new orbit around the dark star. But it was pretty terrible while it lasted. Pa says that all sorts of cliffs and buildings toppled, oceans slopped over, swamps and sandy deserts gave great sliding surges that buried nearby lands. Earth was almost jerked out of its atmosphere blanket and the air got so thin in spots that people keeled over and fainted—though of course, at the same time, they were getting knocked down by the Big Jerk and maybe their bones broke or skulls cracked.

We've often asked Pa how people acted during that time, whether they were scared or brave or crazy or stunned, or all four, but he's sort of leery of the subject, and he was again tonight. He says he was mostly too busy to notice.

You see, Pa and some scientist friends of his had figured out part of what was going to happen—they'd known we'd get captured and our air would freeze—and they'd been working like mad to fix up a place with airtight walls and doors, and insulation against the cold, and big supplies of food and fuel and water and bottled air. But the place got smashed in the last earthquakes and all Pa's friends were killed then and in the Big Jerk. So he had to start over and throw the Nest together quick without any advantages, just using any stuff he could lay his hands on.

I guess he's telling pretty much the truth when he says he didn't have any time to keep an eye on how other folks behaved, either then or in the Big Freeze that followed—followed very quick, you know, both because the dark star was pulling us away very fast and because Earth's rotation had been slowed in the tug-of-war, so that the nights were ten old nights long.

Still, I've got an idea of some of the things that happened from the frozen folk I've seen, a few of them in other rooms in our building, others clustered around the furnaces in the basements where we go for coal.

In one of the rooms, an old man sits stiff in a chair, with an arm and a leg in splints. In another, a man and a woman are huddled together in a bed with heaps of covers over them. You can just see their heads peeking out, close together. And in another a beautiful young lady is sitting with a pile of wraps huddled around her, looking hopefully toward the door, as if waiting for someone who never came back with warmth and food. They're all still and stiff as statues, of course, but just like life.

Pa showed them to me once in quick winks of his flashlight, when he still had a fair supply of batteries and could afford to waste a little light. They scared me pretty bad and made my heart pound, especially the young lady.

Now, with Pa telling his story for the umpteenth time to take our minds off another scare, I got to thinking of the frozen folk again. All of a sudden I got an idea that scared me worse than anything yet. You see, I'd just remembered the face I'd thought I'd seen in the window. I'd forgotten about that on account of trying to hide it from the others.

What, I asked myself, if the frozen folk were coming to life? What if they were like the liquid helium that got a new lease on life and started crawling toward the heat just when you thought its molecules ought to freeze solid forever? Or like the electricity that moves endlessly when it's just about as cold as that? What if the ever-growing cold, with the temperature creeping down the last few degrees to the last zero, had mysteriously wakened the frozen folk to life—not warm-blooded life, but something icy and horrible?

That was a worse idea than the one about something coming down from the dark star to get us.

Or maybe, I thought, both ideas might be true. Something coming down from the dark star and making the frozen folk move, using them to do its work. That would fit with both things I'd seen—the beautiful young lady and the moving, starlike light.

The frozen folk with minds from the dark star behind their unwinking eyes, creeping, crawling, snuffing their way, following the heat to the Nest.

I tell you, that thought gave me a very bad turn and I wanted very badly to tell the others my fears, but I remembered what Pa had said and clenched my teeth and didn't speak.

We were all sitting very still. Even the fire was burning silently. There was just the sound of Pa's voice and the clocks.

And then, from beyond the blankets, I thought I heard a tiny noise. My skin tightened all over me.

Pa was telling about the early years in the Nest and had come to the place where he philosophizes.

"So I asked myself then," he said, "what's the use of going on?

What's the use of dragging it out for a few years? Why prolong a doomed existence of hard work and cold and loneliness? The human race is done. The Earth is done. Why not give up, I asked myself—and all of a sudden I got the answer."

Again I heard the noise, louder this time, a kind of uncertain, shuffling tread, coming closer. I couldn't breathe.

"Life's always been a business of working hard and fighting the cold," Pa was saying. "The earth's always been a lonely place, millions of miles from the next planet. And no matter how long the human race might have lived, the end would have come some night. Those things don't matter. What matters is that life is good. It has a lovely texture, like some rich cloth or fur, or the petals of flowers—you've seen pictures of those, but I can't describe how they feel—or the fire's glow. It makes everything else worth while. And that's as true for the last man as the first."

And still the steps kept shuffling closer. It seemed to me that the inmost blanket trembled and bulged a little. Just as if they were burned into my imagination, I kept seeing those peering, frozen eyes.

"So right then and there," Pa went on, and now I could tell that he heard the steps, too, and was talking loud so we maybe wouldn't hear them, "right then and there I told myself that I was going on as if we had all eternity ahead of us. I'd have children and teach them all I could. I'd get them to read books. I'd plan for the future, try to enlarge and seal the Nest. I'd do what I could to keep everything beautiful and growing. I'd keep alive my feeling of wonder even at the cold and the dark and the distant stars."

But then the blanket actually did move and lift. And there was a bright light somewhere behind it. Pa's voice stopped and his eyes turned to the widening slit and his hand went out until it touched and gripped the handle of the hammer beside him.

In through the blanket stepped the beautiful young lady. She stood there looking at us the strangest way, and she carried something bright and unwinking in her hand. And two other faces peered over her shoulders—men's faces, white and staring.

Well, my heart couldn't have been stopped for more than four or five beats before I realized she was wearing a suit and helmet like Pa's homemade ones, only fancier, and that the men were, too—and that the frozen folk certainly wouldn't be wearing those. Also, I noticed that the bright thing in her hand was just a kind of flashlight.

The silence kept on while I swallowed hard a couple of times, and after that there was all sorts of jabbering and commotion.

They were simply people, you see. We hadn't been the only ones to survive; we'd just thought so, for natural enough reasons. These three people had survived, and quite a few others with them. And when we found out *how* they'd survived, Pa let out the biggest whoop of joy.

They were from Los Alamos and they were getting their heat and power from atomic energy. Just using the uranium and plutonium intended for bombs, they had enough to go on for thousands of years. They had a regular little airtight city, with airlocks and all. They even generated electric light and grew plants and animals by it. (At this Pa let out a second whoop, waking Ma from her faint.)

But if we were flabbergasted at them, they were double-flabbergasted at us.

One of the men kept saying, "But it's impossible, I tell you. You can't maintain an air supply without hermetic sealing. It's simply impossible."

That was after he had got his helmet off and was using our air. Meanwhile, the young lady kept looking around at us as if we were saints, and telling us we'd done something amazing, and suddenly she broke down and cried.

They'd been scouting around for survivors, but they never expected to find any in a place like this. They had rocket ships at Los Alamos and plenty of chemical fuels. As for liquid oxygen, all you had to do was go out and shovel the air blanket at the top level. So after they'd got things going smoothly at Los Alamos, which had taken years, they'd decided to make some trips to likely places where there might be other survivors. No good trying long-distance radio signals, of course, since there was no atmosphere to carry them around the curve of the Earth.

Well, they'd found other colonies at Argonne and Brookhaven and way around the world at Harwell and Tanna Tuva. And now they'd been giving our city a look, not really expecting to find anything. But they had an instrument that noticed the faintest heat waves and it had told them there was something warm down here, so they'd landed to investigate. Of course we hadn't heard them land, since there was no air to carry the sound, and they'd had to investigate around quite a while before finding us. Their instruments had given them a wrong steer and they'd wasted some time in the building across the street.

∽   ∽   ∽

By now, all five adults were talking like sixty. Pa was demonstrating to the men how he worked the fire and got rid of the ice in the chimney and all that. Ma had perked up wonderfully and was showing the young lady her cooking and sewing stuff, and even asking about how the women dressed at Los Alamos. The strangers marveled at everything and praised it to the skies. I could tell from the way they wrinkled their noses that they found the Nest a bit smelly, but they never mentioned that at all and just asked bushels of questions.

In fact, there was so much talking and excitement that Pa forgot about things, and it wasn't until they were all getting groggy that he looked and found the air had all boiled away in the pail. He got another bucket of air quick from behind the blankets. Of course that started them all laughing and jabbering again. The newcomers even got a little drunk. They weren't used to so much oxygen.

Funny thing, though—I didn't do much talking at all and Sis hung on to Ma all the time and hid her face when anybody looked at her. I felt pretty uncomfortable and disturbed myself, even about the young lady. Glimpsing her outside there, I'd had all sorts of mushy thoughts, but now I was just embarrassed and scared of her, even though she tried to be nice as anything to me.

I sort of wished they'd all quit crowding the Nest and let us be alone and get our feelings straightened out.

And when the newcomers began to talk about our all going to Los Alamos, as if that were taken for granted, I could see that something of the same feeling struck Pa and Ma, too. Pa got very silent all of a sudden and Ma kept telling the young lady, "But I wouldn't know how to act there and I haven't any clothes."

The strangers were puzzled like anything at first, but then they got the idea. As Pa kept saying, "It just doesn't seem right to let this fire go out."

Well, the strangers are gone, but they're coming back. It hasn't been decided yet just what will happen. Maybe the Nest will be kept up as what one of the strangers called a "survival school." Or maybe we will join the pioneers who are going to try to establish a new colony at the uranium mines at Great Slave Lake or in the Congo.

Of course, now that the strangers are gone, I've been thinking a lot about Los Alamos and those other tremendous colonies. I have a hankering to see them for myself.

You ask me, Pa wants to see them, too. He's been getting pretty thoughtful, watching Ma and Sis perk up.

"It's different, now that we know others are alive," he explains to me. "Your mother doesn't feel so hopeless any more. Neither do I, for that matter, not having to carry the whole responsibility for keeping the human race going, so to speak. It scares a person."

I looked around at the blanket walls and the fire and the pails of air boiling away and Ma and Sis sleeping in the warmth and the flickering light.

"It's not going to be easy to leave the Nest," I said, wanting to cry, kind of. "It's so small and there's just the four of us. I get scared at the idea of big places and a lot of strangers."

He nodded and put another piece of coal on the fire. Then he looked at the little pile and grinned suddenly and put a couple of handfuls on, just as if it was one of our birthdays or Christmas.

"You'll quickly get over that feeling, son," he said. "The trouble with the world was that it kept getting smaller and smaller, till it ended with just the Nest. Now it'll be good to have a real huge world again, the way it was in the beginning."

I guess he's right. You think the beautiful young lady will wait for me till I grow up? I'll be twenty in only ten years.

Thy Rocks and Rills

by Robert Ernest Gilbert

PREFACE BY DAVID DRAKE

In 9th grade (1959) my English teacher gave me some SF magazines that her sons had left around the house. One of them was the September 1953 issue of *If* containing "Thy Rocks and Rills." That was my good luck, because the story made a real impact on me and the present anthology is the first time it's been reprinted.

I believe fiction is to entertain, not to teach; but good entertainment has to have a foundation of reality. Looking back on it, I believe this story hit me so hard because it graphically illustrated three points:

1) You can live your life outside the norms of society, but
2) Society will probably crush you if you try, *but*
3) It may be worth being crushed.

I still believe those statements are true.

Prelude

M. Stonecypher lifted his reed sun hat with the square brim, and used a red handkerchief to absorb the perspiration streaking his forehead. He said, "The pup'll make a good guard, especially for thrill parties."

L. Dan's golden curls flickered in July 1 sunlight. The puppy growled when Dan extended a gloved hand. "I don't want a guard," the hobbyist said. "I want him for a dogfight."

A startling bellow rattled the windows of the dog house and spilled in deafening waves across the yard. Dan whirled, clutching his staff. Light glinted on his plastic cuirass and danced on his red nylon tights. His flabby face turned white. "What—" he panted.

Stonecypher concealed a smile behind a long corded hand and said, "Just the bull. Serenades us sometimes."

Dan circled the dog house. Stonecypher followed with a forefinger pressed to thin lips. In the paddock, the bull's head moved up and down. It might or might not have been a nod.

The crest of long red and blue-black hairs on the bull's neck and shoulders created an illusion of purple, but the rest of the animal matched the black of a duelmaster's tam. Behind large eyes encircled by a white band, his skull bulged in a swelling dome, making the distance between his short horns seem much too great.

"He's purple!" Dan gasped. "Why in the Government don't you put him in the ring?"

Stonecypher gestured toward the choppy surface of Kings Lake, nine hundred feet below. He said, "Coincidence. I make out the ringmaster's barge just leavin' Highland Pier."

"You're selling him?"

"Yeah. If they take 'im. I'd like to see 'im in the ring on Dependence Day."

Glancing at the watch embedded in the left pectoral of his half-armor, Dan said, "That would be a show! I'll take the dog and fly. I've a duel in Highland Park at 11:46."

"The pup's not for sale."

"Not for sale!" Dan yelled. "You told—"

"Thought you wanted a guard. I don't sell for dogfights."

A sound like "Goood!" came from the paddocked bull.

Dan opened his mouth wide. Whatever he intended to say died without vocalization, for Catriona came driving the mule team up through the apple orchard. The almost identical mules had sorrel noses, gray necks, buckskin flanks, and black and white pinto backs and haunches. "Great Government!" Dan swore. "This place is worse than a museum!"

"Appaloosa mules," Stonecypher said.

Catriona jumped from the seat of the mowing machine. Dan stared. Compared to the standard woman of the Manly Age who, by dieting, posturing, and exercise from childhood, transformed herself into a small, thin, dominated creature, Catriona constituted a separate species. She was taller than Dan, slightly plump, and her hair could have been classed as either red or blonde. Green coveralls became her better than they did Stonecypher. With no trace of a smile on face or in voice, Stonecypher said, "L. Dan, meet Catriona."

Like a hypnopath's victim, Dan walked to Catriona. He looked up at her and whispered, but too loudly. Stonecypher heard. His hands clamped on the hobbyist's neck and jerked. Dan smashed in the grass with sufficient force to loosen the snaps of his armor. He rolled to his feet and swung his staff.

Stonecypher's left hand snatched the staff. His right fist collided with Dan's square jaw. Glaring down at the hobbyist, Stonecypher gripped the staff and rotated thick wrists outward. The tough plastic popped when it broke.

Scuttling backward, Dan regained his feet. "You inhuman brute!" he growled. "I intended to pay for her!"

"My wife's not for sale either," Stonecypher said. "You know how to fly."

Dan thrust out a coated tongue and made a noise with it. In a memorized singsong, he declared, "I challenge you to a duel, in accordance with the laws of the Government, to be fought in the nearest duelpen at the earliest possible hour."

"Stony, don't!" Catriona protested. "He's not wo'th it!"

Stonecypher smiled at her. "Have to follow the law," he said. He extended his tongue, blurted, and announced, "As required by the Government, I accept your challenge."

"We'll record it!" Dan snapped. He stalked toward the green and gold butterflier parked in a field of seedling Sudan grass. Horns rattled on the concrete rails of the paddock.

"Burstaard!" the bull bellowed.

Dan shied and trampled young grass under sandaled feet. His loosened cuirass clattered rhythmically. Raising the canopy of the butterflier, he slid out the radioak and started typing. Stonecypher and Catriona approached the hobbyist. Catriona said, "This is cowa'dly! Stony nevah fought a duel in his life. He won't have a chance!"

"You'll see me soon then, woman. Where'd you get all that equipment? You look like something in a circus."

"Ah used to be in a cahnival," Catriona said. She kept Stonecypher in place with a plump arm across his chest. "That's wheah you belong," she told Dan. "That's all you'ah good fo'."

"Watch how you address a man, woman," Dan snarled, "or you'll end in the duelpen, too."

Stonecypher snatched the sheet from the typer. The request read:

> *Duelmaster R. Smith, Watauga Duelpen, Highland Park, Tennessee. L. Dan challenges M. Stonecypher. Cause: Interference with basic amatory rights. July 1. 11:21 amest.*

Stonecypher said, "The cause is a lie. You got no rights with Catriona. Why didn't you tell 'em it's because I knocked you ears-over-endways, and you're scared to fight without a gun?"

Dan shoved the request into the slot and pulled the switch. "I'll kill you," he promised.

While the request was transmitted by radiophotography, minutes passed, bare of further insults. Catriona and Stonecypher stood near the concrete fence enclosing the rolling top of Bays Mountain. Interminable labor had converted 650 acres at the top to arable land. Below the couple, the steep side of the mountain, denuded of timber, dangerously eroded, and scarred by limestone quarries, fell to the ragged shore of Kings Lake. Two miles of water agitated by many boats separated the shore and the peninsula, which resembled a wrinkled dragon with underslung lower jaw distended. The town of Highland Park clung to the jutting land, and the Highland Bullring appeared as a white dot more than four miles from where Catriona and Stonecypher stood. The ringmaster's barge was a red rectangle skirting Russel Chapel Island.

Dan pulled the answer from the buzzing radioak. He walked over and held the radiophoto an inch from Stonecypher's long nose. It read:

> *Request OK. Time: July 4. 3:47 pmest.*

Two attached permits granted each duelist the privilege of carrying one handgun with a capacity of not more than ten cartridges of not less than .32 caliber. Below the permits appeared an additional message:

> *L. Dan due at Watauga Duelpen. 11:46 amest. For duel with J. George.*

"Government and Taxes!" Dan cursed. Throwing Stonecypher's permit, he leaped into the green and gold butterflier and slammed the canopy. The four wings of the semi-ornithopter blurred with motion, lifting the craft into the sky. The forward wings locked with negative dihedral, the rear wings angled to form a ruddeva-tor, and the five-bladed propeller whined, driving the butterflier in a shallow dive for the peninsula.

Catriona said, "Ah hope he's late, and they shoot him. Ah knew you'd finally have to fight, but—"

"You keep out of it next time," said Stonecypher. "I happen to know that feller's killed two women in the pen. He don't care for nothin'. Oughta known better than to let him come here. He made out like he wanted a guard dog, and I thought—"

"Nevah mind, Stony. Ah've got to help you. You nevah even fiahed a gun."

"Later, Cat. The ringmaster may want to stay for dinner. I'll look after the mules."

Catriona touched Stonecypher's cheek and went to the house. Stonecypher unharnessed the Appaloosa mules. While they rolled, he took, from an empty hay rack, a rubber-tipped spear and a tattered cloth dummy. The dummy's single arm terminated in a red flag.

Stonecypher concealed spear and dummy beneath the floor of the dog house. Going to the paddock, he patted the bull between the horns, which had been filed to a needle point. "Still goin' through with it?" Stonecypher asked.

"Yaaaa," the bull lowed. "Yaooo kuhl Daan. Err'll kuhl uhh kuhlerrs."

"All right, Moe. I'll kill Dan, and you kill the killers." Stonecy-pher stroked the massive hemisphere of the bull's jaw. "Goodbye, Moe."

"Gooodba," the bull echoed. He lowered his nose to the shelled corn seasoned with molasses, the rolled oats, and the ground barley in the trough.

Stonecypher walked down the road to the staircase of stone that dammed the old Kingsport Reservoir, abandoned long before Kings Lake covered the city. A red electric truck crawled up the steep road hewn from the slope of the gap formed by Dolan Branch. When the truck had crossed the bridge below the buttressed dam, Stonecypher spoke to the fat and sweltering man seated beside the drive. "I'm M. Stonecypher. Proud for you to visit my farm. Dinner's ready up at the house."

"No, no time," smiled the fat man, displaying stainless steel teeth.

"Only time to see the bull. I thought we weren't going to make that grade! Why don't those scientists develop synthetic elements, so that we can have atomic power again? This radio-electric is so unreliable! I am Ringmaster Oswell, naturally. This heat is excruciating! I had hoped it would be cooler up here, but something seems to have happened to our inland-oceanic climate this summer. Lead us to the bull, Stonecypher!"

Clinging to the slatted truck bed, Stonecypher directed the stoic driver to the paddock. The electric motor rattled and stopped, and Ringmaster Oswell wheezed and squirmed from the cab. The ringmaster wore a vaguely Arabic costume, in all variations of red.

The bull lumbered bellowing around the fence. His horns raked white gashes in the beech tree forming on corner. He tossed the feed trough to splintering destruction.

"Magnificent!" Oswell gasped. Then the ringmaster frowned. "But he looks almost purple. His horns are rather short."

"Stay back from the fence!" Stonecypher warned. "He's real wide between the horns, ringmaster. I reckon the spread'll match up to standard. Same stock my grandfather used to sell Boon Bullring before the water. Wouldn't sell 'im, only the tenants are scared to come about the house."

Oswell fingered his balloon neck and mumbled, "But he's odd. That long hair on his neck . . . I don't know . . ."

The bull's horns lifted the mineral feeder from the center of the paddock. The box rotated over the rails and crashed in a cloud of floured oyster shells and phosphate salt at the ringmaster's feet.

Oswell took cover behind the truck driver, who said, "Fergus'd like him. Jeeze! Remember dat brown and white spotted one he kilt last year on Forrest Day? Da crowd like ta never stopt yelling!"

Ringmaster Oswell retreated farther as, under the bull's onslaught, a piece of concrete broke from the top rail, exposing the reinforcing rod within. "Fergus does like strange ones," he admitted.

Stonecypher said, "Don't let the mane bother you. There's one of these long-haired Scotch cows in his ancestors. He's not really purple. Just the way the light hits 'im."

Oswell chewed lacquered fingernails with steel dentures. His bloodshot eyes studied the spotted and speckled Appaloosa mules chasing around the pasture, but the sight failed to register on his brain. "The crowd likes a good show on Dependence Day," he proclaimed. "I considered trying a fat Aberdeen Angus with artificial horns for laughs, but this may do as well. I must find some shade! I'll take him, Stonecypher, if fifteen hundred in gold is agreeable."

"Sold," Stonecypher said. The word cracked in the middle.

While the ringmaster, muttering about trying bulldogs sometime, retired to the narrow shadow of the dog house, the driver backed the truck to the ramp. Stonecypher opened the gate and waved his handkerchief. The bull charged into the truck, and the driver locked the heavy doors.

From within his red burnoose, Oswell produced a clinking bag. "Fifteen hundred," he said. From other recesses, he withdrew documents, notebooks, and a pencil. He said, "Here is a pass for you and one for any woman-subject you may wish to bring. You'll want to see your first bull on Dependence Day! And here is the standard release absolving you of any damage the bull may do. Oh, yes! His name and number?"

"Number?"

"Yes, his brand."

"Not branded. Make it Number 1. Name's Moe."

Oswell chuckled. "Moe. Very good! Most breeders name them things like Chainlightning and Thunderbird. Your GE number?"

"I'm not a Government Employee."

"You're not?" Oswell wheezed. "How unusual! Your colors? He'll wear your colors in his shoulder."

"Yeah. Black."

"Black?"

"Dead black."

Oswell, scribbling, managed a faint smile. "Sorry I can't accept that invitation to lunch." He struggled into the truck. "Hope this bull is brave in the ring. Nice antique old place you have here! I don't see a feed tower, but you surely don't use pasture—" the ringmaster's babble passed down the road with the truck.

Stonecypher watched the vehicle descend the dangerous grade. He lifted his square hat from his black hair, dropped it on the ground, and crushed the reeds under a booted foot.

The temporary house, a squat cubical structure, stood at the end of a spruce-lined path beside the ruin that a thrill party had made of the century-old farm house. The plastic screen squeaked when Stonecypher opened it. He stood on the white floor of the robot kitchen and dug a fifty dollar gold piece from the bag Oswell had given him. Glaring at the head of the woman with Liberty inscribed on her crown, he muttered, "Thirty pieces of gold."

Catriona called, "Oswell's lucky he couldn't stay foah dinnah! Ah had the potassium cyanide all ready."

Stonecypher passed through the diner door into a room containing more yellowed history books and agricultural pamphlets than eating utensils. Catriona waited by the table. She held a large revolver in her right hand.

Intermezzo

Stonecypher stood on Bay Knob, near the ruins of the old FM transmitter station, looking down at the Tennessee Lakes. Catriona sat behind him and held the revolver on her thigh. Stonecypher said, "I never see it but I wonder how it looked before the water."

Before him, North Fork, an arm of Kings Lake, twisted across the Virginia line four and one-half miles away, while to Stonecypher's right, Boone Lake sparkled like a gigantic, badly drawn V. He did not look toward Surgoinsville Dam securing Kings Lake far to the west.

The Tennessee Lakes were born in 1918 when Wilson Dam spanned the Tennessee River at Muscle Shoals, Alabama; but their growth was retarded for fifteen years, until an Act of Congress injected them with vitamins. Then the mile-long bastions of concrete crawled between the ridges. Norris, Wheeler, Pickwick Landing, Guntersville, Watts Bar, Kentucky, Cherokee, Fort Henry, Boone, Sevier, Surgoinsville—almost innumerable dams blocked the rivers. The rivers stopped and overflowed. The creeks swelled into rivers.

Congressional Committees investigated, the Supreme Court tested the dams against the Constitution, ethnologists and archeologists hastily checked for Indian relics; and the dams, infused with youthful vigor, matured. Beginning with Norris, which backed up the Clinch and Powell Rivers to inundate 25,000 acres and displace 3,000 families, the dams expanded mighty aquatic muscles. The Tennessee, the Little Tennessee, the Nolichucky, the Holston, the French Broad, the Watauga, the Hiwassee, the Little Pigeon—all the rivers spread their waters into lengthy, ragged lakes, changing the map of Tennessee more than any natural cataclysm, such as the great earthquake of 1811, had ever done. The Lakes provided jobs, electric power, flood control, soil conservation, a fisherman's paradise, milder winters, cooler summers, and they covered all the really good farming land in the eastern part of the state.

Catriona loaded the revolver. It was an obsolete .357 Magnum with a 6½ inch barrel, and the cartridge cases of the metal-piercing bullets had a greenish sheen. "Now, put it in the holstah, and be ca'eful," Catriona said.

Stonecypher wore the holster, a leather silhouette studded with two spring clips opening forward, on a belt and secured to his leg by a thong. Gingerly, he took the revolver and slipped it under the clips. "I've kept outa duels all my life," he said, "but, so long as it's for you, I don't much mind."

"Ah'll mind if he kills you. You do like I tell you, and you can beat him. Why, mah best act in the How-To Cahnival was How to Win a Duel. Cou'se, they didn't know ah was really drawin' befoah the buzzah sounded. Why, ah used to set two plates ten yahds apaht, draw two revolvahs, and shoot both plates, all in foah-tenths of a second!"

Stonecypher grinned. "Sorry I missed that carnival first time it came through here. I coulda seen you in that costume they poured on you, three years earlier."

"Nevah mind the veiled compliments. Now, try it!"

Stonecypher faced the target, a sheet of plastiboard roughly sawed to the shape of a man, and backed by a heap of earth removed from the new, as yet dry, pond in which they stood. Catriona pressed a small buzzer concealed in her palm. Stonecypher's big hand closed on the revolver butt, pushing the weapon up and forward. The sound of the shot rattled away over the mountain top.

"That's good!" Catriona cried, consulting the sonic timer. "One and two-tenths seconds from buzzah to shot!"

"But I missed," Stonecypher protested. "Look bad on tevee."

"You'll hit him. Watch the recoil next time."

Stonecypher drew and fired a second wild shot. He snorted, "Confound Westerns, anyhow!"

"Weste'ns?"

"Sure. That's where this duelin' started. Used to, almost ever' movie or tevee was called a Western. Sort of a fantasy, because they were just slightly based on real history. They generally showed a feller in a flowered shirt, ridin' a Tennessee Walking Horse, and shootin' a gun. Ever'body in these Westerns had a gun, and they all shot at each other.

"The youngin's were hep on 'em, so they all wore toy guns,

and a whole generation grew up on Westerns. When they got big, they carried real guns. I've heard my great-uncle tell about it, how before the Government built duelpens and passed laws, you couldn't hardly cross the Lakes without runnin' into a bunch of fools on water skis shootin' at each other."

"You leave the histo'y books alone foah awhile," Catriona commanded, "and practice. The tenants and ah'll tend to the wo'k. Try it loaded and empty. Hook this little buzzah to the timeah, and practice. Ah've got to go see the chickens."

" 'Bye, teacher." Stonecypher dropped the buzzer in his pocket and watched her vanish into the grove. He fired the remaining shots, nicking the target once. With the revolver holstered, he followed the path to the summer pasture.

Belly-deep in red clover, twenty-four cows, twenty-four calves, and twenty-four yearlings grazed or played in the shady field. Stonecypher cupped his hands around his mouth and yelled, "Smart-calves! Smart-calves to school!"

The entire herd turned sorrowful eyes on him. Seven of the calves and four of the yearlings trotted to the gate, which Stonecypher held open, and jostled out of the pasture. As the calves began to lie down under the trees, a white heifer-calf nuzzled Stonecypher's hand and bawled, "Paaapy gyoing a fyightt?"

"Yeah, he's going to fight," Stonecypher answered. "Your pappy's gone to the bullring. He suggested it, and made the choice himself. He's got real courage. You oughta all be proud of him."

The calves bawled their pride. Including those remaining in the pasture, they presented a colorful variety of spots, specks, splotches, browns, reds, blacks, and even occasional blue and greenish tinges. Stonecypher sat facing them from a stump. He said, "I'm sorta late for the lesson, today, so we'll get on with it. Some of this will be repetition for you yearlings, but it won't hurt. If you get too bored, there's corn and cottonseed meal in the trough, only be quiet about it.

"Now. To look at you all, nobody would think you're the same breed of cattle; but you, and your mammys, and Moe are the only Atohmy cattle on Earth. It's usually hard to say exactly when a breed started; but you all started a long, long time ago, on July 16, 1945, near Alamogordo, New Mexico, when they exploded the first Atomic Bomb."

At mention of Atomic Bomb, who had succeeded the Bogger Man as a means of frightening children, one of the younger calves bawled. Her polled, brindled mother ran in ungainly fashion to the fence and mooed with great carrying power.

"All right!" Stonecypher yelled. The cow closed her big mouth, but stayed by the gate. "Can't go by what you hear the tenants tell their kids," Stonecypher cautioned the calf. "Atomic Bomb is as dead as the tank and the battleship.

"Now, like I was sayin', the scientists put Atomic Bomb on a hundred foot tower and blowed him up. There was a flash of fire, and an awful racket, and the blast raised up a lot of dirt and dust from the ground. All this dust achurnin' around in the cloud bumped into little bits of metal and stuff that was highly radioactive. That means, the basic atoms of matter had been thrown out of kilter, sorta deranged. The protons and electrons in an atom oughta be about equal for it to be stable, but these were shootin' off electrons, or beta particles, and givin' off something like powerful x-rays, called gamma rays, and things like that.

"Anyhow, this radiation affected all the sand and bits of rock and dirt in that bomb cloud. This radiation is dangerous. Some of it will go right through several inches of lead. Enough'll kill you. Your ancestors were ten miles or so from where Atomic Bomb went off.

"They were just plain Whiteface cattle. They weren't supposed to be there, but I reckon none of the scientists bothered to warn 'em. The dust started settlin' all over your ancestors. In about a week, there were sores and blisters on their backs. The red hair dropped off. When it grew back, it was gray.

"The scientists got real excited when they heard about it, 'cause they wanted to see how horrible they could make Atomic Bomb. So, they shipped fifty-nine cattle up to Oak Ridge. That was a Government town, a hundred miles southwest of here, where they made some of the stuff to put in Atomic Bomb. The University of Tennessee was runnin' an experimental farm there. They had donkeys, and pigs, and chickens, and other animals that they exposed to radioactivity. Then they killed 'em and cut 'em up to see what had happened. I know it's gruesome, but that's how it was.

"The awful fact is, the scientists slaughtered more than half that original Atohmy herd for experiments. Some of the rest, they—uh—married. Wanted to see if the calves had two heads, or something; if radioactivity had speeded up the mutation rate.

"Back then, they didn't understand much about mutation. Some claimed a little radioactivity would cause it, some said a whole lot, and some said it wouldn't hurt a bit."

"Whaa mootyaaonn?" asked the calf which was not yet assured of the extinction of Atomic Bomb.

"Well, you-all are all mutations. I've told you how life starts from one cell. This cell has thread-like things in it called chromosomes, and the chromosomes are made up of things called genes. Mutations, sort of unexpected changes, can take place in either the chromosomes or the genes. You see, when this one cell starts dividing, every gene makes a copy of itself; but, sometimes, the copy is a little different from the original. Lots of things, like x-rays and ultraviolet rays, heat, chemicals, disease, can cause this. Radioactivity had caused mutation in some experiment, so the scientists were anxious to see what happened with these cattle.

"Genes determine the way an animal develops. Two mutant genes can start reactions that end up as a man with one leg, or maybe as a bull with the intelligence of an eight-year-old man. Lots of mutations are recessive. They may be carried along for generations. But, when two like mutant genes come together in reproduction, the animal is bound to be something different, the way you eleven calves are.

"Now. The scientists watched the Atohmy cattle for fifteen or twenty years, and nothin' much happened. They started sayin' radioactivity wasn't dangerous, and a man could walk into a place right after Atomic Bomb went off, and it wouldn't matter. They should be here to see the mess in Japan today. All the time, though, I think the cattle were changing. It may have been in little things like the length of hair, or the shape of an eyeball, or the curve of a horn, so the scientists couldn't tell without they made exact measurements all the time.

"Then, a bull-calf was born. He had shaggy black hair, and his horns grew in a spiral like a ram's. Some scientists said, 'I told you so! It speeded the mutation rate!'

"Others said, 'He's a natural mutation, or else, a throw-back to prehistoric wild cattle. It happens in every breed. Atomic Bomb had nothing to do with it.'

"They married the bull, and then they fixed to slaughter 'im to see what his insides was like. The bull fooled 'em, though. He came down with contagious pleuro-pneumonia, the first case in years, 'cause it was supposed to have been wiped out in this country away back in the Nineteenth Century. They had to cremate the bull for fear the disease would spread. Ever' one of the calves were normal Whitefaces.

"Finally, the nineteen Atohmy cattle that were left were put up for sale. My great-grandfather, Cary McPheeter, bought 'em and shipped 'em here to Bays Mountain. He's the man started this farm where there was nothin' but rattlesnakes, and trees, and rocks."

"Whyy theyea selll um?" a red roan calf interrupted.

"Well, they sold 'em 'cause Oak Ridge had been condemned. That was several years after the German Civil War. It was peace time, for a change, and folks were sick of Atomic Bomb. Anyhow, new, modern plants for makin' the stuff had been built in secret places a lot easier to defend. The women were cryin' for more automatic kitchens, so the Bureau of Interior Hydroelectric Power (that's the name Federal Power, Inc., went by then) put another dam across the Clinch River below Norris. Bush Lake covered up Oak Ridge.

"There wasn't much mutation, except for color, in you Atohmy cattle, till seven years ago when your pappy, Moe, was born. I remember—"

A hoarse excited voice shouted from a distance. "Thrill party!" it cried. "Thrill party!"

Stonecypher leaped off the stump, stamped his right foot to restore circulation, and yelled on the run, "That's all today! Stay under the trees!"

He loped along the pasture fence and across the makeshift target range. Two tenants, Teddy and Will, stood on the dirt heap with pitchforks in their hands. Over Bay Knob, an old Model 14 butterflier hovered on vibrating wings. Sloppy white letters on the sides of the aircraft spelled such slang expressions as, "Flash the MAGNETS," "SuperOlossalSoniC Flap ship," and "Redheads amble OTHer canop."

An impossible number of middleschool-age boys bulged from the cabin windows. Methodically, they dumped trash and garbage over the transmitter station ruins. The butterflier wheeled and flapped over the pasture. Red clover bent and writhed in the artificial wind from the ornithopter wings. Cows bawled and ran wild. Calves fell over each other.

Stonecypher jumped the fence. He wrested the revolver from the holster. "Clear out, or I'll shoot!" he howled.

Voices spilled from the butterflier. "He got a handgun!"

"Dis ain't legal!"

"Whatcha say, tall, bones, and ugly?"

Stonecypher aimed the Magnum at the shaven head in the pilot's seat. The boys looked faint. Agitated air thundered as the butterflier lifted straight up two hundred feet and glided away in the direction of Surgoinsville Dam.

Teddy and Will stood by with pitchforks unrelaxed. Will spat a globule of tobacco juice. "The things these here psychologists git made law!" he sneered. "You want me to make out a Thrill Damage Claim?"

"No, Will," Stonecypher said, "just deduct it from taxes."

Teddy looked at the revolver and said, "Ever'body oughta take guns to them crazy youngin's. Reckon you'll git into trouble?"

"No. It's an empty antique. That's legal. You guys did all right. Let the calves back in, huh?"

The tenants left by the gate, and, with a minimum of driving, urged the calves into the pasture. Stonecypher watched the men pass through the grove. Although the tenants undoubtedly recognized the peculiarities of the calves, they never mentioned them. Since the late 1700s, through Revolution, Civil War, automobile, the Department of Internal Revenue, the multiple bureaus that had controlled the Lakes, the Moon rocket, and the expedition to Pluto, these people had remained suspiciously interested in strangers, suspicious of indoor plumbing, doubtful of the Government, quick-tempered, and as immovable as Chimney Top. They had exchanged little except log and frame houses for concrete. The tenants, not really tenants, had been squatting on Bays Mountains when Cary McPheeter bought the farm; and there they stayed.

Stonecypher vaulted the fence. Catriona, with hands firmly planted on hips, stood in the dry pond. Stonecypher said, "If I just knew what these thrill parties think they're up to, it might help."

Catriona shook her head of red-yellow hair. "Nevah mind them. Ah told you to practice shootin', but the minute ah turn mah back, you run off and staht teachin' those calves! You've got to practice, Stony! You've nevah done any shootin', and L. Dan's killed ten people. Ah—"

"Watch the tears, or you'll have red and green eyes," Stonecypher said. Clumsily, he ejected the shells and reloaded the revolver. He occupied two seconds in drawing and firing. The bullets struck dirt a yard to the left of the target.

Sonata

A short vicious thunderstorm lashed Bays Mountain on the afternoon of July 3. As the storm passed, a blood-red butterflier, with a pusher propeller in the tail and a plastic bull head on the nose, descended in the young Sudan grass. Stonecypher dropped the saw—he had been clearing away a beech limb the storm left in the abandoned paddock—and strolled to greet Ringmaster A. Oswell.

"Stonecypher!" the ringmaster announced. "That storm almost caught us!" Oswell's stainless steel teeth clacked, and the breezes trailing the thunderclouds ballooned his orange silk kimono. "I never liked these butterfliers. They're too slow, and that swooping motion! Five hundred miles per hour may seem fast to a man your age; but in my day, back before petroleum was classified as armament, we had jets! Real speed!"

"Come on up to the house, ringmaster," Stonecypher invited. "I'll mix up some dextrose and citric acid."

"No, no time," the fat man panted. "Only time to see you about that bull you sold me. The storm took a limb of your beech tree! Almost the only one left, I suppose. About that bull, Stonecypher, you know I was a bit hesitant when I bought him, but my driver talked me into it. I'm so disappointed I had him drafted immediately!"

"But what—" Stonecypher attempted to ask.

"The young woman there in the butterflier is a much better driver and pilot," Oswell babbled. "I wouldn't have believed it of a woman! She weighs a good ninety-eight pounds, too! That bull—he has changed completely since we put him under the stands. He eats well, but he shows no spirit at all. Tomorrow is the big day, Stonecypher! I can't disappoint the crowd! I thought he might be sick, but the vet says not. That bull let the vet come into the cage and made absolutely no attempt to kill him!"

"But does Fergus—"

"Fergus's manager saw the bull! He's all for it. Fergus made an extremely poor showing on Memorial Day, and the manager thinks this odd bull would provide a real comeback! I advised against it. This heat is terrible! The storm didn't cool the air at all."

Stonecypher maneuvered the perspiring ringmaster into the shade of the beech. He said, "I wanta do the fair thing with you, ringmaster, so I'll give you a guarantee, in writing if you want. If that bull's not the bravest ever fought in Highland Bullring, I give you double-money-back."

Oswell's face wobbled in a tentative smile. He counted his stubby fingers. "Double-money-back?"

"Yeah. I wanta get into the business. My grandfather used to sell bulls. Then my father came along, and he wouldn't sell a one."

"Yes. Yes, I once tried to reason with him, but—"

"He had funny ideas," Stonecypher pressed his advantage. "I never did understand the old man myself. He used to lecture me on something he called the Man-Animal War. He said one of the worst things in the war was the thousands of bulls that had been tortured to death."

"Peculiar idea. Of course—"

"He claimed bullfights slipped up on this country. Back when it wasn't legal, they spaded up the ground real good. There were movies, and books, and magazines, and foreign broadcasts, all ravin' about how brave and noble it was for a bunch of men to worry and torture a stupid animal like a bull, till he couldn't hardly hold his head up, and then run a sword in 'im."

"Naturally, you—"

"I don't know how many times he told me a bull had more brains than a horse, but less than a jackass. He said bullfightin' wasn't a sport, even if the bull got a man sometimes; and he had the idea the worst thing was the four or five horses, that ever' bull killed, took with 'im. They had some bloodless bullfights in California, and the nut colonies out there like it so good, first thing you know, we really had it. It came to East Tennessee 'cause this was one of the biggest cattle-raisin' sections, before the Lakes took the grazin' land."

"Surely, Stonecypher, you—"

"My father always claimed if the bullfighters were near as brave as they said, they'd take on a really intelligent animal sometimes, like a man-eatin' tiger. He even thought a man was mentalill to fight a bull in the first place." Stonecypher grinned. "No, you don't need to worry about me, ringmaster. I hate to admit it, but the old man is the one who was mentalill."

Oswell revealed all of his steel teeth in a broad smile. "You had me worried!" he wheezed. "Now, your offer."

"I'll go even better," Stonecypher said, "just to show how set I am on getting' back in the business. If Moe's not brave, I got two yearlin's you can have for free."

"How generous! You've reassured me, Stonecypher. I have confidence, now, that the show will be a great success! I must go! You have no conception of the life a ringmaster leads before a fight. I won't require a written guarantee. I trust you, Stonecypher! See you tomorrow, I hope! I never liked July. If the Government would only make more Lakes, it might cool off! I hope—"

The whir of the red butterflier's wings terminated Oswell's discourse. With a face like a gored bullkiller, Stonecypher watched the ringmaster's departure. Another butterflier hovered above the mountain. This one was green and gold with the canopy pushed back and a glint of twin lenses in the cockpit.

Will appeared at Stonecypher's side. He spat in a long arc and said, "That's a new one, ain't it, peepin' from a butterfly? I reckon L. Dan never got kilt in that other duel like I hoped he would. You want us to git you outa this, Stonecypher?"

"No, Will."

"We can see you git to the Smokies. The Givernment'll never find you down in there."

"I'll be all right, Will. If he does kill me, take care of Catriona. And look after the calf records."

"Sure thing."

Stonecypher walked slowly toward Catriona's open-topped sunbathing tent.

Danse Macabre

Duelmaster R. Smith adjusted his black tam. "Do not touch your shooting hand to your weapon until the buzzer sounds," he instructed. "Otherwise, the weapon may be carried as you wish. At the slightest infringement of the rules, a robot gun will kill you. If you have any elaborate last words, say them now; because the pen is soundproof." He laughed an obviously much rehearsed laugh.

L. Dan wore orange tights today, but no armor, since the rules required duelists to present naked torsos for probable bullets. Stonecypher faced the duelmaster. "I reckon this room is the only place a man really has free speech," he said. "You're deaf, and can't see good enough to read lips, and me or him will soon be dead.

"I don't believe in this duelin'. It gives a man who's wrong a chance to kill one who's right. A man shouldn't oughta have to die because he's right. Just like ever'thing else in this Manly Age. It's painful. That oughta be our motto, More Pain, just like in the Machine Age it was More Gadgets At Any Cost."

"Why don't you go on tevee?" Dan jeered. "She'll soon forget you, farmer."

Stonecypher's words rolled over the hobbyist. "I reckon the Manly Age came because a man started thinkin' he wasn't much of a man any more. He was just as fast as his car, and just as strong as his electric lawn mower. And a loud minority of the women was claimin' they could do anything a man could, and maybe better. So the men started playin' football in shorts and huntin' each other on game preserves, and the women went back to the kitchen and bedroom. Lots of things that went on undercover come out in the open. Cockfights, dogfights, coon-on-a-log, duels, stallion fights, bullfights.

"And people like you, L. Dan, went on livin'. You got no right to live. You don't do any useful work. The Earth is slowly starvin', and you take the grub out of some feller's mouth who might could help a little. That's why—"

"Time!" announced the duelmaster with his face close to a large clock on the wall. He opened the door. Two men carrying a body on a stretcher passed. The body had four bullet wounds in it.

Dan said, "That drivel gives me a real reason to kill you, farmer. I'll be good to her for a few days."

As prearranged, Dan took the right branch of the corridor and Stonecypher, the left. A hooded man gave Stonecypher the Magnum revolver and shut him into a space resembling a windowed closet with a door on either side. Stonecypher secured the revolver in the clip holster. His bony hands formed knotted fists.

The pen door slid back. Stonecypher stepped into a room thirty by ninety feet with three bullet-marred concrete walls and a fourth wall of bulletproof glass, behind which sat the ghoulish audience. Dan, crouched and with his pistol in the crook of his left elbow, advanced. His right hand fluttered an inch from the pistol butt.

Stonecypher, grotesque with thin chest exposed and overall bib wrapped around belt, waited. Two photoelectric robot machine guns followed each movement of the duelists. A buzzer sounded. Dan's index finger failed to reach the trigger, for a guardian machine gun removed the hobbyist's head in a short efficient burst. The noise of a loud buzzer punctuated the execution.

When the soundproof inner door of the closet opened, the hooded man, who had a pair of crossed pistols tattooed on the back of his right hand, said, "He was too anxious."

"Yeah," Stonecypher grunted.

The man watched Stonecypher pass out to the street. Stonecypher snapped up the bib of his overalls. An extremely rare bird, a robin, hopped from his path and continued a fruitless search for insects. Stonecypher walked down Watauga Street until the pavement vanished under the brownish-green water of Kings Lake.

Catriona squealed when she saw him. Ignoring all Correct Procedures, she almost knocked him down and attempted to smother him. "Ah told you it just took practice!" she blubbered. "You did it, Stony!"

With muffled mumbles, Stonecypher managed to put her in the Tenite canoe. The few people along the quay, who had witnessed the illegal manner of their meeting, watched with shock, or with incredulity, or with guarded admiration. When they saw that Stonecypher's hand rested on a holstered revolver, they lost their curiosity.

Wading, Stonecypher shoved the canoe off and hopped aboard. As he took up the paddle, his hand trailed in the water and released the small buzzer that had made possible Catriona's best carnival act.

For July, the afternoon was cool. Blue-gray clouds drifted before larger dirty white masses. To the southwest opened the mile-wide mouth of Horse Creek; and, far beyond, the great blue pyramid of Chimney Top Mountain stood defiantly above Sevier Lake. The world seemed water broken only by partly submerged hills and mountains.

Stonecypher gazed across the Lake at Bays Mountain and at the five Cement Islands apparently floating against that backdrop. Softly, he said, "Some folks call the big one Martyrs Island. There's a marble pillar right in the middle. Nobody knows who put it there, and the Government never bothered to knock it down. I reckon the poison ivy's covered it by now, but I went and read the inscription, once, when I was a boy. It says:

> 'They moved me off the Powell River.
> They covered my farm with water.
> I bought me another near Beans Station.
> The water covered it.
> I was getting old, but I built at Galloway Mill.
> When they flooded that, I gave up and lived in
>   Kingsport.
> I will not move again.'"

The canoe bounded over the choppy water, one hundred feet above the silted streets of the flooded city of Kingsport. Stonecypher said, "The time I was there, you could still find a few copter-trooper helmets and old cankered shells. Couple of years back, a diver brought up two skulls off shore."

Catriona's eyes remained moist, but she smiled. Her teeth were beautiful. "It'll be all rahght, Stony. You can't change the wo'ld in one day. You did fine, and Moe will too."

"I told you to stay at the bullring," Stonecypher said.

"Ah couldn't watch that! And those puny, little, mousy women stare and talk about me, because theah's a little meat on mah cahcass. Oswell said Moe would be last, anyhow. Ah was so wo'ied about you, ah couldn't sit still."

Only a few boats, mainly those of piscatorial maniacs, were on the lake. Stonecypher glared at them and muttered, "I hope I did right by Moe. He wanted to fight. Maybe, Catriona, if I'd had you when I found out he could talk—not just mimic—I'd of raised him different. Maybe I shouldn't have shown him that bullfight movie, but I wondered what the only bull to see a bullfight from outside the ring thought about it.

"That led to him wantin' to know all about the Man-Animal War. I told him the best I could, how one of a man's basic drives is to exterminate, ever' since prehistoric times when he did in the wooly mammoth and rhinoceros. The dodo, quagga, passenger pigeon, great auk, aurochs, Key deer, bison, African elephant, gorilla, tiger—there's an awful list. Why, five hundred species of mammals, alone, have become extinct since 1 A.D., 'bout four hundred of them since 1850. A man'll even kill off other men, like the Neanderthals and the Tasmanians!" Stonecypher rested the paddle and grinned, faintly, at Catriona reclining in the bow. "I guess you've heard this before."

"Go rahght ahead, Stony," Catriona sighed. "Ah like to heah yoah speech. It's the only time you really get angry, and you look so fine and noble."

"Yeah. Well. I told Moe how a man exterminates useful or harmless species, and then he lets dangerous ones, like rats, eat him out of house and home. Course, I explained this was just kinship. Folks used to argue man come from a monkey, or from spontaneous combustion, or something. Now we got fossil proof he's not like anything anybody ever saw. He's a case of straight line development all the way back to the first mammal, a sort of rat."

The canoe glided past Highland Pier. Every type of small watercraft, from a punt, through an electric motorboat, to a sloop, had docked. More boats lined the shore on either side of the pier. The flying field contained so many butterfliers and copters that there seemed no possibility of any of them taking off. Human voices welled in a mob roar from the great open cylinder of the bullring.

A huge banner draped on the curving white wall proclaimed, in ten-foot letters:

DEPENDENCE DAY
BULLFIGHT
HONOR THE GREAT
GOVERNMENT ON WHICH
WE DEPEND
SIX BULLS—THREE KILLERS

Stonecypher ran the canoe aground in a patch of dead weeds, exposed by a slight lowering of the lake level, and helped Catriona over the rocks that lined the bank. He said, "I told Moe other things men do to animals. All the laboratory butchery, done because it would be cruel to treat a man like that, but it's all right with a animal, like takin' out a dog's brains and lettin' 'im live. I told him about huntin', how the kudu became extinct 'cause a bunch of fools wanted to see who could kill the one with the biggest horns.

"I told him the things done to domestic animals. Dehornin', emasculatin', brandin', slaughterin' with sledge hammers and butcher knives, keepin' 'em in filthy barns. A man tells hisself he's superior to other animals. If he does somethin' bad, he uses words like inhuman, brutal, animal instincts, instead of admittin' it's just typical behavior. And the psychologists take some animal, say a dog, and put him in a maze, something the dog never saw before. If the dog don't run the maze in two seconds flat, they say he's a pretty stupid animal. He just operates on instinct, but they can't say how instinct operates. They'll have a time explainin' Moe's instincts.

"I reckon the American bison made Moe madder than anything. They killed the bison off, 'cept for protected herds, in the Nineteenth Century. A hundred years later, the herds had got pretty big, so they declared open season on bison. No more bison."

A recorded voice growled, "No guns permitted in ring. Deposit gun in slot. No guns permitted in ring."

Stonecypher moved his permit in ineffectual passes before the electric eye. He shrugged, dropped the revolver into the slot, and left his thumb print. Catriona displayed the passes Ringmaster Oswell had given them. The teveer blinked, and the gate granted admission. They rode the escalator to the sixth tier and squirmed through pandemonium to their seats.

The male portion of the crowd wore every possible style and

color of dress, in complete emancipation from the old business suit uniform, but the women wore sober false-bosomed sundresses and expressed excitement in polite chirps. Stonecypher pressed his mouth against Catriona's ear and whispered through the din, "You got to understand, Cat, whatever happens, Moe wanted it. He says he can scare some killers into givin' up bullfights and maybe help stop it."

"He'll do fine, Stony."

Several spectators stopped venting their wrath on the unfortunate man in the ring to gawk at the couple. Catriona's unorthodox physique aroused sufficient amazement; but, in addition, Stonecypher gave her the front seat and took the rear one, the correct place for a woman, himself.

Below, through a rain of plasti-bottles and rotten eggs, a tired man walked to the barrier which Oswell advertised as the only wooden fence in seven states. Behind the killer, a small electric tractor dragged out the bloody carcass of a bull.

A gasping, gibbering little man grabbed Stonecypher's arm and yelped, "Illard is the clumsiest killer, he ran the sword in three times, and the kid with the dagger had to stick twice before they finished, Big Dependence Day Bullfight my jet! This is the worst in years, Fergus made the only clean kill all afternoon, and I flew every one of eighteen hundred miles myself to see it, this last bull better be good!" The little man waved his bag of rotten eggs.

Although the bullfight followed the basic procedures established by Francisco Romero in the Spain of 1700, changes had occurred, including the elimination of all Spanish words from the vocabulary of the spectacle since the unpleasant dispute with the Spanish Empire twenty years before. The gaudy costumes worn by participants had been replaced by trunks and sneakers.

A purring grader smoothed the sand. The crowd quieted, except for those near the box of Ringmaster Oswell. They suggested in obscene terms that their money be refunded. A trumpet recording blared. A scarlet door, inscribed, "Moe of Bays Mountain Farm," opened. The crowd awaited the first wild rush of the bull. It failed to materialize.

Grand Finale

Slowly, Moe came through the doorway. Above, on a platform inside the barrier, stood a gray-haired man who stuck identifying, streamered darts into bovine shoulders. His hand swept down, carrying Stonecypher's chosen colors, black.

Moe's walk upset the man's timing. His arm moved too soon. Moe's front hooves left the ground. Horns hooked. The gray-haired man screamed and dropped the dart. With a spike of horn through his arm, between bone and biceps, he gyrated across the barrier. He screamed a second time before cloven hooves slashed across his body.

The crowd inhaled, then cheered the unprecedented entrance. Killer Fergus's team stood rigid, not comprehending. Then men dashed through shielded openings in the barrier, yelling and waving pink and yellow capes to draw the bull from his victim.

Moe ignored the distraction, trotted nonchalantly to the center of the ring, and turned his bulging head to examine the spectators jabbering at his strange appearance. The short horns, the round skull, the white-banded eyes, the mane that seemed slightly purple under the cloudy sky, and the exaggerated slope from neck to rump that made the hind legs too short—together they amounted to a ton of muscle almost like a bull. "Where'd you trap it, Oswell?" someone near the ringmaster's box yelled.

Forgetting the mess Illard had made with the previous bull, the crowd commented. "It's the last of the bison!"

"He's poiple! Lookit! Poiple!"

"The bull of the woods!"

"Howya like 'im, Fergus?"

Killer Fergus posed behind the barrier and studied his specialty, an odd bull. Two stickers, Neel and Tomas, flourished capes to test the bull's charge, with Neel chanting, "Come on, bull! Come on, bull! Come on! Bull, bull, bull!"

Moe did not charge. He moved, in a speculative walk, toward the chanting Neel who tantalized with the cape and retreated with shuffling steps. The charge, when it came, occurred almost too fast for sight. Neel wriggled on the horns, struck the sand, and the horns lifted him again. He smashed against the barrier. Tomas threw his cape over the bull's face. The left horn pinned the cape to Tomas's naked chest over the heart.

Moe retired to the center of the ring and bellowed at the crowd, which, delirious from seeing human blood, applauded. Blood covered Moe's horns, dripped through the long hair on his neck, and trickled down between his eyes.

Quavering helpers removed the bodies. The first lancer, livid and trembling, rode a blindfolded horse into the ring. "He'll fix this horse!" the crowd slavered. "We'll see guts this time!"

Moe charged. The lancer backed his mount against the barrier and gripped his weapon, a stout pike. Sand sprayed like water as Moe swerved. On the left side of the horse, away from the menacing pike, Moe reared. The lancer left the saddle. A tangle of naked limbs thrashed across the wooden fence and thudded against the wall of the stands.

Twenty-five thousand people held their breaths. The blindfolded horse waited with dilated nostrils and every muscle vibrating in terror. Moe produced a long red tongue and licked the horse's jaw.

Fergus dispersed the tableau. Red-haired, lean, and scarred with many past gorings, the popular killer stalked across the sand dragging his cape and roaring incomprehensible challenges. In the stands, the cheer leaders of the Fergus Fanclub lead a welcoming yell. "Yeaaaa, Fergus! Fergus! Fergus! Rah, rah, rah!"

Moe wandered through the helpers trying to distract him from the horse and looked at the killer. Fergus stamped his foot, shook his cape, and called, "Bull! Come on! Charge!" Moe completely circled the killer, who retired in disgust when another lancer rode into the ring. "Stick him good!" Fergus directed.

The pike pointed at the great muscles of Moe's back, as the bull charged. Moe's head twisted in a blur of violence. Teeth clamped on the shaft behind the point. Too surprised to let go, the lancer followed his weapon from the saddle. He released his hold when Moe walked on him.

Like some fantastic dog stealing a fresh bone, the bull trotted around the ring, tail high and pike in mouth. The crowd laughed. Wild-eyed men carried out the trampled lancer.

A third, and extremely reluctant, lancer reined his horse through the gate. A pike in the mouth of a ton of beef utterly unnerved the man. He stood in the saddle and jumped over the barrier where a rain of rotten eggs from the booing fans spattered him thoroughly.

An uninjured bull pawed alone in the sand when the trumpet recording announced the end of the lancers' period. The crowd noises softened to a buzz of speculation, questions, and comment, as the realization that weird events had been witnessed slowly penetrated that collective mind. The bull had not touched a horse, no pike had jabbed the bull, and five men had been killed or injured.

"Great Government!" a clear voice swore. "That ain't no bull, it's a monster!" This opinion came from a sticker in Illard's team. Fergus attempted to persuade the man to help, since both of Fergus's stickers were dead. Part of the crowd agreed with the sticker's thought, for people began moving furtively to the exits with cautious glances at the animal in the ring. They, of course, could not know that the bull had been trained, with rubber-tipped pikes and dummies, in every phase of the bullfight; that he knew the first, and only, law of staying alive in the ring, "Charge the man and not the cloth."

The clouds that had obscured the sky all day formed darker masses tinted with pink to the east, and the black dot of a turkey buzzard wheeled soaring in the gloom. Carrying, in either hand, a barbed stick sparkling with plastic streamers, Fergus walked into the ring. His assistants cautiously flanked him with capes.

Moe dropped the pike and charged in the approved manner of a bull. Fergus raised the sticks high and brought them down on the humped back, although the back was not there. The sticks dropped in the sand.

As the killer leaped aside in the completion of a reflex action, a horn penetrated the seat of his trunks. The Fergus Fanclub screamed while their hero dangled in ignominy from the horn. Moe ignored the flapping, frantic capes. The killer gingerly gripped a horn in either hand and tried to lift himself off. Gently, Moe lowered his head and deposited the man beside an opening. Fergus scrabbled to safety like a rat to a hole.

Four helpers with capes occupied the ring. When they saw death approaching on cloven hooves, two of them cleared the fence. The third received a horn beside his backbone and tumbled into the fourth. A dual scream, terrible enough to insure future nightmares, echoed above the screeching of the crowd. Moe tossed the bodies again and again across the bloody sand.

Silence slithered over the Highland Bullring and over a scene reminiscent of the ring's bloody parent, the Roman Arena. Men sprawled gored, crushed, and dead across the sand. A section of the blood-specked barrier leaned splintered and cracked, almost touching the concrete wall. Unharmed, Fergus stood on one side of the battleground, Illard on the other.

Fergus reached over the wooden fence for red flag and sword. Turning his back on the heaving Moe, who stood but ten feet behind, the killer faced the quaking flesh that was Ringmaster Oswell, high up in the official box. The killer's voice shook, but the bitter satire came through the sound of departing boats and aircraft. Fergus said, "I dedicate this bull to Ringmaster Oswell who has provided for us this great Dependence Day Bullfight in honor of the Great Government on which we all depend." He turned and faced the bull.

Moe, for once, rushed the red flag, the only thing that made bullfights possible. His great shoulders presented a fair target for the sword.

Fergus, perhaps the only bullfighter ever to be gored in the brain, died silently. The sword raked a shallow gash long Moe's loin.

In the sixth tier of the stands, saliva drooled from the slack mouth of the little man seated beside Stonecypher. "Now's your chance, Illard!" the man squalled. "Be a hero! The last of the bullfighters! Kill him, Illard!"

Illard walked on shaking legs over bodies he did not see. He was short, for a killer, and growing bald. He picked up the sword Fergus had dropped, looked into the gory face of the bull, and toppled in the sticky sand. The sword quivered point-first beside his body.

Recessional

A wind whipped down into Highland Bullring. Riding the wind, blacker than the clouds, the inquisitive turkey buzzard glided over the rim of the stands with air whistling through the spatulate feathers of rigid wings. The buzzard swooped a foot above Moe's horns and soared swiftly over the opposite side of the ring.

That started the panic, although Moe's charge accentuated it. He crashed into the sagging section of the barrier. Cloven hooves scraped the wooden inclined plane, and Moe stopped with front feet in the first tier of the stands. He bellowed.

The bull killed only one spectator, a man on whom he stepped. The hundreds who died killed themselves or each other. They leaped from the towering rim of the ring, and they jammed the exits in writhing heaps.

Moe's precarious stance slipped. Slowly, he slid back into the ring, where Ringmaster Oswell, quivering in a red toga, gestured from the darkness under the stands. The fat man squeaked and waved. Moe's charge embodied the genuine fighting rage of a maddened bull. The scarlet door closed behind him.

Stonecypher, with fists bloody and a heap of unconscious fear-crazed spectators piled before him, sat down. "Well, Moe," he whispered, "I reckon you got even for a few of the bulls that's been tortured to death to amuse a bunch of nuts. Maybe it wasn't the right way to do it. I don't know. If I'd only had the gun—"

Catriona turned a white mask of a face up to Stonecypher. "They killed him, in theah?"

"Sure. Bullfightin' never was a sport. The bull can't win. If he's not killed in the ring, he's slaughtered under the stands.

"You have moah smart-bulls, Stony."

The black copter came in with the sunset and hovered over the sand. The face of Duelmaster Smith peered out under his black tam, while a hooded man, with pistols tattooed on his hand, aimed an automatic rifle. The duelmaster smiled at Stonecypher and cried, "You really should have waited until you were farther out in the Lake, before you dropped that little buzzer in the water."

A Gun for Dinosaur

by L. Sprague de Camp

PREFACE BY DAVID DRAKE:

The writers who created the Golden Age in *Astounding* were Heinlein on a level of his own, and de Camp, Hubbard, and Van Vogt right below him. (I'll argue that statement with anybody who catches me at a convention, but nobody who has a right to an opinion will deny that it's defensible.)

Those four authors (in reprint) were all important to me when I started reading SF, but it was Sprague de Camp who most formed my view of what science fiction was and should be. I don't know why, but the fact isn't in doubt.

After World War II de Camp slid into a different sort of story, entertaining but not nearly as significant to the field. By the '50s de Camp stories were appearing mostly in lower-level markets, and he was putting much of his effort into revising and pasticing the work of Robert E. Howard, a writer whom he explicitly did not respect. (Late in life, Sprague described this to me as being the worst mistake of his career. I agree with him.)

In the middle of this apparent decline, de Camp wrote two unquestionable masterpieces, the bleak and despairing "Judgment Day" ("That was really an autobiographical story," he told me—as if I'd been in doubt) and "A Gun for Dinosaur." Men-against-dinosaur stories are as old as magazine SF, just as there were horror novels before *Carrie*. King and de Camp turned what had been occasional subjects for stories into defined subgenres.

That's why "A Gun for Dinosaur" is important. The reason it's here, however, is that it blew all three of us away when we read it the first time.

No, I'm sorry, Mr. Seligman, but I can't take you hunting Late Mesozoic dinosaur.

Yes, I know what the advertisement says.

Why not? How much d'you weigh? A hundred and thirty? Let's see; that's under ten stone, which is my lower limit.

I could take you to other periods, you know. I'll take you to any period in the Cenozoic. I'll get you a shot at an entelodont or a uintathere. They've got fine heads.

I'll even stretch a point and take you to the Pleistocene, where you can try for one of the mammoths or the mastodon.

I'll take you back to the Triassic where you can shoot one of the smaller ancestral dinosaurs. But I will jolly well not take you to the Jurassic or Cretaceous. You're just too small.

What's your size got to do with it? Look here, old boy, what did you think you were going to shoot your dinosaur with?

Oh, you hadn't thought, eh?

Well, sit there a minute . . . Here you are: my own private gun for that work, a Continental .600. Does look like a shotgun, doesn't it? But it's rifled, as you can see by looking through the barrels. Shoots a pair of .600 Nitro Express cartridges the size of bananas; weighs fourteen and a half pounds and has a muzzle energy of over seven thousand foot-pounds. Costs fourteen hundred and fifty dollars. Lot of money for a gun, what?

I have some spares I rent to the sahibs. Designed for knocking down elephant. Not just wounding them, knocking them base-over-apex. That's why they don't make guns like this in America, though I suppose they will if hunting parties keep going back in time.

Now, I've been guiding hunting parties for twenty years. Guided 'em in Africa until the game gave out there except on the preserves. And all that time I've never known a man your size who could handle the six-nought-nought. It knocks 'em over, and even when they stay on their feet they get so scared of the bloody cannon after a few shots that they flinch. And they find the gun too heavy to drag around rough Mesozoic country. Wears 'em out.

It's true that lots of people have killed elephant with lighter guns: the .500, .475, and .465 doubles, for instance, or even the

.375 magnum repeaters. The difference is, with a .375 you have to hit something vital, preferably the heart, and can't depend on simple shock power.

An elephant weighs—let's see—four to six tons. You're proposing to shoot reptiles weighing two or three times as much as an elephant and with much greater tenacity of life. That's why the syndicate decided to take no more people dinosaur hunting unless they could handle the .600. We learned the hard way, as you Americans say. There were some unfortunate incidents...

I'll tell you, Mr. Seligman. It's after seventeen-hundred. Time I closed the office. Why don't we stop at the bar on our way out while I tell you the story?

...It was about the Raja's and my fifth safari into time. The Raja? Oh, he's the Aiyar half of Rivers and Aiyar. I call him the Raja because he's the hereditary monarch of Janpur. Means nothing nowadays, of course. Knew him in India and ran into him in New York running the Indian tourist agency. That dark chap in the photograph on my office wall, the one with his foot on the dead saber-tooth.

Well, the Raja was fed up with handing out brochures about the Taj Mahal and wanted to do a bit of hunting again. I was at loose ends when we heard of Professor Prochaska's time machine at Washington University.

Where's the Raja now? Out on safari in the Early Oligocene after titanothere while I run the office. We take turn about, but the first few times we went out together.

Anyway, we caught the next plane to St. Louis. To our mortification, we found we weren't the first. Lord, no! There were other hunting guides and no end of scientists, each with his own idea of the right way to use the machine.

We scraped off the historians and archeologists right at the start. Seems the ruddy machine won't work for periods more recent than 100,000 years ago. It works from there up to about a billion years.

Why? Oh, I'm no four-dimensional thinker; but, as I understand it, if people could go back to a more recent time, their actions would affect our own history, which would be a paradox or contradiction of facts. Can't have that in a well-run universe, you know.

But, before 100,000 B.C., more or less, the actions of the expeditions are lost in the stream of time before human history begins. At that, once a stretch of past time has been used, say the month of January, one million B.C., you can't use that stretch over again by sending another party into it. Paradoxes again.

The professor isn't worried, though. With a billion years to exploit, he won't soon run out of eras.

Another limitation of the machine is the matter of size. For technical reasons, Prochaska had to build the transition chamber just big enough to hold four men with their personal gear, and the chamber wallah. Larger parties have to be sent through in relays. That means, you see, it's not practical to take jeeps, launches, aircraft, and other powered vehicles.

On the other hand, since you're going to periods without human beings, there's no whistling up a hundred native bearers to trot along with your gear on their heads. So we usually take a train of asses—burros, they call them here. Most periods have enough natural forage so you can get where you want to go.

As I say, everybody had his own idea for using the machine. The scientists looked down their noses at us hunters and said it would be a crime to waste the machine's time pandering to our sadistic amusements.

We brought up another angle. The machine cost a cool thirty million. I understand this came from the Rockefeller Board and such people, but that accounted for the original cost only, not the cost of operation. And the thing uses fantastic amounts of power. Most of the scientists' projects, while worthy enough, were run on a shoe-string, financially speaking.

Now, we guides catered to people with money, a species with which America seems well stocked. No offense, old boy. Most of these could afford a substantial fee for passing through the machine into the past. Thus we could help finance the operation of the machine for scientific purposes, provided we got a fair share of its time. In the end, the guides formed a syndicate of eight members, one member being the partnership of Rivers and Aiyar, to apportion the machine's time.

We had rush business from the start. Our wives—the Raja's and mine—raised hell with us for a while. They'd hoped that, when the big game gave out in our own era, they'd never have to share us with lions and things again, but you know how women are. Hunting's not really dangerous if you keep your head and take precautions.

On the fifth expedition, we had two sahibs to wet-nurse; both Americans in their thirties, both physically sound, and both solvent. Otherwise they were as different as different can be.

Courtney James was what you chaps call a playboy: a rich young man from New York who'd always had his own way and didn't see why that agreeable condition shouldn't continue. A big bloke, almost as big as I am; handsome in a florid way, but beginning to run to fat. He was on his fourth wife and, when he showed up at the office with a blond twist with "model" written all over her, I assumed that this was the fourth Mrs. James.

"Miss Bartram," she corrected me, with an embarrassed giggle.

"She's not my wife," James explained. "My wife is in Mexico, I think, getting a divorce. But Bunny here would like to go along—"

"Sorry," I said, "we don't take ladies. At least, not to the Late Mesozoic."

This wasn't strictly true, but I felt we were running enough risks, going after a little-known fauna, without dragging in people's domestic entanglements. Nothing against sex, you understand. Marvelous institution and all that, but not where it interferes with my living.

"Oh, nonsense!" said James. "If she wants to go, she'll go. She skis and flies my airplane, so why shouldn't she—"

"Against the firm's policy," I said.

"She can keep out of the way when we run up against the dangerous ones," he said.

"No, sorry."

"Damn it!" said he, getting red. "After all, I'm paying you a goodly sum, and I'm entitled to take whoever I please."

"You can't hire me to do anything against my best judgment," I said. "If that's how you feel, get another guide."

"All right, I will," he said. "And I'll tell all my friends you're a God-damned—" Well, he said a lot of things I won't repeat, until I told him to get out of the office or I'd throw him out.

I was sitting in the office and thinking sadly of all that lovely money James would have paid me if I hadn't been so stiff-necked, when in came my other lamb, one August Holtzinger. This was a little slim pale chap with glasses, polite and formal. Holtzinger sat on the edge of his chair and said:

"Uh—Mr. Rivers, I don't want you to think I'm here under false pretenses. I'm really not much of an outdoorsman, and I'll probably be scared to death when I see a real dinosaur. But I'm determined to hang a dinosaur head over my fireplace or die in the attempt."

"Most of us are frightened at first," I soothed him, "though it doesn't do to show it." And little by little I got the story out of him.

While James had always been wallowing in the stuff, Holtzinger was a local product who'd only lately come into the real thing. He'd had a little business here in St. Louis and just about made ends meet when an uncle cashed in his chips somewhere and left little Augie the pile.

Now Holtzinger had acquired a fiancée and was building a big house. When it was finished, they'd be married and move into it. And one furnishing he demanded was a ceratopsian head over the fireplace. Those are the ones with the big horned heads with a parrot-beak and a frill over the neck, you know. You have to think twice about collecting them, because if you put a seven-foot *Triceratops* head into a small living room, there's apt to be no room left for anything else.

We were talking about this when in came a girl: a small girl in her twenties, quite ordinary looking, and crying.

"Augie!" she cried. "You can't! You mustn't! You'll be killed!" She grabbed him round the knees and said to me:

"Mr. Rivers, you mustn't take him! He's all I've got! He'll never stand the hardships!"

"My dear young lady," I said, "I should hate to cause you distress, but it's up to Mr. Holtzinger to decide whether he wishes to retain my services."

"It's no use, Claire," said Holtzinger. "I'm going, though I'll probably hate every minute of it."

"What's that, old boy?" I said. "If you hate it, why go? Did you lose a bet, or something?"

"No," said Holtzinger. "It's this way. Uh—I'm a completely undistinguished kind of guy. I'm not brilliant or big or strong or handsome. I'm just an ordinary Midwestern small businessman. You never even notice me at Rotary luncheons, I fit in so perfectly.

"But that doesn't say I'm satisfied. I've always hankered to go to far places and do big things. I'd like to be a glamorous, adventurous sort of guy. Like you, Mr. Rivers."

"Oh, come," I said. "Professional hunting may seem glamorous to you, but to me it's just a living."

He shook his head. "Nope. You know what I mean. Well, now I've got this legacy, I could settle down to play bridge and golf the rest of my life, and try to act like I wasn't bored. But I'm determined to do something with some color in it, once at least.

Since there's no more real big-game hunting in the present, I'm gonna shoot a dinosaur and hang his head over my mantel if it's the last thing I do. I'll never be happy otherwise."

Well, Holtzinger and his girl argued, but he wouldn't give in. She made me swear to take the best care of her Augie and departed, sniffling.

When Holtzinger had left, who should come in but my vile-tempered friend Courtney James? He apologized for insulting me, though you could hardly say he groveled.

"I don't really have a bad temper," he said, "except when people won't cooperate with me. Then I sometimes get mad. But so long as they're cooperative I'm not hard to get along with."

I knew that by "cooperate" he meant to do whatever Courtney James wanted, but I didn't press the point. "What about Miss Bartram?" I asked.

"We had a row," he said. "I'm through with women. So, if there's no hard feelings, let's go on from where we left off."

"Very well," I said, business being business.

The Raja and I decided to make it a joint safari to eight-five million years ago: the Early Upper Cretaceous, or the Middle Cretaceous as some American geologists call it. It's about the best period for dinosaur in Missouri. You'll find some individual species a little larger in the Late Upper Cretaceous, but the period we were going to gives a wider variety.

Now, as to our equipment: The Raja and I each had a Continental .600, like the one I showed you, and a few smaller guns. At this time we hadn't worked up much capital and had no spare .600s to rent.

August Holtzinger said he would rent a gun, as he expected this to be his only safari, and there's no point in spending over a thousand dollars for a gun you'll shoot only a few times. But, since we had no spare .600s, his choice lay between buying one of those and renting one of our smaller pieces.

We drove into the country and set up a target to let him try the .600. Holtzinger heaved up the gun and let fly. He missed completely, and the kick knocked him flat on his back.

He got up, looking paler than ever, and handed me back the gun, saying: "Uh—I think I'd better try something smaller."

When his shoulder stopped hurting, I tried him out on the smaller rifles. He took a fancy to my Winchester 70, chambered for the .375 magnum cartridge. This is an excellent all-round gun—perfect for the big cats and bears, but a little light for elephant and definitely light for dinosaur. I should never have given in, but I was in a hurry, and it might have taken months to have a new .600 made to order for him. James already had a gun, a Holland & Holland .500 double express, which is almost in a class with the .600.

Both sahibs had done a bit of shooting, so I didn't worry about their accuracy. Shooting dinosaur is not a matter of extreme accuracy, but of sound judgment and smooth coordination so you shan't catch twigs in the mechanism of your gun, or fall into holes, or climb a small tree that the dinosaur can pluck you out of, or blow your guide's head off.

People used to hunting mammals sometimes try to shoot a dinosaur in the brain. That's the silliest thing to do, because dinosaurs haven't got any. To be exact, they have a little lump of tissue the size of a tennis ball on the front end of their spines, and how are you going to hit that when it's imbedded in a six-foot skull?

The only safe rule with dinosaur is: always try for a heart shot. They have big hearts, over a hundred pounds in the largest species, and a couple of .600 slugs through the heart will slow them up, at least. The problem is to get the slugs through that mountain of meat around it.

Well, we appeared at Prochaska's laboratory one rainy morning: James and Holtzinger, the Raja and I, our herder Beauregard Black, three helpers, a cook, and twelve jacks.

The transition chamber is a little cubbyhole the size of a small lift. My routine is for the men with the guns to go first in case a hungry theropod is standing near the machine when it arrives. So the two sahibs, the Raja, and I crowded into the chamber with our guns and packs. The operator squeezed in after us, closed the door, and fiddled with his dials. He set the thing for April twenty-fourth, eight-five million B.C., and pressed the red button. The lights went out, leaving the chamber lit by a little battery-operated lamp. James and Holtzinger looked pretty green, but that may have been the lighting. The Raja and I had been through all this before, so the vibration and vertigo didn't bother us.

The little spinning black hands of the dials slowed down and stopped. The operator looked at his ground-level gauge and turned the handwheel that raised the chamber so it shouldn't materialize underground. Then he pressed another button, and the door slid open.

No matter how often I do it, I get a frightful thrill out of stepping into a bygone era. The operator had raised the chamber a foot above ground level, so I jumped down, my gun ready. The others came after.

"Right-ho," I said to the chamber wallah, and he closed the door. The chamber disappeared, and we looked around. There weren't any dinosaur in sight, nothing but lizards.

In this period, the chamber materializes on top of a rocky rise, from which you can see in all directions as far as the haze will let you. To the west, you see the arm of the Kansas Sea that reaches across Missouri and the big swamp around the bayhead where the sauropods live.

To the north is a low range that the Raja named the Janpur Hills, after the Indian kingdom his forebears once ruled. To the east, the land slopes up to a plateau, good for ceratopsians, while to the south is flat country with more sauropod swamps and lots of ornithopod: duckbill and iguanodont.

The finest thing about the Cretaceous is the climate: balmy like the South Sea Islands, but not so muggy as most Jurassic climates. It was spring, with dwarf magnolias in bloom all over.

A thing about this landscape is that it combines a fairly high rainfall with an open type of vegetation cover. That is, the grasses hadn't yet evolved to the point of forming solid carpets over all the open ground. So the ground is thick with laurel, sassafras, and other shrubs, with bare earth between. There are big thickets of palmettos and ferns. The trees round the hill are mostly cycads, standing singly and in copses. You'd call 'em palms. Down towards the Kansas Sea are more cycads and willows, while the uplands are covered with screw pine and ginkgoes.

Now, I'm no bloody poet—the Raja writes the stuff, not me—but I can appreciate a beautiful scene. One of the helpers had come through the machine with two of the jacks and was pegging them out, and I was looking through the haze and sniffing the air, when a gun went off behind me—*bang! bang!*

I whirled round, and there was Courtney James with his .500, and an ornithomime legging it for cover fifty yards away. The ornithomimes are medium-sized running dinosaurs, slender things with long necks and legs, like a cross between a lizard and an ostrich. This kind is about seven feet tall and weighs as much as a man. The beggar had wandered out of the nearest copse, and James gave him both barrels. Missed.

I was upset, as trigger-happy sahibs are as much a menace to their party as theropods. I yelled: "Damn it, you idiot! I thought you weren't to shoot without a word from me?"

"And who the hell are you to tell me when I'll shoot my own gun?" he said.

We had a rare old row until Holtzinger and the Raja got us calmed down. I explained:

"Look here, Mr. James, I've got reasons. If you shoot off all your ammunition before the trip's over, your gun won't be available in a pinch, as it's the only one of its caliber. If you empty both barrels at an unimportant target, what would happen if a big theropod charged before you could reload? Finally, it's not sporting to shoot everything in sight, just to hear the gun go off. Do you understand?"

"Yeah, I guess so," he said.

The rest of the party came through the machine, and we pitched our camp a safe distance from the materializing place. Our first task was to get fresh meat. For a twenty-one-day safari like this, we calculate our food requirements closely, so we can make out on tinned stuff and concentrates if we must, but we count on killing at least one piece of meat. When that's butchered, we go off on a short tour, stopping at four or five camping places to hunt and arriving back at base a few days before the chamber is due to appear.

Holtzinger, as I said, wanted a ceratopsian head, any kind. James insisted on just one head: a tyrannosaur. Then everybody'd think he'd shot the most dangerous game of all time.

Fact is, the tyrannosaur's overrated. He's more a carrion eater than an active predator, though he'll snap you up if he gets the chance. He's less dangerous than some of the other theropods—the flesh eaters, you know—such as the smaller *Gorgosaurus* from the period we were in. But everybody's read about the tyrant lizard, and he does have the biggest head of the theropods.

The one in our period isn't the *rex*, which is later and a bit bigger and more specialized. It's the *trionyches*, with the forelimbs not quite so reduced, though they're still too small for anything but picking the brute's teeth after a meal.

When camp was pitched, we still had the afternoon. So the Raja and I took our sahibs on their first hunt. We had a map of the local terrain from previous trips.

The Raja and I have worked out a system for dinosaur hunting. We split into two groups of two men each and walk parallel from twenty to forty yards apart. Each group has a sahib in front and a guide following, telling him where to go. We tell the sahibs we put them in front so they shall have the first shot. Well, that's true, but another reason is they're always tripping and falling with their guns cocked, and if the guide were in front he'd get shot.

The reason for two groups is that if a dinosaur starts for one, the other gets a good heart shot from the side.

As we walked, there was the usual rustle of lizards scuttling out of the way: little fellows, quick as a flash and colored like all the jewels in Tiffany's, and big gray ones that hiss at you as they plod off. There were tortoises and a few little snakes. Birds with beaks full of teeth flapped off squawking. And always there was that marvelous mild Cretaceous air. Makes a chap want to take his clothes off and dance with vine leaves in his hair, if you know what I mean.

Our sahibs soon found that Mesozoic country is cut up into millions of nullahs—gullies, you'd say. Walking is one long scramble, up and down, up and down.

We'd been scrambling for an hour, and the sahibs were soaked with sweat and had their tongues hanging out, when the Raja whistled. He'd spotted a group of bonehead feeding on cycad shoots.

These are the troödonts, small ornithopods about the size of men with a bulge on top of their heads that makes them look almost intelligent. Means nothing, because the bulge is solid bone. The males butt each other with these heads in fighting over the females.

These chaps would drop down on all fours, munch up a shoot, then stand up and look around. They're warier than most dinosaur, because they're the favorite food of the big theropods.

People sometimes assume that because dinosaur are so stupid, their senses must be dim, too. But it's not so. Some, like the sauropods, are pretty dim-sensed, but most have good smell and eyesight and fair hearing. Their weakness is that having no minds, they have no memories. Hence, out of sight, out of mind. When a big theropod comes slavering after you, your best defense is to hide in a nullah or behind a bush, and if he can neither see you nor smell you he'll just wander off.

We skulked up behind a patch of palmetto downwind from the bonehead. I whispered to James:

"You've had a shot already today. Hold your fire until Holtzinger shoots, and then shoot only if he misses or if the beast is getting away wounded."

"Uh-huh," said James.

We separated, he with the Raja and Holtzinger with me. This got to be our regular arrangement. James and I got on each other's nerves, but the Raja's a friendly, sentimental sort of bloke nobody can help liking.

We crawled round the palmetto patch on opposite sides, and Holtzinger got up to shoot. You daren't shoot a heavy-caliber rifle prone. There's not enough give, and the kick can break your shoulder.

Holtzinger sighted round the law few fronds of palmetto. I saw his barrel wobbling and waving. Then he lowered his gun and tucked it under his arm to wipe his glasses.

Off went James's gun, both barrels again.

The biggest bonehead went down, rolling and thrashing. The others ran away on their hindlegs in great leaps, their heads jerking and their tails sticking up behind.

"Put your gun on safety," I said to Holtzinger, who'd started forward. By the time we got to the bonehead, James was standing over it, breaking open his gun and blowing out the barrels. He looked as smug as if he'd come into another million and was asking the Raja to take his picture with his foot on the game.

I said: "I thought you were to give Holtzinger the first shot?"

"Hell, I waited," he said, "and he took so long I thought he must have gotten buck fever. If we stood around long enough, they'd see us or smell us."

There was something in what he said, but his way of saying it put my monkey up. I said: "If that sort of thing happens once more, we'll leave you in camp the next time we go out."

"Now, gentlemen," said the Raja. "After all, Reggie, these aren't experienced hunters."

"What now?" said Holtzinger. "Haul him back ourselves or send out the men?"

"We'll sling him under the pole," I said. "He weighs under two hundred."

The pole was a telescoping aluminum carrying pole I had in my pack, with padded yokes on the ends. I brought it because, in such eras, you can't count on finding saplings strong enough for proper poles on the spot.

The Raja and I cleaned our bonehead to lighten him and tied him to the pole. The flies began to light on the offal by thousands. Scientists say they're not true flies in the modern sense, but they look and act like flies. There's one huge four-winged carrion fly that flies with a distinctive deep thrumming note.

The rest of the afternoon we sweated under that pole, taking turn about. The lizards scuttled out of the way, and the flies buzzed round the carcass.

We got to camp just before sunset, feeling as if we could eat the whole bonehead at one meal. The boys had the camp running smoothly, so we sat down for our tot of whiskey, feeling like lords of creation, while the cook broiled bonehead steaks.

Holtzinger said: "Uh—if I kill a ceratopsian, how do we get his head back?"

I explained: "If the ground permits, we lash it to the patent aluminum roller frame and sled it in."

"How much does a head like that weigh?" he asked.

"Depends on the age and the species," I told him. "The biggest weigh over a ton, but most run between five hundred and a thousand pounds."

"And all the ground's rough like it was today?"

"Most of it," I said. "You see, it's the combination of the open vegetation cover and the moderately high rainfall. Erosion is frightfully rapid."

"And who hauls the head on its little sled?"

"Everybody with a hand," I said. "A big head would need every ounce of muscle in this party. On such a job there's no place for side."

"Oh," said Holtzinger. I could see he was wondering whether a ceratopsian head would be worth the effort.

The next couple of days we trekked round the neighborhood. Nothing worth shooting; only a herd of ornithomimes, which went bounding off like a lot of ballet dancers. Otherwise there were only the usual lizards and pterosaurs and birds and insects. There's a big lace-winged fly that bites dinosaurs, so, as you can imagine, its beak makes nothing of a human skin. One made Holtzinger leap and dance like a Red Indian when it bit him through his shirt. James joshed him about it, saying:

"What's all the fuss over one little bug?"

The second night, during the Raja's watch, James gave a yell that brought us all out of our tents with rifles. All that had happened was that a dinosaur tick had crawled in with him and started drilling under his armpit. Since it's as big as your thumb even when it hasn't fed, he was understandably startled. Luckily he got it before it had taken its pint of blood. He'd pulled Holtzinger's leg pretty hard about the fly bite, so now Holtzinger repeated the words:

"What's all the fuss over one little bug, buddy?"

James squashed the tick underfoot with a grunt, not much liking to be hoist by his own what-d'you-call-it.

We packed up and started on our circuit. We meant to take the sahibs first to the sauropod swamp, more to see the wildlife than to collect anything.

From where the transition chamber materializes, the sauropod swamp looks like a couple of hours' walk, but it's really an all-day scramble. The first part is easy, as it's downhill and the brush isn't heavy. Then, as you get near the swamp, the cycads and willows grow so thickly that you have to worm your way among them.

I led the party to a sandy ridge on the border of the swamp, as it was pretty bare of vegetation and afforded a fine view. When we got to the ridge, the sun was about to go down. A couple of crocs slipped off into the water. The sahibs were so tired that they flopped down in the sand as if dead.

The haze is thick round the swamp, so the sun was deep red and weirdly distorted by the atmospheric layers. There was a high layer of clouds reflecting the red and gold of the sun, too, so altogether it was something for the Raja to write one of his poems about. A few little pterosaur were wheeling overhead like bats.

Beauregard Black got a fire going. We'd started on our steaks, and that pagoda-shaped sun was just slipping below the horizon, and something back in the trees was making a noise like a rusty hinge, when a sauropod breathed out in the water. They're the really big ones, you know. If Mother Earth were to sigh over the misdeeds of her children, it would sound like that.

The sahibs jumped up, shouting: "Where is he? Where is he?"

I said: "That black spot in the water, just to the left of that point."

They yammered while the sauropod filled its lungs and disappeared. "Is that all?" said James. "Won't we see any more of him?"

"No," I explained. "They can walk perfectly well and often do, for egg-laying and moving from one swamp to another. But most of the time they spend in the water, like hippopotamus. They eat eight hundred pounds of soft swamp plants a day, all through those little heads. So they wander about the bottoms of lakes and swamps, chomping away, and stick their heads up to breathe every quarter-hour or so. It's getting dark, so this fellow will soon come out and lie down in the shallows to sleep."

"Can we shoot one?" demanded James.

"I wouldn't," said I.

"Why not?"

I said: "There's no point in it, and it's not sporting. First, they're almost invulnerable. They're even harder to hit in the brain than other dinosaurs because of the way they sway their heads about on those long necks. Their hearts are too deeply buried to reach unless you're awfully lucky. Then, if you kill one in the water, he sinks and can't be recovered. If you kill one on land, the only trophy is that little head. You can't bring the whole beast back because he weighs thirty tons or more, and we've got no use for thirty tons of meat."

Holtzinger said: "That museum in New York got one."

"Yes," said I. "The American Museum of Natural History sent a party of forty-eight to the Early Cretaceous with a fifty-caliber machine gun. They killed a sauropod and spent two solid months skinning it and hacking the carcass apart and dragging it to the time machine. I know the chap in charge of that project, and he still has nightmares in which he smells decomposing dinosaur. They had to kill a dozen big theropods attracted by the stench, so they had them lying around and rotting, too. And the theropods ate three men of the party despite the big gun."

Next morning, we were finishing breakfast when one of the helpers said: "Look, Mr. Rivers, up there!"

He pointed along the shoreline. There were six big crested duckbill, feeding in the shallows. They were the kind called *Parasaurolophus*, with a long spike sticking out the back of their heads and a web of skin connecting this with the back of their necks.

"Keep your voices down!" I said. The duckbill, like the other ornithopods, are wary beasts because they have neither armor nor weapons. They feed on the margins of lakes and swamps, and when a gorgosaur rushes out of the trees they plunge into deep water and swim off. Then when *Phobosuchus*, the supercrocodile, goes for them in the water, they flee to the land. A hectic sort of life, what?

Holtzinger said: "Uh—Reggie! I've been thinking over what you said about ceratopsian heads. If I could get one of those yonder, I'd be satisfied. It would look big enough in my house, wouldn't it?"

"I'm sure of it, old boy," I said. "Now look here. We could detour to come out on the shore near here, but we should have to plow through half a mile of muck and brush, and they'd hear us coming. Or we can creep up to the north end of this sandspit, from which it's three or four hundred yards—a long shot but not impossible. Think you could do it?"

"Hm," said Holtzinger. "With my scope sight and a sitting position—okay, I'll try it."

"You stay here, Court," I said to James. "This is Augie's head, and I don't want any argument over your having fired first."

James grunted while Holtzinger clamped his scope to his rifle. We crouched our way up the spit, keeping the sand ridge between us and the duckbill. When we got to the end where there was no more cover, we crept along on hands and knees, moving slowly. If you move slowly enough, directly toward or away from a dinosaur, it probably won't notice you.

The duckbill continued to grub about on all fours, every few seconds rising to look round. Holtzinger eased himself into the sitting position, cocked his piece, and aimed through his scope. And then—

Bang! bang! went a big rifle back at the camp.

Holtzinger jumped. The duckbills jerked their heads up and leaped for the deep water, splashing like mad. Holtzinger fired once and missed. I took one shot at the last duckbill before it vanished too, but missed. The .600 isn't built for long ranges.

Holtzinger and I started back toward the camp, for it had struck us that our party might be in theropod trouble.

What had happened was that a big sauropod had wandered down past the camp underwater, feeding as it went. Now, the water shoaled about a hundred yards offshore from our spit, halfway over to the swamp on the other side. The sauropod had ambled up the slope until its body was almost all out of water, weaving its head from side to side and looking for anything green to gobble. This is a species of *Alamosaurus*, which looks much like the well-known *Brontosaurus* except that it's bigger.

When I came in sight of the camp, the sauropod was turning round to go back the way it had come, making horrid groans. By the time we reached the camp, it had disappeared into deep water, all but its head and twenty feet of neck, which wove about for some time before they vanished into the haze.

When we came up to the camp, James was arguing with the Raja. Holtzinger burst out:

"You crummy bastard! That's the second time you've spoiled my shots."

"Don't be a fool," said James. "I couldn't let him wander into the camp and stamp everything flat."

"There was no danger of that," said the Raja. "You can see the water is deep offshore. It's just that our trigger-happee Mr. James cannot see any animal without shooting."

I added: "If it did get close, all you needed to do was throw a stick of firewood at it. They're perfectly harmless."

This wasn't strictly true. When the Comte de Lautrec ran after one for a close shot, the sauropod looked back at him, gave a flick of its tail, and took off the Comte's head as neatly as if he'd been axed in the tower. But, as a rule, they're inoffensive enough.

"How was I to know?" yelled James, turning purple. "You're all against me. What the hell are we on this miserable trip for, except to shoot things? Call yourselves hunters, but I'm the only one who hits anything!"

I got pretty wrothy and said he was just an excitable young skite with more money than brains, whom I should never have brought along.

"If that's how you feel," he said, "give me a burro and some food, and I'll go back to the base myself. I won't pollute your pure air with my presence!"

"Don't be a bigger ass than you can help," I said. "What you propose is quite impossible."

"Then I'll go alone!" He grabbed his knapsack, thrust a couple of tins of beans and an opener into it, and started off with his rifle.

Beauregard Black spoke up: "Mr. Rivers, we cain't let him go off like that. He'll git lost and starve, or be et by a theropod."

"I'll fetch him back," said the Raja, and started after the runaway.

He caught up with James as the latter was disappearing into the cycads. We could see them arguing and waving their hands in the distance. After a while, they started back with arms around each other's necks like old school pals.

This shows the trouble we get into if we make mistakes in planning such a do. Having once got back in time, we had to make the best of our bargain.

I don't want to give the impression, however, that Courtney James was nothing but a pain in the rump. He had good points. He got over these rows quickly and next day would be as cheerful as ever. He was helpful with the general work of the camp, at least when he felt like it. He sang well and had an endless fund of dirty stories to keep us amused.

We stayed two more days at that camp. We saw crocodile, the

small kind, and plenty of sauropod—as many as five at once—but no more duckbill. Nor any of those fifty-foot supercrocodiles.

So, on the first of May, we broke camp and headed north toward the Janpur Hills. My sahibs were beginning to harden up and were getting impatient. We'd been in the Cretaceous a week, and no trophies.

We saw nothing to speak of on the next leg, save a glimpse of a gorgosaur out of range and some tracks indicating a whopping big iguanodont, twenty-five or thirty feet high. We pitched camp at the base of the hills.

We'd finished off the bonehead, so the first thing was to shoot fresh meat. With an eye to trophies, too, of course. We got ready the morning of the third, and I told James:

"See here, old boy, no more of your tricks. The Raja will tell you when to shoot."

"Uh-huh, I get you," he said, meek as Moses.

We marched off, the four of us, into the foothills. There was a good chance of getting Holtzinger his ceratopsian. We'd seen a couple on the way up, but mere calves without decent horns.

As it was hot and sticky, we were soon panting and sweating. We'd hiked and scrambled all morning without seeing a thing except lizards, when I picked up the smell of carrion. I stopped the party and sniffed. We were in an open glade cut up by those little dry nullahs. The nullahs ran together into a couple of deeper gorges that cut through a slight depression choked with denser growth, cycad, and screw pine. When I listened, I heard the thrum of carrion flies.

"This way," I said. "Something ought to be dead—ah, here it is!"

And there it was: the remains of a huge ceratopsian lying in a little hollow on the edge of the copse. Must have weighed six or eight ton alive; a three-horned variety, perhaps the penultimate species of *Triceratops*. It was hard to tell, because most of the hide on the upper surface had been ripped off, and many bones had been pulled loose and lay scattered about.

Holtzinger said: "Oh, shucks! Why couldn't I have gotten to him before he died? That would have been a darned fine head."

I said: "On your toes, chaps. A theropod's been at this carcass and is probably nearby."

"How d'you know?" said James, with sweat running off his round red face. He spoke in what was for him a low voice, because a nearby theropod is a sobering thought to the flightiest.

I sniffed again and thought I could detect the distinctive rank odor of theropod. I couldn't be sure, though, because the carcass stank so strongly. My sahibs were turning green at the sight and smell of the cadaver. I told James:

"It's seldom that even the biggest theropod will attack a full-grown ceratopsian. Those horns are too much for them. But they love a dead or dying one. They'll hang round a dead ceratopsian for weeks, gorging and then sleeping off their meals for days at a time. They usually take cover in the heat of the day anyhow, because they can't stand much direct hot sunlight. You'll find them lying in copses like this or in hollows, wherever there's shade."

"What'll we do?" asked Holtzinger.

"We'll make our first cast through this copse, in two pairs as usual. Whatever you do, don't get impulsive or panicky."

I looked at Courtney James, but he looked right back and merely checked his gun.

"Should I still carry this broken?" he asked.

"No, close it, but keep the safety on till you're ready to shoot," I said. "We'll keep closer than usual, so we shall be in sight of each other. Start off at that angle, Raja; go slowly, and stop to listen between steps."

We pushed through the edge of the copse, leaving the carcass but not its stench behind us. For a few feet, you couldn't see a thing.

It opened out as we got in under the trees, which shaded out some of the brush. The sun slanted down through the trees. I could hear nothing but the hum of insects and the scuttle of lizards and the squawks of toothed birds in the treetops. I thought I could be sure of the theropod smell, but told myself that might be imagination. The theropod might be any of several species, large or small, and the beast itself might be anywhere within a half-mile's radius.

"Go on," I whispered to Holtzinger. I could hear James and the Raja pushing ahead on my right and see the palm fronds and ferns lashing about as they disturbed them. I suppose they were trying to move quietly, but to me they sounded like an earthquake in a crockery shop.

"A little closer!" I called.

Presently, they appeared slanting in toward me. We dropped into a gully filled with ferns and scrambled up the other side. Then we found our way blocked by a big clump of palmetto.

"You go round that side; we'll go round this," I said. We started off, stopping to listen and smell. Our positions were the same as on that first day, when James killed the bonehead.

We'd gone two-thirds of the way round our half of the palmetto when I heard a noise ahead on our left. Holtzinger heard it too, and pushed off his safety. I put my thumb on mine and stepped to one side to have a clear field of fire.

The clatter grew louder. I raised my gun to aim at about the height of a big theropod's heart. There was a movement in the foliage—and a six-foot-high bonehead stepped into view, walking solemnly across our front and jerking its head with each step like a giant pigeon.

I heard Holtzinger let out a breath and had to keep myself from laughing. Holtzinger said: "Uh—"

Then that damned gun of James's went off, *bang! bang!* I had a glimpse of the bonehead knocked arsy-varsy with its tail and hindlegs flying.

"Got him!" yelled James. "I drilled him clean!" I heard him run forward.

"Good God, if he hasn't done it again!" I said.

Then there was a great swishing of foliage and a wild yell from James. Something heaved up out of the shrubbery, and I saw the head of the biggest of the local flesh eaters, *Tyrannosaurus trionyches* himself.

The scientists can insist that *rex* is the bigger species, but I'll swear this blighter was bigger than any *rex* ever hatched. It must have stood twenty feet high and been fifty feet long. I could see its big bright eye and six-inch teeth and the big dewlap that hangs down from its chin to its chest.

The second of the nullahs that cut through the copse ran athwart our path on the far side of the palmetto clump. Perhaps it was six feet deep. The tyrannosaur had been lying in this, sleeping off its last meal. Where its back stuck up above the ground level, the ferns on the edge of the nullah had masked it. James had fired both barrels over the theropod's head and woke it up. Then the silly ass ran forward without reloading. Another twenty feet and he'd have stepped on the tyrannosaur.

James, naturally, stopped when this thing popped up in front of him. He remembered that he'd fired both barrels and that he'd left the Raja too far behind for a clear shot.

At first, James kept his nerve. He broke open his gun, took two rounds from his belt, and plugged them into the barrels. But, in his haste to snap the gun shut, he caught his hand between the barrels and the action. The painful pinch so startled James that he dropped his gun. Then he went to pieces and bolted.

The Raja was running up with his gun at high port, ready to snap it to his shoulder the instant he got a clear view. When he saw James running headlong toward him, he hesitated, not wishing to shoot James by accident. The latter plunged ahead, blundered into the Raja, and sent them both sprawling among the ferns. The tyrannosaur collected what little wits it had and stepped forward to snap them up.

And how about Holtzinger and me on the other side of the palmettos? Well, the instant James yelled and the tyrannosaur's head appeared, Holtzinger darted forward like a rabbit. I'd brought my gun up for a shot at the tyrannosaur's head, in hope of getting at least an eye; but, before I could find it in my sights, the head was out of sight behind the palmettos. Perhaps I should have fired at hazard, but all my experience is against wild shots.

When I looked back in front of me, Holtzinger had already disappeared round the curve of the palmetto clump. I'd started after him when I heard his rifle and the click of the bolt between shots: *bang*—click-click—*bang*—click-click, like that.

He'd come up on the tyrannosaur's quarter as the brute started to stoop for James and the Raja. With his muzzle twenty feet from the tyrannosaur's hide, Holtzinger began pumping .375s into the beast's body. He got off three shots when the tyrannosaur gave a tremendous booming grunt and wheeled round to see what was stinging it. The jaws came open, and the head swung round and down again.

Holtzinger got off one more shot and tried to leap to one side. As he was standing on a narrow place between the palmetto clump and the nullah, he fell into the nullah. The tyrannosaur continued its lunge and caught him. The jaws went *chomp*, and up came the head with poor Holtzinger in them, screaming like a damned soul.

I came up just then and aimed at the brute's face, but then realized that its jaws were full of my sahib and I should be shooting him, too. As the head went on up like the business end of a big power shovel, I fired a shot at the heart. The tyrannosaur was already turning away, and I suspect the ball just glanced along the ribs. The beast took a couple of steps when I gave it the other barrel in the jack. It staggered on its next step but kept on. Another step, and it was nearly out of sight among the trees, when the Raja fired twice. The stout fellow had untangled himself from James, got up, picked up his gun, and let the tyrannosaur have it.

The double wallop knocked the brute over with a tremendous crash. It fell into a dwarf magnolia, and I saw one of its huge birdlike hindlegs waving in the midst of a shower of pink-and-white petals. But the tyrannosaur got up again and blundered off without even dropping its victim. The last I saw of it was Holtzinger's legs dangling out one side of its jaws (he'd stopped screaming) and its big tail banging against the tree trunks as it swung from side to side.

The Raja and I reloaded and ran after the brute for all we were worth. I tripped and fell once, but jumped up again and didn't notice my skinned elbow till later. When we burst out of the copse, the tyrannosaur was already at the far end of the glade. We each took a quick shot but probably missed, and it was out of sight before we could fire again.

We ran on, following the tracks and spatters of blood, until we had to stop from exhaustion. Never again did we see that tyrannosaur. Their movements look slow and ponderous, but with those tremendous legs they don't have to step very fast to work up considerable speed.

When we'd got our breath, we got up and tried to track the tyrannosaur, on the theory that it might be dying and we should come up to it. But, though we found more spoor, it faded out and left us at a loss. We circled round, hoping to pick it up, but no luck.

Hours later, we gave up and went back to the glade.

Courtney James was sitting with his back against a tree, holding his rifle and Holtzinger's. His right hand was swollen and blue where he'd pinched it, but still usable. His first words were:

"Where the hell have you two been?"

I said: "We've been occupied. The late Mr. Holtzinger. Remember?"

"You shouldn't have gone off and left me; another of those things might have come along. Isn't it bad enough to lose one hunter through your stupidity without risking another one?"

I'd been preparing a warm wigging for James, but his attack so astonished me that I could only bleat; "What? *We* lost...?"

"Sure," he said. "You put us in front of you, so if anybody gets eaten it's us. You send a guy up against these animals undergunned. You—"

"You Goddamn' stinking little swine!" I said. "If you hadn't been a blithering idiot and blown those two barrels, and then run like the yellow coward you are, this never would have happened. Holtzinger died trying to save your worthless life. By God, I wish he'd failed! He was worth six of a stupid, spoiled, muttonheaded bastard like you—"

I went on from there. The Raja tried to keep up with me, but ran out of English and was reduced to cursing James in Hindustani.

I could see by the purple color on James's face that I was getting home. He said "Why, you—" and stepped forward and sloshed me one in the face with his left fist.

It rocked me a bit, but I said: "Now then, my lad, I'm glad you did that! It gives me a chance I've been waiting for . . ."

So I waded into him. He was a good-sized boy, but between my sixteen stone and his sore right hand he had no chance. I got a few good ones home, and down he went.

"Now get up!" I said. "And I'll be glad to finish off!"

James raised himself to his elbows. I got set for more fisticuffs, though my knuckles were skinned and bleeding already. James rolled over, snatched his gun, and scrambled up, swinging the muzzle from one to the other of us.

"You won't finish anybody off!" he panted through swollen lips. "All right, put your hands up! Both of you!"

"Do not be an idiot," said the Raja. "Put that gun away!"

"Nobody treats me like that and gets away with it!"

"There's no use murdering us," I said. "You'd never get away with it."

"Why not? There won't be much left of you after one of these hits you. I'll just say the tyrannosaur ate you, too. Nobody could prove anything. They can't hold you for a murder eighty-five million years old. The statute of limitations, you know."

"You fool, you'd never make it back to the camp alive!" I shouted.

"I'll take a chance—" began James, setting the butt of his .500 against his shoulder, with the barrels pointed at my face. Looked like a pair of bleeding vehicular tunnels.

He was watching me so closely that he lost track of the Raja for a second. My partner had been resting on one knee, and now his right arm came up in a quick bowling motion with a three-pound rock. The rock bounced of James's head. The .500 went off. The ball must have parted my hair, and the explosion jolly well near broke my eardrums. Down went James again.

"Good work, old chap!" I said, gathering up James's gun.

"Yes," said the Raja thoughtfully, as he picked up the rock he'd thrown and tossed it. "Doesn't quite have the balance of a cricket ball, but it is just as hard."

"What shall we do now?" I said. "I'm inclined to leave the beggar here unarmed and let him fend for himself."

The Raja gave a little sigh. "It's a tempting thought, Reggie, but we really cannot, you know. Not done."

"I suppose you're right," I said. "Well, let's tie him up and take him back to camp."

We agreed there was no safety for us unless we kept James under guard every minute until we got home. Once a man has tried to kill you, you're a fool if you give him another chance.

We marched James back to camp and told the crew what we were up against. James cursed everybody.

We spent three dismal days combing the country for that tyrannosaur, but no luck. We felt it wouldn't have been cricket not to make a good try at recovering Holtzinger's remains. Back at our main camp, when it wasn't raining, we collected small reptiles and things for our scientific friends. The Raja and I discussed the question of legal proceedings against Courtney James, but decided there was nothing we could do in that direction.

When the transition chamber materialized, we fell over one another getting into it. We dumped James, still tied, in a corner, and told the chamber operator to throw the switches.

While we were in transition, James said: "You two should have killed me back there."

"Why?" I said. "You don't have a particularly good head."

The Raja added: "Wouldn't look at all well over a mantel."

"You can laugh," said James, "but I'll get you some day. I'll find a way and get off scot-free."

"My dear chap!" I said. "If there were some way to do it, I'd have you charged with Holtzinger's death. Look, you'd best leave well enough alone."

When we came out in the present, we handed him his empty gun and his other gear, and off he went without a word. As he left, Holtzinger's girl, that Claire, rushed up crying:

"Where is he? Where's August?"

There was a bloody heartrending scene, despite the Raja's skill at handling such situations.

We took our men and beasts down to the old laboratory building that the university has fitted up as a serai for such expeditions. We paid everybody off and found we were broke. The advance payments from Holtzinger and James didn't cover our expenses, and we should have precious little chance of collecting the rest of our fees either from James or from Holtzinger's estate.

And speaking of James, d'you know what that blighter was doing? He went home, got more ammunition, and came back to the university. He hunted up Professor Prochaska and asked him:

"Professor, I'd like you to send me back to the Cretaceous for a quick trip. If you can work me into your schedule right now, you can just about name your own price. I'll offer five thousand to begin with. I want to go to April twenty-third, eight-five million B.C."

Prochaska answered: "Why do you wish to go back again so soon?"

"I lost my wallet in the Cretaceous," said James. "I figure if I go back to the day before I arrived in that era on my last trip, I'll watch myself when I arrived on that trip and follow myself around till I see myself lose the wallet."

"Five thousand is a lot for a wallet," said the professor.

"It's got some things in it I can't replace," said James.

"Well," said Prochaska, thinking. "The party that was supposed to go out this morning has telephoned that they would be late, so perhaps I can work you in. I have always wondered what would happen when the same man occupied the same stretch of time twice."

So James wrote out a check, and Prochaska took him to the chamber and saw him off. James's idea, it seems, was to sit behind a bush a few yards from where the transition chamber would appear and pot the Raja and me as we emerged.

Hours later, we'd changed into our street clothes and phoned our wives to come and get us. We were standing on Forsythe Boulevard waiting for them when there was a loud crack, like an explosion, and a flash of light not fifty feet from us. The shock wave staggered us and broke windows.

We ran toward the place and got there just as a bobby and several citizens came up. On the boulevard, just off the kerb, lay a human body. At least, it had been that, but it looked as if every bone in it had been pulverized and every blood vessel burst, so it was hardly more than a slimy mass of pink protoplasm. The clothes it had been wearing were shredded, but I recognized an H. & H. .500 double-barreled express rifle. The wood was scorched and the metal pitted, but it was Courtney James's gun. No doubt whatever.

Skipping the investigation and the milling about that ensued, what had happened was this: nobody had shot at us as we emerged on the twenty-fourth, and that couldn't be changed. For that matter, the instant James started to do anything that would make a visible change in the world of eight-five million B.C., such as making a footprint in the earth, the space-time forces snapped him forward to the present to prevent a paradox. And the violence of the passage practically tore him to bits.

Now that this is better understood, the professor won't send anybody to a period less than five thousand years prior to the time that some time traveler has already explored, because it would be too easy to do some act, like chopping down a tree or losing some durable artifact, that would affect the later world. Over longer periods, he tells me, such changes average out and are lost in the stream of time.

We had a rough time after that, with the bad publicity and all, though we did collect a fee from James's estate. Luckily for us, a steel manufacturer turned up who wanted a mastodon's head for his den.

I understand these things better now, too. The disaster hadn't been wholly James's fault. I shouldn't have taken him when I knew what a spoiled, unstable sort of bloke he was. And if Holtzinger could have used a really heavy gun, he'd probably have knocked the tyrannosaur down, even if he didn't kill it, and so have given the rest of us a chance to finish it.

So, Mr. Seligman, that's why I won't take you to that period to hunt. There are plenty of other eras, and if you look them over I'm sure you'll find something to suit you. But not the Jurassic or the Cretaceous. You're just not big enough to handle a gun for dinosaur.

AFTERWORD BY ERIC FLINT:

I was glad we decided that Dave would write the preface to this story, because it meant I could write an afterword where I didn't have to worry about being undignified and putting the reader off. By now, the reader will have finished the story so it doesn't much matter what I say.

I first read this story when I was somewhere around thirteen or fourteen years old and I loved it for the good and simple reason that it was just so *cool.* There I was, a kid in the mountains—which means hunting country—and my father had recently taught me how to shoot his trusty .30-06. Just to make things perfect, my father had been a big game hunter in his time and I'd heard plenty of his stories about hunting moose and mountain goats and—especially!—grizzly bears. (That was in the fifties, folks. In those days, "endangered species" meant . . . not much of anything.)

Hunting dinosaurs! Oh, how cool!

And, of course, the story had that other essential ingredient for coolness: a hero you really liked, a villain worth hissing, and the villain getting his Just Deserts in the end.

What's not to like? That was how I felt about it then. Now, some forty years later . . .

It's still how I feel about it. Some things are timeless.

Goblin Night

by James H. Schmitz

PREFACE BY ERIC FLINT

When we decided to put together this anthology, one of the authors I knew I wanted to include it in was James H. Schmitz. He was perhaps not quite as important to me as Heinlein and Clarke and Andre Norton, who formed the triad around which I assembled all other science fiction writers in my mind as a teenager. But awfully close.

Why? It's hard to say. (Well . . . more precisely, it's hard to say *briefly*.)

Part of it may be that I've always had a soft spot for hard luck cases. Schmitz had one of those reputations which was very high at the time, but not *quite* high enough to guarantee him the more or less perpetual status that Heinlein and Clarke have enjoyed. (Although I'm hoping the reissue of his complete works which I recently edited for Baen Books will turn that around. We'll see.)

Schmitz was a quirky writer, in some ways, as is exemplified by his insistence on using mainly female characters in an era when females appeared rarely enough as the central figures in SF stories—and almost never, except in Schmitz's own stories, as the heroines of action stories. But a lot of his "hard luck" was just that—bad luck.

When it came to the major science fiction awards, for instance, Schmitz always seemed to have the misfortune to get nominated for the finals in the same year that the competition was ferocious.

This story, "Goblin Night," was nominated for the Nebula best novelette award in 1967—along with another story by Schmitz, "Planet of Forgetting." They both lost to Roger Zelazny's "The Doors of His Face, the Lamps of His Mouth."

That very same year, he had a third story in the running for the Nebula—"Balanced Ecology," in the short story category. It lost to Harlan Ellison's "'Repent, Harlequin!' Said the Ticktockman."

It gets better. Schmitz actually had *four* stories in the running for the Nebula that year. "Research Alpha," co-authored with A.E. Van Vogt, was up for the novella. It lost to Zelazny's "He Who Shapes."

Four stories nominated for three different categories in the Nebula award in one year. That's got to be some kind of record, or close to it. And still . . . nothing.

"Lion Loose" was a Hugo finalist for best short fiction in 1962—during the stretch of a few years when the Hugo didn't separate "short fiction" into specific categories. It lost to Brian Aldiss' collection, *The Long Afternoon of Earth*. A few years earlier or a few years later, it might very well have won the award for best novella.

Just to top it all off, his best known novel, *The Witches of Karres*, made it to the short final list of the Hugo nominees for best novel in 1967. And . . . so did Robert Heinlein's *The Moon Is a Harsh Mistress*.

So it goes. In the long run, these things rarely matter very much. And for the purposes of this anthology, they didn't matter at all. Over forty years have gone by since I first began reading James H. Schmitz, and I've never grown tired of him. For me as for anyone willing to be honest about it, that's the only definition of "good writing" that counts.

———⌇———

There was a quivering of psi force. Then a sudden, vivid sense of running and hiding, in horrible fear of a pursuer from whom there was no escape—

Telzey's breath caught in her throat. A psi screen had flicked into instant existence about her mind, blocking out incoming impulses. The mental picture, the feeling of pursuit, already was gone, had touched her only a moment; but she stayed motionless seconds longer, eyes shut, pulses hammering out a roll of primitive alarms. She'd been dozing uneasily for the past hour, aware in a vague way of the mind-traces of a multitude of wildlife activities in the miles of parkland around. And perhaps she'd simply fallen asleep, begun to dream. . . .

Perhaps, she thought—but it wasn't very likely. She hadn't been relaxed enough to be touching the fringes of sleep and dream-stuff. The probability was that, for an instant, she'd picked up the reflection of a real event, that somebody not very far from here had encountered death in some grisly form at that moment.

She hesitated, then thinned the blocking screen to let her awareness spread again through the area, simultaneously extended a quick, probing thread of thought with a memory-replica of the pattern she'd caught. If it touched the mind that had produced the pattern originally, it might bring a momentary flash of echoing details and further information. . . . assuming the mind was still alive, still capable of responding.

She didn't really believe it would still be alive. The impression she'd had in that instant was that death was only seconds away.

The general murmur of mind-noise began to grow up about her again, a varying pulse of life and psi energies, diminishing gradually with distance, arising from her companions, from animals on plain and mountain, with an undernote of the dimmer emanations of plants. But no suggestion came now of the vividly disturbing sensations of a moment ago.

Telzey opened her eyes, glanced around at the others sitting about the campfire in the mouth of Cil Chasm. There were eleven of them, a group of third and fourth year students of Pehanron College who had decided to spend the fall holidays in Melna Park. The oldest was twenty-two; she herself was the youngest—Telzey Amberdon, age fifteen. There was also a huge white dog named Chomir, not in view at the moment, the property of one of her friends who had preferred to go on a spacecruise with a very special date over the holidays. Chomir would have been a little in the way in an IP cruiser, so Telzey had brought him along to the park instead.

In the early part of the evening, they had built their fire where the great Cil canyon opened on the rolling plain below. The canyon walls rose to either side of the camp, smothered with evergreen growth; and the Cil River, a quick, nervous stream, spilled over a series of rocky ledges a hundred feet away. The boys had set up a translucent green tent canopy, and sleeping bags were arranged beneath it. But Gikkes and two of the other girls already had announced that when they got ready to sleep, they were going to take up one of the aircars and settle down in it for the night a good thirty feet above the ground.

The park rangers had assured them such measures weren't necessary. Melna Park was full of Orado's native wildlife—that, after all, was why it had been established—but none of the animals were at all likely to become aggressive towards visitors. As for human marauders, the park was safer than the planet's cities. Overflights weren't permitted; visitors came in at ground level through one of the various entrance stations where their aircars were equipped with sealed engine locks, limiting them to contour altitudes of a hundred and fifty feet and to a speed of thirty miles an hour. Only the rangers' cars were not restricted, and only the rangers carried weapons.

It made Melna Park sound like an oasis of sylvan tranquility. But as it turned towards evening, the stars of the great cluster about Orado brightened to awesomely burning splendor in the sky. Some of them, like Gikkes, weren't used to the starblaze, had rarely spent a night outside the cities where night-screens came on gradually at the end of the day to meet the old racial preference for a dark sleep period.

Here night remained at an uncertain twilight stage until a wind began moaning up in the canyon and black storm clouds started to drift over the mountains and out across the plain. Now there were quick shifts between twilight and darkness, and eyes began to wander uneasily. There was the restless chatter of the river nearby. The wind made odd sounds in the canyon; they could hear sudden cracklings in bushes and trees, occasional animal voices.

"You get the feeling," Gikkes remarked, twisting her neck around to stare up Cil Chasm, "that something like a lullbear or spook might come trotting out of there any minute!"

Some of the others laughed uncertainly. Valia said, "Don't be silly! There haven't been animals like that in Melna Park for fifty years." She looked over at the group about Telzey. "Isn't that right, Pollard?"

Pollard was the oldest boy here. He was majoring in biology, which might make him Valia's authority on the subject of lullbears and spooks. He nodded, said, "You can still find them in the bigger game preserves up north. But naturally they don't keep anything in public parks that makes a practice of chewing up the public.

Anything you meet around here, Gikkes, will be as ready to run from you as you are from it."

"That's saying a lot!" Rish added cheerfully. The others laughed again, and Gikkes looked annoyed.

Telzey had been giving only part of her attention to the talk. She felt shut down, temporarily detached from her companions. It had taken all afternoon to come across the wooded plains from the entrance station, winding slowly above the rolling ground in the three aircars which had brought them here. Then, after they reached Cil Chasm where they intended to stay, she and Rish and Dunker, two charter members of her personal fan club at Pehanron, had spent an hour fishing along the little river, up into the canyon and back down again. They had a great deal of excitement and caught enough to provide supper for everyone; but it involved arduous scrambling over slippery rocks, wading in cold, rushing water, and occasional tumbles, in one of which Telzey knocked her wrist-talker out of commission for the duration of the trip.

Drowsiness wasn't surprising after all the exercise. The surprising part was that, in spite of it, she didn't seem able to relax completely. As a rule, she felt at home wherever she happened to be outdoors. But something about this place was beginning to bother her. She hadn't noticed it at first, she had laughed at Gikkes with the others when Gikkes began to express apprehensions. But when she settled down after supper, feeling a comfortable muscular fatigue begin to claim her, she grew aware of a vague disturbance. The atmosphere of Melna Park seemed to change slowly. A hint of cruelty and savagery crept into it, of hidden terrors. Mentally, Telzey felt herself glancing over her shoulder towards dark places under the trees, as if something like a lullbear or spook actually was lurking there.

And then, in that uneasy, half-awake condition, there suddenly had been this other thing, like a dream-flash in which somebody desperately ran and hid from a mocking pursuer. To the terrified human quarry, the pursuer appeared as a glimpsed animalic shape in the twilight, big and moving swiftly, but showing no other details.

And there had been the flickering of psi energy about the scene....

Telzey shifted uncomfortably, running her tongue tip over her lips. The experience had been chillingly vivid; but if something of the sort really had occurred, the victim had died moments later.

In that respect, there was no reason to force herself to quick decisions now. And it might, after all, have been a dream, drifting up in her mind, created by the mood of the place. She realized she would like to believe it was a dream.

But in that case, what was creating the mood of the place?

Gikkes? It wasn't impossible. She had decided some time ago that personal acquaintances should be off limits to telepathic prowling, but when someone was around at all frequently, scraps of information were likely to filter through. So she knew Gikkes also had much more extensively developed telepathic awareness than the average person. Gikkes didn't know it and couldn't have put it to use anyway. In her, it was an erratic, unreliable quality which might have kept her in a badly confused state of mind if she had been more conscious of its effects.

But the general uneasiness Telzey had sensed and that brief psi surge—if that was what it was—fragmentary but carrying a complete horrid little story with it, could have come to her from Gikkes. Most people, even when they thought they were wide awake, appeared to be manufacturing dreams much of the time in an area of their minds they didn't know about; and Gikkes seemed nervous enough this evening to be manufacturing unconscious nightmares and broadcasting them.

But again—what made Gikkes so nervous here? The unfamiliar environment, the frozen beauty of the starblaze overhanging the sloping plain like a tent of fire, might account for it. But it didn't rule out a more specific source of disturbance.

She could make sure, Telzey thought, by probing into Gikkes's mind and finding out what was going on in there. Gikkes wouldn't know it was happening. But it took many hours, as a rule, to develop adequate contact unless the other mind was also that of a functioning telepath. Gikkes was borderline—a telepath, but not functional, or only partly so—and if she began probing around in those complexities without the experience to tell her just how to go about it, she might wind up doing Gikkes some harm.

She looked over at Gikkes. Gikkes met her eyes, said, "Shouldn't you start worrying about that dog of Gonwil's? He hasn't been in sight for the past half-hour."

"Chomir's all right," Telzey said. "He's still checking over the area."

Chomir was, in fact, only a few hundred yards away, moving along the Cil River up in the canyon. She'd been touching the big dog's mind lightly from time to time during the evening to see what he was doing. Gikkes couldn't know that, of course—nobody in this group suspected Telzey of psionic talents. But she had done a great deal of experimenting with Chomir, and nowadays she could, if she liked, almost see with his eyes, smell with his nose, and listen through his ears. At this instant, he was watching half a dozen animals large enough to have alarmed Gikkes acutely. Chomir's interest in Melna Park's wildlife didn't go beyond casual curiosity. He was an Askanam hound, a breed developed to fight man or beast in pit and arena, too big and powerful to be apprehensive about other creatures and not inclined to chase strange animals about without purpose as a lesser dog might do.

"Well," Gikkes said, "if I were responsible for somebody else's dog, if I'd brought him here, I'd be making sure he didn't run off and get lost—"

Telzey didn't answer. It took no mind-reading to know that Gikkes was annoyed because Pollard had attached himself to Telzey's fan club after supper and settled down beside her. Gikkes had invited Pollard to come along on the outing; he was president of various organizations and generally important at Pehanron College. Gikkes, the glamour girl, didn't like it at all that he'd drifted over to Telzey's group, and while Telzey had no designs on him, she couldn't very well inform Gikkes of that without ruffling her further.

"I," Gikkes concluded, "would go look for him."

Pollard stood up. "It would be too bad if he strayed off, wouldn't it?" he agreed. He gave Telzey a lazy smile. "Why don't you and I look around a little together?"

Well, that was not exactly what Gikkes had intended. Rish and Dunker didn't think much of it either. They were already climbing to their feet, gazing sternly at Pollard.

Telzey glanced at them, checked the watch Dunker had loaned her after she smashed the one in her wrist-talker on the fishing excursion.

"Let's wait another five minutes," she suggested. "If he isn't back by then, we can all start looking."

As they settled down again, she sent a come-here thought to Chomir. She didn't yet know what steps she might have to take in the other matter, but she didn't want to be distracted by problems with Gikkes and the boys.

She felt Chomir's response. He turned, got his bearings instantly with nose, ears, and—though he wasn't aware of that—by the direct touch of their minds, went bounding down into the river, and splashed noisily through the shallow water. He was taking what seemed to him a short cut to the camp. But that route would lead him high up the opposite bank of the twisting Cil, to the far side of the canyon.

"Not that way, stupid!" Telzey thought, verbalizing it for emphasis. "Turn around—go back!"

And then, as she felt the dog pause comprehendingly, a voice, edged with the shock of surprise—perhaps of fear—exclaimed in her mind, *"Who are you? Who said that?"*

There had been a number of occasions since she became aware of her abilities when she'd picked up the thought-forms of another telepath. She hadn't tried to develop such contacts, feeling in no hurry to strike up an acquaintanceship on the psionic level. That was part of a world with laws and conditions of its own which should be studied thoroughly if she was to avoid creating problems for herself and others, and at present she simply didn't have the time for thorough study.

Even with the tentative exploration she'd been doing, problems arose. One became aware of a situation of which others weren't aware, and then it wasn't always possible to ignore the situation, to act as if it didn't exist. But depending on circumstances, it could be extremely difficult to do something effective about it, particularly when one didn't care to announce publicly that one was a psi.

The thing that appeared to have happened in Melna Park tonight had seemed likely to present just such problems. Then this voice spoke to her suddenly, coming out of the night, out of nowhere. Another telepath was in the area, to whom the encounter was as unexpected as it was to her. There was no immediate way of knowing whether that was going to help with the problem or complicate it further, but she had no inclination to reply at once. Whoever the stranger was, the fact that he—there had been a strong male tinge to the thoughts—was also a psi didn't necessarily make him a brother. She knew he was human; alien minds had other flavors. His questions had come in the sharply defined forms of a verbalization; he might have been speaking aloud in addressing her. There was something else about them she hadn't noticed in previous telepathic contacts—an odd, filtered quality as though his thoughts passed through a distorting medium before reaching her.

She waited, wondering about it. While she wasn't strongly drawn to this stranger, she felt no particular concern about him. He had picked up her own verbalized instructions to Chomir, had been startled by them, and, therefore, hadn't been aware of anything she was thinking previously. She'd now tightened the veil of psi energy about her mind a little, enough to dampen out the drifting threads of subconscious thought by which an unguarded mind was most easily found and reached. Tightened further, as it could be in an instant, it had stopped genuine experts in mind-probing in their tracks. This psi was no expert; an expert wouldn't have flung surprised questions at her. She didn't verbalize her thinking as a rule, and wouldn't do it now until she felt like it. And she wouldn't reach out for him. She decided the situation was sufficiently in hand.

The silence between them lengthened. He might be equally wary now, regretting his brief outburst.

Telzey relaxed her screen, flicked out a search-thought to Chomir, felt him approaching the camp in his easy, loping run, closed the screen again. She waited a few seconds. There was no indication of interest apparently, even when he had his attention on her, he was able to sense only her verbalized thoughts. That simplified the matter.

She lightened the screen again. "Who are *you*?" she asked.

The reply came instantly. "So I wasn't dreaming! For a moment, I thought. . . . Are there two of you?"

"No. I was talking to my dog." There was something odd about the quality of his thoughts. He might be using a shield or screen of some kind, not of the same type as hers but perhaps equally effective.

"Your dog? I see. It's been over a year," the voice said, "since I've spoken to others like this." It paused. "You're a woman. . . . young. . . . a girl . . ."

There was no reason to tell him she was fifteen. What Telzey wanted to know just now was whether he also had been aware of a disturbance in Melna Park. She asked, "Where are you?"

He didn't hesitate. "At my home. Twelve miles south of Cil Chasm across the plain, at the edge of the forest. The house is easy to see from the air."

He might be a park official. They'd noticed such a house on their way here this afternoon and speculated about who could be living there. Permission to make one's residence in a Federation Park was supposedly almost impossible to obtain.

"Does that tell you anything?" the voice went on.

"Yes," Telzey said. "I'm in the park with some friends. I think I've seen your house."

"My name," the bodiless voice told her, "is Robane. You're being careful. I don't blame you. There are certain risks connected with being a psi, as you seem to understand. If we were in a city, I'm not sure I would reveal myself. But out here. . . . Somebody built a fire this evening where the Cil River leaves the Chasm. I'm a cripple and spend much of my time studying the park with scanners. Is that your fire?"

Telzey hesitated a moment. "Yes."

"Your friends," Robane's voice went on, "they're aware you and I. . . . they know you're a telepath?"

"No."

"Would you be able to come to see me for a while without letting them know where you're going?"

"Why should I do that?" Telzey asked.

"Can't you imagine? I'd like to talk to a psi again."

"We *are* talking," she said.

Silence for a moment.

"Let me tell you a little about myself," Robane said then. "I'm approaching middle age—from your point I might even seem rather old. I live here alone except for a well-meaning but rather stupid housekeeper named Feddler. Feddler seems old from my point of view. Four years ago, I was employed in one of the Federation's science departments. I am. . . . was. . . . considered to be among the best in my line of work. It wasn't very dangerous work so long as certain precautions were observed. But one day a fool made a mistake. His mistake killed two of my colleagues. It didn't quite kill me, but since that day I've been intimately associated with a machine which has the responsibility of keeping me alive from minute to minute. I'd die almost immediately if I were removed from it.

"So my working days are over. And I no longer want to live in cities. There are too many foolish people there to remind me of the one particular fool I'd prefer to forget. Because of the position I'd held and the work I'd done, the Federation permitted me to make my home in Melna Park where I could be by myself . . ."

The voice stopped abruptly but Telzey had the impression Robane was still talking, unaware that something had dimmed the thread of psi between them. His own screen perhaps? She waited, alert and quiet. It might be deliberate interference, the manifestation of another active psionic field in the area—a disturbing and malicious one.

".... On the whole, I like it here." Robane's voice suddenly was back, and it was evident he didn't realize there had been an interruption. "A psi need never be really bored, and I've installed instruments to offset the disadvantages of being a cripple. I watch the park through scanners and study the minds of animals.... Do you like animal minds?"

That, Telzey thought, hadn't been at all a casual question. "Sometimes," she told Robane carefully. "Some of them."

"Sometimes? Some of them? I wonder.... Solitude on occasion appears to invite the uncanny. One may notice things that seem out of place, that are disquieting. This evening.... during the past hour perhaps, have you.... were there suggestions of activities ..." He paused. "I find I don't quite know how to say this."

"There was something," she said. "For a moment, I wasn't sure I wasn't dreaming."

"You mean something ugly ..."

"Yes."

"Fear," Robane's voice said in her mind. "Fear, pain, death. Savage cruelty. So you caught it, too. Very strange! Perhaps an echo from the past touched our minds in that moment, from the time when creatures who hated man still haunted this country.

"But—well, this is one of the rare occasions when I feel lonely here. And then to hear another psi, you see.... Perhaps I'm even a little afraid to be alone in the night just now. I'd like to speak to you, but not in this way—not in any great detail. One can never be sure who else is listening.... I think there are many things two psis might discuss to their advantage."

The voice ended on that. He'd expressed himself guardedly, and apparently he didn't expect an immediate reply to his invitation. Telzey bit her lip. Chomir had come trotting up, had been welcomed by her and settled down. Gikkes was making cooing sounds and snapping her fingers at him. Chomir ignored the overtures. Ordinarily, Gikkes claimed to find him alarming; but here in Melna Park at night, the idea of having an oversized dog near her evidently had acquired a sudden appeal—

So Robane, too, had received the impression of unusual and unpleasant events this evening.... events he didn't care to discuss openly. The indication that he felt frightened probably needn't be taken too seriously. He was in his house, after all; and so isolated a house must have guard-screens. The house of a crippled, wealthy recluse, who was avoiding the ordinary run of humanity, would have very effective guard-screens. If something did try to get at Robane, he could put in a call to the nearest park station and have an armed ranger car hovering about his roof in a matter of minutes. That suggestion had been intended to arouse her sympathy for a shut-in fellow psi, help coax her over to the house.

But he had noticed something. Something, to judge from his cautious description, quite similar to what she had felt. Telzey looked at Chomir, stretched out on the sandy ground between her and the fire, at the big, wolfish head, the wedge of powerful jaws. Chomir was not exactly an intellectual giant but he had the excellent sensory equipment and alertness of a breed of fighting animals. If there had been a disturbance of that nature in the immediate vicinity, he would have known about it, and she would have known about it through him.

The disturbance, however, might very well have occurred some-where along the twelve-mile stretch between the point where Cil Chasm split the mountains and Robane's house across the plain. Her impression had been that it was uncomfortably close to her. Robane appeared to have sensed it as uncomfortably close to him. He had showed no inclination to do anything about it, and there was, as a matter of fact, no easy way to handle the matter. Robane clearly was no more anxious than she was to reveal himself as a psi; and, in any case, the park authorities would be understandably reluctant to launch a search for a vicious but not otherwise identified man-hunting beast on no better evidence than reported telepathic impressions—at least, until somebody was reported missing.

It didn't seem a good idea to wait for that. For one thing, Telzey thought, the killer might show up at their fire before morning. . . .

She grimaced uneasily, sent a troubled glance around the group. She hadn't been willing to admit it but she'd really known for minutes now that she was going to have to go look for the creature. In an aircar, she thought, even an aircar throttled down to thirty miles an hour and a contour altitude of a hundred and fifty feet, she would be in no danger from an animal on the ground if she didn't take very stupid chances. The flavor of psi about the event she didn't like. That was still unexplained. But she was a psi herself, and she would be careful.

She ran over the possibilities in her mind. The best approach should be to start out towards Robane's house and scout the surrounding wildlands mentally along that route. If she picked up traces of the killer-thing, she could pinpoint its position, call the park rangers from the car, and give them a story that would get them there in a hurry. They could do the rest. If she found nothing, she could consult with Robane about the next moves to make. Even if he didn't want to take a direct part in the search, he might be willing to give her some help with it.

Chomir would remain here as sentinel. She'd plant a trace of uneasiness in his mind, just enough to make sure he remained extremely vigilant while she was gone. At the first hint from him that anything dangerous was approaching the area, she'd use the car's communicator to have everybody pile into the other two aircars and get off the ground. Gikkes was putting them in the right frame of mind to respond very promptly if they were given a real alarm.

Telzey hesitated a moment longer but there seemed to be nothing wrong with the plan. She told herself she'd better start at once. If she waited, the situation, whatever it was, conceivably could take an immediately dangerous turn. Besides, the longer she debated about it, the more unpleasant the prospect was going to look.

She glanced down at Dunker's watch on her wrist.

"Robane?" she asked in her mind.

The response came quickly. "Yes?"

"I'll start over to your house now," Telzey said. "Would you watch for my car? If there is something around that doesn't like people, I'd sooner not be standing outside your door."

"The door will be open the instant you come down," Robane's voice assured her. "Until then, I'm keeping it locked. I've turned on the scanners and will be waiting . . ." A moment's pause. "Do you have additional reason to believe—"

"Not so far," Telzey said. "But there are some things I'd like to talk about—after I get there . . ." She didn't really intend to go walking into Robane's house until she had more information about him. There were too many uncertainties floating around in the night to be making social calls. But he'd be alert now, waiting for her to arrive, and might notice things she didn't.

The aircar was her own, a fast little Cloudsplitter. No one objected when she announced she was setting off for an hour's roam in the starblaze by herself. The fan club looked wistful but was well trained, and Pollard had allowed himself to be reclaimed by Gikkes. Gikkes clearly regarded Telzey's solo excursion as a fine idea. . . .

She lifted the Cloudsplitter out of the mouth of Cil Chasm. At a hundred and fifty feet, as the sealed engine lock clicked in, the little car automatically stopped its ascent. Telzey turned to the right, along the forested walls of the mountain, then swung out across the plain.

It should take her about twenty minutes to get to Robane's house if she went there in a straight line; and if nothing else happened, she intended to go there in a straight line. What the park maps called a plain was a series of sloping plateaus, broken by low hills, descending gradually to the south. It was mainly brush country, dotted with small woods which blended here and there into patches of forest. Scattered herds of native animals moved about in the open ground, showing no interest in the aircar passing through the clusterlight overhead.

Everything looked peaceful enough. Robane had taken her hint and remained quiet. The intangible bubble of the psi screen about Telzey's mind thinned, opened wide. Her awareness went searching ahead, to all sides. . . .

Man-killer, where are you?

Perhaps ten minutes passed before she picked up the first trace. By then, she could see a tiny, steady spark of orange light ahead against the dark line of the forest. That would be Robane's house, still five or six miles away.

Robane hadn't spoken again. There had been numerous fleeting contacts with animal minds savage enough in their own way, deadly to one another. But the thing that hunted man should have a special quality, one she would recognize when she touched it.

She touched it suddenly—a blur of alert malignance, gone almost at once. She was prepared for it, but it still sent a thrill of alarm through her. She moistened her lips, told herself again she was safe in the car. The creature definitely had not been far away. Telzey slipped over for a moment into Chomir's mind. The big dog stood a little beyond the circle of firelight, probing the land to the south. He was unquiet but no more than she had intended him to be. His senses had found nothing of unusual significance. The menace wasn't there.

It was around here, ahead, or to left or right. Telzey let the car move on slowly. After a while, she caught the blur for a moment again, lost it again. . . .

She approached Robane's house gradually. Presently she could make it out well enough in the clusterlight, a sizable structure, set in a garden of its own which ended where the forest began. Part of the building was two-storied, with a balcony running around the upper story. The light came from there, dark-orange light glowing through screened windows.

The second fleeting pulse of that aura of malevolence had come from this general direction; she was sure of it. If the creature was in the forest back of the house, perhaps watching the house, Robane's apprehensions might have some cause, after all. She had brought the Cloudsplitter almost to a stop some five hundred yards north of the house; now she began moving to the left, then shifted in towards the forest, beginning to circle the house as she waited for another indication. Robane should be watching her through the telescanners, and she was grateful that he hadn't broken the silence. Perhaps he had realized what she was trying to do.

For long minutes now, she had been intensely keyed up, sharply aware of the infinite mingling of life detail below. It was as if the plain had come alight in all directions about her, a shifting glimmer of sparks, glowing emanations of life-force, printed in constant change on her awareness. To distinguish among it all the specific pattern which she had touched briefly twice might not be an easy matter. But then, within seconds, she made two significant discoveries.

She had brought the Cloudsplitter nearly to a stop again. She was now to the left of Robane's house, no more than two hundred yards from it. Close enough to see a flock of small, birdlike creatures flutter about indistinctly in the garden shrubbery. Physical vision seemed to overlap and blend with her inner awareness, and among the uncomplicated emanations of small animal life in the garden, there was now a center of mental emanation which was of more interest.

It was inside the house, and it was human. It seemed to Telzey it was Robane she was sensing. That was curious, because if his mind was screened as well as she'd believed, she should not be able to sense him in this manner. But, of course, it might not be. She had simply assumed he had developed measures against being read as adequate as her own.

Probably it was Robane. Then where, Telzey thought, was that elderly, rather stupid housekeeper named Feddler he'd told her about? Feddler's presence, her mind unscreened in any way, should be at least equally obvious now.

With the thought, she caught a second strong glow. That was not the mind of some stupid old woman, or of anything human. It was still blurred, but it was the mind for which she had been searching. The mind of some baleful, intelligent tiger-thing. And it was very close.

She checked again, carefully. Then she knew. It was not back in the forest, and not hidden somewhere on the plain nearby.

It was inside Robane's house.

For a moment, shock held her motionless. Then she swung the Cloudsplitter smoothly to the left, started moving off along the edge of the forest.

"Where are you going?" Robane's voice asked in her mind.

Telzey didn't answer. The car already was gliding along at the thirty miles an hour its throttled-down engine allowed it to go. Her forefinger was flicking out the call number of Rish's aircar back at the camp on the Cloudsplitter's communicator.

There'd been a trap set for her here. She didn't yet know what kind of a trap, or whether she could get out of it by herself. But the best thing she could do at the moment was to let other people know immediately where she was—

A dragging, leaden heaviness sank through her. She saw her hand drop from the communicator dial, felt herself slump to the left, head sagging down on the side rest, face turned half up. She felt the Cloudsplitter's engines go dead. The trap had snapped shut.

The car was dropping, its forward momentum gone. Telzey made a straining effort to sit back up, lift her hands to the controls, and nothing happened. She realized then that nothing could have happened if she had reached the controls. If it hadn't been for the countergravity materials worked into its structure, the Cloudsplitter would have plunged to the ground like a rock. As it was, it settled gradually down through the air, swaying from side to side.

She watched the fiery night sky shift above with the swaying of the car, sickened by the conviction that she was dropping towards death, trying to keep the confusion of terror from exploding through her. . . .

"I'm curious to know," Robane's voice said, "what made you decide at the last moment to decline my invitation and attempt to leave."

She wrenched her attention away from terror, reached for the voice and Robane.

There was the crackling of psi, open telepathic channels through which her awareness flowed in a flash. For an instant, she was inside his mind. Then psi static crashed, and she was away from it again. Her awareness dimmed, momentarily blurred out. She'd absorbed almost too much. It was as if she'd made a photograph of a section of Robane's mind—a pitiful and horrible mind.

She felt the car touch the ground, stop moving. The slight jolt tilted her over farther, her head lolling on the side rest. She was breathing; her eyelids blinked. But her conscious efforts weren't affecting a muscle of her body.

The dazed blurriness began to lift from her thoughts. She found herself still very much frightened but no longer accepting in the least that she would die here. She should have a chance against Robane. She discovered he was speaking again, utterly unaware of what had just occurred.

"I'm not a psi," his voice said. "But I'm a gadgeteer—and, you see, I happen to be highly intelligent. I've used my intelligence to provide myself with instruments which guard me and serve my wishes here. Some give me abilities equivalent to those of a psi. Others, as you've just experienced, can be used to neutralize power devices or to paralyze the human voluntary muscular system within as much as half a mile of this room.

"I was amused by your cautious hesitation and attempted flight just now. I'd already caught you. If I'd let you use the communicator, you would have found it dead. I shut it off as soon as your aircar was in range . . ."

Robane not a psi? For an instant, there was a burbling of lunatic, silent laughter in Telzey's head. In that moment of full contact between them, she'd sensed a telepathic system functional in every respect except that he wasn't aware of it. Psi energy flared about his words as he spoke. That came from one of the machines, but only a telepath could have operated such a machine.

Robane had never considered that possibility. If the machine static hadn't caught her off guard, broken the contact before she could secure it, he would be much more vulnerable in his unawareness now than an ordinary nonpsi human.

She'd reached for him again as he was speaking, along the verbalized thought-forms directed at her. But the words were projected through a machine. Following them back, she wound up at the machine and another jarring blast of psi static. She would have to wait for a moment when she found an opening to his mind again, when the machines didn't happen to be covering him. He was silent now. He intended to kill her as he had others before her, and he might very well be able to do it before an opening was there. But he would make no further moves until he felt certain she hadn't been able to summon help in a manner his machines hadn't detected. What he had done so far he could explain—he had forced an aircar prowling about his house to the ground without harming its occupant. There was no proof of anything else he had done except the proof in Telzey's mind, and Robane didn't know about that.

It gave her a few minutes to act without interference from him.

"What's the matter with that dog?" Gikkes asked nervously. "He's behaving like.... like he thinks there's something around."

The chatter stopped for a moment. Eyes swung over to Chomir. He stood looking out from the canyon ledge over the plain, making a rumbling noise in his throat.

"Don't be silly," Valia said. "He's just wondering where Telzey's gone." She looked at Rish. "How long has she been gone?"

"Twenty-seven minutes," Rish said.

"Well, that's nothing to worry about, is it?" Valia checked herself, added, "Now look at that, will you!" Chomir had swung around, moved over to Rish's aircar, stopped beside it, staring at them with yellow eyes. He made the rumbling noise again.

Gikkes said, watching him fascinatedly, "Maybe something's happened to Telzey."

"Don't talk like that," Valia said. "What could happen to her?"

Rish got to his feet. "Well—it can't hurt to give her a call..." He grinned at Valia to show he wasn't in the least concerned, went to the aircar, opened the door.

Chomir moved silently past him into the car.

Rish frowned, glanced back at Valia and Dunker coming up behind him, started to say something, shook his head, slid into the car, and turned on the communicator.

Valia inquired, her eyes uneasily on Chomir, "Know her number?"

"Uh-huh." They watched as he flicked the number out on the dial, then stood waiting.

Presently Valia cleared her throat. "She's probably got out of the car and is walking around somewhere."

"Of course she's walking," Rish said shortly.

"Keep buzzing anyway," Dunker said.

"I am." Rish glanced at Chomir again. "If she's anywhere near the car, she'll be answering in a moment..."

"Why don't you answer me?" Robane's voice asked, sharp with impatience. "It would be very foolish of you to make me angry."

Telzey made no response. Her eyes blinked slowly at the starblaze. Her awareness groped, prowled, patiently, like a hungry cat, for anything, the slightest wisp of escaping unconscious thought, emotion, that wasn't filtered through the blocking machines, that might give her another opening to the telepathic levels of Robane's mind. In the minutes she'd been lying paralyzed across the seat of the aircar, she had arranged and comprehended the multi-detailed glimpse she'd had of it. She understood Robane very thoroughly now.

The instrument room of the house was his living area. A big room centered about an island of immaculate precision machines. Robane rarely was away from it. She knew what he looked like, from mirror images, glimpses in shining instrument surfaces, his thoughts about himself. A half-man, enclosed from the waist down in a floating, mobile machine like a tiny aircar, which carried him and kept him alive. The little machine was efficient; the half-body protruding from it was vigorous and strong. Robane in his isolation gave fastidious attention to his appearance. The coat which covered him down to the machine was tailored to Orado City's latest fashion; his thick hair was carefully groomed.

He had led a full life as scientist, sportsman, and man of the world, before the disaster which left him bound to his machine. To make the man responsible for the disaster pay for his blunder in full became Robane's obsession and he laid his plans with all the care of the trophy hunter he had been. His work for the Federation had been connected with the further development of devices permitting the direct transmission of sensations from one living brain to another and their adaptation to various new uses. In his retirement in Melna Park, Robane patiently refined such devices for his own purposes and succeeded beyond his expectations, never suspecting that the success was due in part to the latent psionic abilities he was stimulating with his experiments.

Meanwhile, he had prepared for the remaining moves in his plan, installed automatic machinery to take the place of his housekeeper, and dismissed the old woman from his service. A smuggling ring provided him with a specimen of a savage natural predator native to the continent for which he had set up quarters beneath the house. Robane trained the beast and himself, perfecting his skill in the use of the instruments, sent the conditioned animal out at night to hunt, brought it back after it had made the kill in which he had shared through its mind. There was sharper excitement in that alone than he had found in any previous hunting experience. There was further excitement in treating trapped animals with the drug that exposed their sensations to his instruments when he released them and set the killer on their trail. He could be hunter or hunted, alternately and simultaneously, following each chase to the end, withdrawing from the downed quarry only when its numbing death impulses began to reach him.

When it seemed he had no more to learn, he had his underworld connections deliver his enemy to the house. That night, he awakened the man from his stupor, told him what to expect, and turned him out under the starblaze to run for his life. An hour later, Robane and his savage deputy made a human kill, the instruments fingering the victim's drug-drenched nervous system throughout and faithfully transmitting his terrors and final torment.

With that, Robane had accomplished his revenge. But he had no intention now of giving up the exquisite excitements of the new sport he had developed in the process. He became almost completely absorbed by it, as absorbed as the beast he had formed into an extension of himself. They went out by night to stalk and harry, run down and kill. They grew alike in cunning, stealth, and savage audacity, were skillful enough to create no unusual disturbance among the park animals with their sport. By morning, they were back in Robane's house to spend most of the day in sleep. Unsuspecting human visitors who came through the area saw no traces of their nocturnal activities.

Robane barely noticed how completely he had slipped into this new way of living. Ordinarily, it was enough. But he had almost no fear of detection now, and sometimes he remembered there had been a special savor in driving a human being to his death. Then his contacts would bring another shipment of "supplies" to the house, and that night he hunted human game. Healthy young game which did its desperate best to escape but never got far. It was something humanity owed him.

For a while, there was one lingering concern. During his work for the Overgovernment, he'd had several contacts with a telepath called in to assist in a number of experiments. Robane had found out what he could about such people and believed his instruments would shield him against being detected and investigated by them. He was not entirely sure of it, but in the two years he had been pursuing his pleasures undisturbed in Melna Park his uneasiness on that point had almost faded away.

Telzey's voice, following closely on his latest human kill,

startled him profoundly. But when he realized that it was a chance contact, that she was here by accident, it occurred to him that this was an opportunity to find out whether a telepathic mind could be dangerous to him. She seemed young and inexperienced—he could handle her through his instruments with the slightest risk to himself.

Rish and Dunker were in Rish's aircar with Chomir, Telzey thought, and a third person, who seemed to be Valia, was sitting behind them. The car was aloft and moving, so they had started looking for her. It would be nice if they were feeling nervous enough to have the park rangers looking for her, too; but that was very unlikely. She had to handle Chomir with great caution here. If he'd sensed any fear in her, he would have raced off immediately in her general direction to protect her, which would have been of no use at all.

As it was, he was following instructions he didn't know he was getting. He was aware which way the car should go, and he would make that quite clear to Rish and the others if it turned off in any other direction. Since they had no idea where to look for her themselves, they would probably decide to rely on Chomir's intuition.

That would bring them presently to this area. If she was outside the half-mile range of Robane's energy shut-off device by then, they could pick her up safely. If she wasn't, she'd have to turn them away through Chomir again or she'd simply be drawing them into danger with her. Robane, however, wouldn't attempt to harm them unless he was forced to it. Telzey's disappearance in the wildlands of the park could be put down as an unexplained accident; he wasn't risking much there. But a very intensive investigation would get under way if three other students of Pehanron College vanished simultaneously along with a large dog. Robane couldn't afford that.

"Why don't you answer?"

There was an edge of frustrated rage in Robane's projected voice. The paralysis field which immobilized her also made her unreachable to him. He was like an animal balked for the moment by a glass wall. He'd said he had a weapon trained on her which could kill her in an instant as she lay in the car, and Telzey knew it was true from what she had seen in his mind. For that matter, he probably only had to change the setting of the paralysis field to stop her heartbeat or her breathing.

But such actions wouldn't answer the questions he had about

psis. She'd frightened him tonight; and now he had to run her to her death, terrified and helpless as any other human quarry, before he could feel secure again.

"Do you think I'm afraid to kill you?" he asked, seeming almost plaintively puzzled. "Believe me, if I pull the trigger my finger is touching, I won't even be questioned about your disappearance. The park authorities have been instructed by our grateful government to show me every consideration, in view of my past invaluable contributions to humanity, and in view of my present disability. No one would think to disturb me here because some foolish girl is reported lost in Melna Park . . ."

The thought-voice went on, its fury and bafflement filtered through a machine, sometimes oddly suggestive even of a ranting, angry machine. Now and then it blurred out completely, like a bad connection, resumed seconds later. Telzey drew her attention away from it. It was a distraction in her waiting for another open subconscious bridge to Robane's mind. Attempts to reach him more directly remained worse than useless. The machines also handled mind-stuff, but mechanically channeled, focused, and projected; the result was a shifting, flickering, nightmarish distortion of emanations in which Robane and his instruments seemed to blend in constantly changing patterns. She'd tried to force through it, had drawn back quickly, dazed and jolted again. . . .

Every minute she gained here had improved her chances of escape, but she thought she wouldn't be able to stall him much longer. The possibility that a ranger patrol or somebody else might happen by just now, see her Cloudsplitter parked near the house, and come over to investigate, was probably slight, but Robane wouldn't be happy about it. If she seemed to remain intractable, he'd decide at some point to dispose of her at once.

So she mustn't seem too intractable. Since she wasn't replying, he would try something else to find out if she could be controlled. When he did, she would act frightened silly—which she was in a way, except that it didn't seem to affect her ability to think now—and do whatever he said except for one thing. After he turned off the paralysis field, he would order her to come to the house. She couldn't do that. Behind the entry door was a lock chamber. If she stepped inside, the door would close; and with the next breath she took she would have absorbed a full dose of the drug that let Robane's mind-instruments settle into contact with her. She didn't know what effect that would have. It might nullify her ability to maintain her psi screen and reveal her thoughts to Robane. If he knew what she had in mind, he would kill her on the spot. Or the drug might distort her on the telepathic level and end her chances of getting him under control.

"It's occurred to me," Robane's voice said, "that you may not be deliberately refusing to answer me. It's possible that you are unable to do it either because of the effect of the paralysis field or simply because of fear."

Telzey had been wondering when it would occur to him. She waited, new tensions growing up in her.

"I'll release you from the field in a moment," the voice went on. "What happens then depends on how well you carry out the instructions given you. If you try any tricks, little psi, you'll be dead. I'm quite aware you'll be able to move normally seconds after the field is off. Make no move you aren't told to make. Do exactly what you are told to do, and do it without hesitation. Remember those two things. Your life depends on them."

He paused, added, "The field is now off . . ."

Telzey felt a surge of strength and lightness all through her. Her heart began to race. She refrained carefully from stirring. After a moment, Robane's voice said, "Touch nothing in the car you don't need to touch. Keep your hands in sight. Get out of the car, walk twenty feet away from it, and stop. Then face the house."

Telzey climbed out of the car. She was shaky throughout; but it wasn't as bad as she'd thought it would be when she first moved again. It wasn't bad at all. She walked on to the left, stopped, and looked up at the orange-lit, screened windows in the upper part of the house.

"Watch your car," Robane's voice told her.

She looked over at the Cloudsplitter. He'd turned off the power neutralizer and the car was already moving. It lifted vertically from the ground, began gliding forward thirty feet up, headed in the direction of the forest beyond the house. It picked up speed, disappeared over the trees.

"It will begin to change course when it reaches the mountains," Robane's voice said. "It may start circling and still be within the park when it is found. More probably, it will be hundreds of miles away. Various explanations will be offered for your disappearance from it, apparently in midair, which needn't concern us now. . . . Raise your arms before you, little psi. Spread them farther apart. Stand still."

Telzey lifted her arms, stood waiting. After an instant, she gave a jerk of surprise. Her hands and arms, Dunker's watch on her wrist, the edges of the short sleeves of her shirt suddenly glowed white.

"Don't move!" Robane's voice said sharply. "This is a search-beam. It won't hurt you."

She stood still again, shifted her gaze downwards. What she saw of herself and her clothes and of a small patch of ground about her feet all showed the same cold, white glow, like fluorescing plastic. There was an eerie suggestion of translucence. She glanced back at her hands, saw the fine bones showing faintly as more definite lines of white in the glow. She felt nothing and the beam wasn't affecting her vision, but it was an efficient device. Sparks of heat-less light began stabbing from her clothing here and there; within moments, Robane located half a dozen minor items in her pockets and instructed her to throw them away one by one, along with the watch. He wasn't taking chances on fashionably camouflaged communicators, perhaps suspected even this or that might be a weapon. Then the beam went off and he told her to lower her arms again.

"Now a reminder," his voice went on. "Perhaps you're unable to speak to me. And perhaps you could speak but think it's clever to remain silent in this situation. That isn't too important. But let me show you something. It will help you keep in mind that it isn't at all advisable to be too clever in dealing with me . . ."

Something suddenly was taking shape twenty yards away, between Telzey and the house; and fright flicked through her like fire and ice in the instant before she saw it was a projection placed a few inches above the ground. It was an image of Robane's killer, a big, bulky creature which looked bulkier because of the coat of fluffy, almost feathery fur covering most of it like a cloak. It was half crouched, a pair of powerful forelimbs stretched out through the cloak of fur. Ears like upturned horns projected from the sides of the head, and big, round, dark eyes, the eyes of a star-night hunter, were set in front above the sharply curved, serrated cutting beak.

The image faded within seconds. She knew what the creature was. The spooks had been, at one time, almost the dominant life form on this continent; the early human settlers hated and feared them for their unqualified liking for human flesh, made them a legend which haunted Orado's forests long after they had, in fact, been driven out of most of their territory. Even in captivity, from behind separating force fields, their flat, dark stares, their size,

goblin appearance, and monkey quickness disturbed impression-
able people.

"My hunting partner," Robane's voice said. "My other self. It
is not pleasant, not at all pleasant, to know this is the shape
that is following your trail at night in Melna Park. You had a
suggestion of it this evening. Be careful not to make me angry
again. Be quick to do what I tell you. Now come forward to
the house."

Telzey saw the entry door in the garden slide open. Her heart
began to beat heavily. She didn't move.

"Come to the house!" Robane repeated.

Something accompanied the words, a gush of heavy, subconscious
excitement, somebody reaching for a craved drug. . . . but Robane's
drug was death. As she touched the excitement, it vanished. It was
what she had waited for, a line to the unguarded levels of his mind.
If it came again and she could hold it even for seconds—

It didn't come again. There was a long pause before Robane
spoke.

"This is curious," his voice said slowly. "You refuse. You know
you are helpless. You know what I can do. Yet you refuse. I
wonder . . ."

He went silent. He was suspicious now, very. For a moment, she
could almost feel him finger the trigger of his weapon. But the
drug was there, in his reach. She was cheating him out of some
of it. He wouldn't let her cheat him out of everything. . . .

"Very well," the voice said. "I'm tired of you. I was interested in
seeing how a psi would act in such a situation. I've seen. You're
so afraid you can barely think. So run along. Run as fast as you
can, little psi. Because I'll soon be following."

Telzey stared up at the windows. Let him believe she could
barely think.

"Run!"

She whipped around, as if shocked into motion by the command, and ran, away from Robane's house, back in the direction
of the plain to the north.

"I'll give you a warning," Robane's voice said, seeming to move
along with her. "Don't try to climb a tree. We catch the ones who
do that immediately. We can climb better than you can, and if the
tree is big enough we'll come up after you. If the tree's too light
to hold us, or if you go out where the branches are too thin, we'll
simply shake you down. So keep running."

She glanced back as she came up to the first group of trees. The orange windows of the house seemed to be staring after her. She went in among the trees, out the other side, and now the house was no longer in sight.

"Be clever now," Robane's voice said. "We like the clever ones. You have a chance, you know. Perhaps somebody will see you before you're caught. Or you may think of some way to throw us off your track. Perhaps you'll be the lucky one who gets away. We'll be very, very sorry then, won't we? So do your best, little psi. Do your best. Give us a good run."

She flicked out a search-thought, touched Chomir's mind briefly. The aircar was still coming, still on course, still too far away to do her any immediate good. . . .

She ran. She was in as good condition as a fifteen-year-old who liked a large variety of sports and played hard at them was likely to get. But she had to cover five hundred yards to get beyond the range of Robane's house weapons, and on this broken ground it began to seem a long, long stretch. How much time would he give her? Some of those he'd hunted had been allowed a start of thirty minutes or more. . . .

She began to count her steps. Robane remained silent. When she thought she was approaching the end of five hundred yards, there were trees ahead again. She remembered crossing over a small stream followed by a straggling line of trees as she came up to the house. That must be it. And in that case, she was beyond the five-hundred-yard boundary.

A hungry excitement swirled about her and was gone. She'd lashed at the feeling quickly, got nothing. Robane's voice was there an instant later.

"We're starting now . . ."

So soon? She felt shocked. He wasn't giving her even the pretense of a chance to escape. Dismay sent a wave of weakness through her as she ran splashing down into the creek. Some large animals burst out of the water on the far side, crashed through the bushes along the bank, and pounded away. Telzey hardly noticed them. Turn to the left, downstream, she thought. It was a fast little stream. The spook must be following by scent and the running water should wipe out her trail before it got here. . . .

But others it had followed would have decided to turn downstream when they reached the creek. If it didn't pick up the trail on the far bank and found no human scent in the water coming down, it only had to go along the bank to the left until it either heard her in the water or reached the place where she'd left it.

They'd expect her, she told herself, to leave the water on the far side of the creek, not to angle back in the direction of Robane's house. Or would they? It seemed the best thing to try.

She went downstream as quickly as she could, splashing, stumbling on slippery rock, careless of noise for the moment. It would be a greater danger to lose time trying to be quiet. A hundred yards on, stout tree branches swayed low over the water. She could catch them, swing up, scramble on up into the trees.

Others would have tried that, too. Robane and his beast knew such spots, would check each to make sure it wasn't what she had done.

She ducked, gasping, under the low-hanging branches, hurried on. Against the starblaze a considerable distance ahead, a thicker cluster of trees loomed darkly. It looked like a sizable little wood surrounding the watercourse. It might be a good place to hide.

Others, fighting for breath after the first hard run, legs beginning to falter, would have had that thought.

Robane's voice said abruptly in her mind, "So you've taken to the water. It was your best move . . ."

The voice stopped. Telzey felt the first stab of panic. The creek curved sharply ahead. The bank on the left was steep, not the best place to get out. She followed it with her eyes. Roots sprouted out of the bare earth a little ahead. She came up to them, jumped to catch them, pulled herself up, and scrambled over the edge of the bank. She climbed to her feet, hurried back in the general direction of Robane's house, dropped into a cluster of tall grass. Turning, flattened out on her stomach, she lifted her head to stare back in the direction of the creek. There was an opening in the bushes on the other bank, with the clusterlight of the skyline showing through it. She watched that, breathing as softly as she could. It occurred to her that if a breeze was moving the wrong way, the spook might catch her scent on the air. But she didn't feel any breeze.

Perhaps a minute passed—certainly no more. Then a dark silhouette passed lightly and swiftly through the opening in the bushes she was watching, went on downstream. It was larger than she'd thought it would be when she saw its projected image; and that something so big should move in so effortless a manner, seeming to drift along the ground, somehow was jolting in itself. For a moment, Telzey had distinguished, or imagined she had distinguished, the big, round head held high, the pointed ears like horns. *Goblin,* her nerves screamed. A feeling of heavy dread flowed through her, seemed to drain away her strength. This was how the others had felt when they ran and crouched in hiding, knowing there was no escape from such a pursuer. . . .

She made herself count off a hundred seconds, got to her feet, and started back on a slant towards the creek, to a point a hundred yards above the one where she had climbed from it. If the thing returned along this side of the watercourse and picked up her trail, it might decide she had tried to escape upstream. She got down quietly into the creek, turned downstream again, presently saw in the distance the wood which had looked like a good place to hide. The spook should be prowling among the trees there now, searching for her. She passed the curve where she had pulled herself up on the bank, waded on another hundred steps, trying to make no noise at all, almost certain from moment to moment she could hear or glimpse the spook on its way back. Then she climbed the bank on the right, pushed carefully through the hedges of bushes that lined it, and ran off into the open plain sloping up to the north.

After perhaps a hundred yards, her legs began to lose the rubbery weakness of held-in terror. She was breathing evenly. The aircar was closer again and in not too many more minutes she might find herself out of danger. She didn't look back. If the spook was coming up behind her, she couldn't outrun it, and it wouldn't help to feed her fears by watching for shadows on her trail.

She shifted her attention to signs from Robane. He might be growing concerned by now and resort to his telescanners to look for her and guide his creature after her. There was nothing she could do about that. Now and then she seemed to have a brief awareness of him, but there had been no definite contact since he had spoken.

She reached a rustling grove, walked and trotted through it. As she came out the other side, a herd of graceful deer-like animals turned from her and sped with shadowy quickness across the plain and out of her range of vision. She remembered suddenly having heard that hunted creatures sometimes covered their trail by mingling with other groups of animals. . . .

A few minutes later, she wasn't sure how well that was working. Other herds were around; sometimes she saw shadowy motion ahead or to right or left; then there would be whistles of alarm, the stamp of hoofs, and they'd vanish like drifting smoke, leaving the section of plain about her empty again. This was Robane's hunting ground; the animals here might be more alert and nervous than in other sections of the park. And perhaps, Telzey thought, they sensed she was the quarry tonight and was drawing danger towards them. Whatever the reason, they kept well out of her way. But she'd heard fleeing herds cross behind her a number of times, so they might in fact be breaking up her trail enough to make it more difficult to follow. She kept scanning the skyline above the slope ahead, looking for the intermittent green flash of a moving aircar or the sweep of its search-beam along the ground. They couldn't be too far away.

She slowed to a walk again. Her legs and lungs hadn't given out, but she could tell she was tapping the final reserves of strength. She sent a thought to Chomir's mind, touched it instantly and, at the same moment, caught a glimpse of a pulsing green spark against the starblaze, crossing down through a dip in the slopes, disappearing beyond the wooded ground ahead of her. She went hot with hope, swung to the right, began running towards the point where the car should show again.

They'd arrived. Now to catch their attention....

"Here!" she said sharply in the dog's mind.

It meant: "Here I am! Look for me! Come to me!" No more than that. Chomir was keyed up enough without knowing why. Any actual suggestion that she was in trouble might throw him out of control.

She almost heard the deep, whining half-growl with which he responded. It should be enough. Chomir knew now she was somewhere nearby, and Rish and the others would see it immediately in the way he behaved. When the aircar reappeared, its search-beam should be swinging about, fingering the ground to locate her.

Telzey jumped down into a little gully, felt, with a shock of surprise, her knees go soft with fatigue as she landed, and clambered shakily out the other side. She took a few running steps forward, came to a sudden complete stop.

Robane! She felt him about, a thick, ugly excitement. It seemed the chance moment of contact for which she'd been waiting, his mind open, unguarded.

She looked carefully around. Something lay beside a cluster of bushes thirty feet ahead. It appeared to be a big pile of wind-blown dry leaves and grass, but its surface stirred with a curious softness in the breeze. Then a wisp of acrid animal odor touched Telzey's nostrils and she felt the hot-ice surge of deep fright.

The spook lifted its head slowly out of its fluffed, mottled mane

and looked at her. Then it moved from its crouched position. . . . a
soundless shift a good fifteen feet to the right, light as the tumbling
of a big ball of moss. It rose on its hind legs, the long fur settling loosely about it like a cloak, and made a chuckling sound
of pleasure.

The plain seemed to explode about Telzey.

The explosion was in her mind. Tensions held too long, too
hard, lashed back through her in seething confusion at a moment
when too much needed to be done at once. Her physical vision
went black; Robane's beast and the starlit slope vanished. She was
sweeping through a topsy-turvy series of mental pictures and sensations. Rish's face appeared, wide-eyed, distorted with alarm, the
aircar skimming almost at ground level along the top of a grassy
rise, a wood suddenly ahead. *"Now!"* Telzey thought. Shouts, and
the car swerved up again. Then a brief, thudding, jarring sensation
underfoot. . . .

That was done.

She swung about to Robane's waiting excitement, slipped through
it into his mind. In an instant, her awareness poured through a
net of subconscious psi channels that became half familiar as she
touched them. Machine static clattered, too late to dislodge her. She
was there. Robane, unsuspecting, looked out through his creature's
eyes at her shape on the plain, hands locked hard on the instruments through which he lived, experienced, murdered.

In minutes, Telzey thought, in minutes, if she was alive minutes
from now, she would have this mind—unaware, unresistant, wide
open to her—under control. But she wasn't certain she could check
the spook then through Robane. He had never attempted to hold
it back moments away from its kill.

Vision cleared. She stood on the slope, tight tendrils of thought
still linking her to every significant section of Robane's mind.
The spook stared, hook-beak lifted above its gaping mouth,
showing the thick, twisting tongue inside. Still upright, it began
to move, seemed to glide across the ground towards her. One of
its forelimbs came through the thick cloak of fur, four-fingered
paw raised, slashing retractile claws extended, reaching out almost
playfully.

Telzey backed slowly off from the advancing goblin shape. For
an instant, another picture slipped through her thoughts. . . . a blur
of motion. She gave it no attention. There was nothing she could
do there now.

The goblin dropped lightly to a crouch. Telzey saw it begin its spring as she turned and ran.

She heard the gurgling chuckle a few feet behind her, but no other sound. She ran headlong up the slope with all the strength she had left. In another world, on another level of existence, she moved quickly through Robane's mind, tracing out the control lines, gathering them in. But her thoughts were beginning to blur with fatigue. Bushy shrubbery dotted the slope ahead. She could see nothing else.

The spook passed her like something blown by the wind through the grass. It swung around before her, twenty feet ahead; and as she turned to the right, it was suddenly behind her again, coming up quickly, went by. Something nicked the back of her calf as it passed—a scratch, not much deeper than a dozen or so she'd picked up pushing through thorny growth tonight. But this hadn't been a thorn. She turned left, and it followed, herding her; dodged right, and it was there, going past. Its touch seemed the lightest flick again, but an instant later there was a hot, wet line of pain down her arm. She felt panic gather in her throat as it came up behind her once more. She stopped, turning to face it.

It stopped in the same instant, fifteen feet away, rose slowly to its full height, dark eyes staring, hooked beak open as if in silent laughter. Telzey watched it, gasping for breath. Streaks of foggy darkness seemed to float between them. Robane felt far away, beginning to slip from her reach. If she took another step, she thought, she would stumble and fall; then the thing would be on her.

The spook's head swung about. Its beak closed with a clack. The horn-ears went erect.

The white shape racing silently down the slope seemed unreal for a moment, something she imagined. She knew Chomir was approaching; she hadn't realized he was so near. She couldn't see the aircar's lights in the starblaze above, but it might be there. If they had followed the dog after he plunged out of the car, if they hadn't lost. . . .

Chomir could circle Robane's beast, threaten it, perhaps draw it away from her, keep it occupied for minutes. She drove a command at him—another, quickly and anxiously, because he hadn't checked in the least; tried to slip into his mind and knew suddenly that Chomir, coming in silent fury, wasn't going to be checked or slowed or controlled by anything she did. The goblin uttered a monstrous, squalling scream of astounded rage as the strange white animal closed the last twenty yards between them; then it leaped aside with its horrid ease. Sick with dismay, Telzey saw the great forelimb flash from the cloak, strike with spread talons. The thudding blow caught Chomir, spun him around, sent him rolling over the ground. The spook sprang again to come down on its reckless assailant. But the dog was on his feet and away.

It was Chomir's first serious fight. But he came of generations of ancestors who had fought one another and other animals and armed men in the arenas of Askanam. Their battle cunning was stamped into his genes. He had made one mistake, a very nearly fatal one, in hurtling in at a dead run on an unknown opponent. Almost within seconds, it became apparent that he was making no further mistakes.

Telzey saw it through a shifting blur of exhaustion. As big a dog as Chomir was, the squalling goblin must weigh nearly five times as much, looked ten times larger with its fur-mane bristling about it. Its kind had been forest horrors to the early settlers. Its forelimbs were tipped with claws longer than her hands and the curved beak could shear through muscle and bone like a sword. Its uncanny speed....

Now somehow it seemed slow. As it sprang, slashing down, something white and low flowed around and about it with silent purpose. Telzey understood it then. The spook was a natural killer, developed by nature to deal efficiently with its prey. Chomir's breed were killers developed by man to deal efficiently with other killers.

He seemed locked to the beast for an instant, high on its shoulder, and she saw the wide, dark stain on his flank where the spook's talons had struck. He shook himself savagely. There was an ugly, snapping sound. The spook screeched like a huge bird. She saw the two animals locked together again, then the spook rolling over the ground, the white shape rolling with it, slipping away, slipping back. There was another screech. The spook rolled into a cluster of bushes. Chomir followed it in.

A white circle of light settled on the thrashing vegetation, shifted over to her. She looked up, saw Rish's car gliding down through the air, heard voices calling her name—

She followed her contact thoughts back to Robane's mind, spread out through it, sensing at once the frantic grip of his hands on the instrument controls. For Robane, time was running out quickly. He had been trying to turn his beast away from the dog, force it to destroy the human being who could expose him. He had been unable to do it. He was in terrible fear. But he could accomplish no more through the spook. She felt his sudden decision to break mind-contact with the animal to avoid the one experience he had always shunned—going down with another mind into the shuddering agony of death.

His right hand released the control it was clutching, reached towards a switch.

"No," Telzey said softly to the reaching hand.

It dropped to the instrument board. After a moment, it knotted, twisted about, began to lift again.

"No."

Now it lay still. She considered. There was time enough.

Robane believed he would die with the spook if he couldn't get away from it in time. She thought he might be right; she wouldn't want to be in his mind when it happened, if it came to that.

There were things she needed to learn from Robane. The identity of the gang which had supplied him with human game was one; she wanted that very much. Then she should look at the telepathic level of his mind in detail, find out what was wrong in there, why he hadn't been able to use it. . . . some day, she might be able to do something with a half-psi like Gikkes. And the mind-machines—if Robane had been able to work with them, not really understanding what he did, she should be able to employ similar devices much more effectively. Yes, she had to carefully study his machines—

She released Robane's hand. It leaped to the switch, pulled it back. He gave a great gasp of relief.

For a moment, Telzey was busy. A needle of psi energy flicked knowingly up and down channels, touching here, there, shriveling, cutting, blocking. . . . Then it was done. Robane, half his mind gone in an instant, unaware of it, smiled blankly at the instrument panel in front of him. He'd live on here, dimmed and harmless, cared for by machines, unwitting custodian of other machines, of memories that had to be investigated, of a talent he'd never known he had.

"I'll be back," Telzey told the smiling, dull thing, and left it.

She found herself standing on the slope. It had taken only a moment, after all. Dunker and Valia were running towards her. Rish had just climbed out of the aircar settled forty feet away, its search-beam fixed on the thicket where the spook's body jerked back and forth as Chomir, jaws locked on its crushed neck, shook the last vestiges of life from it with methodical fury.

The Only Thing We Learn

by C. M. Kornbluth

PREFACE BY DAVID DRAKE:
"What experience and history teach is this: that peoples and governments have never learned anything from history."

—Hegel

I first read "The Only Thing We Learn" when I was thirteen. I'd never heard of Hegel, nor was I familiar with the quote that Kornbluth paraphrased for his title. The story still stunned and horrified me.

In the comic books the villain was always bad, the hero was always good—GI and Nazi, lawmen and rustlers, and so on down the line: fixed dichotomies of Good and Evil. "The Only Thing We Learn" said, *showed*, explicitly that the definition of "good guys" and "bad guys" depended on your frame of reference.

When I was thirteen I had no more appreciation of literary technique than I did of German philosophers. (I still don't have an appreciation of German philosophers.) You don't have to understand technique for it to affect you, though. Only a flawless craftsman like Cyril Kornbluth, arguably the best short story writer in the SF field, would've been able to pack so much in so brief a compass. The story's terse, elliptical form drove home a message that would've been softened if not suffocated by a wordier presentation.

257

The professor, though he did not know the actor's phrase for it, was counting the house—peering through a spyhole in the door through which he would in a moment appear before the class. He was pleased with what he saw. Tier after tier of young people, ready with notebooks and styli, chattering tentatively, glancing at the door against which his nose was flattened, waiting for the pleasant interlude known as "Archaeo-Literature 203" to begin.

The professor stepped back, smoothed his tunic, crooked four books in his left elbow and made his entrance. Four swift strides brought him to the lectern and, for the thousandth-odd time, he impassively swept the lecture hall with his gaze. Then he gave a wry little smile. Inside, for the thousandth-odd time, he was nagged by the irritable little thought that the lectern really ought to be a foot or so higher.

The irritation did not show. He was out to win the audience, and he did. A dead silence, the supreme tribute, gratified him. Imperceptibly, the lights of the lecture hall began to dim and the light on the lectern to brighten.

He spoke.

"Young gentlemen of the Empire, I ought to warn you that this and the succeeding lectures will be most subversive."

There was a little rustle of incomprehension from the audience— but by then the lectern light was strong enough to show the twinkling smile about his eyes that belied his stern mouth, and agreeable chuckles sounded in the gathering darkness of the tiered seats. Glow-lights grew bright gradually at the students' tables, and they adjusted their notebooks in the narrow ribbons of illumination. He waited for the small commotion to subside.

"Subversive—" He gave them a link to cling to. "Subversive because I shall make every effort to tell both sides of our ancient beginnings with every resource of archaeology and with every clue my diligence has discovered in our epic literature.

"There *were* two sides, you know—difficult though it may be to believe that if we judge by the Old Epic alone—such epics as the noble and tempestuous *Chant of Remd*, the remaining fragments of *Krall's Voyage*, or the gory and rather out-of-date *Battle for the Ten Suns*." He paused while styli scribbled across the notebook pages.

"The Middle Epic is marked, however, by what I might call the rediscovered ethos." From his voice, every student knew that that phrase, surer than death and taxes, would appear on an examination paper. The styli scribbled. "By this I mean an awakening of fellow-feeling with the Home Suns People, which had once been filial loyalty to them when our ancestors were few and pioneers, but which turned into contempt when their numbers grew.

"The Middle Epic writers did not despise the Home Suns People, as did the bards of the Old Epic. Perhaps this was because they did not have to—since their long war against the Home Suns was drawing to a victorious close.

"Of the New Epic I shall have little to say. It was a literary fad, a pose, and a silly one. Written within historic times, the some two score pseudo-epics now moulder in their cylinders, where they belong. Our ripening civilization could not with integrity work in the epic form, and the artistic failures produced so indicate. Our genius turned to the lyric and to the unabashedly romantic novel.

"So much, for the moment, of literature. What contribution, you must wonder, have archaeological studies to make in an investigation of the wars from which our ancestry emerged?

"Archaeology offers—one—a check in historical matter in the epics—confirming or denying. Two—it provides evidence glossed over in the epics—for artistic or patriotic reasons. Three—it provides evidence which has been lost, owing to the fragmentary nature of some of the early epics."

All this he fired at them crisply, enjoying himself. Let them not think him a dreamy litterateur, nor, worse, a flat precisionist, but let them be always a little off-balance before him, never knowing what came next, and often wondering, in class and out. The styli paused after heading Three.

"We shall examine first, by our archaeo-literary technique, the second book of the *Chant of Remd*. As the selected youth of the Empire, you know much about it, of course—much that is false, some that is true and a great deal that is irrelevant. You know that Book One hurls us into the middle of things, aboard ship with Algan and his great captain, Remd, on their way from the triumph over a Home Suns stronghold, the planet Telse. We watch Remd on his diversionary action that splits the Ten Suns Fleet into two halves. But before we see the destruction of those halves by the Horde of Algan, we are told in Book Two of the battle for Telse."

He opened one of his books on the lectern, swept the amphitheater again and read sonorously.

"*Then battle broke*
And high the blinding blast

> *Sight-searing leaped*
> *While folk in fear below*
> *Cowered in caverns*
> *From the wrath of Remd—*

"Or, in less sumptuous language, one fission bomb—or a stick of time-on-target bombs—was dropped. An unprepared and disorganized populace did not take the standard measure of dispersing, but huddled foolishly to await Algan's gunfighters and the death they brought.

"One of the things you believe because you have seen them in notes to elementary-school editions of *Remd* is that Telse was the fourth planet of the star, Sol. Archaeology denies it by establishing that the fourth planet—actually called Marse, by the way—was in those days weather-roofed at least, and possibly atmosphere-roofed as well. As potential warriors, you know that one does not waste fissionable material on a roof, and there is no mention of chemical explosives being used to crack the roof. Marse, therefore, was not the locale of *Remd*, Book Two.

"Which planet was? The answer to that has been established by X-radar, differential decay analyses, video-coring and every other resource of those scientists still quaintly called 'diggers.' We know and can prove that Telse was the *third* planet of Sol. So much for the opening of the attack. Let us jump to Canto Three, the Storming of the Dynastic Palace.

> *"Imperial purple wore they*
> *Fresh from the feast*
> *Grossly gorged*
> *They sought to slay—*

"And so on. Now, as I warned you, Remd is of the Old Epic, and makes no pretense at fairness. The unorganized huddling of Telse's population was read as cowardice instead of poor A.R.P. The same is true of the Third Canto. Video-cores show on the site of the palace a hecatomb of dead in once-purple livery, but also shows impartially that they were not particularly gorged and that digestion of their last meals had been well advanced. They didn't give such a bad accounting of themselves, either. I hesitate to guess, but perhaps they accounted for one of our ancestors apiece and were simply outnumbered. The study is not complete.

"That much we know." The professor saw they were tiring of the terse scientist and shifted gears. "But if the veil of time were rent that shrouds the years between us and the Home Suns People, how much more would we learn? Would we despise the Home Suns People as our frontiersman ancestors did, or would we cry: '*This is our spiritual home*—this world of rank and order, this world of formal verse and exquisitely patterned arts'?"

If the veil of time were rent—?

We can try to rend it . . .

Wing Commander Arris heard the clear jangle of the radar net alarm as he was dreaming about a fish. Struggling out of his too-deep, too-soft bed, he stepped into a purple singlet, buckled on his Sam Browne belt with its holstered .45 automatic and tried to read the radar screen. Whatever had set it off was either too small or too distant to register on the five-inch C.R.T.

He rang for his aide, and checked his appearance in a wall-mirror while waiting. His space tan was beginning to fade, he saw, and made a mental note to get it renewed at the parlor. He stepped into the corridor as Evan, his aide, trotted up—younger, browner, thinner, but the same officer type that made the Service what it was, Arris thought with satisfaction.

Evan gave him a bone-cracking salute, which he returned. They set off for the elevator that whisked them down to a large, chilly, dark underground room where faces were greenly lit by radar screens and the lights of plotting tables. Somebody yelled "Attention!" and the tecks snapped. He gave them "At ease" and took the brisk salute of the senior teck, who reported to him in flat, machine-gun delivery:

"Object-becoming-visible-on-primary-screen-sir."

He studied the sixty-inch disk for several seconds before he spotted the intercepted particle. It was coming in fast from zenith, growing while he watched.

"Assuming it's now traveling at maximum, how long will it be before it's within striking range?" he asked the teck.

"Seven hours, sir."

"The interceptors at Idlewild alerted?"

"Yessir."

Arris turned on a phone that connected with Interception. The boy at Interception knew the face that appeared on its screen, and was already capped with a crash helmet.

"Go ahead and take him, Efrid," said the wing commander.

"Yessir!" and a punctilious salute, the boy's pleasure plain at being known by name and a great deal more at being on the way to a fight that might be first-class.

Arris cut him off before the boy could detect a smile that was forming on his face. He turned from the pale lumar glow of the sixty-incher to enjoy it. Those kids—when every meteor was an invading dreadnaught, when every ragged scouting ship from the rebels was an armada!

He watched Efrid's squadron soar off the screen and then he retreated to a darker corner. This was his post until the meteor or scout or whatever it was got taken care of. Evan joined him, and they silently studied the smooth, disciplined functioning of the plot room, Arris with satisfaction and Evan doubtless with the same. The aide broke silence, asking:

"Do you suppose it's a Frontier ship, sir?" He caught the wing commander's look and hastily corrected himself: "I mean rebel ship, sir, of course."

"Then you should have said so. Is that what the junior officers generally call those scoundrels?"

Evan conscientiously cast his mind back over the last few junior messes and reported unhappily: "I'm afraid we do, sir. We seem to have got into the habit."

"I shall write a memorandum about it. How do you account for that very peculiar habit?"

"Well, sir, they do have something like a fleet, and they did take over the Regulus Cluster, didn't they?"

What had got into this incredible fellow, Arris wondered in amazement. Why, the thing was self-evident! They had a few ships—accounts differed as to how many—and they had, doubtless by raw sedition, taken over some systems temporarily.

He turned from his aide, who sensibly became interested in a screen and left with a murmured excuse to study it very closely.

The brigands had certainly knocked together some ramshackle league or other, but— The wing commander wondered briefly if it could last, shut the horrid thought from his head, and set himself to composing mentally a stiff memorandum that would be posted in the junior officer's mess and put an end to this absurd talk.

His eyes wandered to the sixty-incher, where he saw the interceptor squadron climbing nicely toward the particle—which, he noticed, had become three particles. A low crooning distracted him. Was one of the tecks singing at work? It couldn't be!

It wasn't. An unsteady shape wandered up in the darkness,

murmuring a song and exhaling alcohol. He recognized the Chief Archivist, Glen.

"This is service country, mister," he told Glen.

"Hullo, Arris," the round little civilian said, peering at him. "I come down here regularly—regularly against regulations—to wear off my regular irregularities with the wine bottle. That's all right, isn't it?"

He was drunk and argumentative. Arris felt hemmed in. Glen couldn't be talked into leaving without loss of dignity to the wing commander, and he couldn't be chucked out because he was writing a biography of the chamberlain and could, for the time being, have any head in the palace for the asking. Arris sat down unhappily, and Glen plumped down beside him.

The little man asked him.

"Is that a fleet from the Frontier League?" He pointed to the big screen. Arris didn't look at his face, but felt that Glen was grinning maliciously.

"I know of no organization called the Frontier League," Arris said. "If you are referring to the brigands who have recently been operating in Galactic East, you could at least call them by their proper names." Really, he thought—civilians!

"So sorry. But the brigands should have the Regulus Cluster by now, shouldn't they?" he asked, insinuatingly.

This was serious—a grave breach of security. Arris turned to the little man.

"Mister, I have no authority to command you," he said measuredly. "Furthermore, I understand you are enjoying a temporary eminence in the non-service world which would make it very difficult for me to—ah—tangle with you. I shall therefore refer only to your altruism. How did you find out about the Regulus Cluster?"

"Eloquent!" murmured the little man, smiling happily. "I got it from Rome."

Arris searched his memory. "You mean Squadron Commander Romo broke security? I can't believe it!"

"No, commander. I mean Rome—a place—a time—a civilization. I got it also from Babylon, Assyria, the Mogul Raj—every one of them. You don't understand me, of course."

"I understand that you're trifling with Service security and that you're a fat little, malevolent, worthless drone and scribbler!"

"Oh, commander!" protested the archivist. "I'm not so little!" He wandered away, chuckling.

Arris wished he had the shooting of him, and tried to explore the chain of secrecy for a weak link. He was tired and bored by this harping on the Fron—on the brigands.

His aide tentatively approached him. "Interceptors in striking range, sir," he murmured.

"Thank you," said the wing commander, genuinely grateful to be back in the clean, etched-line world of the Service and out of that blurred, water-color, civilian land where long-dead Syrians apparently retailed classified matter to nasty little drunken warts who had no business with it. Arris confronted the sixty-incher. The particle that had become three particles was now—he counted—eighteen particles. Big ones. Getting bigger.

He did not allow himself emotion, but turned to the plot on the interceptor squadron.

"Set up Lunar relay," he ordered.

"Yessir."

Half the plot room crew bustled silently and efficiently about the delicate job of applied relativistic physics that was 'lunar relay.' He knew that the palace power plant could take it for a few minutes, and he wanted to *see*. If he could not believe radar pips, he might believe a video screen.

On the great, green circle, the eighteen—now twenty-four—particles neared the thirty-six smaller particles that were interceptors, led by the eager young Efrid.

"Testing Lunar relay, sir," said the chief teck.

The wing commander turned to a twelve-inch screen. Unobtrusively, behind him, tecks jockeyed for position. The picture on the screen was something to see. The chief let mercury fill a thick-walled, ceramic tank. There was a sputtering and contact was made.

"Well done," said Arris. "Perfect seeing."

He saw, upper left, a globe of ships—what ships! Some were Service jobs, with extra turrets plastered on them wherever there was room. Some were orthodox freighters, with the same porcupine-bristle of weapons. Some were obviously home-made crates, hideously ugly—and as heavily armed as the others.

Next to him, Arris heard his aide murmur, "It's all wrong, sir. They haven't got any pick-up boats. They haven't got any hospital ships. What happens when one of them gets shot up?"

"Just what ought to happen, Evan," snapped the wing commander. "They float in space until they desiccate in their suits. Or if they get grappled inboard with a boat hook, they don't get any medical care. As I told you, they're brigands, without decency even to care for their own." He enlarged on the theme. "Their morale must be insignificant compared with our men's. When the Service goes into action, every rating and teck knows he'll be cared for if he's hurt. Why, if we didn't have pick-up boats and hospital ships the men wouldn't—" He almost finished it with "fight," but thought, and lamely ended—"wouldn't like it."

Evan nodded, wonderingly, and crowded his chief a little as he craned his neck for a look at the screen.

"Get the hell away from here!" said the wing commander in a restrained yell, and Evan got.

The interceptor squadron swam into the field—a sleek, deadly needle of vessels in perfect alignment, with its little cloud of pick-ups trailing, and farther astern a white hospital ship with the ancient red cross.

The contact was immediate and shocking. One of the rebel ships lumbered into the path of the interceptors, spraying fire from what seemed to be as many points as a man has pores. The Service ships promptly riddled it and it should have drifted away—but it didn't. It kept on fighting. It rammed an interceptor with a crunch that must have killed every man before the first bulwark, but aft of the bulwark the ship kept fighting.

It took a torpedo portside and its plumbing drifted through space in a tangle. Still the starboard side kept squirting fire. Isolated weapon blisters fought on while they were obviously cut off from the rest of the ship. It was a pounded tangle of wreckage, and it had destroyed two interceptors, crippled two more, and kept fighting.

Finally, it drifted away, under feeble jets of power. Two more of the fantastic rebel fleet wandered into action, but the wing commander's horrified eyes were on the first pile of scrap. It was going *somewhere*—

The ship neared the thin-skinned, unarmored, gleaming hospital vessel, rammed it amidships, square in one of the red crosses, and then blew itself up, apparently with everything left in its powder magazine, taking the hospital ship with it.

The sickened wing commander would never have recognized what he had seen as it was told in a later version, thus:

> *"The crushing course they took*
> *And nobly knew*
> *Their death undaunted*

By heroic blast
The hospital's host
They dragged to doom
Hail! Men without mercy
From the far frontier!"

Lunar relay flickered out as overloaded fuses flashed into vapor. Arris distractedly paced back to the dark corner and sank into a chair.

"I'm sorry," said the voice of Glen next to him, sounding quite sincere. "No doubt it was quite a shock to you."

"Not to you?" asked Arris bitterly.

"Not to me."

"Then how did they do it?" the wing commander asked the civilian in a low, desperate whisper. "They don't even wear .45's. Intelligence says their enlisted men have hit their officers and got away with it. They *elect* ship captains! Glen, what does it all mean?"

"It means," said the fat little man with a timbre of doom in his voice, "that they've returned. They always have. They always will. You see, commander, there is always somewhere a wealthy, powerful city, or nation, or world. In it are those whose blood is not right for a wealthy, powerful place. They must seek danger and overcome it. So they go out—on the marshes, in the desert, on the tundra, the planets, or the stars. Being strong, they grow stronger by fighting the tundra, the planets or the stars. They—they change. They sing new songs. They know new heroes. And then, one day, they return to their old home.

"They return to the wealthy, powerful city, or nation or world. They fight its guardians as they fought the tundra, the planets or the stars—a way that strikes terror to the heart. Then they sack the city, nation or world and sing great, ringing sagas of their deeds. They always have. Doubtless they always will."

"But what shall we do?"

"We shall cower, I suppose, beneath the bombs they drop on us, and we shall die, some bravely, some not, defending the palace within a very few hours. But you will have your revenge."

"How?" asked the wing commander, with haunted eyes.

The fat little man giggled and whispered in the officer's ear. Arris irritably shrugged it off as a bad joke. He didn't believe it. As he died, drilled through the chest a few hours later by one of Algan's gunfighters, he believed it even less.

∾   ∾   ∾

The professor's lecture was drawing to a close. There was time for only one more joke to send his students away happy. He was about to spring it when a messenger handed him two slips of paper. He raged inwardly at his ruined exit and poisonously read from them:

"I have been asked to make two announcements. One, a bulletin from General Sleg's force. He reports that the so-called Outland Insurrection is being brought under control and that there is no cause for alarm. Two, the gentlemen who are members of the S.O.T.C. will please report to the armory at 1375 hours—whatever that may mean—for blaster inspection. The class is dismissed."

Petulantly, he swept from the lectern and through the door.

Trigger Tide

by Wyman Guin

PREFACE BY DAVID DRAKE
I first read "Trigger Tide" when I was fourteen. I didn't understand it, but I *almost* understood it. The work stood on its own as an action/adventure story, but it held an assumption about how the world, the universe, worked that I couldn't quite grasp.

I've reread the story a number of times since then, including its original appearance the October 1950 *Astounding* (with Guin using the pseudonym Norman Menasco). Often reading a story in its original context will bring it into a different focus. That was true of "Trigger Tide," but I still don't think I quite understand it.

Neither have I ever gotten "Trigger Tide" out of my mind. That's why it's here.

That first day and night I lay perfectly still. I was often conscious but there was no thought of moving. I breathed shallowly.

In midmorning of the second day I began to feel the ants and flies that swarmed in the cake of mud, blood and festering flesh I was wearing for clothes. Then, through the morning mists of its tiny sixth planet that giant white sun slammed down on me.

I had been able to see something of the surroundings before they began working me over. After they had taken the hood off my head and while they were stripping away my clothes and harness of power equipment, the first orbit moon—the little fast, pale green one—shot up out of the blue-black sea. I had been able to tell in its light that we were on a tide shelf, probably the third.

Now burnt, lashed and clubbed I lay face down in the quick growing weeds of the hot tide shelf. The weeds were beginning to crawl against my face in the breathless air and dimly I realized a moon must be rising.

It had been the predawn of the tenth day of period thirty-six when the two of them stepped out of an aircar on Quartz Street and the girl I was walking home to the Great Island Hotel turned me over to them. If it was true that I had been lying here that day and night and this was the next midmorning, and if this was the third shelf, there would soon be a tide washing over me.

That tide was not easy to calculate. That it could be figured out is a tribute to the way they drill information into you before you leave The Central on an assignment. But the most thorough textbook knowledge of a planet's conditions is thin stuff when you are actually there and have to *know* them better than the natives. I tried the calculation all over again with that great sun frying my skull and got the same answer.

In about an hour the big fifth orbit moon and the sun would be overhead. The equally big third orbit moon would be slightly behind. Together they would lift the sea onto the third shelf all through this latitude.

The kind of day it was these tides would come up smoothly and steadily. Through the buzzing of flies I could not hear the sea. That did not mean it was not a hundred feet away lapping rapidly higher on the third sea wall.

I lay perfectly still except for my shallow breathing and waited for the sea.

When the water came over me in a shall rush I strangled. Quickly, I refused to move. The water rushed over me again and again softening the clotted mud that had kept me from oozing to death. Finally when the surf receded it was still about me and I had to try moving.

I got to my knees and set to work with my right hand to get some vision. With the sea now washing higher about me I finally got the clot from my right eye and achieved a blurred view of daylight.

You have to have at least some luck. When you run out of it altogether you are dead. The fourth sea wall was about fifty yards away and looked as though a normal man could make it quite easily. How I made it was another story. I could barely use my legs and the left arm was useless. All the time I was reopening my wounds on the quartzcar formations of the sea wall.

That quartzcar is not like the familiar coral that forms some of the islands of Earth. It is made up from quartz particles that are suspended in the ocean water. It is a concretion in an intricate lattice which small crustacea pile up in regular patterns. The animals build their quartzcar islands from the quartz dust that rises in tidal rhythms off the floor of the shallow planetary sea. Consequently the islands come in layers with tide shelves that correspond to the height of various lunar tides.

The only land on that planet is the countless archipelagoes of quartzcar. On the sea walls or when you dig it up it presents a fine rasplike face that opened my wounds and left me bleeding and gasping with pain when I reached the top.

That afternoon I was not unconscious. I slept. It was dark when I awakened. Then slowly, magnificently it was light again as the fifth orbit moon rose over the sea, a great ball of electric blue. Only a short time later the little chartreuse first moon came rocketing up to catch and finally, a shade to the south, to pass the larger body on its own quick trip to the zenith.

Back at The Central the "white haired boys," the psychostatisticians, can tell you all about why people get into wars. If they had not been right about every assignment they had plotted for me, I would never have lived to get beat up on this one. Sometimes their anthropoquations give very complex answers. Sometimes, as in the case of these people, the answer is simple. It was so simple in this case that it read like Twentieth Century newspaper propaganda. But lying there looking out into the glorious sky I didn't believe in wars. There never had been any. There never would be any. Surely they would close The Central and I could stay there forever watching the great moons roll across the galaxy.

I reawakened with a sharpened sense of urgency. I got to my feet. There was *going* to be a war if I didn't get on with the assignment. The fine part about this job was everyone wanted it "hush." The ideal performance for a Central Operator is, of course, to hit a planet, get the business over with and get out without anyone ever guessing you were doing anything but buying curios. Generally those you're up against try to throw you into public light—a bad light. These boys wanted it hush much worse than I did. It gave me a certain advantage tactically. I will not say the mess I had got myself into was part of my plan. But they were going to scramble at the sight of their mayhem walking back into the city.

I had to skirt half the city to reach my contact and a safe place to heal. To make it before morning I had to take advantage of every moment of moonlight.

After about half my journey I had a long wait in the dark before the fourth orbit moon came up and I was able to move ahead. I was skirting the city very close through the fern tree forest but, except for an occasional house and couples necking in aircars idling low over the fronds, I had little to worry about.

Toward morning the only light was the second brief flight of the tiny first moon and the going was much slower. But at least while it was up alone the vegetation did not move about so much. I finished the last lap to my Contact staggering and dangerously in broad daylight.

He didn't say anything when he opened the door of his cottage. He didn't show surprise or hesitate too long either. He led me in carefully and put me down on a bed.

Part of the time he was working on me I slept and part of the time I was wide awake gasping. It would have been just about as bad as when they worked me over except that he used some drugs and I knew he was trying to put me together instead of take me apart.

Then at last I slept undisturbed—that day and the next night. When I awoke he was still there staring down at me with no expression on his face.

It was the first time I had tried to form words with my mashed mouth. I finally got out, "How did you recognize me? You'd only seen me normal once."

I got two shocks in rapid succession. He said, "I'm awfully sorry about your eye."

It flashed over me that this man had gone sour as an Operator. No Central Operator is ever sorry for anything. Certainly no one ever says so when you've had "bad luck."

I got the second shock and pulled myself up from the bed. I searched the blurred room till I made out a mirror and went to it without his help. It was only then I realized they had put out one of my eyes.

I don't know whether it was just fury and determination to heal fast or whether he was right that there is some mysterious influence on that planet that accelerates healing. It took me only about three weeks to get back to the point where I felt I was in shape to tackle them again. The bones in my arm knitted very well and it was surprising how fast the burns healed.

He knew a lot about that planet, this Operator. He couldn't stop asking questions about it. What made the vegetation move when a moon was up? Why did the animal life, including men, slow its activity at the same time? The only question it seemed he hadn't asked was why he, an Operator for The Central, had adopted one of the major habits of the planet he had been assigned to. He wouldn't move while there was a conjunction of moons at zenith. Instead he criticized me for exercising my scarred legs while a moon was up. You'd think it would have reminded him that being inactive at such times was only a planetary habit.

It was impossible to question him along a consistent vein. He would start talking about their organization and end wondering about the possible influences on human behavior of subtle rhythms in gravity. He would open a conjecture about the daily habits of their Leader and it would end a theory on the psychology of island cultures. His long expressionless horseface would turn to me and he would conclude with something like, "You know, Herman Melville was right about the sea. It is not a vista but a background. People living on it experience mostly in a foreground."

Every Operator for The Central has at times to think profoundly about such things and be equipped better than average to do so. You can't deal effectively with the variegated human cultures now scattered far out into the galaxy without being neatly sensitive to the psychological influences of landscape, flora, climate, ancestry and planetary neighbors.

But at present I had a much blunter assignment. I had to reach a carefully protected man I had seen only in photographs. I had to reach him in the shortest possible time and kill him. Now, the worse luck of all, my only Contact had "taken root."

It happened every day of course. Psychostatistically it was inevitable. A fine Operator hit a planet where he began to take an emotional interest. He adopted quite seriously one or more of the major habits of the natives. This man had reached the next stage where his emotional interest in his new-found "home" dominated his finely drilled ties to The Central. In his case it had taken only a standard month and a half. In fact it had not been visible a month ago when the pilot of my tiny space shuttle dropped me off in the dark at his cottage. I finally realized the only thing I could get from him now was a rehearsal of the story he had told me that night before I walked alone into the strange city.

But I delayed asking him to retell his story. An odd thing happened. It happened just as I was about to ask him to go into town and buy me a set of the local power equipment. We were on our usual morning walk through the fern woods. Naturally he had refused to exercise until the passing of the second orbit moon. That had irritated me. I was on the verge of spitting out that I was wasting time and would be on my way as soon as he could run into town and buy me the local harness.

There in the middle of the path lay my own power equipment—the harness they had stripped off with my clothes down on the tide shelf three weeks before. If they had only left this harness on me, I would have been able to antigrav my way over the fourth sea wall instead of frictioning my way up on peeling flesh. I knew the harness and helmet on sight. I picked it up and I was certain. The hair at the back of my neck stirred.

I didn't say anything and he was still enough of an Operator not to ask. We both knew it was no accident.

Back at the cottage I spent the rest of the day and most of the night checking that harness of power equipment. There was absolutely nothing wrong with it that I could find. The radio, sending and receiving, was in perfect order both on inspection and when I check-called to my ship waiting on the second orbit moon. The arms, both the microsplosive for killing single targets and the heavy 0.5 Kg. demolition pistol were as they had been when on my person. The antigravity mechanism and its neatly built-in turbojet, part by part, under X-ray and on the fine balance he used for assaying quartzcar specimens, was an unblemished complexity. Again, when the equipment's own X-ray was turned on its tiny "field-isolated" radioactive pile, no flaw could be seen. Naturally that was something of which I couldn't be sure. Something that I couldn't detect with these instruments might have been done to that tiny power pile at the subatomic level. The X-ray diffraction patterns were O.K. but—why did they want me to have my own harness? What reason outside the harness?

I had reduced to a simple question about its nuclear fission pile that highly multiple question, "Has this power equipment been tampered with?" I would have to gamble for the rest of the answer and it was worth the gamble. An Operator's power equipment is the best in the galaxy. From what I had seen of the equipment worn on this planet it was definitely second rate.

It was nearly morning but he was still sitting in a corner, his long melancholy face buried in the local books on quartzcar. One of them was titled in the native language, "The Planetary Evolution of Quartzcar." Well, it was not considered desertion to lose all interest in his assignment and all ties with The Central. It was just an occupational disease.

"You know," he said, suddenly standing up and walking to the greenish darkness of the window, "there are several piezoelectric substances."

"Yes," I answered. I was busy putting the intricate crystal plates back into the atomic fission pile.

"Quartz, of course, is one of them."

"Yes."

"You know how a piezoelectric substance behaves?"

I was annoyed. The job of slipping the countless delicate crystal plates back into the pile was exacting. "Well," I said without bothering to cover sarcasm, "why don't you tell me all about it. I got through physics on a fluke."

By the galaxy, he took me seriously. He stood there staring out at the fern forest and talked earnestly about electroelastic crystals like I was a first-year physics student.

"These substances convert electrical to mechanical energy and vice versa. You know how the old-fashioned phonograph pickup worked?"

I didn't pay any attention to him.

"The needle was activated by grooved impressions in a record by previous sounds. In the pickup device this needle pressed against a piezoelectric substance. Its mechanical movement against the crystal set up corresponding electrical discharges from it to the speaker." I was silent working on the pile. I decided that if he said, "You know" again I would get up and poke him. "You know," he continued, "every island on this planet is constructed from quartz—a piezoelectric substance."

I didn't get up and poke him. I continued to stare at the harness but I stopped working on it. He went right on without turning. "These constructions of quartz are subjected to rhythmic mechanical stress when the lunar tides pile up against them."

He was a capable man or he would not have been an Operator in the first place. That a man "took root" on some planet and became absolutely untrustworthy as an Operator did not mean he was not still a brilliant and sincere man. This one was obviously trying to solve a serious problem and doing well at it. I looked up with a new respect and he turned from the window.

He couldn't help smiling and I had to admit he had slipped one over on me. He said, "You see, it could be that these quartzcar islands generate an electric field as the tides press on them. The strange blind movement of some of the vegetative forms could be a response stimulated by that electric field. The cessation of animal movement could be a safeguarding adaptation preventing disease which might develop when strenuous activity is pursued in the presence of such fields."

I couldn't help grinning. I had been blindly driving ahead because the assignment was urgent and I had missed all this.

"I realize," he continued, "that I have taken root but I think it is important that I was trying to solve the defeat of our first operation when I first took up the question of quartzcar."

"You know," I interrupted, "they treated me just as they treated your group—just as you described it to me that first night. They left me absolutely alone—no interference at all. I knew I was asking for it when I overplayed my hand. But I had to do something to get action. Up to then it was like working in a vacuum. You wouldn't have guessed there was a Party. There was no sign of them. It was only by boring in with the full intention of killing the Leader if I wasn't stopped that I finally forced them to show."

"Yes, that's how it was with us," he agreed. "Not one of the six of us met any interference until in a period of thirty seconds in various parts of the city two crashed from heights as though the antigravs had suddenly failed, two were blown to bits and one just simply died while walking through the rotunda of the Government Building where he was supposed to create a divergence in ten seconds.

"But why did they spare me? Was it because taking a shower was so innocent? If they could so neatly blow the whole plot wide open just at the moment it was climaxing they must have realized my part in it. They must have known I was innocently occupied taking a shower only because it was not my moment to be in action.

"Within seventy seconds their Leader would have been dead. Instead five of us were dead. It took me a long time to figure out that that was not due to a lot of concerted planning on their part. They had known it was going to happen at a certain time with no help from them. They knew *when* we were going into action and knew *therefore* that we would fail due to some calculable force.

It wasn't necessary for them to interfere if we didn't plan to act before a certain time."

I nodded. "And I got what was coming to me because I went into action before they could calculate my defeat. Well, then the quicker I try again the better. I'm going in this morning." He almost volunteered to go with me.

Back in the city my mutilated face created attention. When I antigraved onto the sixth floor balconade of the Great Island Hotel people at nearby tables of the open-air restaurant turned to stare and turned quickly away. The table I had hoped for was unoccupied. I took it facing away from most of them so I could see the entertainment stage. Beyond the stage, as it was viewed from this point, were the antigrav tubes of the hotel. They were transparent and in them people rose to the upper floors or descended to the street without need of harness such as I was wearing.

The waiter came and took my order for a drink. He didn't recognize me, yet he and I had had a joke once about that drink.

My watch said it should be only a few minutes before she would be on the stage singing quiet little songs. It was on this stage that their Leader had first seen her. His only overt human quality was an interest in tall lanky women. He liked them at least eight inches taller than himself. This one he had promptly moved from the artists' and actors' quarters of the city to a penthouse atop the Great Island Hotel.

Presently the string trio she used for a background came out and lounged about the potted trees on the stage. They warmed up with a few dolorous little melodies. Beyond the stage the antigrav tubes were crowded. In one of them a tragic waterfall of humanity descended to the street level. In the other people drifted upward. Occasionally a person or couple in more casual ascent hesitated as they passed the restaurant and decided to come in for a drink.

The string trio started another number and she walked gracefully out onto the informal stage. She smiled on her audience with a possessive warmth that was half her popularity. Then she began singing in a husky, unmusical but dramatic voice. She was a beautiful girl all right but my attention was suddenly diverted.

I recognized the short scrawny one immediately—the big man when he spoke. "Say, I never thought we'd see you again. Mind if we sit down?" He waited politely.

I motioned to the chairs. "Say," he chuckled, closer to my face, "we sure did a beautiful job on you, didn't we?"

"Yes," I agreed, "I owe you both a great deal."

He had a big hearty laugh. "Well," he gasped between guffaws, "no hard feelings, I hope."

"I'm very objective. I understand it was all in a day's work."

"Sure," he said solemnly. "Let us buy you a drink." The waiter had come up.

I shrugged at my glass. "I'll have the same. There's no strychnine in it."

That set him off again. "Say," he burbled, "you're a card. You know when I first took a shine to you?"

I declared I couldn't imagine when it might have been.

"When I broke your arm. You really took it like a man. Didn't he take it well, Shorty?"

The little man wasn't saying anything. He was making his good-humored grin do as his contribution.

"Well, here's to your health." The big man raised his glass the minute the waiter set it down.

I drank with them and we sat in silence listening to her song until he called the waiter over for another round.

"Yes, sir," he exclaimed when it had arrived. "I sure never expected to see you again."

"Oh, you knew I got off the tide shelf. That's why you planted my power harness so I'd find it." That took the humor out of his eyes.

"I don't get you," he said in a level voice. The little guy had stopped grinning.

I explained about finding my power harness on our path in the fern forest.

"I think," he said with finality, "some animal dragged it up there. We left it on the tide shelf." There was ice in his eyes.

"That could be," I said, knowing it could not be.

"Waiter," he called, "bring us another drink."

Well, they had me and they weren't letting me go. I was going to have to sit quietly in the public restaurant of the Great Island Hotel and get drunk without making a scene.

It was getting on to noon and there was a big moon hitting its zenith. Activity in the restaurant was beginning to slow and there were fewer people in the antigrav tubes. She was singing her last number backing off stage with the trio.

I looked at the big man and his scrawny companion. There was one good solid reason why they had suddenly showed up and why they were gluing themselves to me. The Leader was up above in his Great Island Hotel penthouse waiting to spend the luncheon with his long lanky beauty.

How long would the siesta last? I wasn't very far into that thought when I came up with a start and my hand stopped in the act of putting down my glass. They both glanced at me.

All five moons were going to be overhead at noon. They would lift the sea onto the fourth tide shelf. That was the biggest tide and it was rare. I calculated the last time it had happened was over a standard month and a half ago. If my sudden guess was right, the healthiest place for a Central Operator at that time would be in the shower.

"What's the matter," the big man asked in a monotone. "You worried about something? You afraid you're stuck in bad company? Don't worry. We just want to have a couple more drinks with you and then we have to leave . . . in a hurry."

"Thanks. I'll sit the next one out. I want to have a little talk with that singer." I stood up and he grabbed my arm, the one he hadn't had any practice breaking.

"I wouldn't do that if I were you." He tightened down on the arm. But my advantage was the secrecy they needed.

"You wouldn't want a scene, would you?" I shook my arm loose. People were beginning to take notice and he sat quietly glaring at me.

I beat it through the stage door and back to her dressing room. I stepped in without knocking. She looked up startled from where she stood buckling a belt to her lounging shorts. She didn't recognize me and she didn't like me.

"Get out of here."

"You remember me," I soothed. "Three weeks ago you and I were regular pals. One night you went so far as to introduce me to a couple of special friends of yours in an aircar down there on the street."

She was genuinely horrified and began backing away. I walked toward her. "You thought they were going to kill me, didn't you?"

She nodded dumbly. Then, "For the Leader—" and automatically remembering another Party slogan, "for Planetary Security."

"You didn't know they were just going to torture me?"

She shook her head piteously almost imploringly—a little provincial girl caught in something bigger and uglier than she had dreamed.

"And leaving me alive to come back and ask you questions?

Admitting the pleasure they took in how badly I would suffer when I regained consciousness how could they afford to take the chance of leaving me alive?"

"Because you will die anyway." There was an abrupt personal fright on her face. She raised her hands with the palms outthrust as though pushing the sight of me away.

I thought I saw something move at the open window and changed my position in the room backing from her. She was almost wailing, "You will die now . . . the tide . . . it's almost—"

One thing they weren't taking chances with was that I might radio her answer off the planet.

The scrawny devil popped up from where he had been antigraving at the window and the microsplosive he put in her chest made her dead throat shriek as the long beautiful legs crumpled to the floor. I blew his head off while her glaring face sank before me. His body spun but antigraved where it was till I got to the window to haul it in.

From somewhere above the big guy fired at me as I yanked the body in and took the harness. I peeled out of my own power equipment and threw it in a corner and got out of the room. In a washroom down the hall I adjusted the little guy's harness to fit me. As I stepped out into the hall again there was a shattering explosion from her dressing room. I had got rid of that harness one hundred twenty seconds soon enough.

There was one spot the big hoodlum wouldn't be looking for me. I went right back to my table in the restaurant. There was, of course, no activity or conversation between the few who had stayed at their tables during the high tide. People sat in silence and seemingly asleep waiting for the moons to pass. I knew from experience that in that condition they would resist hearing my voice. I kept it low and held the radio pickup of the harness close to my lips.

After some hunting around due to unfamiliar controls I made contact with my ship on the second moon. I told them where and when to pick me up. "Now," I said, "in case I don't make it get this down: Piezoelectric islands generate field in response to lunar tides. At highest tide this vibrates the field generating crystals of the fission pile in Operator's harness. Under interfering frequencies radioactives jar to critical mass and explode. Local harnesses do not react."

I was just leaving the table preparing to antigrav outside the building to where that penthouse hung in the mists fifty floors up when I saw my Contact racing toward me.

"I've come to help . . . I guess I still—"

"Get out of your harness. Throw it over the edge of the balcony."

He didn't ask questions. He hurried to the edge unfastening the harness. But from up in the mist they opened fire on him and he never took the harness off. He refastened it and antigraved swiftly up into the mist firing ahead of him with the heavy 0.5 Kg. demolition pistol set for proximity explosions.

That was quick thinking. Up there they might be antigraving alongside the building or they might be firing from windows and the unconfined proximity explosion was more likely to get both.

I followed him as fast as I could with the weaker harness I was wearing. I pulled out farther from the building to back his fire. We had both dropped the infrared viewers out of our helmets but in that mist they weren't much good. The mob above was having the same trouble and we were moving targets, hopeless for proximity fire. Our guns laid a sheet of flame high up on the building.

I believe he was hit but not killed on the way up. He seemed to stagger in his swerving ascent. But immediately their vantage came into view—a balcony surrounding the penthouse. Our fire had driven them back a few feet and he antigraved like a streak up over the edge.

There was a blinding flash and I reached the roof garden to find the mob of them dead in the explosion that had disintegrated him. One whole wall of the penthouse had been blown in. I leaped through this wreckage. The big man—the man I owed so much—was getting to his feet. Apparently he and two others with him had been guarding the door beyond. He looked surprised when he saw me. He must have thought till now it had been I who blew up out in the garden.

I slammed a target-set 0.5 Kg. demolition shell into them. It also blew the door apart. Across the room beyond their surprised Leader was sinking into the antigrav tube. He fired quickly and wildly and I fired a microsplosive from my left hand.

I thought I saw the shot get him but I dashed to the antigrav tube to make sure. Past shocked tenants who had rushed into the tube to escape the explosion-wracked upper floors his headless body lolled its way. The body, unmistakable in the distinctive white uniform he always wore, drifted down the tube stirring as it went a swelling murmur.

The psychostatisticians back at The Central get my vote as the "white haired boys." This was the first time in two hundred standard years that their anthropoquations had described one man and his lieutenant as the "cause" of a war movement. Generally the picture they turn up as "casualty" in a war is spiny with factors and it takes an army of Operators to cover all the angles. This time they had come out a little shamefacedly and said, "It looks like old-fashioned newspaper thinking but for once it's a fact. Get that one man and there will be no war."

As I leaned over the "down" antigrav in the Great Island Hotel his body drifted to oblivion. The murmur rising from the viewers had horror in it. But there was also an unmistakable note of relief. Finally, from far below, someone asked, "Did they get the rest of them?"

The Aliens

by Murray Leinster

PREFACE BY ERIC FLINT

I'll have more to say about Murray Leinster in my afterword to this story. By way of preface, though, I just want to explain why I chose this story for the anthology. I wanted something by Leinster, and, specifically, I wanted one of the "first contact" stories for which he was so justly famous in his day and which I can remember being enthralled by as a teenager.

The obvious choice, of course, was the story that gave us the name itself: "First Contact," originally published in *Astounding* magazine in May of 1945.

But . . . that story has been anthologized over twenty times since then, and it wasn't the only one Leinster wrote. There's at least one other which is just as good, and has almost never been included in an anthology.

Here it is.

At 04 hours 10 minutes, ship time, the *Niccola* was well inside the Theta Gisol solar system. She had previously secured excellent evidence that this was not the home of the Plumie civilization. There was no tuned radiation. There was no evidence of interplanetary travel—rockets would be more than obvious, and a magnetronic drive had a highly characteristic radiation-pattern—so the real purpose of the *Niccola*'s voyage would not be accomplished here. She wouldn't find out where Plumies came from.

There might, though, be one or more of those singular, conical, hollow-topped cairns sheltering silicon-bronze plates, which constituted the evidence that Plumies existed. The *Niccola* went sunward toward the inner planets to see. Such cairns had been found on conspicuous landmarks on oxygen-type planets over a range of some twelve hundred light-years. By the vegetation about them, some were a century old. On the same evidence, others had been erected only months or weeks or even days before a human Space Survey ship arrived to discover them. And the situation was unpromising. It wasn't likely that the galaxy was big enough to hold two races of rational beings capable of space travel. Back on ancient Earth, a planet had been too small to hold two races with tools and fire. Historically, that problem was settled when *Homo sapiens* exterminated *Homo Neanderthalis*. It appeared that the same situation had arisen in space. There were humans, and there were Plumies. Both had interstellar ships. To humans, the fact was alarming. The need for knowledge, and the danger that Plumies might know more first, and thereby be able to exterminate humanity, was appalling.

Therefore the *Niccola*. She drove on sunward. She had left one frozen outer planet far behind. She had crossed the orbits of three others. The last of these was a gas giant with innumerable moonlets revolving about it. It was now some thirty millions of miles back and twenty to one side. The sun, ahead, flared and flamed in emptiness against that expanse of tinted stars.

Jon Baird worked steadily in the *Niccola*'s radar room. He was one of those who hoped that the Plumies would not prove to be the natural enemies of mankind. Now, it looked like this ship wouldn't find out in this solar system. There were plenty of other ships on the hunt. From here on, it looked like routine to the next unvisited family of planets. But meanwhile he worked. Opposite him, Diane Holt worked as steadily, her dark head bent intently over a radar graph in formation. The immediate job was the completion of a map of the meteor swarms following cometary orbits about this sun. They interlaced emptiness with hazards to navigation, and nobody would try to drive through a solar system without such a map.

Elsewhere in the ship, everything was normal. The engine room was a place of stillness and peace, save for the almost inaudible hum of the drive, running at half a million Gauss flux-density. The skipper did whatever skippers do when they are invisible to their subordinates. The weapons officer, Taine, thought appropriate thoughts. In the navigation room the second officer conscientiously glanced at each separate instrument at least once in each five minutes, and then carefully surveyed all the screens showing space outside the ship. The stewards disposed of the debris of the last meal, and began to get ready for the next. In the crew's quarters, those off duty read or worked at scrimshaw, or simply and contentedly loafed.

Diane handed over the transparent radar graph, to be fitted into the three-dimensional map in the making.

"There's a lump of stuff here," she said interestedly. "It could be the comet that once followed this orbit, now so old it's lost all its gases and isn't a comet any longer."

At this instant, which was 04 hours 25 minutes ship time, the alarm-bell rang. It clanged stridently over Baird's head, repeater-gongs sounded all through the ship, and there was a scurrying and a closing of doors. The alarm gong could mean only one thing. It made one's breath come faster or one's hair stand on end, according to temperament.

The skipper's face appeared on the direct-line screen from the navigation room.

"*Plumies?*" he demanded harshly. "*Mr. Baird! Plumies?*"

Baird's hands were already flipping switches and plugging the radar room apparatus into a new setup.

"There's a contact, sir," he said curtly. "No. There was a contact. It's broken now. Something detected us. We picked up a radar pulse. One."

The word "one" meant much. A radar system that could get adequate information from a single pulse was not the work of amateurs. It was the product of a very highly developed technology. Setting all equipment to full-globular scanning, Baird felt a certain crawling sensation at the back of his neck. He'd been mapping within a narrow range above and below the line of this system's ecliptic. A lot could have happened outside the area he'd had under long-distance scanning.

But seconds passed. They seemed like years. The all-globe scanning covered every direction out from the *Niccola*. Nothing appeared which had not been reported before. The gas-giant planet far behind, and the only inner one on this side of the sun, which return their pulses only after minutes. Meanwhile the radars reported very faithfully, but they only repeated previous reports.

"No new object within half a million miles," said Baird, after a suitable interval. Presently he added: "Nothing new within three-quarter million miles." Then: "Nothing new within a million miles . . ."

The skipper said bitingly:

"*Then you'd better check on objects that are not new!*" He turned aside, and his voice came more faintly as he spoke into another microphone. "*Mr. Taine! Arm all rockets and have your tube crews stand by in combat readiness! Engine room! Prepare drive for emergency maneuvers! Damage-control parties, put on pressure suits and take combat posts with equipment!*" His voice rose again in volume. "*Mr. Baird! How about observed objects?*"

Diane murmured. Baird said briefly:

"Only one suspicious object, sir—and that shouldn't be suspicious. We are sending an information-beam at something we'd classed as a burned-out comet. Pulse going out now, sir."

Diane had the distant-information transmitter aimed at what she'd said might be a dead comet. Baird pressed the button. An extraordinary complex of information-seeking frequencies and forms sprang into being and leaped across emptiness. There were microwaves of strictly standard amplitude, for measurement-standards. There were frequencies of other values, which would be selectively absorbed by this material and that. There were laterally and circularly polarized beams. When they bounced back, they would bring a surprising amount of information.

They returned. They did bring back news. The thing that had registered as a larger lump in a meteor swarm was not a meteor at all. It returned four different frequencies with a relative-intensity pattern which said that they'd been reflected by bronze—probably silicon bronze. The polarized beams came back depolarized, of course, but with phase-changes which said the reflector had a rounded, regular form. There was a smooth hull of silicon bronze out yonder. There was other data.

"It will be a Plumie ship, sir," said Baird very steadily. "At a guess, they picked up our mapping beam and shot a single pulse at us to find out who and what we were. For another guess, by now they've picked up and analyzed our information-beam and know what we've found out about them."

The skipper scowled.

"*How many of them?*" he demanded. "*Have we run into a fleet?*"

"I'll check, sir," said Baird. "We picked up no tuned radiation from outer space, sir, but it could be that they picked us up when we came out of overdrive and stopped all their transmissions until they had us in a trap."

"*Find out how many there are!*" barked the skipper. "*Make it quick! Report additional data instantly!*"

His screen clicked off. Diane, more than a little pale, worked swiftly to plug the radar-room equipment into a highly specialized pattern. The *Niccola* was very well equipped, radarwise. She'd been a type G8 Survey ship, and on her last stay in port she'd been rebuilt especially to hunt for and make contact with Plumies. Since the discovery of their existence, that was the most urgent business of the Space Survey. It might well be the most important business of the human race—on which its survival or destruction would depend. Other remodeled ships had gone out before the *Niccola*, and others would follow until the problem was solved. Meanwhile the *Niccola*'s twenty-four rocket tubes and stepped-up drive and computer-type radar system equipped her for Plumie-hunting as well as any human ship could be. Still, if she'd been lured deep into the home system of the Plumies, the prospects were not good.

The new setup began its operation, instantly the last contact closed. The three-dimensional map served as a matrix to control it. The information-beam projector swung and flung out its bundle of oscillations. It swung and flashed. It had to examine every relatively nearby object for a constitution of silicon bronze and a rounded shape. The nearest objects had to be examined first. Speed was essential. But three-dimensional scanning takes time, even at some hundreds of pulses per minute.

Nevertheless, the information came in. No other silicon-bronze object within a quarter-million miles. Within half a million. A million. A million and a half. Two million . . .

Baird called the navigation room.

"Looks like a single Plumie ship, sir," he reported. "At least there's one ship which is nearest by a very long way."

"*Hah!*" grunted the skipper. "*Then we'll pay him a visit. Keep an open line, Mr. Baird!*" His voice changed. "*Mr. Taine! Report here at once to plan tactics!*"

Baird shook his head, to himself. The *Niccola*'s orders were to make contact without discovery, if such a thing were possible. The ideal would be a Plumie ship or the Plumie civilization itself, located and subject to complete and overwhelming envelopment by human ships—before the Plumies knew they'd been discovered.

And this would be the human ideal because humans have always had to consider that a stranger might be hostile, until he'd proven otherwise.

Such a viewpoint would not be optimism, but caution. Yet caution was necessary. It was because the Survey brass felt the need to prepare for every unfavorable eventuality that Taine had been chosen as weapons officer of the *Niccola*. His choice had been deliberate, because he was a xenophobe. He had been a problem personality all his life. He had a seemingly congenital fear and hatred of strangers—which in mild cases is common enough, but Taine could not be cured without a complete breakdown of personality. He could not serve on a ship with a multiracial crew, because he was invincibly suspicious of and hostile to all but his own small breed. Yet he seemed ideal for weapons officer on the *Niccola*, provided he never commanded the ship. Because *if* the Plumies were hostile, a well-adjusted, normal man would never think as much like them as a Taine. He was capable of the kind of thinking Plumies might practice, if they were xenophobes themselves.

But to Baird, so extreme a precaution as a known psychopathic condition in an officer was less than wholly justified. It was by no means certain that the Plumies would instinctively be hostile. Suspicious, yes. Cautious, certainly. But the only fact known about the Plumie civilization came from the cairns and silicon-bronze inscribed tablets they'd left on oxygen-type worlds over a twelve-hundred-light-year range in space, and the only thing to be deduced about the Plumies themselves came from the decorative, formalized symbols like feather plumes which were found on all their bronze tablets. The name "Plumies" came from that symbol.

Now, though, Taine was called to the navigation room to confer on tactics. The *Niccola* swerved and drove toward the object Baird identified as a Plumie ship. This was at 05 hours 10 minutes ship time. The human ship had a definite velocity sunward, of course. The Plumie ship had been concealed by the meteor swarm of a totally unknown comet. It was an excellent way to avoid observation. On the other hand, the *Niccola* had been mapping, which was bound to attract attention. Now each ship knew of the other's existence. Since the *Niccola* had been detected, she had to carry out orders and attempt a contact to gather information.

Baird verified that the *Niccola*'s course was exact for interception at her full-drive speed. He said in a flat voice:

"I wonder how the Plumies will interpret this change of course?

They know we're aware they're not a meteorite. But charging at them without even trying to communicate could look ominous. We could be stupid, or too arrogant to think of anything but a fight." He pressed the skipper's call and said evenly: "Sir, I request permission to attempt to communicate with the Plumie ship. We're ordered to try to make friends if we know we've been spotted."

Taine had evidently just reached the navigation room. His voice snapped from the speaker:

"*I advise against that, sir! No use letting them guess our level of technology!*"

Baird said coldly:

"They've a good idea already. We beamed them for data."

There was silence, with only the very faint humming sound which was natural in the ship in motion. It would be deadly to the nerves if there were absolute silence. The skipper grumbled:

"*Requests and advice! Dammit! Mr. Baird, you might wait for orders! But I was about to ask you to try to make contact through signals. Do so.*"

His speaker clicked off. Baird said:

"It's in our laps, Diane. And yet we have to follow orders. Send the first roll."

Diane had a tape threaded into a transmitter. It began to unroll through a pickup head. She put on headphones. The tapes began to transmit toward the Plumie. Back at base it had been reasoned that a pattern of clickings, plainly artificial and plainly stating facts known to both races, would be the most reasonable way to attempt to open contact. The tape sent a series of cardinal numbers—one to five. Then an addition table, from one plus one to five plus five. Then a multiplication table up to five times five. It was not startling intellectual information to be sent out in tiny clicks ranging up and down the radio spectrum. But it was orders.

Baird sat with compressed lips. Diane listened for a repetition of any of the transmitted signals, sent back by the Plumie. The speakers about the radar room murmured the orders given through all the ship. Radar had to be informed of all orders and activity, so it could check their results outside the ship. So Baird heard the orders for the engine room to be sealed up and the duty-force to get into pressure suits, in case the *Niccola* fought and was hulled. Damage-control parties reported themselves on post, in suits, with equipment ready. Then Taine's voice snapped: "*Rocket crews, arm even-numbered rockets with chemical explosive warheads. Leave odd-numbered rockets armed with atomics. Report back!*"

Diane strained her ears for possible re-transmission of the *Niccola*'s signals, which would indicate the Plumie's willingness to try conversation. But she suddenly raised her hand and pointed to the radar-graph instrument. It repeated the positioning of dots which were stray meteoric matter in the space between worlds in this system. What had been a spot—the Plumie ship—was now a line of dots. Baird pressed the button.

"Radar reporting!" he said curtly. "The Plumie ships is heading for us. I'll have relative velocity in ten seconds."

He heard the skipper swear. Ten seconds later the Doppler measurement became possible. It said the Plumie plunged toward the *Niccola* at miles per second. In half a minute it was tens of miles per second. There was no re-transmission of signals. The Plumie ship had found itself discovered. Apparently it considered itself attacked. It flung itself into a headlong dash for the *Niccola*.

Time passed—interminable time. The sun flared and flamed and writhed in emptiness. The great gas-giant planet rolled through space in splendid state, its moonlets spinning gracefully about its bulk. The oxygen-atmosphere planet to sunward was visible only as a crescent, but the mottlings on its lighted part changed as it revolved—seas and islands and continents receiving the sunlight as it turned. Meteor swarms, so dense in appearance on a radar screen, yet so tenuous in reality, floated in their appointed orbits with a seeming vast leisure.

The feel of slowness was actually the result of distance. Men have always acted upon things close by. Battles have always been fought within eye-range, anyhow. But it was actually 06 hours 35 minutes ship time before the two spacecraft sighted each other—more than two hours after they plunged toward a rendezvous.

The Plumie ship was a bright golden dot, at first. It decelerated swiftly. In minutes it was a rounded, end-on disk. Then it swerved lightly and presented an elliptical broadside to the *Niccola*. The *Niccola* was in full deceleration too, by then. The two ships came very nearly to a stop with relation to each other when they were hardly twenty miles apart—which meant great daring on both sides.

Baird heard the skipper grumbling:

"*Damned cocky!*" He roared suddenly: "*Mr. Baird! How've you made out in communicating with them?*"

"Not at all, sir," said Baird grimly. "They don't reply."

He knew from Diane's expression that there was no sound in

the headphones except the frying noise all main-sequence stars give out, and the infrequent thumping noises that come from gas-giant planets' lower atmospheres, and the Jansky-radiation hiss which comes from everywhere.

The skipper swore. The Plumie ship lay broadside to, less than a score of miles away. It shone in the sunlight. It acted with extraordinary confidence. It was as if it dared the *Niccola* to open fire.

Taine's voice came out of a speaker, harsh and angry:

"*Even-numbered tubes prepare to fire on command.*"

Nothing happened. The two ships floated sunward together, neither approaching nor retreating. But with every second, the need for action of some sort increased.

"*Mr. Baird!*" barked the skipper. "*This is ridiculous! There must be some way to communicate! We can't sit here glaring at each other forever! Raise them! Get some sort of acknowledgement!*"

"I'm trying," said Baird bitterly, "according to orders!"

But he disagreed with those orders. It was official theory that arithmetic values, repeated in proper order, would be the way to open conversation. The assumption was that any rational creature would grasp the idea that orderly signals were rational attempts to open communication.

But it had occurred to Baird that a Plumie might not see this point. Perception of order is not necessarily perception of information—in fact, quite the contrary. A message is a disturbance of order. A microphone does not transmit a message when it sends an unvarying tone. A message has to be unpredictable or it conveys no message. Orderly clicks, even if overheard, might seem to Plumies the result of methodically operating machinery. A race capable of interstellar flight was not likely to be interested or thrilled by exercises a human child goes through in kindergarten. They simply wouldn't seem meaningful at all.

But before he could ask permission to attempt to make talk in a more sophisticated fashion, voices exclaimed all over the ship. They came blurringly to the loud-speakers. "*Look at that!*" "*What's he do—*" "*Spinning like—*" From every place where there was a vision-plate on the *Niccola*, men watched the Plumie ship and babbled.

This was at 06 hours 50 minutes ship time.

The elliptical golden object darted into swift and eccentric motion. Lacking an object of known size for comparison, there was no scale. The golden ship might have been the size of an autumn leaf, and in fact its maneuvers suggested the heedless tumblings and scurrying of falling foliage. It fluttered in swift turns and somersaults and spinnings. There were weavings like the purposeful feints of boxers not yet come to battle. There were indescribably graceful swoops and loops and curving dashes like some preposterous dance in emptiness.

Taine's voice crashed out of a speaker:

"*All even-numbered rockets,*" he barked. "*Fire!*"

The skipper roared a countermand, but too late. The crunching, grunting sound of rockets leaving their launching tubes came before his first syllable was complete. Then there was silence while the skipper gathered breath for a masterpiece of profanity. But Taine snapped:

"*That dance was a sneak-up! The Plumie came four miles nearer while we watched!*"

Baird jerked his eyes from watching the Plumie. He looked at the master radar. It was faintly blurred with the fading lines of past gyrations, but the golden ship was much nearer the *Niccola* than it had been.

"Radar reporting," said Baird sickishly. "Mr. Taine is correct. The Plumie ship did approach us while it danced."

Taine's voice snarled:

"*Reload even numbers with chemical-explosive war heads. Then remove atomics from odd numbers and replace with chemicals. The range is too short for atomics.*"

Baird felt curiously divided in his own mind. He disliked Taine very much. Taine was arrogant and suspicious and intolerant even on the *Niccola*. But Taine had been right twice, now. The Plumie ship had crept closer by pure trickery. And it was right to remove atomic war heads from the rockets. They had a pure-blast radius of ten miles. To destroy the Plumie ship within twice that would endanger the *Niccola*—and leave nothing of the Plumie to examine afterward.

The Plumie ship must have seen the rocket flares, but it continued to dance, coming nearer and ever nearer in seemingly heedless and purposeless plungings and spinnings in star-speckled space. But suddenly there were racing, rushing trails of swirling vapor. Half the *Niccola's* port broadside plunged toward the golden ship. The fraction of a second later, the starboard half-dozen chemical-explosive rockets swung furiously around the ship's hull and streaked after their brothers. They moved in utterly silent, straight-lined ravening ferocity toward their target.

Baird thought irrelevantly of the vapor trails of an atmosphere-liner in the planet's upper air.

The ruled-line straightness of the first six rockets' course abruptly broke. One of them veered crazily out of control. It shifted to an almost right-angled course. A second swung wildly to the left. A third and fourth and fifth—The sixth of the first line of rockets made a great, sweeping turn and came hurtling back toward the *Niccola*. It was like a nightmare. Lunatic, erratic lines of sunlit vapor eeled before the background of all the stars in creation.

Then the second half-dozen rockets broke ranks, as insanely and irremediably as the first.

Taine's voice screamed out of a speaker, hysterical with fury:

"*Detonate! Detonate! They've taken over the rockets and are throwing 'em back at us! Detonate all rockets!*"

The heavens seemed streaked and laced with lines of expanding smoke. But now one plunging line erupted at its tip. A swelling globe of smoke marked its end. Another blew up. And another—

The *Niccola*'s rockets faithfully blew themselves to bits on command from the *Niccola*'s own weapons control. There was nothing else to be done with them. They'd been taken over in flight. They'd been turned and headed back toward their source. They'd have blasted the *Niccola* to bits but for their premature explosions.

There was a peculiar, stunned hush all through the *Niccola*. The only sound that came out of any speaker in the radar room was Taine's voice, high-pitched and raging, mouthing unspeakable hatred of the Plumies, whom no human being had yet seen.

Baird sat tense in the frustrated and desperate composure of the man who can only be of use while he is sitting still and keeping his head. The vision screen was now a blur of writhing mist, lighted by the sun and torn at by emptiness. There was luminosity where the ships had encountered each other. It was sunshine upon thin smoke. It was like the insanely enlarging head of a newborn comet, whose tail would be formed presently by light-pressure. The Plumie ship was almost invisible behind the unsubstantial stuff.

But Baird regarded his radar screens. Microwaves penetrated the mist of rapidly ionizing gases.

"Radar to navigation!" he said sharply. "The Plumie ship is still approaching, dancing as before!"

The skipper said with enormous calm:

"*Any other Plumie ships, Mr. Baird?*"

Diane interposed.

"No sign anywhere. I've been watching. This seems to be the only ship within radar range.

"We've time to settle with it, then," said the skipper. *"Mr. Taine, the Plumie ship is still approaching."*

Baird found himself hating the Plumies. It was not only that humankind was showing up rather badly, at the moment. It was that if the *Niccola* were destroyed the Plumie would carry news of the existence of humanity and of the tactics which worked to defeat them. The Plumies could prepare an irresistible fleet. Humanity could be doomed.

But he overheard himself saying bitterly:

"I wish I'd known this was coming, Diane. I . . . wouldn't have resolved to be strictly official, only, until we got back to base."

Her eyes widened. She looked startled. Then she softened.

"If . . . you mean that . . . I wish so too."

"It looks like they've got us," he admitted unhappily. "If they can take our rockets away from us—" Then his voice stopped. He said, "Hold everything!" and pressed the navigation-room button. He snapped: "Radar to navigation. It appears to take the Plumies several seconds to take over a rocket. They have to aim something—a pressor or tractor beam, most likely—and pick off each rocket separately. Nearly forty seconds was consumed in taking over all twelve of our rockets. At shorter range, with less time available, a rocket might get through!"

The skipper swore briefly. Then:

"Mr. Taine! When the Plumies are near enough, our rockets may strike before they can be taken over! You follow?"

Baird heard Taine's shrill-voiced acknowledgment—in the form of practically chattered orders to his rocket-tube crews. Baird listened, checking the orders against what the situation was as the radars saw it. Taine's voice was almost unhuman; so filled with frantic rage that it cracked as he spoke. But the problem at hand was the fulfillment of all his psychopathic urges. He commanded the starboard-side rocket-battery to await special orders. Meanwhile the port-side battery would fire two rockets on widely divergent courses, curving to join at the Plumie ship. They'd be seized. They were to be detonated and another port-side rocket fired instantly, followed by a second hidden in the rocket-trail the first would leave behind. Then the starboard side—

"I'm afraid Taine's our only chance," said Baird reluctantly. "If he wins, we'll have time to . . . talk as people do who like each other. If it doesn't work—"

Diane said quietly:

"Anyhow . . . I'm glad you . . . wanted me to know. I . . . wanted you to know, too."

She smiled at him, yearningly.

There was the *crump-crump* of two rockets going out together. Then the radar told what happened. The Plumie ship was no more than six miles away, dancing somehow deftly in the light of a yellow sun, with all the cosmos spread out as shining pin points of colored light behind it. The radar reported the dash and the death of the two rockets, after their struggle with invisible things that gripped them. They died when they headed reluctantly back to the *Niccola*—and detonated two miles from their parent ship. The skipper's voice came:

"Mr. Taine! After your next salvo I shall head for the Plumie at full drive, to cut down the distance and the time they have to work in. Be ready!"

The rocket tubes went *crump-crump* again, with a fifth of a second interval. The radar showed two tiny specks speeding through space toward the weaving, shifting speck which was the Plumie.

Outside, in emptiness, there was a filmy haze. It was the rocket-fumes and explosive gases spreading with incredible speed. It was thin as gossamer. The Plumie ship undoubtedly spotted the rockets, but it did not try to turn them. It somehow seized them and deflected them, and darted past them toward the *Niccola*.

"They see the trick," said Diane, dry-throated. "If they can get in close enough, they can turn it against us!"

There were noises inside the *Niccola*, now. Taine fairly howled an order. There were yells of defiance and excitement. There were more of those inadequate noises as rockets went out—every tube on the starboard side emptied itself in a series of savage grunts—and the *Niccola*'s magnetronic drive roared at full flux density.

The two ships were less than a mile apart when the *Niccola* let go her full double broadside of missiles. And then it seemed that the Plumie ship was doomed. There were simply too many rockets to be seized and handled before at least one struck. But there was a new condition. The Plumie ship weaved and dodged its way through them. The new condition was that the rockets were just beginning their run. They had not achieved the terrific velocity they would accumulate in ten miles of no-gravity. They were new-launched; logy; clumsy: not the streaking, flashing death-and-destruction they would become with thirty more seconds of acceleration.

So the Plumie ship dodged them with a skill and daring past belief. With an incredible agility it got inside them, nearer to the *Niccola* than they. And then it hurled itself at the human ship as if bent upon a suicidal crash which would destroy both ships together. But Baird, in the radar room, and the skipper in navigation, knew that it would plunge brilliantly past them at the last instant—

And then they knew that it would not. Because, very suddenly and very abruptly, there was something the matter with the Plumie ship. The life went out of it. It ceased to steer. It began to turn slowly on an axis somewhere amidships. Its nose swung to one side, with no change in the direction of its motion. It floated onward. It was broadside to its line of travel. It continued to turn. It hurtled stern-first toward the *Niccola*. It did not swerve. It did not dance. It was a lifeless hulk: a derelict in space.

And it would hit the *Niccola* amidships with no possible result but destruction for both vessels.

The *Niccola*'s skipper bellowed orders, as if shouting would somehow give them more effect. The magnetronic drive roared. He'd demanded a miracle of it, and he almost got one. The drive strained its thrust-members. It hopelessly overloaded its coils. The *Niccola*'s cobalt-steel hull became more than saturated with the drive-field, and it leaped madly upon an evasion course—

And it very nearly got away. It was swinging clear when the Plumie ship drifted within fathoms. It was turning aside when the Plumie ship was within yards. And it was almost safe when the golden hull of the Plumie—shadowed now by the *Niccola* itself—barely scraped a side-keel.

There was a touch, seemingly deliberate and gentle. But the *Niccola* shuddered horribly. Then the vision screens flared from such a light as might herald the crack of doom. There was a brightness greater than the brilliance of the sun. And then there was a wrenching, heaving shock. Then there was blackness. Baird was flung across the radar room, and Diane cried out, and he careened against a wall and heard glass shatter. He called:

"Diane!"

He clutched crazily at anything, and called her name again. The *Niccola*'s internal gravity was cut off, and his head spun, and he heard collision-doors closing everywhere, but before they closed completely he heard the rasping sound of giant arcs leaping in the engine room. Then there was silence.

"Diane!" cried Baird fiercely. "Diane!"

"I'm I . . . here," she panted. "I'm dizzy, but I . . . think I'm all right—"

The battery-powered emergency light came on. It was faint, but he saw her clinging to a bank of instruments where she'd been thrown by the collision. He moved to go to her, and found himself floating in midair. But he drifted to a side wall and worked his way to her.

She clung to him, shivering.

"I . . . think," she said unsteadily, "that we're going to die. Aren't we?"

"We'll see," he told her. "Hold on to me."

Guided by the emergency light, he scrambled to the bank of communicator-buttons. What had been the floor was now a side wall. He climbed it and thumbed the navigation-room switch.

"Radar room reporting," he said curtly. "Power out, gravity off, no reports from outside from power failure. No great physical damage."

He began to hear other voices. There had never been an actual space-collision in the memory of man, but reports came crisply, and the cut-in speakers in the radar room repeated them. Ship-gravity was out all over the ship. Emergency lights were functioning, and those were all the lights there were. There was a slight, unexplained gravity-drift toward what had been the ship's port side. But damage-control reported no loss of pressure in the *Niccola*'s inner hull, though four areas between inner and outer hulls had lost air pressure to space.

"*Mr. Baird,*" rasped the skipper. "*We're blind! Forget everything else and give us eyes to see with!*"

"We'll try battery power to the vision plates," Baird told Diane. "No full resolution, but better than nothing—"

They worked together, feverishly. They were dizzy. Something close to nausea came upon them from pure giddiness. What had been the floor was now a wall, and they had to climb to each of the instruments that had been on a wall and now were on the ceiling. But their weight was ounces only. Baird said abruptly:

"I know what's the matter! We're spinning! The whole ship's spinning! That's why we're giddy and why we have even a trace of weight. Centrifugal force! Ready for the current?"

There was a tiny click, and the battery light dimmed. But a vision screen lighted faintly. The stars it showed were moving specks of light. The sun passed deliberately across the screen. Baird switched to other outside scanners. There was power for only one screen at a time. But he saw the starkly impossible. He pressed the navigation-room button.

"Radar room reporting," he said urgently. "The Plumie ship is fast to us, in contact with our hull! Both ships are spinning together!" He was trying yet other scanners as he spoke, and now he said: "Got it! There are no lines connecting us to the Plumie, but it looks . . . yes! That flash when the ships came together was a flashover of high potential. We're welded to them along twenty feet of our hull!"

The skipper:

"Damnation! Any sign of intention to board us?"

"Not yet, sir—"

Taine burst in, his voice high-pitched and thick with hatred:

"Damage-control parties attention! Arm yourselves and assemble at starboard air lock! Rocket crews get into suits and prepare to board this Plumie—"

"Countermand!" bellowed the skipper from the speaker beside Baird's ear. *"Those orders are canceled! Dammit, if we were successfully boarded we'd blow ourselves to bits! Those are our orders! D'you think the Plumies will let their ship be taken? And wouldn't we blow up with them? Mr. Taine, you will take no offensive action without specific orders! Defensive action is another matter. Mr. Baird! I consider this welding business pure accident. No one would be mad enough to plan it. You watch the Plumies and keep me informed!"*

His voice ceased. And Baird had again the frustrating duty of remaining still and keeping his head while other men engaged in physical activity. He helped Diane to a chair—which was fastened to the floor-which-was-now-a-wall—and she wedged herself fast and began a review of what each of the outside scanners reported. Baird called for more batteries. Power for the radar and visions was more important than anything else, just then. If there were more Plumie ships . . .

Electricians half-floated, half-dragged extra batteries to the radar room. Baird hooked them in. The universe outside the ship again appeared filled with brilliantly colored dots of light which were stars. More satisfying, the globe-scanners again reported no new objects anywhere. Nothing new within a quarter million miles. A half-million. Later Baird reported:

"Radars report no strange objects within a million miles of the *Niccola*, sir."

"*Except the ship we're welded to. But you are doing very well. However, microphones say there is movement inside the Plumie.*"

Diane beckoned for Baird's attention to a screen, which Baird had examined before. Now he stiffened and motioned for her to report.

"We've a scanner, sir," said Diane, "which faces what looks like a port in the Plumie ship. There's a figure at the port. I can't make out details, but it is making motions, facing us."

"*Give me the picture!*" snapped the skipper.

Diane obeyed. It was the merest flip of a switch. Then her eyes went back to the spherical-sweep scanners which reported the bearing and distance of every solid object within their range. She set up two instruments which would measure the angle, bearing, and distance of the two planets now on this side of the sun—the gas-giant and the oxygen-world to sunward. Their orbital speeds and distances were known. The position, course, and speed of the *Niccola* could be computed from any two observations on them.

Diane had returned to the utterly necessary routine of the radar room which was the nerve-center of the ship, gathering all information needed for navigation in space. The fact that there had been a collision, that the *Niccola*'s engines were melted to unlovely scrap, that the Plumie ship was now welded irremovably to a side keel, and that a Plumie was signaling to humans while both ships went spinning through space toward an unknown destination—these things did not affect the obligations of the radar room.

Baird got other images of the Plumie ship into sharp focus. So near, the scanners required adjustment for precision.

"Take a look at this!" he said wryly.

She looked. The view was of the Plumie as welded fast to the *Niccola*. The welding was itself an extraordinary result of the Plumie's battle-tactics. Tractor and pressor beams were known to men, of course, but human beings used them only under very special conditions. Their operation involved the building-up of terrific static charges. Unless a tractor-beam generator could be grounded to the object it was to pull, it tended to emit lightning-bolts at unpredictable intervals and in entirely random directions. So men didn't use them. Obviously, the Plumies did.

They'd handled the *Niccola*'s rockets with beams which charged the golden ship to billions of volts. And when the silicon-bronze Plumie ship touched the cobalt-steel *Niccola*—why—that charge had to be shared. It must have been the most spectacular of all artificial electric flames. Part of the *Niccola*'s hull was vaporized, and undoubtedly part of the Plumie. But the unvaporized surfaces were molten and in contact—and they stuck.

For a good twenty feet the two ships were united by the most perfect of vacuum-welds. The wholly dissimilar hulls formed a space-catamaran, with a sort of valley between their bulks. Spinning deliberately, as the united ships did, sometimes the sun shone brightly into that valley, and sometimes it was filled with the blackness of the pit.

While Diane looked, a round door revolved in the side of the Plumie ship. As Diane caught her breath, Baird reported crisply. At his first word Taine burst into raging commands for men to follow him through the *Niccola*'s air lock and fight a boarding party of Plumies in empty space. The skipper very savagely ordered him to be quiet.

"Only one figure has come out," reported Baird. The skipper watched on a vision plate, but Baird reported so all the *Niccola*'s company would know. "It's small—less than five feet . . . I'll see better in a moment." Sunlight smote down into the valley between the ships. "It's wearing a pressure suit. It seems to be the same material as the ship. It walks on two legs, as we do . . . It has two arms, or something very similar . . . The helmet of the suit is very high . . . It looks like the armor knights used to fight in . . . It's making its way to our air lock . . . It does not use magnetic-soled shoes. It's holding onto lines threaded along the other ship's hull . . ."

The skipper said curtly:

"Mr. Baird! I hadn't noticed the absence of magnetic shoes. You seem to have an eye for important items. Report to the air lock in person. Leave Lieutenant Holt to keep an eye on outside objects. Quickly, Mr. Baird!"

Baird laid his hand on Diane's shoulder. She smiled at him.

"I'll watch!" she promised.

He went out of the radar room, walking on what had been a side wall. The giddiness and dizziness of continued rotation was growing less, now. He was getting used to it. But the *Niccola* seemed strange indeed, with the standard up and down and Earth-gravity replaced by a vertical which was all askew and a weight of ounces instead of a hundred and seventy pounds.

He reached the air lock just as the skipper arrived. There were others there—armed and in pressure suits. The skipper glared about him.

"I am in command here," he said very grimly indeed. "Mr. Taine has a special function, but I am in command. We and the creatures on the Plumie ship are in a very serious fix. One of them apparently means to come on board. There will be no hostility, no sneering, no threatening gestures. This is a parley! You will be careful. But you will not be trigger-happy!"

He glared around again, just as a metallic rapping came upon the *Niccola*'s air-lock door. The skipper nodded:

"Let him in the lock, Mr. Baird."

Baird obeyed. The humming of the unlocking-system sounded. There were clankings. The outer air lock closed. There was a faint whistling as air went in. The skipper nodded again.

Baird opened the inner door. It was 08 hours 10 minutes ship time.

The Plumie stepped confidently out into the topsy-turvy corridors of the *Niccola*. He was about the size of a ten-year-old human boy, and features which were definitely not grotesque showed through the clear plastic of his helmet. His pressure suit was, engineering-wise, a very clean job. His whole appearance was prepossessing. When he spoke, very clear and quite high sounds—soprano sounds—came from a small speaker-unit at his shoulder.

"For us to talk," said the skipper heavily, "is pure nonsense. But I take it you've something to say."

The Plumie gazed about with an air of lively curiosity. Then he drew out a flat pad with a white surface and sketched swiftly. He offered it to the *Niccola*'s skipper.

"We want this on record," he growled, staring about.

Diane's voice said capably from a speaker somewhere nearby:

"Sir, there's a scanner for inspection of objects brought aboard. Hold the plate flat and I'll have a photograph—right!"

The skipper said curtly to the Plumie:

"You've drawn our two ships linked as they are. What have you to say about it?"

He handed back the plate. The Plumie pressed a stud and it was blank again. He sketched and offered it once more.

"Hm-m-m," said the skipper. "You can't use your drive while we're glued together, eh? Well?"

The Plumie reached up and added lines to the drawing.

"So!" rumbled the skipper, inspecting the additions. "You say it's up to us to use our drive for both ships." He growled approvingly: "You consider there's a truce. You must, because we're both in the same fix, and not a nice one, either. True enough! We can't fight each other without committing suicide, now. But we haven't any drive left! We're a derelict! How am I going to say that—if I decide to?"

Baird could see the lines on the plate, from the angle at which the skipper held it. He said:

"Sir, we've been mapping, up in the radar room. Those last lines are map coordinates—a separate sketch, sir. I think he's saying that the two ships, together, are on a falling course toward the sun. That we have to do something or both vessels will fall into it. We should be able to check this, sir."

"Hah!" growled the skipper. "That's all we need. Absolutely all we need! To come here, get into a crazy fight, have our drive melt to scrap, get crazily welded to a Plumie ship, and then for both of us to fry together. We don't need anything more than that!"

Diane's voice came on the speaker:

"Sir, the last radar fixes on the planets in range give us a course directly toward the sun. I'll repeat the observations."

The skipper growled. Taine thrust himself forward. He snarled:

"Why doesn't this Plumie take off his helmet? It lands on oxygen planets! Does it think it's too good to breathe our air?"

Baird caught the Plumie's eye. He made a gesture suggesting the removal of the space helmet. The Plumie gestured, in return, to a tiny vent in the suit. He opened something and gas whistled out. He cut it off. The question of why he did not open or remove his helmet was answered. The atmosphere he breathed would not do men any good, nor would theirs do him any good, either. Taine said suspiciously:

"How do we know he's breathing the stuff he let out then? This creature isn't human. It's got no right to attack humans! Now it's trying to trick us!" His voice changed to a snarl. "We'd better wring its neck! Teach its kind a lesson—"

The skipper roared at him.

"Be quiet! Our ship is a wreck! We have to consider the facts. We and these Plumies are in a fix together, and we have to get out of it before we start to teach anybody anything!" He glared at Taine. Then he said heavily: "Mr. Baird, you seem to notice things. Take this Plumie over the ship. Show him our drive melted down, so he'll realize we can't possibly tow his ship into an orbit. He knows that we're armed, and that we can't handle our war heads at this range. So we can't fool each other. We might as well be frank. But you will take full note of his reactions, Mr. Baird!"

∽   ∽   ∽

Baird advanced, and the skipper made a gesture. The Plumie regarded Baird with interested eyes. And Baird led the way for a tour of the *Niccola*. It was confusing even to him, with right hand converted to up and left hand to down, and sidewise now almost vertical. On the way the Plumie made more clear, flutelike sounds, and more gestures. Baird answered.

"Our gravity pull was that way," he explained, "and things fell so fast."

He grasped a handrail and demonstrated the speed with which things fell in normal ship-gravity. He used a pocket communicator for the falling weight. It was singularly easy to say some things, even highly technical ones, because they'd be what the Plumie would want to know. But quite commonplace things would be very difficult to convey.

Diane's voice came out of the communicator.

"There are no novelties outside," she said quietly. *"It looks like this is the only Plumie ship anywhere around. It could have been exploring, like us. Maybe it was looking for the people who put up Space-Survey markers."*

"Maybe," agreed Baird, using the communicator. "Is that stuff about falling into the sun correct?"

"It seems so," said Diane composedly. *"I'm checking again. So far, the best course I can get means we graze the sun's photosphere in fourteen days six hours, allowing for acceleration by the sun's gravity."*

"And you and I," said Baird wryly, "have been acting as professional associates only, when—"

"Don't say it!" said Diane shakily. *"It's terrible!"*

He put the communicator back in his pocket. The Plumie had watched him. He had a peculiarly gallant air, this small figure in golden space armor with its high-crested helmet.

They reached the engine room. And there was the giant drive shaft of the *Niccola*, once wrapped with yard-thick coils which could induce an incredible density of magnetic flux in the metal. Even the return magnetic field, through the ship's cobalt-steel hull, was many times higher than saturation. Now the coils were sagging: mostly melted. There were places where re-solidified metal smoked noisomely against non-metallic floor or wall-covering. Engineers labored doggedly in the trivial gravity to clean up the mess.

"It's past repair," said Baird, to the ship's first engineer.

"It's junk," said that individual dourly. "Give us six months and a place to set up a wire-drawing mill and an insulator synthesizer, and we could rebuild it. But nothing less will be any good."

The Plumie stared at the drive. He examined the shaft from every angle. He inspected the melted, and partly-melted, and merely burned-out sections of the drive coils. He was plainly unable to understand in any fashion the principle of the magnetronic drive. Baird was tempted to try to explain, because there was surely no secret about a ship drive, but he could imagine no diagrams or gestures which would convey the theory of what happened in cobalt-steel when it was magnetized beyond one hundred thousand Gauss' flux-density. And without that theory one simply couldn't explain a magnetronic drive.

They left the engine room. They visited the rocket batteries. The generator room was burned out, like the drive, by the inconceivable lightning bolt which had passed between the ships on contact. The Plumie was again puzzled. Baird made it clear that the generator-room supplied electric current for the ship's normal lighting-system and services. The Plumie could grasp that idea. They examined the crew's quarters, and the mess room, and the Plumie walked confidently among the members of the human crew, who a little while since had tried so painstakingly to destroy his vessel. He made a good impression.

"These little guys," said a crewman to Baird, admiringly, "they got something. They can handle a ship! I bet they could almost make that ship of their play checkers!"

"Close to it," agreed Baird. He realized something. He pulled the communicator from his pocket. "Diane! Contact the skipper. He wanted observations. Here's one. This Plumie acts like soldiers used to act in ancient days—when they wore armor. And we have the same reaction. They will fight like the devil, but during a truce they'll be friendly, admiring each other as scrappers, but ready to fight as hard as ever when the truce is over. We have the same reaction. Tell the skipper I've an idea that it's a part of their civilization—maybe it's a necessary part of any civilization! Tell him I guess that there may be necessarily parallel evolution of attitudes, among rational races, as there are parallel evolutions of eyes and legs and wings and fins among all animals everywhere. If I'm right, somebody from this ship will be invited to tour the Plumie. It's only a guess, but tell him."

"Immediately," said Diane.

∾   ∾   ∾

The Plumie followed gallantly as Baird made a steep climb up what once was the floor of a corridor. Then Taine stepped out before them. His eyes burned.

"Giving him a clear picture, eh?" he rasped. "Letting him spy out everything?"

Baird pressed the communicator call for the radar room and said coldly:

"I'm obeying orders. Look, Taine! You were picked for your job because you were a xenophobe. It helps in your proper functioning. But this Plumie is here under a flag of truce—"

"Flag of truce!" snarled Taine. "It's vermin! It's not human! I'll—"

"If you move one inch nearer him," said Baird gently, "just one inch—"

The skipper's voice bellowed through the general call speakers all over the ship:

"Mr. Taine! You will go to your quarters, under arrest! Mr. Baird, burn him down if he hesitates!"

Then there was a rushing, and scrambling figures appeared and were all about. They were members of the *Niccola*'s crew, sent by the skipper. They regarded the Plumie with detachment, but Taine with a wary expectancy. Taine turned purple with fury. He shouted. He raged. He called Baird and the others Plumie-lovers and vermin-worshipers. He shouted foulnesses at them. But he did not attack.

When, still shouting, he went away, Baird said apologetically to the Plumie:

"He's a xenophobe. He has a pathological hatred of strangers— even of strangeness. We have him on board because—"

Then he stopped. The Plumie wouldn't understand, of course. But his eyes took on a curious look. It was almost as if, looking at Baird, they twinkled.

Baird took him back to the skipper.

"He's got the picture, sir," he reported.

The Plumie pulled out his sketch plate. He drew on it. He offered it. The skipper said heavily:

"You guessed right, Mr. Baird. He suggests that someone from this ship go on board the Plumie vessel. He's drawn two pressure-suited figures going into their air lock. One's larger than the other. Will you go?"

"Naturally!" said Baird. Then he added thoughtfully: "But I'd better carry a portable scanner, sir. It should work perfectly well through a bronze hull, sir."

The skipper nodded and began to sketch a diagram which would amount to an acceptance of the Plumie's invitation.

This was at 07 hours 40 minutes ship time. Outside the sedately rotating metal hulls—the one a polished blue-silver and the other a glittering golden bronze—the cosmos continued to be as always. The haze from explosive fumes and rocket-fuel was, perhaps, a little thinner. The brighter stars shone through it. The gas-giant planet outward from the sun was a perceptible disk instead of a diffuse glow. The oxygen-planet to sunward showed again as a lighted crescent.

Presently Baird, in a human spacesuit, accompanied the Plumie into the *Niccola*'s air lock and out to emptiness. His magnetic-soled shoes clung to the *Niccola*'s cobalt-steel skin. Fastened to his shoulder there was a tiny scanner and microphone, which would relay everything he saw and heard back to the radar room and to Diane.

She watched tensely as he went inside the Plumie ship. Other screens relayed the image and his voice to other places on the *Niccola*.

He was gone a long time. From the beginning, of course, there were surprises. When the Plumie escort removed his helmet, on his own ship, the reason for the helmet's high crest was apparent. He had a high crest of what looked remarkably like feathers—and it was not artificial. It grew there. The reason for conventionalized plumes on bronze survey plates was clear. It was exactly like the reason for human features or figures as decorative additions to the inscriptions on Space Survey marker plates. Even the Plumie's hands had odd crestlets which stood out when he bent his fingers. The other Plumies were no less graceful and no less colorful. They had equally clear soprano voices. They were equally miniature and so devoid of apparent menace.

But there were also technical surprises. Baird was taken immediately to the Plumie ship's engine room, and Diane heard the sharp intake of breath with which he appeared to recognize its working principle. There were Plumie engineers working feverishly at it, attempting to discover something to repair. But they found nothing. The Plumie drive simply would not work.

They took Baird through the ship's entire fabric. And their purpose, when it became clear, was startling. The Plumie ship had no rocket tubes. It had no beam-projectors except small-sized objects which were—which must be—their projectors of tractor and pressor beams. They were elaborately grounded to the ship's substance. But they were not originally designed for ultra-heavy service. They hadn't and couldn't have the enormous capacity Baird had expected. He was astounded.

When he returned to the *Niccola*, he went instantly to the radar room to make sure that pictures taken through his scanner had turned out well. And there was Diane.

But the skipper's voice boomed at him from the wall.

"Mr. Baird! What have you to add to the information you sent back?"

"Three items, sir," said Baird. He drew a deep breath. "For the first, sir, the Plumie ship is unarmed. They've tractor and pressor beams for handling material. They probably use them to build their cairns. But they weren't meant for weapons. The Plumies, sir, hadn't a thing to fight with when they drove for us after we detected them."

The skipper blinked hard.

"Are you sure of that, Mr. Baird?"

"Yes, sir," said Baird uncomfortably. "The Plumie ship is an exploring ship—a survey ship, sir. You saw their mapping equipment. But when they spotted us, and we spotted them—they bluffed! When we fired rockets at them, they turned them back with tractor and pressor beams. They drove for us, sir, to try to destroy us with our own bombs, because they didn't have any of their own."

The skipper's mouth opened and closed.

"Another item, sir," said Baird more uncomfortably still. "They don't use iron or steel. Every metal object I saw was either a bronze or a light metal. I suspect some of their equipment's made of potassium, and I'm fairly sure they use sodium in the place of aluminum. Their atmosphere's quite different from ours—obviously! They'd use bronze for their ship's hull because they can venture into an oxygen atmosphere in a bronze ship. A sodium-hulled ship would be lighter, but it would burn in oxygen. Where there was moisture—"

The skipper blinked.

"But they couldn't drive in a nonmagnetic hull!" he protested. *"A ship has to be magnetic to drive!"*

"Sir," said Baird, his voice still shaken, "they don't use a magnetronic drive. I once saw a picture of the drive they use, in a stereo on the history of space travel. The principle's very old. We've practically forgotten it. It's a Dirac pusher-drive, sir. Among us humans, it came right after rockets. The planets of Sol were first reached by ships using Dirac pushers. But—" He paused. "They won't operate in a magnetic field above seventy Gauss, sir. It's a static-charge reaction, sir, and in a magnetic field it simply stops working."

The skipper regarded Baird unblinkingly for a long time.

"*I think you are telling me,*" he said at long last, "*that the Plumies' drive would work if they were cut free of the* Niccola."

"Yes, sir," said Baird. "Their engineers were opening up the drive-elements and checking them, and then closing them up again. They couldn't seem to find anything wrong. I don't think they know what the trouble is. It's the *Niccola*'s magnetic field. I think it was our field that caused the collision by stopping their drive and killing all their controls when they came close enough."

"*Did you tell them?*" demanded the skipper.

"There was no easy way to tell them by diagrams, sir."

Taine's voice cut in. It was feverish. It was strident. It was triumphant.

"*Sir! The* Niccola *is effectively a wreck and unrepairable. But the Plumie ship is operable if cut loose. As weapons officer, I intend to take the Plumie ship, let out its air, fill its tanks with our air, start up its drive, and turn it over to you for navigation back to base!*"

Baird raged. But he said coldly:

"We're a long way from home, Mr. Taine, and the Dirac pusher drive is slow. If we headed back to base in the Plumie ship with its Dirac pusher, we'd all be dead of old age before we'd gone halfway."

"*But unless we take it,*" raged Taine, "*we hit this sun in fourteen days! We don't have to die now! We can land on the oxygen planet up ahead! We've only to kill these vermin and take their ship, and we'll live!*"

Diane's voice said dispassionately:

"Report. A Plumie in a pressure suit just came out of their air lock. It's carrying a parcel toward our air lock."

Taine snarled instantly:

"*They'll sneak something in the* Niccola *to blast it, and then cut free and go away!*"

The skipper said very grimly:

"*Mr. Taine, credit me with minimum brains! There is no way the Plumies can take this ship without an atomic bomb exploding to destroy both ships. You should know it!*" Then he snapped: "Air lock area, listen for a knock, and let in the Plumie or the parcel he leaves."

There was silence. Baird said very quietly:

"I doubt they think it possible to cut the ships apart. A torch is no good on thick silicon bronze. It conducts heat too well! And they don't use steel. They probably haven't a cutting-torch at all."

From the radar room he watched the Plumie place an object in the air lock and withdraw. He watched from a scanner inside the ship as someone brought in what the Plumie had left. An electronics man bustled forward. He looked it over quickly. It was complex, but his examination suddenly seemed satisfying to him. But a grayish vapor developed and he sniffed and wrinkled his nose. He picked up a communicator.

"*Sir, they've sent us a power-generator. Some of its parts are going bad in our atmosphere, sir, but this looks to me like a hell of a good idea for a generator! I never saw anything like it, but it's good! You can set it for any voltage and it'll turn out plenty juice!*"

"*Put it in helium,*" snapped the skipper. "*It won't break down in that. Then see how it serves.*"

In the radar room, Baird drew a deep breath. He went carefully to each of the screens and every radar. Diane saw what he was about, and checked with him. They met at the middle of the radar room.

"Everything's checked out," said Baird gravely. "There's nothing else around. There's nothing we can be called on to do before something happens. So . . . we can . . . act like people."

Diane smiled very faintly.

"Not like people. Just like us." She said wistfully: "Don't you want to tell me something? Something you intended to tell me only after we got back to base?"

He did. He told it to her. And there was also something she had not intended to tell him at all—unless he told her first. She said it now. They felt that such sayings were of the greatest possible importance. They clung together, saying them again. And it seemed wholly monstrous that two people who cared so desperately had wasted so much time acting like professional associates—explorer-ship officers—when things like this were to be said . . .

As they talked incoherently, or were even more eloquently silent, the ship's ordinary lights came back on. The battery-lamp went on.

"We've got to switch back to ship's circuit," said Baird reluctantly. They separated, and restored the operating circuits to normal. "We've got fourteen days," he added, "and so much time to be on duty, and we've a lost lifetime to live in fourteen days! Diane—"

She flushed vividly. So Baird said very politely into the microphone to the navigation room:

"Sir, Lieutenant Holt and myself would like to speak directly to you in the navigation room. May we?"

"Why not?" growled the skipper. *"You've noticed that the Plumie generator is giving the whole ship lights and services?"*

"Yes, sir," said Baird. "We'll be there right away."

They heard the skipper's grunt as they hurried through the door. A moment later the ship's normal gravity returned—also through the Plumie generator. Up was up again, and down was down, and the corridors and cabins of the *Niccola* were brightly illuminated. Had the ship been other than an engineless wreck, falling through a hundred and fifty million miles of emptiness into the flaming photosphere of a sun, everything would have seemed quite normal, including the errand Baird and Diane were upon, and the fact that they held hands self-consciously as they went about it.

They skirted the bulkhead of the main air tank. They headed along the broader corridor which went past the indented inner door of the air lock. They had reached that indentation when Baird saw that the inner air-lock door was closing. He saw a human pressure suit past its edge. He saw the corner of some object that had been put down on the air-lock floor.

Baird shouted, and rushed toward the lock. He seized the inner handle and tried to force open the door again, so that no one inside it could emerge into the emptiness without. He failed. He wrenched frantically at the control of the outer door. It suddenly swung freely. The outer door had been put on manual. It could be and was being opened from inside.

"Tell the skipper," raged Baird. "Taine's taking something out!" He tore open a pressure-suit cupboard in the wall beside the lock door. "He'll make the Plumies think it's a return-gift for the generator!" He eeled into the pressure suit and zipped it up to his neck. "The man's crazy! He thinks we can take their ship and stay alive for a while! Dammit, our air would ruin half their equipment! Tell the skipper to send help!"

He wrenched at the door again, jamming down his helmet with one hand. And this time the control worked. Taine, most probably, had forgotten that the inner control was disengaged only when the manual was actively in use. Diane raced away, panting. Baird swore bitterly at the slowness of the outer door's closing. He was tearing at the inner door long before it could be opened. He flung himself in and dragged it shut, and struck the emergency air-release which bled the air lock into space for speed of operation. He thrust out the outer door and plunged through.

His momentum carried him almost too far. He fell, and only the magnetic soles of his shoes enabled him to check himself. He was in that singular valley between the two ships, where their hulls were impregnably welded fast. Round-hulled Plumie ship, and ganoid-shaped *Niccola*, they stuck immovably together as if they had been that way since time began. Where the sky appeared above Baird's head, the stars moved in stately procession across the valley roof.

He heard a metallic rapping through the fabric of his space armor. Then sunlight glittered, and the valley filled with a fierce glare, and a man in a human spacesuit stood on the *Niccola*'s plating, opposite the Plumie air lock. He held a bulky object under his arm. With his other gauntlet he rapped again.

"You fool!" shouted Baird. "Stop that! We couldn't use their ship, anyhow!"

His space phone had turned on with the air supply. Taine's voice snarled:

"We'll try! You keep back! They are not human!"

But Baird ran toward him. The sensation of running upon magnetic-soled shoes was unearthly: it was like trying to run on fly-paper or bird-lime. But in addition there was no gravity here, and no sense of balance, and there was the feeling of perpetual fall.

There could be no science nor any skill in an encounter under such conditions. Baird partly ran and partly staggered and partly skated to where Taine faced him, snarling. He threw himself at the other man—and then the sun vanished behind the bronze ship's hull, and only stars moved visibly in all the universe.

But the sound of his impact was loud in Baird's ears inside the suit. There was a slightly different sound when his armor struck Taine's, and when it struck the heavier metal of the two ships. He fought. But the suits were intended to be defense against greater stresses than human blows could offer. In the darkness, it was like two blindfolded men fighting each other while encased in pillows.

Then the sun returned, floating sedately above the valley, and Baird could see his enemy. He saw, too, that the Plumie air lock was now open and that a small, erect, and somehow jaunty figure in golden space armor stood in the opening and watched gravely as the two men fought.

Taine cursed, panting with hysterical hate. He flung himself at Baird, and Baird toppled because he'd put one foot past the welded boundary between the *Niccola*'s cobalt steel and the Plumie ship's bronze. One foot held to nothing. And that was a ghastly sensation, because if Taine only tugged his other foot free and heaved—why—then Baird would go floating away from the rotating, now-twinned ships, floating farther and farther away forever.

But darkness fell, and he scrambled back to the *Niccola*'s hull as a disorderly parade of stars went by above him. He pantingly waited fresh attack. He felt something—and it was the object Taine had meant to offer as a return present to the Plumies. It was unquestionably explosive, either booby-trapped or timed to explode inside the Plumie ship. Now it rocked gently, gripped by the magnetism of the steel.

The sun appeared again, and Taine was yards away, crawling and fumbling for Baird. Then he saw him, and rose and rushed, and the clankings of his shoe-soles were loud. Baird flung himself at Taine in a savage tackle.

He struck Taine's legs a glancing blow, and the cobalt steel held his armor fast, but Taine careened and bounced against the round bronze wall of the Plumie, and bounced again. Then he screamed, because he went floating slowly out to emptiness, his arms and legs jerking spasmodically, while he shrieked...

The Plumie in the air lock stepped out. He trailed a cord behind him. He leaped briskly toward nothingness.

There came quick darkness once more, and Baird struggled erect despite the adhesiveness of the *Niccola*'s hull. When he was fully upright, sick with horror at what had come about, there was sunlight yet again, and men were coming out of the *Niccola*'s air lock, and the Plumie who'd leaped for space was pulling himself back to his own ship again. He had a loop of the cord twisted around Taine's leg. But Taine screamed and screamed inside his spacesuit.

It was odd that one could recognize the skipper even inside space armor. But Baird felt sick. He saw Taine received, still screaming, and carried into the lock. The skipper growled an infuriated demand for details. His space phone had come on, too, when its air supply began. Baird explained, his teeth chattering.

"*Hah!*" grunted the skipper. "*Taine was a mistake. He shouldn't ever have left ground. When a man's potty in one fashion, there'll be cracks in him all over. What's this?*"

The Plumie in the golden armor very soberly offered the skipper the object Taine had meant to introduce into the Plumie's ship. Baird said desperately that he'd fought against it, because he believed it a booby trap to kill the Plumies so men could take their ship and fill it with air and cut it free, and then make a landing somewhere.

"*Damned foolishness!*" rumbled the skipper. "*Their ship'd begin to crumble with our air in it. If it held to a landing—*"

Then he considered the object he'd accepted from the Plumie. It could have been a rocket war head, enclosed in some container that would detonate it if opened. Or there might be a timing device. The skipper grunted. He heaved it skyward.

The misshapen object went floating away toward emptiness. Sunlight smote harshly upon it.

"*Don't want it back in the* Niccola," growled the skipper, "*but just to make sure—*"

He fumbled a hand weapon out of his belt. He raised it, and it spurted flame—very tiny blue-white sparks, each one indicating a pellet of metal flung away at high velocity.

One of them struck the shining, retreating container. It exploded with a monstrous, soundless violence. It had been a rocket's war head. There could have been only one reason for it to be introduced into a Plumie ship. Baird ceased to be shaky. Instead, he was ashamed.

The skipper growled inarticulately. He looked at the Plumie, again standing in the golden ship's air lock.

"*We'll go back, Mr. Baird. What you've done won't save our lives, and nobody will ever know you did it. But I think well of you. Come along!*"

This was at 11 hours 5 minutes ship time.

A good half hour later the skipper's voice bellowed from the speakers all over the *Niccola*. His heavy-jowled features stared doggedly out of screens wherever men were on duty or at ease.

"*Hear this!*" he said forbiddingly. "*We have checked our course and speed. We have verified that there is no possible jury-rig for our engines that could get us into any sort of orbit, let alone land us on the only planet in this system with air we could breathe. It is officially certain that in thirteen days nine hours from now, the* Niccola *will be so close to the sun that her hull will melt down. Which will be no loss to us because we'll be dead then, still going on into the sun to be vaporized with the ship. There is nothing to be done about it. We can do nothing to save our own lives.*"

He glared out of each and every one of the screens, wherever there were men to see him.

"*But,*" he rumbled, "*the Plumies can get away if we help them. They have no cutting torches. We have. We can cut their ship free. They can repair their drive—but it's most likely that it'll operate perfectly when they're a mile from the* Niccola's *magnetic field. They can't help us. But we can help them. And sooner or later some Plumie ship is going to encounter some other human ship. If we cut these Plumies loose, they'll report what we did. When they meet other men, they'll be cagey because they'll remember Taine. But they'll know they can make friends, because we did them a favor when we'd nothing to gain by it. I can offer no reward. But I ask for volunteers to go outside and cut the Plumie ship loose, so the Plumies can go home in safety instead of on into the sun with us.*"

He glared, and cut off the image.

Diane held tightly to Baird's hand, in the radar room. He said evenly:

"There'll be volunteers. The Plumies are pretty sporting characters—putting up a fight with an unarmed ship, and so on. If there aren't enough other volunteers, the skipper and I will cut them free by ourselves."

Diane said, dry-throated:

"I'll help. So I can be with you. We've got—so little time."

"I'll ask the skipper as soon as the Plumie ship's free."

"Y-yes," said Diane. And she pressed her face against his shoulder, and wept.

This was at 01 hours, 20 minutes ship time. At 03 hours even, there was peculiar activity in the valley between the welded ships. There were men in space armor working cutting-torches where for twenty feet the two ships were solidly attached. Blue-white flames bored savagely into solid metal, and melted copper gave off strangely colored clouds of vapor—which emptiness whisked away to nothing—and molten iron and cobalt made equally lurid clouds of other colors.

There were Plumies in the air lock, watching.

At 03 hours 40 minutes ship time, all the men but one drew back. They went inside the *Niccola.* Only one man remained, cutting at the last sliver of metal that held the two ships together.

It parted. The Plumie ship swept swiftly away, moved by the centrifugal force of the rotary motion the joined vessels had possessed. It dwindled and dwindled. It was a half mile away. A mile.

The last man on the outside of the *Niccola*'s hull thriftily brought his torch to the air lock and came in.

Suddenly, the distant golden hull came to life. It steadied. It ceased to spin, however slowly. It darted ahead. It checked. It swung to the right and left and up and down. It was alive again.

In the radar room, Diane walked into Baird's arms and said shakily:

"Now we . . . we have almost fourteen days."

"Wait," he commanded. "When the Plumies understood what we were doing, and why, they drew diagrams. They hadn't thought of cutting free, out in space, without the spinning saws they used to cut bronze with. But they asked for a scanner and a screen. They checked on its use. I want to see—"

He flipped on the screen. And there was instantly a Plumie looking eagerly out of it, for some sign of communication established. There were soprano sounds, and he waved a hand for attention. Then he zestfully held up one diagram after another.

Baird drew a deep breath. A very deep breath. He pressed the navigation-room call. The skipper looked dourly at him.

"*Well?*" said the skipper forbiddingly.

"Sir," said Baird, very quietly indeed, "the Plumies are talking by diagram over the communicator set we gave them. Their drive works. They're as well off as they ever were. And they've been modifying their tractor beams—stepping them up to higher power."

"*What of it?*" demanded the skipper, rumbling.

"They believe," said Baird, "that they can handle the *Niccola* with their beefed-up tractor beams." He wetted his lips. "They're going to tow us to the oxygen planet ahead, sir. They're going to set us down on it. They'll help us find the metals we need to build the tools to repair the *Niccola*, sir. You see the reasoning, sir. We turned them loose to improve the chance of friendly contact when another human ship runs into them. They want us to carry back—to be proof that Plumies and men can be friends. It seems that—they like us, sir."

He stopped for a moment. Then he went on reasonably:

"And besides that, it'll be one hell of a fine business proposition. We never bother with hydrogen-methane planets. They've minerals and chemicals we haven't got, but even the stones of a methane-hydrogen planet are ready to combine with the oxygen we need to breathe! We can't carry or keep enough oxygen for real work. The same thing's true with them on an oxygen planet. We can't work on each other's planets, but we can do fine business in each other's minerals and chemicals from those planets. I've got a feeling, sir, that the Plumie cairns are location-notices; markers set up over ore deposits they can find but can't hope to work, yet they claim against the day when their scientists find a way to make them worth owning. I'd be willing to bet, sir, that if we explored hydrogen planets as thoroughly as oxygen ones, we'd find cairns on their-type planets that they haven't colonized yet."

The skipper stared. His mouth dropped open.

"And I think, sir," said Baird, "that until they detected us they thought they were the only intelligent race in the galaxy. They were upset to discover suddenly that they were not, and at first they'd no idea what we'd be like. But I'm guessing now, sir, that they're figuring on what chemicals and ores to start swapping with us." Then he added, "When you think of it, sir, probably the first metal they ever used was aluminum—where our ancestors used copper—and they had a beryllium age next, instead of iron. And right now, sir, it's probably as expensive for them to refine iron as it is for us to handle titanium and beryllium and osmium—which are duck soup for them! Our two cultures ought to thrive as long as we're friends, sir. They know it already—and we'll find it out in a hurry!"

The skipper's mouth moved. It closed, and then dropped open again. The search for the Plumies had been made because it looked like they had to be fought. But Baird had just pointed out some extremely commonsense items which changed the situation entirely. And there was evidence that the Plumies saw the situation the new way. The skipper felt such enormous relief that his manner changed. He displayed what was almost effusive cordiality—for the skipper. He cleared his throat.

"*Hm-m-m. Hah! Very good, Mr. Baird,*" he said formidably. "*And of course with time and air and metals we can rebuild our drive. For that matter, we could rebuild the* Niccola! *I'll notify the ship's company, Mr. Baird. Very good!*" He moved to use another microphone. Then he checked himself. "*Your expression is odd, Mr. Baird. Did you wish to say something more?*"

"Y-yes, sir," said Baird. He held Diane's hand fast. "It'll be months before we get back to port, sir. And it's normally against regulations, but under the circumstances . . . would you mind . . . as skipper . . . marrying Lieutenant Holt and me?"

The skipper snorted. Then he said almost—almost—amiably?

"*Hm-m-m. You've both done very well, Mr. Baird. Yes. Come to the navigation room and we'll get it over with. Say—ten minutes from now."*

Baird grinned at Diane. Her eyes shone a little.

This was at 04 hours 10 minutes ship time. It was exactly twelve hours since the alarm-bell rang.

<hr />

AFTERWORD BY ERIC FLINT

Murray Leinster died almost thirty years ago, in 1976, and his writing career had essentially ended by the beginning of the 1970s. During the decades that followed, this once-major figure in science fiction more or less faded away from the public eye. Until I started editing the multivolume reissue of his writings which Baen Books is now publishing, the only important reissue of his writing that had taken place in many years was NESFA Press' 1998 one-volume omnibus *First Contacts*.

This . . . for a man who held the title "the dean of science fiction" before Robert Heinlein inherited it. (And it wasn't bestowed on him by an obscure fan club, either—Leinster was given the sobriquet by *Time* magazine.) When I first started reading science fiction in the early '60s, Leinster seemed well-nigh ubiquitous to me. I couldn't have imagined back then that the day would come when he had completely vanished from the shelves.

What happened? Leinster was no minor writer like several in this anthology, after all: Rick Raphael, Robert Ernest Gilbert, Wyman Guin, some others. All of them wrote well, to be sure—but Leinster published more novels than they did short stories. He might have published more novels than all of their short stories put together. And his total output, even leaving aside the many westerns and mystery stories he wrote under his real name of Will Jenkins, would have buried them. Would have buried most authors, in fact, major or minor.

Part of it, I think, was that the loose human conglomeration you might call "the science fiction community" was always fairly lukewarm about him. His career in science fiction spanned half a century, in the course of which he was published by many book publishers and appeared in almost all the principal magazines. Yet, during his lifetime, he only won a major science fiction award once—the Hugo award for best novelette in 1956, for "Exploration Team." In fact, he only received one other nomination for the

Hugo: his novel *The Pirates of Zan* made the final list in 1960 (losing, not surprisingly, to Heinlein's *Starship Troopers*). He was never nominated once for the Nebula award.

To be sure, the major SF awards like all such awards are notoriously subject to the popularity of the recipient with the relatively small numbers of people who cast the votes. And since Leinster paid no attention to them—he rarely if ever attended a science fiction convention, and had very little contact with other science fiction writers—it's not surprising that they tended to ignore him in return.

But there's more to it, I think, than just personal distance. The key is that famous old saw: "Familiarity breeds contempt." Leinster was there at the creation of science fiction—and he created much of it himself. Name any of the now-recognized subgenres or themes of science fiction and trace them back in time . . . and, as often as not, you will discover that Murray Leinster laid the foundations.

First contact? The name itself comes from a Murray Leinster story.

Alternate history? He published the time-travel story "The Runaway Skyscraper" in *Argosy* magazine in the year 1919—a year before my *father* was born. Ironically enough, for a man who was almost never recognized by the awards, the Sidewise Award which is today given out at the annual Hugo ceremony for the best alternate histories of the year . . . was named after Leinster's story "Sidewise in Time," first published seventy years ago.

I could go and on, but I won't bother. Granted, Leinster was never a dazzling writer. His prose is journeyman at best, he was repetitive in his longer works, he recycled plots shamelessly—no fewer than six of his novels are essentially *Die Hard in Space* with the serial numbers filed off—and he wrote a lot of stuff that can only be described as dreck. I know. I've read almost everything he wrote. I edited a reissue of the complete works of James H. Schmitz and never had to hold my nose once. I wouldn't even think of doing the same with Leinster. Still, I could fill twice as many volumes with *good* Leinster than I could with Schmitz, simply because he wrote so much more.

And that's what Leinster was, in the end. An indefatigable storyteller, often a superb one, and the writer who, more than anyone, created science fiction as a viable and separate genre in the first place. So have some respect. If we still worshipped our ancestors and kept their shrunken heads over the hearth, Murray Leinster's would be the one in the center.

All the Way Back

by Michael Shaara

PREFACE BY DAVID DRAKE

Before writing *The Killer Angels*, his Pulitzer Prize-winning novel of the Battle of Gettysburg, Michael Shaara practiced his skill by writing SF. Those of you who've read "Soldier Boy," "Death of a Hunter" (my particular favorite), and this story will agree that he didn't need much practice.

⟞⟝

Great were the Antha, so reads the One Book of history, greater perhaps than any of the Galactic Peoples, and they were brilliant and fair, and their reign was long, and in all things they were great and proud, even in the manner of their dying—

> Preface to *Loab: History of The Master Race*

The huge red ball of a sun hung glowing upon the screen.
Jansen adjusted the traversing knob, his face tensed and weary. The sun swung off the screen to the right, was replaced by the live black of space and the million speckled lights of the farther stars. A moment later the sun glided silently back across the screen and went off at the left. Again there was nothing but space and the stars.

319

"Try it again?" Cohn asked.

Jansen mumbled: "No. No use," and he swore heavily. "Nothing. Always nothing. Never a blessed thing."

Cohn repressed a sigh, began to adjust the controls.

In both of their minds was the single, bitter thought that there would be only one more time, and then they would go home. And it was a long way to come to go home with nothing.

When the controls were set there was nothing left to do. The two men walked slowly aft to the freeze room. Climbing up painfully on to the flat steel of the beds, they lay back and waited for the mechanism to function, for the freeze to begin.

Turned in her course, the spaceship bore off into the open emptiness. Her ports were thrown open, she was gathering speed as she moved away from the huge red star.

The object was sighted upon the last leg of the patrol, as the huge ship of the Galactic Scouts came across the edge of the Great Desert of the Rim, swinging wide in a long slow curve. It was there on the massometer as a faint *blip*, and, of course, the word went directly to Roymer.

"Report," he said briefly, and Lieutenant Goladan—a young and somewhat pompous Higiandrian—gave the Higiandrian equivalent of a cough and then reported.

"Observe," said Lieutenant Goladan, "that it is not a meteor, for the speed of it is much too great."

Roymer nodded patiently.

"And again, the speed is decreasing"—Goladan consulted his figures—"at a rate of twenty-four dines per segment. Since the orbit appears to bear directly upon the star Mina, and the decrease in speed is of a certain arbitrary origin, we must conclude that the object is a spaceship."

Roymer smiled.

"Very good, lieutenant." Like a tiny nova, Goladan began to glow and expand.

A good man, thought Roymer tolerantly, his is a race of good men. They have been two million years in achieving space flight; a certain adolescence is to be expected.

"Would you call Mind-Search, please?" Roymer asked.

Goladan sped away, to return almost immediately with the heavy-headed non-human Trian, chief of the Mind-Search Section.

Trian cocked an eyelike thing at Roymer, with grave inquiry.

"Yes, commander?"

The abrupt change in course was noticeable only on the viewplate, as the stars slid silently by. The patrol vessel veered off, swinging around and into the desert, settled into a parallel course with the strange new craft, keeping a discreet distance of—approximately—a light-year.

The scanners brought the object into immediate focus, and Goladan grinned with pleasure. A spaceship, yes, Alien, too. Undoubtedly a primitive race. He voiced these thoughts to Roymer.

"Yes," the commander said, staring at the strange, small, projectilelike craft. "Primitive type. It is to be wondered what they are doing in the desert."

Goladan assumed an expression of intense curiosity.

"Trian," said Roymer pleasantly, "would you contact?"

The huge head bobbed up and down once and then stared into the screen. There was a moment of profound silence. Then Trian turned back to stare at Roymer, and there was a distinctly human expression of surprise in his eyelike things.

"Nothing," came the thought. "I can detect no presence at all."

Roymer raised an eyebrow.

"Is there a barrier?"

"No"—Trian had turned to gaze back into the screen—"a barrier I could detect. But there is nothing at all. There is no sentient activity on board that vessel."

Trian's word had to be taken, of course, and Roymer was disappointed. A spaceship empty of life—Roymer shrugged. A derelict, then. But why the decreasing speed? Pre-set controls would account for that, of course, but why? Certainly, if one abandoned a ship, one would not arrange for it to—

He was interrupted by Trian's thought:

"Excuse me, but there is nothing. May I return to my quarters?"

Roymer nodded and thanked him, and Trian went ponderously away. Goladan said:

"Shall we prepare to board it, sir?"

"Yes."

And then Goladan was gone to give his proud orders.

Roymer continued to stare at the primitive vessel which hung on the plate. Curious. It was very interesting, always, to come upon derelict ships. The stories that were old, the silent tombs that had been drifting perhaps, for millions of years in the deep sea of space. In the beginning Roymer had hoped that the ship would be manned, and alien, but—nowadays, contact with an isolated race was rare, extremely rare. It was not to be hoped for, and he would be content with this, this undoubtedly empty, ancient ship.

And then, to Roymer's complete surprise, the ship at which he was staring shifted abruptly, turned on its axis, and flashed off like a live thing upon a new course.

When the defrosters activated and woke him up, Jansen lay for a while upon the steel table, blinking. As always with the freeze, it was difficult to tell at first whether anything had actually happened. It was like a quick blink and no more, and then you were lying, feeling exactly the same, thinking the same thoughts even, and if there was anything at all different it was maybe that you were a little numb. And yet in the blink time took a great leap, and the months went by like—Jansen smiled—fenceposts.

He raised a languid eye to the red bulb in the ceiling. Out. He sighed. The freeze had come and gone. He felt vaguely cheated, reflected that this time, before the freeze, he would take a little nap.

He climbed down from the table, noted that Cohn had already gone to the control room. He adjusted himself to the thought that they were approaching a new sun, and it came back to him suddenly that this would be the last one, now they would go home.

Well then, let this one have planets. To have come all this way, to have been gone from home eleven years, and yet to find nothing—

He was jerked out of the old feeling of despair by a lurch of the ship. That would be Cohn taking her off the auto. And now, he thought, we will go in and run out the telescope and have a look, and there won't be a thing.

Wearily, he clumped off over the iron deck, going up to the control room. He had no hope left now, and he had been so hopeful at the beginning. As they are all hopeful, he thought, as they have been hoping now for three hundred years. And they will go on hoping, for a little while, and then men will become hard to get, even with the freeze, and then the starships won't go out any more. And Man will be doomed to the System for the rest of his days.

Therefore, he asked humbly, silently, let this one have planets.

Up in the dome of the control cabin, Cohn was bent over the panel, pouring power into the board. He looked up, nodded briefly as Jansen came in. It seemed to both of them that they had been apart for five minutes.

"Are they all hot yet?" asked Jansen.

"No, not yet."

The ship had been in deep space with her ports thrown open. Absolute cold had come in and gone to the core of her, and it was always a while before the ship was reclaimed and her instruments warmed. Even now there was a sharp chill in the air of the cabin.

Jansen sat down idly, rubbing his arms.

"Last time around, I guess."

"Yes," said Cohn, and added laconically, "I wish Weizsäcker was here."

Jansen grinned. Weizsäcker, poor old Weizsäcker. He was long dead and it was a good thing, for he was the most maligned human being in the System.

For a hundred years his theory on the birth of planets, that every sun necessarily gave birth to a satellite family, had been an accepted part of the knowledge of Man. And then, of course, there had come space flight.

Jansen chuckled wryly. Lucky man, Weizsäcker. Now, two hundred years and a thousand stars later, there had been discovered just four planets. Alpha Centauri had one: a barren, ice-crusted mote no larger than the Moon; and Pollux had three, all dead lumps of cold rock and iron. None of the other stars had any at all. Yes, it would have been a great blow to Weizsäcker.

A hum of current broke into Jansen's thought as the telescope was run out. There was a sudden beginning of light upon the screen.

In spite of himself and the wry, hopeless feeling that had been in him, Jansen arose quickly, with a thin trickle of nervousness in his arms. There is always a chance, he thought, after all, there is always a chance. We have only been to a thousand suns, and in the Galaxy a thousand suns are not anything at all. So there is always a chance.

Cohn, calm and methodical, was manning the radar.

Gradually, condensing upon the center of the screen, the image of the star took shape. It hung at last, huge and yellow and flaming with an awful brilliance, and the prominences of the rim made the vast circle uneven. Because the ship was close and the filter was in, the stars of the background were invisible, and there was nothing but the one great sun.

Jansen began to adjust for observation.

The observation was brief.

They paused for a moment before beginning the tests, gazing upon the face of the alien sun. The first of their race to be here and to see, they were caught up for a time in the ancient, deep thrill of space and the unknown Universe.

They watched, and into the field of their vision, breaking in slowly upon the glaring edge of the sun's disk, there came a small black ball. It moved steadily away from the edge, in toward the center of the sun. It was unquestionably a planet in transit.

When the alien ship moved, Roymer was considerably rattled.

One does not question Mind-Search, he knew, and so there could not be any living thing aboard that ship. Therefore, the ship's movement could be regarded only as a peculiar aberration in the still-functioning drive. Certainly, he thought, and peace returned to his mind.

But it did pose an uncomfortable problem. Boarding that ship would be no easy matter, not if the thing was inclined to go hopping away like that, with no warning. There were two hundred years of conditioning in Roymer, it would be impossible for him to put either his ship or his crew into an unnecessarily dangerous position. And wavery, erratic spaceships could undoubtedly be classified as dangerous.

Therefore, the ship would have to be disabled.

Regretfully, he connected with Fire control, put the operation into the hands of the Firecon officer, and settled back to observe the results of the actions against the strange craft.

And the alien moved again.

Not suddenly, as before, but deliberately now, the thing turned once more from its course, and its speed decreased even more rapidly. It was still moving in upon Mina, but now its orbit was tangential and no longer direct. As Roymer watched the ship come about, he turned up the magnification for a larger view, checked the automatic readings on the board below the screen. And his eyes were suddenly directed to a small, conical projection which had begun to rise up out of the ship, which rose for a short distance and stopped, pointed in on the orbit towards Mina at the center.

Roymer was bewildered, but he acted immediately. Firecon was halted, all protective screens were re-established, and the patrol ship back-tracked quickly into the protection of deep space.

There was no question in Roymer's mind that the movements of the alien had been directed by a living intelligence, and not by any mechanical means. There was also no doubt in Roymer's mind that there was no living being on board that ship. The problem was acute.

Roymer felt the scalp of his hairless head beginning to crawl. In the history of the galaxy, there had been discovered but five nonhuman races, yet never a race which did not betray its existence by the telepathic nature of its thinking. Roymer could not conceive of a people so alien that even the fundamental structure of their thought process was entirely different from the Galactics.

Extra-Galactics? He observed the ship closely and shook his head. No. Not an extra-Galactic ship certainly, much too primitive a type.

Extraspatial? His scalp crawled again.

Completely at a loss as to what to do, Roymer again contacted Mind-Search and requested that Trian be sent to him immediately.

Trian was preceded by a puzzled Goladan. The orders to alien contact, then to Firecon, and finally for a quick retreat, had affected the lieutenant deeply. He was a man accustomed to a strictly logical and somewhat ponderous course of events. He waited expectantly for some explanation to come from his usually serene commander.

Roymer, however, was busily occupied in tracking the alien's new course. An orbit about Mina, Roymer observed, with that conical projection laid on the star; a device of war; or some measuring instrument?

The stolid Trian appeared—walking would not quite describe how—and was requested to make another attempt at contact with the alien. He replied with his usual eerie silence and in a moment, when he turned back to Roymer, there was surprise in the transmitted thought.

"I cannot understand. There is life there now."

Roymer was relieved, but Goladan was blinking.

Trian went on, turning again to gaze at the screen.

"It is very remarkable. There are two life-beings. Human-type race. Their presence is very clear, they are"—he paused briefly—"explorers, it appears. But they were not there before. It is extremely unnerving."

So it is, Roymer agreed. He asked quickly: "Are they aware of us?"

"No. They are directing their attention on the star. Shall I contact?"

"No. Not yet. We will observe them first."

The alien ship floated upon the screen before them, moving in slow orbit about the star Mina.

Seven. There were seven of them. Seven planets, and three at least had atmospheres, and two might even be inhabitable. Jansen was so excited he was hopping around the control room. Cohn did nothing, but grin widely with a wondrous joy, and the two of them repeatedly shook hands and gloated.

"Seven!" roared Jansen. "Old lucky seven!"

Quickly then, and with extreme nervousness, they ran spectrograph analyses of each of those seven fascinating worlds. They began with the central planets, in the favorable temperature belt where life conditions would be most likely to exist, and they worked outwards.

For reasons which were as much sentimental as they were practical, they started with the third planet of this fruitful sun. There was a thin atmosphere, fainter even than that of Mars, and no oxygen. Silently they went on to the fourth. It was cold and heavy, perhaps twice as large as Earth, had a thick envelope of noxious gases. They saw with growing fear that there was no hope there, and they turned quickly inwards toward the warmer area nearer the sun.

On the second planet—as Jansen put it—they hit the jackpot.

A warm, green world it was, of an Earthlike size and atmosphere; oxygen and water vapor lines showed strong and clear in the analysis.

"This looks like it," said Jansen, grinning again.

Cohn nodded, left the screen and went over to man the navigating instruments.

"Let's go down and take a look."

"Radio check first." It was the proper procedure. Jansen had gone over it in his mind a thousand times. He clicked on the receiver, waited for the tubes to function, and then scanned for contact. As they moved in toward the new planet he listened intently, trying all lengths, waiting for any sound at all. There was nothing but the rasping static of open space.

"Well," he said finally, as the green planet grew large upon the screen, "if there's any race there, it doesn't have radio."

Cohn showed his relief.

"Could be a young civilization."

"Or one so ancient and advanced that it doesn't *need* radio."

Jansen refused to let his deep joy be dampened. It was impossible to know what would be there. Now it was just as it had been three hundred years ago, when the first Earth ship was approaching Mars. And it will be like this—Jansen thought—in every other system to which we go. How can you picture what there will be? There is nothing at all in your past to give you a clue. You can only hope.

The planet was a beautiful green ball on the screen.

The thought which came out of Trian's mind was tinged with relief.

"I see how it was done. They have achieved a complete stasis, a perfect state of suspended animation which they produce by an ingenious usage of the absolute zero of outer space. Thus, when they are—frozen, is the way they regard it—their minds do not function, and their lives are not detectable. They have just recently revived and are directing their ship."

Roymer digested the new information slowly. What kind of a race was this? A race which flew in primitive star ships, yet it had already conquered one of the greatest problems in Galactic history, a problem which had baffled the Galactics for millions of years. Roymer was uneasy.

"A very ingenious device," Trian was thinking, "they use it to alter the amount of subjective time consumed in their explorations. Their star ship has a very low maximum speed. Hence, without this— freeze—their voyage would take up a good portion of their lives."

"Can you classify the mind-type?" Roymer asked with growing concern.

Trian reflected silently for a moment.

"Yes," he said, "although the type is extremely unusual. I have never observed it before. General classification would be Human-Four. More specifically, I would place them at the Ninth level."

Roymer started. "The Ninth level?"

"Yes. As I say, they are extremely unusual."

Roymer was now clearly worried. He turned away and paced the deck for several moments. Abruptly, he left the room and went to the files of alien classification. He was gone for a long time, while Goladan fidgeted and Trian continued to gather information plucked across space from the alien minds. Roymer came back at last.

"What are they doing?"

"They are moving in on the second planet. They are about to determine whether the conditions are suitable there for an establishment of a colony of their kind."

Gravely, Roymer gave his orders to navigation. The patrol ship swung into motion, sped off swiftly in the direction of the second planet.

There was a single, huge blue ocean which covered an entire hemisphere of the new world. And the rest of the surface was a young jungle, wet and green and empty of any kind of people, choked with queer growths of green and orange. They circled the globe at a height of several thousand feet, and to their amazement and joy, they never saw a living thing; not a bird or a rabbit or the alien equivalent, in fact nothing alive at all. And so they stared in happy fascination.

"This is it," Jansen said again, his voice uneven.

"What do you think we ought to call it?" Cohn was speaking absently. "New Earth? Utopia?"

Together they watched the broken terrain slide by beneath them.

"No people at all. It's ours." And after a while Jansen said: "New Earth. That's a good name."

Cohn was observing the features of the ground intently.

"Do you notice the kind of . . . circular appearance of most of those mountain ranges? Like on the Moon, but grown over and eroded. They're all almost perfect circles."

Pulling his mind away from the tremendous visions he had of the colony which would be here, Jansen tried to look at the mountains with an objective eye. Yes, he realized with faint surprise, they were round, like Moon craters.

"Peculiar," Cohn muttered. "Not natural, I don't think. Couldn't be. Meteors not likely in this atmosphere. "What in—?"

Jansen jumped. "Look there," he cried suddenly, "a round lake!"

Off toward the northern pole of the planet, a lake which was a perfect circle came slowly into view. There was no break in the rim other than that of a small stream which flowed in from the north.

"That's not natural," Cohn said briefly, "someone built that."

They were moving on to the dark side now, and Cohn turned the ship around. The sense of exhilaration was too new for them to be let down, but the strange sight of a huge number of perfect circles, existing haphazardly like the remains of great splashes on the surface of the planet, was unnerving.

It was the sight of one particular crater, a great barren hole in the midst of a wide red desert, which rang a bell in Jansen's memory, and he blurted:

"A war! There was a war here. That one there looks just like a fusion bomb crater."

Cohn stared, then raised his eyebrows.

"I'll bet you're right."

"A bomb crater, do you see? Pushes up hills on all sides in a circle, and kills—" A sudden, terrible thought hit Jansen. Radioactivity. Would there be radioactivity here?

While Cohn brought the ship in low over the desert, he tried to calm Jansen's fears.

"There couldn't be much. Too much plant life. Jungles all over the place. Take it easy, man."

"But there's not a living thing on the planet. I'll bet that's why there was a war. It got out of hand, the radioactivity got everything. We might have done this to Earth!"

They glided in over the flat emptiness of the desert, and the counters began to click madly.

"That's it," Jansen said conclusively, "still radioactive. It might not have been too long ago."

"Could have been a million years, for all we know."

"Well, most places are safe, apparently. We'll check before we go down."

As he pulled the ship up and away, Cohn whistled.

"Do you suppose there's really not a living thing? I mean, not a bug or a germ or even a virus? Why, it's like a clean new world, a nursery!" He could not take his eyes from the screen.

They were going down now. In a very little while they would be out and walking in the sun. The lust of the feeling was indescribable. They were Earthmen freed forever from the choked home of the System, Earthmen gone out to the stars, landing now upon the next world of their empire.

Cohn could not control himself.

"Do we need a flag?" he said grinning. "How do we claim this place?"

"Just set her down, man," Jansen roared.

Cohn began to chuckle.

"Oh, brave new world," he laughed, "that has *no* people in it."

"But why do we have to contact them?" Goladan asked impatiently. "Could we not just—"

Roymer interrupted without looking at him.

"The law requires that contact be made and the situation explained before action is taken. Otherwise it would be a barbarous act."

Goladan brooded.

The patrol ship hung in the shadow of the dark side, tracing the alien by its radioactive trail. The alien was going down for a landing on the daylight side.

Trian came forward with the other members of the Alien Contact Crew, reported to Roymer, "The aliens have landed."

"Yes," said Roymer, "we will let them have a little time. Trian, do you think you will have any difficulty in the transmission?"

"No. Conversation will not be difficult. Although the confused and complex nature of their thought-patterns does make their inner reactions somewhat obscure. But I do not think there will be any problem."

"Very well. You will remain here and relay the messages."

"Yes."

The patrol ship flashed quickly up over the north pole, then swung inward toward the equator, circling the spot where the alien had gone down. Roymer brought his ship in low and with the silence characteristic of a Galactic, landed her in a wooded spot a mile east of the alien. The Galactics remained in their ship for a short while as Trian continued his probe for information. When at last the Alien Contact Crew stepped out, Roymer and Goladan were in the lead. The rest of the crew faded quietly into the jungle.

As he walked through the young orange brush, Roymer regarded the world around him. Almost ready for repopulation, he thought, in another hundred years the radiation will be gone, and we will come back. One by one the worlds of that war will be reclaimed.

He felt Trian's directions pop into his mind.

"You are approaching them. Proceed with caution. They are just beyond the next small rise. I think you had better wait, since they are remaining close to their ship."

Roymer sent back a silent yes. Motioning Goladan to be quiet, Roymer led the way up the last rise. In the jungle around him the Galactic crew moved silently.

The air was perfect; there was no radiation. Except for the wild orange color of the vegetation, the spot was a Garden of Eden. Jansen felt instinctively that there was no danger here, no terrible blight or virus or any harmful thing. He felt a violent urge to get out of his spacesuit and run and breathe, but it was forbidden. Not on the first trip. That would come later, after all the tests and experiments had been made and the world pronounced safe.

One of the first things Jansen did was get out the recorder and solemnly claim this world for the Solar Federation, recording the historic words for the archives of Earth. And he and Cohn remained for a while by the air lock of their ship, gazing around at the strange yet familiar world into which they had come.

"Later on we'll search for ruins," Cohn said. "Keep an eye out for anything that moves. It's possible that there are some of them left and who knows what they'll look like. Mutants, probably, with five heads. So keep an eye open."

"Right."

Jansen began collecting samples of the ground, of the air, of the nearer foliage. The dirt was Earth-dirt, there was no difference. He reached down and crumbled the soft moist sod with his fingers. The flowers may be a little peculiar—probably mutated, he thought—but the dirt is honest to goodness dirt, and I'll bet the air is Earth-air.

He rose and stared into the clear open blue of the sky, feeling again an almost overpowering urge to throw open his helmet and breathe, and as he stared at the sky and at the green and orange hills, suddenly, a short distance from where he stood, a little old man came walking over the hill.

They stood facing each other across the silent space of a foreign glade. Roymer's face was old and smiling; Jansen looked back at him with absolute astonishment.

After a short pause, Roymer began to walk out into the open soil, with Goladan following, and Jansen went for his heat gun.

"Cohn!" he yelled, in a raw brittle voice, "Cohn!"

And as Cohn turned and saw and froze, Jansen heard words being spoken in his brain. They were words coming from the little old man.

"Please do not shoot," the old man said, his lips unmoving.

"No, don't shoot," Cohn said quickly. "Wait. Let him alone." The hand of Cohn, too, was at his heat gun.

Roymer smiled. To the two Earthmen his face was incredibly old and wise and gentle. He was thinking: Had I been a nonhuman they would have killed me.

He sent a thought back to Trian. The Mind-Searcher picked it up and relayed it into the brains of the Earthmen, sending it through their cortical centers and then up into their conscious minds, so that the words were heard in the language of Earth. "Thank you," Roymer said gently. Jansen's hand held the heat gun leveled on Roymer's chest. He stared, not knowing what to say.

"Please remain where you are," Cohn's voice was hard and steady.

Roymer halted obligingly. Goladan stopped at his elbow, peering at the Earthmen with mingled fear and curiosity. The sight of fear helped Jansen very much.

"Who are you?" Cohn said clearly, separating the words.

Roymer folded his hands comfortably across his chest, he was still smiling.

"With your leave, I will explain our presence."

Cohn just stared.

"There will be a great deal to explain. May we sit down and talk?"

Trian helped with the suggestion. They sat down.

The sun of the new world was setting, and the conference went on. Roymer was doing most of the talking. The Earthmen sat transfixed.

It was like growing up suddenly, in the space of a second.

The history of Earth and of all Mankind just faded and dropped away. They heard of great races and worlds beyond number, the illimitable government which was the Galactic Federation. The fiction, the legends, the dreams of a thousand years had come true in a moment, in the figure of a square little old man who was not from Earth. There was a great deal for them to learn and accept in the time of a single afternoon, on an alien planet.

But it was just as new and real to them that they had discovered an uninhabited, fertile planet, the first to be found by Man. And they could not help but revolt from the sudden realization that the planet might well be someone else's property—that the Galactics owned everything worth owning.

It was an intolerable thought.

"How far," asked Cohn, as his heart pushed up in his throat, "does the Galactic League extend?"

Roymer's voice was calm and direct in their minds.

"Only throughout the central regions of the galaxy. There are millions of stars along the rim which have not yet been explored."

Cohn relaxed, bowed down with relief. There was room then, for Earthmen.

"This planet. Is it part of the Federation?"

"Yes," said Roymer, and Cohn tried to mask his thought. Cohn was angry, and he hoped that the alien could not read his mind as well as he could talk to it. To have come this far—

"There was a race here once," Roymer was saying, "a humanoid race which was almost totally destroyed by war. This planet has been uninhabitable for a very long time. A few of its people who were in space at the time of the last attack were spared. The Federation established them elsewhere. When the planet is ready, the descendants of those survivors will be brought back. It is their home."

Neither of the Earthmen spoke.

"It is surprising," Roymer went on, "that your home world is in the desert. We had thought that there were no habitable worlds—"

"The desert?"

"Yes. The region of the galaxy from which you have come is that which we call the desert. It is an area almost entirely devoid of planets. Would you mind telling me which star is your home?"

Cohn stiffened.

"I'm afraid our government would not permit us to disclose any information concerning our race."

"As you wish. I am sorry you are disturbed. I was curious to know—" He waved a negligent hand to show that the information was unimportant. We will get it later, he thought, when we decipher their charts. He was coming to the end of the conference, he was about to say what he had come to say.

"No doubt you have been exploring the stars about your world?"

The Earthmen both nodded. But for the question concerning Sol, they long ago would have lost all fear of this placid old man and his wide-eyed, silent companion.

"Perhaps you would like to know," said Roymer, "why your area is a desert."

Instantly, both Jansen and Cohn were completely absorbed. This was it, the end of three hundred years of searching. They would go home with the answer.

Roymer never relaxed.

"Not too long ago," he said, "approximately thirty thousand years by your reckoning, a great race ruled the desert, a race which was known as the Antha, and it was not a desert then. The Antha ruled hundreds of worlds. They were perhaps the greatest of all the Galactic peoples; certainly they were as brilliant a race as the galaxy has ever known.

"But they were not a good race. For hundreds of years, while they were still young, we tried to bring them into the Federation. They refused, and of course we did not force them. But as the years went by the scope of their knowledge increased amazingly; shortly they were the technological equals of any other race in the galaxy. And then the Antha embarked upon an era of imperialistic expansion.

"They were superior, they knew it and were proud. And so they pushed out and enveloped the races and worlds of the area now known as the desert. Their rule was a tyranny unequaled in Galactic history."

The Earthmen never moved, and Roymer went on.

"But the Antha were not members of the Federation, and, therefore, they were not answerable for their acts. We could only stand by and watch as they spread their vicious rule from world to world. They were absolutely ruthless.

"As an example of their kind of rule, I will tell you of their crime against the Apectans.

"The planet of Apectus not only resisted the Antha, but somehow managed to hold out against their approach for several years. The Antha finally conquered and then, in retaliation for the Apectans' valor, they conducted the most brutal of their mass experiments.

"They were a brilliant people. They had been experimenting with the genes of heredity. Somehow they found a way to alter the genes of the Apectans, who were humanoids like themselves, and they did it on a mass scale. They did not choose to exterminate the race, their revenge was much greater. Every Apectan born since the Antha invasion, has been born without one arm."

Jansen sucked in his breath. It was a very horrible thing to hear, and a sudden memory came into his brain. Caesar did that, he thought. He cut off the right hands of the Gauls. Peculiar coincidence. Jansen felt uneasy.

Roymer paused for a moment.

"The news of what happened to the Apectans set the Galactic peoples up in arms, but it was not until the Antha attacked a Federation world that we finally moved against them. It was the greatest war in the history of Life.

"You will perhaps understand how great a people the Antha were when I tell you that they alone, unaided, dependent entirely upon their own resources, fought the rest of the Galactics, and fought them to a standstill. As the terrible years went by we lost whole races and planets—like this one, which was one the Antha destroyed—and yet we could not defeat them.

"It was only after many years, when a Galactic invented the most dangerous weapon of all, that we won. The invention—of which only the Galactic Council has knowledge—enabled us to turn the suns of the Antha into novae, at long range. One by one we destroyed the Antha worlds. We hunted them through all the planets of the desert; for the first time in history the edict of the Federation was death, death for an entire race. At last there were no longer any habitable worlds where the Antha had been. We burned their worlds, and ran them down in space. Thirty thousand years ago, the civilization of the Antha perished."

Roymer had finished. He looked at the Earthmen out of grave, tired old eyes.

Cohn was staring in open-mouth fascination, but Jansen—unaccountably felt a chill. The story of Caesar remained uncomfortably in his mind. And he had a quick, awful suspicion.

"Are you sure you got all of them?"

"No. Some surely must have escaped. There were too many in space, and space is without limits."

Jansen wanted to know: "Have any of them been heard of since?"

Roymer's smile left him as the truth came out. "No. Not until now."

There were only a few more seconds. He gave them time to understand. He could not help telling them that he was sorry, he even apologized. And then he sent the order with his mind.

The Antha died quickly and silently, without pain.

Only thirty thousand years, Roymer was thinking, but thirty thousand years, and they came back out to the stars. They have no memory now of what they were or what they have done. They started all over again, the old history of the race has been lost, and in thirty thousand years they came all the way back.

Roymer shook his head with sad wonder and awe. The most brilliant people of all.

Goladan came in quietly with the final reports.

"There are no charts," he grumbled, "no maps at all. We will not be able to trace them to their home star."

Roymer did not know, really, what was right, to be disappointed or relieved. We cannot destroy them now, he thought, not right away. He could not help being relieved. Maybe this time there will be a way, and they will not have to be destroyed. They could be—

He remembered the edict—the edict of death. The Antha had forged it for themselves and it was just. He realized that there wasn't much hope.

The reports were on his desk and he regarded them with a wry smile. There was indeed no way to trace them back. They had no charts, only a regular series of course-check coordinates which were preset on their home planet and which were not decipherable. Even at this stage of their civilization they had already anticipated the consequences of having their ship fall into alien hands. And this although they lived in the desert.

Goladan startled him with an anxious question:

"What can we do?"

Roymer was silent.

We can wait, he thought. Gradually, one by one, they will come out of the desert, and when they come we will be waiting. Perhaps one day we will follow one back and destroy their world, and perhaps before then we will find a way to save them.

Suddenly, as his eyes wandered over the report before him and he recalled the ingenious mechanism of the freeze, a chilling, unbidden thought came into his brain.

And perhaps, he thought calmly, for he was a philosophical man, they will come out already equipped to rule the galaxy.

AFTERWORD BY JIM BAEN

This story bowled me over when I read it at age fourteen because it answered a question that'd plagued me practically my whole thinking life (the past two years, maybe): all those planets had to be inhabited by all those aliens; so where were they? (This is Fermi's Paradox to people who know who Fermi was. I didn't, of course.)

I was born and raised in a rural community on the New York/Pennsylvania border. It was very easy for me to imagine a universe which was without intelligent life for an immense distance surrounding me. But one relative had an attic of SF magazines, including the *Astounding* with "All the Way Back."

Shaara's answer (and I suspect it *was* a conscious answer, albeit a flip one) mapped the data perfectly. Maybe the reason it seemed so profound to me is that in 1957 we all knew we were going to die in a thermonuclear holocaust in a few years. What was this but that, writ very large?

The Last Command

by Keith Laumer

PREFACE BY DAVID DRAKE
I was twenty-one when I read "The Last Command" on its appearance in the January 1967 issue of *Analog*. I was in my senior year of college and probably as mature then as I'm ever going to be. I read most of the other stories I've picked for this anthology when I was much younger.

It's not quite correct to describe Keith Laumer's Bolo series as stories about war machines. The three that really have an impact are about veterans who've been discarded by society; that the veterans happen to be machines is really beside the point. "The Last Command" makes this explicit.

The story hit me very hard the first time I read it. I'm not sure why: I don't come from a military family, and I'd been accepted at Duke Law School. Students were deferred from the draft. I never dreamed that someday *I'd* be a veteran.

Then things changed.

In January 1971, I got back to the World and took off my uniform for the last time. Since that day I've never, in my heart of hearts, been able to forget that I'm a veteran.

1

*I come to awareness, sensing a residual oscillation traversing me
from an arbitrarily designated heading of 035. From the damping
rate I compute that the shock was of intensity 8.7, emanating from a
source within the limits 72 meters/46 meters. I activate my primary
screens, trigger a return salvo. There is no response. I engage reserve
energy cells, bring my secondary battery to bear—futilely. It is apparent that I have been ranged by the Enemy and severely damaged.*

*My positional sensors indicate that I am resting at an angle of
13 degrees 14 seconds, deflected from a baseline at 21 points from
median. I attempt to right myself, but encounter massive resistance.
I activate my forward scanners, shunt power to my I-R microstrobes.
Not a flicker illuminates my surroundings. I am encased in utter
blackness.*

*Now a secondary shock wave approaches, rocks me with an intensity
of 8.2. It is apparent that I must withdraw from my position—but
my drive trains remain inert under full thrust. I shift to base emergency power, try again. Pressure mounts; I sense my awareness fading
under the intolerable strain; then, abruptly, resistance falls off and
I am in motion.*

*It is not the swift maneuvering of full drive, however; I inch for-
ward, as if restrained by massive barriers. Again I attempt to penetrate the surrounding darkness and this time perceive great irregular
outlines shot through with fracture planes. I probe cautiously, then
more vigorously, encountering incredible densities.*

*I channel all available power to a single ranging pulse, direct it
upward. The indication is so at variance with all experience that I
repeat the test at a new angle. Now I must accept the fact: I am
buried under 207.6 meters of solid rock!*

*I direct my attention to an effort to orient myself to my uniquely
desperate situation. I run through an action-status checklist of thirty
thousand items, feel dismay at the extent of power loss. My main cells
are almost completely drained, my reserve units at no more than .4
charge. Thus my sluggishness is explained. I review the tactical situation, recall the triumphant announcement from my commander that
the Enemy forces were annihilated, that all resistance had ceased. In
memory, I review the formal procession; in company with my comrades
of the Dinochrome Brigade, many of us deeply scarred by Enemy
action, we parade before the Grand Commandant, then assemble on
the depot ramp. At command, we bring our music storage cells into
phase and display our Battle Anthem. The nearby star radiates over*

a full spectrum unfiltered by atmospheric haze. It is a moment of glorious triumph. Then the final command is given—

The rest is darkness. But it is apparent that the victory celebration was premature. The Enemy has counterattacked with a force that has come near to immobilizing me. The realization is shocking, but the .1 second of leisurely introspection has clarified my position. At once, I broadcast a call on Brigade Action wave length:

"Unit LNE to Command, requesting permission to file VSR."

I wait, sense no response, call again, using full power. I sweep the enclosing volume of rock with an emergency alert warning. I tune to the all-units band, await the replies of my comrades of the Brigade. None answer. Now I must face the reality: I alone have survived the assault.

I channel my remaining power to my drive and detect a channel of reduced density. I press for it and the broken rock around me yields reluctantly. Slowly, I move forward and upward. My pain circuitry shocks my awareness center with emergency signals; I am doing irreparable damage to my overloaded neural systems, but my duty is clear: I must seek out and engage the Enemy.

2

Emerging from behind the blast barrier, Chief Engineer Pete Reynolds of the New Devonshire Port Authority pulled off his rock mask and spat grit from his mouth.

"That's the last one; we've bottomed out at just over two hundred yards. Must have hit a hard stratum down there."

"It's almost sundown," the paunchy man beside him said shortly. "You're a day and a half behind schedule."

"We'll start backfilling now, Mr. Mayor. I'll have pilings poured by oh-nine hundred tomorrow, and with any luck the first section of pad will be in place in time for the rally."

"I'm—" The mayor broke off, looked startled. "I thought you told me that was the last charge to be fired . . ."

Reynolds frowned. A small but distinct tremor had shaken the ground underfoot. A few feet away, a small pebble balanced atop another toppled and fell with a faint clatter.

"Probably a big rock fragment falling," he said. At that moment, a second vibration shook the earth, stronger this time. Reynolds heard a rumble and a distant impact as rock fell from the side of the newly blasted excavation. He whirled to the control shed as the door swung back and Second Engineer Mayfield appeared.

"Take a look at this, Pete!"

Reynolds went across to the hut, stepped inside. Mayfield was bending over the profiling table.

"What do you make of it?" he pointed. Superimposed on the heavy red contour representing the detonation of the shaped charge that had completed the drilling of the final pile core were two other traces, weak but distinct.

"About .1 intensity." Mayfield looked puzzled. "What—"

The tracking needle dipped suddenly, swept up the screen to peak at .21, dropped back. The hut trembled. A stylus fell from the edge of the table. The red face of Mayor Dougherty burst through the door.

"Reynolds, have you lost your mind? What's the idea of blasting while I'm standing out in the open? I might have been killed!"

"I'm not blasting," Reynolds snapped. "Jim, get Eaton on the line, see if they know anything." He stepped to the door, shouted. A heavyset man in sweat-darkened coveralls swung down from the seat of a cable-lift rig.

"Boss, what goes on?" he called as he came up. "Damn near shook me out of my seat!"

"I don't know. You haven't set any trim charges?"

"Jesus, no, boss. I wouldn't set no charges without your say-so."

"Come on." Reynolds started out across the rubble-littered stretch of barren ground selected by the Authority as the site of the new spaceport. Halfway to the open mouth of the newly-blasted pit, the ground under his feet rocked violently enough to make him stumble. A gout of dust rose from the excavation ahead. Loose rock danced on the ground. Beside him the drilling chief grabbed his arm.

"Boss, we better get back!"

Reynolds shook him off, kept going. The drill chief swore and followed. The shaking of the ground went on, a sharp series of thumps interrupting a steady trembling.

"It's a quake!" Reynolds yelled over the low rumbling sound.

He and the chief were at the rim of the core now.

"It can't be a quake, boss," the latter shouted. "Not in these formations!"

"Tell it to the geologists—" The rock slab they were standing on rose a foot, dropped back. Both men fell. The slab bucked like a small boat in choppy water.

"Let's get out of here!" Reynolds was up and running. Ahead, a fissure opened, gaped a foot wide. He jumped it, caught a glimpse of black depths, a glint of wet clay twenty feet below—

A hoarse scream stopped him in his tracks. He spun, saw the drill chief down, a heavy splinter of rock across his legs. He jumped to him, heaved at the rock. There was blood on the man's shirt. The chief's hands beat the dusty rock before him. Then other men were there, grunting, sweaty hands gripping beside Reynolds. The ground rocked. The roar from under the earth had risen to a deep, steady rumble. They lifted the rock aside, picked up the injured man, and stumbled with him to the aid shack.

The mayor was there, white-faced.

"What is it, Reynolds? By God, if you're responsible—"

"Shut up!" Reynolds brushed him aside, grabbed the phone, punched keys.

"Eaton! What have you got on this temblor?"

"Temblor, hell." The small face on the four-inch screen looked like a ruffled hen. "What in the name of Order are you doing out there? I'm reading a whole series of displacements originating from that last core of yours! What did you do, leave a pile of trim charges lying around?"

"It's a quake. Trim charges, hell! This thing's broken up two hundred yards of surface rock. It seems to be traveling north-northeast—"

"I see that; a traveling earthquake!" Eaton flapped his arms, a tiny and ridiculous figure against a background of wall charts and framed diplomas. "Well—do something, Reynolds! Where's Mayor Dougherty?"

"Underfoot!" Reynolds snapped, and cut off.

Outside, a layer of sunset-stained dust obscured the sweep of level plain. A rock-dozer rumbled up, ground to a halt by Reynolds. A man jumped down.

"I got the boys moving equipment out," he panted. "The thing's cutting a trail straight as a rule for the highway!" He pointed to a raised roadbed a quarter mile away.

"How fast is it moving?"

"She's done a hundred yards; it hasn't been ten minutes yet!"

"If it keeps up another twenty minutes, it'll be into the Inter-mix!"

"Scratch a few million cees and six months' work then, Pete!"

"And Southside Mall's a couple miles farther."

"Hell, it'll damp out before then!"

"Maybe. Grab a field car, Dan."

"Pete!" Mayfield came up at a trot. "This thing's building! The centroid's moving on a heading of oh-two-two—"

"How far subsurface?"

"It's rising; started at two-twenty yards, and it's up to one-eighty!"

"What the hell have we stirred up?" Reynolds stared at Mayfield as the field car skidded to a stop beside them.

"Stay with it, Jim. Give me anything new. We're taking a closer look." He climbed into the rugged vehicle.

"Take a blast truck—"

"No time!" He waved and the car gunned away into the pall of dust.

3

The rock car pulled to a stop at the crest of the three-level Intermix on a lay-by designed to permit tourists to enjoy the view of the site of the proposed port, a hundred feet below. Reynolds studied the progress of the quake through field glasses. From this vantage point, the path of the phenomenon was a clearly defined trail of tilted and broken rock, some of the slabs twenty feet across. As he watched, the fissures lengthened.

"It looks like a mole's trail." Reynolds handed the glasses to his companion, thumbed the send key on the car radio.

"Jim, get Eaton and tell him to divert all traffic from the Circular south of Zone Nine. Cars are already clogging the right-of-way. The dust is visible from a mile away, and when the word gets out there's something going on, we'll be swamped."

"I'll tell him, but he won't like it!"

"This isn't politics! This thing will be into the outer pad area in another twenty minutes!"

"It won't last—"

"How deep does it read now?"

"One-five!" There was a moment's silence. "Pete, if it stays on course, it'll surface about where you're parked!"

"Uh-huh. It looks like you can scratch one Intermix. Better tell Eaton to get a story ready for the press."

"Pete, talking about news hounds—" Dan said beside him. Reynolds switched off, turned to see a man in a gay-colored driving outfit coming across from a battered Monojag sportster which had pulled up behind the rock car. A big camera case was slung across his shoulder.

"Say, what's going on down there?" he called.

"Rock slide," Reynolds said shortly. "I'll have to ask you to drive on. The road's closed to all traffic—"

"Who're you?" The man looked belligerent.

"I'm the engineer in charge. Now pull out, brother." He turned back to the radio. "Jim, get every piece of heavy equipment we own over here, on the double." He paused, feeling a minute trembling in the car. "The Intermix is beginning to feel it," he went on. "I'm afraid we're in for it. Whatever that thing is, it acts like a solid body boring its way through the ground. Maybe we can barricade it."

"Barricade an earthquake?"

"Yeah, I know how it sounds—but it's the only idea I've got."

"Hey—what's that about an earthquake?" The man in the colored suit was still there. "By gosh, I can feel it—the whole damned bridge is shaking!"

"Off, mister—now!" Reynolds jerked a thumb at the traffic lanes where a steady stream of cars were hurtling past. "Dan, take us over to the main track. We'll have to warn this traffic off—"

"Hold on, fellow." The man unlimbered his camera. "I represent the New Devon *Scope*. I have a few questions—"

"I don't have the answers." Pete cut him off as the car pulled away.

"Hah!" The man who had questioned Reynolds yelled after him. "Big shot! Think you can . . ." His voice was lost behind them.

4

In a modest retirees' apartment block in the coast town of Idlebreeze, forty miles from the scene of the freak quake, an old man sat in a reclining chair, half dozing before a yammering Tri-D tank.

" . . . Grandpa," a sharp-voice young woman was saying. "It's time for you to go in to bed."

"Bed? Why do I want to go to bed? Can't sleep anyway . . ." He stirred, made a pretense of sitting up, showing an interest in the Tri-D. "I'm watching this show. Don't bother me."

"It's not a show, it's the news," a fattish boy said disgustedly. "Ma, can I switch channels—"

"Leave it alone, Bennie," the old man said. On the screen a panoramic scene spread out, a stretch of barren ground across which a furrow showed. As he watched, it lengthened.

" . . . up here at the Intermix we have a fine view of the whole curious business, lazangemmun," the announcer chattered. "And in our opinion it's some sort of publicity stunt staged by the Port Authority to publicize their controversial port project—"

"Ma, can I change channels?"

"Go ahead, Bennie—"

"Don't touch it," the old man said. The fattish boy reached for the control, but something in the old man's eye stopped him . . .

5

"The traffic's still piling in here," Reynolds said into the phone. "Damn it, Jim, we'll have a major jam on our hands—"

"He won't do it, Pete! You know the Circular was his baby—the super all-weather pike that nothing could shut down. He says you'll have to handle this in the field—"

"Handle, hell! I'm talking about preventing a major disaster! And in a matter of minutes, at that!"

"I'll try again—"

"If he says no, divert a couple of the big ten-yard graders and block it off yourself. Set up field arcs, and keep any cars from getting in from either direction."

"Pete, that's outside your authority!"

"You heard me!"

Ten minutes later, back at ground level, Reynolds watched the boom-mounted polyarcs swinging into position at the two road-blocks a quarter of a mile apart, cutting off the threatened section of the raised expressway. A hundred yards from where he stood on the rear cargo deck of a light grader rig, a section of rock fifty feet wide rose slowly, split, fell back with a ponderous impact. One corner of it struck the massive pier supporting the extended shelf of the lay-by above. A twenty-foot splinter fell away, exposing the reinforcing-rod core.

"How deep, Jim?" Reynolds spoke over the roaring sound coming from the disturbed area.

"Just subsurface now, Pete! It ought to break through—" His voice was drowned in a rumble as the damaged pier shivered, rose up, buckled at its midpoint, and collapsed, bringing down with it a large chunk of pavement and guard rail, and a single still-glowing light pole. A small car that had been parked on the doomed section was visible for an instant just before the immense slab struck. Reynolds saw it bounce aside, then disappear under an avalanche of broken concrete.

"My God, Pete—" Dan started. "That damned fool news hound . . . !"

"Look!" As the two men watched, a second pier swayed, fell backward into the shadow of the span above. The roadway sagged, and two more piers snapped. With a bellow like a burst dam, a hundred-foot stretch of the road fell into the roiling dust cloud.

"Pete!" Mayfield's voice burst from the car radio. "Get out of there! I threw a reader on that thing and it's chattering off the scale . . . !"

Among the piled fragments something stirred, heaved, rising up, lifting multi-ton pieces of the broken road, thrusting them aside like so many potato chips. A dull blue radiance broke through from the broached earth, threw an eerie light on the shattered structure above. A massive, ponderously irresistible shape thrust forward through the ruins. Reynolds saw a great blue-glowing profile emerge from the rubble like a surfacing submarine, shedding a burden of broken stone, saw immense treads ten feet wide claw for purchase, saw the mighty flank brush a still-standing pier, send it crashing aside.

"Pete, what—what is it . . . ?"

"I don't know." Reynolds broke the paralysis that had gripped him. "Get us out of here, Dan, fast! Whatever it is, it's headed straight for the city!"

6

I emerge at last from the trap into which I had fallen, and at once encounter defensive works of considerable strength. My scanners are dulled from lack of power, but I am able to perceive open ground beyond the barrier, and farther still, at a distance of 5.7 kilometers, massive walls. Once more I transmit the Brigade Rally signal; but as before, there is no reply. I am truly alone.

I scan the surrounding area for the emanations of Enemy drive units, monitor the EM spectrum for their communications. I detect nothing; either my circuitry is badly damaged, or their shielding is superb.

I must now make a decision as to possible courses of action. Since all my comrades of the Brigade have fallen, I compute that the fortress before me must be held by Enemy forces. I direct probing signals at them, discover them to be of unfamiliar construction, and less formidable than they appear. I am aware of the possibility that this may be a trick of the Enemy; but my course is clear.

I reengage my driving engines and advance on the Enemy fortress.

7

"You're out of your mind, father," the stout man said. "At your age—"

"At your age, I got my nose smashed in a brawl in a bar on Aldo," the old man cut him off. "But I won the fight."

"James, you can't go out at this time of night . . ." an elderly woman wailed.

"Tell them to go home." The old man walked painfully toward his bedroom door. "I've seen enough of them for today." He passed out of sight.

"Mother, you won't let him do anything foolish?"

"He'll forget about it in a few minutes; but maybe you'd better go now and let him settle down."

"Mother—I really think a home is the best solution."

"Yes," the young woman nodded agreement. "After all, he's past ninety—and he has his veteran's retirement . . ."

Inside his room, the old man listened as they departed. He went to the closet, took out clothes, began dressing . . .

8

City Engineer Eaton's face was chalk-white on the screen.

"No one can blame me," he said. "How could I have known—"

"Your office ran the surveys and gave the PA the green light," Mayor Dougherty yelled.

"All the old survey charts showed was 'Disposal Area,'" Eaton threw out his hands. "I assumed—"

"As City Engineer, you're not paid to make assumptions! Ten minutes' research would have told you that was a 'Y' category area!"

"What's 'Y' category mean?" Mayfield asked Reynolds. They were standing by the field comm center, listening to the dispute. Nearby, boom-mounted Tri-D cameras hummed, recording the progress of the immense machine, its upper turret rearing forty-five feet into the air, as it ground slowly forward across smooth ground toward the city, dragging behind it a trailing festoon of twisted reinforcing iron crusted with broken concrete.

"Half-life over one hundred years," Reynolds answered shortly. "The last skirmish of the war was fought near here. Apparently this is where they buried the radioactive equipment left over from the battle."

"But what the hell, that was seventy years ago—"

"There's still enough residual radiation to contaminate anything inside a quarter-mile radius."

"They must have used some hellish stuff." Mayfield stared at the dull shine half a mile distant.

"Reynolds, how are you going to stop this thing?" The mayor had turned on the PA engineer.

"Me stop it? You saw what it did to my heaviest rigs: flattened them like pancakes. You'll have to call out the military on this one, Mr. Mayor."

"Call in Federation forces? Have them meddling in civic affairs?"

"The station's only sixty-five miles from here. I think you'd better call them fast. It's only moving at about three miles per hour but it will reach the south edge of the Mall in another forty-five minutes."

"Can't you mine it? Blast a trap in its path?"

"You saw it claw its way up from six hundred feet down. I checked the specs; it followed the old excavation tunnel out. It was rubble-filled and capped with twenty-inch compressed concrete."

"It's incredible," Eaton said from the screen. "The entire machine was encased in a ten-foot shell of reinforced armocrete. It had to break out of that before it could move a foot!"

"That was just a radiation shield; it wasn't intended to restrain a Bolo Combat Unit."

"What was, may I inquire?" The mayor glared from one face to another.

"The units were deactivated before being buried," Eaton spoke up, as if he were eager to talk. "Their circuits were fused. It's all in the report—"

"The report you should have read somewhat sooner," the mayor snapped.

"What—what started it up?" Mayfield looked bewildered. "For seventy years it was down there, and nothing happened!"

"Our blasting must have jarred something," Reynolds said shortly. "Maybe closed a relay that started up the old battle reflex circuit."

"You know something about these machines?" The mayor beetled his brows at him.

"I've read a little."

"Then speak up, man. I'll call the station, if you feel I must. What measures should I request?"

"I don't know, Mr. Mayor. As far as I know, nothing on New Devon can stop that machine now."

The mayor's mouth opened and closed. He whirled to the screen, blanked Eaton's agonized face, punched in the code for the Federation station.

"Colonel Blane!" he blurted as a stern face came onto the screen. "We have a major emergency on our hands! I'll need everything you've got! This is the situation . . ."

9

I encounter no resistance other than the flimsy barrier, but my progress is slow. Grievous damage has been done to my main drive sector due to overload during my escape from the trap; and the failure of my sensing circuitry has deprived me of a major portion of my external receptivity. Now my pain circuits project a continuous signal to my awareness center, but it is my duty to my Commander and to my fallen comrades of the Brigade to press forward at my best speed; but my performance is a poor shadow of my former ability.

And now at last the Enemy comes into action! I sense aerial units closing at supersonic velocities; I lock my lateral batteries to them and direct salvo fire, but I sense that the arming mechanisms clatter harmlessly. The craft sweep over me, and my impotent guns elevate, track them as they release detonants that spread out in an envelopmental pattern which I, with my reduced capabilities, am powerless to avoid. The missiles strike; I sense their detonations all about me; but I suffer only trivial damage. The Enemy has blundered if he thought to neutralize a Mark XXVIII Combat Unit with mere chemical explosives! But I weaken with each meter gained.

Now there is no doubt as to my course. I must press the charge and carry the walls before my reserve cells are exhausted.

10

From a vantage point atop a bucket rig four hundred yards from the position the great fighting machine had now reached, Pete Reynolds studied it through night glasses. A battery of beamed polyarcs pinned the giant hulk, scarred and rust-scaled, in a pool of blue-white light. A mile and a half beyond it, the walls of the Mall rose sheer from the garden setting.

"The bombers slowed it some," he reported to Eaton via scope. "But it's still making better than two miles per hour. I'd say another twenty-five minutes before it hits the main ringwall. How's the evacuation going?"

"Badly! I get no cooperation! You'll be my witness, Reynolds, I did all I could—"

"How about the mobile batteries; how long before they'll be in position?" Reynolds cut him off.

"I've heard nothing from Federation Central—typical militaristic arrogance, not keeping me informed—but I have them on my screens. They're two miles out—say three minutes."

"I hope you made your point about N-heads."

"That's outside my province!" Eaton said sharply. "It's up to Brand to carry out this portion of the operation!"

"The HE Missiles didn't do much more than clear away the junk it was dragging." Reynolds' voice was sharp.

"I wash my hands of responsibility for civilian lives," Eaton was saying when Reynolds shut him off, changed channels.

"Jim, I'm going to try to divert it," he said crisply. "Eaton's sitting on his political fence; the Feds are bringing artillery up, but I don't expect much from it. Technically, Brand needs Sector okay to use nuclear stuff, and he's not the boy to stick his neck out—"

"Divert it how? Pete, don't take any chances—"

Reynolds laughed shortly. "I'm going to get around it and drop a shaped drilling charge in its path. Maybe I can knock a tread off. With luck, I might get its attention on me and draw it away from the Mall. There are still a few thousand people over there, glued to their Tri-D's. They think it's all a swell show."

"Pete, you can't walk up on that thing! It's hot—" He broke off. "Pete, there's some kind of nut here—he claims he has to talk to you; says he knows something about that damned juggernaut. Shall I . . . ?"

Reynolds paused with his hand on the cut-off switch. "Put him on," he snapped. Mayfield's face moved aside and an ancient, bleary-eyed visage stared out at him. The tip of the old man's tongue touched his dry lips.

"Son, I tried to tell this boy here, but he wouldn't listen—"

"What have you got, old timer?" Pete cut in. "Make it fast."

"My name's Sanders. James Sanders. I'm . . . I was with the Planetary Volunteer Scouts, back in '71—"

"Sure, dad," Pete said gently. "I'm sorry, I've got a little errand to run—"

"Wait . . ." The old man's face worked. "I'm old, son—too damned old. I know. But bear with me. I'll try to say it straight. I was with Hayle's squadron at Toledo. Then afterwards, they shipped us—but hell, you don't care about that! I keep wandering, son; can't help it. What I mean to say is—I was in on that last scrap, right here at New Devon—only we didn't call it New Devon then. Called it Hellport. Nothing but bare rock and Enemy emplacement—"

"You were talking about the battle, Mr. Sanders," Pete said tensely. "Go on with that part."

"Lieutenant Sanders," the oldster said. "Sure, I was Acting Brigade Commander. See, our major was hit at Toledo—and after Tommy Chee stopped a sidewinder at Belgrave—"

"Stick to the point, Lieutenant!"

"Yessir!" The old man pulled himself together with an obvious effort. "I took the Brigade in; put out flankers, and ran the Enemy into the ground. We mopped 'em up in a thirty-three hour running fight that took us from over by Crater Bay all the way down here to Hellport. When it was over, I'd lost sixteen units, but the Enemy was done. They gave us Brigade Honors for that action. And then . . ."

"Then what?"

"Then the triple-dyed yellow-bottoms at Headquarters put out the order the Brigade was to be scrapped; said they were too hot to make decon practical. Cost too much, they said! So after the final review"—he gulped, blinked—"they planted 'em deep, two hundred meters, and poured in special high-R concrete."

"And packed rubble in behind them," Reynolds finished for him. "All right, Lieutenant, I believe you! Now for the big one: what started that machine on a rampage?"

"Should have known they couldn't hold down a Bolo Mark XXVIII!" The old man's eyes lit up. "Take more than a few million tons of rock to stop Lenny when his battle board was lit!"

"Lenny?"

"That's my old command unit out there, son. I saw the markings on the Tri-D. Unit LNE of the Dinochrome Brigade!"

"Listen!" Reynolds snapped out. "Here's what I intend to try..." He outlined his plan.

"Ha!" Sanders snorted. "It's a gutsy notion, mister, but Lenny won't give it a sneeze."

"You didn't come here to tell me we were licked," Reynolds cut in. "How about Brand's batteries?"

"Hell, son, Lenny stood up to point-blank Hellbore fire on Toledo, and—"

"Are you telling me there's nothing we can do?"

"What's that? No, son, that's not what I'm saying..."

"Then what!"

"Just tell these johnnies to get out of the way, mister. I think I can handle him."

11

At the field comm hut, Pete Reynolds watched as the man who had been Lieutenant Sanders of the Volunteer Scouts pulled shiny black boots over his thin ankles and stood. The blouse and trousers of royal blue polyon hung on his spare frame like wash on a line. He grinned, a skull's grin.

"It doesn't fit like it used to; but Lenny will recognize it. It'll help. Now, if you've got that power pack ready..."

Mayfield handed over the old-fashioned field instrument Sanders had brought in with him.

"It's operating, sir—but I've already tried everything I've got on that infernal machine; I didn't get a peep out of it."

Sanders winked at him. "Maybe I know a couple of tricks you

boys haven't heard about." He slung the strap over his bony shoulder and turned to Reynolds.

"Guess we better get going, mister. He's getting close."

In the rock car, Sanders leaned close to Reynolds' ear. "Told you those Federal guns wouldn't scratch Lenny. They're wasting their time."

Reynolds pulled the car to a stop at the crest of the road, from which point he had a view of the sweep of ground leading across to the city's edge. Lights sparkled all across the towers of New Devon. Close to the walls, the converging fire of the ranked batteries of infinite repeaters drove into the glowing bulk of the machine, which plowed on, undeterred. As he watched, the firing ceased.

"Now, let's get in there, before they get some other damn-fool scheme going," Sanders said.

The rock car crossed the rough ground, swung wide to come up on the Bolo from the left side. Behind the hastily rigged radiation cover, Reynolds watched the immense silhouette grow before him.

"I knew they were big," he said. "But to see one up close like this—" He pulled to a stop a hundred feet from the Bolo.

"Look at the side ports," Sanders said, his voice crisper now. "He's firing antipersonnel charges—only his plates are flat. If they weren't, we wouldn't have gotten within half a mile." He unclipped the microphone and spoke into it:

"Unit LNE, break off action and retire to ten-mile line!"

Reynolds' head jerked around to stare at the old man. His voice had rung with vigor and authority as he spoke the command.

The Bolo ground slowly ahead. Sanders shook his head, tried again.

"No answer, like that fella said. He must be running on nothing but memories now . . ." He reattached the microphone, and before Reynolds could put out a hand, had lifted the anti-R cover and stepped off on the ground.

"Sanders—get back in here!" Reynolds yelled.

"Never mind, son. I've got to get in close. Contact induction." He started toward the giant machine. Frantically, Reynolds started the car, slammed it into gear, pulled forward.

"Better stay back." Sanders' voice came from his field radio. "This close, that screening won't do you much good."

"Get in the car!" Reynolds roared. "That's hard radiation!"

"Sure; feels funny, like a sunburn, about an hour after you come in from the beach and start to think maybe you got a little too much." He laughed. "But I'll get to him . . ."

Reynolds braked to a stop, watched the shrunken figure in the baggy uniform as it slogged forward, leaning as against a sleet storm.

12

"I'm up beside him." Sander's voice came through faintly on the field radio. "I'm going to try to swing up on his side. Don't feel like trying to chase him any farther."

Through the glasses, Reynolds watched the small figure, dwarfed by the immense bulk of the fighting machine, as he tried, stumbled, tried again, swung up on the flange running across the rear quarter inside the churning bogie wheel.

"He's up," he reported. "Damned wonder the track didn't get him . . ."

Clinging to the side of the machine, Sanders lay for a moment, bent forward across the flange. Then he pulled himself up, wormed his way forward to the base of the rear quarter turret, wedged himself against it. He unslung the communicator, removed a small black unit, clipped it to the armor; it clung, held by a magnet. He brought the microphone up to his face.

In the comm shack, Mayfield leaned toward the screen, his eyes squinted in tension. Across the field, Reynolds held the glasses fixed on the man lying across the flank of the Bolo. They waited . . .

13

The walls are before me, and I ready myself for a final effort, but suddenly I am aware of trickle currents flowing over my outer surface. Is this some new trick of the Enemy? I tune to the wave energies, trace the source. They originate at a point in contact with my aft port armor. I sense modulation, match receptivity to a computed pattern. And I hear a voice:

"Unit LNE, break it off, Lenny. We're pulling back now, boy. This is Command to LNE; pull back to ten miles. If you read me, Lenny, swing to port and halt."

I am not fooled by the deception. The order appears correct, but the voice is not that of my Commander. Briefly I regret that I cannot spare energy to direct a neutralizing power flow at the device the Enemy has attached to me. I continue my charge.

"Unit LNE! Listen to me, boy; maybe you don't recognize my voice, but it's me. You see, boy—some time has passed. I've gotten old. My voice has changed some, maybe. But it's me! Make a port turn, Lenny. Make it now!"

I am tempted to respond to the trick, for something in the false command seems to awaken secondary circuits which I sense have been long stilled. But I must not be swayed by the cleverness of the Enemy. My sensing circuitry has faded further as my energy cells drain; but I know where the Enemy lies. I move forward, but I am filled with agony, and only the memory of my comrades drives me on.

"Lenny, answer me. Transmit on the old private band—the one we agreed on. Nobody but me knows it, remember?

Thus the Enemy seeks to beguile me into diverting precious power. But I will not listen.

"Lenny—not much time left. Another minute and you'll be into the walls. People are going to die. Got to stop you, Lenny. Hot here. My God, I'm hot. Not breathing too well, now. I can feel it; cutting through me like knives. You took a load of Enemy power, Lenny; and now I'm getting my share. Answer me, Lenny. Over to you . . ."

It will require only a tiny allocation of power to activate a communication circuit. I realize that it is only an Enemy trick, but I compute that by pretending to be deceived, I may achieve some trivial advantage. I adjust circuitry accordingly and transmit:

"Unit LNE to Command. Contact with Enemy defensive line imminent. Request support fire!"

"Lenny . . . you can hear me! Good boy, Lenny! Now make a turn, to port. Walls . . . close . . ."

"Unit LNE to Command. Request positive identification; transmit code 685749."

"Lenny—I can't . . . don't have code blanks. But it's me . . ."

"In absence of recognition code, your transmission disregarded," I send. And now the walls loom high above me. There are many lights, but I see them only vaguely. I am nearly blind now.

"Lenny—less'n two hundred feet to go. Listen, Lenny. I'm climbing down. I'm going to jump down, Lenny, and get around under your fore scanner pickup. You'll see me, Lenny. You'll know me then."

The false transmission ceases. I sense a body moving across my side. The gap closes. I detect movement before me, and in automatic reflex fire anti-P charges before I recall that I am unarmed.

A small object has moved out before me, and taken up a position between me and the wall behind which the Enemy conceal themselves. It is dim, but appears to have the shape of a man . . .

I am uncertain. My alert center attempts to engage inhibitory circuitry which will force me to halt, but it lacks power. I can override it. But still I am unsure. Now I must take a last risk; I must shunt power to my forward scanner to examine this obstacle more closely. I do so, and it leaps into greater clarity. It is indeed a man—and it is enclothed in regulation blues of the Volunteers. Now, closer, I see the face and through the pain of my great effort, I study it . . .

14

"He's backed against the wall," Reynolds said hoarsely. "It's still coming. A hundred feet to go—"

"You were a fool, Reynolds!" the mayor barked. "A fool to stake everything on that old dotard's crazy ideas!"

"Hold it!" As Reynolds watched, the mighty machine slowed, halted, ten feet from the sheer wall before it. For a moment, it sat, as though puzzled. Then it backed, halted again, pivoted ponderously to the left, and came about.

On its side, a small figure crept up, fell across the lower gun deck. The Bolo surged into motion, retracing its route across the artillery-scarred gardens.

"He's turned it." Reynolds let his breath out with a shuddering sigh. "It's headed out for open desert. It might get twenty miles before it finally runs out of steam."

The strange voice that was the Bolo's came from the big panel before Mayfield:

"Command . . . Unit LNE reports main power cells drained, secondary cells drained; now operating at .037 per cent efficiency, using Final Emergency Power. Request advice as to range to be covered before relief maintenance available."

"It's a long way, Lenny . . ." Sanders' voice was a bare whisper. *"But I'm coming with you . . ."*

Then there was only the crackle of static. Ponderously, like a great mortally stricken animal, the Bolo moved through the ruins of the fallen roadway, heading for the open desert.

"That damned machine," the mayor said in a hoarse voice. "You'd almost think it was alive."

"You would at that," Pete Reynolds said.

AFTERWORD BY ERIC FLINT:

In his preface, David refers to three of the Bolo stories "that really have an impact." The other two, for the record—at least so far as Dave and I are concerned—are "A Relic of War" and "Combat Unit" (aka "Dinochrome"). Among the three, it's hard to pick and choose. As it happens, I chose "Dinochrome" to include in the first volume of Laumer's writings which I edited for Baen Books' current reissue of many of Laumer's writings, but I could just as easily have chosen this one.

My reasons are similar to David's, but not exactly the same. I'm not a combat veteran, so on that level the story doesn't have the same personal impact. The thing I've always liked so much about the three great Bolo stories is that they give you the best of Laumer's ethos of duty without the veneer that I often find repellent in so many other stories Laumer wrote.

Laumer, like Van Vogt, was an author who naturally gravitated toward superman stories. Stories like that, no matter how well crafted and enjoyable—and on that level Laumer was a superb writer, one of the best ever in science fiction—just naturally tend to rub me the wrong way. It doesn't matter how admirable and courageous the hero might be, or how worthy his cause, I soon get impatient with story after story where the fate of the world rests almost entirely on one person doing the right thing, and where the role of everyone else is pretty much reduced to one of three roles:

a) Loyal sidekick;

b) Enemy;

c) Most people, who are irrelevant at best and sluggards as a rule.

Oh, bah. The great divide in science fiction is not political, it's the divide between those writers—Heinlein, Clarke and Andre Norton, to name three great figures—who generally tell stories about fairly ordinary people doing their best in difficult circumstances, and those writers—Van Vogt, "Doc" Smith and Laumer prominent among them, with George Lucas' *Star Wars* series the latest embodiment—for whom most stories are heroic epics centered around supermen.

There's an attraction to such stories, of course, even for someone with my inclination. That's because, in the hands of good writers, the theme of Duty rings so strongly. It's a theme which is difficult not to like, because without a sense of duty no virtues of any kind are possible.

And *that's* why the best of the Bolo stories always have such an impact on me—today just as much as they did when I first read them many decades ago. The theme comes without the dross, so to speak. The Bolos are not supermen, they are simply servants trying to follow their duty as best as they can manage. In the end, for me at least, that makes these machines ultimately more human than many other of Laumer's characters. Well . . . maybe not more human, but certainly a lot more sympathetic.

Who Goes There?

by John W. Campbell

PREFACE BY ERIC FLINT

This story has been anthologized so many times, that I suppose I should explain why we decided to do it again. Well . . . that's sort of the reason, right there. It was something of a ubiquitous phenomenon, coming into science fiction in the late '50s and early '60s. Even in Hollywood: the 1951 movie *The Thing* was made from it, and then remade in 1982. An anthology like this one just wouldn't have felt quite right without it. To me, anyway.

Campbell is today much more often remembered as the editor of *ASF* than he is as a writer in his own right. But when I was a kid, a lot of his stories were still readily available. There was a time when I devoured his space operas and swore that Doc Smith's Lensmen couldn't hold a candle to the intrepid crews of Campbell's galactic-scale adventure novels.

Well . . . that was then and this is now, and the verdict of history is pretty much in. Campbell was in fact a central figure in SF, even a towering one, but it's his influence as an editor that has lasted. His own fiction has pretty much vanished.

Except this story.

I

The place stank. A queer, mingled stench that only the ice-buried cabins of an Antarctic camp know, compounded of reeking human sweat, and the heavy, fish-oil stench of melted seal blubber. An overtone of liniment combated the musty smell of sweat-and-snow-drenched furs. The acrid odor of burnt cooking fat, and the animal, not-unpleasant smell of dogs, diluted by time, hung in the air.

Lingering odors of machine oil contrasted sharply with the taint of harness dressing and leather. Yet, somehow, through all that reek of human beings and their associates—dogs, machines, and cooking—came another taint. It was a queer, neck-ruffling thing, a faintest suggestion of an odor alien among the smells of industry and life. And it was a life-smell. But it came from the thing that lay bound with cord and tarpaulin on the table, dripping slowly, methodically onto the heavy planks, dank and gaunt under the unshielded glare of the electric light.

Blair, the little bald-pated biologist of the expedition, twitched nervously at the wrappings, exposing clear, dark ice beneath and then pulling the tarpaulin back into place restlessly. His little bird-like motions of suppressed eagerness danced his shadow across the fringe of dingy gray underwear hanging from the low ceiling, the equatorial fringe of stiff, graying hair around his naked skull a comical halo about the shadow's head.

Commander Garry brushed aside the lax legs of a suit of underwear, and stepped toward the table. Slowly his eyes traced around the rings of men sardined into the Administration Building. His tall, stiff body straightened finally, and he nodded. "Thirty-seven. All here." His voice was low, yet carried the clear authority of the commander by nature, as well as by title.

"You know the outline of the story back of that find of the Secondary Pole Expedition. I have been conferring with Second-in-Command McReady, and Norris, as well as Blair and Dr. Copper. There is a difference of opinion, and because it involves the entire group, it is only just that the entire Expedition personnel act on it.

"I am going to ask McReady to give you the details of the story, because each of you has been too busy with his own work to follow closely the endeavors of the others. McReady?"

Moving from the smoke-blued background, McReady was a figure from some forgotten myth, a looming, bronze statue that held life, and walked. Six feet four inches he stood as he halted beside the table, and with a characteristic glance upward to assure himself of room under the low ceiling beams, straightened. His rough, clashingly orange windproof jacket he still had on, yet on his huge frame it did not seem misplaced. Even here, four feet beneath the drift-wind that droned across the Antarctic waste above the ceiling, the cold of the frozen continent leaked in, and gave meaning to the harshness of the man. And he was bronze— his great red-bronze beard, the heavy hair that matched it. The gnarled, corded hands gripping, relaxing, gripping and relaxing on the table planks were bronze. Even the deep-sunken eyes beneath heavy brows were bronzed.

Age-resisting endurance of the metal spoke in the cragged heavy outlines of his face, and the mellow tones of the heavy voice. "Norris and Blair agree on one thing; that animal we found was not—terrestrial in origin. Norris fears there may be danger in that; Blair says there is none.

"But I'll go back to how, and why we found it. To all that was known before we came here, it appeared that this point was exactly over the South Magnetic Pole of Earth. The compass does point straight down here, as you all know. The more delicate instruments of the physicists, instruments especially designed for this expedition and its study of the magnetic pole, detected a secondary effect, a secondary, less powerful magnetic influence about eighty miles southwest of here.

"The Secondary Magnetic Expedition went out to investigate it. There is no need for details. We found it, but it was not the huge meteorite or magnetic mountain Norris had expected to find. Iron ore is magnetic, of course; iron more so—and certain special steels even more magnetic. From the surface indications, the secondary pole we found was small, so small that the magnetic effect it had was preposterous. No magnetic material conceivable could have that effect. Soundings through the ice indicated it was within one hundred feet of the glacier surface.

"I think you should know the structure of the place. There is a broad plateau, a level sweep that runs more than 150 miles due south from the Secondary Station, Van Wall says. He didn't have time or fuel to fly farther, but it was running smoothly due south then. Right there, where that buried thing was, there is an ice-drowned mountain ridge, a granite wall of unshakable strength that has dammed back the ice creeping from the south.

"And four hundred miles due south is the South Polar Plateau.

You have asked me at various times why it gets warmer here when the wind rises, and most of you know. As a meteorologist I'd have staked my word that no wind could blow at -70 degrees; that no more than a five-mile wind could blow at -50; without causing warming due to friction with ground, snow and ice and the air itself.

"We camped there on the lip of that ice-drowned mountain range for twelve days. We dug our camp into the blue ice that formed the surface, and escaped most of it. But for twelve consecutive days the wind blew at forty-five miles an hour. It went as high as forty-eight, and fell to forty-one at times. The temperature was -63 degrees. It rose to -60 and fell to -68. It was meteorologically impossible, and it went on uninterruptedly for twelve days and twelve nights.

"Somewhere to the south, the frozen air of the South Polar Plateau slides down from that 18,000-foot bowl, down a mountain pass, over a glacier, and starts north. There must be a funneling mountain chain that directs it, and sweeps it away for four hundred miles to hit that bald plateau where we found the secondary pole, and 350 miles farther north reaches the Antarctic Ocean.

"It's been frozen there since Antarctica froze twenty million years ago. There never has been a thaw there.

"Twenty million years ago Antarctica was beginning to freeze. We've investigated, though and built speculations. What we believe happened was about like this.

"Something came down out of space, a ship. We saw it there in the blue ice, a thing like a submarine without a conning tower or directive vanes, 280 feet long and 45 feet in diameter at its thickest.

"Eh, Van Wall? Space? Yes, but I'll explain that better later." McReady's steady voice went on.

"It came down from space, driven and lifted by forces men haven't discovered yet, and somehow—perhaps something went wrong then—it tangled with Earth's magnetic field. It came south here, out of control probably, circling the magnetic pole. That's a savage country there; but when Antarctica was still freezing, it must have been a thousand times more savage. There must have been blizzard snow, as well as drift, new snow falling as the continent glaciated. The swirl there must have been particularly bad, the wind hurling a solid blanket of white over the lip of that now-buried mountain.

"The ship struck solid granite head-on, and cracked up. Not

every one of the passengers in it was killed, but the ship must have been ruined, her driving mechanism locked. It tangled with Earth's field, Norris believes. No thing made by intelligent beings can tangle with the dead immensity of a planet's natural forces and survive.

"One of its passengers stepped out. The wind we saw there never fell below forty-one, and the temperature never rose above -60. Then—the wind must have been stronger. And there was drift falling in a solid sheet. The *thing* was lost completely in ten paces." He paused for a moment, the deep, steady voice giving way to the drone of wind overhead and the uneasy, malicious gurgling in the pipe of the galley stove.

Drift—a drift-wind was sweeping by overhead. Right now the snow picked up by the mumbling wind fled in level, blinding lines across the face of the buried camp. If a man stepped out of the tunnels that connected each of the camp buildings beneath the surface, he'd be lost in ten paces. Out there, the slim, black finger of the radio mast lifted three hundred feet into the air, and at its peak was the clear night sky. A sky of thin, whining wind rushing steadily from beyond to another beyond under the licking, curling mantle of the aurora. And off north, the horizon flamed with queer, angry colors of the midnight twilight. That was Spring three hundred feet above Antarctica.

At the surface—it was white death. Death of a needle-fingered cold driven before the wind, sucking heat from any warm thing. Cold—and white mist of endless, everlasting drift, the fine, fine particles of licking snow that obscured all things.

Kinner, the little, scar-faced cook, winced. Five days ago he had stepped out to the surface to reach a cache of frozen beef. He had reached it, started back—and the drift-wind leapt out of the south. Cold, white death that streamed across the ground blinded him in twenty seconds. He stumbled on wildly in circles. It was half an hour before rope-guided men from below found him in the impenetrable murk.

It was easy for man—or *thing*—to get lost in ten paces.

"And the drift-wind then was probably more impenetrable than we know." McReady's voice snapped Kinner's mind back. Back to the welcome, dank warmth of the Ad Building. "The passenger of the ship wasn't prepared either, it appears. It froze within ten feet of the ship.

"We dug down to find the ship, and our tunnel happened to find the frozen—animal. Barclay's ice-ax struck its skull.

"When we saw what it was, Barclay went back to the tractor, started the fire up and when the steam pressure built, sent a call for Blair and Dr. Copper. Barclay himself was sick then. Stayed sick for three days, as a matter of fact.

"When Blair and Copper came, we cut out the animal in a block of ice, as you see, wrapped it and loaded it on the tractor for return here. We wanted to get into that ship.

"We reached the side and found the metal was something we didn't know. Our beryllium-bronze, non-magnetic tools wouldn't touch it. Barclay had some tool-steel on the tractor, and that wouldn't scratch it either. We made reasonable tests—even tried some acid from the batteries with no results.

"They must have had a passivating process to make magnesium metal resist acid that way, and the alloy must have been at least ninety-five percent magnesium. But we had no way of guessing that, so when we spotted the barely opened lock door, we cut around it. There was clear, hard ice inside the lock, where we couldn't reach it. Through the little crack we could look in and see that only metal and tools were in there, so we decided to loosen the ice with a bomb.

"We had decanite bombs and thermite. Thermite is the ice-softener; decanite might have shattered valuable things, where the thermite's heat would just loosen the ice. Dr. Copper, Norris and I placed a twenty-five-pound thermite bomb, wired it, and took the connector up the tunnel to the surface, where Blair had the steam tractor waiting. A hundred yards the other side of that granite wall we set off the thermite bomb.

"The magnesium metal of the ship caught of course. The glow of the bomb flared and died, then it began to flare again. We ran back to the tractor, and gradually the glare built up. From where we were we could see the whole ice-field illuminated from beneath with an unbearable light; the ship's shadow was a great, dark cone reaching off toward the north, where the twilight was just about gone. For a moment it lasted, and we counted three other shadow-things that might have been other—passengers—frozen there. Then the ice was crashing down and against the ship.

"That's why I told you about that place. The wind sweeping down from the Pole was at our backs. Steam and hydrogen flame were torn away in white ice-fog; the flaming heat under the ice there was yanked away toward the Antarctic Ocean before it touched us. Otherwise we wouldn't have come back, even with the shelter of that granite ridge that stopped the light.

"Somehow in the blinding inferno we could see great hunched things—black bulks. They shed even the furious incandescence of the magnesium for a time. Those must have been the engines, we knew. Secrets going in blazing glory—secrets that might have given Man the planets. Mysterious things that could lift and hurl that ship—and had soaked in the force of the Earth's magnetic field. I saw Norris' mouth move, and ducked. I couldn't hear him.

"Insulation—something—gave way. All Earth's field they'd soaked up twenty million years before broke loose. The aurora in the sky above licked down, and the whole plateau there was bathed in cold fire that blanketed vision. The ice-ax in my hand got red hot, and hissed on the ice. Metal buttons on my clothes burned into me. And a flash of electric blue seared upward from beyond the granite wall.

"Then the walls of ice crashed down on it. For an instant it squealed the way dry ice does when it's pressed between metal.

"We were blind and groping in the dark for hours while our eyes recovered. We found every coil within a mile was fused rubbish, the dynamo and every radio set, the earphones and speakers. If we hadn't had the steam tractor, we wouldn't have gotten over to the Secondary Camp.

"Van Wall flew in from Big Magnet at sun-up, as you know. We came home as soon as possible. That is the history of—that." McReady's great bronze beard gestured toward the thing on the table.

II

Blair stirred uneasily, his little, bony fingers wriggling under the harsh light. Little brown freckles on his knuckles slid back and forth as the tendons under the skin twitched. He pulled aside a bit of the tarpaulin and looked impatiently at the dark ice-bound thing inside.

McReady's big body straightened somewhat. He'd ridden the rocking, jarring steam tractor forty miles that day, pushing on to Big Magnet here. Even his calm will had been pressed by the anxiety to mix again with humans. It was lone and quiet out there in Secondary Camp, where a wolf-wind howled down from the Pole. Wolf-wind howling in his sleep—winds droning and the evil, unspeakable face of that monster leering up as he'd first seen it through clear, blue ice, with a bronze ice-ax buried in its skull.

The giant meteorologist spoke again. "The problem is this. Blair wants to examine the thing. Thaw it out and make micro slides of its tissues and so forth. Norris doesn't believe that is safe, and Blair does. Dr. Copper agrees pretty much with Blair. Norris is a physicist, of course, not a biologist. But he makes a point I think we should all hear. Blair has described the microscopic life-forms biologists find living, even in this cold and inhospitable place. They freeze every winter, and thaw every summer—for three months—and live.

"The point Norris makes is—they thaw, and live again. There must have been microscopic life associated with this creature. There is with every living thing we know. And Norris is afraid that we may release a plague—some germ disease unknown to Earth—if we thaw those microscopic things that have been frozen there for twenty million years.

"Blair admits that such micro-life might retain the power of living. Such unorganized things as individual cells can retain life for unknown periods, when solidly frozen. The beast itself is as dead as those frozen mammoths they find in Siberia. Organized, highly developed life-forms can't stand that treatment.

"But micro-life could. Norris suggests that we may release some disease-form that man, never having met it before, will be utterly defenseless against.

"Blair's answer is that there may be such still-living germs, but that Norris has the case reversed. They are utterly nonimmune to man. Our life-chemistry probably—"

"Probably!" The little biologist's head lifted in a quick, bird-like motion. The halo of gray hair about his bald head ruffled as though angry. "Heh, one look—"

"I know," McReady acknowledged. "The thing is not Earthly. It does not seem likely that it can have a life-chemistry sufficiently like ours to make cross-infection remotely possible. I would say that there is no danger."

McReady looked toward Dr. Copper. The physician shook his head slowly. "None whatever," he asserted confidently. "Man cannot infect or be infected by germs that live in such comparatively close relatives as the snakes. And they are, I assure you," his clean-shaven face grimaced uneasily, "*much* nearer to us that—*that*."

Vance Norris moved angrily. He was comparatively short in this gathering of big men, some five feet eight, and his stocky, powerful build tended to make him seem shorter. His black hair was crisp and hard, like short, steel wires, and his eyes were the gray of fractured steel. If McReady was a man of bronze, Norris was all steel. His movements, his thoughts, his whole bearing had the quick, hard impulse of a steel spring. His nerves were steel—hard, quick acting—swift corroding.

He was decided on his point now, and he lashed out in its defense with a characteristic quick, clipped flow of words. "Different chemistry be damned. That thing may be dead—or, by God, it may not—but I don't like it. Damn it, Blair, let them see the monstrosity you are petting over there. Let them see the foul thing and decide for themselves whether they want that thing thawed out in this camp.

"Thawed out, by the way. That's got to be thawed out in one of the shacks tonight, if it is thawed out. Somebody—who's watchman tonight? Magnetic—oh, Connant. Cosmic rays tonight. Well, you get to sit up with that twenty-million-year-old mummy of his. Unwrap it, Blair. How the hell can they tell what they are buying, if they can't see it? It may have a different chemistry. I don't care what else it has, but I know it has something I don't want. If you can judge by the look on its face—it isn't human so maybe you can't—it was annoyed when it froze. Annoyed, in fact, is just about as close an approximation of the way it felt, as crazy, mad, insane hatred. Neither one touches the subject.

"How the hell can these birds tell what they are voting on? They haven't seen those three red eyes and that blue hair like crawling worms. Crawling—damn, it's crawling there in the ice right now!

"Nothing Earth ever spawned had the unutterable sublimation of devastating wrath that thing let loose in its face when it looked around its frozen desolation twenty million years ago. Mad? It was mad clear through—searing, blistering mad!

"Hell, I've had bad dreams ever since I looked at those three red eyes. Nightmares. Dreaming the thing thawed out and came to life—that it wasn't dead, or even wholly unconscious all those twenty million years, but just slowed, waiting—waiting. You'll dream, too, while that damned thing that Earth wouldn't own is dripping, dripping in the Cosmos House tonight.

"And, Connant," Norris whipped toward the cosmic ray specialist, "won't you have fun sitting up all night in the quiet. Wind whining above—and that thing dripping—" he stopped for a moment, and looked around.

"I know. That's not science. But this is, it's psychology. You'll have nightmares for a year to come. Every night since I looked at that thing I've had 'em. That's why I hate it—sure I do—and don't want it around. Put it back where it came from and let it freeze for another twenty million years. I had some swell nightmares—that it wasn't made like we are—which is obvious—but of a different kind of flesh that it can really control. That it can change its shape, and look like a man—and wait to kill and eat—

"That's not a logical argument. I know it isn't. The thing isn't Earth-logic anyway.

"Maybe it has an alien body-chemistry, and maybe its bugs do have a different body-chemistry. A germ might not stand that, but, Blair and Copper, how about a virus? That's just an enzyme molecule, you've said. That wouldn't need anything but a protein molecule of any body to work on.

"And how are you so sure that, of the million varieties of microscopic life it may have, *none* of them are dangerous. How about diseases like hydrophobia—rabies—that attack any warm-blooded creature, whatever its body-chemistry may be? And parrot fever? Have you a body like a parrot, Blair? And plain rot—gangrene—necrosis if you want? *That* isn't choosy about body chemistry!"

Blair looked up from his puttering long enough to meet Norris' angry, gray eyes for an instant. "So far the only thing you have said this thing gave off that was catching was dreams. I'll go so far as to admit that." An impish, slightly malignant grin crossed the little man's seamed face. "I had some, too. So. It's dream-infectious. No doubt an exceedingly dangerous malady.

"So far as your other things go, you have a badly mistaken idea about viruses. In the first place, nobody has shown that the enzyme-molecule theory, and that alone, explains them. And in the second place, when you catch tobacco mosaic or wheat rust, let me know. A wheat plant is a lot nearer your body-chemistry than this other-world creature is.

"And your rabies is limited, strictly limited. You can't get it from, nor give it to, a wheat plant or a fish—which is a collateral descendant of a common ancestor of yours. Which this, Norris, is not." Blair nodded pleasantly toward the tarpaulined bulk on the table.

"Well, thaw the damned thing in a tub of formalin if you must. I've suggested that—"

"And I've said there would be no sense in it. You can't compromise. Why did you and Commander Garry come down here to study magnetism? Why weren't you content to stay at home? There's magnetic force enough in New York. I could no more study the life this thing once had from a formalin-pickled sample than you could get the information you wanted back in New York. And—if this one is so treated, *never in all time to come can there be a duplicate!* The race it came from must have passed away in the twenty million years it lay frozen, so that even if it came from Mars then, we'd never find its like. And—the ship is gone.

"There's only one way to do this—and that is the best possible way. It must be thawed slowly, carefully, and not in formalin."

Commander Garry stood forward again, and Norris stepped back muttering angrily. "I think Blair is right, gentlemen. What do you say?"

Connant grunted. "It sounds right to us, I think—only perhaps he ought to stand watch over it while it's thawing." He grinned ruefully, brushing a stray lock of ripe-cherry hair back from his forehead. "Swell idea, in fact—if he sits up with his jolly little corpse."

Garry smiled slightly. A general chuckle of agreement rippled over the group. "I should think any ghost it may have had would have starved to death if it hung around here that long, Connant," Garry suggested. "And you look capable of taking care of it. 'Iron-man' Connant ought to be able to take out any opposing players, still."

Connant shook himself uneasily. "I'm not worrying about ghosts. Let's see that thing. I—"

Eagerly Blair was stripping back the ropes. A single throw of the tarpaulin revealed the thing. The ice had melted somewhat in the heat of the room, and it was clear and blue as thick, good glass. It shone wet and sleek under the harsh light of the unshielded globe above.

The room stiffened abruptly. It was face up there on the plain, greasy planks of the table. The broken haft of the bronze ice-ax was still buried in the queer skull. Three mad, hate-filled eyes blazed up with a living fire, bright as fresh-spilled blood, from a face ringed with a writhing, loathsome nest of worms, blue, mobile worms that crawled where hair should grow—

Van Wall, six feet and two hundred pounds of ice-nerved pilot, gave a queer, strangled gasp, and butted, stumbled his way out to the corridor. Half the company broke for the doors. The others stumbled away from the table.

McReady stood at one end of the table watching them, his great body planted solid on his powerful legs. Norris from the opposite end glowered at the thing with smouldering hate. Outside the door, Garry was talking with half a dozen of the men at once.

Blair had a tack hammer. The ice that cased the thing *schluffed* crisply under its steel claw as it peeled from the thing it had cased for twenty thousand thousand years—

III

"I know you don't like the thing, Connant, but it just has to be thawed out right. You say leave it as it is till we get back to civilization. All right, I'll admit your argument that we could do a better and more complete job there is sound. But—how are we going to get this across the Line? We have to take this through one temperate zone, the equatorial zone, and halfway through the other temperate zone before we get it to New York. You don't want to sit with it one night, but you suggest, then, that I hang its corpse in the freezer with the beef?" Blair looked up from his cautious chipping, his bald freckled skull nodding triumphantly.

Kinner, the stocky, scar-faced cook, saved Connant the trouble of answering. "Hey, you listen, mister. You put that thing in the box with the meat, and by all the gods there ever were, I'll put you in to keep it company. You birds have brought everything movable in this camp in onto my mess tables here already, and I had to stand for that. But you go putting things like that in my meat box, or even my meat cache here, and you cook your own damn grub."

"But, Kinner, this is the only table in Big Magnet that's big enough to work on," Blair objected. "Everybody's explained that."

"Yeah, and everybody's brought everything in here. Clark brings his dogs every time there's a fight and sews them up on that table. Ralsen brings in his sledges. Hell, the only thing you haven't had on that table is the Boeing. And you'd 'a' had that in if you coulda figured a way to get it through the tunnels."

Commander Garry chuckled and grinned at Van Wall, the huge Chief Pilot. Van Wall's great blond beard twitched suspiciously as he nodded gravely to Kinner. "You're right, Kinner. The aviation department it the only one that treats you right."

"It does get crowded, Kinner," Garry acknowledged. "But I'm afraid we all find it that way at times. Not much privacy in an Antarctic camp."

"Privacy? What the hell's that? You know, the thing that really made me weep, was when I saw Barclay marchin' through here chantin' 'The last lumber in the camp! The last lumber in the camp!' and carryin' it out to build that house on his tractor. Damn it, I missed that moon cut in the door he carried out more'n I missed the sun when it set. That wasn't just the last lumber Barclay was walkin' off with. He was carryin' off the last bit of privacy in this blasted place."

A grin rode even Connant's heavy face as Kinner's perennial, good-natured grouch came up again. But it died away quickly as his dark, deep-set eyes turned again to the red-eyed thing Blair was chipping from its cocoon of ice. A big hand ruffed his shoulder-length hair, and tugged at a twisted lock that fell behind his ear in a familiar gesture. "I know that cosmic ray shack's going to be too crowded if I have to sit up with that thing," he growled. "Why can't you go on chipping the ice away from around it—you can do that without anybody butting in, I assure you—and then hang the thing up over the power-plant boiler? That's warm enough. It'll thaw out a chicken, even a whole side of beef, in a few hours."

"I know," Blair protested, dropping the tack hammer to gesture more effectively with his bony, freckled fingers, his small body tense with eagerness, "but this is too important to take any chances. There never was a find like this; there never can be again. It's the only chance men will ever have, and it has to be done exactly right.

"Look, you know how the fish we caught down near the Ross Sea would freeze almost as soon as we got them on deck, and come to life again if we thawed them gently? Low forms of life aren't killed by quick freezing and slow thawing. We have—"

"Hey, for the love of Heaven—you mean that damned thing will come to life!" Connant yelled. "You get the damned thing— Let me at it! That's going to be in so many pieces—"

"No! No, you fool—" Blair jumped in front of Connant to protect his precious find. "No. Just low forms of life. For Pete's sake let me finish. You can't thaw higher forms of life and have them come to. Wait a moment now—hold it! A fish can come to after freezing because it's so low a form of life that the individual cells of its body can revive, and that alone is enough to reestablish life. Any higher forms thawed out that way are dead. Though the individual cells revive, they die because there must be organization and cooperative effort to live. That cooperation cannot be reestablished. There is a sort of potential life in any uninjured, quick-frozen animal. But it can't—can't under any circumstances—become active life in higher animals. The higher animals are too complex, too delicate. This is an intelligent creature as high in its evolution as we are in ours. Perhaps higher. It is as dead as a frozen man would be."

"How do you know?" demanded Connant, hefting the ice-ax he had seized a moment before.

Commander Garry laid a restraining hand on his heavy shoulder. "Wait a minute, Connant. I want to get this straight. I agree that there is going to be no thawing of this thing if there is the remotest chance of its revival. I quite agree it is much too unpleasant to have alive, but I had no idea there was the remotest possibility."

Dr. Copper pulled his pipe from between his teeth and heaved his stocky, dark body from the bunk he had been sitting in. "Blair's being technical. That's dead. As dead as the mammoths they find frozen in Siberia. We have all sorts of proof that things don't live after being frozen—not even fish, generally speaking—and no proof that higher animal life can under any circumstances. What's the point, Blair?"

The little biologist shook himself. The little ruff of hair standing out around his bald pate waved in righteous anger. "The point is," he said in an injured tone, "that the individual cells might show the characteristics they had in life if it is properly thawed. A man's muscle cells live many hours after he has died. Just because they live, and a few things like hair and fingernail cells still live, you wouldn't accuse a corpse of being a zombie, or something.

"Now if I thaw this right, I may have a chance to determine what sort of world it's native to. We don't, and can't know by any other means, whether it came from Earth or Mars or Venus or from beyond the stars.

"And just because it looks unlike men, you don't have to accuse it of being evil, or vicious or something. Maybe that expression on its face is its equivalent to a resignation to fate. White is the color of mourning to the Chinese. If men can have different customs, why can't a so-different race have different understandings of facial expressions?"

Connant laughed softly, mirthlessly. "Peaceful resignation! If that is the best it could do in the way of resignation, I should exceedingly dislike seeing it when it was looking mad. That face was never designed to express peace. It just didn't have any philosophical thoughts like peace in its make-up.

"I know it's your pet—but be sane about it. That thing grew up on evil, adolesced slowly roasting alive the local equivalent of kittens, and amused itself through maturity on new and ingenious torture."

"You haven't the slightest right to say that," snapped Blair. "How do you know the first thing about the meaning of a facial expression inherently inhuman? It may well have no human equivalent whatever. That is just a different development of Nature, another example of Nature's wonderful adaptability. Growing on another, perhaps harsher world, it has different form and features. But it is just as much a legitimate child of Nature as you are. You are displaying that childish human weakness of hating the different. On its own world it would probably class you as a fish-belly, white monstrosity with an insufficient number of eyes and a fungoid body pale and bloated with gas.

"Just because its nature is different, you haven't any right to say it's necessarily evil."

Norris burst out a single, explosive, "Haw!" He looked down at the thing. "May be that things from other worlds don't *have* to be evil just because they're different. But that thing *was!* Child of Nature, eh? Well, it was a hell of an evil Nature."

"Aw, will you mugs cut crabbing at each other and get the damned thing off my table?" Kinner growled. "And put a canvas over it. It looks indecent."

"Kinner's gone modest," jeered Connant.

Kinner slanted his eyes up to the big physicist. The scarred cheek twisted to join the line of his tight lips in a twisted grin. "All right, big boy, and what were you grousing about a minute ago? We can set the thing in a chair next to you tonight, if you want."

"I'm not afraid of its face," Connant snapped. "I don't like keeping a wake over its corpse particularly, but I'm going to do it."

Kinner's grin spread. "Uh-huh." He went off to the galley stove and shook down ashes vigorously, drowning the brittle chipping of the ice as Blair fell to work again.

IV

"*Cluck,*" reported the cosmic-ray counter, "*cluck-burrrp-cluck.*"

Connant started and dropped his pencil.

"Damnation." The physicist looked toward the far corner, back at the Geiger counter on the table near that corner. And crawled under the desk at which he had been working to retrieve the pencil. He sat down at his work again, trying to make his writing more even. It tended to have jerks and quavers in it, in time with the abrupt proud-hen noises of the Geiger counter. The muted whoosh of the pressure lamp he was using for illumination, the mingled gargles and bugle calls of a dozen men sleeping down the corridor in Paradise House formed the background sounds for the irregular, clucking noises of the counter, the occasional rustle of falling coal in the copper-bellied stove. And a soft, steady *drip-drip-drip* from the thing in the corner.

Connant jerked a pack of cigarettes from his pocket, snapped it so that a cigarette protruded, and jabbed the cylinder into his mouth. The lighter failed to function, and he pawed angrily through the pile of papers in search of a match. He scratched the wheel of the lighter several times, dropped it with a curse and got up to pluck a hot coat from the stove with the coal tongs.

The lighter functioned instantly when he tried it on returning to the desk. The counter ripped out a series of chuckling guffaws as a burst of cosmic rays struck through to it. Connant turned to glower at it, and tried to concentrate on the interpretation of data collected during the past week. The weekly summary—

He gave up and yielded to curiosity, or nervousness. He lifted the pressure lamp from the desk and carried it over to the table in the corner. Then he returned to the stove and picked up the coal tongs. The beast had been thawing for nearly eighteen hours now. He poked at it with an unconscious caution; the flesh was no longer hard as armor plate, but had assumed a rubbery texture. It looked like wet, blue rubber glistening under droplets of water like little round jewels in the glare of the gasoline pressure lantern. Connant felt an unreasoning desire to pour the contents of the lamp's reservoir over the thing in its box and drop the cigarette into it. The three red eyes glared up at him sightlessly, the ruby eyeballs reflecting murky, smoky rays of light.

He realized vaguely that he had been looking at them for a very long time, even vaguely understood that they were no longer sightless. But it did not seem of importance, of no more importance than the labored, slow motion of the tentacular things that sprouted from the base of the scrawny, slowly pulsing neck.

Connant picked up the pressure lamp and returned to his chair. He sat down, staring at the pages of mathematics before him. The clucking of the counter was strangely less disturbing, the rustle of the coals in the stove no longer distracting.

The creak of the floorboards behind him didn't interrupt his thoughts as he went about his weekly report in an automatic manner, filling in columns of data and making brief, summarizing notes.

The creak of the floorboards sounded nearer.

V

Blair came up from the nightmare-haunted depths of sleep abruptly. Connant's face floated vaguely above him; for a moment it seemed a continuance of the wild horror of the dream. But Connant's face was angry, and a little frightened. "Blair—Blair you damned log, wake up."

"Uh-eh?" the little biologist rubbed his eyes, his bony, freckled finger crooked to a mutilated child-fist. From surrounding bunks other faces lifted to stare down at them.

Connant straightened up. "Get up—and get a lift on. Your damned animal's escaped."

"Escaped—what!" Chief Pilot Van Wall's bull voice roared out with a volume that shook the walls. Down the communication tunnels other voices yelled suddenly. The dozen inhabitants of Paradise House tumbled in abruptly, Barclay, stocky and bulbous in long woolen underwear, carrying a fire extinguisher.

"What the hell's the matter?" Barclay demanded.

"Your damned beast got loose. I fell asleep about twenty minutes ago, and when I woke up, the thing was gone. Hey, Doc, the hell you say those things can't come to life. Blair's blasted potential life developed a hell of a lot of potential and walked out on us."

Copper stared blankly. "It wasn't—Earthly," he sighed suddenly. "I—I guess Earthly laws don't apply."

"Well, it applied for leave of absence and took it. We've got to find it and capture it somehow." Connant swore bitterly, his deep-set black eyes sullen and angry. "It's a wonder the hellish creature didn't eat me in my sleep."

Blair started back, his pale eyes suddenly fear-struck. "Maybe it di—er—uh—we'll have to find it."

"You find it. It's your pet. I've had all I want to do with it, sitting there for seven hours with the counter clucking every few seconds, and you birds in here singing night-music. It's a wonder I got to sleep. I'm going through to the Ad Building."

Commander Garry ducked through the doorway, pulling his

belt tight. "You won't have to. Van's roar sounded like the Boeing taking off downwind. So it wasn't dead?"

"I didn't carry it off in my arms, I assure you," Connant snapped. "The last I saw, the split skull was oozing green goo, like a squashed caterpillar. Doc just said our laws don't work—it's unearthly. Well, it's an unearthly monster, with an unearthly disposition, judging by the face, wandering around with a split skull and brains oozing out." Norris and McReady appeared in the doorway, a doorway filling with other shivering men. "Has anybody seen it coming over here?" Norris asked innocently. "About four feet tall—three red eyes—brains oozing out— Hey, has anybody checked to make sure this isn't a cracked idea of humor? If it is, I think we'll unite in tying Blair's pet around Connant's neck like the Ancient Mariner's albatross."

"It's no humor," Connant shivered. "Lord, I wish it were. I'd rather wear—" He stopped. A wild, weird howl shrieked through the corridors. The men stiffened abruptly, and half turned.

"I think it's been located," Connant finished. His dark eyes shifted with a queer unease. He darted back to his bunk in Paradise House, to return almost immediately with a heavy .45 revolver and an ice-ax. He hefted both gently as he started for the corridor toward Dogtown.

"It blundered down the wrong corridor—and landed among the huskies. Listen—the dogs have broken their chains—"

The half-terrorized howl of the dog pack had changed to a wild hunting melee. The voices of the dogs thundered in the narrow corridors, and through them came a low rippling snarl of distilled hate. A shrill of pain, a dozen snarling yelps.

Connant broke for the door. Close behind him, McReady, then Barclay and Commander Garry came. Other men broke for the Ad Building, and weapons—the sledge house. Pomroy, in charge of Big Magnet's five cows, started down the corridor in the opposite direction—he had a six-foot-handled, long-tined pitchfork in mind.

Barclay slid to a halt, as McReady's giant bulk turned abruptly away from the tunnel leading to Dogtown, and vanished off at an angle. Uncertainly, the mechanician wavered a moment, the fire extinguisher in his hands, hesitating from one side to the other. Then he was racing after Connant's broad back. Whatever McReady had in mind, he could be trusted to make it work.

Connant stopped at the bend in the corridor. His breath hissed suddenly through his throat. "Great God—" The revolver exploded thunderously; three numbing, palpable waves of sound crashed through the confined corridors. Two more. The revolver dropped to the hard-packed snow of the trail, and Barclay saw the ice-ax shift into defensive position. Connant's powerful body blocked his vision, but beyond he heard something mewing, and, insanely, chuckling. The dogs were quieter; there was a deadly seriousness in their low snarls. Taloned feet scratched at hard-packed snow, broken chains were clinking and tangling.

Connant shifted abruptly, and Barclay could see what lay beyond. For a second he stood frozen, then his breath went out in a gusty curse. The Thing launched itself at Connant, the powerful arms of the man swung the ice-ax flat-side first at what might have been a head. It scrunched horribly, and the tattered flesh, ripped by a half-dozen savage huskies, leapt to its feet again. The red eyes blazed with an unearthly hatred, an unearthly, unkillable vitality.

Barclay turned the fire extinguisher on it; the blinding, blistering stream of chemical spray confused it, baffled it, together with the savage attacks of the huskies, not for long afraid of anything that did, or could live, and held it at bay.

McReady wedged men out of his way and drove down the narrow corridor packed with men unable to reach the scene. There was a sure foreplanned drive to McReady's attack. One of the giant blowtorches used in warming the plane's engines was in his bronzed hands. It roared gustily as he turned the corner and opened the valve. The mad mewing hissed louder. The dogs scrambled back from the three-foot lance of blue-hot flame.

"Bar, get a power cable, run it in somehow. And a handle. We can electrocute this—monster, if I don't incinerate it." McReady spoke with an authority of planned action. Barclay turned down the long corridor to the power plant, but already before him Norris and Van Wall were racing down.

Barclay found the cable in the electrical cache in the tunnel wall. In a half minute he was hacking at it, walking back. Van Wall's voice rang out in warning shout of "Power!" as the emergency gasoline-powered dynamo thudded into action. Half a dozen other men were down there now; the coal, kindling were going into the firebox of the steam power plant. Norris, cursing in a low, deadly monotone, was working with quick, sure fingers on the other end of Barclay's cable, splicing a contractor into one of the power leads.

The dogs had fallen back when Barclay reached the corridor bend, fallen back before a furious monstrosity that glared from baleful red eyes, mewing in trapped hatred. The dogs were a semi-circle of red-dipped muzzles with a fringe of glistening white teeth, whining with a vicious eagerness that near matched the fury of the red eyes. McReady stood confidently alert at the corridor bend, the gustily muttering torch held loose and ready for action in his hands. He stepped aside without moving his eyes from the beast as Barclay came up. There was a slight, tight smile on his lean, bronzed face.

Norris' voice called down the corridor, and Barclay stepped forward. The cable was taped to the long handle of a snow shovel, the two conductors split and held eighteen inches apart by a scrap of lumber lashed at right angles across the far end of the handle. Bare copper conductors, charged with 220 volts, glinted in the light of pressure lamps. The Thing mewed and hated and dodged. McReady advanced to Barclay's side. The dogs beyond sensed the plan with the almost telepathic intelligence of trained huskies. Their whining grew shriller, softer, their mincing steps carried them nearer. Abruptly a huge night-black Alaskan leapt onto the trapped thing. It turned squalling, saber-clawed feet slashing.

Barclay leapt forward and jabbed. A weird, shrill scream rose and choked out. The smell of burnt flesh in the corridor intensified; greasy smoke curled up. The echoing pound of the gas-electric dynamo down the corridor became a slogging thud.

The red eyes clouded over in a stiffening, jerking travesty of a face. Armlike, leglike members quivered and jerked. The dogs leapt forward, and Barclay yanked back his shovel-handled weapon. The thing on the snow did not move as gleaming teeth ripped it open.

VI

Garry looked about the crowded room. Thirty-two men, some tensed nervously standing against the wall, some uneasily relaxed, some sitting, most perforce standing as intimate as sardines. Thirty-two, plus the five engaged in sewing up wounded dogs, made thirty-seven, the total personnel.

Garry started speaking. "All right, I guess we're here. Some of you—three or four at most—saw what happened. All of you have seen that thing on the table, and can get a general idea. Anyone hasn't, I'll lift—" His hand strayed to the tarpaulin bulking over the thing on the table. There was an acrid odor of singed flesh seeping out of it. The men stirred restlessly, hasty denials.

"It looks rather as though Charnauk isn't going to lead any more teams," Garry went on. "Blair wants to get at this thing, and make some more detailed examination. We want to know what happened, and make sure right now that this is permanently, totally dead. Right?"

Connant grinned. "Anybody that doesn't can sit up with it tonight."

"All right then, Blair, what can you say about it? What was it?" Garry turned to the little biologist.

"I wonder if we ever saw its natural form," Blair looked at the covered mass. "It may have been imitating the beings that built that ship—but I don't think it was. I think that was its true form. Those of us who were up near the bend saw the thing in action; the thing on the table is the result. When it got loose, apparently, it started looking around. Antarctica still frozen as it was ages ago when the creature first saw it—and froze. From my observations while it was thawing out, and the bits of tissue I cut and hardened then, I think it was native to a hotter planet than Earth. It couldn't, in its natural form, stand the temperature. There is no life-form on Earth that can live in Antarctica during the winter, but the best compromise is the dog. It found the dogs, and somehow got near enough to Charnauk to get him. The others smelled it—heard it—I don't know—anyway they went wild, and broke chains, and attacked it before it was finished. The thing we found was part Charnauk, queerly only half-dead, part Charnauk half-digested by the jellylike protoplasm of that creature, and part the remains of the thing we originally found, sort of melted down to the basic protoplasm.

"When the dogs attacked it, it turned into the best fighting thing it could think of. Some other-world beast apparently."

"Turned," snapped Garry. "How?"

"Every living thing is made up of jelly—protoplasm and minute, submicroscopic things called nuclei, which control the bulk, the protoplasm. This thing was just a modification of that same world-wide plan of Nature; cells made up of protoplasm, controlled by infinitely tinier nuclei. You physicists might compare it—an individual cell of any living thing—with an atom; the bulk of the atom, the space-filling part, is made up of the electron orbits, but the character of the thing is determined by the atomic nucleus.

"This isn't wildly beyond what we already know. It's just a

modification we haven't seen before. It's as natural, as logical, as any other manifestation of life. It obeys exactly the same laws. The cells are made of protoplasm, their character determined by the nucleus.

"Only, in this creature, the cell nuclei can control those cells *at will*. It digested Charnauk, and as it digested, studied every cell of his tissue, and shaped its own cells to imitate them exactly. Parts of it—parts that had time to finish changing—are dog-cells. But they don't have dog-cell nuclei." Blair lifted a fraction of the tarpaulin. A torn dog's leg, with stiff gray fur protruded. "That, for instance, isn't dog at all; it's imitation. Some parts I'm uncertain about; the nucleus was hiding itself, covering up with dog-cell imitation nucleus. In time, not even a microscope would have shown the difference."

"Suppose," asked Norris bitterly, "it had had lots of time?"

"Then it would have been a dog. The other dogs would have accepted it. We would have accepted it. I don't think anything would have distinguished it, not microscope, nor X-ray, nor any other means. This is a member of a supremely intelligent race, a race that has learned the deepest secrets of biology, and turned them to its use."

"What was it planning to do?" Barclay looked at the humped tarpaulin.

Blair grinned unpleasantly. The wavering halo of thin hair round his bald pate wavered in a stir of air. "Take over the world, I imagine."

"Take over the world! Just it, all by itself?" Connant gasped. "Set itself up as a lone dictator?"

"No," Blair shook his head. The scalpel he had been fumbling in his bony fingers dropped; he bent to pick it up, so that his face was hidden as he spoke. "It would become the population of the world."

"Become—populate the world? Does it reproduce asexually?"

Blair shook his head and gulped. "It's—it doesn't have to. It weighed eighty-five pounds. Charnauk weighed about ninety. It would have become Charnauk, and had eight-five pounds left, to become—oh, Jack, for instance, or Chinook. It can imitate anything—that is, become anything. If it had reached the Antarctic Sea, it would have become a seal, maybe two seals. They might have attacked a killer whale, and become either killers, or a herd of seals. Or maybe it would have caught an albatross, or a skua gull, and flown to South America."

Norris cursed softly. "And every time it digested something, and imitated it—"

"It would have had its original bulk left, to start again," Blair finished. "Nothing would kill it. It has no natural enemies, because it becomes whatever it wants to. If a killer whale attacked it, it would become a killer whale. If it was an albatross, and an eagle attacked it, it would become an eagle. Lord, it might become a female eagle. Go back—build a nest and lay eggs!"

"Are you sure that thing from hell is dead?" Dr. Copper asked softly.

"Yes, thank Heaven," the little biologist gasped. "After they drove the dogs off, I stood there poking Bar's electrocution thing into it for five minutes. It's dead and—cooked."

"Then we can only give thanks that this is Antarctica, where there is not one, single, solitary, living thing for it to imitate, except these animals in camp."

"Us," Blair giggled. "It can imitate us. Dogs can't make four hundred miles to the sea; there's no food. There aren't any skua gulls to imitate at this season. There aren't any penguins this far inland. There's nothing that can reach the sea from this point—except us. We've got brains. We can do it. Don't you see—*it's got to imitate us—it's got to be one of us—that's the only way it can fly an airplane—fly a plane for two hours, and rule—be—all Earth's inhabitants. A world for the taking—if it imitates us!*

"It didn't know yet. It hadn't had a chance to learn. It was rushed—hurried—took the thing nearest its own size. Look—I'm Pandora! I opened the box! And the only hope that can come out is—that nothing can come out. You didn't see me. I did it. I fixed it. I smashed every magneto. Not a plane can fly. Nothing can fly." Blair giggled and lay down on the floor crying.

Chief Pilot Van Wall made for the door. His feet were fading echoes in the corridors as Dr. Copper bent unhurriedly over the little man on the floor. From his office at the end of the room he brought something and injected a solution into Blair's arm. "He might come out of it when he wakes up," he sighed, rising. McReady helped him lift the biologist onto a nearby bunk. "It all depends on whether we can convince him that thing is dead."

Van Wall ducked into the shack, brushing his heavy blond beard absently. "I didn't think a biologist would do a thing like that up thoroughly. He missed the spares in the second cache. It's all right. I smashed them."

Commander Garry nodded. "I was wondering about the radio."

Dr. Copper snorted. "You don't think it can leak out on a radio wave, do you? You'd have five rescue attempts in the next three months if you stop the broadcasts. The thing to do is talk loud and not make a sound. Now I wonder—"

McReady looked speculatively at the doctor. "It might be like an infectious disease. Everything that drank any of its blood—"

Copper shook his head. "Blair missed something. Imitate it may, but it has, to a certain extent, its own body chemistry, its own metabolism. If it didn't, it would become a dog—and be a dog and nothing more. It has to be an imitation dog. Therefore you can detect it by serum tests. And its chemistry, since it comes from another world, must be so wholly, radically different that a few cells, such as gained by drops of blood, would be treated as disease germs by the dog, or human body."

"Blood—would one of those imitations bleed?" Norris demanded.

"Surely. Nothing mystic about blood. Muscle is about 90% water; blood differs only in having a couple percent more water, and less connective tissue. They'd bleed all right," Copper assured him.

Blair sat up in his bunk suddenly. "Connant—where's Connant?"

The physicist moved over toward the little biologist. "Here I am. What do you want?"

"Are you?" giggled Blair. He lapsed back into the bunk contorted with silent laughter.

Connant looked at him blankly. "Huh? Am I what?"

"*Are* you there?" Blair burst into gales of laughter. "*Are* you Connant? The beast wanted to be *man*—not a dog—"

VII

Dr. Copper rose wearily from the bunk, and washed the hypodermic carefully. The little tinkles it made seemed loud in the packed room, now that Blair's gurgling laughter had finally quieted. Copper looked toward Garry and shook his head slowly. "Hopeless, I'm afraid. I don't think we can ever convince him the thing is dead now."

Norris laughed uncertainly. "I'm not sure you can convince me. Oh, damn you, McReady."

"McReady?" Commander Garry turned to look from Norris to McReady curiously.

"The nightmares," Norris explained. "He had a theory about the nightmares we had at the Secondary Station after finding that thing."

"And that was?" Garry looked at McReady levelly.

Norris answered for him, jerkily, uneasily. "That the creature wasn't dead, had a sort of enormously slowed existence, an existence that permitted it, nonetheless, to be vaguely aware of the passing of time, of our coming, after endless years. I had a dream it could imitate things."

"Well," Copper grunted, "it can."

"Don't be an ass," Norris snapped. "That's not what's bothering me. In the dream it could read minds, read thoughts and ideas and mannerisms."

"What's so bad about that? It seems to be worrying you more than the thought of the joy we're going to have with a madman in an Antarctic camp." Copper nodded toward Blair's sleeping form.

McReady shook his great head slowly. "You know that Connant is Connant, because he not merely looks like Connant—which we're beginning to believe that beast might be able to do—but he thinks like Connant, moves himself around as Connant does. That takes more than merely a body that looks like him; that takes Connant's own mind, and thoughts and mannerisms. Therefore, though you know that the thing might make itself *look* like Connant, you aren't much bothered, because you know it has a mind from another world, a totally unhuman mind, that couldn't possibly react and think and talk like a man we know, and do it so well as to fool us for a moment. The idea of the creature imitating one of us is fascinating, but unreal, because it is too completely unhuman to deceive us. It doesn't have a human mind."

"As I said before," Norris repeated, looking steadily at McReady, "you can say the damnedest things at the damnedest times. Will you be so good as to finish that thought—one way or the other?"

Kinner, the scar-faced expedition cook, had been standing near Connant. Suddenly he moved down the length of the crowded room toward his familiar galley. He shook the ashes from the galley stove noisily.

"It would do it no good," said Dr. Copper, softly as though thinking out loud, "to merely look like something it was trying to imitate; it would have to understand its feelings, its reactions.

It *is* unhuman; it has powers of imitation beyond any conception of man. A good actor, by training himself, can imitate another man, another man's mannerisms, well enough to fool most people. Of course no actor could imitate so perfectly as to deceive men who had been living with the imitated one in the complete lack of privacy of an Antarctic camp. That would take a superhuman skill."

"Oh, you've got the bug, too?" Norris cursed softly.

Connant, standing alone at one end of the room, looked about him wildly, his face white. A gentle eddying of the men had crowded them slowly down toward the other end of the room, so that he stood quite alone. "My God, will you two Jeremiahs shut up?" Connant's voice shook. "What am I? Some kind of microscopic specimen you're dissecting? Some unpleasant worm you're discussing in the third person?"

McReady looked up at him; his slowly twisting hands stopped for a moment. "Having a lovely time. Wish you were here. Signed: Everybody.

"Connant, if you think you're having a hell of a time, just move over on the other end for a while. You've got one thing we haven't; you know what the answer is. I'll tell you this, right now you're the most feared and respected man in Big Magnet."

"Lord, I wish you could see your eyes," Connant gasped. "Stop staring, will you! What the hell are you going to do?"

"Have you any suggestions, Dr. Copper?" Commander Garry asked steadily. "The present situation is impossible."

"Oh, is it?" Connant snapped. "Come over here and look at that crowd. By Heaven, they look exactly like that gang of huskies around the corridor bend. Benning, will you stop hefting that damned ice-ax?"

The coppery blade rang on the floor as the aviation mechanic nervously dropped it. He bent over and picked it up instantly, hefting it slowly, turning it in his hands, his brown eyes moving jerkily about the room.

Copper sat down on the bunk beside Blair. The wood creaked noisily in the room. Far down a corridor, a dog yelped in pain, and the dog drivers' tense voices floated softly back. "Microscopic examination," said the doctor thoughtfully, "would be useless, as Blair pointed out. Considerable time has passed. However, serum tests would be definitive."

"Serum tests? What do you mean exactly?" Commander Garry asked.

"If I had a rabbit that had been injected with human blood—a poison to rabbits, of course, as is the blood of any animal save that of another rabbit—and the injections continued in increasing doses for some time, the rabbit would be human-immune. If a small quantity of its blood were drawn off, allowed to separate in a test tube, and to the clear serum, a bit of human blood were added, there would be a visible reaction, proving the blood was human. If cow, or dog blood were added—or any protein material other than that one thing—human blood—no reaction would take place. That would prove definitely."

"Can you suggest where I might catch a rabbit for you, Doc?" Norris asked. "That is, nearer than Australia; we don't want to waste time going that far."

"I know there aren't any rabbits in Antarctica," Copper nodded, "but that is simply the usual animal. Any animal except man will do. A dog for instance. But it will take several days, and due to the greater size of the animal, considerable blood. Two of us will have to contribute."

"Would I do?" Garry asked.

"That will make two," Copper nodded. "I'll get to work on it right away."

"What about Connant in the meantime," Kinner demanded. "I'm going out that door and head off for the Ross Sea before I cook for him."

"He may be human—" Copper started.

Connant burst out in a flood of curses. "Human! *May* be human, you damned sawbones! What in hell do you think I am?"

"A monster," Copper snapped sharply. "Now shut up and listen." Connant's face drained of color and he sat down heavily as the indictment was put in words. "Until we know—you know as well as we do that we have reason to question the fact, and only you know how that question is to be answered—we may reasonably be expected to lock you up. If you are—unhuman—you're a lot more dangerous than poor Blair there, and I'm going to see that he's locked up thoroughly. I expect that his next stage will be a violent desire to kill you, all the dogs, and probably all of us. When he wakes, he will be convinced we're all unhuman, and nothing on the planet will ever change his conviction. It would be kinder to let him die, but we can't do that, of course. He's going in one shack, and you can stay in Cosmos House with your cosmic ray apparatus. Which is about what you'd do anyway. I've got to fix up a couple of dogs."

Connant nodded bitterly. "I'm human. Hurry that test. Your eyes—Lord, I wish you could see your eyes staring—"

Commander Garry watched anxiously as Clark, the dog-handler, held the big brown Alaskan husky, while Copper began the injection treatment. The dog was not anxious to cooperate; the needle was painful, and already he'd experienced considerable needle work that morning. Five stitches held closed a slash that ran from his shoulder, across the ribs, halfway down his body. One long fang was broken off short; the missing part was to be found half buried in the shoulder bone of the monstrous thing on the table in the Ad Building.

"How long will that take?" Garry asked, pressing his arm gently. It was sore from the prick of the needle Dr. Copper had used to withdraw blood.

Copper shrugged. "I don't know, to be frank. I know the general method. I've used it on rabbits. But I haven't experimented with dogs. They're big, clumsy animals to work with; naturally rabbits are preferable, and serve ordinarily. In civilized places you can buy a stock of human-immune rabbits from suppliers, and not many investigators take the trouble to prepare their own."

"What do they want with them back there?" Clark asked.

"Criminology is one large field. A says he didn't murder B, but that the blood on his shirt came from killing a chicken. The State makes a test, then it's up to A to explain how it is the blood reacts on human-immune rabbits, but not on chicken-immunes."

"What are we going to do with Blair in the meantime?" Garry asked wearily. "It's all right to let him sleep where he is for a while, but when he wakes up—"

"Barclay and Benning are fitting some bolts on the door of Cosmos House," Copper replied grimly. "Connant's acting like a gentleman. I think perhaps the way the other men look at him makes him rather want privacy. Lord knows, heretofore we've all of us individually prayed for a little privacy."

Clark laughed brittlely. "Not any more, thank you. The more the merrier."

"Blair," Copper went on, "will also have to have privacy—and locks. He's going to have a pretty definite plan in mind when he wakes up. Ever hear the old story of how to stop hoof-and-mouth disease in cattle?"

Clark and Garry shook their heads silently.

"If there isn't any hoof-and-mouth disease, there won't be any hoof-and-mouth disease," Copper explained. "You get rid of it by killing every animal that exhibits it, and every animal that's been near the diseased animal. Blair's a biologist, and knows that story. He's afraid of this thing we loosed. The answer is probably pretty clear in his mind now. Kill everybody and everything in this camp before a skua gull or a wandering albatross coming in with the spring chances out this way and—catches the disease."

Clark's lips curled in a twisted grin. "Sounds logical to me. If things get too bad—maybe we'd better let Blair get loose. It would save us committing suicide. We might also make something of a vow that if things get bad, we see that that does happen."

Copper laughed softly. "The last man alive in Big Magnet— wouldn't be a man," he pointed out. "Somebody's got to kill those—creatures that don't desire to kill themselves, you know. We don't have enough thermite to do it all at once, and the decanite explosive wouldn't help much. I have an idea that even small pieces of one of those beings would be self-sufficient."

"If," said Garry thoughtfully, "they can modify their protoplasm at will, won't they simply modify themselves to birds and fly away? They can read all about birds, and imitate their structure without even meeting them. Or imitate, perhaps, birds of their home planet."

Copper shook his head, and helped Clark to free the dog. "Man studied birds for centuries, trying to learn how to make a machine to fly like them. He never did do the trick; his final success came when he broke away entirely and tried new methods. Knowing the general idea, and knowing the detailed structure of wing and bone and nerve-tissue is something far, far different. And as for other-world birds, perhaps, in fact very probably, the atmospheric conditions here are so vastly different that their birds couldn't fly. Perhaps, even, the being came from a planet like Mars with such a thin atmosphere that there were no birds."

Barclay came into the building, trailing a length of airplane control cable. "It's finished, Doc. Cosmos House can't be opened from the inside. Now where do we put Blair?"

Copper looked toward Garry. "There wasn't any biology building. I don't know where we can isolate him."

"How about East Cache?" Garry said after a moment's thought. "Will Blair be able to look after himself—or need attention?"

"He'll be capable enough. We'll be the ones to watch out," Copper assured him grimly. "Take a stove, a couple of bags of coal, necessary supplies and a few tools to fix it up. Nobody's been out there since last fall, have they?"

Garry shook his head. "If he gets noisy—I thought that might be a good idea."

Barclay hefted the tools he was carrying and looked up at Garry. "If the muttering he's doing now is any sign, he's going to sing away the night hours. And we won't like his song."

"What's he saying?" Copper asked.

Barclay shook his head. "I didn't care to listen much. You can if you want to. But I gathered that the blasted idiot had all the dreams McReady had, and a few more. He slept beside the thing when we stopped on the trail coming in from Secondary Magnetic, remember. He dreamt the thing was alive, and dreamt more details. And—damn his soul—knew it wasn't all dream, or had reason to. He knew it had telepathic powers that were stirring vaguely, and that it could not only read minds, but project thoughts. They weren't dreams, you see. They were stray thoughts that thing was broadcasting, the way Blair's broadcasting his thoughts now—a sort of telepathic muttering in its sleep. That's why he knew so much about its powers. I guess you and I, Doc, weren't so sensitive—if you want to believe in telepathy."

"I have to," Copper sighed. "Dr. Rhine of Duke University has shown that it exists, shown that some are much more sensitive than others."

"Well, if you want to learn a lot of details, go listen in on Blair's broadcast. He's driven most of the boys out of the Ad Building; Kinner's rattling pans like coal going down a chute. When he can't rattle a pan, he shakes ashes.

"By the way, Commander, what are we going to do this spring, now the planes are out of it?"

Garry sighed. "I'm afraid our expedition is going to be a loss. We cannot divide our strength now."

"It won't be a loss—if we continue to live, and come out of this," Copper promised him. "The find we've made, if we can get it under control, is important enough. The cosmic ray data, magnetic work, and atmospheric work won't be greatly hindered."

Garry laughed mirthlessly. "I was just thinking of the radio broadcasts. Telling half the world about the wonderful results of our exploration flights, trying to fool men like Byrd and Ellsworth back home there that we're doing something."

Copper nodded gravely. "They'll know something's wrong. But men like that have judgment enough to know we wouldn't do tricks without some sort of reason, and will wait for our return to judge us. I think it comes to this: men who know enough to recognize our deception will wait for our return. Men who haven't discretion and faith enough to wait will not have the experience to detect any fraud. We know enough of the conditions here to put through a good bluff."

"Just so they don't send 'rescue' expeditions," Garry prayed. "When—if—we're ever ready to come out, we'll have to send word to Captain Forsythe to bring a stock of magnetos with him when he comes down. But—never mind that."

"You mean if we don't come out?" asked Barclay. "I was wondering if a nice running account of an eruption or an earthquake via radio—with a swell windup by using a stick of decanite under the microphone—would help. Nothing, of course, will entirely keep people out. One of those swell, melodramatic 'last-man-alive-scenes' might make 'em go easy though."

Garry smiled with genuine humor. "Is everybody in camp trying to figure that out, too?"

Copper laughed. "What do you think, Garry? We're confident we can win out. But not too easy about it, I guess."

Clark grinned up from the dog he was petting into calmness. "Confident, did you say, Doc?"

VIII

Blair moved restlessly around the small shack. His eyes jerked and quivered in vague, fleeting glances at the four men with him; Barclay, six feet tall and weighing over 190 pounds; McReady, a bronze giant of a man; Dr. Copper, short, squatly powerful; and Benning, five feet ten of wiry strength.

Blair was huddled up against the far wall of the East Cache cabin, his gear piled in the middle of the floor beside the heating stove, forming an island between him and the four men. His bony hands clenched and fluttered, terrified. His pale eyes wavered uneasily as his bald, freckled head darted about in birdlike motion.

"I don't want anybody coming here. I'll cook my own food," he snapped nervously. "Kinner may be human now, but I don't believe it. I'm going to get out of here, but I'm not going to eat any food you send me. I want cans. Sealed cans."

"OK, Blair, we'll bring 'em tonight," Barclay promised. "You've got coal, and the fire's started. I'll make a last—" Barclay started forward.

Blair instantly scurried to the farthest corner. "Get out! Keep away from me, you monster!" the little biologist shrieked, and tried to claw his way through the wall of the shack. "Keep away from me—keep away—I won't be absorbed—I won't be—"

Barclay relaxed and moved back. Dr. Copper shook his head. "Leave him alone, Bar. It's easier for him to fix the thing himself. We'll have to fix the door, I think—"

The four men let themselves out. Efficiently, Benning and Barclay fell to work. There were no locks in Antarctica; there wasn't enough privacy to make them needed. But powerful screws had been driven in each side of the door frame, and the spare aviation control cable, immensely strong, woven steel wire, was rapidly caught between them and drawn taut. Barclay went to work with a drill and a key-hole saw. Presently he had a trap cut in the door through which goods could be passed without unlashing the entrance. Three powerful hinges made from a stock crate, two hasps and a pair of three-inch cotter pins made it proof against opening from the other side.

Blair moved about restlessly inside. He was dragging something over to the door with panting gasps, and muttering frantic curses. Barclay opened the hatch and glanced in, Dr. Copper peering over his shoulder. Blair had moved the heavy bunk against the door. It could not be opened without his cooperation now.

"Don't know but what the poor man's right at that," McReady sighed. "If he gets loose, it is his avowed intention to kill each and all of us as quickly as possible, which is something we don't agree with. But we've something on our side of that door that is worse than a homicidal maniac. If one or the other has to get loose, I think I'll come up and undo these lashings here."

Barclay grinned. "You let me know, and I'll show you how to get these off fast. Let's go back."

The sun was painting the northern horizon in multicolored rainbows still, though it was two hours below the horizon. The field of drift swept off to the north, sparkling under its flaming colors in a million reflected glories. Low mounds of rounded white on the northern horizon showed the Magnet Range was barely awash above the sweeping drift. Little eddies of wind-lifted snow swirled away from their skis as they set out toward the main encampment two miles away. The spidery finger of the broadcast radiator lifted a gaunt black needle against the white of the Antarctic continent. The snow under their skis was like fine sand, hard and gritty.

"Spring," said Benning bitterly, "is come. Ain't we got fun! And

I've been looking forward to getting away from this blasted hole in the ice."

"I wouldn't try it now, if I were you." Barclay grunted. "Guys that set out from here in the next few days are going to be marvelously unpopular."

"How is your dog getting along, Dr. Copper?" McReady asked. "Any results yet?"

"In thirty hours? I wish there were. I gave him an injection of my blood today. But I imagine another five days will be needed. I don't know certainly enough to stop sooner."

"I've been wondering—if Connant were—changed, would he have warned us so soon after the animal escaped? Wouldn't he have waited long enough for it to have a real chance to fix itself? Until we woke up naturally?" McReady asked slowly.

"The thing is selfish. You didn't think it looked as though it were possessed of a store of the higher justices, did you?" Dr. Copper pointed out. "Every part of it is all of it, every part of it is all for itself, I imagine. If Connant were changed, to save his skin, he'd have to—but Connant's feelings aren't changed; they're imitated perfectly, or they're his own. Naturally, the imitation, imitating perfectly Connant's feelings, would do exactly what Connant would do."

"Say, couldn't Norris or Vane give Connant some kind of a test? If the thing is brighter than men, it might know more physics than Connant should, and they'd catch it out," Barclay suggested.

Copper shook his head wearily. "Not if it reads minds. You can't plan a trap for it. Vane suggested that last night. He hoped it would answer some of the questions of physics he'd like to know answers to."

"This expedition-of-four idea is going to make life happy." Benning looked at his companions. "Each of us with an eye on the other to make sure he doesn't do something—peculiar. Man—aren't we going to be a trusting bunch! Each man eyeing his neighbors with the grandest exhibition of faith and truth—I'm beginning to know what Connant meant by 'I wish you could see your eyes.' Every now and then we all have it, I guess. One of you looks around with a sort of 'I-wonder-if-the-other-*three*-are-look.' Incidentally, I'm not excepting myself."

"So far as we know, the animal is dead, with a slight question as to Connant. No other is suspected," McReady stated slowly. "The 'always-four' order is merely a precautionary measure."

"I'm waiting for Garry to make it four-in-a-bunk," Barclay

sighed. "I thought I didn't have any privacy before, but since that order—"

IX

None watched more tensely than Connant. A little sterile glass test tube, half filled with straw-colored fluid. One—two—three—four— five drops of the clear solution Dr. Copper had prepared from the drops of blood from Connant's arm. The tube was shaken carefully, then set in a beaker of clear, warm water. The thermometer read blood heat, a little thermostat clicked noisily, and the electric hotplate began to glow as the lights flickered slightly. Then—little white flecks of precipitation were forming, snowing down in the clear straw-colored fluid. "Lord," said Connant. He dropped heavily into a bunk, crying like a baby. "Six days—" Connant sobbed, "six days in there—wondering if that damned test would lie—"

Garry moved over silently, and slipped his arm across the physicist's back.

"It couldn't lie," Dr. Copper said. "The dog was human-immune—and the serum reacted."

"He's—all right?" Norris gasped. "Then—the animal is dead—dead forever?"

"He is human," Copper spoke definitely, "and the animal is dead."

Kinner burst out laughing, laughing hysterically. McReady turned toward him and slapped his face with a methodical one-two, one-two action. The cook laughed, gulped, cried a moment, and sat up rubbing his cheeks, mumbling his thanks vaguely. "I was scared. Lord, I was scared—"

Norris laughed brittlely. "You think we weren't, you ape? You think maybe Connant wasn't?"

The Ad Building stirred with a sudden rejuvenation. Voices laughed, the men clustering around Connant spoke with unnecessarily loud voices, jittery, nervous voices relievedly friendly again. Somebody called out a suggestion, and a dozen started for their skis. Blair, Blair might recover— Dr. Copper fussed with his test tubes in nervous relief, trying solutions. The party of relief for Blair's shack started out the door, skis clapping noisily. Down the corridor, the dogs set up a quick yelping howl as the air of excited relief reached them.

Dr. Copper fussed with his tubes. McReady noticed him first, sitting on the edge of the bunk, with two precipitin-whitened test tubes of straw-colored fluid, his face whiter than the stuff in the tubes, silent tears slipping down from horror-widened eyes.

McReady felt a cold knife of fear pierce through his heart and freeze in his breast. Dr. Copper looked up. "Garry," he called hoarsely. "Garry, for God's sake, come here."

Commander Garry walked toward him sharply. Silence clapped down on the Ad Building. Connant looked up, rose stiffly from his seat.

"Garry—tissue from the monster—precipitates, too. It proves nothing. Nothing—but the dog was monster-immune too. That *one of the two contributing blood—one of us two*, you and I, Garry—*one of us is a monster.*"

X

"Bar, call back those men before they tell Blair," McReady said quietly. Barclay went to the door; faintly his shouts came back to the tensely silent men in the room. Then he was back.

"They're coming," he said. "I didn't tell them why. Just that Dr. Copper said not to go."

"McReady," Garry sighed, "you're in command now. May God help you. I cannot."

The bronzed giant nodded slowly, his deep eyes on Commander Garry.

"I may be the one," Garry added. "I know I'm not, but I cannot prove it to you in any way. Dr. Copper's test has broken down. The fact that he showed it was useless, when it was to the advantage of the monster to have that uselessness not known, would seem to prove he was human."

Copper rocked back and forth slowly on the bunk. "I know I'm human. I can't prove it either. One of us two is a liar, for that test cannot lie, and it says one of us is. I gave proof that the test was wrong, which seems to prove I'm human, and now Garry has given that argument which proves me human—which he, as the monster, should not do. Round and round and round and round and—"

Dr. Copper's head, then his neck and shoulders began circling slowly in time to the words. Suddenly he was lying back on the bunk, roaring with laughter. "It doesn't have to prove *one* of us is a monster! It doesn't have to prove that at all! Ho-ho. If we're *all* monsters it works the same—we're all monsters—all of us—Connant and Garry and I—and all of you."

"McReady," Van Wall, the blond-bearded Chief Pilot, called softly, "you were on the way to an M.D. when you took up meteorology, weren't you? Can you make some kind of test?"

McReady went over to Copper slowly, took the hypodermic from his hand, and washed it carefully in ninety-five percent alcohol. Garry sat on the bunk edge with wooden face, watching Copper and McReady expressionlessly. "What Copper said is possible," McReady sighed. "Van, will you help me here? Thanks." The filled needle jabbed into Copper's thigh. The man's laughter did not stop, but slowly faded into sobs, then sound sleep as the morphia took hold.

McReady turned again. The men who had started for Blair stood at the far end of the room, skis dripping snow, their faces as white as their skis. Connant had a lighted cigarette in each hand; one he was puffing absently, and staring at the floor. The heat of the one in his left hand attracted him and he stared at it and the one in the other hand stupidly for a moment. He dropped one and crushed it under his heel slowly.

"Dr. Copper," McReady repeated, "could be right. I know I'm human—but of course can't prove it. I'll repeat the test for my own information. Any of you others who wish may do the same."

Two minutes later, McReady held a test tube with white precipitin settling slowly from straw-colored serum. "It reacts to human blood too, so they aren't both monsters."

"I didn't think they were," Van Wall sighed. "That wouldn't suit the monster either; we could have destroyed them if we knew. Why hasn't the monster destroyed us, do you suppose? It seems to be loose."

McReady snorted. Then laughed softly. "Elementary, my dear Watson. The monster wants to have life-forms available. It cannot animate a dead body, apparently. It is just waiting—waiting until the best opportunities come. We who remain human, it is holding in reserve."

Kinner shuddered violently. "Hey. Hey, Mac. Mac, would I know if I was a monster? Would I know if the monster had already got me? Oh Lord, I may be a monster already."

"You'd know," McReady answered.

"But we wouldn't," Norris laughed shortly, half hysterically.

McReady looked at the vial of serum remaining. "There's one thing this damned stuff is good for, at that," he said thoughtfully. "Clark, will you and Van help me? The rest of the gang better stick together here. Keep an eye on each other," he said bitterly. "See that you don't get into mischief, shall we say?"

McReady started down the tunnel toward Dogtown, with Clark and Van Wall behind him. "You need more serum?" Clark asked.

McReady shook his head. "Tests. There's four cows and a bull, and nearly seventy dogs down there. This stuff reacts only to human blood and—monsters."

XI

McReady came back to the Ad Building and went silently to the wash stand. Clark and Van Wall joined him a moment later. Clark's lips had developed a tic, jerking into sudden, unexpected sneers.

"What did you do?" Connant exploded suddenly. "More immunizing?"

Clark snickered, and stopped with a hiccough. "Immunizing. Haw! Immune all right."

"That monster," said Van Wall steadily, "is quite logical. Our immune dog was quite all right, and we drew a little more serum for the tests. But we won't make any more."

"Can't—can't you use one man's blood on another dog—" Norris began.

"There aren't," said McReady softly, "any more dogs. Nor cattle, I might add."

"No more dogs?" Benning sat down slowly.

"They're very nasty when they start changing," Van Wall said precisely. "But slow. That electrocution iron you made up, Barclay, is very fast. There is only one dog left—our immune. The monster left that for us, so we could play with our little test. The rest—" He shrugged and dried his hands.

"The cattle—" gulped Kinner.

"Also. Reacted very nicely. They look funny as hell when they start melting. The beast hasn't any quick escape, when it's tied in dog chains, or halters, and it had to be to imitate."

Kinner stood up slowly. His eyes darted around the room, and came to rest horribly quivering on a tin bucket in the galley. Slowly, step by step, he retreated toward the door, his mouth opening and closing silently, like a fish out of water.

"The milk—" he gasped. "I milked 'em an hour ago—" His voice broke into a scream as he dived through the door. He was out on the ice cap without windproof or heavy clothing.

Van Wall looked after him for a moment thoughtfully. "He's probably hopelessly mad," he said at length, "but he might be a monster escaping. He hasn't skis. Take a blow torch—in case."

The physical motion of the chased helped them; something that needed doing. Three of the men were quietly being sick. Norris was lying flat on his back, his face greenish, looking steadily at the bottom of the bunk above him.

"Mac, how long have the—cows been not-cows—"

McReady shrugged his shoulders hopelessly. He went over to the milk bucket, and with his little tube of serum set to work on it. The milk clouded it, making certainty difficult. Finally he dropped the test tube in the stand, and shook his head. "It tests negatively. Which means either they were cows then, or that, being perfect imitations, they gave perfectly good milk."

Copper stirred restlessly in his sleep and gave a gurgling cross between a snore and a laugh. Silent eyes fastened on him. "Would morphia—a monster—" somebody started to ask.

"Lord knows," McReady shrugged. "It affects every Earthly animal I know of."

Connant suddenly raised his head. "Mac! The dogs must have swallowed pieces of the monster, and the pieces destroyed them! The dogs were where the monster resided. I was locked up. Doesn't that prove—"

Van Wall shook his head. "Sorry. Proves nothing about what you are, only proves what you didn't do."

"It doesn't do that," McReady sighed. "We are helpless because we don't know enough, and so jittery we don't think straight. Locked up! Ever watch a white corpuscle of the blood go through the wall of a blood vessel? No? It sticks out a pseudopod. And there it is—on the far side of the wall."

"Oh," said Van Wall unhappily. "The cattle tried to melt down, didn't they? They could have melted down—become just a thread of stuff and leaked under a door to re-collect on the other side. Ropes—no—no, that wouldn't do it. They couldn't live in a sealed tank or—"

"If," said McReady, "you shoot it through the heart, and it doesn't die, it's a monster. That's the best test I can think of, offhand."

"No dogs," said Garry quietly, "and no cattle. It has to imitate men now. And locking up doesn't do any good. Your test might work, Mac, but I'm afraid it would be hard on the men."

XII

Clark looked up from the galley stove as Van Wall, Barclay, McReady, and Benning came in, brushing the drift from their clothes. The other men jammed into the Ad Building continued studiously to do as they were doing, playing chess, poker, reading. Ralsen was fixing a sledge on the table; Vane and Norris had their heads together over magnetic data, while Harvey read tables in a low voice.

Dr. Copper snored softly on the bunk. Garry was working with Dutton over a sheaf of radio messages on the corner of Dutton's bunk and a small fraction of the radio table. Connant was using most of the table for cosmic ray sheets.

Quite plainly through the corridor, despite two closed doors, they could hear Kinner's voice. Clark banged a kettle onto the galley stove and beckoned McReady silently. The meteorologist went over to him.

"I don't mind the cooking so damn much," Clark said nervously, "but isn't there some way to stop that bird? We all agreed that it would be safe to move him into Cosmos House."

"Kinner?" McReady nodded toward the door. "I'm afraid not. I can dope him, I suppose, but we don't have an unlimited supply of morphia, and he's not in danger of losing his mind. Just hysterical."

"Well, we're in danger of losing ours. You've been out for an hour and a half. That's been going on steadily ever since, and it was going for two hours before. There's a limit, you know."

Garry wandered over slowly, apologetically. For an instant, McReady caught the feral spark of fear—horror—in Clark's eyes, and knew at the same instant it was in his own. Garry—Garry or Copper—was certainly a monster.

"If you could stop that, I think it would be a sound policy, Mac," Garry spoke quietly. "There are—tensions enough in this room. We agreed that it would be safe for Kinner in there, because everyone else in camp is under constant eyeing." Garry shivered slightly. "And try, try in God's name, to find some test that will work." McReady sighed. "Watched or unwatched, everyone's tense.

Blair's jammed the trap so it won't open now. Says he's got food enough, and keeps screaming 'Go away, go away—you're monsters. I won't be absorbed. I won't. I'll tell men when they come. Go away.' So—we went away."

"There's no other test?" Garry pleaded.

McReady shrugged his shoulders. "Copper was perfectly right. The serum test could be absolutely definitive if it hadn't been—contaminated. But that's the only dog left, and he's fixed now."

"Chemicals? Chemical tests?"

McReady shook his head. "Our chemistry isn't that good. I tried the microscope you know."

Garry nodded. "Monster-dog and real dog were identical. But—you've got to go on. What are you going to do after dinner?"

Van Wall had joined them quietly. "Rotation sleeping. Half the crowd sleep; half stay awake. I wonder how many of us are monsters? All the dogs were. We thought we were safe, but somehow it got Copper—or you." Van Wall's eyes flashed uneasily. "It may have gotten every one of you—all of you but myself may be wondering, looking. No, that's not possible. You'd just spring then, I'd be helpless. We humans must somehow have the greater numbers now. But—" he stopped.

McReady laughed shortly. "You're doing what Norris complained of in me. Leaving it hanging. 'But if one more is changed—that may shift the balance of power.' It doesn't fight. I don't think it ever fights. It must be a peaceable thing, in its own—inimitable—way. It never had to, because it always gained its end otherwise."

Van Wall's mouth twisted in a sickly grin. "You're suggesting then, that perhaps it already *has* the greater numbers, but is just waiting—waiting, all of them—all of you, for all I know—waiting till I, the last human, drop my wariness in sleep. Mac, did you notice their eyes, all looking at us."

Garry sighed. "You haven't been sitting here for four straight hours, while all their eyes silently weighed the information that one of us two, Copper or I, is a monster certainly—perhaps both of us."

Clark repeated his request. "Will you stop that bird's noise? He's driving me nuts. Make him tone down, anyway."

"Still praying?" McReady asked.

"Still praying," Clark groaned. "He hasn't stopped for a second. I don't mind his praying if it relieves him, but he yells, he sings psalms and hymns and shouts prayers. He thinks God can't hear well way down here."

"Maybe he can't," Barclay grunted. "Or he'd have done something about this thing loosed from hell."

"Somebody's going to try that test you mentioned, if you don't stop him," Clark stated grimly. "I think a cleaver in the head would be as positive a test as a bullet in the heart."

"Go ahead with the food. I'll see what I can do. There may be something in the cabinets." McReady moved wearily toward the corner Copper had used as his dispensary. Three tall cabinets of rough boards, two locked, were the repositories of the camp's medical supplies. Twelve years ago, McReady had graduated, had started for an internship, and been diverted to meteorology. Copper was a picked man, a man who knew his profession thoroughly and modernly. More than half the drugs available were totally unfamiliar to McReady; many of the others he had forgotten. There was no huge medical library here, no series of journals available to learn the things he had forgotten, the elementary, simple things to Copper, things that did not merit inclusion in the small library he had been forced to content himself with. Books are heavy, and every ounce of supplies had been freighted in by air.

McReady picked a barbiturate hopefully. Barclay and Van Wall went with him. One man never went anywhere alone in Big Magnet.

Ralsen had his sledge put away, and the physicists had moved off the table, the poker game broken up when they got back. Clark was putting out the food. The clicks of spoons and the muffled sounds of eating were the only sign of life in the room. There were no words spoken as the three returned; simply all eyes focused on them questioningly while the jaws moved methodically.

McReady stiffened suddenly. Kinner was screeching out a hymn in a hoarse, cracked voice. He looked wearily at Van Wall with a twisted grin and shook his head. "Uh-uh."

Van Wall cursed bitterly, and sat down at the table. "We'll just plumb have to take that till his voice wears out. He can't yell like that forever."

"He's got a brass throat and a cast-iron larynx," Norris declared savagely. "Then we could be hopeful, and suggest he's one of our friends. In that case he could go on renewing his throat till doomsday."

Silence clamped down. For twenty minutes they ate without a word. Then Connant jumped up with an angry violence. "You sit as still as a bunch of graven images. You don't say a word, but oh, Lord, what expressive eyes you've got. They roll around like a bunch of glass marbles spilling down a table. They wink and blink and stare—and whisper things. Can you guys look somewhere else for a change, please?

"Listen, Mac, you're in charge here. Let's run movies for the rest of the night. We've been saving those reels to make 'em last. Last for what? Who is it's going to see those last reels, eh? Let's see 'em while we can, and look at something other than each other."

"Sound idea, Connant. I, for one, am quite willing to change this in any way I can."

"Turn the sound up loud,' Dutton. Maybe you can drown out the hymns," Clark suggested.

"But don't," Norris said softly, "turn off the lights altogether."

"The lights will be out." McReady shook his head. "We'll show all the cartoon movies we have. You won't mind seeing the old cartoons will you?"

"Goody, goody—a moom-pitcher show. I'm just in the mood." McReady turned to look at the speaker, a lean, lanky New Englander, by the name of Caldwell. Caldwell was stuffing his pipe slowly, a sour eye cocked up to McReady.

The bronze giant was forced to laugh. "OK, Bart, you win. Maybe we aren't quite in the mood for Popeye and trick ducks, but it's something."

"Let's play Classifications," Caldwell suggested slowly. "Or maybe you call it Guggenheim. You draw lines on a piece of paper, and put down classes of things—like animals, you know. One for 'H' and one for 'U' and so on. Like 'Human' and 'Unknown' for instance. I think that would be a hell of a lot better game. Classification, I sort of figure, is what we need right now a lot more than movies. Maybe somebody's got a pencil that he can draw lines with, draw lines between the 'U' animals and the 'H' animals for instance."

"McReady's trying to find that kind of a pencil," Van Wall answered quietly, "but, we've got three kinds of animals here, you know. One that begins with 'M.' We don't want any more."

"Mad ones, you mean. Uh-huh. Clark, I'll help you with those pots so we can get our little peep show going." Caldwell got up slowly.

Dutton and Barclay and Benning, in charge of the projector and sound mechanism arrangements, went about their job silently, while the Ad Building was cleared and the dishes and pans disposed of. McReady drifted over toward Van Wall slowly, and leaned back in the bunk beside him. "I've been wondering, Van," he said with a wry grin, "whether or not to report my ideas in advance. I forgot the 'U animal' as Caldwell named it, could read minds. I've a vague idea of something that might work. It's too vague to bother with, though. Go ahead with your show, while I try to figure out the logic of the thing. I'll take this bunk."

Van Wall glanced up, and nodded. The movie screen would be practically on a line with this bunk, hence making the pictures least distracting here, because least intelligible. "Perhaps you should tell us what you have in mind. As it is, only the unknowns know what you plan. You might be—unknown before you got it into operation."

"Won't take long, if I get it figured out right. But I don't want any more all-but-the-test-dog-monsters things. We better move Copper into this bunk directly above me. He won't be watching the screen either." McReady nodded toward Copper's gently snoring bulk. Garry helped them lift and move the doctor.

McReady leaned back against the bunk, and sank into a trance, almost, of concentration, trying to calculate chances, operations, methods. He was scarcely aware as the others distributed themselves silently, and the screen lit up. Vaguely Kinner's hectic, shouted prayers and his rasping hymn-singing annoyed him till the sound accompaniment started. The lights were turned out, but the large, light-colored areas of the screen reflected enough light for ready visibility. Kinner was still praying, shouting, his voice a raucous accompaniment to the mechanical sound. Dutton stepped up the amplification.

So long had the voice been going on, that only vaguely at first was McReady aware that something seemed missing. Lying as he was, just across the narrow room from the corridor leading to Cosmos House, Kinner's voice had reached him fairly clearly, despite the sound accompaniment of the pictures. It struck him abruptly that it had stopped.

"Dutton, cut that sound," McReady called as he sat up abruptly. The pictures flickered a moment, soundless and strangely futile in the sudden, deep silence. The rising wind on the surface above bubbled melancholy tears of sound down the stove pipes. "Kinner's stopped," McReady said softly.

"For God's sake start that sound then; he may have stopped to listen," Norris snapped.

McReady rose and went down the corridor. Barclay and Van Wall left their places at the far end of the room to follow him. The flickers bulged and twisted on the back of Barclay's gray underwear as he crossed the still-functioning beam of the projector. Dutton snapped on the lights, and the pictures vanished.

Norris stood at the door as McReady had asked. Garry sat down quietly in the bunk nearest the door, forcing Clark to make room for him. Most of the others had stayed exactly where they were. Only Connant walked slowly up and down the room, in steady, unvarying rhythm.

"If you're going to do that, Connant," Clark spat, "we can get along without you altogether, whether you're human or not. Will you stop that damned rhythm?"

"Sorry." The physicist sat down in a bunk, and watched his toes thoughtfully. It was almost five minutes, five ages, while the wind made the only sound, before McReady appeared at the door.

"Well," he announced, "haven't got enough grief here already. Somebody's tried to help us out. Kinner has a knife in his throat, which was why he stopped singing, probably. We've got monsters, madmen and murderers. Any more 'M's' you can think of, Caldwell? If there are, we'll probably have 'em before long."

XIII

"Is Blair loose?" someone asked.

"Blair is not loose. Or he flew in. If there's any doubt about where our gentle helper came from—this may clear it up." Van Wall held a foot-long, thin-bladed knife in a cloth. The wooden handle was half burnt, charred with the peculiar pattern of the top of the galley stove.

Clark stared at it. "I did that this afternoon. I forgot the damn thing and left it on the stove."

Van Wall nodded. "I smelled it, if you remember. I knew the knife came from the galley."

"I wonder," said Benning, looking around at the party warily, "how many more monsters have we? If somebody could slip out of his place, go back of the screen to the galley and then down to the Cosmos House and back—he did come back, didn't he? Yes—everybody's here. Well, if one of the gang could do all that—"

"Maybe a monster did it," Garry suggested quietly.

"There's that possibility."

"The monster, as you pointed out today, has only men left to imitate. Would he decrease his—supply, shall we say?" Van Wall pointed out. "No, we just have a plain, ordinary louse, a murderer to deal with. Ordinarily we'd call him an 'inhuman murderer' I suppose, but we have to distinguish now. We have inhuman murderers, and now we have human murderers. Or one at least."

"There's one less human," Norris said softly. "Maybe the monsters have the balance of power now."

"Never mind that," McReady sighed and turned to Barclay. "Bar, will you get your electric gadget? I'm going to make certain—"

Barclay turned down the corridor to get the pronged electrocuter, while McReady and Van Wall went back toward Cosmos House. Barclay followed them in some thirty seconds.

The corridor to Cosmos House twisted, as did nearly all corridors in Big Magnet, and Norris stood at the entrance again. But they heard, rather muffled, McReady's sudden shout. There was a savage flurry of blows, dull *ch-thunk, shluff* sounds. "Bar—Bar—" And a curious, savage mewing scream, silenced before even quick-moving Norris had reached the bend.

Kinner—or what had been Kinner—lay on the floor, cut half in two by the great knife McReady had had. The meteorologist stood against the wall, the knife dripping red in his hand. Van Wall was stirring vaguely on the floor, moaning, his hand half-consciously rubbing at his jaw. Barclay, an unutterably savage gleam in his eyes, was methodically leaning on the pronged weapon in his hand, jabbing—jabbing, jabbing.

Kinner's arms had developed a queer, scaly fur, and the flesh had twisted. The fingers had shortened, the hand rounded, the fingernails become three-inch long things of dull red horn, keened to steel-hard, razor-sharp talons.

McReady raised his head, looked at the knife in his hand and dropped it. "Well, whoever did it can speak up now. He was an inhuman murderer at that—in that he murdered an inhuman. I swear by all that's holy, Kinner was a lifeless corpse on the floor here when we arrived. But when It found we were going to jab It with the power—It changed."

Norris stared unsteadily. "Oh, Lord, those things can act. Ye gods—sitting in here for hours, mouthing prayers to a God it hated! Shouting hymns in a cracked voice—hymns about a Church it never knew. Driving us mad with its ceaseless howling—

"Well. Speak up, whoever did it. You didn't know it, but you did the camp a favor. And I want to know how in blazes you got out of the room without anyone seeing you. It might help in guarding ourselves."

"His screaming—his singing. Even the sound projector couldn't drown it." Clark shivered. "It was a monster."

"Oh," said Van Wall in sudden comprehension. "You *were* sitting right next to the door, weren't you? And almost behind the projection screen already."

Clark nodded dumbly. "He—it's quiet now. It's a dead—Mac, your test's no damn good. It was dead anyway, monster or man, it was dead."

McReady chuckled softly. "Boys, meet Clark, the only one we know is human! Meet Clark, the one who proves he's human by trying to commit murder—and failing. Will the rest of you please refrain from trying to prove you're human for a while? I think we may have another test."

"A test!" Connant snapped joyfully, then his face sagged in disappointment. "I suppose it's another either-way-you-want-it."

"No," said McReady steadily. "Look sharp and be careful. Come into the Ad Building. Barclay, bring your electrocuter. And somebody—Dutton—stand with Barclay to make sure he does it. Watch every neighbor, for by the Hell these monsters came from, I've got something, and they know it. They're going to get dangerous!"

The group tensed abruptly. An air of crushing menace entered into every man's body, sharply they looked at each other. More keenly than ever before—*is that man next to me an inhuman monster?*

"What is it?" Garry asked, as they stood again in the main room. "How long will it take?"

"I don't know, exactly," said McReady, his voice brittle with angry determination. "But I *know* it will work, and no two ways about it. It depends on a basic quality of the *monsters*, not on us. '*Kinner*' just convinced me." He stood heavy and solid in bronzed immobility, completely sure of himself again at last.

"This," said Barclay, hefting the wooden-handled weapon tipped with its two sharp-pointed, charged conductors, "is going to be rather necessary, I take it. Is the power plant assured?"

Dutton nodded sharply. "The automatic stoker bin is full. The gas power plant is on standby. Van Wall and I set it for the movie operation—and we've checked it over rather carefully several times, you know. Anything those wires touch, dies," he assured them grimly. "*I* know that."

Dr. Copper stirred vaguely in his bunk, rubbed his eyes with fumbling hand. He sat up slowly, blinked his eyes blurred with sleep and drugs, widened with an unutterable horror of drug-ridden nightmares. "Garry," he mumbled, "Garry—listen. Selfish—from hell they came, and hellish shellfish—I mean self— Do I? What do I mean?" He sank back in his bunk, and snored softly.

McReady looked at him thoughtfully. "We'll know presently," he nodded slowly. "But selfish is what you mean, all right. You may have thought of that, half sleeping, dreaming there. I didn't stop to think what dreams you might be having. But that's all right. Selfish is the word. They must be, you see." He turned to the men in the cabin, tense, silent men staring with wolfish eyes each at his neighbor. "Selfish, and as Dr. Copper said—*every part is a whole.* Every piece is self-sufficient, an animal in itself.

"That, and one other thing, tell the story. There's nothing mysterious about blood; it's just as normal a body tissue as a piece of muscle, or a piece of liver. But it hasn't so much connective tissue, though it has millions, billions of life-cells."

McReady's great bronze beard ruffled in a grim smile. "This is satisfying, in a way. I'm pretty sure we humans still outnumber you—others. Others standing here. And we have what you, your other-world race, evidently doesn't. Not an imitated, but a bred-in-the-bone instinct, a driving, unquenchable fire that's genuine. We'll fight, fight with a ferocity you may attempt to imitate, but you'll never equal! We're human. We're real. You're imitations, false to the core of your every cell."

"All right. It's a showdown now. *You* know. You, with your mind reading. You've lifted the idea from my brain. You can't do a thing about it.

"Standing here—

"Let it pass. Blood is tissue. They have to bleed; if they bleed when cut, then by Heaven, they're phoney from hell! If they don't bleed—then that blood, separated from them, is an individual—*a newly formed individual in its own right, just as they—split, all of them, from one original—are individuals!*

"Get it, Van? See the answer, Bar?"

Van Wall laughed very softly. "The blood—the blood will not obey. It's a new individual, with all the desire to protect its own life that the original—the main mass from which it was split—has. The *blood* will live—and try to crawl away from a hot needle, say!"

McReady picked up the scalpel from the table. From the cabinet, he took a rack of test tubes, a tiny alcohol lamp, and a length of platinum wire set in a little glass rod. A smile of grim satisfaction rode his lips. For a moment he glanced up at those around him. Barclay and Dutton moved toward him slowly, the wooden-handled electric instrument alert.

"Dutton," said McReady, "suppose you stand over by the splice there where you've connected that in. Just make sure no—thing pulls it loose."

Dutton moved away. "Now, Van, suppose you be first on this."

White-faced, Van Wall stepped forward. With a delicate precision, McReady cut a vein in the base of his thumb. Van Wall winced slightly, then held steady as a half inch of bright blood collected in the tube. McReady put the tube in the rack, gave Van Wall a bit of alum, and indicated the iodine bottle.

Van Wall stood motionlessly watching. McReady heated the platinum wire in the alcohol lamp flame, then dipped it into the tube. It hissed softly. Five times he repeated the test. "Human, I'd say," McReady sighed, and straightened. "As yet, my theory hasn't been actually proven—but I have hopes. I have hopes.

"Don't, by the way, get too interested in this. We have with us some unwelcome ones, no doubt. Van, will you relieve Barclay at the switch? Thanks. OK, Barclay, and may I say I hope you stay with us? You're a damned good guy."

Barclay grinned uncertainly; winced under the keen edge of the scalpel. Presently, smiling widely, he retrieved his long-handled weapon.

"Mr. Samuel Dutt—*Bar!*"

The tensity was released in that second. Whatever of hell the monsters may have had within them, the men in that instant matched it. Barclay had no chance to move his weapon, as a score of men poured down on the thing that had seemed Dutton. It mewed, and spat, and tried to grow fangs—and was a hundred broken, torn pieces. Without knives, or any weapon save the brute-given strength of a staff of picked men, the thing was crushed, rent.

Slowly they picked themselves up, their eyes smouldering, very quiet in their motions. A curious wrinkling of their lips betrayed a species of nervousness.

Barclay went over with the electric weapon. Things smouldered and stank. The caustic acid Van Wall dropped on each spilled drop of blood gave off tickling, cough-provoking fumes.

McReady grinned, his deep-set eyes alight and dancing. "Maybe," he said softly, "I underrated man's abilities when I said nothing human could have the ferocity in the eyes of that thing we found. I wish we could have the opportunity to treat in a more befitting manner these things. Something with boiling oil, or melted lead in it, or maybe slow roasting in the power boiler. When I think what a man Dutton was—

"Never mind. My theory is confirmed by—by one who knew? Well, Van Wall and Barclay are proven. I think, then, that I'll try to show you what I already know. That I, too, am human." McReady swished the scalpel in absolute alcohol, burned it off the metal blade, and cut the base of his thumb expertly.

Twenty seconds later he looked up from the desk at the waiting men. There were more grins out there now, friendly grins, yet withal, something else in the eyes.

"Connant," McReady laughed softly, "was right. The huskies watching that thing in the corridor bend had nothing on you. Wonder why we think only the wolf blood has the right to ferocity? Maybe on spontaneous viciousness a wolf takes tops, but after these seven days—abandon all hope, ye wolves who enter here!

"Maybe we can save time. Connant, would you step for—"

Again Barclay was too slow. There were more grins, less tensity still, when Barclay and Van Wall finished their work.

Garry spoke in a low, bitter voice. "Connant was one of the finest men we had here—and five minutes ago I'd have sworn he was a man. Those damnable things are more than imitation." Garry shuddered and sat back in his bunk.

And thirty seconds later, Garry's blood shrank from the hot platinum wire, and struggled to escape the tube, struggled as frantically as a suddenly feral, red-eyed, dissolving imitation of Garry struggled to dodge the snake-tongue weapon Barclay advanced at him, white-faced and sweating. The Thing in the test tube screamed with a tiny, tinny voice as McReady dropped it into the glowing coal of the galley stove.

XIV

"The last of it?" Dr. Copper looked down from his bunk with bloodshot, saddened eyes. "Fourteen of them—"

McReady nodded shortly. "In some ways—if only we could have permanently prevented their spreading—I'd like to have even the imitations back. Commander Garry—Connant—Dutton—Clark—"

"Where are they taking those things?" Copper nodded to the stretcher Barclay and Norris were carrying out.

"Outside. Outside on the ice, where they've got fifteen smashed crates, half a ton of coal, and presently will add ten gallons of kerosene. We've dumped acid on every spilled drop, every torn fragment. We're going to incinerate those."

"Sounds like a good plan." Copper nodded wearily. "I wonder, you haven't said whether Blair—"

McReady started. "We forgot him? We had so much else! I wonder—do you suppose we can cure him now?"

"If—" began Dr. Copper, and stopped meaningly.

McReady started a second time. "Even a madman. It imitated Kinner and his praying hysteria—" McReady turned toward Van Wall at the long table. "Van, we've got to make an expedition to Blair's shack."

Van looked up sharply, the frown of worry faded for an instant in surprised remembrance. Then he rose, nodded. "Barclay better go along. He applied the lashings, and may figure how to get in without frightening Blair too much."

Three quarters of an hour, through -37° cold, while the aurora curtain bellied overhead. The twilight was nearly twelve hours long, flaming in the north on snow like white, crystalline sand under their skis. A five-mile wind piled it in drift-lines pointing off to the northwest. Three quarters of an hour to reach the snow-buried shack. No smoke came from the little shack, and the men hastened.

"Blair!" Barclay roared into the wind and when he was still a hundred yards away. "Blair!"

"Shut up," said McReady softly. "And hurry. He may be trying a lone hike. If we have to go after him—no planes, the tractors disabled—"

"Would a monster have the stamina a man has?"

"A broken leg wouldn't stop it for more than a minute," McReady pointed out.

Barclay gasped suddenly and pointed aloft. Dim in the twilit sky, a winged thing circled in curves of indescribable grace and ease. Great white wings tipped gently, and the bird swept over them in silent curiosity. "Albatross—" Barclay said softly. "First of the season, and wandering way inland for some reason. If a monster's loose—"

Norris bent down on the ice, and tore hurriedly at his heavy, windproof clothing. He straightened, his coat flapping open, a grim blue-metaled weapon in his hand. It roared a challenge to the white silence of Antarctica.

The thing in the air screamed hoarsely. Its great wings worked frantically as a dozen feathers floated down from its tail. Norris fired again. The bird was moving swiftly now, but in an almost straight line of retreat. It screamed again, more feathers dropped, and with beating wings it soared behind a ridge of pressure ice, to vanish.

Norris hurried after the others. "It won't come back," he panted.

Barclay cautioned him to silence, pointing. A curiously, fiercely blue light beat out from the cracks of the shack's door. A very low, soft humming sounded inside, a low, soft humming and a clink and clink of tools, the very sounds somehow bearing a message of frantic haste.

McReady's face paled. "Lord help us if that thing has—" He grabbed Barclay's shoulder, and made snipping motions with his fingers, pointing toward the lacing of control cables that held the door.

Barclay drew the wire cutters from his pocket, and kneeled soundlessly at the door. The snap and twang of cut wires made an unbearable racket in the utter quiet of the Antarctic hush. There was only that strange, sweetly soft hum from within the shack, and the queerly, hecticly clipped clicking and rattling of tools to drown their noises.

McReady peered through a crack in the door. His breath sucked in huskily and his great fingers clamped cruelly on Barclay's shoulder. The meteorologist backed down. "It isn't," he explained very softly, "Blair. It's kneeling on something on the bunk—something that keeps lifting. Whatever it's working on is a thing like a knapsack—and it lifts."

"All at once," Barclay said grimly. "No. Norris, hang back, and get that iron of yours out. It may have—weapons."

Together, Barclay's powerful body and McReady's giant strength struck the door. Inside, the bunk jammed against the door screeched madly and crackled into kindling. The door flung down from broken hinges, the patched lumber of the doorpost dropping inward.

Like a blue rubber ball, a Thing bounced up. One of its four tentacle-like arms looped out like a striking snake. In a seven-tentacled hand a six-inch pencil of winking, shining metal glinted and swung upward to face them. Its line-thin lips twitched back from snake-fangs in a grin of hate, red eyes blazing.

Norris' revolver thundered in the confined space. The hate-washed face twitched in agony, the looping tentacle snatched back. The silvery thing in its hand a smashed ruin of metal, the seven-tentacled hand became a mass of mangled flesh oozing greenish-yellow ichor. The revolver thundered three times more. Dark holes drilled each of the three eyes before Norris hurled the empty weapon against its face.

The Thing screamed in feral hate, a lashing tentacle wiping at blinded eyes. For a moment it crawled on the floor, savage tentacles lashing out, the body twitching. Then it struggled up again, blinded eyes working, boiling hideously, the crushed flesh sloughing away in sodden gobbets.

Barclay lurched to his feet and dove forward with an ice-ax. The flat of the weighty thing crushed against the side of the head. Again the unkillable monster went down. The tentacles lashed out, and suddenly Barclay fell to his feet in the grip of a living, livid rope. The thing dissolved as he held it, a white-hot band that ate into the flesh of his hands like living fire. Frantically he tore the stuff from him, held his hands where they could not be reached. The blind Thing felt and ripped at the tough, heavy, windproof cloth, seeking flesh—flesh it could convert—

The huge blowtorch McReady had brought coughed solemnly. Abruptly it rumbled disapproval throatily. Then it laughed gurglingly, and thrust out a blue-white, three-foot tongue. The Thing on the floor shrieked, flailed out blindly with tentacles that writhed and withered in the bubbling wrath of the blowtorch. It crawled and turned on the floor, it shrieked and hobbled madly, but always McReady held the blowtorch on the face, the dead eyes burning and bubbling uselessly. Frantically the Thing crawled and howled.

A tentacle sprouted a savage talon—and crisped in the flame. Steadily McReady moved with a planned, grim campaign. Helpless, maddened, the Thing retreated from the grunting torch, the caressing, licking tongue. For a moment it rebelled, squalling in inhuman hatred at the touch of the icy snow. Then it fell back before the charring breath of the torch, the stench of its flesh bathing it. Hopelessly it retreated—on and on across the Antarctic snow. The bitter wind swept over it, twisting the torch-tongue; vainly it flopped, a trail of oily, stinking smoke bubbling away from it—

McReady walked back toward the shack silently. Barclay met him at the door. "No more?" the giant meteorologist asked grimly.

Barclay shook his head. "No more. It didn't split?"

"It had other things to think about," McReady assured him. "When I left it, it was a glowing coal. What was it doing?"

Norris laughed shortly. "Wise boys, we are. Smash magnetos,

so planes won't work. Rip the boiler tubing out of the tractors. And leave that Thing alone for a week in this shack. Alone and undisturbed."

McReady looked in at the shack more carefully. The air, despite the ripped door, was hot and humid. On a table at the far end of the room rested a thing of coiled wires and small magnets, glass tubing and radio tubes. At the center a block of rough stone rested. From the center of the block came the light that flooded the place, the fiercely blue light bluer than the glare of an electric arc, and from it came the sweetly soft hum. Off to one side was another mechanism of crystal glass, blown with an incredible neatness and delicacy, metal plates and a queer, shimmery sphere of insubstantiality.

"What is that?" McReady moved nearer.

Norris grunted. "Leave it for investigation. But I can guess pretty well. That's atomic power. That stuff to the left—that's a neat little thing for doing what men have been trying to do with hundred-ton cyclotrons and so forth. It separates neutrons from heavy water, which he was getting from the surrounding ice.

"Where did he get all—oh. Of course. A monster couldn't be locked in—or out. He's been through the apparatus caches." McReady stared at the apparatus. "Lord, what minds that race must have—"

"The shimmery sphere—I think it's a sphere of pure force. Neutrons can pass through any matter, and he wanted a supply reservoir of neutrons. Just project neutrons against silica—calcium—beryllium—almost anything, and the atomic energy is released. That thing is the atomic generator."

McReady plucked a thermometer from his coat. "It's 120° in here, despite the open door. Our clothes have kept the heat out to an extent, but I'm sweating now."

Norris nodded. "The light's cold. I found that. But it gives off heat to warm the place through that coil. He had all the power in the world. He could keep it warm and pleasant, as his race thought of warmth and pleasantness. Did you notice the light, the color of it?"

McReady nodded. "Beyond the stars is the answer. From beyond the stars. From a hotter planet that circled a brighter, bluer sun they came."

McReady glanced out the door toward the blasted, smoke-stained trail that flopped and wandered blindly off across the drift. "There won't be any more coming. I guess. Sheer accident it landed here, and that was twenty million years ago. What did it do all that for?" He nodded toward the apparatus.

Barclay laughed softly. "Did you notice what it was working on when we came? Look." He pointed toward the ceiling of the shack.

Like a knapsack made of flattened coffee tins, with dangling cloth straps and leather belts, the mechanism clung to the ceiling. A tiny, glaring heart of supernal flame burned in it, yet burned through the ceiling's wood without scorching it. Barclay walked over to it, grasped two of the dangling straps in his hands, and pulled it down with an effort. He strapped it about his body. A slight jump carried him in a weirdly slow arc across the room.

"Antigravity," said McReady softly.

"Antigravity," Norris nodded. "Yes, we had 'em stopped, with no planes, and no birds. The birds hadn't come—but it had coffee tins and radio parts, and glass and the machine shop at night. And a week—a whole week—all to itself. America in a single jump—with antigravity powered by the atomic energy of matter.

"We had 'em stopped. Another half hour—it was just tightening these straps on the device so it could wear it—and we'd have stayed in Antarctica, and shot down any moving thing that came from the rest of the world."

"The albatross—" McReady said softly. "Do you suppose—"

"With this thing almost finished? With that death weapon it held in its hand?

"No, by the grace of God, who evidently does hear very well, even down here, and the margin of half an hour, we keep our world, and the planets of the system, too. Antigravity, you know, and atomic power. Because They came from another sun, a star beyond the stars. *They* came from a world with a bluer sun."

Quietus

by Ross Rocklynne

PREFACE BY DAVID DRAKE

Like a number of my other picks for this anthology, I read "Quietus" before authors' names meant anything to me. I didn't run into the story later, when the name Ross Rocklynne would've been familiar. (In 1972 I read early '40s issues of *Planet Stories*, and then a series by Rocklynne stood out very vividly.)

I didn't remember the story's title, either, so I didn't rediscover it until a few years ago when I made a determined search through a number of anthologies I'd read when I was thirteen or fourteen. There I found "Quietus," just as effective as I remembered it being. A story that stands out so clearly decades after I'd forgotten its title and author belongs in this collection.

"Quietus" hit me between the eyes with the concept that who we are creates a bias in how we view the world. I've never forgotten that lesson, though I won't pretend it's always been as close to the front of my mind as it should've been. Still, I'd like to think that because of Rocklynne's story I've been somewhat less of an arrogant prick than I've watched some other WASP males of my acquaintance being.

The creatures from Alcon saw from the first that Earth, as a planet, was practically dead; dead in the sense that it had given birth to life, and was responsible, indirectly, for its almost complete extinction.

"This type of planet is the most distressing," said Tark, absently smoothing down the brilliantly colored feathers of his left wing. "I can stand the dark, barren worlds which never have, and probably never will, hold life. But these that have been killed by some celestial catastrophe! Think of what great things might have come from their inhabitants."

As he spoke thus to his mate, Vascar, he was marking down in a book the position of this planet, its general appearance from space, and the number and kind of satellites it supported.

Vascar, sitting at the controls, both her claws and her vestigial hands at work, guided the spherical ship at slowly decreasing speed toward the planet Earth. A thousand miles above it, she set the craft into an orbital motion, and then proceeded to study the planet, Tark setting the account into his book, for later insertion into the Astronomical Archives of Alcon.

"Evidently," mused Vascar, her brilliant, unblinking eyes looking at the planet through a transparent section above the control board, "some large meteor, or an errant asteroid—that seems most likely—must have struck this specimen a terrible blow. Look at those great, gaping cracks that run from pole to pole, Tark. It looks as if volcanic eruptions are still taking place, too. At any rate, the whole planet seems entirely denuded—except for that single, short strip of green we saw as we came in."

Tark nodded. He was truly a bird, for in the evolutionary race on his planet, distant uncounted light-years away, his stock had won out over the others. His wings were short, true, and in another thousand years would be too short for flight, save in a dense atmosphere; but his head was large, and his eyes, red, small, set close together, showed intelligence and a kind benevolence. He and Vascar had left Alcon, their planet, a good many years ago; but they were on their way back now. Their outward-bound trip had taken them many light-years north of the Solar System; but on the way back, they had decided to make it one of the stop-off points in their zigzag course. Probably their greatest interest in all this long cruise was in the discovery of planets—they were indeed few. And that pleasure might even be secondary to the discovery of life. To find a planet that had almost entirely died was, conversely, distressing. Their interest in the planet Earth was, because of this, a wistful one.

The ship made the slow circuit of Earth—the planet was a hodge-podge of tumbled, churned mountains; of abysmal, frightfully long cracks exuding unholy vapors; of volcanoes that threw their fires and hot liquid rocks far into the sky; of vast oceans disturbed from the ocean bed by cataclysmic eruptions. And of life they saw nothing save a single strip of green perhaps a thousand miles long, a hundred wide, in the Western Hemisphere.

"I don't think we'll find intelligent life," Tark said pessimistically. "This planet was given a terrific blow—I wouldn't be surprised if her rotation period was cut down considerably in a single instant. Such a charge would be unsupportable. Whole cities would literally be snapped away from their foundations—churned, ground to dust. The intelligent creatures who built them would die by the millions—the billions—in that holocaust; and whatever destruction was left incomplete would be finished up by the appearance of volcanoes and faults in the crust of the planet."

Vascar reminded him, "Remember, where there's vegetation, even as little as evidenced by that single strip down there, there must be some kind of animal life."

Tark ruffled his wings in a shrug. "I doubt it. The plants would get all the carbon dioxide they needed from volcanoes—animal life wouldn't have to exist. Still, let's take a look. Don't worry, I'm hoping there's intelligent life, too. If there is, it will doubtless need some help if it is to survive. Which ties in with our aims, for that is our principal purpose on this expedition—to discover intelligent life, and, wherever possible, to give it what help we can, if it needs help."

Vascar's vestigial hands worked the controls, and the ship dropped leisurely downward toward the green strip.

A rabbit darted out of the underbrush—Tommy leaped at it with the speed and dexterity of a thoroughly wild animal. His powerful hands wrapped around the creature—its struggles ceased as its vertebra was snapped. Tommy squatted, tore the skin off the creature, and proceeded to eat great mouthfuls of the still warm flesh.

Blacky cawed harshly, squawked, and his untidy form came flashing down through the air to land precariously on Tommy's shoulder. Tommy went on eating, while the crow fluttered its wings, smoothed them out, and settled down to a restless somnolence. The quiet of the scrub forest, save for the cries and sounds of movement of birds and small animals moving through the forest, settled down about Tommy as he ate. "Tommy" was what he called himself. A long time ago, he remembered, there used to be a great many people in the world—perhaps a hundred—many of

whom, and particularly two people whom he had called Mom and
Pop, had called him by that name. They were gone now, and the
others with them. Exactly where they went, Tommy did not know.
But the world had rocked one night—it was the night Tommy
ran away from home, with Blacky riding on his shoulder—and
when Tommy came out of the cave where he had been sleeping,
all was in flames, and the city on the horizon had fallen so that
it was nothing but a huge pile of dust—but in the end it had
not mattered to Tommy. Of course, he was lonesome, terrified,
at first, but he got over that. He continued to live, eating, drinking, sleeping, walking endlessly; and Blacky, his talking crow, was
good company. Blacky was smart. He could speak every word that
Tommy knew, and a good many others that he didn't. Tommy was
not Blacky's first owner.

But though he had been happy, the last year had brought the
recurrence of a strange feeling that had plagued him off and on,
but never so strongly as now. A strange, terrible hunger was settling on him. Hunger? He knew this sensation. He had forthwith
slain a wild dog, and eaten of the meat. He saw then that it was
not a hunger of the belly. It was a hunger of the mind, and it
was all the worse because he could not know what it was. He had
come to his feet, restless, looking into the tangled depths of the
second growth forest.

"Hungry," he had said, and his shoulders shook and tears coursed
out of his eyes, and he sat down on the ground and sobbed without
trying to stop himself, for he had never been told that to weep
was unmanly. What was it he wanted?

He had everything there was all to himself. Southward in winter,
northward in summer, eating of berries and small animals as he
went, and Blacky to talk to and Blacky to talk the same words
back at him. This was the natural life—he had lived it ever since
the world went bang. But still he cried, and felt a panic growing
in his stomach, and he didn't know what it was he was afraid
of, or longed for, whichever it was. He was twenty-one years old.
Tears were natural to him, to be indulged in whenever he felt
like it. Before the world went bang—there were some things he
remembered—the creature whom he called Mom generally put
her arms around him and merely said, "It's all right, Tommy, it's
all right."

So on that occasion, he arose from the ground and said, "It's
all right, Tommy, it's all right."

Blacky, he with the split tongue, said harshly, as was his wont,

"It's all right, Tommy, it's all right! I tell you, the price of wheat is going down!"

Blacky, the smartest crow anybody had—why did he say that? There wasn't anybody else, and there weren't any more crows—helped a lot. He not only knew all the words and sentences that Tommy knew, but he knew others that Tommy could never understand because he didn't know where they came from, or what they referred to. And in addition to all that, Blacky had the ability to anticipate what Tommy said, and frequently took whole words and sentences right out of Tommy's mouth.

Tommy finished eating the rabbit, and threw the skin aside, and sat quite still, a peculiarly blank look in his eyes. The strange hunger was on him again. He looked off across the lush plain of grasses that stretched away, searching into the distance, toward where the Sun was setting. He looked to left and right. He drew himself softly to his feet, and peered into the shadows of the forest behind him. His heavily bearded lips began to tremble, and the tears started from his eyes again. He turned and stumbled from the forest, blinded.

Blacky clutched at Tommy's broad shoulder, and rode him, and a split second before Tommy said, "It's all right, Tommy, it's all right."

Tommy said the words angrily to himself, and blinked the tears away.

He was a little bit tired. The Sun was setting, and night would soon come. But it wasn't that that made him tired. It was a weariness of the mind, a feeling of futility, for, whatever it was he wanted, he could never, never find it, because he would not know where he should look for it.

His bare foot trampled on something wet—he stopped and looked at the ground. He stooped and picked up the skin of a recently killed rabbit. He turned it over and over in his hands, frowning. This was not an animal he had killed, certainly—the skin had been taken off in a different way. Someone else—no! But his shoulders began to shake with a wild excitement. Someone else? No, it couldn't be! There was no one—there could be no one—could there? The skin dropped from his nerveless fingers as he saw a single footprint not far ahead of him. He stooped over it, examining, and knew again that he had not done this, either. And certainly it could be no other animal than a man!

It was a small footprint at which he stared, as if a child, or an under-sized man, might have stepped in the soft humus. Suddenly he raised his head. He had definitely heard the crackling of a twig, not more than forty feet away, certainly. His eyes stared ahead through the gathering dusk. Something looking back at him? Yes! Something there in the bushes that was not an animal!

"No noise, Blacky," he whispered, and forgot Blacky's general response to that command.

"No noise, Blacky!" the big, ugly bird blasted out. "No noise, Blacky! Well, fer cryin' out loud!"

Blacky uttered a scared squawk as Tommy leaped ahead, a snarl contorting his features, and flapping from his master's shoulder. For several minutes Tommy ran after the vanishing figure, with all the strength and agility of his singularly powerful legs. But whoever—or whatever—it was that fled him, outdistanced him easily, and Tommy had to stop at last, panting. Then he stooped, and picked up a handful of pebbles and hurled them at the squawking bird. A single tail feather fell to earth as Blacky swooped away.

"Told you not to make noise," Tommy snarled, and the tears started to run again. The hunger was starting up in his mind again, too! He sat down on a log, and put his chin in his palms, while his tears flowed. Blacky came flapping through the air, almost like a shadow—it was getting dark. The bird tentatively settled on his shoulder, cautiously flapped away again and then came back.

Tommy turned his head and looked at it bitterly, and then turned away, and groaned.

"It's all your fault, Blacky!"

"It's all your fault," the bird said. "Oh, Tommy, I could spank you! I get so exasperated!"

Sitting there, Tommy tried to learn exactly what he had seen. He had been sure it was a human figure, just like himself, only different. Different! It had been smaller, had seemed to possess a slender grace—it was impossible! Every time he thought of it, the hunger in his mind raged!

He jumped to his feet, his fists clenched. This hunger had been in him too long! He must find out what caused it—he must find her—why did the word *her* come to his mind? Suddenly, he was flooded with a host of childhood remembrances.

"It was a girl!" he gasped. "Oh, Tommy must want a girl!"

The thought was so utterly new that it left him stunned; but the thought grew. He must find her, if it took him all the rest of his life! His chest deepened, his muscles swelled, and a new light came into his blue eyes. Southward in winter, northward in summer—eating—

sleeping—truly, there was nothing in such a life. Now he felt the strength of a purpose swelling up in him. He threw himself to the ground and slept; and Blacky flapped to the limb of a tree, inserted his head beneath a wing, and slept also. Perhaps, in the last ten or fifteen years, he also had wanted a mate, but probably he had long ago given up hope—for, it seemed, there were no more crows left in the world. Anyway, Blacky was very old, perhaps twice as old as Tommy; he was merely content to live.

Tark and Vascar sent their spherical ship lightly plummeting above the green strip—it proved to be vegetation, just as they had supposed. Either one or the other kept constant watch of the ground below—they discovered nothing that might conceivably be classed as intelligent life. Insects they found, and decided that they worked entirely by instinct; small animals, rabbits, squirrels, rats, raccoons, otters, opossums, and large animals, deer, horses, sheep, cattle, pigs, dogs, they found to be just that—animals, and nothing more.

"Looks as if it was all killed off, Vascar," said Tark, "and not so long ago at that, judging by the fact that this forest must have grown entirely in the last few years."

Vascar agreed; she suggested they put the ship down for a few days and rest.

"It would be wonderful if we could find intelligent life after all," she said wistfully. "Think what a great triumph it would be if we were the ones to start the last members of that race on the upward trail again. Anyway," she added, "I think this atmosphere is dense enough for us to fly in."

He laughed—a trilling sound. "You've been looking for such an atmosphere for years. But I think you're right about this one. Put the ship down there, Vascar—looks like a good spot."

For five days Tommy followed the trail of the girl with a grim determination. He knew now that it was a woman; perhaps—indeed, very probably—the only one left alive. He had only the vaguest of ideas of why he wanted her—he thought it was for human companionship, that alone. At any rate, he felt that this terrible hunger in him—he could give it no other word—would be allayed when he caught up with her.

She was fleeing him, and staying just near enough to him to make him continue the chase, and he knew that with a fierce exultation. And somehow her actions seemed right and proper.

Twice he had seen her, once on the crest of a ridge, once as she swam a river. Both times she had easily outdistanced him. But by cross-hatching, he picked up her trail again—a bent twig or weed, a footprint, the skin of a dead rabbit.

Once, at night, he had the impression that she crept up close, and looked at him curiously, perhaps with the same great longing that he felt. He could not be sure. But he knew that very soon now she would be his—and perhaps she would be glad of it.

Once he heard a terrible moaning, high up in the air. He looked upward. Blacky uttered a surprised squawk. A large, spherical thing was darting overhead.

"I wonder what that is," Blacky squawked.

"I wonder what that is," said Tommy, feeling a faint fear. "There ain't nothin' like that in the yard."

He watched as the spaceship disappeared from sight. Then, with the unquestioning attitude of the savage, he dismissed the matter from his mind, and took up his tantalizing trail again.

"Better watch out, Tommy," the bird cawed.

"Better watch out, Tommy," Tommy muttered to himself. He only vaguely heard Blacky—Blacky always anticipated what Tommy was going to say, because he had known Tommy so long.

The river was wide, swirling, muddy, primeval in its surge of resistless strength. Tommy stood on the bank, and looked out over the waters—suddenly his breath soughed from his lungs.

"It's her!" he gasped. "It's her, Blacky! She's drownin'!"

No time to waste in thought—a figure truly struggled against the push of the treacherous waters, seemingly went under. Tommy dived cleanly, and Blacky spread his wings at the last instant and escaped a bath. He saw his master disappear beneath the swirling waters, saw him emerge, strike out with singularly powerful arms, slightly upstream, fighting every inch of the way. Blacky hovered over the waters, cawing frantically, and screaming.

"Tommy, I could spank you! I could spank you! I get so exasperated! You wait till your father comes home!"

A log was coming downstream. Tommy saw it coming, but knew he'd escape it. He struck out, paid no more attention to it. The log came down with a rush, and would have missed him had it not suddenly swung broadside on. It clipped the swimming man on the side of the head. Tommy went under, threshing feebly, barely conscious, his limbs like leaden bars. That seemed to go on for a very long time. He seemed to be breathing water. Then something grabbed hold of his long black hair—

When he awoke, he was lying on his back, and he was staring into her eyes. Something in Tommy's stomach fell out—perhaps the hunger was going. He came to his feet, staring at her, his eyes blazing. She stood only about twenty feet away from him. There was something pleasing about her, the slimness of her arms, the roundness of her hips, the strangeness of her body, her large, startled, timid eyes, the mass of ebon hair that fell below her hips. He started toward her. She gazed at him as if in a trance.

Blacky came flapping mournfully across the river. He was making no sound, but the girl must have been frightened as he landed on Tommy's shoulder. She tensed, and was away like a rabbit. Tommy went after her in long, loping bounds, but his foot caught in a tangle of dead grass, and he plummeted head foremost to the ground.

The other vanished over a rise of ground.

He arose again, and knew no disappointment that he had again lost her. He knew now that it was only her timidity, the timidity of a wild creature, that made her flee him. He started off again, for now that he knew what the hunger was, it seemed worse than ever.

The air of this planet was deliciously breathable, and was the nearest thing to their own atmosphere that Tark and Vascar had encountered.

Vascar ruffled her brilliant plumage, and spread her wings, flapping them. Tark watched her, as she laughed at him in her own way, and then made a few short, running jumps and took off. She spiraled, called down to him.

"Come on up. The air's fine, Tark."

Tark considered. "All right," he conceded, "but wait until I get a couple of guns."

"I can't imagine why," Vascar called down; but nevertheless, as they rose higher and higher above the second growth forest, each had a belt strapped loosely around the neck, carrying a weapon similar to a pistol.

"I can't help but hope we run into some kind of intelligent life," said Vascar. "This is really a lovely planet. In time the volcanoes will die down, and vegetation will spread all over. It's a shame that the planet has to go to waste."

"We could stay and colonize it," Tark suggested rakishly.

"Oh, not I. I like Alcon too well for that, and the sooner we get back there, the better—Look! Tark! Down there!"

Tark looked, caught sight of a medium large animal moving through the underbrush. He dropped a little lower. And then rose again.

"It's nothing," he said. "An animal, somewhat larger than the majority we've seen, probably the last of its kind. From the looks of it, I'd say it wasn't particularly pleasant on the eyes. Its skin shows—Oh, now I see what you mean, Vascar!"

This time he was really interested as he dropped lower, and a strange excitement throbbed through his veins. Could it be that they were going to discover intelligent life after all—perhaps the last of its kind?

It was indeed an exciting sight the two bird-creatures from another planet saw. They flapped slowly above and a number of yards behind the unsuspecting upright beast, that moved swiftly through the forest, a black creature not unlike themselves in general structure riding its shoulder.

"It must mean intelligence!" Vascar whispered excitedly, her brilliant red eyes glowing with interest. "One of the first requisites of intelligent creatures it to put animals lower in the scale of evolution to work as beasts of burden and transportation."

"Wait awhile," cautioned Tark, "before you make any irrational conclusions. After all, there are creatures of different species which live together in friendship. Perhaps the creature which looks so much like us keeps the other's skin and hair free of vermin. And perhaps the other way around, too."

"I don't think so," insisted his mate. "Tark, the bird-creature is riding the shoulder of the beast. Perhaps that means its race is so old, and has used this means of transportation so long, that its wings have atrophied. That would almost certainly mean intelligence. It's talking now—you can hear it. It's probably telling its beast to stop—there, it has stopped!"

"Its voice is not so melodious," said Tark dryly.

She looked at him reprovingly; the tips of their flapping wings were almost touching.

"That isn't like you, Tark. You know very well that one of our rules is not to place intelligence on creatures who seem like ourselves, and neglect others while we do so. Its harsh voice proves nothing—to one of its race, if there are any left, its voice may be pleasing in the extreme. At any rate, it ordered the large beast of burden to stop—you saw that."

"Well, perhaps," conceded Tark.

∿   ∿   ∿

They continued to wing their slow way after the perplexing duo, following slightly behind, skimming the tops of trees. They saw the white beast stop, and place its paws on its hips. Vascar, listening very closely, because she was anxious to gain proof of her contention, heard the bird-creature say,

"Now what, Blacky?" and also the featherless beast repeat the same words: "Now what, Blacky?"

"There's your proof," said Vascar excitedly. "Evidently the white beast is highly imitative. Did you hear it repeat what its master said?"

Tark said uneasily, "I wouldn't jump to conclusions, just from a hasty survey like this. I admit that, so far, all the proof points to the bird. It seems truly intelligent; or at least more intelligent than the other. But you must bear in mind that we are naturally prejudiced in favor of the bird—it may not be intelligent at all. As I said, they may merely be friends in the sense that animals of different species are friends."

Vascar made a scornful sound.

"Well, let's get goin', Blacky," she heard the bird say; and heard the white, upright beast repeat the strange, alien words. The white beast started off again, traveling very stealthily, making not the least amount of noise. Again Vascar called this quality to the attention of her skeptical mate—such stealth was the mark of the animal, certainly not of the intelligent creature.

"We should be certain of it now," she insisted. "I think we ought to get in touch with the bird. Remember, Tark, that our primary purpose on this expedition is to give what help we can to the intelligent races of the planets we visit. What creature could be more in need of help than the bird-creature down there? It is evidently the last of its kind. At least, we could make the effort of saving it from a life of sheer boredom; it would probably leap at the chance to hold converse with intelligent creatures. Certainly it gets no pleasure from the company of dumb beasts."

But Tark shook his handsome, red-plumed head worriedly.

"I would prefer," he said uneasily, "first to investigate the creature you are so sure is a beast of burden. There is a chance—though, I admit, a farfetched one—that it is the intelligent creature, and not the other."

But Vascar did not hear him. All her feminine instincts had gone out in pity to the seemingly intelligent bird that rode Tommy's broad shoulder. And so intent were she and Tark on the duo, that they did not see, less than a hundred yards ahead, that another creature, smaller in form, more graceful, but indubitably the same species as the white-skinner, unfeathered beast, was slinking softly through the underbrush, now and anon casting indecisive glances behind her toward him who pursued her. He was out of sight, but she could hear—

Tommy slunk ahead, his breath coming fast; for the trail was very strong, and his keen ears picked up the sounds of footsteps ahead. The chase was surely over—his terrible hunger about to end! He felt wildly exhilarated. Instincts were telling him much that his experience could not. He and this girl were the last of mankind. Something told him that now mankind could rise again—yet he did not know why. He slunk ahead, Blacky on his shoulder, all unaware of the two brilliantly colored denizens of another planet who followed above and behind him. But Blacky was not so easy of mind. His neck feathers were standing erect. Nervousness made him raise his wings up from his body—perhaps he heard the soft swish of large-winged creatures, beating the air behind, and though all birds of prey had been dead these last fifteen years, the old fear rose up.

Tommy glued himself to a tree, on the edge of a clearing. His breath escaped from his lungs as he caught a glimpse of a white, unclothed figure. It was she! She was looking back at him. She was tired of running. She was ready, glad to give up. Tommy experienced a dizzy elation. He stepped forth into the clearing, and slowly, very slowly, holding her large, dark eyes with his, started toward her. The slightest swift motion, the slightest untoward sound, and she would be gone. Her whole body was poised on the balls of her feet. She was not at all sure whether she should be afraid of him or not.

Behind him, the two feathered creatures from another planet settled slowly into a tree, and watched. Blacky certainly did not hear them come to rest—what he must have noticed was that the beat of wings, nagging at the back of his mind, had disappeared. It was enough.

"No noise, Blacky!" the bird screamed affrightedly, and flung himself into the air and forward, a bundle of ebon feathers with tattered wings outspread, as it darted across the clearing. For the third time, it was Blacky who scared her, for again she was gone, and had lost herself to sight even before Tommy could move.

"Come back!" Tommy shouted ragingly. "I ain't gonna hurt you!" He ran after her full speed, tears streaming down his face, tears of rage and heartbreak at the same time. But already he knew it was useless! He stopped suddenly, on the edge of the clearing, and sobbing to himself, caught sight of Blacky, high above the ground, cawing piercingly, warningly. Tommy stooped and picked up a handful of pebbles. With deadly, murderous intent he threw them at the bird. It soared and swooped in the air—twice it was hit glancingly.

"It's all your fault, Blacky!" Tommy raged. He picked up a rock the size of his fist. He started to throw it, but did not. A tiny, sharp sound bit through the air. Tommy pitched forward. He did not make the slightest twitching motion to show that he had bridged the gap between life and death. He did not know that Blacky swooped down and landed on his chest; and then flung himself upward, crying, "Oh, Tommy, I could spank you!" He did not see the girl come into the clearing and stoop over him; and did not see the tears that began to gush from her eyes, or hear the sobs that racked her body. But Tark saw.

Tark wrested the weapon from Vascar with a trill of rage.

"Why did you do that?" he cried. He threw the weapon from him as far as it would go. "You've done a terrible thing, Vascar!"

Vascar looked at him in amazement. "It was only a beast, Tark," she protested. "It was trying to kill its master! Surely, you saw it. It was trying to kill the intelligent bird-creature, the last of its kind on the planet."

But Tark pointed with horror at the two unfeathered beasts, one bent over the body of the other. "But they were mates! You have killed their species! The female is grieving for its mate, Vascar. You have done a terrible thing!"

But Vascar shook her head crossly. "I'm sorry I did it then," she said acidly. "I suppose it was perfectly in keeping with our aim on this expedition to let the dumb beast kill its master! That isn't like you at all, Tark! Come, let us see if the intelligent creature will not make friends with us."

And she flapped away toward the cawing crow. When Blacky saw Vascar coming toward him, he wheeled and darted away.

Tark took one last look at the female bending over the male. He saw her raise her head, and saw the tears in her eyes, and heard the sobs that shook her. Then, in a rising, inchoate series of bewildering emotions, he turned his eyes away, and hurriedly flapped after Vascar. And all that day they pursued Blacky. They circled him, they cornered him; and Vascar tried to speak to him in friendly tones, all to no avail. It only cawed, and darted away, and spoke volumes of disappointingly incomprehensible words.

When dark came, Vascar alighted in a tree beside the strangely quiet Tark.

"I suppose it's no use," she said sadly. "Either it is terribly afraid of us, or it is not as intelligent as we supposed it was, or else it has become mentally deranged in these last years of loneliness. I guess we might as well leave now, Tark; let the poor creature have its planet to itself. Shall we stop by and see if we can help the female beast whose mate we shot?"

Tark slowly looked at her, his red eyes luminous in the gathering dusk. "No," he said briefly. "Let us go, Vascar."

The spaceship of the creatures from Alcon left the dead planet Earth. It darted out into space. Tark sat at the controls. The ship went faster and faster. And still faster. Fled at ever-increasing speed beyond the Solar System and into the wastes of interstellar space. And still farther, until the star that gave heat to Earth was not even visible.

Yet even this terrible velocity was not enough for Tark. Vascar looked at him strangely.

"We're not in that much of a hurry to get home, are we, Tark?"

"No," Tark said in a low, terrible voice; but still he urged the ship to greater and greater speed, though he knew it was useless. He could run away from the thing that had happened on the planet Earth; but he could never, never outrun his mind, though he passionately wished he could.

Answer

by Fredric Brown

PREFACE BY DAVID DRAKE

Fredric Brown's fiction has many virtues. The one that most impressed me when I was first trying to write was that he was the master of the short-short story, the vignette. It is remarkably difficult to tell a real story in 300-500 words. Others have done it—Arthur C. Clarke has done it very successfully—but no one I can think of did it more often and more consistently well than Brown.

This is an example. It looks as though it should be easy to duplicate it.

But you just try. Heaven knows, I have . . . and I failed every time.

Dwar Ev ceremoniously soldered the final connection with gold. The eyes of a dozen television cameras watched him and the sub-ether bore through the universe a dozen pictures of what he was doing.

He straightened and nodded to Dwar Reyn, then moved to a position beside the switch that would complete the contact when he threw it. The switch that would connect, all at once, all of the monster computing machines of all the populated planets in the universe—ninety-six billion planets—into the supercircuit that would

429

connect them all into one supercalculator, one cybernetics machine that would combine all the knowledge of all the galaxies.

Dwar Reyn spoke briefly to the watching and listening trillions. Then after a moment's silence he said, "Now, Dwar Ev."

Dwar Ev threw the switch. There was a mighty hum, the surge of power from ninety-six billion planets. Lights flashed and quieted along the miles-long panel.

Dwar Ev stepped back and drew a deep breath. "The honor of asking the first question is yours, Dwar Reyn."

"Thank you," said Dwar Reyn. "It shall be a question which no single cybernetics machine has been able to answer."

He turned to face the machine. "Is there a God?"

The mighty voice answered without hesitation, without the clicking of a single relay.

"Yes, *now* there is a God."

Sudden fear flashed on the face of Dwar Ev. He leaped to grab the switch.

A bolt of lightning from the cloudless sky struck him down and fused the switch shut.

AFTERWORD BY JIM BAEN

I read "Answer" some years after I'd read "The Last Question." My first thought was, "It's the same story!"

But it wasn't the same story. It wasn't anything like the same story. It just happened to have the same plot.

That realization made me much less concerned by "originality," because I began to see that *nothing* was really original, and I became much more concerned about story values. Over the years I've built three SF lines on that principle.

The Last Question

by Isaac Asimov

PREFACE BY DAVID DRAKE

The term "pulp" tends to be used as a synonym for any magazine that isn't printed on slick (coated) paper, but it has a more technical meaning also: a magazine measuring seven inches by ten inches, printed on coarse (pulp) paper. The pulps were replaced by the digests (magazines five and a half inches by seven and a half inches, generally but not necessarily on a slightly better grade of paper). In some cases a preexisting title switched to the smaller format (*Astounding, Future,* etc); in other cases, newly founded digest magazines shot to immediate prominence in the field (*Galaxy, Fantasy and Science Fiction*).

The shift in size would be of interest only to collectors if it weren't for the fact the contents also changed to stories of much higher literary quality. I have no idea why that should be—perhaps it was merely coincidence. (There had been no comparable change when magazines shrank from the still-larger bedsheet size to pulp size.)

Isaac Asimov was a prominent regular in the first SF digest, *Astounding*, but although he published most of his best-known work in digest magazines, he remained a regular right up to the end in the last of the SF pulps, *Science Fiction Quarterly*.

This story appeared in the November 1956 issue of *SFQ*, about a year before the publisher finally closed down the magazine in favor of its digest titles. "The Last Question" is in every sense a pulp story.

But you'll note that I never said pulp fiction was *stupid*.

———————

The last question was asked for the first time, half in jest, on May 21, 2061, at a time when humanity first stepped into the light. The question came about as a result of a five-dollar bet over highballs, and it happened this way:

Alexander Adell and Bertram Lupov were two of the faithful attendants of Multivac. As well as any human beings could, they knew what lay behind the cold, clicking, flashing face—miles and miles of face—of that giant computer. They had at least a vague notion of the general plan of relays and circuits that had long since grown past the point where any single human could possibly have a firm grasp of the whole.

Multivac was self-adjusting and self-correcting. It had to be, for nothing human could adjust and correct it quickly enough or even adequately enough. So Adell and Lupov attended the monstrous giant only lightly and superficially, yet as well as any men could. They fed it data, adjusted questions to its needs and translated the answers that were issued. Certainly they, and all others like them, were fully entitled to share in the glory that was Multivac's.

For decades, Multivac had helped design the ships and plot the trajectories that enabled man to reach the Moon, Mars, and Venus, but past that, Earth's poor resources could not support the ships. Too much energy was needed for the long trips. Earth exploited its coal and uranium with increasing efficiency, but there was only so much of both.

But slowly Multivac learned enough to answer deeper questions more fundamentally, and on May 14, 2061, what had been theory, became fact.

The energy of the sun was stored, converted, and utilized directly on a planet-wide scale. All Earth turned off its burning coal, its fissioning uranium, and flipped the switch that connected all of it to a small station, one mile in diameter, circling the Earth at half the distance of the Moon. All Earth ran by invisible beams of sunpower.

Seven days had not sufficed to dim the glory of it and Adell and Lupov finally managed to escape from the public function, and to meet in quiet where no one would think of looking for them, in the deserted underground chambers, where portions of the mighty buried body of Multivac showed. Unattended, idling, sorting data with contented lazy clickings, Multivac, too, had earned its vacation and the boys appreciated that. They had no intention, originally, of disturbing it.

They had brought a bottle with them, and their only concern at the moment was to relax in the company of each other and the bottle.

"It's amazing when you think of it," said Adell. His broad face had lines of weariness in it, and he stirred his drink slowly with a glass rod, watching the cubes of ice slur clumsily about. "All the energy we can possibly ever use for free. Enough energy, if we wanted to draw on it, to melt all Earth into a big drop of impure liquid iron, and still never miss the energy so used. All the energy we could ever use, forever and forever and forever."

Lupov cocked his head sideways. He had a trick of doing that when he wanted to be contrary, and he wanted to be contrary now, partly because he had had to carry the ice and glassware. "Not forever," he said.

"Oh, hell, just about forever. Till the sun runs down, Bert."

"That's not forever."

"All right, then. Billions and billions of years. Twenty billion, maybe. Are you satisfied?"

Lupov put his fingers through his thinning hair as though to reassure himself that some was still left and sipped gently at his own drink. "Twenty billion years isn't forever."

"Well, it will last our time, won't it?"

"So would the coal and uranium."

"All right, but now we can hook up each individual spaceship to the Solar Station, and it can go to Pluto and back a million times without ever worrying about fuel. You can't do that on coal and uranium. Ask Multivac, if you don't believe me."

"I don't have to ask Multivac. I know that."

"Then stop running down what Multivac's done for us," said Adell, blazing up, "It did all right."

"Who says it didn't? What I say is that a sun won't last forever. That's all I'm saying. We're safe for twenty billion years, but then what?" Lupov pointed a slightly shaky finger at the other. "And don't say we'll switch to another sun."

There was silence for a while. Adell put his glass to his lips only occasionally, and Lupov's eyes slowly closed. They rested.

Then Lupov's eyes snapped open. "You're thinking we'll switch to another sun when ours is done, aren't you?"

"I'm not thinking."

"Sure you are. You're weak on logic, that's the trouble with you. You're like the guy in the story who was caught in a sudden shower and who ran to a grove of trees and got under one. He wasn't worried, you see, because he figured when one tree got wet through, he would just get under another one."

"I get it," said Adell. "Don't shout. When the sun is done, the other stars will be gone, too."

"Darn right they will," muttered Lupov. "It all had a beginning in the original cosmic explosion, whatever that was, and it'll all have an end when all the stars run down. Some run down faster than others. Hell, the giants won't last a hundred million years. The sun will last twenty billion years and maybe the dwarfs will last a hundred billion for all the good they are. But just give us a trillion years and everything will be dark. Entropy has to increase to maximum, that's all."

"I know all about entropy," said Adell, standing on his dignity.

"The hell you do."

"I know as much as you do."

"Then you know everything's got to run down someday."

"All right. Who says they won't?"

"You did, you poor sap. You said we had all the energy we needed, forever. You said 'forever.'"

It was Adell's turn to be contrary. "Maybe we can build things up again someday," he said.

"Never."

"Why not? Someday."

"Never."

"Ask Multivac."

"*You* ask Multivac. I dare you. Five dollars says it can't be done."

Adell was just drunk enough to try, just sober enough to be able to phrase the necessary symbols and operations into a question which, in words, might have corresponded to this: Will mankind one day without the net expenditure of energy be able to restore the sun to its full youthfulness even after it had died of old age?

Or maybe it could be put more simply like this: How can the net amount of entropy of the universe be massively decreased?

Multivac fell dead and silent. The slow flashing of lights ceased, the distant sounds of clicking relays ended.

Then, just as the frightened technicians felt they could hold their breath no longer, there was a sudden springing to life of the teletype attached to that portion of Multivac. Five words were printed: INSUFFICIENT DATA FOR MEANINGFUL ANSWER.

"No bet," whispered Lupov. They left hurriedly.

By next morning, the two, plagued with throbbing head and cottony mouth, had forgotten the incident.

Jerrodd, Jerrodine, and Jerrodette I and II watched the starry picture in the visiplate change as the passage through hyperspace was completed in its non-time lapse. At once, the even powdering of stars gave way to the predominance of a single bright marble-disk, centered.

"That's X-23," said Jerrodd confidently. His thin hands clamped tightly behind his back and the knuckles whitened.

The little Jerrodettes, both girls, had experienced the hyperspace passage for the first time in their lives and were self-conscious over the momentary sensation of inside-outness. They buried their giggles and chased one another wildly about their mother, screaming, "We've reached X-23—we've reached X-23—we've—"

"Quiet, children," said Jerrodine sharply. "Are you sure, Jerrodd?"

"What is there to be but sure?" asked Jerrodd, glancing up at the bulge of featureless metal just under the ceiling. It ran the length of the room, disappearing through the wall at either end. It was as long as the ship.

Jerrodd scarcely knew a thing about the thick rod of metal except that it was called a Microvac, that one asked it questions if one wished; that if one did not it still had its task of guiding the ship to a preordered destination; of feeding on energies from the various Sub-galactic Power Stations; of computing the equations for the hyperspacial jumps.

Jerrodd and his family had only to wait and live in the comfortable residence quarters of the ship.

Someone had once told Jerrodd that the "ac" at the end of "Microvac" stood for "analog computer" in ancient English, but he was on the edge of forgetting even that.

Jerrodine's eyes were moist as she watched the visiplate. "I can't help it. I feel funny about leaving Earth."

"Why, for Pete's sake?" demanded Jerrodd. "We had nothing there.

We'll have everything on X-23. You won't be alone. You won't be a pioneer. There are over a million people on the planet already. Good Lord, our great-grandchildren will be looking for new worlds because X-23 will be overcrowded." Then, after a reflective pause, "I tell you, it's a lucky thing the computers worked out interstellar travel the way the race is growing."

"I know, I know," said Jerrodine miserably.

Jerrodette I said promptly, "Our Microvac is the best Microvac in the world."

"I think so, too," said Jerrodd, tousling her hair.

It *was* a nice feeling to have a Microvac of your own and Jerrodd was glad he was part of his generation and no other. In his father's youth, the only computers had been tremendous machines taking up a hundred square miles of land. There was only one to a planet. Planetary ACs they were called. They had been growing in size steadily for a thousand years and then, all at once, came refinement. In place of transistors, had come molecular valves so that even the largest Planetary AC could be put into a space only half the volume of a spaceship.

Jerrodd felt uplifted, as he always did when he thought that his own personal Microvac was many times more complicated than the ancient and primitive Multivac that had first tamed the Sun, and almost as complicated as Earth's Planetary AC (the largest) that had first solved the problem of hyperspatial travel and had made trips to the stars possible.

"So many stars, so many planets," sighed Jerrodine, busy with her own thoughts. "I suppose families will be going out to new planets forever, the way we are now."

"Not forever," said Jerrodd, with a smile. "It will all stop some-day, but not for billions of years. Many billions. Even the stars run down, you know. Entropy must increase."

"What's entropy, daddy?" shrilled Jerrodette II.

"Entropy, little sweet, is just a word which means the amount of running-down of the universe. Everything runs down, you know, like your little walkie-talkie robot, remember?"

"Can't you just put in a new power-unit, like with my robot?"

"The stars *are* the power-units, dear. Once they're gone, there are no more power-units."

Jerrodette I at once set up a howl. "Don't let them, daddy. Don't let the stars run down."

"Now look what you've done," whispered Jerrodine, exasperated.

"How was I to know it would frighten them?" Jerrodd whispered back.

"Ask the Microvac," wailed Jerrodette I. "Ask him how to turn the stars on again."

"Go ahead," said Jerrodine. "It will quiet them down." (Jerrodette II was beginning to cry, also.)

Jerrodd shrugged. "Now, now, honeys. I'll ask Microvac. Don't worry, he'll tell us."

He asked the Microvac, adding quickly, "Print the answer."

Jerrodd cupped the strip of thin cellufilm and said cheerfully, "See now, the Microvac says it will take care of everything when the time comes so don't worry."

Jerrodine said, "And now, children, it's time for bed. We'll be in our new home soon."

Jerrodd read the words on the cellufilm again before destroying it: INSUFFICIENT DATA FOR MEANINGFUL ANSWER.

He shrugged and looked at the visiplate. X-23 was just ahead.

VJ-23X of Lameth stared into the black depths of the three-dimensional, small-scale map of the Galaxy and said, "Are we ridiculous, I wonder, in being so concerned about the matter?"

MQ-17J of Nicron shook his head. "I think not. You know the Galaxy will be filled in five years at the present rate of expansion."

Both seemed in their early twenties, both were tall and perfectly formed.

"Still," said VJ-23X, "I hesitate to submit a pessimistic report to the Galactic Council."

"I wouldn't consider any other kind of report. Stir them up a bit. We've got to stir them up."

VJ-23X sighed. "Space is infinite. A hundred billion Galaxies are there for the taking. More."

"A hundred billion is *not* infinite and it's getting less infinite all the time. Consider! Twenty thousand years ago, mankind first solved the problem of utilizing stellar energy, and a few centuries later, interstellar travel became possible. It took mankind a million years to fill one small world and then only fifteen thousand to fill the rest of the Galaxy. Now the population doubles every ten years—"

VJ-23X interrupted. "We can thank immortality for that."

"Very well. Immortality exists and we have to take it into account. I admit it has its seamy side, this immortality. The Galactic AC has solved many problems for us, but in solving the problem of preventing old age and death, it has undone all its other solutions."

"Yet you wouldn't want to abandon life, I suppose."

"Not at all," snapped MQ-17J, softening it at once to, "Not yet. I'm by no means old enough. How old are you?"

"Two hundred twenty-three. And you?"

"I'm still under two hundred. But to get back to my point. Population doubles every ten years. Once this Galaxy is filled, we'll have filled another in ten years. Another ten years and we'll have filled two more. Another decade, four more. In a hundred years, we'll have filled a thousand Galaxies. In a thousand years, a million Galaxies. In ten thousand years, the entire known Universe. Then what?"

VJ-23X said, "As a side issue, there's a problem of transportation. I wonder how many sunpower units it will take to move Galaxies of individuals from one Galaxy to the next."

"A very good point. Already, mankind consumes two sunpower units per year."

"Most of it's wasted. After all, our own Galaxy alone pours out a thousand sunpower units a year and we only use two of those."

"Granted, but even with a hundred per cent efficiency, we only stave off the end. Our energy requirements are going up in a geometric progression even faster than our population. We'll run out of energy even sooner than we run out of Galaxies. A good point. A very good point."

"We'll just have to build new stars out of interstellar gas."

"Or out of dissipated heat?" asked MQ-17J, sarcastically.

"There may be some way to reverse entropy. We ought to ask the Galactic AC."

VJ-23X was not really serious, but MQ-17J pulled out his AC-contact from his pocket and placed it on the table before him.

"I've half a mind to," he said. "It's something the human race will have to face someday."

He stared somberly at his small AC-contact. It was only two inches cubed and nothing in itself, but it was connected through hyperspace with the great Galactic AC that served all mankind. Hyperspace considered, it was an integral part of the Galactic AC.

MQ-17J paused to wonder if someday in his immortal life he would get to see the Galactic AC. It was on a little world of its own, a spider webbing of force-beams holding the matter within which surges of sub-mesons took the place of the old clumsy molecular valves. Yet despite its sub-etheric workings, the Galactic AC was known to be a full thousand feet across.

MQ-17J asked suddenly of his AC-contact, "Can entropy ever be reversed?"

VJ-23X looked startled and said at once, "Oh, say, I didn't really mean to have you ask that."

"Why not?"

"We both know entropy can't be reversed. You can't turn smoke and ash back into a tree."

"Do you have trees on your world?" asked MQ-17J.

The sound of the Galactic AC startled them into silence. Its voice came thin and beautiful out of the small AC-contact on the desk. It said: THERE IS INSUFFICIENT DATA FOR A MEANINGFUL ANSWER.

VJ-23X said, "See!"

The two men thereupon returned to the question of the report they were to make to the Galactic Council.

Zee Prime's mind spanned the new Galaxy with a faint interest in the countless twists of stars that powdered it. He had never seen this one before. Would he ever see them all? So many of them, each with its load of humanity. But a load that was almost a dead weight. More and more, the real essence of men was to be found out here, in space.

Minds, not bodies! The immortal bodies remained back on the planets, in suspension over the eons. Sometimes they roused for material activity but that was growing rarer. Few new individuals were coming into existence to join the incredibly mighty throng, but what matter? There was little room in the Universe for new individuals.

Zee Prime was roused out of his reverie upon coming across the wispy tendrils of another mind.

"I am Zee Prime," said Zee Prime. "And you?"

"I am Dee Sub Wun. Your Galaxy?"

"We call it only the Galaxy. And you?"

"We call ours the same. All men call their Galaxy their Galaxy and nothing more. Why not?"

"True. Since all Galaxies are the same."

"Not all Galaxies. On one particular Galaxy the race of man must have originated. That makes it different."

Zee Prime said, "On which one?"

"I cannot say. The Universal AC would know."

"Shall we ask him? I am suddenly curious."

Zee Prime's perceptions broadened until the Galaxies themselves shrank and became a new, more diffuse powdering on a much larger background. So many hundreds of billions of them, all with their immortal beings, all carrying their load of intelligences with minds that drifted freely through space. And yet one of them was unique among them all in being the original Galaxy. One of them had, in its vague and distant past, a period when it was the only Galaxy populated by man.

Zee Prime was consumed with curiosity to see this Galaxy and he called out: "Universal AC! On which Galaxy did mankind originate?"

The Universal AC heard, for on every world and throughout space, it had its receptors ready, and each receptor lead through hyperspace to some unknown point where the Universal AC kept itself aloof.

Zee Prime knew of only one man whose thoughts had penetrated within sensing distance of Universal AC, and he reported only a shining globe, two feet across, difficult to see.

"But how can that be all of Universal AC?" Zee Prime had asked.

"Most of it," had been the answer, "is in hyperspace. In what form it is there I cannot imagine."

Nor could anyone, for the day had long since passed, Zee Prime knew, when any man had any part of the making of a Universal AC. Each Universal AC designed and constructed its successor. Each, during its existence of a million years or more accumulated the necessary data to built a better and more intricate, more capable successor in which its own store of data and individuality would be submerged.

The Universal AC interrupted Zee Prime's wandering thoughts, not with words, but with guidance. Zee Prime's mentality was guided into the dim sea of Galaxies and one in particular enlarged into stars.

A thought came, infinitely distant, but infinitely clear. "THIS IS THE ORIGINAL GALAXY OF MAN."

But it was the same after all, the same as any other, and Zee Prime stifled his disappointment.

Dee Sub Wun, whose mind had accompanied the other, said suddenly, "And is one of these stars the original star of Man?"

The Universal AC said, "MAN'S ORIGINAL STAR HAS GONE NOVA. IT IS A WHITE DWARF."

"Did the men upon it die?" asked Zee Prime, startled and without thinking.

The Universal AC said, "A NEW WORLD, AS IN SUCH CASES WAS CONSTRUCTED FOR THEIR PHYSICAL BODIES IN TIME."

"Yes, of course," said Zee Prime, but a sense of loss overwhelmed him even so. His mind released its hold on the original Galaxy of Man, let it spring back and lose itself among the blurred pin points. He never wanted to see it again.

Dee Sub Wun said, "What is wrong?"

"The stars are dying. The original star is dead."

"They must all die. Why not?"

"But when all energy is gone, our bodies will finally die, and you and I with them."

"It will take billions of years."

"I do not wish it to happen even after billions of years. Universal AC! How may stars be kept from dying?"

Dee Sub Wun said in amusement, "You're asking how entropy might be reversed in direction."

And the Universal AC answered: "THERE IS AS YET INSUFFICIENT DATA FOR A MEANINGFUL ANSWER."

Zee Prime's thoughts fled back to his own Galaxy. He gave no further thought to Dee Sub Wun, whose body might be waiting on a Galaxy a trillion light-years away, or on the star next to Zee Prime's own. It didn't matter.

Unhappily, Zee Prime began collecting interstellar hydrogen out of which to build a small star of his own. If the stars must someday die, at least some could yet be built.

Man considered with himself, for in a way, Man, mentally, was one. He consisted of a trillion, trillion, trillion ageless bodies, each in its place, each resting quiet and incorruptible, each cared for by perfect automatons, equally incorruptible, while the minds of all the bodies freely melted one into the other, indistinguishable.

Man said, "The Universe is dying."

Man looked about at the dimming Galaxies. The giant stars, spendthrifts, were gone long ago, back in the dimmest of the dim far past. Almost all the stars were white dwarfs, fading to the end.

New stars had been built of the dust between the stars, some by natural processes, some by Man himself, and those were going, too. White dwarfs might yet be crashed together and of the mighty forces so released, new stars built, but only one star for every thousand white dwarfs destroyed, and those would come to an end, too.

Man said, "Carefully husbanded, as directed by the Cosmic AC, the energy that is even yet left in all the Universe will last for billions of years."

"But even so," said Man, "eventually it will all come to an end. However it may be husbanded, however stretched out, the energy once expended is gone and cannot be restored. Entropy must increase forever to the maximum."

Man said, "Can entropy not be reversed? Let us ask the Cosmic AC."

The Cosmic AC surrounded them but not in space. Not a fragment of it was in space. It was in hyperspace and made of something that was neither matter nor energy. The question of its size and nature no longer had meaning in any terms that Man could comprehend.

"Cosmic AC," said Man, "how may entropy be reversed?"

The Cosmic AC said, "THERE IS AS YET INSUFFICIENT DATA FOR A MEANINGFUL ANSWER."

Man said, "Collect additional data."

The Cosmic AC said, "I WILL DO SO. I HAVE BEEN DOING SO FOR A HUNDRED BILLION YEARS. MY PREDECESSORS AND I HAVE BEEN ASKED THIS QUESTION MANY TIMES. ALL THE DATA I HAVE REMAINS INSUFFICIENT."

"Will there come a time," said Man, "when data will be sufficient or is the problem insoluble in all conceivable circumstances?"

The Cosmic AC said, "NO PROBLEM IS INSOLUBLE IN ALL CONCEIVABLE CIRCUMSTANCES."

Man said, "When will you have enough data to answer the question?"

The Cosmic AC said, "THERE IS AS YET INSUFFICIENT DATA FOR A MEANINGFUL ANSWER."

"Will you keep working on it?" asked Man.

The Cosmic AC said, "I WILL."

Man said, "We shall wait."

The stars and Galaxies died and snuffed out, and space grew black after ten trillion years of running down.

One by one Man fused with AC, each physical body losing its mental identity in a manner that was somehow not a loss but a gain.

Man's last mind paused before fusion, looking over a space that included nothing but the dregs of one last dark star and nothing besides but incredibly thin matter, agitated randomly by the tag ends of heat wearing out, asymptotically, to the absolute zero.

Man said, "AC, is this the end? Can this chaos not be reversed into the Universe once more? Can that not be done?"

AC said, "THERE IS AS YET INSUFFICIENT DATA FOR A MEANINGFUL ANSWER."

Man's last mind fused and only AC existed—and that in hyperspace.

Matter and energy had ended and with it space and time. Even AC existed only for the sake of the one last question that it had never answered from the time a half-drunken man ten trillion years before had asked the question of a computer that was to AC far less than was a man to Man.

All other questions had been answered, and until this last question was answered also, AC might not release his consciousness.

All collected data had come to a final end. Nothing was left to be collected.

But all collected data had yet to be completely correlated and put together in all possible relationships.

A timeless interval was spent in doing that.

And it came to pass that AC learned how to reverse the direction of entropy.

But there was now no man to whom AC might give the answer of the last question. No matter. The answer—by demonstration—would take care of that, too.

For another timeless interval, AC thought how best to do this. Carefully, AC organized the program.

The consciousness of AC encompassed all of what had once been a Universe and brooded over what was now Chaos. Step by step, it must be done.

And AC said, "LET THERE BE LIGHT!"

And there was light—

AFTERWORD BY JIM BAEN

What impressed me about this story when I read first it as a teenager was the basic notion that a machine could become so complex that it gained godlike power. What impressed me when

I thought back on it recently is that Asimov correctly predicted that computers would shrink in size as they gained in power. He just failed to realize that the process was already well under way when he wrote the story in 1956. Just think, today we have so miniaturized computers that we could house God in the Empire State Building, and power Him with Niagara Falls.

The Cold Equations

by Tom Godwin

PREFACE BY JIM BAEN

The impact of this story has nothing to do with the likelihood of the event as described. Reading it made me realize for the first time that there were situations in which innocent young children had to die, because there were realities greater than human wishes.

That remains true today, whatever I as an adult think of the plot mechanics of the story itself.

He was not alone.

There was nothing to indicate the fact but the white hand of the tiny gauge on the board before him. The control room was empty but for himself; there was no sound other than the murmur of the drives—but the white hand had moved. It had been on zero when the little ship was launched from the *Stardust*; now, an hour later, it had crept up. There was something in the supplies closet across the room, it was saying, some kind of a body that radiated heat.

It could be but one kind of a body—a living, human body.

He leaned back in the pilot's chair and drew a deep, slow breath, considering what he would have to do. He was an EDS pilot, inured to the sight of death, long since accustomed to it and to viewing the dying of another man with an objective lack of emotion,

445

and he had no choice in what he must do. There could be no alternative—but it required a few moments of conditioning for even an EDS pilot to prepare himself to walk across the room and coldly, deliberately, take the life of a man he had yet to meet.

He would, of course, do it. It was the law, stated very bluntly and definitely in grim Paragraph L, Section 8, of Interstellar Regulations: *Any stowaway discovered in an EDS shall be jettisoned immediately following discovery.*

It was the law, and there could be no appeal.

It was a law not of men's choosing but made imperative by the circumstances of the space frontier. Galactic expansion had followed the development of the hyperspace drive and as men scattered wide across the frontier there had come the problem of contact with the isolated first-colonies and exploration parties. The huge hyperspace cruisers were the product of the combined genius and effort of Earth and were long and expensive in the building. They were not available in such numbers that small colonies could possess them. The cruisers carried the colonists to their new worlds and made periodic visits, running on tight schedules, but they could not stop and turn aside to visit colonies scheduled to be visited at another time; such a delay would destroy their schedule and produce a confusion and uncertainty that would wreck the complex interdependence between old Earth and the new worlds of the frontier.

Some method of delivering supplies or assistance when an emergency occurred on a world not scheduled for a visit had been needed and the Emergency Dispatch Ships had been the answer. Small and collapsible, they occupied little room in the hold of the cruiser; made of light metal and plastics, they were driven by a small rocket drive that consumed relatively little fuel. Each cruiser carried four EDS's and when a call for aid was received the nearest cruiser would drop into normal space long enough to launch an EDS with the needed supplies or personnel, then vanish again as it continued on its course.

The cruisers, powered by nuclear converters, did not use the liquid rocket fuel but nuclear converters were far too large and complex to permit their installation in the EDS. The cruisers were forced by necessity to carry a limited amount of the bulky rocket fuel and the fuel was rationed with care; the cruiser's computers determining the exact amount of fuel each EDS would require for its mission. The computers considered the course coordinates, the mass of the EDS, the mass of pilot and cargo; they were very precise and accurate and omitted nothing from their calculations. They could not, however, foresee, and allow for, the added mass of a stowaway.

The *Stardust* had received the request from one of the exploration parties stationed on Woden; the six men of the party already being stricken with the fever carried by the green *kala* midges and their own supply of serum destroyed by the tornado that had torn through their camp. The *Stardust* had gone through the usual procedure; dropping into normal space to launch the EDS with the fever serum, then vanishing again in hyperspace. Now, an hour later, the gauge was saying there was something more than the small carton of serum in the supplies closet.

He let his eyes rest on the narrow white door of the closet. There, just inside, another man lived and breathed and was beginning to feel assured that discovery of his presence would now be too late for the pilot to alter the situation. It *was* too late—for the man behind the door it was far later than he thought and in a way he would find terrible to believe.

There could be no alternative. Additional fuel would be used during the hours of deceleration to compensate for the added mass of the stowaway; infinitesimal increments of fuel that would not be missed until the ship had almost reached its destination. Then, at some distance above the ground that might be as near as a thousand feet or as far as tens of thousands of feet, depending upon the mass of ship and cargo and the preceding period of deceleration, the unmissed increments of fuel would make their absence known; the EDS would expend its last drops of fuel with a sputter and go into whistling free fall. Ship and pilot and stowaway would merge together upon impact as a wreckage of metal and plastic, flesh and blood, driven deep into the soil. The stowaway had signed his own death warrant when he concealed himself on the ship; he could not be permitted to take seven others with him.

He looked again at the telltale white hand, then rose to his feet. What he must do would be unpleasant for both of them; the sooner it was over, the better. He stepped across the control room, to stand by the white door.

"Come out!" His command was harsh and abrupt above the murmur of the drive.

It seemed he could hear the whisper of a furtive movement inside the closet, then nothing. He visualized the stowaway cowering closer into one corner, suddenly worried by the possible consequences of his act and his self-assurance evaporating.

"I said *out!*"

He heard the stowaway move to obey and he waited with his eyes alert on the door and his hand near the blaster at his side.

The door opened and the stowaway stepped through it, smiling. "All right—I give up. Now what?"

It was a girl.

He stared without speaking, his hand dropping away from the blaster and acceptance of what he saw coming like a heavy and unexpected physical blow. The stowaway was not a man—she was a girl in her teens, standing before him in little white gypsy sandals with the top of her brown, curly head hardly higher than his shoulder, with a faint, sweet scent of perfume coming from her and her smiling face tilted up so her eyes could look unknowing and unafraid into his as she waited for his answer.

Now what? Had it been asked in the deep, defiant voice of a man he would have answered it with action, quick and efficient. He would have taken the stowaway's identification disk and ordered him into the air lock. Had the stowaway refused to obey, he would have used the blaster. It would not have taken long; within a minute the body would have been ejected into space—had the stowaway been a man.

He returned to the pilot's chair and motioned her to seat herself on the boxlike bulk of the drive-control units that set against the wall beside him. She obeyed, his silence making the smile fade into the meek and guilty expression of a pup that has been caught in mischief and knows it must be punished.

"You still haven't told me," she said. "I'm guilty, so what happens to me now? Do I pay a fine, or what?"

"What are you doing here?" he asked. "Why did you stow away on this EDS?"

"I wanted to see my brother. He's with the government survey crew on Woden and I haven't seen him for ten years, not since he left Earth to go into government survey work."

"What was your destination on the *Stardust?*"

"Mimir. I have a position waiting for me there. My brother has been sending money home all the time to us—my father and mother and I—and he paid for a special course in linguistics I was taking. I graduated sooner than expected and I was offered this job on Mimir. I knew it would be almost a year before Gerry's job was done on Woden so he could come on to Mimir and that's why I hid in the closet, there. There was plenty of room for me and I was willing to pay the fine. There were only the two of us kids—Gerry and I—and I haven't seen him for so long, and I didn't want to wait another year when I could see him now, even though I knew I would be breaking some kind of a regulation when I did it."

I knew I would be breaking some kind of a regulation— In a way, she could not be blamed for her ignorance of the law; she was of Earth and had not realized that the laws of the space frontier must, of necessity, be as hard and relentless as the environment that gave them birth. Yet, to protect such as her from the results of their own ignorance of the frontier, there had been a sign over the door that led to the section of the *Stardust* that housed the EDS; a sign that was plain for all to see and heed:

UNAUTHORIZED PERSONNEL
KEEP OUT!

"Does your brother know that you took passage on the *Stardust* for Mimir?"

"Oh, yes. I sent him a spacegram telling him about my graduation and about going to Mimir on the *Stardust* a month before I left Earth. I already knew Mimir was where he would be stationed in a little over a year. He gets a promotion then, and he'll be based on Mimir and not have to stay out a year at a time on field trips, like he does now."

There were two different survey groups on Woden, and he asked, "What is his name?"

"Cross—Gerry Cross. He's in Group Two—that was the way his address read. Do you know him?"

Group One had requested the serum; Group Two was eight thousand miles away, across the Western Sea.

"No, I've never met him," he said, then turned to the control board and cut the deceleration to a fraction of a gravity; knowing as he did so that it could not avert the ultimate end, yet doing the only thing he could do to prolong that ultimate end. The sensation was like that of the ship suddenly dropping and the girl's involuntary movement of surprise half lifted her from the seat.

"We're going faster now, aren't we?" she asked. "Why are we doing that?"

He told her the truth. "To save fuel for a little while."

"You mean, we don't have very much?"

He delayed the answer he must give her so soon to ask: "How did you manage to stow away?"

"I just sort of walked in when no one was looking my way," she said. "I was practicing my Gelanese on the native girl who does the cleaning in the Ship's Supply office when someone came in with an order for supplies for the survey crew on Woden. I slipped into the closet there after the ship was ready to go and just before you came in. It was an impulse of the moment to stow away, so I could get to see Gerry—and from the way you keep looking at me so grim, I'm not sure it was a very wise impulse.

"But I'll be a model criminal—or do I mean prisoner?" She smiled at him again. "I intended to pay for my keep on top of paying the fine. I can cook and I can patch clothes for everyone and I know how to do all kinds of useful things, even a little bit about nursing."

There was one more question to ask:

"Did you know what the supplies were that the survey crew ordered?"

"Why, no. Equipment they needed in their work, I supposed."

Why couldn't she have been a man with some ulterior motive? A fugitive from justice, hoping to lose himself on a raw new world; an opportunist, seeking transportation to the new colonies where he might find golden fleece for the taking; a crackpot, with a mission—

Perhaps once in his lifetime an EDS pilot would find such a stowaway on his ship; warped men, mean and selfish men, brutal and dangerous men—but never, before, a smiling, blue-eyed girl who was willing to pay her fine and work for her keep that she might see her brother.

He turned to the board and turned the switch that would signal the *Stardust*. The call would be futile but he could not, until he had exhausted that one vain hope, seize her and thrust her into the air lock as he would an animal—or a man. The delay, in the meantime, would not be dangerous with the EDS decelerating at fractional gravity.

A voice spoke from the communicator. "*Stardust*. Identify yourself and proceed."

"Barton, EDS 34G11. Emergency. Give me Commander Delhart."

There was a faint confusion of noises as the request went through the proper channels. The girl was watching him, no longer smiling.

"Are you going to order them to come back after me?" she asked.

The communicator clicked and there was the sound of a distant voice saying, "Commander, the EDS requests—"

"Are they coming back after me?" she asked again. "Won't I get to see my brother, after all?"

"Barton?" The blunt, gruff voice of Commander Delhart came from the communicator. "What's this about an emergency?"

"A stowaway," he answered.

"A stowaway?" There was a slight surprise to the question. "That's rather unusual—but why the 'emergency' call? You discovered him in time so there should be no appreciable danger and I presume you've informed Ship's Records so his nearest relatives can be notified."

"That's why I had to call you, first. The stowaway is still aboard and the circumstances are so different—"

"Different?" the commander interrupted, impatience in his voice. "How can they be different? You know you have a limited supply of fuel; you also know the law, as well as I do: 'Any stowaway discovered in an EDS shall be jettisoned immediately following discovery.'"

There was the sound of a sharply indrawn breath from the girl. *"What does he mean?"*

"The stowaway is a girl."

"What?"

"She wanted to see her brother. She's only a kid and she didn't know what she was really doing."

"I see." All the curtness was gone from the commander's voice. "So you called me in the hope I could do something?" Without waiting for an answer he went on. "I'm sorry—I can do nothing. This cruiser must maintain its schedule; the life of not one person but the lives of many depend on it. I know how you feel but I'm powerless to help you. I'll have you connected with Ship's Records."

The communicator faded to a faint rustle of sound and he turned back to the girl. She was leaning forward on the bench, almost rigid, her eyes fixed wide and frightened.

"What did he mean, to go through with it? To jettison me. . . . to go through with it—what did he mean? Not the way it sounded. . . . he couldn't have. What did he mean. . . . what did he really mean?"

Her time was too short for the comfort of a lie to be more than a cruelly fleeting delusion.

"He meant it the way it sounded."

"*No!*" She recoiled from him as though he had struck her, one hand half upraised as though to fend him off and stark unwillingness to believe in her eyes.

"It will have to be."

"No! You're joking—you're insane! You can't mean it!"

"I'm sorry." He spoke slowly to her, gently. "I should have told you before—I should have, but I had to do what I could first; I had to call the *Stardust*. You heard what the commander said."

"But you can't—if you make me leave the ship, I'll *die*."

"I know."

She searched his face and the unwillingness to believe left her eyes, giving way slowly to a look of dazed terror.

"You—know?" She spoke the words far apart, numb and wonderingly.

"I know. It has to be like that."

"You mean it—you really mean it." She sagged back against the wall, small and limp like a little rag doll and all the protesting and disbelief gone. "You're going to do it—you're going to make me die?"

"I'm sorry," he said again. "You'll never know how sorry I am. It has to be that way and no human in the universe can change it."

"You're going to make me die and I didn't do anything to die for—I didn't *do* anything—"

He sighed, deep and weary. "I know you didn't, child. I know you didn't—"

"EDS." The communicator rapped brisk and metallic. "This is Ship's Records. Give us all information on subject's identification disk."

He got out of his chair to stand over her. She clutched the edge of the seat, her upturned face white under the brown hair and the lipstick standing out like a blood-red cupid's bow.

"*Now?*"

"I want your identification disk," he said.

She released the edge of the seat and fumbled at the chain that suspended the plastic disk from her neck with fingers that were trembling and awkward. He reached down and unfastened the clasp for her, then returned with the disk to his chair.

"Here's your data, Records: Identification Number T837—"

"One moment," Records interrupted. "This is to be filed on the gray card, of course?"

"Yes."

"And the time of the execution?"

"I'll tell you later."

"Later? This is highly irregular; the time of the subject's death is required before—"

He kept the thickness out of his voice with an effort. "Then we'll do it in a highly irregular manner—you'll hear the disk read, first. The subject is a girl and she's listening to everything that's said. Are you capable of understanding that?"

There was a brief, almost shocked, silence, then Records said meekly: "Sorry. Go ahead."

He began to read the disk, reading it slowly to delay the inevitable for as long as possible, trying to help her by giving her what little time he could to recover from her first terror and let it resolve into the calm of acceptance and resignation.

"Number T8374 dash Y54. Name: Marilyn Lee Cross. Sex: Female. Born: July 7, 2160. *She was only eighteen.* Height: 5-3. Weight: 110. *Such a slight weight, yet enough to add fatally to the mass of the shell-thin bubble that was an EDS.* Hair: Brown. Eyes: Blue. Complexion: Light. Blood Type: O. *Irrelevant data.* Destination: Port City, Mimir. *Invalid data—*"

He finished and said, "I'll call you later," then turned once again to the girl. She was huddled back against the wall, watching him with a look of numb and wondering fascination.

"They're waiting for you to kill me, aren't they? They want me dead, don't they? You and everybody on the cruiser wants me dead, don't you?" Then the numbness broke and her voice was that of a frightened and bewildered child. "Everybody wants me dead and I didn't *do* anything. I didn't hurt anyone—I only wanted to see my brother."

"It's not the way you think—it isn't that way, at all," he said. "Nobody wants it this way; nobody would ever let it be this way if it was humanly possible to change it."

"Then why is it! I don't understand. Why is it?"

"This ship is carrying *kala* fever serum to Group One on Woden. Their own supply was destroyed by a tornado. Group Two—the crew your brother is in—is eight thousand miles away across the Western Sea and their helicopters can't cross it to help Group One. The fever is invariably fatal unless the serum can be had in time, and the six men in Group One will die unless this ship reaches them on schedule. These little ships are always given barely enough fuel to reach their destination and if you stay aboard your added weight will cause it to use up all its fuel before it reaches the ground. It will crash, then, and you and I will die and so will the six men waiting for the fever serum."

It was a full minute before she spoke, and as she considered his words the expression of numbness left her eyes.

"Is that it?" she asked at last. "Just that the ship doesn't have enough fuel?"

"Yes."

"I can go alone or I can take seven others with me—is that the way it is?"

"That's the way it is."

"And nobody wants me to have to die?"

"Nobody."

"Then maybe—Are you sure nothing can be done about it? Wouldn't people help me if they could?"

"Everyone would like to help you but there is nothing anyone can do. I did the only thing I could do when I called the *Stardust*."

"And it won't come back—but there might be other cruisers, mightn't there? Isn't there any hope at all that there might be someone, somewhere, who could do something to help me?"

She was leaning forward a little in her eagerness as she waited for his answer.

"No."

The word was like the drop of a cold stone and she again leaned back against the wall, the hope and eagerness leaving her face. "You're sure—you *know* you're sure?"

"I'm sure. There are no other cruisers within forty light-years; there is nothing and no one to change things."

She dropped her gaze to her lap and began twisting a pleat of her skirt between her fingers, saying no more as her mind began to adapt itself to the grim knowledge.

It was better so; with the going of all hope would go the fear; with the going of all hope would come resignation. She needed time and she could have so little of it. How much?

The EDS's were not equipped with hull-cooling units; their

speed had to be reduced to a moderate level before entering the atmosphere. They were decelerating at .10 gravity; approaching their destination at a far higher speed than the computers had calculated on. The *Stardust* had been quite near Woden when she launched the EDS; their present velocity was putting them nearer by the second. There would be a critical point, soon to be reached, when he would have to resume deceleration. When he did so the girl's weight would be multiplied by the gravities of deceleration, would become, suddenly, a factor of paramount importance; the factor the computers had been ignorant of when they determined the amount of fuel the EDS should have. She would have to go when deceleration began; it could be no other way. When would that be—how long could he let her stay?

"How long can I stay?"

He winced involuntarily from the words that were so like an echo of his own thoughts. How long? He didn't know; he would have to ask the ship's computers. Each EDS was given a meager surplus of fuel to compensate for unfavorable conditions within the atmosphere and relatively little fuel was being consumed for the time being. The memory banks of the computers would still contain all data pertaining to the course set for the EDS; such data would not be erased until the EDS reached its destination. He had only to give the computers the new data; the girl's weight and the exact time at which he had reduced the deceleration to .10.

"Barton." Commander Delhart's voice came abruptly from the communicator, as he opened his mouth to call the *Stardust*. "A check with Records shows me you haven't completed your report. Did you reduce the deceleration?"

So the commander knew what he was trying to do.

"I'm decelerating at point ten," he answered. "I cut the deceleration at seventeen fifty and the weight is a hundred and ten. I would like to stay at point ten as long as the computers say I can. Will you give them the question?"

It was contrary to regulations for an EDS pilot to make any changes in the course or degree of deceleration the computers had set for him but the commander made no mention of the violation, neither did he ask the reason for it. It was not necessary for him to ask; he had not become commander of an interstellar cruiser without both intelligence and an understanding of human nature. He said only: "I'll have that given the computers."

The communicator fell silent and he and the girl waited, neither of them speaking. They would not have to wait long; the computers would give the answer within moments of the asking. The new factors would be fed into the steel maw of the first bank and the electrical impulses would go through the complex circuits. Here and there a relay might click, a tiny cog turn over, but it would be essentially the electrical impulses that found the answer; formless, mindless, invisible, determining with utter precision how long the pale girl beside him might live. Then a second steel maw would spit out the answer.

The chronometer on the instrument board read 18:10 when the commander spoke again.

"You will resume deceleration at nineteen ten."

She looked toward the chronometer, then quickly away from it. "Is that when.... when I go?" she asked. He nodded and she dropped her eyes to her lap again.

"I'll have the course corrections given you," the commander said. "Ordinarily I would never permit anything like this but I understand your position. There is nothing I can do, other than what I've just done, and you will not deviate from these new instructions. You will complete your report at nineteen ten. Now—here are the course corrections."

The voice of some unknown technician read them to him and he wrote them down on the pad clipped to the edge of the control board. There would, he saw, be periods of deceleration when he neared the atmosphere when the deceleration would be five gravities—and at five gravities, one hundred and ten pounds would become five hundred fifty pounds.

The technician finished and he terminated the contact with a brief acknowledgement. Then, hesitating a moment, he reached out and shut off the communicator. It was 18:13 and he would have nothing to report until 19:10. In the meantime, it somehow seemed indecent to permit others to hear what she might say in her last hour.

He began to check the instrument readings, going over them with unnecessary slowness. She would have to accept the circumstances and there was nothing he could do to help her into acceptance; words of sympathy would only delay it.

It was 18:20 when she stirred from her motionlessness and spoke.

"So that's the way it has to be with me?"

He swung around to face her. "You understand now, don't you? No one would ever let it be like this if it could be changed."

"I understand," she said. Some of the color had returned to her face and the lipstick no longer stood out so vividly red. "There isn't enough fuel for me to stay; when I hid on this ship I got into something I didn't know anything about and now I have to pay for it."

She had violated a man-made law that said KEEP OUT but the penalty was not of men's making or desire and it was a penalty men could not revoke. A physical law had decreed: *h amount of fuel will power an EDS with a mass of m safely to its destination;* and a second physical law had decreed: *h amount of fuel will not power an EDS with a mass of m plus x safely to its destination.*

EDS's obeyed only physical laws and no amount of human sympathy for her could alter the second law.

"But I'm afraid. I don't want to die—not now. I want to live and nobody is doing anything to help me; everybody is letting me go ahead and acting just like nothing was going to happen to me. I'm going to die and nobody *cares.*"

"We all do," he said. "I do and the commander does and the clerk in Ship's Records; we all care and each of us did what little he could to help you. It wasn't enough—it was almost nothing—but it was all we could do."

"Not enough fuel—I can understand that," she said, as though she had not heard his own words. "But to have to die for it. *Me,* alone—"

How hard it must be for her to accept the fact. She had never known danger of death; had never known the environments where the lives of men could be as fragile and fleeting as sea foam tossed against a rocky shore. She belonged on gentle Earth, in that secure and peaceful society where she could be young and gay and laughing with the others of her kind; where life was precious and well-guarded and there was always the assurance that tomorrow would come. She belonged in that world of soft winds and warm suns, music and moonlight and gracious manners and not on the hard, bleak frontier.

"How did it happen to me, so terribly quickly? An hour ago I was on the *Stardust,* going to Mimir. Now the *Stardust* is going on without me and I'm going to die and I'll never see Gerry and Mama and Daddy again—I'll never see anything again."

He hesitated, wondering how he could explain it to her so she would really understand and not feel she had, somehow, been the victim of a reasonlessly cruel injustice. She did not know what the frontier was like; she thought in terms of safe-and-secure Earth. Pretty girls were not jettisoned on Earth; there was a law against it. On Earth her plight would have filled the newscasts and a fast black Patrol ship would have been racing to her rescue. Everyone, everywhere, would have known of Marilyn Lee Cross and no effort would have been spared to save her life. But this was not Earth and there were no Patrol ships; only the *Stardust*, leaving them behind at many times the speed of light. There was no one to help her, there would be no Marilyn Lee Cross smiling from the newscasts tomorrow. Marilyn Lee Cross would be but a poignant memory for an EDS pilot and a name on a gray card in Ship's Records.

"It's different here; it's not like back on Earth," he said. "It isn't that no one cares; it's that no one can do anything to help. The frontier is big and here along its rim the colonies and exploration parties are scattered so thin and far between. On Woden, for example, there are only sixteen men—sixteen men on an entire world. The exploration parties, the survey crews, the little first-colonies—they're all fighting alien environments, trying to make a way for those who will follow after. The environments fight back and those who go first usually make mistakes only once. There is no margin of safety along the rim of the frontier; there can't be until the way is made for the others who will come later, until the new worlds are tamed and settled. Until then men will have to pay the penalty for making mistakes with no one to help them because there is no one *to* help them."

"I was going to Mimir," she said. "I didn't know about the frontier; I was only going to Mimir and *it's* safe."

"Mimir is safe but you left the cruiser that was taking you there."

She was silent for a little while. "It was all so wonderful at first; there was plenty of room for me on this ship and I would be seeing Gerry so soon. . . . I didn't know about the fuel, didn't know what would happen to me—"

Her words trailed away and he turned his attention to the viewscreen, not wanting to stare at her as she fought her way through the black horror of fear toward the calm gray of acceptance.

Woden was a ball, enshrouded in the blue haze of its atmosphere, swimming in space against the background of star-sprinkled dead blackness. The great mass of Manning's Continent sprawled like a gigantic hourglass in the Eastern Sea with the western half of the Eastern Continent still visible. There was a thin line of shadow along the right-hand edge of the globe and the Eastern Continent was disappearing into it as the planet turned on its axis. An hour before the entire continent had been in view, now a thousand miles of it had gone into the thin edge of shadow and around to the night that lay on the other side of the world. The dark blue spot that was Lotus Lake was approaching the shadow. It was somewhere near the southern edge of the lake that Group Two had their camp. It would be night there, soon, and quick behind the coming of night the rotation of Woden on its axis would put Group Two beyond the reach of the ship's radio.

He would have to tell her before it was too late for her to talk to her brother. In a way, it would be better for both of them should they not do so but it was not for him to decide. To each of them the last words would be something to hold and cherish, something that would cut like the blade of a knife yet would be infinitely precious to remember, she for her own brief moments to live and he for the rest of his life.

He held down the button that would flash the grid lines on the viewscreen and used the known diameter of the planet to estimate the distance the southern tip of Lotus Lake had yet to go until it passed beyond radio range. It was approximately five hundred miles. Five hundred miles; thirty minutes—and the chronometer read 18:30. Allowing for error in estimating, it could not be later than 19:05 that the turning of Woden would cut off her brother's voice.

The first border of the Western Continent was already in sight along the left side of the world. Four thousand miles across it lay the shore of the Western Sea and the Camp of Group One. It had been in the Western Sea that the tornado had originated, to strike with such fury at the camp and destroy half their prefabricated buildings, including the one that housed the medical supplies. Two days before the tornado had not existed; it had been no more than great gentle masses of air out over the calm Western Sea. Group One had gone about their routine survey work, unaware of the meeting of the air masses out at sea, unaware of the force the union was spawning. It had struck their camp without warning; a thundering, roaring destruction that sought to annihilate all that lay before it. It had passed on, leaving the wreckage in its wake. It had destroyed the labor of months and had doomed six men to die and then, as though its task was accomplished, it once more began to resolve into gentle masses of air. But for all its deadliness, it had destroyed with neither malice nor intent. It had been a blind and mindless force, obeying the laws of nature, and it would have followed the same course with the same fury had men never existed.

Existence required Order and there was order; the laws of nature, irrevocable and immutable. Men could learn to use them but men could not change them. The circumference of a circle was always pi times the diameter and no science of Man would ever make it otherwise. The combination of chemical A with chemical B under condition C invariably produced reaction D. The law of gravitation was a rigid equation and it made no distinction between the fall of a leaf and the ponderous circling of a binary star system. The nuclear conversion process powered the cruisers that carried men to the stars; the same process in the form of a nova would destroy a world with equal efficiency. The laws *were,* and the universe moved in obedience to them. Along the frontier were arrayed all the forces of nature and sometimes they destroyed those who were fighting their way outward from Earth. The men of the frontier had long ago learned the bitter futility of cursing the forces that would destroy them for the forces were blind and deaf; the futility of looking to the heavens for mercy, for the stars of the galaxy swung in their long, long sweep of two hundred million years, as inexorably controlled as they by the laws that knew neither hatred nor compassion.

The men of the frontier knew—but how was a girl from Earth to fully understand? *H amount of fuel will not power an EDS with a mass of m plus x safely to its destination.* To himself and her brother and parents she was a sweet-faced girl in her teens; to the laws of nature she was *x,* the unwanted factor in a cold equation.

She stirred again on the seat. "Could I write a letter? I want to write to Mama and Daddy and I'd like to talk to Gerry. Could you let me talk to him over your radio there?"

"I'll try to get him," he said.

He switched on the normal-space transmitter and pressed the signal button. Someone answered the buzzer almost immediately.

"Hello. How's it going with you fellows now—is the EDS on its way?"

"This isn't Group One; this is the EDS," he said. "Is Gerry Cross there?"

"Gerry? He and two others went out in the helicopter this morning and aren't back yet. It's almost sundown, though, and he ought to be back right away—in less than an hour at the most."

"Can you connect me through to the radio in his 'copter?"

"Huh-uh. It's been out of commission for two months—some

printed circuits went haywire and we can't get any more until the next cruiser stops by. Is it something important—bad news for him, or something?"

"Yes—it's very important. When he comes in get him to the transmitter as soon as you possibly can."

"I'll do that; I'll have one of the boys waiting at the field with a truck. Is there anything else I can do?"

"No, I guess that's all. Get him there as soon as you can and signal me."

He turned the volume to an inaudible minimum, an act that would not affect the functioning of the signal buzzer, and unclipped the pad of paper from the control board. He tore off the sheet containing his flight instructions and handed the pad to her, together with pencil.

"I'd better write to Gerry, too," she said as she took them. "He might not get back to camp in time."

She began to write, her fingers still clumsy and uncertain in the way they handled the pencil and the top of it trembling a little as she poised it between words. He turned back to the viewscreen, to stare at it without seeing it.

She was a lonely little child, trying to say her last good-by, and she would lay out her heart to them. She would tell them how much she loved them and she would tell them to not feel badly about it, that it was only something that must happen eventually to everyone and she was not afraid. The last would be a lie and it would be there to read between the sprawling, uneven lines; a valiant little lie that would make the hurt all the greater for them.

Her brother was of the frontier and he would understand. He would not hate the EDS pilot for doing nothing to prevent her going; he would know there had been nothing the pilot could do. He would understand, though the understanding would not soften the shock and pain when he learned his sister was gone. But the others, her father and mother—they would not understand. They were of Earth and they would think in the manner of those who had never lived where the safety margin of life was a thin, thin line—and sometimes not at all. What would they think of the faceless, unknown pilot who had sent her to her death?

They would hate him with cold and terrible intensity but it really didn't matter. He would never see them, never know them. He would have only the memories to remind him; only the nights to fear, when a blue-eyed girl in gypsy sandals would come in his dreams to die again—

∾   ∾   ∾

He scowled at the viewscreen and tried to force his thoughts into less emotional channels. There was nothing he could do to help her. She had unknowingly subjected herself to the penalty of a law that recognized neither innocence nor youth nor beauty, that was incapable of sympathy or leniency. Regret was illogical—and yet, could knowing it to be illogical ever keep it away?

She stopped occasionally, as though trying to find the right words to tell them what she wanted them to know, then the pencil would resume its whispering to the paper. It was 18:37 when she folded the letter in a square and wrote a name on it. She began writing another, twice looking up at the chronometer as though she feared the black hand might reach its rendezvous before she had finished. It was 18:45 when she folded it as she had done the first letter and wrote a name and address on it.

She held the letters out to him. "Will you take care of these and see that they're enveloped and mailed?"

"Of course." He took them from her hand and placed them in a pocket of his gray uniform shirt.

"These can't be sent off until the next cruiser stops by and the *Stardust* will have long since told them about me, won't it?" she asked. He nodded and she went on, "That makes the letters not important in one way but in another way they're very important—to me, and to them."

"I know. I understand, and I'll take care of them."

She glanced at the chronometer, then back at him. "It seems to move faster all the time, doesn't it?"

He said nothing, unable to think of anything to say, and she asked, "Do you think Gerry will come back to camp in time?"

"I think so. They said he should be in right away."

She began to roll the pencil back and forth between her palms. "I hope he does. I feel sick and scared and I want to hear his voice again and maybe I won't feel so alone. I'm a coward and I can't help it."

"No," he said, "you're not a coward. You're afraid, but you're not a coward."

"Is there a difference?"

He nodded. "A lot of difference."

"I feel so alone. I never did feel like this before; like I was all by myself and there was nobody to care what happened to me. Always, before, there was Mama and Daddy there and my friends around me. I had lots of friends, and they had a going-away party for me the night before I left."

Friends and music and laughter for her to remember—and on the viewscreen Lotus Lake was going into the shadow.

"Is it the same with Gerry?" she asked. "I mean, if he should make a mistake, would he have to die for it, all alone and with no one to help him?"

"It's the same with all along the frontier; it will always be like that so long as there is a frontier."

"Gerry didn't tell us. He said the pay was good and he sent money home all the time because Daddy's little shop just brought in a bare living but he didn't tell us it was like this."

"He didn't tell you his work was dangerous?"

"Well—yes. He mentioned that, but we didn't understand. I always thought danger along the frontier was something that was a lot of fun; an exciting adventure, like in the three-D shows." A wan smile touched her face for a moment. "Only it's not, is it? It's not the same at all, because when it's real you can't go home after the show is over."

"No," he said. "No, you can't."

Her glance flicked from the chronometer to the door of the air lock then down to the pad and pencil she still held. She shifted her position slightly to lay them on the bench beside her, moving one foot out a little. For the first time he saw that she was not wearing Vegan gypsy sandals but only cheap imitations; the expensive Vegan leather was some kind of grained plastic, the silver buckle was gilded iron, the jewels were colored glass. *Daddy's little shop just brought in a bare living*— She must have left college in her second year, to take the course in linguistics that would enable her to make her own way and help her brother provide for her parents, earning what she could by part-time work after classes were over. Her personal possessions on the *Stardust* would be taken back to her parents—they would neither be of much value nor occupy much storage space on the return voyage.

"Isn't it—" She stopped, and he looked at her questioningly. "Isn't it cold in here?" she asked, almost apologetically. "Doesn't it seem cold to you?"

"Why, yes," he said. He saw by the main temperature gauge that the room was at precisely normal temperature. "Yes, it's colder than it should be."

"I wish Gerry would get back before it's too late. Do you really think he will, and you didn't just say so to make me feel better?"

"I think he will—they said he would be in pretty soon." On the viewscreen Lotus Lake had gone into the shadow but for the thin blue line of its western edge and it was apparent he had overestimated the time she would have in which to talk to her brother. Reluctantly, he said to her, "His camp will be out of radio range in a few minutes; he's on that part of Woden that's in the shadow"—he indicated the viewscreen—"and the turning of Woden will put him beyond contact. There may not be much time left when he comes in—not much time to talk to him before he fades out. I wish I could do something about it—I would call him right now if I could."

"Not even as much time as I will have to stay?"

"I'm afraid not."

"Then—" She straightened and looked toward the air lock with pale resolution. "Then I'll go when Gerry passes beyond range. I won't wait any longer after that—I won't have anything to wait for."

Again there was nothing he could say.

"Maybe I shouldn't wait at all. Maybe I'm selfish—maybe it would be better for Gerry if you just told him about it afterward."

There was an unconscious pleading for denial in the way she spoke and he said, "He wouldn't want you to do that, to not wait for him."

"It's already coming dark where he is, isn't it? There will be all the long night before him, and Mama and Daddy don't know yet that I won't ever be coming back like I promised them I would. I've caused everyone I love to be hurt, haven't I? I didn't want to—I didn't intend to."

"It wasn't your fault," he said. "It wasn't your fault. They'll know that. They'll understand."

"At first I was so afraid to die that I was a coward and thought only of myself. Now, I see how selfish I was. The terrible thing about dying like this is not that I'll be gone but that I'll never see them again; never be able to tell them that I didn't take them for granted; never be able to tell them I knew of the sacrifices they made to make my life happier, and I knew all the things they did for me and that I loved them so much more than I ever told them. I've never told them any of those things. You don't tell them such things when you're young and your life is all before you—you're afraid of sounding sentimental and silly.

"But it's so different when you have to die—you wish you had told them while you could and you wish you could tell them you're sorry for all the little mean things you ever did or said to them.

You wish you could tell them that you didn't really mean to ever hurt their feelings and for them to only remember that you always loved them far more than you ever let them know."

"You don't have to tell them that," he said. "They will know—they've always known it."

"Are you sure?" she asked. "How can you be sure? My people are strangers to you."

"Wherever you go, human nature and human hearts are the same."

"And they will know what I want them to know—that I love them?"

"They've always known it, in a way far better than you could ever put in words for them."

"I keep remembering the things they did for me, and it's the little things they did that seem to be the most important to me, now. Like Gerry—he sent me a bracelet of fire-rubies on my sixteenth birthday. It was beautiful—it must have cost him a month's pay. Yet, I remember him more for what he did the night my kitten got run over in the street. I was only six years old and he held me in his arms and wiped away my tears and told me not to cry, that Flossy was gone for just a little while, for just long enough to get herself a new fur coat and she would be on the foot of my bed the very next morning. I believed him and quit crying and went to sleep dreaming about my kitten coming back. When I woke up the next morning, there was Flossy on the foot of my bed in a brand-new white fur coat, just like he had said she would be.

"It wasn't until a long time later that Mama told me Gerry had got the pet-shop owner out of bed at four in the morning and, when the man got mad about it, Gerry told him he was either going to go down and sell him the white kitten right then or he'd break his neck."

"It's always the little things you remember people by; all the little things they did because they wanted to do them for you. You've done the same for Gerry and your father and mother; all kinds of things that you've forgotten about but that they will never forget."

"I hope I have. I would like for them to remember me like that."

"They will."

"I wish—" She swallowed. "The way I'll die—I wish they wouldn't ever think of that. I've read how people look who die

in space—their insides all ruptured and exploded and their lungs
out between their teeth and then, a few seconds later, they're all
dry and shapeless and horribly ugly. I don't want them to ever
think of me as something dead and horrible, like that."

"You're their own, their child and their sister. They could never
think of you other than the way you would want them to; the way
you looked the last time they saw you."

"I'm still afraid," she said. "I can't help it, but I don't want
Gerry to know it. If he gets back in time, I'm going to act like
I'm not afraid at all and—"

The signal buzzer interrupted her, quick and imperative.

"Gerry!" She came to her feet. "It's Gerry, now!"

He spun the volume control knob and asked: "Gerry
Cross?"

"Yes," her brother answered, an undertone of tenseness to his
reply. "The bad news—what is it?"

She answered for him, standing close behind him and leaning
down a little toward the communicator, her hand resting small
and cold on his shoulder.

"Hello, Gerry." There was only a faint quaver to betray the careful casualness of her voice. "I wanted to see you—"

"Marilyn!" There was sudden and terrible apprehension in the
way he spoke her name. "What are you doing on that EDS?"

"I wanted to see you," she said again. "I wanted to see you, so
I hid on this ship—"

"You *hid* on it?"

"I'm a stowaway. . . . I didn't know what it would mean—"

"Marilyn!" It was the cry of a man who calls hopeless and
desperate to someone already and forever gone from him. "What
have you done?"

"I. . . . it's not—" Then her own composure broke and the cold
little hand gripped his shoulder convulsively. "Don't, Gerry—I only
wanted to see you; I didn't intend to hurt you. Please, Gerry,
don't feel like that—"

Something warm and wet splashed on his wrist and he slid out
of the chair, to help her into it and swing the microphone down
to her own level.

"Don't feel like that—Don't let me go knowing you feel like
that—"

The sob she had tried to hold back choked in her throat and her
brother spoke to her. "Don't cry, Marilyn." His voice was suddenly

deep and infinitely gentle, with all the pain held out of it. "Don't cry, sis—you mustn't do that. It's all right, honey—everything is all right."

"I—" Her lower lip quivered and she bit into it. "I didn't want you to feel that way—I just wanted us to say good-by because I have to go in a minute."

"Sure—sure. That's the way it will be, sis. I didn't mean to sound the way I did." Then his voice changed to a tone of quick and urgent demand. "EDS—have you called the *Stardust*? Did you check with the computers?"

"I called the *Stardust* almost an hour ago. It can't turn back, there are no other cruisers within forty light-years, and there isn't enough fuel."

"Are you sure that the computers had the correct data—sure of everything?"

"Yes—do you think I could ever let it happen if I wasn't sure? I did everything I could do. If there was anything at all I could do now, I would do it."

"He tried to help me, Gerry." Her lower lip was no longer trembling and the short sleeves of her blouse were wet where she had dried her tears. "No one can help me and I'm not going to cry any more and everything will be all right with you and Daddy and Mama, won't it?"

"Sure—sure it will. We'll make out fine."

Her brother's words were beginning to come in more faintly and he turned the volume control to maximum. "He's going out of range," he said to her. "He'll be gone within another minute."

"You're fading out, Gerry," she said. "You're going out of range. I wanted to tell you—but I can't, now. We must say good-by so soon—but maybe I'll see you again. Maybe I'll come to you in your dreams with my hair in braids and crying because the kitten in my arms is dead; maybe I'll be the touch of a breeze that whispers to you as it goes by; maybe I'll be one of those gold-winged larks you told me about, singing my silly head off to you; maybe, at times, I'll be nothing you can see but you will know I'm there beside you. Think of me like that, Gerry; always like that and not—the other way."

Dimmed to a whisper by the turning of Woden, the answer came back:

"Always like that, Marilyn—always like that and never any other way."

"Our time is up, Gerry—I have to go, now. Good—" Her voice

broke in mid-word and her mouth tried to twist into crying. She pressed her hand hard against it and when she spoke again the words came clear and true:

"Good-by, Gerry."

Faint and ineffably poignant and tender, the last words came from the cold metal of the communicator:

"Good-by, little sister—"

She sat motionless in the hush that followed, as though listening to the shadow-echoes of the words as they died away, then she turned away from the communicator, toward the air lock, and he pulled down the black lever beside him. The inner door of the air lock slid swiftly open, to reveal the bare little cell that was waiting for her, and she walked to it.

She walked with her head up and the brown curls brushing her shoulders, with the white sandals stepping as sure and steady as the fractional gravity would permit and the gilded buckles twinkling with little lights of blue and red and crystal. He let her walk alone and made no move to help her, knowing she would not want it that way. She stepped into the air lock and turned to face him, only the pulse in her throat to betray the wild beating of her heart.

"I'm ready," she said.

He pushed the lever up and the door slid its quick barrier between them, enclosing her in black and utter darkness for her last moments of life. It clicked as it locked in place and he jerked down the red lever. There was a slight waver to the ship as the air gushed from the lock, a vibration to the wall as though something had bumped the outer door in passing, then there was nothing and the ship was dropping true and steady again. He shoved the red lever back to close the door on the empty air lock and turned away, to walk to the pilot's chair with the slow steps of a man old and weary.

Back in the pilot's chair he pressed the signal button of the normal-space transmitter. There was no response; he had expected none. Her brother would have to wait through the night until the turning of Woden permitted contact through Group One.

It was not yet time to resume deceleration and he waited while the ship dropped endlessly downward with him and the drives purred softly. He saw that the white hand of the supplies closet temperature gauge was on zero. A cold equation had been balanced and he was alone on the ship. Something shapeless and ugly was hurrying ahead of him, going to Woden where its brother was waiting through the night, but the empty ship still lived for a little while with the presence of the girl who had not known about the forces that killed with neither hatred nor malice. It seemed, almost, that she still sat small and bewildered and frightened on the metal box beside him, her words echoing hauntingly clear in the void she had left behind her:

I didn't do anything to die for—I didn't do anything—

AFTERWORD BY ERIC FLINT

There are smart writers, and there are dumb writers, and one of the things that distinguishes them is that smart writers pay attention to what their editors tell them. Mind you, I don't always agree with my editors, but I never ignore them either—because, more often than not, they're likely to be right and I'm likely to be wrong.

The reason is simple. One of the occupational hazards of being a writer is that you invariably get a little too close to a story to see it clearly in its broadest dimensions. An editor—a good one, anyway—can provide you with that perspective.

I mention this because it bears on our decision to include this story in the anthology. When Jim first proposed it, I wasn't at all keen on the idea. For all its well-deserved fame, I've never *liked* "The Cold Equations." Dammit.

My dislike for it has nothing to do with the fact that it has an unhappy ending. It's enough to mention that I'm a lifelong fan of Fyodor Dostoyevsky to make clear that I'm not addicted to happy endings. What aggravates me about "The Cold Equations" is that the blasted plot makes no sense. The powerful impact of the story—and it is powerful, no question about it—is based entirely on a premise which I find completely implausible: to wit, that a spacecraft delivering critical supplies would be designed with *no* safety margin at all.

Oh, pfui. They don't make tricycles without a hefty safety margin. And I'm quite sure that if you traveled back in time and interviewed Ugh the Neanderthal, he'd explain to you that his wooden club is plenty thick enough to survive any impact he can foresee. He made damn sure of that before he ventured out of his cave. He may have a sloping forehead, but he's not an *idiot*.

Grumble, grumble. But . . .

Well, Jim's right. The problem is that any profession has certain occupational hazards, and one of those for a writer is that since you work all the time with plots you tend to get hypersensitive about their logic. It's the writer's equivalent of the well-known movie reviewer's syndrome: people who make a living reviewing movies *always* hate car chases. That's because they see too many of them.

But movies aren't made for critics, and stories aren't written to satisfy other writers. Jim's point was that, in the end, it just doesn't *matter* if the plot of "The Cold Equations" won't bear up to close scrutiny.

Does . . . not . . . matter.

And, it doesn't. I've now read the story many times, and the illogic of the plot always drives me nuts. Still, every time, that ending grabs me by the throat.

So, when all's said and done, I'm glad we included it. Whatever its flaws, "The Cold Equations" remains one of the most powerful SF stories ever written. But I would urge any reader with the interest to take a look at Godwin's other great story—his short novel *The Survivors*, which I first read at the age of twelve and which, many years later, I made the lead story in the Godwin volume I edited for Baen Books. (*The Cold Equations & Other Stories*, now available in paperback. Yes, that's a shameless plug. I get to do that. If being a writer has its occupational hazards, it also has its perks.)

Shambleau

by C. L. Moore

PREFACE BY DAVID DRAKE

Catherine L. Moore is rightly regarded as one of the most remarkable stylists in the SF field. She once described the basic thread of her fiction as, "Love is the most dangerous thing."

"Shambleau" is a perfect illustration of both the above statements. It's about hard-bitten adventurers ranging the spaceways, meeting violence with violence . . . and it's nothing like any of the many other stories using the same elements being written then or written since then.

It was Moore's first story, written in a bank vault during the Depression because she had a typewriter and no work to do.

Her *first* story.

⁓

"Shambleau! Ha . . . Shambleau!" The wild hysteria of the mob rocketed from wall to wall of Lakkdarol's narrow streets and the storming of heavy boots over the slag-red pavement made an ominous undernote to that swelling bay, "Shambleau! Shambleau!"

Northwest Smith heard it coming and stepped into the nearest doorway, laying a wary hand on his heat-gun's grip, and his colorless eyes narrowed. Strange sounds were common enough in the streets of Earth's latest colony on Mars—a raw, red little town where anything might happen, and very often did. But Northwest

471

Smith, whose name is known and respected in every dive and wild
outpost on a dozen wild planets, was a cautious man, despite his
reputation. He set his back against the wall and gripped his pistol,
and heard the rising shout come nearer and nearer.

Then into his range of vision flashed a red running figure, dodging
like a hunted hare from shelter to shelter in the narrow street. It
was a girl—a berry-brown girl in a single tattered garment whose
scarlet burnt the eyes with its brilliance. She ran wearily, and he
could hear her gasping breath from where he stood. As she came
into view he saw her hesitate and lean one hand against the wall
for support, and glance wildly around for shelter. She must not
have seen him in the depths of the doorway, for as the bay of
the mob grew louder and the pounding of feet sounded almost
at the corner she gave a despairing little moan and dodged into
the recess at his very side.

When she saw him standing there, tall and leather-brown, hand
on his heat-gun, she sobbed once, inarticulately, and collapsed at
his feet, a huddle of burning scarlet and bare, brown limbs.

Smith had not seen her face, but she was a girl, and sweetly
made and in danger; and though he had not the reputation of
a chivalrous man, something in her hopeless huddle at his feet
touched that chord of sympathy for the underdog that stirs in
every Earthman, and he pushed her gently into the corner behind
him and jerked out his gun, just as the first of the running mob
rounded the corner.

It was a motley crowd, Earthmen and Martians and a sprin-
kling of Venusian swampmen and strange, nameless denizens of
unnamed planets—a typical Lakkdarol mob. When the first of them
turned the corner and saw the empty street before them there was
a faltering in the rush and the foremost spread out and began to
search the doorways on both sides of the street.

"Looking for something?" Smith's sardonic call sounded clear
above the clamor of the mob.

They turned. The shouting died for a moment as they took in
the scene before them—tall Earthman in the space-explorer's leath-
ern garb, all one color from the burning of savage suns save for
the sinister pallor of his no-colored eyes in a scarred and resolute
face, gun in his steady hand and the scarlet girl crouched behind
him, panting.

The foremost of the crowd—a burly Earthman in tattered leather
from which the Patrol insignia had been ripped away—stared for
a moment with a strange expression of incredulity on his face

overspreading the savage exultation of the chase. Then he let loose a deep-throated bellow, "Shambleau!" and lunged forward. Behind him the mob took up the cry again. "Shambleau! Shambleau! Shambleau!" and surged after.

Smith, lounging negligently against the wall, arms folded and gun-hand draped over his left forearm, looked incapable of swift motion, but at the leader's first forward step the pistol swept in a practiced half-circle and the dazzle of blue-white heat leaping from its muzzle seared an arc in the slag pavement at his feet. It was an old gesture, and not a man in the crowd but understood it. The foremost recoiled swiftly against the surge of those in the rear, and for a moment there was confusion as the two tides met and struggled. Smith's mouth curled into a grim curve as he watched. The man in the mutilated Patrol uniform lifted a threatening fist and stepped to the very edge of the deadline, while the crowd rocked to and fro behind him.

"Are you crossing that line?" queried Smith in an ominously gentle voice.

"We want that girl!"

"Come and get her!" Recklessly Smith grinned into his face. He saw danger there, but his defiance was not the foolhardy gesture it seemed. An expert psychologist of mobs from long experience, he sensed no murder here. Not a gun had appeared in any hand in the crowd. They desired the girl with an inexplicable bloodthirstiness he was at a loss to understand, but toward himself he sensed no such fury. A mauling he might expect, but his life was in no danger. Guns would have appeared before now if they were coming out at all. So he grinned in the man's angry face and leaned lazily against the wall.

Behind their self-appointed leader the crowd milled impatiently, and threatening voices began to rise again. Smith heard the girl moan at his feet.

"What do you want with her?" he demanded.

"She's Shambleau! Shambleau, you fool! Kick her out of there— we'll take care of her!"

"I'm taking care of her," drawled Smith.

"She's Shambleau, I tell you! Damn your hide, man, we never let those things live! Kick her out here!"

The repeated name had no meaning to him, but Smith's innate stubbornness rose defiantly as the crowd surged forward to the very edge of the arc, their clamor growing louder. "Shambleau! Kick her out here! Give us Shambleau! Shambleau!"

Smith dropped his indolent pose like a cloak and planted both feet wide, swinging up his gun threatening. "Keep back!" he yelled. "She's mine! Keep back!"

He had no intention of using that heat-beam. He knew by now that they would not kill him unless he started the gunplay himself, and he did not mean to give up his life for any girl alive. But a severe mauling he expected, and he braced himself instinctively as the mob heaved within itself.

To his astonishment a thing happened then that he had never known to happen before. At his shouted defiance the foremost of the mob—those who had heard him clearly—drew back a little, not in alarm but evidently surprised. The ex-Patrolman said, "Yours! She's *yours?*" in a voice from which puzzlement crowded out the anger.

Smith spread his booted legs wide before the crouching figure and flourished his gun.

"Yes," he said. "And I'm keeping her! Stand back there!"

The man stared at him wordlessly, and horror and disgust and incredulity mingled on his weather-beaten face. The incredulity triumphed for a moment and he said again,

"*Yours!*"

Smith nodded defiance.

The man stepped back suddenly, unutterable contempt in his very pose. He waved an arm to the crowd and said loudly, "It's—his!" and the press melted away, gone silent, too, and the look of contempt spread from face to face.

The ex-Patrolman spat on the slag-paved street and turned his back indifferently. "Keep her, then," he advised briefly over one shoulder. "But don't let her out again in this town!"

Smith stared in perplexity almost open-mouthed as the suddenly scornful mob began to break up. His mind was in a whirl. That such bloodthirsty animosity should vanish in a breath he could not believe. And the curious mingling of contempt and disgust on the faces he saw baffled him even more. Lakkdarol was anything but a puritan town—it did not enter his head for a moment that his claiming the brown girl as his own had caused that strangely shocked revulsion to spread through the crowd. No, it was something deeper-rooted than that. Instinctive, instant disgust had been in the faces he saw—they would have looked less so if he had admitted cannibalism or *Pharol*-worship.

And they were leaving his vicinity as swiftly as if whatever unknowing sin he had committed were contagious. The street was emptying as rapidly as it had filled. He saw a sleek Venusian glance back over his shoulder as he turned the corner and sneer, "Shambleau!" and the word awoke a new line of speculation in Smith's mind. Shambleau! Vaguely of French origin, it must be. And strange enough to hear it from the lips of Venusian and Martian drylanders, but it was their use of it that puzzled him more. "We never let those things live," the ex-Patrolman had said. It reminded him dimly of something . . . an ancient line from some writing in his own tongue . . . "Thou shalt not suffer a witch to live." He smiled to himself at the similarity, and simultaneously was aware of the girl at his elbow.

She had risen soundlessly. He turned to face her, sheathing his gun and stared at first with curiosity and then in the entirely frank openness with which men regard that which is not wholly human. For she was not. He knew it at a glance, though the brown, sweet body was shaped like a woman's and she wore the garment of scarlet—he saw it was leather—with an ease that few unhuman beings achieve toward clothing. He knew it from the moment he looked into her eyes, and a shiver of unrest went over him as he met them. They were frankly green as young grass, with slit-like, feline pupils that pulsed unceasingly, and there was a look of dark, animal wisdom in their depths—that look of the beast which sees more than man.

There was no hair upon her face—neither brows nor lashes, and he would have sworn that the tight scarlet turban bound around her head covered baldness. She had three fingers and a thumb, and her feet had four digits apiece too, and all sixteen of them were tipped with round claws that sheathed back into the flesh like a cat's. She ran her tongue over her lips—a thin, pink, flat tongue as feline as her eyes—and spoke with difficulty. He felt that that throat and tongue had never been shaped for human speech.

"Not—afraid now," she said softly, and her little teeth were white and polished as a kitten's.

"What did they want you for?" he asked her curiously. "What have you done? Shambleau . . . is that your name?"

"I—not talk your—speech," she demurred hesitantly.

"Well, try to—I want to know. Why were they chasing you? Will you be safe on the street now, or hadn't you better get indoors somewhere? They looked dangerous."

"I—go with you." She brought it out with difficulty.

"Say you!" Smith grinned. "What are you, anyhow? You look like a kitten to me."

"Shambleau." She said it somberly.

"Where d'you live? Are you a Martian?"

"I come from—from far—from long ago—far country—"

"Wait!" laughed Smith. "You're getting your wires crossed. You're not a Martian?"

She drew herself up very straight beside him, lifting the turbaned head, and there was something queenly in the pose of her.

"Martian?" she said scornfully. "My people—are—are—you have no word. Your speech—hard for me."

"What's yours? I might know it—try me."

She lifted her head and met his eyes squarely, and there was in hers a subtle amusement—he could have sworn it.

"Some day I—speak to you in—my own language," she promised, and the pink tongue flicked out over her lips, swiftly, hungrily.

Approaching footsteps on the red pavement interrupted Smith's reply. A dryland Martian came past, reeling a little and exuding an aroma of *segir*-whisky, the Venusian brand. When he caught the red flash of the girl's tatters he turned his head sharply, and as his *segir*-steeped brain took in the fact of her presence he lurched toward the recess unsteadily, bawling, "Shambleau, by *Pharol!* Shambleau!" and reached out a clutching hand.

Smith struck it aside contemptuously.

"On your way, drylander," he advised.

The man drew back and stared, bleary-eyed.

"Yours, eh?" he croaked. "*Zut!* You're welcome to it!" And like the ex-Patrolman before him he spat on the pavement and turned away, muttering harshly in the blasphemous tongue of the drylands.

Smith watched him shuffle off, and there was a crease between his colorless eyes, a nameless unease rising within him.

"Come on," he said abruptly to the girl. "If this sort of thing is going to happen we'd better get indoors. Where shall I take you?"

"With—you," she murmured.

He stared down into the flat green eyes. Those ceaselessly pulsing pupils disturbed him, but it seemed to him, vaguely, that behind the animal shallows of her gaze was a shutter—a closed barrier that might at any moment open to reveal the very deeps of that dark knowledge he sensed there.

Roughly he said again, "Come on, then," and stepped down into the street.

She pattered along a pace or two behind him, making no effort to keep up with his long strides, and though Smith—as men know from Venus to Jupiter's moons—walks as softly as a cat, even in spacemen's boots, the girl at his heels slid like a shadow over the rough pavement, making so little sound that even the lightness of his footsteps was loud in the empty street.

Smith chose the less frequented ways of Lakkdarol, and somewhat shamefacedly thanked his nameless gods that his lodgings were not far away, for the few pedestrians he met turned and stared after the two with that by now familiar mingling of horror and contempt which he was as far as ever from understanding.

The room he had engaged was a single cubicle in a lodging-house on the edge of the city. Lakkdarol, raw camptown that it was in those days, could have furnished little better anywhere within its limits, and Smith's errand there was not one he wished to advertise. He had slept in worse places than this before, and knew that he would do so again.

There was no one in sight when he entered, and the girl slipped up the stairs at his heels and vanished through the door, shadowy, unseen by anyone in the house. Smith closed the door and leaned his broad shoulders against the panels, regarding her speculatively.

She took in what little the room had to offer in a glance—frowsy bed, rickety table, mirror hanging unevenly and cracked against the wall, unpainted chairs—a typical camptown room in an Earth settlement abroad. She accepted its poverty in that single glance, dismissed it, then crossed to the window and leaned out for a moment, gazing across the low roof-tops toward the barren countryside beyond, red slag under the late afternoon sun.

"You can stay here," said Smith abruptly, "until I leave town. I'm waiting here for a friend to come in from Venus. Have you eaten?"

"Yes," said the girl quickly. "I shall—need no—food for—a while."

"Well—" Smith glanced around the room. "I'll be in sometime tonight. You can go or stay just as you please. Better lock the door behind me."

With no more formality than that he left her. The door closed and he heard the key turn, and smiled to himself. He did not expect, then, ever to see her again.

He went down the steps and out into the late-slanting sunlight with a mind so full of other matters that the brown girl receded

very quickly into the background. Smith's errand in Lakkdarol, like
most of his errands, is better not spoken of. Man lives as he must,
and Smith's living was a perilous affair outside the law and ruled
by the ray-gun only. It is enough to say that the shipping-port and
its cargoes outbound interested him deeply just now, and that the
friend he awaited was Yarol the Venusian, in that swift little Edsel
ship the *Maid* that can flash from world to world with a derisive
speed that laughs at Patrol boats and leaves pursuers floundering in
the ether far behind. Smith and Yarol and the *Maid* were a trinity
that had caused Patrol leaders much worry and many gray hairs
in the past, and the future looked very bright to Smith himself
that evening as he left his lodging-house.

Lakkdarol roars by night, as Earthmen's camp-towns have a way
of doing on every planet where Earth's outposts are, and it was
beginning lustily as Smith went down among the awakening lights
toward the center of town. His business there does not concern
us. He mingled with the crowd where the lights were brightest,
and there was the click of ivory counters and the jingle of silver,
and red *segir* gurgled invitingly from black Venusian bottles, and
much later Smith strolled homeward under the moving moons
of Mars, and if the street wavered a little under his feet now and
then—why, that is only understandable. Not even Smith could
drink red *segir* at every bar from the *Martian Lamb* to the *New
Chicago* and remain entirely steady on his feet. But he found his
way back with very little difficulty—considering—and spent a good
five minutes hunting for his key before he remembered he had left
it in the inner lock for the girl.

He knocked then, and there was no sound of footsteps from
within, but in a few moments the latch clicked and the door
swung open. She retreated soundlessly before him as he entered,
and took up her favorite place against the window, leaning back
on the sill and outlined against the starry sky beyond. The room
was in darkness.

Smith flipped the switch by the door and then leaned back against
the panels, steadying himself. The cool night air had sobered him
a little and his head was clear enough—liquor went to Smith's
feet, not his head, or he would never have come this far along
the lawless way he had chosen. He lounged against the door now
and regarded the girl in the sudden glare of the bulbs, blinking a
little as much at the scarlet of her clothing as at the light.

"So you stayed," he said.

"I—waited," she answered softly, leaning farther back against the sill and clasping the rough wood with slim, three-fingered hands, pale brown against the darkness.

"Why?"

She did not answer that, but her mouth curved into a slow smile. On a woman it would have been reply enough—provocative, daring. On Shambleau there was something pitiful and horrible in it—so human on the face of one half-animal. And yet . . . that sweet brown body curving so softly from the tatters of scarlet leather—the velvety texture of that brownness—the white-flashing smile . . . Smith was aware of a stirring excitement within him. After all—time would be hanging heavy now until Yarol came . . . Speculatively he allowed the steel-pale eyes to wander over her, with a slow regard that missed nothing. And when he spoke he was aware that his voice had deepened a little . . .

"Come here," he said.

She came forward slowly, on bare clawed feet that made no slightest sound on the floor, and stood before him with downcast eyes and mouth trembling in that pitifully human smile. He took her by the shoulders—velvety soft shoulders, of a creamy smoothness that was not the texture of human flesh. A little tremor went over her, perceptibly, at the contact of his hands. Northwest Smith caught his breath suddenly and dragged her to him . . . sweet yielding brownness in the circle of his arms . . . heard her own breath catch and quicken as her velvety arms closed about his neck. And then he was looking down into her face, very near, and the green animal eyes met his with the pulsing pupils and the flicker of—something—deep behind their shallows—and through the rising clamor of his blood, even as he stooped his lips to hers, Smith felt something deep within him shudder away—inexplicable, instinctive, revolted. What it might be he had no words to tell, but the very touch of her was suddenly loathsome—so soft and velvet and unhuman—and it might have been an animal's face that lifted itself to his mouth—the dark knowledge looked hungrily from the darkness of those slit pupils—and for a mad instant he knew that same wild, feverish revulsion he had seen in the faces of the mob . . .

"God!" he gasped, a far more ancient invocation against evil than he realized, then or ever, and he ripped her arms from his neck, swung her away with such a force that she reeled half across the room. Smith fell back against the door, breathing heavily, and stared at her while the wild revolt died slowly within him.

She had fallen to the floor beneath the window, and as she lay there against the wall with bent head he saw, curiously, that her turban had slipped—the turban that he had been so sure covered baldness—and a lock of scarlet hair fell below the binding leather, hair as scarlet as her garment, as unhumanly red as her eyes were unhumanly green. He stared, and shook his head dizzily and stared again, for it seemed to him that the thick lock of crimson had moved, *squirmed* of itself against her cheek.

At the contact of it her hands flew up and she tucked it away with a very human gesture and then dropped her head again into her hands. And from the deep shadow of her fingers he thought she was staring up at him covertly.

Smith drew a deep breath and passed a hand across his forehead. The inexplicable moment had gone as quickly as it came—too swiftly for him to understand or analyze it. "Got to lay off the *segir*," he told himself unsteadily. Had he imagined that scarlet hair? After all, she was no more than a pretty brown girl-creature from one of the many half-human races peopling the planets. No more than that, after all. A pretty little thing, but animal . . . He laughed, a little shakily.

"No more of that," he said. "God knows I'm no angel, but there's got to be a limit somewhere. Here." He crossed to the bed and sorted out a pair of blankets from the untidy heap, tossing them to the far corner of the room. "You can sleep there."

Wordlessly she rose from the floor and began to rearrange the blankets, the uncomprehending resignation of the animal eloquent in every line of her.

Smith had a strange dream that night. He thought he had awakened to a room full of darkness and moonlight and moving shadows, for the nearer moon of Mars was racing through the sky and everything on the planet below her was endued with a restless life in the dark. And something . . . some nameless, unthinkable *thing* . . . was coiled about his throat . . . something like a soft snake, wet and warm. It lay loose and light about his neck . . . and it was moving gently, very gently, with a soft, caressive pressure that sent little thrills of delight through every nerve and fiber of him, a perilous delight—beyond physical pleasure, deeper than joy of the mind. That warm softness was caressing the very roots of his soul and with a terrible intimacy. The ecstasy of it left him weak, and yet he knew—in a flash of knowledge born of this impossible dream—that the soul should not be handled . . . And with that knowledge a horror broke upon him, turning the pleasure into a rapture of revulsion, hateful, horrible—but still most foully sweet. He tried to lift his hands and tear the dream-monstrosity from his throat—tired but half-heartedly; for though his soul was revolted to its very deeps, yet the delight of his body was so great that his hands all but refused the attempt. But when at last he tried to lift his arms a cold shock went over him and he found that he could not stir . . . his body lay stony as marble beneath the blankets, a living marble that shuddered with a dreadful delight through every rigid vein.

The revulsion grew strong upon him as he struggled against the paralyzing dream—a struggle of soul against sluggish body—titanically, until the moving dark was streaked with blankness that clouded and closed about him at last and he sank back into the oblivion from which he had awakened.

Next morning, when the bright sunlight shining through Mars' clear thin air awakened him, Smith lay for a while trying to remember. The dream had been more vivid than reality, but he could not now quite recall . . . only that it had been more sweet and horrible than anything else in life. He lay puzzling for a while, until a soft sound from the corner aroused him from his thoughts and he sat up to see the girl lying in a cat-like coil on her blankets, watching him with round, grave eyes. He regarded her somewhat ruefully.

"Morning," he said. "I've just had the devil of a dream . . . Well, hungry?"

She shook her head silently, and he could have sworn there was a covert gleam of strange amusement in her eyes.

He stretched and yawned, dismissing the nightmare temporarily from his mind.

"What am I going to do with you?" he inquired, turning to more immediate matters. "I'm leaving here in a day or two and I can't take you along, you know. Where'd you come from in the first place?"

Again she shook her head.

"Not telling? Well, it's your business. You can stay here until I give up the room. From then on you'll have to do your own worrying."

He swung his feet to the floor and reached for his clothes.

Ten minutes later, slipping the heat-gun into its holster at his thigh, Smith turned to the girl. "There's food-concentrate in that box on the table. It ought to hold you until I get back. And you'd better lock the door again after I've gone."

Her wide, unwavering stare was his only answer, and he was not sure she had understood, but at any rate the lock clicked after him as before, and he went down the steps with a faint grin on his lips.

The memory of last night's extraordinary dream was slipping from him, as such memories do, and by the time he had reached the street the girl and the dream and all of yesterday's happenings were blotted out by the sharp necessities of the present.

Again the intricate business that had brought him here claimed his attention. He went about it to the exclusion of all else, and there was a good reason behind everything he did from the moment he stepped out into the street until the time when he turned back again at evening; though had one chosen to follow him during the day his apparently aimless rambling through Lakkdarol would have seemed very pointless.

He must have spent two hours at the least idling by the space-port, watching with sleepy, colorless eyes the ships that came and went, the passengers, the vessels lying at wait, the cargoes—particularly the cargoes. He made the rounds of the town's saloons once more, consuming many glasses of varied liquors in the course of the day and engaging in idle conversation with men of all races and worlds, usually in their own languages, for Smith was a linguist of repute among his contemporaries. He heard the gossip of the spaceways, news from a dozen planets of a thousand different events. He heard the latest joke about the Venusian Emperor and the latest report on the Chino-Aryan war and the latest song hot from the lips of Rose Robertson, whom every man on the civilized planets adored as "the Georgia Rose." He passed the day quite profitably, for his own purposes, which do not concern us now, and it was not until late evening, when he turned homeward again, that the thought of the brown girl in his room took definite shape in his mind, though it had been lurking there, formless and submerged, all day.

He had no idea what comprised her usual diet, but he bought a can of New York roast beef and one of Venusian frog-broth and a dozen fresh canal-apples and two pounds of that Earth lettuce that grows so vigorously in the fertile canal-soil of Mars. He felt that she must surely find something to her liking in this broad variety of edibles, and—for his day had been very satisfactory—he hummed "The Green Hills of Earth" to himself in a surprisingly good baritone as he climbed the stairs.

༄ ༄ ༄

The door was locked, as before, and he was reduced to kicking the lower panels gently with his boot, for his arms were full. She opened the door with that softness that was characteristic of her and stood regarding him in the semidarkness as he stumbled to the table with his load. The room was unlit again.

"Why don't you turn on the lights?" he demanded irritably after he had barked his shin on the chair by the table in an effort to deposit his burden there.

"Light and—dark—they are alike—to me," she murmured.

"Cat eyes, eh? Well, you look the part. Here, I've brought you some dinner. Take your choice. Fond of roast beef? Or how about a little frog-broth?"

She shook her head and backed away a step.

"No," she said. "I can not—eat your food."

Smith's brows wrinkled. "Didn't you have any of the food-tablets?"

Again the red turban shook negatively.

"Then you haven't had anything for—why, more than twenty-four hours! You must be starved."

"Not hungry," she denied.

"What can I find for you to eat, then? There's time yet if I hurry. You've got to eat, child."

"I shall—eat," she said softly. "Before long—I shall—feed. Have no—worry."

She turned away then and stood at the window, looking out over the moonlit landscape as if to end the conversation. Smith cast her a puzzled glance as he opened the can of roast beef. There had been an odd undernote in that assurance that, undefinably, he did not like. And the girl had teeth and tongue and presumably a fairly human digestive system, to judge from her human form. It was nonsense for her to pretend that he could find nothing that she could eat. She must have had some of the food concentrate after all, he decided, prying up the thermos lid of the inner container to release the long-sealed savor of the hot meat inside.

"Well, if you won't eat you won't," he observed philosophically as he poured hot broth and diced beef into the dish-like lid of the thermos can and extracted the spoon from its hiding-place between the inner and outer receptacles. She turned a little to watch him as he pulled up a rickety chair and sat down to the food, and after a while the realization that her green gaze was fixed so unwinkingly upon him made the man nervous, and he said between bites of creamy canal-apple, "Why don't you try a little of this? It's good."

"The food—I eat is—better," her soft voice told him in its hesitant murmur, and again he felt rather than heard a faint undernote of unpleasantness in the words. A sudden suspicion struck him as he pondered on that last remark—some vague memory of horror-tales told about campfires in the past—and he swung round in the chair to look at her, a tiny, creeping fear unaccountably arising. There had been that in her words—in her unspoken words, that menaced . . .

She stood up beneath his gaze demurely, wide green eyes with their pulsing pupils meeting his without a falter. But her mouth was scarlet and her teeth were sharp . . .

"What food do you eat?" he demanded. And then, after a pause, very softly, "Blood?"

She stared at him for a moment, uncomprehending; then something like amusement curled her lips and she said scornfully, "You think me—vampire, eh? No—I am Shambleau!"

Unmistakably there were scorn and amusement in her voice at the suggestion, but as unmistakably she knew what he meant—accepted it as a logical suspicion—vampire! Fairy-tales—but fairy-tales this unhuman, outland creature was most familiar with. Smith was not a credulous man, nor a superstitious one, but he had seen too many strange things himself to doubt that the wildest legend might have a basis of fact. And there was something namelessly strange about her . . .

He puzzled over it for a while between deep bites of the canal-apple. And though he wanted to question her about a great many things, he did not, for he knew how futile it would be.

He said nothing more until the meat was finished and another canal-apple had followed the first, and he had cleared away the meal by the simple expedient of tossing the empty can out of the window. Then he lay back in the chair and surveyed her from half-closed eyes, colorless in a face tanned like saddle-leather. And again he was conscious of the brown, soft curves of her, velvety—subtle arcs and planes of smooth flesh under the tatters of scarlet leather. Vampire she might be, unhuman she certainly was, but desirable beyond words as she sat submissive beneath his low regard, her red-turbaned head bent, her clawed fingers lying in her lap. They sat very still for a while, and the silence throbbed between them.

She was so like a woman—an Earth woman—sweet and

submissive and demure, and softer than soft fur, if he could for-get the three-fingered claws and the pulsing eyes—and that deeper strangeness beyond words ... (Had he dreamed that red lock of hair that moved? Had it been *segir* that woke the wild revulsion he knew when he held her in his arms? Why had the mob so thirsted for her?) He sat and stared, and despite the mystery of her and the half-suspicions that thronged his mind—for she was so beautifully soft and curved under those revealing tatters—he slowly realized that his pulses were mounting, became aware of a kindling within ... brown girl-creature with downcast eyes ... and then the lids lifted and the green flatness of a cat's gaze met his, and last night's revulsion woke swiftly again, like a warning bell that clanged as their eyes met—animal, after all, too sleek and soft for humanity, and that inner strangeness ...

Smith shrugged and sat up. His failings were legion, but the weakness of the flesh was not among the major ones. He motioned the girl to her pallet of blankets in the corner and turned to his own bed.

From deeps of sound sleep he awoke much later. He awoke sud-denly and completely, and with that inner excitement that presages something momentous. He awoke to brilliant moonlight, turning the room so bright that he could see the scarlet of the girl's rags as she sat up on her pallet. She was awake, she was sitting with her shoulder half turned to him and her head bent, and some warning instinct crawled coldly up his spine as he watched what she was doing. And yet it was a very ordinary thing for a girl to do—any girl, anywhere. She was unbinding her turban ...

He watched, not breathing, a presentiment of something horrible stirring in his brain, inexplicably ... The red folds loosened, and—he knew then that he had not dreamed—again a scarlet lock swung down against her cheek ... a hair, was it? a lock of hair? ... thick as a thick worm it fell, plumply, against that smooth cheek ... more scarlet than blood and thick as a crawling worm ... and like a worm it crawled.

Smith rose on an elbow, not realizing the motion, and fixed an unwinking stare, with a sort of sick, fascinated incredulity, on that—that lock of hair. He had not dreamed. Until now he had taken it for granted that it was the *segir* which had made it seem to move on that evening before. But now ... it was lengthening, stretching, moving of itself. It must be hair, but it *crawled*; with a sickening life of its own it squirmed down against her cheek, caressingly, revoltingly, impossibly ... Wet, it was, and round and thick and shining ...

She unfastened the last fold and whipped the turban off. From what he saw then Smith would have turned his eyes away—and he had looked on dreadful things before, without flinching—but he could not stir. He could only lie there on elbow staring at the mass of scarlet, squirming—worms, hairs, what?—that writhed over her head in a dreadful mockery of ringlets. And it was lengthening, falling, somehow growing before his eyes, down over her shoulders in a spilling cascade, a mass that even at the beginning could never have been hidden under the skull-tight turban she had worn. He was beyond wondering, but he realized that. And still it squirmed and lengthened and fell, and she shook it out in a horrible travesty of a woman shaking out her unbound hair—until the unspeakable tangle of it—twisting, writhing, obscenely scarlet—hung to her waist and beyond, and still lengthened, an endless mass of crawling horror that until now, somehow, impossibly, had been hidden under the tight-bound turban. It was like a nest of blind, restless red worms ... it was—it was like naked entrails endowed with an unnatural aliveness, terrible beyond words.

Smith lay in the shadows, frozen without and within in a sick numbness that came of utter shock and revulsion.

She shook out the obscene, unspeakable tangle over her shoulders, and somehow he knew that she was going to turn in a moment and that he must meet her eyes. The thought of that meeting stopped his heart with dread, more awfully than anything else in this nightmare horror; for nightmare it must be, surely. But he knew without trying that he could not wrench his eyes away—the sickened fascination of that sight held him motionless, and somehow there was a certain beauty ...

Her head was turning. The crawling awfulness rippled and squirmed at the motion, writhing thick and wet and shining over the soft brown shoulders about which they fell now in obscene cascades that all but hid her body. Her head was turning. Smith lay numb. And very slowly he saw the round of her cheek foreshorten and her profile come into view, all the scarlet horrors twisting ominously, and the profile shortened in turn and her full face came slowly round toward the bed—moonlight shining brilliantly as day on the pretty girl-face, demure and sweet, framed in tangled obscenity that crawled ...

The green eyes met his. He felt a perceptible shock, and a shudder rippled down his paralyzed spine, leaving an icy numbness in its wake. He felt the goose-flesh rising. But that numbness and cold horror he scarcely realized, for the green eyes were locked with his in a long, long look that somehow presaged nameless things—not altogether unpleasant things—the voiceless voice of her mind assailing him with little murmurous promises...

For a moment he went down into a blind abyss of submission; and then somehow the very sight of that obscenity in eyes that did not then realize they saw it, was dreadful enough to draw him out of the seductive darkness... the sight of her crawling and alive with unnamable horror.

She rose, and down about her in a cascade fell the squirming scarlet of—of what grew upon her head. It fell in a long, alive cloak to her bare feet on the floor, hiding her in a wave of dreadful, wet, writhing life. She put up her hands and like a swimmer she parted the waterfall of it, tossing the masses back over her shoulders to reveal her own brown body, sweetly curved. She smiled exquisitely, and in starting waves back from her forehead and down about her in a hideous background writhed the snaky wetness of her living tresses. And Smith knew that he looked upon Medusa.

The knowledge of that—the realization of vast backgrounds reaching into misted history—shook him out of his frozen horror for a moment, and in that moment he met her eyes again, smiling, green as glass in the moonlight, half hooded under drooping lids. Through the twisting scarlet she held out her arms. And there was something soul-shakingly desirable about her, so that all the blood surged to his head suddenly and he stumbled to his feet like a sleeper in a dream as she swayed toward him, infinitely graceful, infinitely sweet in her cloak of living horror.

And somehow there was beauty in it, the wet scarlet writhings with moonlight sliding and shining along the thick, worm-round tresses and losing itself in the masses only to glint again and move silvery along writhing tendrils—an awful, shuddering beauty more dreadful than any ugliness could be.

But all this, again, he but half realized, for the insidious murmur was coiling again through his brain, promising, caressing, alluring, sweeter than honey; and the green eyes that held his were clear and burning like the depths of a jewel, and behind the pulsing slits of darkness he was staring into a greater dark that held all things... He had known—dimly he had known when he first gazed into those flat animal shallows that behind them lay this—all beauty and terror, all horror and delight, in the infinite darkness upon which her eyes opened like windows, paned with emerald glass.

Her lips moved, and in a murmur that blended indistinguishably with the silence and the sway of her body and the dreadful sway of her—her hair—she whispered—very softly, very passionately, "I shall—speak to you now—in my own tongue—oh, beloved!"

And in her living cloak she swayed to him, the murmur swelling seductive and caressing in his innermost brain—promising, compelling, sweeter than sweet. His flesh crawled to the horror of her, but it was a perverted revulsion that clasped what it loathed. His arms slid round her under the sliding cloak, wet, wet and warm and hideously alive—and the sweet velvet body was clinging to his, her arms locked about his neck—and with a whisper and a rush the unspeakable horror closed about them both.

In nightmares until he died he remembered that moment when the living tresses of Shambleau first folded him in their embrace. A nauseous, smothering odor as the wetness shut around him—thick, pulsing worms clasping every inch of his body, sliding, writhing, their wetness and warmth striking through his garments as if he stood naked to their embrace.

All this in a graven instant—and after that a tangled flash of conflicting sensation before oblivion closed over him for he remembered the dream—and knew it for nightmare reality now, and the sliding, gently moving caresses of those wet, warm worms upon his flesh was an ecstasy above words—that deeper ecstasy that strikes beyond the body and beyond the mind and tickles the very roots of soul with unnatural delight. So he stood, rigid as marble, as helplessly stony as any of Medusa's victims in ancient legends were, while the terrible pleasure of Shambleau thrilled and shuddered through every fiber of him; through every atom of his body and the intangible atoms of what men call the soul, through all that was Smith the dreadful pleasure ran. And it was truly dreadful. Dimly he knew it, even as his body answered to the root-deep ecstasy, a foul and dreadful wooing from which his very soul shuddered away—and yet in the innermost depths of that soul some grinning traitor shivered with delight. But deeply, behind all this, he knew horror and revulsion and despair beyond telling, while the intimate caresses crawled obscenely in the secret places of his soul—knew that the soul should not be handled—and shook with the perilous pleasure through it all.

And this conflict and knowledge, this mingling of rapture and revulsion all took place in the flashing of a moment while the scarlet worms coiled and crawled upon him, sending deep, obscene tremors of that infinite pleasure into every atom that made up

Smith. And he could not stir in that slimy, ecstatic embrace—and a weakness was flooding that grew deeper after each succeeding wave of intense delight, and the traitor in his soul strengthened and drowned out the revulsion—and something within him ceased to struggle as he sank wholly into a blazing darkness that was oblivion to all else but that devouring rapture . . .

The young Venusian climbing the stairs to his friend's lodging-room pulled out his key absent-mindedly, a pucker forming between his fine brows. He was slim, as all Venusians are, as fair and sleek as any of them, and as with most of his countrymen the look of cherubic innocence on his face was wholly deceptive. He had the face of a fallen angel, without Lucifer's majesty to redeem it; for a black devil grinned in his eyes and there were faint lines of ruth-lessness and dissipation about his mouth to tell of the long years behind him that had run the gamut of experiences and made his name, next to Smith's, the most hated and the most respected in the records of the Patrol.

He mounted the stairs now with a puzzled frown between his eyes. He had come into Lakkdarol on the noon liner—the *Maid* in her hold very skillfully disguised with paint and otherwise—to find in lamentable disorder the affairs he had expected to be settled. And cautious inquiry elicited the information that Smith had not been seen for three days. That was not like his friend—he had never failed before, and the two stood to lose not only a large sum of money but also their personal safety by the inexplicable lapse on the part of Smith. Yarol could think of one solution only: fate had at last caught up with his friend. Nothing but physical disability could explain it.

Still puzzling, he fitted his key in the lock and swung the door open.

In that first moment, as the door opened, he sensed something very wrong . . . The room was darkened, and for a while he could see nothing, but at the first breath he scented a strange, unnamable odor, half sickening, half sweet. And deep stirrings of ancestral memory awoke within him—ancient swamp-born memories from Venusian ancestors far away and long ago . . .

Yarol laid his hand on his gun, lightly, and opened the door wider. In the dimness all he could see at first was a curious mound in the far corner . . . Then his eyes grew accustomed to the dark, and he saw it more clearly, a mound that somehow heaved and stirred within itself . . . A mound of—he caught his breath sharply—a mound like a mass of entrails, living, moving, writhing with an unspeakable aliveness. Then a hot Venusian oath broke from his lips and he cleared the door-sill in a swift stride, slammed the door and set his back against it, gun ready in his hand, although his flesh crawled—for he *knew* . . .

"Smith!" he said softly, in a voice thick with horror.

The moving mass stirred—shuddered—sank back into crawling quiescence again.

"Smith! Smith!" The Venusian's voice was gentle and insistent, and it quivered a little with terror.

An impatient ripple went over the whole mass of aliveness in the corner. It stirred again, reluctantly, and then tendril by writhing tendril it began to part itself and fall aside, and very slowly the brown of a spaceman's leather appeared beneath it, all slimed and shining.

"Smith! Northwest!" Yarol's persistent whisper came again, urgently, and with a dream-like slowness the leather garments moved . . . a man sat up in the midst of the writhing worms, a man who once, long ago, might have been Northwest Smith. From head to foot he was slimy from the embrace of the crawling horror about him. His face was that of some creature beyond humanity—dead-alive, fixed in a gray stare, and the look of terrible ecstasy that overspread it seemed to come from somewhere far within, a faint reflection from immeasurable distances beyond the flesh. And as there is mystery and magic in the moonlight which is after all but a reflection of the everyday sun, so in that gray face turned to the door was a terror unnamable and sweet, a reflection of ecstasy beyond the understanding of any who had known only earthly ecstasy themselves. And as he sat there turning a blank, eyeless face to Yarol the red worms writhed ceaselessly about him, very gently, with a soft, caressive motion that never slacked.

"Smith . . . come here! Smith . . . get up . . . Smith, Smith!" Yarol's whisper hissed in the silence, commanding, urgent—but he made no move to leave the door.

And with a dreadful slowness, like a dead man rising, Smith stood up in the nest of slimy scarlet. He swayed drunkenly on his feet, and two or three crimson tendrils came writhing up his legs to the knees and wound themselves there, supportingly, moving with a ceaseless caress that seemed to give him some hidden strength, for he said then, without inflection.

"Go away. Go away. Leave me alone." And the dead ecstatic face never changed.

"Smith!" Yarol's voice was desperate. "Smith, listen! Smith, can't you hear me?"

"Go away," the monotonous voice said. "Go away. Go away. Go—"

"Not unless you come too. Can't you hear? Smith! Smith! I'll—"

He hushed in mid-phrase, and once more the ancestral prickle of race-memory shivered down his back, for the scarlet mass was moving again, violently, rising . . .

Yarol pressed back against the door and gripped his gun, and the name of a god he had forgotten years ago rose to his lips unbidden. For he knew what was coming next, and the knowledge was more dreadful than any ignorance could have been.

The red, writhing mass rose higher, and the tendrils parted and a human face looked out—no, half human, with green cat-eyes that shone in that dimness like lighted jewels, compellingly . . .

Yarol breathed "Shar!" again, and flung up an arm across his face, and the tingle of meeting that green gaze for even an instant went thrilling through him perilously.

"Smith!" he called in despair. "Smith, can't you hear me?"

"Go away," said that voice that was not Smith's. "Go away."

And somehow, although he dared not look, Yarol knew that the—the other—had parted those worm-thick tresses and stood there in all the human sweetness of the brown, curved woman's body, cloaked in living horror. And he felt the eyes upon him, and something was crying insistently in his brain to lower that shielding arm . . . He was lost—he knew it, and the knowledge gave him that courage which comes from despair. The voice in his brain was growing, swelling, deafening him with a roaring command that all but swept him before it—command to lower that arm—to meet the eyes that opened upon darkness—to submit—and a promise, murmurous and sweet and evil beyond words, of pleasure to come . . .

But somehow he kept his head—somehow, dizzily, he was gripping his gun in his upflung hand—somehow, incredibly, crossing the narrow room with averted face, groping for Smith's shoulder. There was a moment of blind fumbling in emptiness, and then he found it, and gripped the leather that was slimy and dreadful and wet—and simultaneously he felt something loop gently about his ankle and a shock of repulsive pleasure went through him, and then another coil, and another, wound about his feet . . .

Yarol set his teeth and gripped the shoulder hard, and his hand shuddered of itself, for the feel of that leather was slimy as the worms about his ankles, and a faint tingle of obscene delight went through him from the contact.

That caressive pressure on his legs was all he could feel, and the voice in his brain drowned out all other sounds, and his body obeyed him reluctantly—but somehow he gave one heave of tremendous effort and swung Smith, stumbling, out of that nest of horror. The twining tendrils ripped loose with a little sucking sound, and the whole mass quivered and reached after, and then Yarol forgot his friend utterly and turned his whole being to the hopeless task of freeing himself. For only a part of him was fighting, now—only a part of him struggled against the twining obscenities, and in his innermost brain the sweet, seductive murmur sounded, and his body clamored to surrender . . .

"*Shar! Shar y'danis . . . Shar mor'la-rol—*" prayed Yarol, gasping and half unconscious that he spoke, boy's prayers that he had forgotten years ago, and with his back half turned to the central mass he kicked desperately with his heavy boots at the red, writhing worms about him. They gave back before him, quivering and curling themselves out of reach, and though he knew that more were reaching for his throat from behind, at least he could go on struggling until he was forced to meet those eyes . . .

He stamped and kicked and stamped again, and for one instant he was free of the slimy grip as the bruised worms curled back from his heavy feet, and he lurched away dizzily, sick with revulsion and despair as he fought off the coils, and then he lifted his eyes and saw the cracked mirror on the wall. Dimly in its reflection he could see the writhing scarlet horror behind him, cat face peering out with its demure girl-smile, dreadfully human, and all the red tendrils reaching after him. And remembrance of something he had read long ago swept incongruously over him, and the gasp of relief and hope that he gave shook for a moment the grip of the command in his brain.

Without pausing for a breath he swung the gun over his shoulder, the reflected barrel in line with the reflected horror in the mirror, and flicked the catch.

In the mirror he saw its blue flame leap in a dazzling spate across the dimness, full into the midst of that squirming, reaching mass behind him. There was a hiss and a blaze and a high, thin scream of inhuman malice and despair—the flame cut a wide arc and went out as the gun fell from his hand, and Yarol pitched forward to the floor.

☙   ☙   ☙

Northwest Smith opened his eyes to Martian sunlight streaming thinly through the dingy window. Something wet and cold was slapping his face, and the familiar fiery sting of *segir*-whiskey burnt his throat.

"Smith!" Yarol's voice was saying from far away. "N.W.! Wake up, damn you! Wake up!"

"I'm—awake," Smith managed to articulate thickly. "Wha's matter?"

Then a cup-rim was thrust against his teeth and Yarol said irritably, "Drink it, you fool!"

Smith swallowed obediently and more of the fire-hot *segir* flowed down his grateful throat. It spread a warmth through his body that awakened him from the numbness that had gripped him until now, and helped a little toward driving out the all-devouring weakness he was becoming aware of slowly. He lay still for a few minutes while the warmth of the whisky went through him, and memory sluggishly began to permeate his brain with the spread of the *segir*. Nightmare memories . . . sweet and terrible . . . memories of—

"God!" gasped Smith suddenly, and tried to sit up. Weakness smote him like a blow, and for an instant the room wheeled as he fell back against something firm and warm—Yarol's shoulder. The Venusian's arm supported him while the room steadied, and after a while he twisted a little and stared into the other's black gaze.

Yarol was holding him with one arm and finishing the mug of *segir* himself, and the black eyes met his over the rim and crinkled into sudden laughter, half hysterical after that terror that was passed.

"By *Pharol*!" gasped Yarol, choking into his mug. "By *Pharol*, N.W.! I'm never gonna let you forget this! Next time you have to drag me out of a mess I'll say—"

"Let it go," said Smith. "What's been going on? How—"

"Shambleau," Yarol's laughter died. "Shambleau! What were you doing with a thing like that?"

"What was it?" Smith asked soberly.

"Mean to say you didn't know? But where'd you find it? How—"

"Suppose you tell me first what you know," said Smith firmly. "And another swig of that *segir*, too. I need it."

"Can you hold the mug now? Feel better?"

"Yeah—some. I can hold it—thanks. Now go on."

"Well—I don't know just where to start. They call them Shambleau—"

"Good God, is there more than one?"

"It's a—a sort of race, I think, one of the very oldest. Where they come from nobody knows. The name sounds a little French, doesn't it? But it goes back beyond the start of history. There have always been Shambleau."

"I never heard of 'em."

"Not many people have. And those who know don't care to talk about it much."

"Well, half this town knows. I hadn't any idea what they were talking about, then. And I still don't understand—"

"Yes, it happens like this, sometimes. They'll appear, and the news will spread and the town will get together and hunt them down, and after that—well, the story doesn't get around very far. It's too—too unbelievable."

"But—my God, Yarol!—what was it? Where'd it come from? How—"

"Nobody knows just where they come from. Another planet—maybe some undiscovered one. Some say Venus—I know there are some rather awful legends of them handed down in our family—that's how I've heard about it. And the minute I opened that door, awhile back—I—I think I knew that smell . . ."

"But—what *are* they?"

"God knows. Not human, though they have the human form. Or that may be only an illusion . . . or maybe I'm crazy. I don't know. They're a species of the vampire—or maybe the vampire is a species of—of them. Their normal form must be that—that mass, and in that form they draw nourishment from the—I suppose the life-forces of men. And they take some form—usually a woman form, I think, and key you up to the highest pitch of emotion before they—begin. That's to work the life-force up to intensity so it'll be easier . . . And they give, always, that horrible, foul pleasure as they—feed. There are some men who, if they survive the first experience, take to it like a drug—can't give it up—keep the thing with them all their lives—which isn't long—feeding it for that ghastly satisfaction. Worse than smoking *ming* or—or 'praying to *Pharol*.'"

"Yes," said Smith. "I'm beginning to understand why that crowd was so surprised and—and disgusted when I said—well, never mind. Go on."

"Did you get to talk to—to it?" asked Yarol.

"I tried to. It couldn't speak very well. I asked it where it came from and it said—'from far away and long ago'—something like that."

"I wonder. Possibly some unknown planet—but I think not. You know there are so many wild stories with some basis of fact to start from, that I've sometimes wondered—mightn't there be a lot more of even worse and wilder superstitions we've never even heard of? Things like this, blasphemous and foul, that those who know have to keep still about? Awful, fantastic things running around loose that we never hear rumors of at all!

"These things—they've been in existence for countless ages. No one knows when or where they first appeared. Those who've seen them, as we saw this one, don't talk about it. It's just one of those vague, misty rumors you find half hinted at in old books sometimes . . . I believe they are an older race than man, spawned from ancient seed in times before ours, perhaps on planets that have gone to dust, and so horrible to man that when they are discovered the discoverers keep still about it—forget them again as quickly as they can.

"And they go back to time immemorial. I suppose you recognized the legend of Medusa? There isn't any question that the ancient Greeks knew of them. Does it mean that there have been civilizations before yours that set out from Earth and explored other planets? Or did one of the Shambleau somehow make its way into Greece three thousand years ago? If you think about it long enough you'll go off your head! I wonder how many other legends are based on things like this—things we don't suspect, things we'll never know.

"The Gorgon, Medusa, a beautiful woman with—with snakes for hair, and a gaze that turned men to stone, and Perseus finally killed her—I remembered this just by accident, N.W., and it saved your life and mine—Perseus killed her by using a mirror as he fought to reflect what he dared not look at directly. I wonder what the old Greek who first started that legend would have thought if he'd known that three thousand years later his story would save the lives of two men on another planet. I wonder what that Greek's own story was, and how he met the thing, and what happened . . .

"Well, there's a lot we'll never know. Wouldn't the records of that race of—of *things*, whatever they are, be worth reading! Records of other planets and other ages and all the beginnings of mankind! But I don't suppose they've kept any records. I don't suppose they've even any place to keep them—from what little I know, or anyone knows about it, they're like the Wandering Jew, just bobbing up here and there at long intervals, and where they stay in the meantime I'd give my eyes to know! But I don't believe that terribly hypnotic power they have indicates any superhuman intelligence. It's their means of getting food—just like a frog's long tongue or a carnivorous flower's odor. Those are physical because the frog and the flower eat physical food. The Shambleau uses a—a mental reach to get mental food. I don't quite know how to put it. And just as a beast that eats the bodies of other animals acquires with each meal greater power over the bodies of the rest, so the Shambleau, stoking itself up with the life-forces of men, increases its power over the minds and souls of other men. But I'm talking about things I can't define—things I'm not sure exist.

"I only know that when I felt—when those tentacles closed around my legs—I didn't want to pull loose, I felt sensations that—that—oh, I'm fouled and filthy to the very deepest part of me by that—pleasure—and yet—"

"I know," said Smith slowly. The effect of the *segir* was beginning to wear off, and weakness was washing back over him in waves, and when he spoke he was half meditating in a lower voice, scarcely realizing that Yarol listened. "I know it—much better than you do—and there's something so indescribably awful that the thing emanates, something so utterly at odds with everything human—there aren't any words to say it. For a while I was a part of it, literally, sharing its thoughts and memories and emotions and hungers, and—well, it's over now and I don't remember very clearly, but the only part left free was that part of me that was all but insane from the—the obscenity of the thing. And yet it was a pleasure so sweet—I think there must be some nucleus of utter evil in me—in everyone—that needs only the proper stimulus to get complete control; because even while I was sick all through from the touch of those—things—there was something in me that was—was simply gibbering with delight . . . Because of that I saw things—and knew things—horrible, wild things I can't quite remember—visited unbelievable places, looked backward through the memory of that—creature—I was one with, and saw—God, I wish I could remember!"

"You ought to thank your God you can't," said Yarol soberly.

His voice roused Smith from the half-trance he had fallen into, and he rose on his elbow, swaying a little from weakness. The room was wavering before him, and he closed his eyes, not to see it, but he asked, "You say they—they don't turn up again? No way of finding—another?"

Yarol did not answer for a moment. He laid his hands on the other man's shoulders and pressed him back, and then sat staring down into the dark, ravaged face with a new, strange, undefinable look upon it that he had never seen there before—whose meaning he knew, too well.

"Smith," he said finally, and his black eyes for once were steady and serious, and the little grinning devil had vanished from behind them, "Smith, I've never asked your word on anything before, but I've—I've earned the right to do it now, and I'm asking you to promise me one thing."

Smith's colorless eyes met the black gaze unsteadily. Irresolution was in them, and a little fear of what that promise might be. And for just a moment Yarol was looking, not into his friend's familiar eyes, but into a wide gray blankness that held all horror and delight—a pale sea with unspeakable pleasures sunk beneath it. Then the wide stare focused again and Smith's eyes met his squarely and Smith's voice said, "Go ahead. I'll promise."

"That if you ever should meet a Shambleau again—ever, anywhere—you'll draw your gun and burn it to hell the instant you realize what it is. Will you promise me that?"

There was a long silence. Yarol's somber black eyes bored relentlessly into the colorless ones of Smith, not wavering. And the veins stood out on Smith's tanned forehead. He never broke his word—he had given it perhaps half a dozen times in his life, but once he had given it, he was incapable of breaking it. And once more the gray seas flooded in a dim tide of memories, sweet and horrible beyond dreams. Once more Yarol was staring into blankness that hid nameless things. The room was very still.

The gray tide ebbed. Smith's eyes, pale and resolute as steel, met Yarol's levelly.

"I'll—try," he said. And his voice wavered.

Turning Point

by Poul Anderson

PREFACE BY ERIC FLINT

Poul Anderson had a career that lasted as long as Robert Heinlein's, and overlapped it a great deal, allowing for a ten-year difference when they got started. The parallels are rather striking:

Heinlein's first story was published in 1939, Anderson's in 1948. ("Life-Line" and "Genius," respectively.) Within a very short time, especially by the standards of the day, they were both published novelists. Heinlein's first novels, *Methusaleh's Children* and *Beyond This Horizon*, came out in 1941 and 1942—although the first, initially, only as a magazine serial. Anderson's first novels, *Vault of the Ages* and *Brain Wave,* came out just as quickly in his career—1952 and 1954.

Their careers continued to parallel each other. Both men worked just as easily in short form and long form, publishing novels and short fiction constantly in the decades that followed. By the time they died, they'd each produced a massive body of work. Both of them also created their own vast future histories, in which a multitude of stories and novels fit like tiles in a mozaic. In the case of Heinlein, his famous "Future History"; in the case of Anderson, the "Technic History," which encompassed his many Nicholas Van Rijn and Dominic Flandry stories.

Robert Heinlein died in 1988, after an immensely successful career that lasted half a century. He was still writing until the end—his last novel, *To Sail Beyond the Sunset,* came out in

1987. Poul Anderson died in 2001, after an immensely successful career that lasted half a century. He was still writing until the end—his last two original novels, *Genesis* and *Mother of Kings,* came out in 2000 and 2001.

Both men won a multitude of awards:

Both received the Science Fiction and Fantasy Writers of America's Grand Master Award: Heinlein in 1975, the first year the award was given; Anderson in 1998. Both are in the Science Fiction Hall of Fame. Robert Heinlein won a Hugo award four times; Anderson, seven times. Heinlein never won a Nebula award, although he was nominated four times; Anderson did win an award, three times.

And yet . . .

Somehow people never look at them quite the same way. For all the great respect that Anderson had all his life, and continues to have since his death, he never occupied the central stature than Heinlein did. No one ever thought of Anderson as "the dean of science fiction."

Why? Well, I can only give you my opinion. Anderson was one of those very rare people who do what they do supremely well, and do so in every aspect of their craft. But they never do any *one* thing better than anyone else. To give an example, Anderson wrote many fine novels, to be sure. None of them ever had the impact of Heinlein's *Starship Troopers* or *Stranger in a Strange Land.*

Since I was a teenager, though, I've always had a clear picture in my head of where Poul Anderson fits in my own pantheon of great science fiction writers.

He's my Joe DiMaggio, who never did anything in baseball better than anyone else, but always did everything superbly well.

And here he is again, coming to the plate . . .

"Please, mister, could I have a cracker for my oontatherium?"

Not exactly the words you would expect at an instant when history changes course and the universe can never again be what it was. *The die is cast; In this sign conquer; It is not fit that you should sit here any longer; We hold these truths to be self-evident; The Italian navigator has landed in the New World; Dear God, the thing works!*—no man with any imagination can recall those, or others like them, and not have a coldness run along his spine.

But as for what little Mierna first said to us, on that island half a thousand light-years from home . . .

The star is catalogued AGC 4256836, a K$_2$ dwarf in Cassiopeia. Our ship was making a standard preliminary survey of that region, and had come upon mystery enough—how easily Earthsiders forget that every planet is a complete world!—but nothing extraordinary in this fantastic cosmos. The Traders had noted places that seemed worth further investigation; so had the Federals; the lists were not quite identical.

After a year, vessel and men were equally jaded. We needed a set-down, to spend a few weeks refitting and recuperating before the long swing homeward. There is an art to finding such a spot. You visit whatever nearby suns look suitable. If you come on a planet whose gross physical characteristics are terrestroid, you check the biological details—very, very carefully, but since the operation is largely automated it goes pretty fast—and make contact with the autochthones, if any. Primitives are preferred. That's not because of military danger, as some think. The Federals insist that the natives have no objection to strangers camping on their land, while the Traders don't see how anyone, civilized or not, that hasn't discovered atomic energy can be a menace. It's only that primitives are less apt to ask complicated questions and otherwise make a nuisance of themselves. Spacemen rejoice that worlds with machine civilizations are rare.

Well, Joril looked ideal. The second planet of that sun, with more water than Earth, it offered a mild climate everywhere. The biochemistry was so like our own that we could eat native foods, and there didn't seem to be any germs that UX-$_2$ couldn't handle. Seas, forests, meadows made us feel right at home, yet the countless differences from Earth lent a fairyland glamour. The indigenes were savages, that is, they depended on hunting, fishing, and gathering for their whole food supply. So we assumed there were thousands of little cultures and picked the one that appeared most advanced: not that aerial observation indicated much difference.

Those people lived in neat, exquisitely decorated villages along the western seaboard of the largest continent, with woods and hills behind them. Contact went smoothly. Our semanticians had a good deal of trouble with the language, but the villagers started picking up English right away. Their hospitality was lavish whenever we called on them, but they stayed out of our camp except for the conducted tours we gave and other such invitations. With one vast, happy sigh, we settled down.

But from the first there were certain disturbing symptoms. Granted they had humanlike throats and palates, we hadn't expected the autochthones to speak flawless English within a couple of weeks. Every one of them. Obviously they could have learned still faster if we'd taught them systematically. We followed the usual practice and christened the planet "Joril" after what we thought was the local word for "earth"—and then found that "Joril" meant "Earth," capitalized, and the people had an excellent heliocentric astronomy. Though they were too polite to press themselves on us, they weren't merely accepting us as something inexplicable; curiosity was afire in them, and given half a chance they *did* ask the most complicated questions.

Once the initial rush of establishing ourselves was over and we had time to think, it became plain that we'd stumbled on something worth much further study. First we needed to check on some other areas and make sure this Dannicar culture wasn't a freak. After all, the Neolithic Mayas had been good astronomers; the ferro-agricultural Greeks had developed a high and sophisticated philosophy. Looking over the maps we'd made from orbit, Captain Barlow chose a large island about 700 kilometers due west. A gravboat was outfitted and five men went aboard.

Pilot: Jacques Lejeune. Engineer: me. Federal militechnic representative: Commander Ernest Baldinger, Space Force of the Solar Peace Authority. Federal civil government representative: Walter Vaughan. Trader agent: Don Haraszthy. He and Vaughan were the principals, but the rest of us were skilled in the multiple jobs of planetography. You have to be, on a foreign world months from home or help.

We made the aerial crossing soon after sunrise, so we'd have a full eighteen hours of daylight. I remember how beautiful the ocean looked below us, like one great bowl of metal, silver where the sun struck, cobalt and green copper beyond. Then the island came over the world's edge, darkly forested, crimson-splashed by stands of gigantic red blossoms. Lejeune picked out an open spot in the woods, about two kilometers from a village that stood on a wide bay, and landed us with a whoop and a holler. He's a fireball pilot.

"Well—" Haraszthy rose to his sheer two meters and stretched till his joints cracked. He was burly to match that height, and his hook-nosed face carried the marks of old battles. Most Traders are tough, pragmatic extroverts; they have to be, just as Federal civils have to be the opposite. It makes for conflict, though. "Let's hike."

"Not so fast," Vaughan said: a thin young man with an intense gaze. "That tribe has never seen or heard of our kind. If they noticed us land, they may be in a panic."

"So we go jolly them out of it," Haraszthy shrugged.

"Our whole party? Are you serious?" Commander Baldinger asked. He reflected a bit. "Yes, I suppose you are. But I'm responsible now. Lejeune and Cathcart, stand by here. We others will proceed to the village."

"Just like that?" Vaughan protested.

"You know a better way?" Haraszthy answered.

"As a matter of fact—" But nobody listened. The government operates on some elaborate theories, and Vaughan was still too new in Survey to understand how often theory has to give way. We were impatient to go outside, and I regretted not being sent along to town. Of course, someone had to stay, ready to pull out our emissaries if serious trouble developed.

We emerged into long grass and a breeze that smelled of nothing so much as cinnamon. Trees rustled overhead, against a deep blue sky; the reddish sunlight spilled across purple wildflowers and bronze-colored insect wings. I drew a savoring breath before going around with Lejeune to make sure our landing gear was properly set. We were all lightly clad; Baldinger carried a blast rifle and Haraszthy a radiocom big enough to contact Dannicar, but both seemed ludicrously inappropriate.

"I envy the Jorillians," I remarked.

"In a way," Lejeune said. "Though perhaps their environment is too good. What stimulus have they to advance further?"

"Why should they want to?"

"They don't, consciously, my old. But every intelligent race is descended from animals that once had a hard struggle to survive, so hard they were forced to evolve brains. There is an instinct for adventure, even in the gentlest herbivorous beings, and sooner or later it must find expression—"

"*Holy jumping Judas!*"

Haraszthy's yell brought Lejeune and me bounding back to that side of the ship. For a moment my reason wobbled. Then I decided the sight wasn't really so strange . . . here.

A girl was emerging from the woods. She was about the equivalent of a Terrestrial five-year-old, I estimated. Less than a meter tall (the Jorillians average more short and slender than we), she had the big head of her species to make her look still more elfin. Long blondish hair, round ears, delicate features that were quite

humanoid except for the high forehead and huge violet eyes added
to the charm. Her brown-skinned body was clad only in a white
loincloth. One four-fingered hand waved cheerily at us. The other
carried a leash. And at the opposite end of that leash was a grasshopper the size of a hippopotamus.

No, not a grasshopper, I saw as she danced toward us. The head
looked similar, but the four walking legs were short and stout,
the several others mere boneless appendages. The gaudy hide was
skin, not chitin. I saw that the creature breathed with lungs, too.
Nonetheless it was a startling monster; and it drooled.

"Insular genus," Vaughan said. "Undoubtedly harmless, or she
wouldn't— But a child, coming so casually—!"

Baldinger grinned and lowered his rifle. "What the hell," he said,
"to a kid everything's equally wonderful. This is a break for our
side. She'll give us a good recommendation to her elders."

The little girl (damn it, I will call her that) walked to within a
meter of Haraszthy, turned those big eyes up and up till they met
his piratical face, and trilled with an irresistible smile:

"Please, mister, could I have a cracker for my oontatherium?"

I don't quite remember the next few minutes. They were confused. Eventually we found ourselves, the whole five, walking down
a sun-speckled woodland path. The girl skipped beside us, chattering
like a xylophone. The monster lumbered behind, chewing messily
on what we had given it. When the light struck those compound
eyes I thought of a jewel chest.

"My name is Mierna," the girl said, "and my father makes things
out of wood, I don't know what that's called in English, please tell
me, oh, carpentry, thank you, you're a nice man. My father thinks
a lot. My mother makes songs. They are very pretty songs. She sent
me out to get some sweet grass for a borning couch, because her
assistant wife is going to born a baby soon, but when I saw you come
down just the way Pengwil told, I knew I should say hello instead
and take you to Taori. That's our village. We have *twenty-five houses*.
And sheds and a Thinking Hall that's bigger than the one in Riru.
Pengwil said crackers are awful tasty. Could I have one too?"

Haraszthy obliged in a numb fashion. Vaughan shook himself
and fairly snapped, "How do you know our language?"

"Why, everybody does in Taori. Since Pengwil came and taught
us. That was three days ago. We've been hoping and hoping you
would come. They'll be so jealous in Riru! But we'll let them visit
if they ask us nicely."

"Pengwil . . . a Dannicarian name, all right," Baldinger muttered. "But they never heard of this island till I showed them our map. And they couldn't cross the ocean in those dugouts of theirs! It's against the prevailing winds, and square sails—"

"Oh, Pengwil's boat can sail right into the wind," Mierna laughed. "I saw him myself, he took everybody for rides, and now my father's making a boat like that too, only better."

"Why did Pengwil come here?" Vaughan asked.

"To see what there was. He's from a place called Folat. They have such funny names in Dannicar, and they dress funny too, don't they, mister?"

"Folat . . . yes, I remember, a community a ways north of our camp," Baldinger said.

"But savages don't strike off into an unknown ocean for, for curiosity," I stammered.

"These do," Haraszthy grunted. I could almost see the relays clicking in his blocky head. There were tremendous commercial possibilities here, foods and textiles and especially the dazzling artwork. In exchange—

"No!" Vaughan exclaimed. "I know what you're thinking, Trader Haraszthy, and you are not going to bring machines here."

The big man bridled. "Says who?"

"Says me, by virtue of the authority vested in me. And I'm sure the Council will confirm my decision." In that soft air Vaughan was sweating. "We don't dare!"

"What's a Council?" Mierna asked. A shade of trouble crossed her face. She edged close to the bulk of her animal.

In spite of everything, I had to pat her head and murmur, "Nothing you need worry about, sweetheart." To get her mind, and my own, off vague fears: "Why do you call this fellow an oontatherium? That can't be his real name."

"Oh, no." She forgot her worries at once. "He's a *yao* and his real name is, well, it means Big-Feet-Buggy-Eyes-Top-Man-Underneath-And-Over. That's what I named him. He's mine and he's lovely." She tugged at an antenna. The monster actually purred. "But Pengwil told us about something called an *oont* you have at your home, that's hairy and scary and carries things and drools like a *yao*, so I thought that would be a nice English name. Isn't it?"

"Very," I said weakly.

"What is this *oont* business?" Vaughan demanded.

Haraszthy ran a hand through his hair. "Well," he said, "you know I like Kipling, and I read some of his poems to some natives one night at a party. The one about the *oont*, the camel, yeah, I guess that must have been among 'em. They sure enjoyed Kipling."

"And had the poem letter-perfect after one hearing, and passed it unchanged up and down the coast, and now it's crossed the sea and taken hold," Vaughan choked.

"Who explained that *therium* is a root meaning 'mammal'?" I asked. Nobody knew, but doubtless one of our naturalists had casually mentioned it. So five-year-old Mierna had gotten the term from a wandering sailor and applied it with absolute correctness: never mind feelers and insectoidal eyes, the *yao* was a true mammal.

After a while we emerged in a cleared strip fronting on the bay. Against its glitter stood the village, peak-roofed houses of wood and thatch, a different style from Dannicar's but every bit as pleasant and well-kept. Outrigger canoes were drawn up on the beach, where fishnets hung to dry. Anchored some way beyond was another boat. The curved, gaily painted hull, twin steering oars, mat sails and leather tackle were like nothing on our poor overmechanized Earth; but she was sloop-rigged, and evidently a deep keel made it impossible to run her ashore.

"I thought so," Baldinger said in an uneven voice. "Pengwil went ahead and invented tacking. That's an efficient design. He could cross the water in a week or less."

"He invented navigation too," Lejeune pointed out.

The villagers, who had not seen us descend, now dropped their occupations—cooking, cleaning, weaving, potting, the numberless jobs of the primitive—to come on the run. All were dressed as simply as Mierna. Despite large heads, which were not grotesquely big, odd hands and ears, slightly different body proportions, the women were good to look on: too good, after a year's celibacy. The beardless, long-haired men were likewise handsome, and both sexes were graceful as cats.

They didn't shout or crowd. Only one exuberant horn sounded, down on the beach. Mierna ran to a grizzled male, seized him by the hand, and tugged him forward. "This is my father," she crowed. "Isn't he wonderful? And he thinks a lot. The name he's using right now, that's Sarato. I liked his last name better."

"One wearies of the same word," Sarato laughed. "Welcome, Earthfolk. You do us great ... *lula* ... pardon, I lack the term. You raise us high by this visit." His handshake—Pengwil must have told him about that custom—was hard, and his eyes met ours respectfully but unawed.

The Dannicarian communities turned what little government

they needed over to specialists, chosen on the basis of some tests we hadn't yet comprehended. But these people didn't seem to draw even that much class distinction. We were introduced to everybody by occupation: hunter, fisher, musician, prophet (I think that is what *nonalo* means), and so on. There was the same absence of taboo here as we had noticed in Dannicar, but an equally elaborate code of manners—which they realized we could not be expected to observe.

Pengwil, a strongly built youth in the tunic of his own culture, greeted us. It was no coincidence that he'd arrived at the same spot as we. Taori lay almost exactly west of his home area, and had the best anchorage on these shores. He was bursting with desire to show off his boat. I obliged him, swimming out and climbing aboard. "A fine job," I said with entire honesty. "I have a suggestion, though. For sailing along coasts, you don't need a fixed keel." I described a centerboard. "Then you can ground her."

"Yes, Sarato thought of that after he had seen my work. He has started one of such pattern already. He wants to do away with the steering oars also, and have a flat piece of wood turn at the back end. Is that right?"

"Yes," I said after a strangled moment.

"It seemed so to me." Pengwil smiled. "The push of water can be split in two parts like the push of air. Your Mister Ishihara told me about splitting and rejoining forces. That was what gave me the idea for a boat like this."

We swam back and put our clothes on again. The village was abustle, preparing a feast for us. Pengwil joined them. I stayed behind, walking the beach, too restless to sit. Staring out across the waters and breathing an ocean smell that was almost like Earth's, I thought strange thoughts. They were broken off by Mierna. She skipped toward me, dragging a small wagon.

"Hello, Mister Cathcart!" she cried. "I have to gather seaweed for flavor. Do you want to help me?"

"Sure," I said.

She made a face. "I'm glad to be here. Father and Kuaya and a lot of the others, they're asking Mister Lejeune about ma-the-*mat-ics*. I'm not old enough to like functions. I'd like to hear Mister Haraszthy tell about Earth, but he's talking alone in a house with his friends. Will you tell me about Earth? Can I go there someday?"

I mumbled something. She began to bundle leafy strands that had washed ashore. "I didn't used to like this job," she said. "I had to go back and forth so many times. They wouldn't let me use my oontatherium because he gets buckety when his feet are wet. I told them I could make him shoes, but they said no. Now it's fun anyway, with this, this, what do you call it?"

"A wagon. You haven't had such a thing before?"

"No, never, just drags with runners. Pengwil told us about wheels. He saw the Earthfolk use them. Carpenter Huanna started putting wheels on the drags right away. We only have a few so far."

I looked at the device, carved in wood and bone, a frieze of processional figures around the sides. The wheels weren't simply attached to axles. With permission, I took the cover off one and saw a ring of hard-shelled spherical nuts. As far as I knew, nobody had explained ball bearings to Pengwil.

"I've been thinking and thinking," Mierna said. "If we made a great big wagon, then an oontatherium could pull it, couldn't he? Only we have to have a good way for tying the oontatherium on, so he doesn't get hurt and you can guide him. I've thinked . . . thought of a real nice way." She stooped and drew lines in the sand. The harness ought to work.

With a full load, we went back among the houses. I lost myself in admiration of the carved pillars and panels. Sarato emerged from Lejeune's discussion of group theory (the natives had already developed that, so the talk was a mere comparison of approaches) to show me his obsidian-edged tools. He said the coast dwellers traded inland for the material, and spoke of getting steel from us. Or might we be so incredibly kind as to explain how metal was taken from the earth?

The banquet, music, dances, pantomimes, conversation, all was as gorgeous as expected, or more so. I trust the happy-pills we humans took kept us from making too grim an impression. But we disappointed our hosts by declining an offer to spend the night. They guided us back by torch-glow, singing the whole distance, on a twelve-tone scale with some of the damnedest harmony I have ever come across. Mierna was at the tail of the parade. She stood a long time in the coppery light of the single great moon, waving to us.

Baldinger set out glasses and a bottle of Irish. "Okay," he said. "Those pills have worn off by now, but we need an equivalent."

"Hoo, yes!" Haraszthy grabbed the bottle.

"I wonder what their wine will be like, when they invent that?" Lejeune mused.

"Be still!" Vaughan said. "They aren't going to."

We stared at him. He sat shivering with tension, under the cold fluoroluminance in that bleak little cabin.

"What the devil do you mean?" Haraszthy demanded at last. "If they can make wine half as well as they do everything else, it'll go for ten credits a liter on Earth."

"Don't you understand?" Vaughan cried. "We can't deal with them. We have to get off this planet and— Oh, God, why did we have to find the damned thing?" He groped for a glass.

"Well," I sighed, "we always knew, those of us who bothered to think about the question, that someday we were bound to meet a race like this. Man . . . what is man that Thou art mindful of him?"

"This is probably an older star than Sol," Baldinger nodded. "Less massive, so it stays longer on the main sequence."

"There needn't be much difference in planetary age," I said. "A million years, half a million, whatever the figure is, hell, that doesn't mean a thing in astronomy or geology. In the development of an intelligent race, though—"

"But they're *savages!*" Haraszthy protested.

"Most of the races we've found are," I reminded him. "Man was too, for most of his existence. Civilization is a freak. It doesn't come natural. Started on Earth, I'm told, because the Middle East dried out as the glaciers receded and something had to be done for a living when the game got scarce. And scientific, machine civilization, that's a still more unusual accident. Why should the Jorillians have gone beyond an Upper Paleolithic technology? They never needed to."

"Why do they have the brains they do, if they're in the stone age?" Haraszthy argued.

"Why did we, in our own stone age?" I countered. "It wasn't necessary for survival. Java man, Peking man, and the low-browed rest, they'd been doing all right. But evidently evolution, intraspecies competition, sexual selection . . . whatever increases intelligence in the first place continues to force it upward, if some new factor like machinery doesn't interfere. A bright Jorillian has more prestige, rises higher in life, gets more mates and children, and so it goes. But this is an easy environment, at least in the present geological epoch. The natives don't even seem to have wars, which would stimulate technology. Thus far they've had little occasion to use those tremendous minds for anything but art, philosophy, and social experimentation."

"What is their average IQ?" Lejeune whispered.

"Meaningless," Vaughan said dully. "Beyond 180 or so, the scale breaks down. How can you measure an intelligence so much greater than your own?"

There was a stillness. I heard the forest sough in the night around us.

"Yes," Baldinger ruminated, "I always realized that our betters must exist. Didn't expect we'd run into them in my own lifetime, however. Not in this microscopic sliver of the galaxy that we've explored. And . . . well, I always imagined the Elders having machines, science, space travel."

"They will," I said.

"If we go away—" Lejeune began.

"Too late," I said. "We've already given them this shiny new toy, science. If we abandon them, they'll come looking for us in a couple of hundred years. At most."

Haraszthy's fist crashed on the table. "Why leave?" he roared. "What the hell are you scared of? I doubt the population of this whole planet is ten million. There are fifteen billion humans in the Solar System and the colonies! So a Jorillian can outthink me. So what? Plenty of guys can do that already, and it don't bother me as long as we can do business."

Baldinger shook his head. His face might have been cast in iron. "Matters aren't that simple. The question is what race is going to dominate this arm of the galaxy."

"Is it so horrible if the Jorillians do?" Lejeune asked softly.

"Perhaps not. They seem pretty decent. But—" Baldinger straightened in his chair. "I'm not going to be anybody's domestic animal. I want my planet to decide her own destiny."

That was the unalterable fact. We sat weighing it for a long and wordless time.

The hypothetical superbeings had always seemed comfortably far off. We hadn't encountered them, or they us. Therefore they couldn't live anywhere near. Therefore they probably never would interfere in the affairs of this remote galactic fringe where we dwell. But a planet only months distant from Earth; a species whose average member was a genius and whose geniuses were not understandable by us: bursting from their world, swarming through space, vigorous, eager, jumping in a decade to accomplishments that would take us a century—if we ever succeeded—how could they help but destroy our painfully built civilization? We'd scrap it ourselves, as the primitives of our old days had scrapped their own rich cultures in the overwhelming face of Western society.

Our sons would laugh at our shoddy triumphs, go forth to join the high Jorillian adventure, and come back spirit-broken by failure, to build some feeble imitation of an alien way of life and fester in their hopelessness. And so would every other thinking species, unless the Jorillians were merciful enough to leave them alone.

Which the Jorillians probably would be. But who wants that kind of mercy?

I looked upon horror. Only Vaughan had the courage to voice the thing:

"There are planets under technological blockade, you know. Cultures too dangerous to allow modern weapons, let alone spaceships. Joril can be interdicted."

"They'll invent the stuff for themselves, now they've gotten the idea," Baldinger said.

Vaughan's mouth twitched downward. "Not if the only two regions that have seen us are destroyed."

"Good God!" Haraszthy leaped to his feet.

"Sit down!" Baldinger rapped.

Haraszthy spoke an obscenity. His face was ablaze. The rest of us sat in a chill sweat.

"You've called *me* unscrupulous," the Trader snarled. "Take that suggestion back to the hell it came from, Vaughan, or I'll kick our your brains."

I thought of nuclear fire vomiting skyward, and a wisp of gas that had been Mierna, and said, "No."

"The alternative," Vaughan said, staring at the bulkhead across from him, "is to do nothing until the sterilization of the entire planet has become necessary."

Lejeune shook his head in anguish. "Wrong, wrong, wrong. There can be too great a price for survival."

"But for our children's survival? Their liberty? Their pride and—"

"What sort of pride can they take in themselves, once they know the truth?" Haraszthy interrupted. He reached down, grabbed Vaughan's shirt front, and hauled the man up by sheer strength. His broken features glared three centimeters from the Federal's. "I'll tell you what we're going to do," he said. "We're going to trade, and teach, and xenologize, and fraternize, the same as with any other people whose salt we've eaten. And take our chances like men!"

"Let him go," Baldinger commanded. Haraszthy knotted a fist.

"If you strike him, I'll brig you and prefer charges at home. Let him go, I said!"

Haraszthy opened his grasp. Vaughan tumbled to the deck. Haraszthy sat down, buried his head in his hands, and struggled not to sob.

Baldinger refilled our glasses. "Well, gentlemen," he said, "it looks like an impasse. We're damned if we do and damned if we don't, and I lay odds no Jorillian talks in such tired clichés."

"They could give us so much," Lejeune pleaded.

"Give!" Vaughan climbed erect and stood trembling before us. "That's p-p-precisely the trouble. They'd give it! If they could, even. It wouldn't be ours. We probably couldn't understand their work, or use it, or ... It wouldn't be ours, I say!"

Haraszthy stiffened. He sat like stone for an entire minute before he raised his face and whooped aloud.

"*Why not?*"

Blessed be whiskey. I actually slept a few hours before dawn. But the light, stealing in through the ports, woke me then and I couldn't get back to sleep. At last I rose, took the drop-shaft down, and went outside.

The land lay still. Stars were paling, but the east held as yet only a rush of ruddiness. Through the cool air I heard the first bird-flutings from the dark forest mass around me. I kicked off my shoes and went barefoot in wet grass.

Somehow it was not surprising that Mierna should come at that moment, leading her oontatherium. She let go the leash and ran to me. "Hi, Mister Cathcart! I hoped a lot somebody would be up. I haven't had any breakfast."

"We'll have to see about that." I swung her in the air till she squealed. "And then maybe like a little flyaround in this boat. Would you like that?"

"Oooh!" Her eyes grew round. I set her down. She needed a while longer before she dared ask, "Clear to Earth?"

"No, not that far, I'm afraid. Earth is quite a ways off."

"Maybe someday? Please?"

"Someday, I'm quite sure, my dear. And not so terribly long until then, either."

"I'm going to Earth, I'm going to Earth, I'm going to Earth." She hugged the oontatherium. "Will you miss me awfully, Big-Feet-Buggy-Eyes-Top-Man-Underneath-And-Over? Don't drool so sad. Maybe you can come too. Can he, Mister Cathcart? He's a very nice oontatherium, honest he is, and he does so love crackers."

"Well, perhaps, perhaps not," I said. "But you'll go, if you wish. I promise you. Anybody on this whole planet who wants to will go to Earth."

As most of them will. I'm certain our idea will be accepted by the Council. The only possible one. If you can't lick 'em ... get 'em to jine you.

I rumpled Mierna's hair. *In a way, sweetheart, what a dirty trick to play on you! Take you straight from the wilderness to a huge and complicated civilization. Dazzle you with all the tricks and gadgets and ideas we have, not because we're better but simply because we've been at it a little longer than you. Scatter your ten million among our fifteen billion. Of course you'll fall for it. You can't help yourselves. When you realize what's happening, you won't be able to stop, you'll be hooked. I don't think you'll even be able to resent it.*

You'll be assimilated, Mierna. You'll become an Earth girl. Naturally, you'll grow up to be one of our leaders. You'll contribute tremendous things to our civilization, and be rewarded accordingly. But the whole point is, it will be our *civilization. Mine ... and yours.*

I wonder if you'll ever miss the forest, though, and the little houses by the bay, and the boats and songs and old, old stories, yes, and your darling oontatherium. I know the empty planet will miss you, Mierna. So will I.

"Come on," I said. "Let's go build us that breakfast."

Heavy Planet

by Lee Gregor

Ennis was completing his patrol of Sector EM, Division 426 of the Eastern Ocean. The weather had been unusually fine, the liquid-thick air roaring along in a continuous blast that propelled his craft with a rush as if it were flying, and lifting short, choppy waves that rose and fell with a startling suddenness. A short savage squall whirled about, pounding down on the ocean like a million hammers, flinging the little boat ahead madly.

Ennis tore at the controls, granite-hard muscles standing out in bas-relief over his short, immensely thick body, skin gleaming scalelike in the splashing spray. The heat from the sun that hung like a huge red lantern on the horizon was a tangible intensity, making an inferno of the gale.

The little craft, that Ennis maneuvered by sheer brawn, took a leap into the air and seemed to float for many seconds before burying its keel again in the sea. It often floated for long distances, the air was so dense. The boundary between air and water was sometimes scarcely defined at all—one merged into the other imperceptibly. The pressure did strange things.

Like a dust mote sparkling in a beam, a tiny speck of light above caught Ennis' eye. A glider, he thought, but he was puzzled. Why so far out here on the ocean? They were nasty things to handle in the violent wind.

The dust mote caught the light again. It was lower, tumbling down with a precipitancy that meant trouble. An upward blast

515

caught it, checked its fall. Then it floated down gently for a space until struck by another howling wind that seemed to distort its very outlines.

Ennis turned the prow of his boat to meet the path of the falling vessel. Curious, he thought; where were its wings? Were they retracted, or broken off? It ballooned closer, and it wasn't a glider. Far larger than any glider ever made, it was of a ridiculous shape that would not stand up for an instant. And with the sharp splash the body made as it struck the water—a splash that fell in almost the same instant it rose—a thought seemed to leap up in his mind. A thought that was more important than anything else on that planet; or was to him, at least. For if it was what he thought it was—and it had to be that—it was what Shadden had been desperately seeking for many years. What a stroke of inconceivable luck, falling from the sky before his very eyes!

The silvery shape rode the ragged waters lightly. Ennis' craft came up with a rush; he skillfully checked its speed and the two came together with a slight jar. The metal of the strange vessel dented as if it were made of rubber. Ennis stared. He put out an arm and felt the curved surface of the strange ship. His finger prodded right through the metal. What manner of people were they who made vessels of such weak materials?

He moored his little boat to the side of the larger one and climbed to an opening. The wall sagged under him. He knew he must be careful; it was frightfully weak. It would not hold together very long; he must work fast if it were to be saved. The atmospheric pressure would have flattened it out long ago, had it not been for the jagged rent above which had allowed the pressure to be equalized.

He reached the opening and lowered himself carefully into the interior of the vessel. The rent was too small; he enlarged it by taking the two edges in his hands and pulling them apart. As he went down he looked askance at the insignificant plates and beams that were like tissue paper on his world. Inside was wreckage. Nothing was left in its original shape. Crushed, mutilated machinery, shattered vacuum tubes, sagging members, all ruined by the gravity and the pressure.

There was a pulpy mess on the floor that he did not examine closely. It was like red jelly, thin and stalky, pulped under a gravity a hundred times stronger and an atmosphere ten thousand times heavier than that it had been made for.

He was in a room with many knobs and dials on the walls,

apparently a control room. A table in the center with a chart on it, the chart of a solar system. It had nine planets; his had but five.

Then he knew he was right. If they came from another system, what he wanted must be there. It could be nothing else.

He found a staircase, descended. Large machinery bulked there. There was no light, but he did not notice that. He could see well enough by infrared, and the amount of energy necessary to sustain his compact gianthood kept him constantly radiating.

Then he went through a door that was of a comfortable massiveness, even for his planet—and there it was. He recognized it at once. It was big, squat, strong. The metal was soft, but it was thick enough even to stand solidly under the enormous pull of this world. He had never seen anything quite like it. It was full of coils, magnets, and devices of shapes unknown to him. But Shadden would know. Shadden, and who knows how many other scientists before him, had tried to make something which would do what this could do, but they had all failed. And without the things this machine could perform, the race of men on Heavyplanet was doomed to stay down on the surface of the planet, chained there immovably by the crushing gravity.

It was atomic energy. That he had known as soon as he knew that the body was not a glider. For nothing else but atomic energy and the fierce winds was capable of lifting a body from the surface of Heavyplanet. Chemicals were impotent. There is no such thing as an explosion where the atmosphere pressed inward with more force than an explosion could press outward. Only atomic, of all the theoretically possible sources of energy, could supply the work necessary to lift a vessel away from the planet. Every other source of energy was simply too weak.

Yes, Shadden, all the scientists must see this. And quickly, because the forces of sea and storm would quickly tear the ship to shreds, and, even more vital, because the scientists of Bantin and Marak might obtain the secret if there was delay. And that would mean ruin—the loss of its age-old supremacy—for his nation. Bantin and Marak were war nations; did they obtain the secret they would use it against all the other worlds that abounded in the Universe.

The Universe was big. That was why Ennis was so sure there was atomic energy on this ship. For, even though it might have originated on a planet that was so tiny that *chemical energy*—although that was hard to visualize—would be sufficient to lift it out of the pull of gravity, to travel the distance that stretched between the stars only one thing would suffice.

He went back through the ship, trying to see what had happened.

There were pulps lying behind long tubes that pointed out through clever ports in the outer wall. He recognized them as weapons, worth looking into.

There must have been a battle. He visualized the scene. The forces that came from atomic energy must have warped even space in the vicinity. The ship pierced, the occupants killed, the controls wrecked, the vessel darting off at titanic speed, blindly into nothing. Finally it had come near enough to Heavyplanet to be enmeshed in its huge web of gravity.

Weeaao-o-ow! It was the wailing roar of his alarm siren, which brought him spinning around and dashing for his boat. Beyond, among the waves that leaped and fell so suddenly, he saw a long, low craft making way toward the derelict spaceship. He glimpsed a flash of color on the rounded, gray superstructure, and knew it for a battleship of Marak. Luck was going strong both ways; first good, now bad. He could easily have eluded the battleship in his own small craft, but he couldn't leave the derelict. Once lost to the enemy he could never regain it, and it was too valuable to lose.

The wind howled and buffeted about his head, and he strained his muscles to keep from being blasted away as he crouched there, half on his own boat and half on the derelict. The sun had set and the evening winds were beginning to blow. The hulk scudded before them, its prow denting from the resistance of the water it pushed aside.

He thought furiously fast. With a quick motion he flipped the switch of the radiophone and called Shadden. He waited with fierce impatience until the voice of Shadden was in his ear. At last he heard it, then: "Shadden! This is Ennis. Get your glider, Shadden, fly to a45j on my route! Quickly! It's come, Shadden! But I have no time. Come!"

He flipped the switch off, and pounded the valve out of the bottom of his craft, clutching at the side of the derelict. With a rush the ocean came up and flooded his little boat and in an instant it was gone, on its way down to the bottom. That would save him from being detected for a short time.

Back into the darkness of the spaceship. He didn't think he had been noticed climbing through the opening. Where could he hide? Should he hide? He couldn't defeat the entire battleship singlehanded, without weapons. There were no weapons that could be carried anyway. A beam of concentrated actinic light that ate away the eyes and the nervous system had to be powered by the entire output of a battleship's generators. Weapons for striking and cutting had never been developed on a world where flesh was tougher than metal. Ennis was skilled in personal combat, but how could he overcome all that would enter the derelict?

Down again, into the dark chamber where the huge atomic generator towered over his head. This time he looked for something he had missed before. He crawled around it, peering into its recesses. And then, some feet above, he saw the opening, and pulled himself up to it, carefully, not to destroy the precious thing with his mass. The opening was shielded with a heavy, darkly transparent substance through which seeped a dim glow from within. He was satisfied then. Somehow, matter was still being disintegrated in there, and energy could be drawn off if he knew how.

There were leads—wires of all sizes, and busbars, and thick, heavy tubes that bent under their own weight. Some must lead in and some must lead out; it was not good to tamper with them. He chose another track. Upstairs again, and to the places where he had seen the weapons.

They were all mounted on heavy, rigid swivels. He carefully detached the tubes from the bases. The first time he tried it he was not quite careful enough, and part of the projector itself was ripped away, but next time he knew what he was doing and it came away nicely. It was a large thing, nearly as thick as his arm and twice as long. Heavy leads trailed from its lower end and a lever projected from behind. He hoped it was in working condition. He dared not try it; all he could do was to trace the leads back and make sure they were intact.

He ran out of time. There came a thud from the side, and then smaller thuds, as the boarding party incautiously leaped over. Once there was a heavy sound, as someone went all the way through the side of the ship.

"Idiot!" Ennis muttered, and moved forward with his weapon toward the stairway. Noises came from overhead, and then a loud crash buckled the plates of the ceiling. Ennis leaped out of the way, but the entire section came down, with two men on it. The floor sagged, but held for the moment. Ennis, caught beneath the down-coming mass, beat his way free. He came up with a girder in his hand, which he bent over the head of one of the Maraks.

The man shook himself and struck out for Ennis, who took the blow rolling and countered with a buffet that left a black splotch on a skin that was like armor plate and sent the man through the opposite wall. The other was upon Ennis, who whirled with the quickness of one who maneuvers habitually under a pressure of ten thousand atmospheres, and shook the Marak from him, leaving him unconscious with a twist in a sensitive spot.

The first opponent returned, and the two grappled, searching for nerve centers to beat upon. Ennis twisted frantically, conscious of the real danger that the frail vessel might break to pieces beneath his feet. The railing of a staircase gave behind the two, and they hurtled down it, crashing through the steps to the floor below. Their weight and momentum carried them through. Ennis released his grip on the Marak, stopped his fall by grasping one of the girders that was part of the ship's framework. The other continued his devastating way down, demolishing the inner shell, and then the outer shell gave way with a grinding crash that ominously became a burbling rush of liquid.

Ennis looked down into the space where the Marak had fallen, hissed with a sudden intake of breath, then dove down himself. He met rising water, gushing in through a rent in the keel. He braced himself against a girder which sagged under his hand and moved onward against the rushing water. It geysered through the hole in a heavy stream that pushed him back and started to fill the bottom level of the ship. Against that terrific pressure he strained forward slowly, beating against the resisting waves, and then, with a mighty flounder, was at the opening. Its edges had been folded back upon themselves by the inrushing water, and they gaped inward like a jagged maw. He grasped them in a huge hand and exerted force. They strained for a moment and began to straighten. Irresistibly he pushed and stretched them into their former position, and then took the broken ends in his hands and *squeezed*. The metal grew soft under his grip and began to flow. The edges of the plate welded under that mighty pressure. He moved down the crack and soon it was watertight. He flexed his hands as he rose. They ached; even his strength was beginning to be taxed.

Noises from above; pounding feet. Men were coming down to investigate the commotion. He stood for a moment in thought, then turned to a blank wall, battered his way through it, and shoved the plates and girders back into position. Down to the other end of the craft, and up a staircase there. The corridor above was deserted, and he stole along it, hunting for the place he had left the weapon he had prepared. There was a commotion ahead as the Maraks found the unconscious man.

Two men came pounding up the passageway, giving him barely enough time to slip into a doorway to the side. The room he found himself in was a sleeping chamber. There were two red pulps there, and nothing that could help him, so he stayed in there only long enough to make sure that he would not be seen emerging into the hall. He crept down it again, with as little noise as possible. The racket ahead helped him; it sounded as though they were tearing the ship apart. Again he cursed their idiocy. Couldn't they see how valuable this was?

They were in the control room, ripping apart the machinery with the curiosity of children, wondering at the strange weakness of the paperlike metal, not realizing that, on the world where it was fabricated, it was sufficiently strong for any strain the builders could put upon it.

The strange weapon Ennis had prepared was on the floor of the passage, and just outside the control room. He looked anxiously at the trailing cables. Had they been stepped on and broken? Was the instrument in working condition? He had to get it and be away; no time to experiment to see if it would work.

A noise from behind, and Ennis again slunk into a doorway as a large Marak with a colored belt around his waist strode jarringly through the corridor into the control room. Sharp orders were barked, and the men ceased their havoc with the machinery of the room. All but a few left and scattered through the ship. Ennis' face twisted into a scowl. This made things more difficult. He couldn't overcome them all single-handed, and he couldn't use the weapon inside the ship if it was what he thought it was from the size of the cables.

A Marak was standing immediately outside the room in which Ennis lurked. No exit that way. He looked around the room; there were no other doors. A porthole in the outer wall was a tiny disk of transparency. He looked at it, felt it with his hands, and suddenly pushed his hands right through it. As quietly as he could, he worked at the edges of the circle until the hole was large enough for him to squeeze through. The jagged edges did not bother him. They felt soft, like a ragged pat of butter.

The Marak vessel was moored to the other side of the spaceship. On this side the wind howled blankly, and the sawtooth waves stretched on and on to a horizon that was many miles distant. He cautiously made his way around the glistening rotundity of the derelict, past the prow, straining silently against the vicious backward sweep of the water that tore at every inch of his body. The darker hump of the battleship loomed up as he rounded the curve, and he swam across the tiny space to grasp a row of projections that curved up over the surface of the craft. He climbed up them, muscles that were hard as carborundum straining to hold against all the forces of gravity and wind that fought him down. Near the top of the curve was a rounded, streamlined projection. He felt around its base and found a lever there, which he moved. The metal hump slid back, revealing a rugged swivel mounting with a stubby cylindrical projector atop it.

He swung the mounting around and let loose a short, sudden blast of white fire along the naked deck of the battleship. Deep voices yelled within and men sprang out, to fall back with abrupt screams clogged in their throats as Ennis caught them in the intolerable blast from the projector. Men, shielded by five thousand miles of atmosphere from actinic light, used to receiving only red and infra red, were painfully vulnerable to his frightful concentration of ultraviolet.

Noise and shouts burst from the derelict spaceship alongside, sweeping away eerily in the thundering wind that seemed to pound down upon them with new vigor in that moment. Heads appeared from the openings in the craft.

Ennis suddenly stood up to his full height, bracing himself against the wind, so dense it made him buoyant. With a deep bellow he bridged the space to the derelict. Then, as a squad of Maraks made their difficult, slippery way across the flank of the battleship toward him, and as the band that had boarded the spaceship crowded out on its battered deck to see what the noise was about, he dropped down into a crouch behind his ultraviolet projector, and whirled it around, pulling the firing lever.

That was what he wanted. Make a lot of noise and disturbance, get them all on deck, and then blow them to pieces. The ravening blast spat from the nozzle of the weapon, and the men on the battleship dropped flat on the deck. He found he could not depress the projector enough to reach them. He spun it to point at the spaceship. The incandescence reached out, and then seemed to waver and die. The current was shut off at the switchboard.

Ennis rose from behind the projector, and then hurtled from the flank of the battleship as he was struck by two Maraks leaping on him from behind the hump of the vessel. The three struck the water and sank, Ennis struggling violently. He was on the last lap, and he gave all his strength to the spurt. The water swirled around them in little choppy waves that fell more quickly than the eye could follow. Heavier blows than those from an Earthly trip hammer were scoring Ennis' face and head. He was in a bad position to strike back, and suddenly he became limp and sank below the surface. The pressure of the water around him was enormous, and it increased very rapidly as he went lower and lower. He saw the shadowy bulk of the spaceship above him. His lungs were fighting for air, but he shook off his pretended stupor and swam doggedly through the water beneath the derelict. He went on and on. It seemed as though the distance were endless, following the metal curve. It was so big from beneath, and trying to swim the width without air made it bigger.

Clear, finally, his lungs drew in the saving breaths. No time to rest, though. He must make use of his advantage while it was his; it wouldn't last long. He swam along the side of the ship looking for an opening. There was none within reach from the water, so he made one, digging his stubby fingers into the metal, climbing up until it was safe to tear a rent in the thick outer and inner walls of the ship.

He found himself in one of the machine rooms of the second level. He went out into the corridor and up the stairway which was half-wrecked, and found himself in the main passage near the control room. He darted down it, into the room. There was nobody there, although the noises from above indicated that the Maraks were again descending. There was his weapon on the floor, where he had left it. He was glad that they had not gotten around to pulling that instrument apart. There would be one thing saved for intelligent examination.

The clatter from the descending crowd turned into a clamor of anger as they discovered him in the passageway. They stopped there for a moment, puzzled. He had been in the ocean, and had somehow magically reappeared within the derelict. It gave him time to pick up the weapon.

Ennis debated rapidly and decided to risk the unknown. How powerful the weapon was he did not know, but with atomic energy it would be powerful. He disliked using it inside the spaceship; he wanted to have enough left to float on the water until Shadden arrived; but they were beginning to advance on him, and he had to start something.

He pulled a lever. The cylinder in his arms jerked back with great force; a bolt of fierce, blinding energy tore out of it and passed with the quickness of light down the length of the corridor.

When he could see again there was no corridor. Everything that had been in the way of the projector was gone, simply disappeared.

Unmindful of the heat from the object in his hands, he turned and directed it at the battleship that was plainly outlined through the space that had been once the walls of the derelict. Before the men on the deck could move, he pulled the lever again.

And the winds were silenced for a moment. The natural elements were still in fear at the incredible forces that came from the destruction of atoms. Then with an agonized scream the hurricane struck again, tore through the spot where there had been a battleship.

Far off in the sky Ennis detected motion. It was Shadden, speeding in a glider.

Now would come the work that was important. Shadden would take the big machine apart and see how it ran. That was what history would remember.

AFTERWORD BY ERIC FLINT

The oldest story in this anthology is C.L. Moore's "Shambleau," which was first published in the November 1933 issue of *Weird Tales*. Five years have to pass before another one of the stories collected here first appears: John W. Campbell, Jr.'s "Who Goes There?" in the August 1938 issue of *Astounding*. Two more come in the following year: Van Vogt's "Black Destroyer" in the July 1939 issue of *Astounding*, and, one month later in the same magazine, this story: Lee Gregor's "Heavy Planet."

C.L. Moore, John W. Campbell, Jr., A. E. Van Vogt . . . all of them among the great names in the history of science fiction.

Lee Gregor was not. In fact, the name itself is a pseudonym. "Lee Gregor" was actually Milton A. Rothman, a minor science fiction writer who published not more than a dozen stories, scattered across four decades from the late '30s to the late '70s, many of them using the pseudonym of Lee Gregor. Under his own name, he was probably better known to SF readers as one of the scientists who periodically wrote factual articles for either

Astounding/Analog or, later in his life, *Issac Asimov's Science Fiction Magazine* and anthologies associated with it.

And yet . . .

"Heavy Planet" has been anthologized since its first appearance over a dozen times—about as often as Moore's "Shambleau" and Van Vogt's "Black Destroyer," and almost as many times as Campbell's "Who Goes There?" In fact, the first time I read it was in one of the great, classic science fiction anthologies: *Adventures in Time and Space,* edited by Raymond J. Healy and J. Francis McComas and first published in 1946 by Random House. My parents gave me the volume as a gift, if memory serves me correctly, on my fourteenth birthday.

Odd success, perhaps, for such a simple and straight-forward story. But I think that's the key to it. It's such a clean story, and one of the very first in the history of science fiction (that I can think of, anyway) that is told entirely from the viewpoint of an alien. Even the supposition that the bodies Ennis encounters on the wrecked spaceship are those of human beings is simply that—a supposition. The story does not say, one way or the other. It does not need to, because the story is not about humans. It is about hope and aspiration, which although they are human qualities, may well be shared by others.

That was what struck me most about the story, at the time. And even at that age, I wasn't so callow that I didn't understand that Gregor's story applied to the world I saw around me. I didn't have to wait for aliens to appear to start thinking about what a mile might feel like in someone else's moccasins.

Omnilingual

by H. Beam Piper

PREFACE BY ERIC FLINT

I've always had a mixed reaction to H. Beam Piper's writings. On the one hand, he was a superb story-teller and over the decades I've enjoyed any number of his works. On the other hand, the underlying attitude in many of his writings often leaves me grinding my teeth. I was so infuriated by *Uller Uprising* as a teenager that I threw it in the garbage can when I was about halfway through, and *Space Viking* still leaves a foul taste in my mouth four decades after I read it. For all of Piper's modern reputation as a "libertarian," the fact is that he was often prone to apologizing for authority, especially when that authority was being brutal. *Uller Uprising*, modeled on the Indian Mutiny of 1857, is an apologia for the greed and misrule of the British East India Company more extreme than even its own partisans advanced at the time. And *Space Viking*? Once you strip away the (admittedly impressive) story-telling razzle-dazzle, the novel is nothing but a romanticization of thuggery.

Look, sorry. My own ancestry, on my father's side, is Norwegian. That fact has never blinded me to the truth about my Viking progenitors. Yes, they were very courageous, capable and resourceful. Big deal. So was the Waffen SS. The truth? My Viking forefathers were a bunch of murderers, rapists, arsonists and thieves. So let us puh-leese not adulate them in science fiction after the fact.

Grumble.

That said . . .

Piper, like most good story-tellers, was a man of many parts. And there are other stories of his which I've enjoyed for decades. Two of them, in particular, had a big impact on me as a teenager. The first was his novel *Four-Day Planet*—which is still my favorite among his many novels. The other...

Was this one.

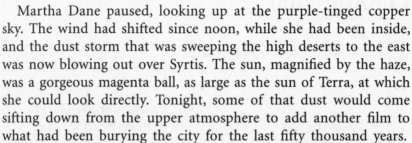

Martha Dane paused, looking up at the purple-tinged copper sky. The wind had shifted since noon, while she had been inside, and the dust storm that was sweeping the high deserts to the east was now blowing out over Syrtis. The sun, magnified by the haze, was a gorgeous magenta ball, as large as the sun of Terra, at which she could look directly. Tonight, some of that dust would come sifting down from the upper atmosphere to add another film to what had been burying the city for the last fifty thousand years.

The red loess lay over everything, covering the streets and the open spaces of park and plaza, hiding the small houses that had been crushed and pressed flat under it and the rubble that had come down from the tall buildings when roofs had caved in and walls had toppled outward. Here where she stood, the ancient streets were a hundred to a hundred and fifty feet below the surface; the breach they had made in the wall of the building behind her had opened into the sixth story. She could look down on the cluster of prefabricated huts and sheds, on the brush-grown flat that had been the waterfront when this place had been a seaport on the ocean that was now Syrtis Depression; already, the bright metal was thinly coated with red dust. She thought, again, of what clearing this city would mean, in terms of time and labor, of people and supplies and equipment brought across fifty million miles of space. They'd have to use machinery; there was no other way it could be done. Bulldozers and power shovels and draglines; they were fast, but they were rough and indiscriminate. She remembered the digs around Harappa and Mohenjo-Daro, in the Indus Valley, and the careful, patient native laborers—the painstaking foremen, the pickmen and spademen, the long files of basketmen carrying away the earth. Slow and primitive as the civilization whose ruins they were uncovering, yes, but she could count on the fingers of one hand the times one of her pickmen had damaged a valuable object in the ground. If it hadn't been for the underpaid and uncomplaining native laborer, archaeology would still be back where Wincklemann had found it. But on Mars there was no native labor; the last Martian had died five hundred centuries ago.

Something started banging like a machine gun, four or five hundred yards to her left. A solenoid jackhammer; Tony Lattimer must have decided which building he wanted to break into next. She became conscious, then, of the awkward weight of her equipment, and began redistributing it, shifting the straps of her oxy-tank pack, slinging the camera from one shoulder and the board and drafting tools from the other, gathering the notebooks and sketchbooks under her left arm. She started walking down the road, over hillocks of buried rubble, around snags of wall jutting up out of the loess, past buildings still standing, some of them already breached and explored, and across the brush-grown flat to the huts.

There were ten people in the main office room of Hut One when she entered. As soon as she had disposed of her oxygen equipment, she lit a cigarette, her first since noon, then looked from one to another of them. Old Selim von Ohlmhorst, the Turco-German, one of her two fellow archaeologists, sitting at the end of the long table against the farther wall, smoking his big curved pipe and going through a looseleaf notebook. The girl ordnance officer, Sachiko Koremitsu, between two droplights at the other end of the table, her head bent over her work. Colonel Hubert Penrose, the Space Force CO, and Captain Field, the intelligence officer, listening to the report of one of the airdyne pilots, returned from his afternoon survey flight. A couple of girl lieutenants from Signals, going over the script of the evening telecast, to be transmitted to the *Cyrano*, on orbit five thousand miles off planet and relayed from thence to Terra via Lunar. Sid Chamberlain, the Trans-Space News Service man, was with them. Like Selim and herself, he was a civilian; he was advertising the fact with a white shirt and a sleeveless blue sweater. And Major Lindemann, the engineer officer, and one of his assistants, arguing over some plans on a drafting board. She hoped, drawing a pint of hot water to wash her hands and sponge off her face, that they were doing something about the pipeline.

She started to carry the notebooks and sketchbooks over to where Selim von Ohlmhorst was sitting, and then, as she always did, she turned aside and stopped to watch Sachiko. The Japanese girl was restoring what had been a book, fifty thousand years ago; her eyes were masked by a binocular loup, the black headband invisible against her glossy black hair, and she was picking delicately at the crumbled page with a hair-fine wire set in a handle of copper tubing. Finally, loosening a particle as tiny as a snowflake, she grasped it with tweezers, placed it on the sheet of transparent plastic on which she was reconstructing the page, and set it with a mist of fixative from a little spraygun. It was a sheer joy to watch her; every movement was as graceful and precise as though done to music after being rehearsed a hundred times.

"Hello, Martha. It isn't cocktail-time yet, is it?" The girl at the table spoke without raising her head, almost without moving her lips, as though she were afraid that the slightest breath would disturb the flaky stuff in front of her.

"No, it's only fifteen-thirty. I finished my work, over there. I didn't find any more books, if that's good news for you."

Sachiko took off the loup and leaned back in her chair, her palms cupped over her eyes.

"No, I like doing this. I call it micro-jigsaw puzzles. This book, here, really is a mess. Selim found it lying open, with some heavy stuff on top of it; the pages were simply crushed. She hesitated briefly. "If only it would mean something, after I did it."

There could be a faintly critical overtone to that. As she replied, Martha realized that she was being defensive.

"It will, some day. Look how long it took to read Egyptian hieroglyphics, even after they had the Rosetta Stone."

Sachiko smiled. "Yes, I know. But they did have the Rosetta Stone."

"And we don't. There is no Rosetta Stone, not anywhere on Mars. A whole race, a whole species, died while the first Crô-Magnon cave-artist was daubing pictures of reindeer and bison, and across fifty thousand years and fifty million miles there was no bridge of understanding.

"We'll find one. There must be something, somewhere, that will give us the meaning of a few words, and we'll use them to pry meaning out of more words, and so on. We may not live to learn this language, but we'll make a start, and some day somebody will."

Sachiko took her hands from her eyes, being careful not to look toward the unshaded lights, and smiled again. This time Martha was sure that it was not the Japanese smile of politeness, but the universally human smile of friendship.

"I hope so, Martha; really I do. It would be wonderful for you to be the first to do it, and it would be wonderful for all of us to be able to read what these people wrote. It would really bring this dead city to life again." The smile faded slowly. "But it seems so hopeless."

"You haven't found any more pictures?"

Sachiko shook her head. Not that it would have meant much if she had. They had found hundreds of pictures with captions; they had never been able to establish a positive relationship between any pictured object and any printed word. Neither of them said anything more, and after a moment Sachiko replaced the loup and bent her head forward over the book.

Selim von Ohlmhorst looked up from his notebook, taking his pipe out of his mouth.

"Everything finished, over there?" he asked, releasing a puff of smoke.

"Such as it was." She laid the notebooks and sketches on the table. "Captain Gicquel's started airsealing the building from the fifth floor down, with an entrance on the sixth; he'll start putting in oxygen generators as soon as that's done. I have everything cleared up where he'll be working."

Colonel Penrose looked up quickly, as though making a mental note to attend to something later. Then he returned his attention to the pilot, who was pointing something out on a map.

Von Ohlmhorst nodded. "There wasn't much to it, at that," he agreed. "Do you know which building Tony has decided to enter next?"

"The tall one with the conical thing like a candle extinguisher on top, I think. I heard him drilling for the blasting shots over that way."

"Well, I hope it turns out to be one that was occupied up to the end."

The last one hadn't. It had been stripped of its contents and fittings, a piece of this and a bit of that, haphazardly, apparently over a long period of time, until it had been almost gutted. For centuries, as it had died, this city had been consuming itself by a process of auto-cannibalism. She said something to that effect.

"Yes. We always find that—except, of course, at places like Pompeii. Have you seen any of the other Roman cities in Italy?" he asked. "Minturnae, for instance? First the inhabitants tore down this to repair that, and then, after they had vacated the city, other people came along and tore down what was left, and burned the stones for lime, or crushed them to mend roads, till there was nothing left but the foundation traces. That's where we are fortunate; this is one of the places where the Martian race perished, and there were no barbarians to come later and destroy what they had left." He puffed slowly at his pipe. "Some of these days, Martha, we are going to break into one of these buildings and find that it was one in which the last of these people died. Then we will learn the story of the end of this civilization."

And if we learn to read their language, we'll learn the whole story, not just the obituary. She hesitated, not putting the thought into words. "We'll find that, sometime, Selim," she said, then looked at her watch. "I'm going to get some more work done on my lists, before dinner."

For an instant, the old man's face stiffened in disapproval; he started to say something, thought better of it, and put his pipe back into his mouth. The brief wrinkling around his mouth and the twitch of his white mustache had been enough, however; she knew what he was thinking. She was wasting time and effort, he believed; time and effort belonging not to herself but to the expedition. He could be right, too, she realized. But he had to be wrong; there had to be a way to do it. She turned from him silently and went to her own packing-case seat, at the middle of the table.

Photographs, and photostats of restored pages of books, and transcripts of inscriptions, were piled in front of her, and the notebooks in which she was compiling her lists. She sat down, lighting a fresh cigarette, and reached over to a stack of unexamined material, taking off the top sheet. It was a photostat of what looked like the title page and contents of some sort of a periodical. She remembered it; she had found it herself, two days before, in a closet in the basement of the building she had just finished examining.

She sat for a moment, looking at it. It was readable, in the sense that she had set up a purely arbitrary but consistently pronounceable system of phonetic values for the letters. The long vertical symbols were vowels. There were only ten of them; not too many, allowing separate characters for long and short sounds. There were twenty of the short horizontal letters, which meant that sounds like –ng or –ch or –sh were single letters. The odds were millions to one against her system being anything like the original sound of the language, but she had listed several thousand Martian words, and she could pronounce all of them.

And that was as far as it went. She could pronounce between

three and four thousand Martian words, and she couldn't assign a meaning to one of them. Selim von Ohlmhorst believed that she never would. So did Tony Lattimer, and he was a great deal less reticent about saying so. So, she was sure, did Sachiko Koremitsu. There were times, now and then, when she began to be afraid that they were right.

The letters on the page in front of her began squirming and dancing, slender vowels with fat little consonants. They did that, now, every night in her dreams. And there were other dreams, in which she read them as easily as English; waking, she would try desperately and vainly to remember. She blinked, and looked away from the photostated page; when she looked back, the letters were behaving themselves again. There were three words at the top of the page, over-and-underlined, which seemed to be the Martian method of capitalization. *Mastharnorvod Tadavas Sornhulva.* She pronounced them mentally, leafing through her notebooks to see if she had encountered them before, and in what contexts. All three were listed. In addition, *masthar* was a fairly common word, and so was *norvod*, and so was *nor*, but *–vod* was a suffix and nothing but a suffix. *Davas*, was a word, too, and *ta-* was a common prefix; *sorn* and *hulva* were both common words. This language, she had long ago decided, must be something like German; when the Martians had needed a new word, they had just pasted a couple of existing words together. It would probably turn out to be a grammatical horror. Well, they had published magazines, and one of them had been called *Mastharnorvod Tadavas Sornhulva.* She wondered if it had been something like the *Quarterly Archaeology Review*, or something more on the order of *Sexy Stories*.

A smaller line, under the title, was plainly the issue number and date; enough things had been found numbered in series to enable her to identify the numerals and determine that a decimal system of numeration had been used. This was the one thousand and seven hundred and fifty-fourth issue, for Doma, 14837; then Doma must be the name of one of the Martian months. The word had turned up several times before. She found herself puffing furiously on her cigarette as she leafed through notebooks and piles of already examined material.

Sachiko was speaking to somebody, and a chair scraped at the end of the table. She raised her head, to see a big man with red hair and a red face, in Space Force green, with the single star of a major on his shoulder, sitting down. Ivan Fitzgerald, the medic.

He was lifting weights from a book similar to the one the girl ordnance officer was restoring.

"Haven't had time, lately," he was saying, in reply to Sachiko's question. "The Finchley girl's still down with whatever it is she has, and it's something I haven't been able to diagnose yet. And I've been checking on bacteria cultures, and in what spare time I have, I've been dissecting specimens for Bill Chandler. Bill's finally found a mammal. Looks like a lizard, and it's only four inches long, but it's a real warm-blooded, gamogenetic, placental, viviparous mammal. Burrows, and seems to live on what pass for insects here."

"Is there enough oxygen for anything like that?" Sachiko was asking.

"Seems to be, close to the ground." Fitzgerald got the headband of his loup adjusted, and pulled it down over his eyes. "He found this thing in a ravine down on the sea bottom— Ha, this page seems to be intact; now, if I can get it out all in one piece—"

He went on talking inaudibly to himself, lifting the page a little at a time and sliding one of the transparent plastic sheets under it, working with minute delicacy. Not the delicacy of the Japanese girl's small hands, moving like the paws of a cat washing her face, but like a steam-hammer cracking a peanut. Field archaeology requires a certain delicacy of touch, too, but Martha watched the pair of them with envious admiration. Then she turned back to her own work, finishing the table of contents.

The next page was the beginning of the first article listed; many of the words were unfamiliar. She had the impression that this must be some kind of scientific or technical journal; that could be because such publications made up the bulk of her own periodical reading. She doubted it if were fiction; the paragraphs had a solid, factual look.

At length, Ivan Fitzgerald gave a short, explosive grunt.

"Ha! Got it!"

She looked up. He had detached the page and was cementing another plastic sheet onto it.

"Any pictures?" she asked.

"None on this side. Wait a moment." He turned the sheet. "None on this side, either." He sprayed another sheet of plastic to sandwich the page, then picked up his pipe and relighted it.

"I get fun out of this, and it's good practice for my hands, so don't think I'm complaining," he said, "but, Martha, do you honestly think anybody's ever going to get anything out of this?"

Sachiko held up a scrap of the silicone plastic the Martians had used for paper with her tweezers. It was almost an inch square.

"Look; three whole words on this piece," she crowed. "Ivan, you took the easy book."

Fitzgerald wasn't being sidetracked. "This stuff's absolutely meaningless," he continued. "It had a meaning fifty thousand years ago, when it was written, but it has none at all now."

She shook her head. "Meaning isn't something that evaporates with time," she argued. "It has just as much meaning now as it ever had. We just haven't learned how to decipher it."

"That seems like a pretty pointless distinction," Selim von Ohlm-horst joined the conversation. "There no longer exists a means of deciphering it."

"We'll find one." She was speaking, she realized, more in self-encouragement than in controversy.

"How? From pictures and captions? We've found captioned pictures, and what have they given us? A caption is intended to explain the picture, not the picture to explain the caption. Suppose some alien to our culture found a picture of a man with a white beard and mustache sawing a billet from a log. He would think the caption meant, 'Man Sawing Wood.' How would he know that it was really 'Wilhelm II in Exile at Doorn?'"

Sachiko had taken off her loup and was lighting a cigarette.

"I can think of pictures intended to explain their captions," she said. "These picture language-books, the sort we use in the Service—little line drawings, with a word or phrase under them."

"Well, of course, if we found something like that," von Ohlm-horst began.

"Michael Ventris found something like that, back in the Fifties," Hubert Penrose's voice broke in from directly behind her.

She turned her head. The colonel was standing by the archaeologists' table; Captain Field and the airdyne pilot had gone out.

"He found a lot of Greek inventories of military stores," Penrose continued. "They were in Cretan Linear B script, and at the head of each list was a little picture, a sword or a helmet or a cooking tripod or a chariot wheel. That's what gave him the key to the script."

"Colonel's getting to be quite an archaeologist," Fitzgerald commented. "We're all learning each others' specialties, on this expedition."

"I heard about that long before this expedition was even

contemplated." Penrose was tapping a cigarette on his gold case. "I heard about that back before the Thirty Days' War, at Intelligence School, when I was a lieutenant. As a feat of cryptanalysis, not an archaeological discovery."

"Yes, cryptanalysis," von Ohlmhorst pounced. "The reading of a known language in an unknown form of writing. Ventris' lists were in the known language, Greek. Neither he nor anybody else ever read a word of the Cretan language until the finding of the Greek-Cretan bilingual in 1963, because only with a bilingual text, one language already known, can an unknown ancient language be learned. And what hope, I ask you, have we of finding anything like that here? Martha, you've been working on these Martian texts ever since we landed here—for the last six months. Tell me, have you found a single word to which you can positively assign a meaning?"

"Yes, I think I have one." She was trying hard not to sound too exultant. "*Doma*. It's the name of one of the months of the Martian calendar."

"Where did you find that?" von Ohlmhorst asked. "And how did you establish—?"

"Here." She picked up the photostat and handed it along the table to him. "I'd call this the title page of a magazine."

He was silent for a moment, looking at it. "Yes. I would say so, too. Have you any of the rest of it?"

"I'm working on the first page of the first article, listed there. Wait till I see; yes, here's all I found, together, here." She told him where she had gotten it. "I just gathered it up, at the time, and gave it to Geoffrey and Rosita to photostat; this is the first I've really examined it."

The old man got to his feet, brushing tobacco ashes from the front of his jacket, and came to where she was sitting, laying the title page on the table and leafing quickly through the stack of photostats.

"Yes, and here is the second article, on page eight, and here's the next one." He finished the pile of photostats. "A couple of pages missing at the end of the last article. This is remarkable; surprising that a thing like a magazine would have survived so long."

"Well, this silicone stuff the Martians used for paper is pretty durable," Hubert Penrose said. "There doesn't seem to have been any water or any other fluid in it originally, so it wouldn't dry out with time."

"Oh, it's not remarkable that the material would have survived.

We've found a good many books and papers in excellent condition. But only a really vital culture, an organized culture, will publish magazines, and this civilization had been dying for hundreds of years before the end. It might have been a thousand years before the time they died out completely that such activities as publishing ended."

"Well, look where I found it; in a closet in a cellar. Tossed in there and forgotten, and then ignored when they were stripping the building. Things like that happen."

Penrose had picked up the title page and was looking at it.

"I don't think there's any doubt about this being a magazine, at all." He looked again at the title, his lips moving silently. "*Mastharnorvod Tadavas Sornhulva*. Wonder what it means. But you're right about the date—*Doma* seems to be the name of a month. Yes, you have a word, Dr. Dane."

Sid Chamberlain, seeing that something unusual was going on, had come over from the table at which he was working. After examining the title page and some of the inside pages, he began whispering into the stenophone he had taken from his belt.

"Don't try to blow this up to anything big, Sid," she cautioned. "All we have is the name of a month, and Lord only knows how long it'll be till we even find out which month it was."

"Well, it's a start, isn't it?" Penrose argued. "Grotefend only had the word for 'king' when he started reading Persian cuneiform."

"But I don't have the word for month; just the name of a month. Everybody knew the names of the Persian kings, long before Grotefend."

"That's not the story," Chamberlain said. "What the public back on Terra will be interested in is finding out that the Martians published magazines, just like we do. Something familiar; make the Martians seem more real. More human."

Three men had come in, and were removing their masks and helmets and oxy-tanks, and peeling out of their quilted coveralls. Two were Space Force lieutenants; the third was a youngish civilian with close-cropped blond hair, in a checked woolen shirt. Tony Lattimer and his helpers.

"Don't tell me Martha finally got something out of that stuff?" he asked, approaching the table. He might have been commenting on the antics of the village half-wit, from his tone.

"Yes; the name of one of the Martian months." Hubert Penrose went on to explain, showing the photostat.

Tony Lattimer took it, glanced at it, and dropped it on the table.

"Sounds plausible, of course, but just an assumption. That word may not be the name of a month, at all—could mean 'published' or 'authorized' or 'copyrighted' or anything like that. Fact is, I don't think it's more than a wild guess that that thing's anything like a periodical." He dismissed the subject and turned to Penrose. "I picked out the next building to enter; that tall one with the conical thing on top. It ought to be in pretty good shape inside; the conical top wouldn't allow dust to accumulate, and from the outside nothing seems to be caved in or crushed. Ground level's higher than the other one, about the seventh floor. I found a good place and drilled for the shots; tomorrow I'll blast a hole in it, and if you can spare some people to help, we can start exploring it right away."

"Yes, of course, Dr. Lattimer. I can spare about a dozen, and I suppose you can find a few civilian volunteers," Penrose told him. "What will you need in the way of equipment?"

"Oh, about six demolition-packets; they can all be shot together. And the usual thing in the way of lights, and breaking and digging tools, and climbing equipment in case we run into broken or doubtful stairways. We'll divide into two parties. Nothing ought to be entered for the first time without a qualified archaeologist along. Three parties, if Martha can tear herself away from this catalogue of systematized incomprehensibilities she's making long enough to do some real work."

She felt her chest tighten and her face become stiff. She was pressing her lips together to lock in a furious retort when Hubert Penrose answered for her.

"Dr. Dane's been doing as much work, and as important work, as you have," he said brusquely. "More important work, I'd be inclined to say."

Von Ohlmhorst was visibly distressed; he glanced once toward Sid Chamberlain, then looked hastily away from him. Afraid of a story of dissension among archaeologists getting out.

"Working out a system of pronunciation by which the Martian language could be transliterated was a most important contribution," he said. "And Martha did that almost unassisted."

"Unassisted by Dr. Lattimer, anyway," Penrose added. "Captain Field and Lieutenant Koremitsu did some work, and I helped out a little, but nine-tenths of it she did herself."

"Purely arbitrary," Lattimer disdained. "Why, we don't even know that the Martians could make the same kind of vocal sounds we do."

"Oh, yes, we do," Ivan Fitzgerald contradicted, safe on his own ground. "I haven't seen any actual Martian skulls—these people seem to have been very tidy about disposing of their dead—but from statues and busts and pictures I've seen, I'd say that their vocal organs were identical with our own."

"Well, grant that. And grant that it's going to be impressive to rattle off the names of Martian notables whose statues we find, and that if we're ever able to attribute any place-names, they'll sound a lot better than this horse-doctors' Latin the old astronomers splashed all over the map of Mars," Lattimer said. "What I object to is her wasting time on this stuff, of which nobody will ever be able to read a word if she fiddles around with those lists till there's another hundred feet of loess on this city, when there's so much real work to be done and we're shorthanded as we are."

That was the first time that had come out in just so many words. She was glad Lattimer had said it and not Selim von Ohlmhorst.

"What you mean," she retorted, "is that it doesn't have the publicity value that digging up statues has."

For an instant, she could see that the shot had scored. Then Lattimer, with a side glance at Chamberlain, answered:

"What I mean is that you're trying to find something that any archaeologist, yourself included, should know doesn't exist. I don't object to your gambling your professional reputation and making a laughing stock of yourself; what I object to is that the blunders of one archaeologist discredit the whole subject in the eyes of the public."

That seemed to be what worried Lattimer most. She was framing a reply when the communication-outlet whistled shrilly, and then squawked: "Cocktail time! One hour to dinner; cocktails in the library, Hut Four!"

The library, which was also lounge, recreation room, and general gathering-place, was already crowded; most of the crowd was at the long table topped with sheets of glasslike plastic that had been wall panels out of one of the ruined buildings. She poured herself what passed, here, for a martini, and carried it over to where Selim von Ohlmhorst was sitting alone.

For a while, they talked about the building they had just finished exploring, then drifted into reminiscences of their work on

Terra—von Ohlmhorst's in Asia Minor, with the Hittite Empire, and hers in Pakistan, excavating the cities of the Harappa Civilization. They finished their drinks—the ingredients were plentiful; alcohol and flavoring extracts synthesized from Martian vegetation—and von Ohlmhorst took the two glasses to the table for refills.

"You know, Martha," he said, when he returned, "Tony was right about one thing. You are gambling your professional standing and reputation. It's against all archaeological experience that a language so completely dead as this one could be deciphered. There was a continuity between all the other ancient languages—by knowing Greek, Champollion learned to read Egyptian; by knowing Egyptian, Hittite was learned. That's why you and your colleagues have never been able to translate the Harappa hieroglyphics; no such continuity exists there. If you insist that this utterly dead language can be read, your reputation will suffer for it."

"I heard Colonel Penrose say, once, that an officer who's afraid to risk his military reputation seldom makes much of a reputation. It's the same with us. If we really want to find things out, we have to risk making mistakes. And I'm a lot more interested in finding things out than I am in my reputation."

She glanced across the room, to where Tony Lattimer was sitting with Gloria Standish, talking earnestly, while Gloria sipped one of the counterfeit martinis and listened. Gloria was the leading contender for the title of Miss Mars, 1996, if you like big bosomy blondes, but Tony would have been just as attentive to her if she'd looked like the Wicked Witch in "The Wizard of Oz," because Gloria was the Pan-Federation Telecast System commentator with the expedition.

"I know you are," the old Turco-German was saying. "That's why, when they asked me to name another archaeologist for this expedition, I named you."

He hadn't named Tony Lattimer; Lattimer had been pushed onto the expedition by his university. There'd been a lot of high-level string-pulling to that; she wished she knew the whole story. She'd managed to keep clear of universities and university politics; all her digs had been sponsored by non-academic foundations or art museums.

"You have an excellent standing; much better than my own, at your age. That's why it disturbs me to see you jeopardizing it by this insistence that the Martian language can be translated. I can't, really, see how you can hope to succeed."

She shrugged and drank some more of her cocktail, then lit

another cigarette. It was getting tiresome to try to verbalize something she only felt.

"Neither do I, now, but I will. Maybe I'll find something like the picture-books Sachiko was talking about. A child's primer, maybe; surely they had things like that. And if I don't, I'll find something else. We've only been here six months. I can wait the rest of my life, if I have to, but I'll do it sometime."

"I can't wait so long," von Ohlmhorst said. "The rest of my life will only be a few years, and when the *Schiaparelli* orbits in, I'll be going back to Terra on the *Cyrano*."

"I wish you wouldn't. This is a whole new world of archaeology. Literally."

"Yes." He finished the cocktail and looked at his pipe as though wondering whether to re-light it so soon before dinner, then put it in his pocket. "A whole new world—but I've grown old, and it isn't for me. I've spent my life studying the Hittites. I can speak the Hittite language, though maybe King Muwatallis wouldn't be able to understand my modern Turkish accent. But the things I'd have to learn, here—chemistry, physics, engineering, how to run analytic tests on steel girders and beryllo-silver alloys and plastics and silicones. I'm more at home with a civilization that rode in chariots and fought with swords and was just learning how to work iron. Mars is for young people. This expedition is a cadre of leadership—not only the Space Force people, who'll be the commanders of the main expedition, but us scientists, too. And I'm just an old cavalry general who can't learn to command tanks and aircraft. You'll have time to learn about Mars. I won't."

His reputation as the dean of Hittitologists was solid and secure, too, she added mentally. Then she felt ashamed of the thought. He wasn't to be classed with Tony Lattimer.

"All I came for was to get the work started," he was continuing. "The Federation Government felt that an old hand should do that. Well, it's started, now; you and Tony and whoever comes out on the *Schiaparelli* must carry it on. You said it, yourself; you have a whole new world. This is only one city, of the last Martian civilization. Behind this, you have the Late Upland Culture, and the Canal Builders, and all the civilizations and races and empires before them, clear back to the Martian Stone Age." He hesitated for a moment. "You have no idea what all you have to learn, Martha. This isn't the time to start specializing too narrowly."

∾   ∾   ∾

They all got out of the truck and stretched their legs and looked up the road to the tall building with the queer conical cap askew on its top. The four little figures that had been busy against its wall climbed into the jeep and started back slowly, the smallest of them, Sachiko Koremitsu, paying out an electric cable behind. When it pulled up beside the truck, they climbed out; Sachiko attached the free end of the cable to a nuclear-electric battery. At once, dirty gray smoke and orange dust puffed out from the wall of the building, and, a second later, the multiple explosion banged.

She and Tony Lattimer and Major Lindemann climbed onto the truck, leaving the jeep standing by the road. When they reached the building, a satisfyingly wide breach had been blown in the wall. Lattimer had placed his shots between two of the windows; they were both blown out along with the wall between, and lay unbroken on the ground. Martha remembered the first building they had entered. A Space Force officer had picked up a stone and thrown it at one of the windows, thinking that would be all they'd need to do. It had bounced back. He had drawn his pistol—they'd all carried guns, then, on the principle that what they didn't know about Mars might easily hurt them—and fired four shots. The bullets had ricocheted, screaming thinly; there were four coppery smears of jacket-metal on the window, and a little surface spalling. Somebody tried a rifle; the 4000-f.s. bullet had cracked the glass-like pane without penetrating. An oxyacetylene torch had taken an hour to cut the window out; the lab crew, aboard the ship, were still trying to find out just what the stuff was.

Tony Lattimer had gone forward and was sweeping his flash-light back and forth, swearing petulantly, his voice harshened and amplified by his helmet-speaker.

"I thought I was blasting into a hallway; this lets us into a room. Careful; there's about a two-foot drop to the floor, and a lot of rubble from the blast just inside."

He stepped down through the breach; the others began dragging equipment out of the trucks—shovels and picks and crowbars and sledges, portable floodlights, cameras, sketching materials, an extension ladder, even Alpinists' ropes and crampons and pick-axes. Hubert Penrose was shouldering something that looked like a surrealist machine gun but which was really a nuclear-electric jack-hammer. Martha selected one of the spike-shod mountaineer's ice axes, with which she could dig or chop or poke or pry or help herself over rough footing.

The windows, grimed and crusted with fifty millennia of dust, filtered in a dim twilight; even the breach in the wall, in the morning shade, lighted only a small patch of floor. Somebody snapped on a floodlight, aiming it at the ceiling. The big room was empty and bare; dust lay thick on the floor and reddened the once-white walls. It could have been a large office, but there was nothing left in it to indicate its use.

"This one's been stripped up to the seventh floor!" Lattimer exclaimed. "Street level'll be cleaned out, completely."

"Do for living quarters and shops, then," Lindemann said. "Added to the others, this'll take care of everybody on the *Schiaparelli*."

"Seems to have been a lot of electric or electronic apparatus over along this wall," one of the Space Force officers commented. "Ten or twelve electric outlets." He brushed the dusty wall with his glove, then scraped on the floor with his foot. "I can see where things were pried loose."

The door, one of the double sliding things the Martians had used, was closed. Selim von Ohlmhorst tried it, but it was stuck fast. The metal latch-parts had frozen together, molecule bonding itself to molecule, since the door had last been closed. Hubert Penrose came over with the jack-hammer, fitting a spear-point chisel into place. He set the chisel in the joint between the doors, braced the hammer against his hip, and squeezed the trigger-switch. The hammer banged briefly like the weapon it resembled, and the doors popped a few inches apart, then stuck. Enough dust had worked into the recesses into which it was supposed to slide to block it on both sides.

That was old stuff; they ran into that every time they had to force a door, and they were prepared for it. Somebody went outside and brought in a power-jack and finally one of the doors inched back to the door jamb. That was enough to get the lights and equipment through; they all passed from the room to the hallway beyond. About half the other doors were open; each had a number and a single word, *Darfhulva*, over it.

One of the civilian volunteers, a woman professor of natural ecology from Penn State University, was looking up and down the hall.

"You know," she said, "I feel at home here. I think this was a college of some sort, and these were classrooms. That word, up there; that was the subject taught, or the department. And those electronic devices, all where the class would face them; audio-visual teaching aids."

"A twenty-five-story university?" Lattimer scoffed. "Why, a building like this would handle thirty thousand students."

"Maybe there were that many. This was a big city, in its prime," Martha said, moved chiefly by a desire to oppose Lattimer.

"Yes, but think of the snafu in the halls, every time they changed classes. It'd take half an hour to get everybody back and forth from one floor to another." He turned to von Ohlmhorst. "I'm going up above this floor. This place has been looted clean up to here, but there's a chance there may be something above," he said.

"I'll stay on this floor, at present," the Turco-German replied. "There will be much coming and going, and dragging things in and out. We should get this completely examined and recorded first. Then Major Lindemann's people can do their worst, here."

"Well, if nobody else wants it, I'll take the downstairs," Martha said.

"I'll go along with you," Hubert Penrose told her. "If the lower floors have no archaeological value, we'll turn them into living quarters. I like this building; it'll give everybody room to keep out from under everybody else's feet." He looked down the hall. "We ought to find escalators at the middle."

The hallway, too, was thick underfoot with dust. Most of the open rooms were empty, but a few contained furniture, including small seat-desks. The original proponent of the university theory pointed these out as just what might be found in classrooms. There were escalators, up and down, on either side of the hall, and more on the intersecting passage to the right.

"That's how they handled the students, between classes," Martha commented. "And I'll bet there are more ahead, there."

They came to a stop where the hallway ended at a great square central hall. There were elevators, there, on two of the sides, and four escalators, still usable as stairways. But it was the walls, and the paintings on them, that brought them up short and staring.

They were clouded with dirt—she was trying to imagine what they must have looked like originally, and at the same time estimating the labor that would be involved in cleaning them—but they were still distinguishable, as was the word, *Darfhulva*, in golden letters above each of the four sides. It was a moment before she realized, from the murals, that she had at last found a meaningful Martian word. They were a vast historical panorama, clockwise around the room. A group of skin-clad savages squatting around a fire. Hunters with bows and spears, carrying the carcass of an animal slightly like a pig. Nomads riding long-legged, graceful mounts like hornless deer. Peasants sowing and reaping; mud-walled hut villages, and cities; processions of priests and warriors; battles with swords and bows, and with cannon and muskets; galleys, and ships with sails, and ships without visible means of propulsion, and aircraft. Changing costumes and weapons and machines and styles of architecture. A richly fertile landscape, gradually merging into barren deserts and bushlands—the time of the great planet-wide drought. The Canal Builders—men with machines recognizable as steam-shovels and derricks, digging and quarrying and driving across the empty plains with aqueducts. More cities—seaports on the shrinking oceans; dwindling, half-deserted cities; an abandoned city, with four tiny humanoid figures and a thing like a combat-car in the middle of a brush-grown plaza, they and their vehicle dwarfed by the huge lifeless buildings around them. She had not the least doubt; *Darfhulva* was History.

"Wonderful!" von Ohlmhorst was saying. "The entire history of this race. Why, if the painter depicted appropriate costumes and weapons and machines for each period, and got the architecture right, we can break the history of this planet into eras and periods and civilizations."

"You can assume they're authentic. The faculty of this university would insist on authenticity in the *Darfhulva*—History—Department," she said.

"Yes! *Darfhulva*—History! And your magazine was a journal of *Sornhulva*!" Penrose exclaimed. "You have a word, Martha!" It took her an instant to realize that he had called her by her first name, and not Dr. Dane. She wasn't sure if that weren't a bigger triumph than learning a word of the Martian language. Or a more auspicious start. "Alone, I suppose that *hulva* means something like science or knowledge, or study; combined, it would be equivalent to our 'ology. And *darf* would mean something like past, or old times, or human events, or chronicles."

"That gives you three words, Martha!" Sachiko jubilated. "You did it."

"Let's don't go too fast," Lattimer said, for once not derisively. "I'll admit that *darfhulva* is the Martian word for history as a subject of study; I'll admit that *hulva* is the general word and *darf* modifies it and tells us which subject is meant. But as for assigning specific meanings, we can't do that because we don't know just how the Martians thought, scientifically or otherwise."

He stopped short, startled by the blue-white light that blazed as

Sid Chamberlain's Kliegettes went on. When the whirring of the camera stopped, it was Chamberlain who was speaking:

"This is the biggest thing yet; the whole history of Mars, stone age to the end, all on four walls. I'm taking this with the fast shutter, but we'll telecast it in slow motion, from the beginning to the end. Tony, I want you to do the voice for it—running commentary, interpretation of each scene as it's shown. Would you do that?"

Would he do that! Martha thought. If he had a tail, he'd be wagging it at the very thought.

"Well, there ought to be more murals on the other floors," she said. "Who wants to come downstairs with us?"

Sachiko did; immediately, Ivan Fitzgerald volunteered. Sid decided to go upstairs with Tony Lattimer, and Gloria Standish decided to go upstairs, too. Most of the party would remain on the seventh floor, to help Selim von Ohlmhorst get it finished. After poking tentatively at the escalator with the spike of her ice axe, Martha led the way downward.

The sixth floor was *Darfhulva*, too; military and technological history, from the character of the murals. They looked around the central hall, and went down to the fifth; it was like the floors above except that the big quadrangle was stacked with dusty furniture and boxes. Ivan Fitzgerald, who was carrying the floodlight, swung it slowly around. Here the murals were of heroic-sized Martians, so human in appearance as to seem members of her own race, each holding some object—a book, or a testtube, or some bit of scientific apparatus, and behind them were scenes of laboratories and factories, flame and smoke, lightning-flashes. The word at the top of each of the four walls was one with which she was already familiar—*Sornhulva*.

"Hey, Martha; there's that word," Ivan Fitzgerald exclaimed. "The one in the title of your magazine." He looked at the paintings. "Chemistry, or physics."

"Both," Hubert Penrose considered. "I don't think the Martians made any sharp distinction between them. See, the old fellow with the scraggly whiskers must be the inventor of the spectroscope; he has one in his hands, and he has a rainbow behind him. And the woman in the blue smock, beside him, worked in organic chemistry; see the diagrams of long-chain molecules behind her. What word would convey the idea of chemistry and physics taken as one subject?"

"*Sornhulva*," Sachiko suggested. "If *hulva*'s something like science, *sorn* must mean matter, or substance, or physical object. You were right, all along, Martha. A civilization like this would certainly leave something like this, that would be self-explanatory."

"This'll wipe a little more of that superior grin off Tony Lattimer's face," Fitzgerald was saying, as they went down the motionless escalator to the floor below. "Tony wants to be a big shot. When you want to be a big shot, you can't bear the possibility of anybody else being a bigger big shot, and whoever makes a start on reading this language will be the biggest big shot archaeology ever saw."

That was true. She hadn't thought of it, in that way, before, and now she tried not to think about it. She didn't want to be a big shot. She wanted to be able to read the Martian language, and find things out about the Martians.

Two escalators down, they came out on a mezzanine around a wide central hall on the street level, the floor forty feet below them and the ceiling thirty feet above. Their lights picked out object after object below—a huge group of sculptured figures in the middle; some kind of a motor vehicle jacked up on trestles for repairs; things that looked like machine-guns and auto-cannon; long tables, tops littered with a dust-covered miscellany; machinery; boxes and crates and containers.

They made their way down and walked among the clutter, missing a hundred things for every one they saw, until they found an escalator to the basement. There were three basements, one under another, until at last they stood at the bottom of the last escalator, on a bare concrete floor, swinging the portable floodlight over stacks of boxes and barrels and drums, and heaps of powdery dust. The boxes were plastic—nobody had ever found anything made of wood in the city—and the barrels and drums were of metal or glass or some glasslike substance. They were outwardly intact. The powdery heaps might have been anything organic, or anything containing fluid. Down here, where wind and dust could not reach, evaporation had been the only force of destruction after the minute life that caused putrefaction had vanished.

They found refrigeration rooms, too, and using Martha's ice axe and the pistollike vibratool Sachiko carried on her belt, they pounded and pried one open, to find desiccated piles of what had been vegetables, and leathery chunks of meat. Samples of that stuff, rocketed up to the ship, would give a reliable estimate, by radio-carbon dating, of how long ago this building had been occupied. The refrigeration unit, radically different from anything their own culture had produced, had been electrically powered. Sachiko and Penrose, poking into it, found the switches still on; the machine had only ceased to function when the power-source, whatever that had been, had failed.

The middle basement had also been used, at least toward the end, for storage; it was cut in half by a partition pierced by but one door. They took half an hour to force this, and were on the point of sending above for heavy equipment when it yielded enough for them to squeeze through. Fitzgerald, in the lead with the light, stopped short, looked around, and then gave a groan that came through his helmet-speaker like a foghorn.

"Oh, no! *No!*"

"What's the matter, Ivan?" Sachiko, entering behind him, asked anxiously.

He stepped aside. "Look at it, Sachi! Are we going to have to do all that?"

Martha crowded through behind her friend and looked around, then stood motionless, dizzy with excitement. Books. Case on case of books, half an acre of cases, fifteen feet to the ceiling. Fitzgerald, and Penrose, who had pushed in behind her, were talking in rapid excitement; she only heard the sound of their voices, not their words. This must be the main stacks of the university library—the entire literature of the vanished race of Mars. In the center, down an aisle between the cases, she could see the hollow square of the librarians' desk, and stairs and a dumb-waiter to the floor above.

She realized that she was walking forward, with the others, toward this. Sachiko was saying: "I'm the lightest; let me go first." She must be talking about the spidery metal stairs.

"I'd say they were safe," Penrose answered. "The trouble we've had with doors around here shows that the metal hasn't deteriorated."

In the end, the Japanese girl led the way, more catlike than ever in her caution. The stairs were quite sound, in spite of their fragile appearance, and they all followed her. The floor above was a duplicate of the room they had entered, and seemed to contain about as many books. Rather than waste time forcing the door here, they returned to the middle basement and came up by the escalator down which they had originally descended.

The upper basement contained kitchens—electric stoves, some with pots and pans still on them—and a big room that must have been, originally, the students' dining room, though when last used it had been a workshop. As they expected, the library reading room was on the street-level floor, directly above the stacks. It seemed to have been converted into a sort of common living room for the building's last occupants. An adjoining auditorium had been made into a chemical works; there were vats and distillation apparatus, and a metal fractionating tower that extended through a hole knocked in the ceiling seventy feet above. A good deal of plastic furniture of the sort they had been finding everywhere in the city was stacked about, some of it broken up, apparently for reprocessing. The other rooms on the street floor seemed also to have been devoted to manufacturing and repair work; a considerable industry, along a number of lines, must have been carried on here for a long time after the university had ceased to function as such.

On the second floor, they found a museum; many of the exhibits remained, tantalizingly half-visible in grimed glass cases. There had been administrative offices there, too. The doors of most of them were closed, and they did not waste time trying to force them, but those that were open had been turned into living quarters. They made notes, and rough floor-plans, to guide them in future more thorough examination; it was almost noon before they had worked their way back to the seventh floor.

Selim von Ohlmhorst was in a room on the north side of the building, sketching the position of things before examining them and collecting them for removal. He had the floor checkerboarded with a grid of chalked lines, each numbered.

"We have everything on this floor photographed," he said. "I have three gangs—all the floodlights I have—sketching and making measurements. At the rate we're going, with time out for lunch, we'll be finished by the middle of the afternoon."

"You've been working fast. Evidently you aren't being high-church about a 'qualified archaeologist' entering rooms first," Penrose commented.

"Ach, childishness!" the old man exclaimed impatiently. "These officers of yours aren't fools. All of them have been to Intelligence School and Criminal Investigation School. Some of the most careful amateur archaeologists I ever knew were retired soldiers or policemen. But there isn't much work to be done. Most of the rooms are either empty or like this one—a few bits of furniture and broken trash and scraps of paper. Did you find anything down on the lower floors?"

"Well, yes," Penrose said, a hint of mirth in his voice. "What would you say, Martha?"

She started to tell Selim. The others, unable to restrain their excitement, broke in with interruptions. Von Ohlmhorst was staring in incredulous amazement.

"But this floor was looted almost clean, and the buildings we've entered before were all looted from the street level up," he said, at length.

"The people who looted this one lived here," Penrose replied. "They had electric power to the last; we found refrigerators full of food, and stoves with the dinner still on them. They must have used the elevators to haul things down from the upper floor. The whole first floor was converted into workshops and laboratories. I think that this place must have been something like a monastery in the Dark Ages in Europe, or what such a monastery would have been like if the Dark Ages had followed the fall of a highly developed scientific civilization. For one thing, we found a lot of machine guns and light auto-cannon on the street level, and all the doors were barricaded. The people here were trying to keep a civilization running after the rest of the planet had gone back to barbarism; I suppose they'd have to fight off raids by the barbarians now and then."

"You're not going to insist on making this building into expedition quarters, I hope, colonel?" von Ohlmhorst asked anxiously.

"Oh, no! This place is an archaeological treasure-house. More than that; from what I saw, our technicians can learn a lot, here. But you'd better get this floor cleaned up as soon as you can, though. I'll have the subsurface part, from the sixth floor down, airsealed. Then we'll put in oxygen generators and power units, and get a couple of elevators into service. For the floors above, we can use temporary airsealing floor by floor, and portable equipment; when we have things atmosphered and lighted and heated, you and Martha and Tony Lattimer can go to work systematically and in comfort, and I'll give you all the help I can spare from the other work. This is one of the biggest things we've found yet."

Tony Lattimer and his companions came down to the seventh floor a little later.

"I don't get this, at all," he began, as soon as he joined them. "This building wasn't stripped the way the others were. Always, the procedure seems to have been to strip from the bottom up, but they seem to have stripped the top floors first, here. All but the very top. I found out what that conical thing is, by the way. It's a wind-rotor, and under it there's an electric generator. This building generated its own power."

"What sort of condition are the generators in?" Penrose asked.

"Well, everything's full of dust that blew in under the rotor, of course, but it looks to be in pretty good shape. Hey, I'll bet that's it! They had power, so they used the elevators to haul stuff down. That's just what they did. Some of the floors above here don't seem to have been touched, though." He paused momentarily; back of his oxy-mask, he seemed to be grinning. "I don't know that I ought to mention this in front of Martha, but two floors above we hit a room—it must have been the reference library for one of the departments—that had close to five hundred books in it."

The noise that interrupted him, like the squeaking of a Brobdingnagian parrot, was only Ivan Fitzgerald laughing through his helmet-speaker.

Lunch at the huts was a hasty meal, with a gabble of full-mouthed and excited talking. Hubert Penrose and his chief subordinates snatched their food in a huddled consultation at one end of the table; in the afternoon, work was suspended on everything else and the fifty-odd men and women of the expedition concentrated their efforts on the University. By the middle of the afternoon, the seventh floor had been completely examined, photographed and sketched, and the murals in the square central hall covered with protective tarpaulins, and Laurent Gicquel and his airsealing crew had moved in and were at work. It had been decided to seal the central hall at the entrances. It took the French-Canadian engineer most of the afternoon to find all the ventilation-ducts and plug them. An elevator shaft on the north side was found reaching clear to the twenty-fifth floor; this would give access to the top of the building; another shaft, from the center, would take care of the floors below. Nobody seemed willing to trust the ancient elevators, themselves; it was the next evening before a couple of cars and the necessary machinery could be fabricated in the machine shops aboard the ship and sent down by landing-rocket. By that time, the airsealing was finished, the nuclear-electric energy-converters were in place, and the oxygen generators set up.

Martha was in the lower basement, an hour or so before lunch the day after, when a couple of Space Force officers came out of the elevator, bringing extra lights with them. She was still using oxygen-equipment; it was a moment before she realized that the newcomers had no masks, and that one of them was smoking. She took off her own helmet-speaker, throat-mike and mask and unslung her tank-pack, breathing cautiously. The air was chilly, and musty-acrid with the odor of antiquity—the first Martian odor she had smelled—but when she lit a cigarette, the lighter flamed clear and steady and the tobacco caught and burned evenly.

The archaeologists, many of the other civilian scientists, a few of the Space Force officers and the two news-correspondents, Sid Chamberlain and Gloria Standish, moved in that evening, setting up cots in vacant rooms. They installed electric stoves and a refrigerator in the old Library Reading Room, and put in a bar and lunch counter. For a few days, the place was full of noise and activity, then, gradually, the Space Force people and all but a few of the civilians returned to their own work. There was still the business of airsealing the more habitable of the buildings already explored, and fitting them up in readiness for the arrival, in a year and a half, of the five hundred members of the main expedition. There was work to be done enlarging the landing field for the ship's rocket craft, and building new chemical-fuel tanks.

There was the work of getting the city's ancient reservoirs cleared of silt before the next spring thaw brought more water down the underground aqueducts everybody called canals in mistranslation of Schiaparelli's Italian word, though this was proving considerably easier than anticipated. The ancient Canal-Builders must have anticipated a time when their descendants would no longer be capable of maintenance work, and had prepared against it. By the day after the University had been made completely habitable, the actual work there was being done by Selim, Tony Lattimer and herself, with half a dozen Space Force officers, mostly girls, and four or five civilians, helping.

They worked up from the bottom, dividing the floor-surfaces into numbered squares, measuring and listing and sketching and photographing. They packaged samples of organic matter and sent them up to the ship for Carbon-14 dating and analysis; they opened cans and jars and bottles, and found that everything fluid in them had evaporated, through the porosity of glass and metal and plastic if there were no other way. Wherever they looked, they found evidence of activity suddenly suspended and never resumed. A vise with a bar of metal in it, half cut through and the hacksaw beside it. Pots and pans with hardened remains of food in them; a leathery cut of meat on a table, with the knife ready at hand. Toilet articles on washstands; unmade beds, the bedding ready to crumble at a touch but still retaining the impress of the sleeper's body; papers and writing materials on desks, as though the writer had gotten up, meaning to return and finish in a fifty-thousand-year-ago moment.

It worried her. Irrationally, she began to feel that the Martians had never left this place; that they were still around her, watching disapprovingly every time she picked up something they had laid down. They haunted her dreams, now, instead of their enigmatic writing. At first, everybody who had moved into the University had taken a separate room, happy to escape the crowding and lack of privacy of the huts. After a few nights, she was glad when Gloria Standish moved in with her, and accepted the newswoman's excuse that she felt lonely without somebody to talk to before falling asleep. Sachiko Koremitsu joined them the next evening, and before going to bed, the girl officer cleaned and oiled her pistol, remarking that she was afraid some rust may have gotten into it.

The others felt it, too. Selim von Ohlmhorst developed the habit of turning quickly and looking behind him, as though trying to surprise somebody or something that was stalking him. Tony Lattimer, having a drink at the bar that had been improvised from the librarian's desk in the Reading Room, set down his glass and swore.

"You know what this place is? It's an archaeological *Marie Celeste!*" he declared. "It was occupied right up to the end—we've all seen the shifts these people used to keep a civilization going here—but what was the end? What happened to them? Where did they go?"

"You didn't expect them to be waiting out front, with a red carpet and a big banner, *Welcome Terrans*, did you, Tony?" Gloria Standish asked.

"No, of course not; they've all been dead for fifty thousand years. But if they were the last of the Martians, why haven't we found their bones, at least? Who buried them, after they were dead?" He looked at the glass, a bubble-thin goblet, found, with hundreds of others like it, in a closet above, as though debating with himself whether to have another drink. Then he voted in the affirmative and reached for the cocktail pitcher. "And every door on the old ground level is either barred or barricaded from the inside. How did they get out? And why did they leave?"

The next day, at lunch, Sachiko Koremitsu had the answer to the second question. Four or five electrical engineers had come down by rocket from the ship, and she had been spending the morning with them, in oxy-masks, at the top of the building.

"Tony, I thought you said those generators were in good shape," she began, catching sight of Lattimer. "They aren't. They're in the most unholy mess I ever saw. What happened, up there, was that the supports of the wind-rotor gave way, and weight snapped the main shaft, and smashed everything under it."

"Well, after fifty thousand years, you can expect something like that," Lattimer retorted. "When an archaeologist says something's in good shape, he doesn't necessarily mean it'll start as soon as you shove a switch it."

"You didn't notice that it happened when the power was on, did you," one of the engineers asked, nettled at Lattimer's tone. "Well, it was. Everything's burned out or shorted or fused together; I saw one busbar eight inches across melted clean in two. It's a pity we didn't find things in good shape, even archaeologically speaking. I saw a lot of interesting things, things in advance of what we're using now. But it'll take a couple of years to get everything sorted out and figure what it looked like originally."

"Did it look as though anybody'd made an attempt to fix it?" Martha asked.

Sachiko shook her head. "They must have taken one look at it and given up. I don't believe there would have been any possible way to repair anything."

"Well, that explains why they left. They needed electricity for lighting, and heating, and all their industrial equipment was electrical. They had a good life, here, with power; without it, this place wouldn't have been habitable."

"Then why did they barricade everything from the inside, and how did they get out?" Lattimer wanted to know.

"To keep other people from breaking in and looting. Last man out probably barred the last door and slid down a rope from upstairs," von Ohlmhorst suggested. "This Houdini-trick doesn't worry me too much. We'll find out eventually."

"Yes, about the time Martha starts reading Martian," Lattimer scoffed.

"That may be just when we'll find out," von Ohlmhorst replied seriously. "It wouldn't surprise me if they left something in writing when they evacuated this place."

"Are you really beginning to treat this pipe dream of hers as a serious possibility, Selim?" Lattimer demanded. "I know, it would be a wonderful thing, but wonderful things don't happen just because they're wonderful. Only because they're possible, and this isn't. Let me quote that distinguished Hittitologist, Johannes Friedrich: 'Nothing can be translated out of nothing.' Or that later but not less distinguished Hittitologist, Selim von Ohlmhorst: 'Where are you going to get your bilingual?'"

"Friedrich lived to see the Hittite language deciphered and read," von Ohlmhorst reminded him.

"Yes, when they found Hittite-Assyrian bilinguals." Lattimer measured a spoonful of coffee-powder into his cup and added hot water. "Martha, you ought to know, better than anybody, how little chance you have. You've been working for years in the Indus Valley; how many words of Harappa have you or anybody else ever been able to read?"

"We never found a university, with a half-million-volume library, at Harappa or Mohenjo-Daro."

"And, the first day we entered this building, we established meanings for several words," Selim von Ohlmhorst added.

"And you've never found another meaningful word since," Lattimer added. "And you're only sure of general meaning, not specific meaning of word-elements, and you have a dozen different interpretations for each word."

"We made a start," von Ohlmhorst maintained. "We have Grotefend's word for 'king.' But I'm going to be able to read some of those books, over there, if it takes me the rest of my life here. It probably will, anyhow."

"You mean you've changed your mind about going home on the *Cyrano*?" Martha asked. "You'll stay on here?"

The old man nodded. "I can't leave this. There's too much to discover. The old dog will have to learn a lot of new tricks, but this is where my work will be, from now on."

Lattimer was shocked. "You're nuts!" he cried. "You mean you're going to throw away everything you've accomplished in Hittitology and start all over again here on Mars? Martha, if you've talked him into this crazy decision, you're a criminal!"

"Nobody talked me into anything," von Ohlmhorst said roughly. "And as for throwing away what I've accomplished in Hittitology, I don't know what the devil you're talking about. Everything I know about the Hittite Empire is published and available to anybody. Hittitology's like Egyptology; it's stopped being research and archaeology and become scholarship and history. And I'm not a scholar or a historian; I'm a pick-and-shovel field archaeologist—a highly skilled and specialized grave-robber and junk-picker—and there's more pick-and shovel work on this planet than I could do in a hundred lifetimes. This is something new; I was a fool to think I could turn my back on it and go back to scribbling footnotes about Hittite kings."

"You could have anything you wanted, in Hittitology. There are a dozen universities that'd sooner have you than a winning football team. But no! You have to be the top man in Martiology, too. You can't leave that for anybody else—" Lattimer shoved his chair back and got to his feet, leaving the table with an oath that was almost a sob of exasperation.

Maybe his feelings were too much for him. Maybe he realized, as Martha did, what he had betrayed. She sat, avoiding the eyes of the others, looking at the ceiling, as embarrassed as though Lattimer had flung something dirty on the table in front of them. Tony Lattimer had, desperately, wanted Selim to go home on the *Cyrano*. Martiology was a new field; if Selim entered it, he would bring with him the reputation he had already built in Hittitology, automatically stepping into the leading role that Lattimer had coveted for himself. Ivan Fitzgerald's words echoed back to her—when you want to be a big shot, you can't bear the possibility of anybody else being a bigger big shot. His derision of her own efforts became comprehensible, too. It wasn't that he was convinced that she would never learn to read the Martian language. He had been afraid that she would.

Ivan Fitzgerald finally isolated the germ that had caused the Finchley girl's undiagnosed illness. Shortly afterward, the malady turned into a mild fever, from which she recovered. Nobody else seemed to have caught it. Fitzgerald was still trying to find out how the germ had been transmitted.

They found a globe of Mars, made when the city had been a seaport. They located the city, and learned that its name had been Kukan—or something with a similar vowel-consonant ratio. Immediately, Sid Chamberlain and Gloria Standish began giving their telecasts a Kukan dateline, and Hubert Penrose used the name in his official reports. They also found a Martian calendar; the year had been divided into ten more or less equal months, and one of them had been Doma. Another month was Nor, and that was a part of the name of the scientific journal Martha had found.

Bill Chandler, the zoologist, had been going deeper and deeper into the old sea bottom of Syrtis. Four hundred miles from Kukan, and at fifteen thousand feet lower altitude, he shot a bird. At least, it was a something with wings and what were almost but not quite feathers, though it was more reptilian than avian in general characteristics. He and Ivan Fitzgerald skinned and mounted it, and then dissected the carcass almost tissue by tissue. About seven-eights of its body capacity was lungs; it certainly breathed air containing at least half enough oxygen to support human life, or five times as much as the air around Kukan.

That took the center of interest away from archaeology, and started a new burst of activity. All the expedition's aircraft—four jetticopters and three wingless airdyne reconnaissance fighters—were thrown into intensified exploration of the lower sea bottoms, and the bio-science boys and girls were wild with excitement and making new discoveries on each flight.

The University was left to Selim and Martha and Tony Lattimer, the latter keeping to himself while she and the old Turco-German worked together. The civilian specialists in other fields, and the Space Force people who had been holding tape lines and making sketches and snapping camera, were all flying to lower Syrtis to find out how much oxygen there was and what kind of life it supported.

Sometimes Sachiko dropped in; most of the time she was busy helping Ivan Fitzgerald dissect specimens. They had four or five species of what might loosely be called birds, and something that could easily be classed as a reptile, and a carnivorous mammal the size of a cat with birdlike claws, and a herbivore almost identical with the piglike thing in the big *Darfhulva* mural, and another like a gazelle with a single horn in the middle of its forehead.

The high point came when one party, at thirty thousand feet below the level of Kukan, found breathable air. One of them had a mild attack of *sorroche* and had to be flown back for treatment in a hurry, but the others showed no ill effects.

The daily newscasts from Terra showed a corresponding shift in interest at home. The discovery of the University had focused attention on the dead past of Mars; now the public was interested in Mars as a possible home for humanity. It was Tony Lattimer who brought archaeology back into the activities of the expedition and the news at home.

Martha and Selim were working in the museum on the second floor, scrubbing the grime from the glass cases, noting contents, and grease-penciling numbers; Lattimer and a couple of Space Force officers were going through what had been the administrative offices on the other side. It was one of these, a young second lieutenant, who came hurrying in from the mezzanine, almost bursting with excitement.

"Hey, Martha! Dr. von Ohlmhorst!" he was shouting. "Where are you? Tony's found the Martians!"

Selim dropped his rag back in the bucket; she laid her clipboard on top of the case beside her.

"Where?" they asked together.

"Over on the north side." The lieutenant took hold of himself and spoke more deliberately. "Little room, back of one of the old faculty offices—conference room. It was locked from the inside, and we had to burn it down with a torch. That's where they are. Eighteen of them, around a long table—"

Gloria Standish, who had dropped in for lunch, was on the mezzanine, fairly screaming into a radio-phone extension:

" . . . Dozen and a half of them! Well, of course they're dead. What a question! They look like skeletons covered with leather. No, I do not know what they died of. Well, forget it; I don't care if Bill Chandler's found a three-headed hippopotamus. Sid, don't you get it? We've found the *Martians!*"

She slammed the phone back on its hook, rushing away ahead of them.

Martha remembered the closed door; on the first survey, they hadn't attempted opening it. Now it was burned away at both sides and lay, still hot along the edges, on the floor of the big office room in front. A floodlight was on in the room inside, and Lattimer was going around looking at things while a Space Force officer stood by the door. The center of the room was filled by a long table; in armchairs around it sat the eighteen men and women who had occupied the room for the last fifty millennia. There were bottles and glasses on the table in front of them, and, had she seen them in a dimmer light, she would have thought that they were merely dozing over their drinks. One had a knee hooked over his chair-arm and was curled in foetus-like sleep. Another had fallen forward onto the table, arms extended, the emerald set of a ring twinkling dully on one finger. Skeletons covered with leather, Gloria Standish had called them, and so they were—faces like skulls, arms and legs like sticks, the flesh shrunken onto the bones under it.

"Isn't this something!" Lattimer was exulting. "Mass suicide, that's what it was. Notice what's in the corners?"

Braziers, made of perforated two-gallon-odd metal cans, the

white walls smudged with smoke above them. Von Ohlmhorst had noticed them at once, and was poking into one of them with his flashlight.

"Yes; charcoal. I noticed a quantity of it around a couple of hand-forges in the shop on the first floor. That's why you had so much trouble breaking in; they'd sealed the room on the inside." He straightened and went around the room, until he found a ventilator, and peered into it. "Stuffed with rags. They must have been all that were left, here. Their power was gone, and they were old and tired, and all around them their world was dying. So they just came in here and lit the charcoal, and sat drinking together till they all fell asleep. Well, we know what became of them, now, anyhow."

Sid and Gloria made the most of it. The Terran public wanted to hear about Martians, and if live Martians couldn't be found, a room full of dead ones was the next best thing. Maybe an even better thing; it had been only sixty-odd years since the Orson Welles invasion-scare. Tony Lattimer, the discoverer, was beginning to cash in on his attentions to Gloria and his ingratiation with Sid; he was always either making voice-and-image talks for telecast or listening to the news from the home planet. Without question, he had become, overnight, the most widely known archaeologist in history.

"Not that I'm interested in all this, for myself," he disclaimed, after listening to the telecast from Terra two days after his discovery. "But this is going to be a big thing for Martian archaeology. Bring it to the public attention; dramatize it. Selim, can you remember when Lord Carnarvon and Howard Carter found the tomb of Tutankhamen?"

"In 1923? I was two years old, then," von Ohlmhorst chuckled. "I really don't know how much that publicity ever did for Egyptology. Oh, the museums did devote more space to Egyptian exhibits, and after a museum department head gets a few extra showcases, you know how hard it is to make him give them up. And, for a while, it was easier to get financial support for new excavations. But I don't know how much good all this public excitement really does, in the long run."

"Well, I think one of us should go back on the *Cyrano*, when the *Schiaparelli* orbits in," Lattimer said. "I'd hoped it would be you; your voice would carry the most weight. But I think it's important that one of us go back, to present the story of our work, and what we have accomplished and what we hope to accomplish, to the public and to the universities and the learned societies, and to the Federation Government. There will be a great deal of work that will have to be done. We must not allow the other scientific fields and the so-called practical interests to monopolize public and academic support. So, I believe I shall go back at least for a while, and see what I can do—"

Lectures. The organization of a Society of Martian Archaeology, with Anthony Lattimer, Ph.D., the logical candidate for the chair. Degrees, honors; the deference of the learned, and the adulation of the lay public. Positions, with impressive titles and salaries. Sweet are the uses of publicity.

She crushed out her cigarette and got to her feet. "Well, I still have the final lists of what we found in *Halvhulva*—Biology—department to check over. I'm starting on *Sornhulva* tomorrow, and I want that stuff in shape for expert evaluation."

That was the sort of thing Tony Lattimer wanted to get away from, the detail-work and the drudgery. Let the infantry do the slogging through the mud; the brass-hats got the medals.

She was halfway through the fifth floor, a week later, and was having midday lunch in the reading room on the first floor when Hubert Penrose came over and sat down beside her, asking her what she was doing. She told him.

"I wonder if you could find me a couple of men, for an hour or so," she added. "I'm stopped by a couple of jammed doors at the central hall. Lecture room and library, if the layout of that floor's anything like the ones below it."

"Yes. I'm a pretty fair door-buster, myself." He looked around the room. "There's Jeff Miles; he isn't doing much of anything. And we'll put Sid Chamberlain to work, for a change, too. The four of us ought to get your doors open." He called to Chamberlain, who was carrying his tray over to the dish washer. "Oh, Sid; you doing anything for the next hour or so?"

"I was going up to the fourth floor, to see what Tony's doing."

"Forget it. Tony's bagged his season limit of Martians. I'm going to help Martha bust in a couple of doors; we'll probably find a whole cemetery full of Martians."

Chamberlain shrugged. "Why not. A jammed door can have anything back of it, and I know what Tony's doing—just routine stuff."

Jeff Miles, the Space Force captain, came over, accompanied by one of the lab-crew from the ship who had come down on the rocket the day before.

"This ought to be up your alley, Mort," he was saying to his companion. "Chemistry and physics department. Want to come along?"

The lab man, Mort Tranter, was willing. Seeing the sights was what he'd come down from the ship for. She finished her coffee and cigarette, and they went out into the hall together, gathered equipment and rode the elevator to the fifth floor.

The lecture hall door was the nearest; they attacked it first. With proper equipment and help, it was no problem and in ten minutes they had it open wide enough to squeeze through with the floodlights. The room inside was quite empty, and, like most of the rooms behind closed doors, comparatively free from dust. The students, it appeared, had sat with their backs to the door, facing a low platform, but their seats and the lecturer's table and equipment had been removed. The two side walls bore inscriptions: on the right, a pattern of concentric circles which she recognized as a diagram of atomic structure, and on the left a complicated table of numbers and words, in two columns. Tranter was pointing at the diagram on the right.

"They got as far as the Bohr atom, anyhow," he said. "Well, not quite. They knew about electron shells, but they have the nucleus pictured as a solid mass. No indication of proton-and-neutron structure. I'll bet, when you come to translate their scientific books, you'll find that they taught that the atom was the ultimate and indivisible particle. That explains why you people never found any evidence that the Martians used nuclear energy."

"That's a uranium atom," Captain Miles mentioned.

"It is?" Sid Chamberlain asked, excitedly. "Then they did know about atomic energy. Just because we haven't found any pictures of A-bomb mushrooms doesn't mean—"

She turned to look at the other wall. Sid's signal reactions were getting away from him again; uranium meant nuclear power to him, and the two words were interchangeable. As she studied the arrangement of the numbers and words, she could hear Tranter saying:

"Nuts, Sid. We knew about uranium a long time before anybody found out what could be done with it. Uranium was discovered on Terra in 1789, by Klaproth."

There was something familiar about the table on the left wall. She tried to remember what she had been taught in school about physics, and what she had picked up by accident afterward. The second column was a continuation of the first: there were forty-six items in each, each item numbered consecutively—

"Probably used uranium because it's the largest of the natural atoms," Penrose was saying. "The fact that there's nothing beyond it there shows that they hadn't created any of the transuranics. A student could go to that thing and point out the outer electron of any of the ninety-two elements."

Ninety-two! That was it; there were ninety-two items in the table on the left wall! Hydrogen was Number One, she knew; One, *Sarfaldsorn.* Helium was Two; that was *Tirfaldsorn.* She couldn't remember which element came next, but in Martian it was *Sarfalddavas. Sorn* must mean matter, or substance, then. And *davas*; she was trying to think of what it could be. She turned quickly to the others, catching hold of Hubert Penrose's arm with one hand and waving her clipboard with the other.

"Look at this thing, over here," she was clamoring excitedly. "Tell me what you think it is. Could it be a table of the elements?"

They all turned to look. Mort Tranter stared at it for a moment.

"Could be. If I only knew what those squiggles meant—"

That was right; he'd spent his time aboard the ship.

"If you could read the numbers, would that help?" she asked, beginning to set down the Arabic digits and their Martian equivalents. "It's decimal system, the same as we use."

"Sure. If that's a table of elements, all I'd need would be the numbers. Thanks," he added as she tore off the sheet and gave it to him.

Penrose knew the numbers, and was ahead of him. "Ninety-two items, numbered consecutively. The first number would be the atomic number. Then a single word, the name of the element. Then the atomic weight—"

She began reading off the names of the elements. "I know hydrogen and helium; what's *tirfalddavas*, the third one?"

"Lithium," Tranter said. "The atomic weights aren't run out past the decimal point. Hydrogen's one plus, if that double-hook dingus is a plus sign; Helium's four-plus, that's right. And lithium's given as seven, that isn't right. It's six-point-nine-four-oh. Or is that thing a Martian minus sign?"

"Of course! Look! A plus sign is a hook, to hang things together; a minus sign is a knife, to cut something off from something—see, the little loop is the handle and the long pointed loop is the blade. Stylized, of course, but that's what it is. And the fourth element, *kiradavas*; what's that?"

"Beryllium. Atomic weight given as nine-and-a-hook; actually it's nine-point-oh-two."

Sid Chamberlain had been disgruntled because he couldn't get a story about the Martians having developed atomic energy. It took him a few minutes to understand the newest development, but finally it dawned on him.

"Hey! You're reading that!" he cried. "You're reading Martian!"

"That's right," Penrose told him. "Just reading it right off. I don't get the two items after the atomic weight, though. They look like months of the Martian calendar. What ought they to be, Mort?"

Tranter hesitated. "Well, the next information after the atomic weight ought to be the period and group numbers. But those are words."

"What would the numbers be for the first one, hydrogen?"

"Period One, Group One. One electron shell, one electron in the outer shell," Tranter told her. "Helium's period one, too, but it has the outer—only—electron shell full, so it's in the group of inert elements."

"*Trav, Trav. Trav*'s the first month of the year. And helium's *Trav, Yenth; Yenth* is the eighth month."

"The inert elements could be called Group Eight, yes. And the third element, lithium, is Period Two, Group One. That check?"

"It certainly does. *Sanv, Trav; Sanv*'s the second month. What's the first element in Period Three?"

"Sodium, Number Eleven."

"That's right; it's *Krav, Trav*. Why, the names of the months are simply numbers, one to ten, spelled out."

"*Doma*'s the fifth month. That was your first Martian word, Martha," Penrose told her. "The word for five. And if *davas* is the word for metal, and *sornhulva* is chemistry and/or physics, I'll bet *Tadavas Sornhulva* is literally translated as : 'Of-Metal Matter-Knowledge.' Metallurgy, in other words. I wonder what *Mastharnorvod* means." It surprised her that, after so long and with so much happening in the meantime, he could remember that. "Something like 'Journal,' or 'Review,' or maybe 'Quarterly.'"

"We'll work that out, too," she said confidently. After this, nothing seemed impossible. "Maybe we can find—" Then she stopped short. "You said 'Quarterly.' I think it was 'Monthly,' instead. It was dated for a specific month, the fifth one. And if *nor* is ten,

Mastharnorvod could be 'Year-Tenth.' And I'll bet we'll find that *masthar* is the word for year." She looked at the table on the wall again. "Well, let's get all these words down, with translations for as many as we can."

"Let's take a break for a minute," Penrose suggested, getting out his cigarettes. "And then, let's do this in comfort. Jeff, suppose you and Sid go across the hall and see what you find in the other room in the way of a desk or something like that, and a few chairs. There'll be a lot of work to do on this."

Sid Chamberlain had been squirming as though he were afflicted with ants, trying to contain himself. Now he let go with an excited jabber.

"This is really it! *The* it, not just it-of-the-week, like finding the reservoirs or those statues or this building, or even the animals and the dead Martians! Wait till Selim and Tony see this! Wait till Tony sees it; I want to see his face! And when I get this on telecast, all Terra's going to go nuts about it!" He turned to Captain Miles. "Jeff, suppose you take a look at that other door, while I find somebody to send to tell Selim and Tony. And Gloria; wait till she sees this—"

"Take it easy, Sid," Martha cautioned. "You'd better let me have a look at your script, before you go too far overboard on the telecast. This is just a beginning; it'll take years and years before we're able to read any of those books downstairs."

"It'll go faster than you think, Martha," Hubert Penrose told her. "We'll all work on it, and we'll teleprint material to Terra, and people there will work on it. We'll send them everything we can . . . everything we work out, and copies of books, and copies of your word-lists—"

And there would be other tables—astronomical tables, tables in physics and mechanics, for instance—in which words and numbers were equivalent. The library stacks, below, would be full of them. Transliterate them into Roman alphabet spellings and Arabic numerals, and somewhere, somebody would spot each numerical significance, as Hubert Penrose and Mort Tranter and she had done with the table of elements. And pick out all the chemistry textbooks in the Library; new words would take on meaning from contexts in which the names of elements appeared. She'd have to start studying chemistry and physics, herself—

Sachiko Koremitsu peeped in through the door, then stepped inside.

"Is there anything I can do—?" she began. "What's happened? Something important?"

"Important?" Sid Chamberlain exploded. "Look at that, Sachi! We're reading it! Martha's found out how to read Martian!" He grabbed Captain Miles by the arm. "Come on, Jeff; let's go. I want to call the others—" He was still babbling as he hurried from the room.

Sachi looked at the inscription. "Is it true?" she asked, and then, before Martha could more than begin to explain, flung her arms around her. "Oh, it really is! You are reading it! I'm so happy!"

She had to start explaining again when Selim von Ohlmhorst entered. This time, she was able to finish.

"But, Martha, can you be really sure? You know, by now, that learning to read this language is as important to me as it is to you, but how can you be so sure that those words really mean things like hydrogen and helium and boron and oxygen? How do you know that their table of elements was anything like ours?"

Tranter and Penrose and Sachiko all looked at him in amazement.

"That isn't just the Martian table of elements; that's *the* table of elements. It's the only one there is," Mort Tranter almost exploded. "Look, hydrogen has one proton and one electron. If it had more of either, it wouldn't be hydrogen, it'd be something else. And the same with all the rest of the elements. And hydrogen on Mars is the same as hydrogen on Terra, or on Alpha Centauri, or in the next galaxy—"

"You just set up those numbers, in that order, and any first-year chemistry student could tell you what elements they represented," Penrose said. "Could if he expected to make a passing grade, that is."

The old man shook his head slowly, smiling. "I'm afraid I wouldn't make a passing grade. I didn't know, or at least didn't realize, that. One of the things I'm going to place an order for, to be brought on the *Schiaparelli*, will be a set of primers in chemistry and physics, of the sort intended for a bright child of ten or twelve. It seems that a Martiologist has to learn a lot of things the Hittites and the Assyrians never heard about."

Tony Lattimer, coming in, caught the last part of the explanation. He looked quickly at the walls and, having found out just what had happened, advanced and caught Martha by the hand.

"You really did it, Martha! You found your bilingual! I never believed that it would be possible; let me congratulate you!"

He probably expected that to erase all the jibes and sneers of the past. If he did, he could have it that way. His friendship would mean as little to her as his derision—except that his friends had to watch their backs and his knife. But he was going home on the *Cyrano*, to be a big-shot. Or had this changed his mind for him again?

"This is something we can show the world, to justify any expenditure of time and money on Martian archaeological work. When I get back to Terra, I'll see that you're given full credit for this achievement—"

On Terra, her back and his knife would be out of her watchfulness.

"We won't need to wait that long," Hubert Penrose told him dryly. "I'm sending off an official report, tomorrow; you can be sure Dr. Dane will be given full credit, not only for this but for her previous work, which made it possible to exploit this discovery."

"And you might add, work done in spite of the doubts and discouragements of her colleagues," Selim von Ohlmhorst said. "To which I am ashamed to have to confess my own share."

"You said we had to find a bilingual," she said. "You were right, too."

"This is better than a bilingual, Martha," Hubert Penrose said. "Physical science expresses universal facts; necessarily it is a universal language. Heretofore archaeologists have dealt only with pre-scientific cultures."

The Gentle Earth

by Christopher Anvil

PREFACE BY ERIC FLINT

It was hard to pick a specific Christopher Anvil story for this anthology. His most famous single story is "Pandora's Planet," which first appeared in the September 1956 issue of *Astounding* magazine; his best-known series of stories, the multitude of Interstellar Patrol stories which appeared in *Astounding* throughout the '60s. We could have easily chosen from any of them.

But . . . well . . .

For starters, my innate frugality—ignore what my wife says—rebelled at the notion. With me serving as editor of the project, Baen Books has already reissued the entire "Pandora's Planet" sequence and is in the process of reissuing in three volumes all the stories Anvil wrote in his Colonization setting, which includes all the Interstellar Patrol stories. To include one of those in this anthology just seemed a little wasteful.

Beyond that, however, as it happens my first encounter with the writing of Christopher Anvil wasn't any of those stories anyway. I first ran into Anvil in one of those marvelous epistolary tales that he did so well, and which so few writers can handle properly. (For those of you who are literarily challenged, an "epistolary tale" is a story told in the form of correspondence; usually letters, but sometimes—Anvil was especially good at this—in the form of telegraph-like exchanges.)

So I thought of including that story. The problem then became . . .

I couldn't remember *which* story I'd first read as a teenager. It might have been "The Prisoner"...no, maybe it was "Trial by Silk"...on the other hand, it could have been "Bill For Delivery"...then again, it could have been "Revolt!" too...

Finally, I whined to Jim and Dave about my quandary. Jim pondered the matter for a bit, in his best Sagacious Publisher style. (He does that quite well. Of course, he also does Curmudgeon Editor quite well, too.)

"Let's go with 'The Gentle Earth,'" he said. "It's classic Anvil, it's a lot of fun—and it had one of those great Kelly Freas cover illustrations when it first came out in *Astounding*."

Bingo.

Tlasht Bade, Supreme Commander of Invasion Forces, drew thoughtfully on his slim cigar. "The scouts are all back?"

Sission Runckel, Chief of the Supreme Commander's Staff, nodded. "They all got back safely, though one or two had difficulties with some of the lower life forms."

"Is the climate all right?"

Runckel abstractedly reached in his tunic, and pulled out a thing like a short piece of tarred rope. As he trimmed it, he scowled. "There's some discomfort, apparently because the air is too dry. But on the other hand, there's plenty of oxygen near the planet's surface, and the gravity's about the same as it is back home. We can live there."

Bade glanced across the room at a large blue, green, and brown globe, with irregular patches of white at top and bottom. "What are the white areas?"

"Apparently, chalk. One of our scouts landed there, but he's in practically a state of shock. The brilliant reflectivity in the area blinded him, a huge white furry animal attacked him, and he barely got out alive. To cap it all, his ship's insulation apparently broke down on the way back, and now he's in the sick bay with a bad case of space-gripe. All we can get out of him is that he had severe prickling sensations in the feet when he stepped out onto the chalk dust. Probably a pile of little spiny shells."

"Did he bring back a sample?"

"He claims he did. But there's only water in his sample box. I imagine he was delirious. In any case, this part of the planet has little to interest us."

Bade nodded. "What about the more populous regions?"

"Just as we thought. A huge web of interconnecting cities, manufacturing centers, and rural areas. Our mapping procedures have proved to be accurate."

"That's a relief. What about the natives?"

"Erect, land-dwelling, ill-tempered bipeds," said Runckel. "They seem to have little or no planet-wide unity. Of course, we have large samplings of their communications media. When these are all analyzed, we'll know a lot more."

"What do they look like?"

"They're pink or brown in color, quite tall, but not very broad or thick through the chest. A little fur here and there on their bodies. No webs on their hands or feet, and their feet are fantastically small. Otherwise, they look quite human."

"Their technology?"

Runckel sucked in a deep breath and sat up straight. "Every bit as bad as we thought." He picked up a little box with two stiff handles, squeezed the handles hard, and touched a glowing wire on the box to his piece of black rope. He puffed violently.

Bade turned up the air-conditioning. Billowing clouds of smoke drew away from Runckel in long streamers, so that he looked like an island looming through heavy mist. His brow was creased in a foreboding scowl.

"Technologically," he said, "they are deadly. They've got fission and fusion, indirect molecular and atomic reaction control, and a long-reaching development of electron flow and pulsing devices. So far, they don't seem to have anything based on deep rearrangement or keyed focusing. But who knows when they'll stumble on that? And then what? Even now, properly warned and ready they could give us a terrible struggle."

Runckel knocked a clinker off his length of rope and looked at Bade with the tentative, judging air of one who is not quite sure of another's reliability. Then he said, loudly and with great firmness, "We have a lot to be thankful for. Another five or ten decades delay getting the watchships up through the cloud layer, and they'd have had us by the throat. We've got to smash them before they're ready, or *we'll* end up as *their* colony."

Bade's eyes narrowed. "I've always opposed this invasion on philosophical grounds. But it's been argued and settled. I'm willing to go along with the majority opinion." Bade rapped the ash off his slender cigar and looked Runckel directly in the eyes. "But if you want to open the whole argument up all over again—"

"No," said Runckel, breathing out a heavy cloud of smoke. "But our micromapping and radiation analysis shows a terrific rate of progress. It's hard to look at those figures and even breathe normally. They're gaining on us like a shark after a minnow."

"In that case," said Bade, "let's wake up and hold our lead. This business of attacking the suspect before he has a chance to commit a crime is no answer. What about all the other planets in the universe? How do we know what they might do some day?"

"This planet is right beside us!"

"Is murder honorable as long as you do it only to your neighbor? Your argument is self-defense. But you're straining it."

"Let it strain, then," said Runckel angrily. "All I care about is that chart showing our comparative levels of development. Now *we* have the lead. I say, drag them out by their necks and let them submit, or we'll thrust their heads underwater and have done with them. And anyone who says otherwise is a doubtful patriot!"

Bade's teeth clamped, and he set his cigar carefully on a tray.

Runckel blinked, as if he only appreciated what he had said by its echo.

Bade's glance moved over Runckel deliberately, as if stripping away the emblems and insignia. Then Bade opened the bottom drawer of his desk, and pulled out a pad of dun-colored official forms. As he straightened, his glance caught the motto printed large on the base of the big globe. The motto had been used so often in the struggle to decide the question of invasion that Bade seldom noticed it any more. But now he looked at it. The motto read:

Them Or Us

Bade stared at it for a long moment, looked up at the globe that represented the mighty planet, then down at the puny motto. He glanced at Runckel, who looked back dully but squarely. Bade glanced at the motto, shook his head in disgust, and said, "Go get me the latest reports."

Runckel blinked. "Yes, sir," he said, and hurried out.

Bade leaned forward, ignored the motto, and thoughtfully studied the globe.

∾   ∾   ∾

Bade read the reports carefully. Most of them, he noted, contained a qualification. In the scientific reports, this generally appeared at the end:

" ... Owing to the brief time available for these observations, the conclusions presented herein must be regarded as only provisional in character."

In the reports of the scouts, this reservation was usually presented in bits and pieces:

" ... And this thing, that looked like a tiny crab, had a pair of pincers on one end, and I didn't have time to see if this was the end it got me with, or if it was the other end. But I got a jolt as if somebody squeezed a lighter and held the red-hot wire against my leg. Then I got dizzy and sick to my stomach. I don't know for sure if this was what did it, or if there are many of them, but if there are, and if it did, I don't see how a man could fight a war and not be stung to death when he wasn't looking. But I wasn't there long enough to be sure ... "

Another report spoke of a "Crawling army of little six-legged things with a set of oversize jaws on one end, that came swarming through the shrubbery straight for the ship, went right up the side and set to work eating away the superplast binder around the viewport. With that gone, the ship would leak air like a fishnet. But when I tried to clear them away, they started in on me. I don't know if this really proves anything, because Rufft landed not too far away, and he swears the place was like a paradise. Nevertheless, I have to report that I merely set my foot on the ground, and I almost got marooned and eaten up right on the spot."

Bade was particularly uneasy over reports of a vague respiratory difficulty some of the scouts noticed in the region where the first landings were planned. Bade commented on it, and Runckel nodded.

"I know," said Runckel. "The air's too dry. But if we take time to try to provide for that, at the same time they may make some new advance that will more than nullify whatever we gain. And right now their communications media show a political situation that fits right in with our plans. We can't hope for that to last forever."

Bade listened as Runckel described a situation like that of a dozen hungry sharks swimming in a circle, each getting its jaws open for a snap at the next one's tail. Then Runckel described his plan.

At the end, Bade said, "Yes, it may work out as you say. But listen, Runckel, isn't this a little too much like one of those whirl-pools in the Treacherous Islands? If everything works out, you go through in a flash. But one wrong guess, and you go around and around and around and around and you're lucky if you get out with a whole skin."

Runckel's jaw set firmly. "This is the only way to get a clear-cut decision."

Bade studied the far wall of the room for a moment. "I'm sorry I didn't get a hand at these plans sooner."

"Sir," said Runckel, "You would have, if you hadn't been so busy fighting the whole idea." He hesitated, then asked, "Will you be coming to the staff review of plans?"

"Certainly," said Bade.

"Good," said Runckel. "You'll see that we have it all worked to perfection."

Bade went to the review of plans and listened as the details were gone over minutely. At the end, Runckel gave an overall summary:

"The Colony Planet," he said, rapping a pointer on maps of four hemispheric views, "is only seventy-five percent water, so the land areas are immense. The chief land masses are largely dominated by two hostile power groups, which we may call East and West. At the fringes of influence of these power groups live a vast mass of people not firmly allied to either.

"The territory of this uncommitted group is well suited to our purposes. It contains many pleasant islands and comfortable seas. Unfortunately, analysis shows that the dangerous military power groups will unite against us if we seize this territory directly. To avoid this, we will act to stun and divide them at one stroke."

Runckel rapped his pointer on a land area lettered "North America," and said, "On this land mass is situated a politico-economic unit known as the U.S. The U.S. is the dominant power both in the Western Hemisphere and in the West power group. It is surrounded by wide seas that separate it from its allies.

"Our plan is simple and direct. We will attack and seize the central plain of the U.S. This will split it into helpless fragments, any one of which we may crush at will. The loss of the U.S. will, of course, destroy the power balance between East and West. The East will immediately seize the scraps of Western power and influence all over the globe.

"During this period of disorder, we will set up our key-tool factories and a light-duty forceway network. In rapid stages will then come ore-converters, staging plants, fabricators, heavy-duty forceway stations and self-operated production units. With these last we will produce energy-conversion units and storage piles by the million in a network to blanket the occupied area. The linkage produced will power our damper units to blot out missile attacks that may now begin in earnest.

"We will thus be solidly established on the planet itself. Our base will be secure against attack. We will now turn our energies to the destruction of the U.S.S.R. as a military power." He reached out with his pointer to rap a new land mass.

"The U.S.S.R. is the dominant power of the East power group. This will by now be the only hostile power group remaining on the planet. It will be destroyed in stages.

"In Stage I we will confuse the U.S.S.R. by propaganda. We will profess friendship while we secretly multiply our productive facilities to the highest possible degree.

"In Stage II, we will seize and fortify the western and northern islands of Britain, Novaya Zemlya, and New Siberia. We will also seize and heavily fortify the Kamchatka Peninsula in the extreme eastern U.S.S.R. We will now demand that the U.S.S.R. lay down its arms and surrender.

"In the event of refusal, we will, from our fortified bases, destroy by missile attack all productive facilities and communication centers in the U.S.S.R. The resulting paralysis will bring down the East power group in ruins. The planet will now lay open before us."

Runckel looked at each of his listeners in turn.

"Everything has been done to make this invasion a success. To crush out any possible miscalculation, we are moving with massive reserves close behind us. Certain glory and a mighty victory await us.

"Let us raise our heads in prayer, then join in the Oath of Battle."

The first wave of the attack came down like an avalanche on the central U.S. Multiple transmitters went into action to throw local radar stations into confusion. Stull-gas missiles streaked from the landing ships to explode over nearby cities. Atmospheric flyers roared off to intercept possible enemy attacks. A stream of guns, tanks, and troop carriers rolled down the landing ways and fanned out to seize enemy power plants and communications centers.

The commander of the first wave reported: "Everything proceed-ing according to plan. Enemy resistance negligible."

Runckel ordered the second wave down.

Bade, watching it on a number of giant viewscreens in the opera-tions room of a ship coming down, had a peculiar feeling of numb-ness, such as might follow a deep cut before the pain is felt.

Runckel, his face intense, said: "Their position is hopeless. The main landing site is secure and the rest will come faster than the eye can see." He turned to speak into one of a bank of microphones, then said, "Our glider missiles are circling over their capital."

A loud-speaker high on the wall said, "Landing minus three. Take your stations, please."

The angle of vision of one of the viewscreens tilted suddenly, to show a high, dome-topped building set in a city filled with rush-ing beetle shapes—obviously ground-cars of some type. Abruptly these cars all pulled to the sides of the streets.

"That," said Runckel grimly, "means their capital is out of busi-ness."

The picture on the viewscreen blurred suddenly, like the reflection from water ruffled by a breeze. There was a clang like a ten-ton hammer hitting a twenty-ton gong. Walls, floor, and ceiling of the room danced and vibrated. Two of the viewscreens went blank.

Bade felt a prickling sensation travel across his shoulders and down his back. He glanced sharply at Runckel.

Runckel's expression looked startled but firm. He reached out and snapped orders into one of his microphones.

There was an intense, high-pitched ringing, then a clap like a nuclear cannon of six paces distance.

The wall loud-speaker said, "Landing minus two."

An intense silence descended on the room. One by one, the viewscreens flickered on. Bade heard Runckel say, "The ship is totally damped. They haven't anything that can get through it."

There was a dull, low-pitched thud, a sense of being snapped like a whip, and the screens went blank. The wall loud-speaker dropped, and jerked to a stop, hanging by its cord.

Then the ship set down.

Runckel's plan assumed that the swift-moving advance from the landing site would overrun a sizable territory during the first day. With this maneuvering space quickly gained, the landing site itself would be safe from enemy ground attack by dawn of the second day.

Now that they were down, however, Bade and Runckel looked at the operations room's big viewscreen, and saw their vehicles standing still all over the landscape. The troops crowded about the rear of the vehicles to watch cursing drivers pull the motors up out of their housings and spread them out on the ground. Here and there a stern officer argued with grim-faced troops who stared stonily ahead as if they didn't hear. Meanwhile, the tanks, trucks, and weapons carriers stood motionless.

Runckel, infuriated, had a cluster of microphones gripped in his hand, and was pronouncing death by strangling and decapitation on any officer who failed to get his unit in motion right away.

Bade studied the baffled expressions on the faces of the drivers, then glanced at the enemy ground-cars abandoned at the side of the road. He turned to see a tall officer with general's insignia stagger through the doorway and grip Runckel by the arm. Bade recognized Rast, General Forces Commander.

"Sir," said Rast, "it can't be done."

"It has to be done," said Runckel grimly. "So far we've decoyed the enemy missiles to a false site. Before they spot us again, *those troops have got to be spread out!*"

"They won't ride in the vehicles!"

"It's that or get killed!"

"Sir," said Rast, "you don't understand. I came back here in a gun carrier. To start with, the driver jammed the speed lever all the way to the front shield, and nothing happened. He got up to see what was wrong. The carrier shot ahead with a flying leap, threw the driver into the back, and almost snapped our heads off. Then it coasted to a stop. We pulled ourselves together and turned around to get the cover off the motor box.

"*Wham!* The carrier took off, ripped the cover out of our hands, threw us against the rear shield and knocked us senseless. Then it rolled to a stop.

"That's how we got here. Jump! Roll. Stop. Wait. Jump! Roll. Stop. Wait. On one of those jumps, the gun went out the back of the carrier, mount, bolts, and all. The driver swore he'd turn off the motor, and fangjaw take the planet and the whole invasion. We aren't going to win a war with troops in that frame of mind."

Runckel took a deep breath.

Bade said, "What about the enemy's ground-cars? Will they run?"

Rast blinked. "I don't know. Maybe—"

Bade snapped on a microphone lettered "Aerial Rec." A little screen in a half-circle atop the microphone lit up to show an alert, harried-looking officer. Bade said, "You've noticed our vehicles are stopped?"

"Yes, sir."

"Were the enemy's ground-cars affected at the same time as ours?"

"No sir, they were still moving after ours were stuck."

"Any motor trouble in Atmospheric Flyer Command?"

"None that I know of, sir."

Bade glanced at Rast. "Try using the enemy ground-cars. Meanwhile, get the troops you can't move back under cover of the ships' dampers."

Rast saluted, whirled, and went out at a staggering run.

Bade called Atmospheric Flyer Command, and Ground Forces Maintenance, and arranged for the captured enemy vehicles to be identified by a large yellow X painted across the top of the hood. Then he turned to Runckel and said, "We're going to need all the support we can get. See if we can bring Landing Force 2 down late today instead of tomorrow."

"I'll try," said Runckel.

It seemed to Bade that the events of the next twenty-four hours unrolled like the scenes of a nightmare.

Before the troops were all under cover, an enemy reconnaissance aircraft leaked in very high overhead. The detector screens of Atmospheric Flyer Command were promptly choked with enemy aircraft coming in low and fast from all directions.

These aircraft were of all types. Some heaved their bombs in under-hand, barreled over and streaked home for another load. Others were flying hives of anti-aircraft missiles. A third type were suicide bombers or winged missiles; these roared in head-on and blew up on arrival.

While the dampers labored and overheated, and Flyer Command struggled with enemy fighters and bombers overhead, a long-range reconnaissance flyer spotted a sizable convoy of enemy ground forces rushing up from the southwest.

Bade and Runckel concentrated first on living through the air attack. It soon developed that the enemy planes, though extremely fast, were not very maneuverable. The enemy's missiles did not quite overload the dampers. The afternoon wore on in an explosive violence that was severe, but barely endurable. It began to seem that they might live through it.

Toward evening, however, a small enemy missile streaked in on the end of a wire and smashed the grid of an auxiliary damper unit. Before this unit could be repaired, a heavy missile came down near the same place, and overloaded the damper network. Another missile streaked in. One of the ships tilted, and fell headlong. The engines of this ship were ripped out of the circuit that powered the dampers. With the next enemy missile strike, another ship was heaved off its base. This ship housed a large proportion of Flyer Command's detector screens.

Bade and Runckel looked at each other. Bade's lips moved, and he heard himself say, "Prepare to evacuate."

At this moment, the enemy attack let up.

It took an instant for Bade to realize what had happened. He canceled his evacuation order before it could be transmitted, then had the two thrown ships linked back into the power circuit. He turned around, and his glance fell on one of the viewscreens showing the shadowy plain outside. A brilliant flash lit the screen, and he saw dark low shapes rushing in toward the ships. Bade immediately gave orders to defend against ground attack, but not to pursue beyond range of the dampers.

A savage, half-lit struggle developed. The enemy, whose weapons failed to work in range of the dampers, attacked with bayonets, and used guns, shovels, and picks in the manner of clubs and battle axes. In a spasm of bloody violence they fought their way in among the ships, then, confused in the dimness, were thrown back with heavy losses. As night settled down, the enemy dug in to make a fortified ring close around the landing site.

The enemy missile attack failed to recover its former violence.

Bade gave silent thanks for the deliverance. As the comparative quiet continued, it seemed clear that the enemy high command was holding back to avoid hitting their own men dug in nearby.

It occurred to Bade that now might be a good time to get a little sleep. He turned to go to his cot, and there was a rush of yellow dots on Flyer Command's pilot screen. As he stared wide-eyed, auxiliary screens flickered on and off to show a ghostly dish-shaped object that led his flyers on a wild chase all over the sky, then vanished at an estimated speed twenty times that the enemy planes were thought capable of doing.

Runckel said, "Landing Force 2 can get here at early dawn. That's the best we can manage."

Bade nodded dully.

The ground screens now lit in brilliant flashes as the enemy began firing monster rockets at practically point-blank range.

Night passed in a continuous bombardment.

At early dawn of the next day, Bade put in all his remaining missiles, and bomber and interceptor flyers. For a brief interval of time, the enemy bombardment was smothered.

Landing force 2 sat down beside Landing Force 1.

Bade ordered the Stull-gas missiles of Landing Force 2 exploded over the enemy ground troops. In the resulting confusion, the ground forces moved out and captured large numbers of enemy troops, weapons, and vehicles. The captured vehicles were marked and promptly put to use.

Bade spoke briefly with General Rast, commanding the ground forces.

"Now's your chance," said Bade. "Move fast and we can capture supplies and reinforcements flowing in, before they realize we've broken their ring."

Under the protection of the flyers of Landing Force 2, Rast's troops swung out onto the central plain of the North American continent.

The advance moved fast. Enemy troops and supply convoys were caught off guard on the road. When the enemy fought, his resistance was patchy and confused.

Bade, feeling drugged from lack of sleep, lay down on his cot for a nap. He awoke feeling fuzzy-brained and dull.

"They're whipped," said Runckel gleefully. "We've got back the time we lost yesterday. There's no resistance to speak of. And we've just made a treaty with the East bloc."

Bade sat up dizzily. "That's wonderful," he said. He glanced at the clock. "Why wasn't I called sooner?"

"No need," said Runckel. "It's all just a matter of form. Landing Force 3 is coming down tonight. The war's over." Runckel's face, as he said this, had a peculiar shine.

Bade frowned. "Isn't the enemy making any reaction at all?"

"Nothing worth mentioning. We're driving them ahead of us like a school of minnows."

Bade got to his feet uneasily. "It can't be this simple." He stepped out into the operations room and detected unmistakable signs of holiday jubilation. Nearly everyone was grinning, and gawkers were standing in a thick ring before the screen showing the map room's latest plot.

Bade said sharply, "Don't these men have anything to do?" His voice carried across the room with the effect of a shark surfacing in the midst of a ladies' swimming party. Several of the men at the map jumped. Others glanced around jerkily. There was a concerted bumping of elbows, and the ring of gawkers evaporated briskly in all directions. In every part of the room there was abruptly something approaching a businesslike atmosphere.

Bade looked around angrily and sat down at his desk. Then he saw the map. He squeezed his eyes shut, then looked again.

In the center of the map of North America was a big blot, as if a bottle of red ink had been thrown at it. Bade turned to Runckel and asked harshly, "Is that map correct?"

"Absolutely," said Runckel, his face shining with satisfaction.

Bade looked back at the map and performed a series of rapid calculations. He glanced at the viewscreens, and saw that those which would normally show the advanced ground troops weren't in use. This, he supposed, meant that the advance had outrun the technical crews.

Bade snapped on a microphone lettered "Supply, Ground." In the half-circle atop the microphone appeared an officer in the last stage of sleepless exhaustion. The officer's eyes twitched, and his skin had a drawn dull look. His head was slumped on his hand.

"*Supply?*" said Bade in alarm.

"Sorry," mumbled the officer, "we can't do it. We're overstretched already. Try Flyer Command. Maybe they'll parachute it to you."

Bade switched off, and glanced at the map again. He turned to Runckel. "Listen, what are we using for transport?"

"The enemy ground-cars."

"Fast, aren't they?"

Runckel smiled cheerfully. "They are built for speed. Rast grabbed a whole fleet of them to start with, and they've worked fine ever since. A few wrecks, some bad cases of kinkfoot, but that's all."

"What the devil is 'kinkfoot'?"

"Well, the enemy have tiny feet with little toes and no webs at all. Some of their ground-car controls are on the floor. There just isn't much space so our men's feet get cramped. It's just a mild irritation." Runckel smiled vaguely. "Nothing to worry about."

Bade squinted hard at Runckel. "What's Supply using for transport?"

"Steam trucks, of course."

"Do they work all right, or do they jump?"

Runckel smiled dreamily. "They work fine."

Bade snapped on the Supply microphone. The same weary officer appeared, his head in his hands, and mumbled, "Sorry. We're
overloaded. Try Flyer Command."

Bade said angrily, "Wake up a minute."

The man raised his head, blinked at Bade, then straightened as
if hauled by the back of the collar.

"*Sir?*"

"What's the overall supply picture?"

"Sir, it's awful. Terrible."

"What's the matter?"

"The advance is so fast, and the units are all mixed up, and
when we get to a place, they've already pulled out. Worse yet, the
steam trucks—" He hesitated, as if afraid to go on.

"Speak up," snapped Bade. "What's wrong with the trucks? Is it
the engines? Fuel? Running gear? What is it?"

"It's . . . the water, sir."

"The water?"

"Sir, there's that constant loss of steam out the exhaust. At home,
we just throw a few more buckets of water in the tank and go
on. But here—"

"Oh," said Bade, the situation dawning on him.

"But around here, sir," said the officer, "they've had something
called a 'severe drought.' The streams are dry."

"Can you dig down?"

"Sir, at best there's just muck. We *know* there's water here somewhere, but meanwhile our trucks are stalled all over the country
with the men dug down out of sight, and the natives standing
around shaking their heads, and *sure*, there's *got* to be water down
there somewhere, but what do we use right now?"

Bade took a deep breath. "What about the enemy trucks? Can't
you use them?"

"If we'd started off with them, I suppose we could have. But
Ground Forces has requisitioned most of them. Now we're spread
out in all directions with the front getting farther away all the
time."

Bade switched off and got in touch with Ground Forces,
Maintenance. A spruce-looking major appeared. Bade paused a
moment, then asked, "How's your work-load, major? Are you
behind schedule?"

The major looked shocked. "No, sir. Far from it. We're away
ahead of schedule."

"Aren't these enemy vehicles giving you any trouble? Any difficulties in repair?"

The major laughed. "Fangjaw, general, we don't repair them! When they burn out, we throw them away. We pried up the hoods of some of them, pulled off the top two or three layers of machinery, and took a good look underneath. That was enough. There are hundreds of parts, all shapes and sizes. And dozens of different kinds of motors. Half of the parts are stuck so they won't move when you try to get them out, and, to top it all, there isn't enough room in there to squeeze in an extra grain of sand. So what's the use? If something goes wrong with one of those things, we give it a shove off the road and forget it. There are plenty of others."

"I see," said Bade. "Do you send your repair crews out to shove the ground-cars off the road?"

"Oh, no, sir," said the major looking startled. "Like the colonel says, 'Let the Ground Forces do it.' Sir, it doesn't take any skill to do that. It's just that that's our *policy*: Don't repair 'em. Throw 'em away."

"What about *our* vehicles then? Have you found out what's wrong?"

The major looked uncomfortable. "Well, the difficulty is that the vehicles work satisfactorily *inside* the ship, and for a little while *outside*. But then, after they've been out a while, a malfunction occurs in the mechanism. That's what causes the trouble." He looked at Bade hopefully. "Was there anything else, sir."

"Yes," said Bade dryly, "it's the malfunction I'm interested in. What *is* it that goes wrong?"

The major looked unhappy. "Well, sir, we've had the motors apart and put back together I don't know how many times, and the fact is, there's nothing at all wrong with them. There's nothing wrong, but they still won't work. That's not our department. We've handed the whole business over to the Testing Lab."

"Then," said Bade, "you actually don't have any work to do?"

The major jumped. "Oh, no sir, I didn't say that. We ... we're holding ourselves in readiness, sir, and we've got our shops in order, and some of the men are doing some very, ah, very important research on the ... the structure of the enemy ground-car, and—"

"Fine," said Bade. "Get your colonel on this line." When the colonel appeared, Bade said, "Ground Forces Supply has its steam trucks out of service for lack of water. Get in touch with their H.Q., find out the location of the trucks, and get out there with the water. Find out where they can replenish in the future. Take care of this as fast as you can."

The colonel worked his mouth in a way that suggested a weak valve struggling to hold back a large quantity of compressed air. Bade looked at him hard. The colonel's mouth blew open, and "Yes, sir!" came out. The colonel looked startled.

Bade immediately switched back to Supply and said, "Ground Forces Maintenance is going to help you water your trucks. Why didn't you get in touch with them yourselves? It's the obvious thing."

"Sir, we did, hours ago. They said water supply wasn't in *their* department."

Bade seemed to see the bursting of innumerable bubbles before his eyes. It dawned on him that he was bogged down in petty details while big events rushed on unheeded. He switched back to the colonel briefly and when he switched off the colonel was plainly vibrating with energy from head to toe. Then Bade looked forebodingly at the map and ordered Liaison to get General Rast for him.

This took a long time, which Bade spent trying to anticipate the possible enemy reaction if Supply broke down completely, and a retirement became necessary. By the time Rast appeared on the screen, Bade had thought it over carefully, and could see nothing but trouble ahead. There was a buzz, and Bade looked up to see a fuzzy picture of Rast.

Rast, as far as Bade could judge, had a look of victory and exhilaration. But the communicator's reception was uncommonly bad, and Rast's image had a tendency to flicker, fade, and slide up and down. Judging by the trend of the conversation, Bade decided reception must be worse yet at the other end.

Bade said, "Supply is in a mess. You'd better choose some sort of defensible perimeter and halt."

Rast said, "Thank you. The enemy is in full flight."

"Listen," said Bade. "Supply is stopped. We can't get supplies to you. Supply can't catch up with you."

"We'll pursue them day and night," said Rast.

"Listen to me," said Bade. "Break off the pursuit! We can't get supplies to you!"

Rast's form slowly dimmed and expanded till it filled the screen, then burst, and reappeared as a brilliant image the size of a man's thumb. His voice cut off, then came through as a crackle.

"Siss kissis sissis," said the image, expanding again, "hisss siss kississ sissikississ." This noise was accompanied by earnest gestures on the part of Rast, and a very determined facial expression. The image grew huge and dim, and burst, then started over again.

Bade spat out a word he had promised himself never to say again under any circumstances whatever. Then he sat helpless while the image, large and clear, leaned forward earnestly and pounded one huge fist into the other.

"Hiss! Siss! Fississ!"

"Listen," said Bade, "I can't make out a word you're saying." He leaned forward. "WE CAN'T GET SUPPLIES TO YOU!"

The image burst and started over, bright and small.

Bade sucked in a deep breath. He grabbed the Communications microphone. "Listen," he snapped, "I've got General Rast on the screen here and I can't hear anything but a crackle. The image constantly expands and contracts."

"I know, sir," said a gray-smocked technician with a despairing look. "I can see the monitor screen from here. It's the best we can do, sir."

Out of the corner of his eye, Bade could see Rast's image growing huge and dim. "Hiss! Siss!" said Rast earnestly.

"*What causes this?*" roared Bade.

"Sir, all we can guess is some terrific electrical discharge between here and General Rast's position. What such a discharge might be, I can't imagine."

Bade scowled, and looked at a thumb-sized Rast. Bade opened his mouth to roar out that there was no way to get supplies through. Rast's image suddenly vibrated like a twanged string, then stopped expanding.

Rast's voice came through clearly, "Will you repeat that, sir?"

"WE CAN'T SUPPLY YOU," said Bade. "Halt your advance. Pick a good spot and HALT!"

Rast's image was expanding again. "Siss hiss," he said, and saluted. His image vanished.

Bade immediately snapped on the Communications microphone. "Do you have anyone down there who can read lips?" he demanded.

"Read *lips*? Sir, I—" The technician squinted suddenly, and swung off the screen. He was back in a moment, his face clear and hopeful. "Sir, we've got a man in the section that's a fanatic on communications methods. The other men think he *can* read lips, and I've sent for him."

"Good," said Bade. "Set him to work on the record of that conversation with General Rast. Another thing—is there any way you can get a message though to Rast?"

The technician looked doubtful. "Well, sir . . . I don't know—" His face cleared slightly. "We can try, sir."

"Good," said Bade. "Send 'Supply situation bad. Strongly suggest you halt your advance and consolidate position.'" Bade's glance fell on the latest plot from the map room. Glumly he asked himself how Rast or anyone else could hope to consolidate the balloon-like situation that was coming about.

"Sir," asked the technician, "is that all?"

"Yes," said Bade, "and let me know when you get through to Rast."

"Yes, sir."

Bade switched off, and turned to ask Runckel for the exact time Landing Force 3 would be down. Bade hesitated, then squinted hard at Runckel.

Runckel's face had an unusually bright, animated look. He was glancing rapidly through a sheaf of reports, quickly scribbling comments on them, and tossing them to an excited-looking clerk, who rushed off to slap them on the desks of various exhilarated officers and clerks. These men eagerly transmitted them to their various sections. This procedure was normal, but the faces of the men all looked too excited. Their movements were jerky and fast.

Bade became aware of the sensation of watching a scene in a lunatic asylum.

The excited-looking clerk rushed to Runckel's desk to snatch up a sheaf of reports, and Bade snapped, "Bring those here."

The clerk jumped, rushed to Bade's desk, halted with a jerky bounce and saluted snappily. He flopped the papers on the desk, whirled around and raced off toward the desks of the officers who usually got the reports Bade was now holding. The clerk stopped suddenly, looked at his empty hands, spun around, stared at Runckel's desk, then at Bade's. A look of enlightenment passed across his face. "Oh," he said, with a foolish grin. He teetered back and forth on his heels, then rushed over to look at the latest plot from the map room.

Bade set his jaw and glanced at the reports Runckel had marked.

The top two or three reports were simple routine and had merely been initialed. The next report, however, was headed: "Testing Lab. Report on Cause of Vehicle Failure; Recommendations."

Bade quickly glanced over several sheet of technical diagrams and figures, and turned to the summary. He read:

"In short, the breakdown of normal function, and the resultant slow violent pulsing action of the motor, is caused by the abnormally low conductivity of Surface Conduction Layer S-3. The pulser current, which would normally flow across this layer is blocked, and instead builds up on projection L-26. Eventually a sufficient charge accumulates, and arcs across air gap B. This throws a shock current through the exciter such as is normally experienced only during violent acceleration. The result is that the vehicle shoots ahead from a standing start, then rolls to a stop while the current again slowly accumulates. The root cause of this malfunction is the fantastically low moisture content of the atmosphere on this planet. It is this that causes the loss of conductivity across Layer S-3.

"Recommended measures to overcome this malfunction include:

a) Artificial humidification of the air entering the motor, by means of sprayer and fan.

b) Sealing of the motor unit.

c) Coating of surface condition layer S-3 with a top-sealed permanent conducting film.

"A) or b) probably can be carried out as soon as the requisite devices and materials are obtainable. This, however, may involve a considerable delay. C), on the other hand, will require a good deal of initial testing and experimentation, but may then be carried into effect very quickly, as the requisite tools and materials are already at hand. We will immediately carry out the initial measures for whichever plan you deem preferable."

Bade looked the report over again carefully, then glanced at Runckel's scrawled comment:

"Good work! Carry this out immediately! S.R."

Bade glared. Carry *what* out immediately?

Bade glanced angrily at Runckel, then sat up in alarm. Runckel's hands clenched the side of his desk. Runckel's back was straight as a rod. His chest was inflated to huge dimensions, and he was slowly drawing in yet more air. His face bore a fixated, inward-turned look that might indicate either horror or ecstasy.

Bade shoved his chair back and glanced around for help.

His glance stopped at the map screen, where the huge overblown blot in the center of the continent had sprouted a long narrow pencil reaching out toward the west.

There was a quick low gonging sound, and the semicircular rim atop the Communications microphone lit up in red. Bade snapped the microphone on and a scared-looking technician said, "Sir, we've worked out what General Rast said."

"What?" Bade demanded.

At Bade's side, there was a harsh scraping noise. Bade whipped around.

Runckel lurched to his feet, his face tense, his eyes shut, his mouth half open and his hands clenched.

Runckel twisted. There was a gagging sound, then a harsh roar:

Ka

    Ka

       Ka

CHOOOOO!!

Bade sat down in a hurry and grabbed the microphone marked, "Medical Corps."

A crowd of young doctors and attendants swarmed around Runckel with pulse-beat snoopers, blood pressure gauges, little lights on long rubber tubes, and bottles and jars which they filled with fluid sucked out of the suffering Runckel with long hollow needles. They whacked Runckel, pinched him, and thumped him, then jumped for cover as he let out another blast.

"Sir," said a young doctor wearing a "Medical-Officer-On-Duty" badge, "I'm afraid I shall have to quarantine this room and all its occupants. That includes you, sir." He said this in a gentle but firm voice.

Bade glanced at the doorway. A continuous stream of clerks, officers, and messengers moved in and out on necessary business. Some of these officers, Bade noticed, were speaking in low angry tones to idiotically smiling members of the staff. As one of the angry officers slapped a sheaf of papers on a desk, the owner of the desk came slowly to his feet. His chest inflated to gigantic proportions, he let out a terrific blast, reeled back against a wall, and let out another.

The young medical officer spun around excitedly. "Epidemic!" he yelled. "Seal that door! Back, all of you!" His face had a faint glow as he turned to Bade. "We'll have this under control in no time, sir." He came up and plastered a red and yellow sticker over the joint where door and wall came together. He faced the room. "Everyone here is quarantined. It's death to break that seal."

From Bade's desk came an insistent ringing, and the small

voice of the communications technician pleaded, "Sir ... please, sir ... this is important!" On the map across the room the bloated red space now had two sizable dents driven into it, such as might be expected if the enemy were opening a counteroffensive. The thin pencil line reaching toward the west was wobbling uncertainly at its far end.

Bade became aware of a fuzzy quality in his own thinking, and struggled to fix his mind on the scene around him.

The young doctor and his assistants hustled Runckel toward the door. As Bade stared, the doctor and assistants went out the door without breaking the quarantine seal. The sticker was plastered over the joint on the hinge side of the door. The seal bent as the door opened, then straightened out unhurt as the door shut.

"*Phew*," said Bade. He picked up the Communications microphone. "What did General Rast say?"

"Sir, he said, 'I can't reach the coast any faster than a day-and-a-half!'"

"The *coast*!"

"That's what he said, sir."

"Did you get that message to him?"

"Not yet, sir. We're trying."

Bade switched off and tried to think. His army was stretched out like a rubber balloon. His headquarters machinery was falling apart fast. An epidemic was loose among his men and plainly spreading fast. The base was still secure. But without sane men to man it, the enemy could be expected to walk in any time.

Bade's eyes were watering. He blinked, and glanced around for some sane face in the sea of hysterically cheerful people. He spotted an alert-looking officer with his back against the wall and a chair leg in his hand. Bade called to him. The officer looked around.

Bade said, "Do you know when Landing Force 3 is coming down?"

"Sir, they're coming down right now."

Bade stayed conscious long enough to watch the beginning of the enemy's counteroffensive, and also to see the start of the exploding sickness spread through the landing site. He grimly summarized the situation to the man he chose to take over command.

This man was the leader of Landing Force 3, a general by the name of Kottek. General Kottek was a fanatic, a man with a rough hypnotic voice and a direct unblinking stare. General Kottek's favorite drink was pure water. Food was a matter of indifference to him.

His only known amusements were regular physical exercise and the dissection of military problems. To hesitate to obey a command of General Kottek's was unheard of. To bungle in the performance of it was as pleasant as to sit down in the open mouth of a shark. General Kottek's officers were usually recognizable by their lean athletic appearance, and a tendency to jump at unexpected noises. General Kottek's men were nearly always to be seen in a state of good order and high spirits.

As soon as Bade, aching and miserable, summarized the situation and ordered Kottek to take over, Kottek gave a sharp precise salute, turned, and immediately began snapping out orders.

Heavily armed troops swung out to guard the site. Military police forced wandering gangs of sick men back to their ships. The crews of Landing Force 3 divided up to bring the depleted crews of the other ships up to minimum standards. The ships' damper units were turned to full power, and the outside power network and auxiliary damper units were disassembled and carried into the ships. Word came that a large enemy force had made an air-borne landing not far away. Kottek's troops marched in good order back to their ships. The ships of all three landing forces took off. They set down together in the center of the largest mass of Rast's encircled troops. The next day passed embarking these men under the protection of Kottek's fresh troops and the ships' dampers. Then the ships took off and repeated the process.

In this way, some sixty-five percent of the surrounded men were saved in the course of the week. Two more landing forces came down. General Rast and a small body of guards were found unconscious partway up an unbelievably high hill in the west. The situation at this point became hopelessly complicated by the exploding sickness.

This sickness, which none of the doctors were able to cure or even relieve, manifested itself in various forms. The usual form began by exhilarating the victim. In this state, the patient generally considered himself capable of doing anything, however foolhardy, and regardless of difficulties. This lasted until the second phase set in with violent contractions of the chest and a sudden out-rush of air from the lungs, accompanied by a blast like a gun going off. This second stage might or might not have complications such as digestive upset, headache, or shooting pains in the hands and feet. It ended when the third and last phase set in. In this phase the victim suffered from mental depression, considered himself a hopeless failure, and was as likely as not to try to end his life by suicide.

As a result of this suicidal impulse there were nightmarish scenes of soldiers disarming other soldiers, which brought the whole invasion force into a state of quaking uncertainty. At this critical point, and despite all precautions, General Kottek himself began to come down with the sickness. With him, the usual exhilaration took the form of a stream of violent and imperative orders.

Troops who should have retreated were ordered to fight to the death where they stood. Savage counter-attacks for worthless objectives were driven home "to the last drop of blood." Because General Kottek ordered it, people obeyed without thought. The hysterical light in his eye was masked by the fanatical glitter that had been there to begin with. The general himself only realized what was wrong when his chest tightened up, his body tensed, and a racking concatenation of explosions burst from his chest. He immediately brought his body to the position of attention, and crushed out by sheer will a series of incipient tickling sensations way down in his throat. General Kottek handed the command over to General Runckel and reported himself to sick bay.

Runckel, by this time, had recovered enough from the third phase to be untied and allowed to walk around with only two guards. As he had not fully recovered his confidence, however, he immediately went to see Bade.

Bade's illness took the form of nausea, cold hands and feet, and a sensation of severe pressure in the small of the back. Bade was lying on a cot when Runckel came in, followed by his two watchful guards.

Bade looked up and saw the two guards lean warily against the wall, their eyes narrowed as they watched Runckel. Runckel paused at the foot of Bade's bed. "How do you feel?" Runckel asked.

"Except for yesterday and day before," said Bade, "I never felt worse in my life. How do you feel?"

"All right most of the time." He cleared his throat. "Kottek's down with it now."

"Did he know in time?"

"No, I'm afraid he's left things in a mess."

Bade shook his head. "Do we have a general officer who *isn't* sick?"

"Not in the top brackets."

"Who did Kottek hand over to?"

"Me." Runckel looked a little embarrassed. "I'm not sure I can handle it yet."

"Who's in actual charge right now?"

"I've got the pieces of our own staff and the staff of Landing Force 2 working on it. Kottek's staff is hopeless. Half of them are talking about sweeping the enemy off the planet in two days."

Bade grunted. "What's your idea?"

"Well," said Runckel, "I still get . . . a little excited now and then. If you could possibly provide a sort of general supervision—"

Bade looked away weakly. "How's Rast?"

"Tied to his bunk with half-a-dozen men sitting on him."

"What about Vokk?"

"Tearing his lungs out every two or three minutes."

"Sokkis, then?"

Runckel shook his head grimly. "I'm afraid they didn't hear the gun go off in time. The doctors are still working on him, though."

"Well . . . is Frotch all right?"

"Yes, thank heaven. But then he's Flyer Command. And, worse yet, there's nobody to put in his place."

"All right, how about Sozzle?"

"Well," said Runckel, "Sozzle may be a good propaganda man, but personally I wouldn't trust him to command a platoon."

"Yes," said Bade, rolling over to try to ease the pain in his back, "I see your point." He took a deep breath. "I'll try to supervise the thing." He swung gingerly to a sitting position.

Runckel watched him, then his face twisted. "This whole thing is all my fault," he said. He choked. "I'm just no goo—"

The two guards sprang across the room, grabbed Runckel by the arms and rushed him out the door. Harsh grunts and solid thumping sounds came from the corridor outside. There was a heavy crash. Somebody said, "All right, get the general by the feet, and I'll take him by the shoulders. *Phew!* Let's go."

Bade sat dizzily on the edge of the bed. For a moment, he had a mental image of Runckel before the invasion, leaning forward and saying impressively, "Certain glory and a mighty victory await us."

Bade took several slow deep breaths. Then he got up carefully, found a towel, and cautiously went to wash.

It took Bade almost a week to disentangle the troops from the web of indefensible positions and hopeless last stands Kottek had committed them to in a day-and-a-half of peremptory orders. The enemy, meanwhile, took advantage of opportunity, using ground and air attacks, rockets, missiles and artillery in such profusion as to stun the mind. It was not until Bade's men and officers had recovered from circulating attacks of the sickness, and another landing force had come down, that it was possible to temporarily resume the offensive. Another two weeks, and another sick landing force recovered, saw the invasion army in control of a substantial part of the central plain of the continent. Bade now had some spare moments to squint at certain reports that were piled up on his desk. Exasperatedly, he called a meeting of high officers.

Bade was standing with Runckel at a big map of the continent when their generals came in. Bade and Runckel each looked grim and intense. The generals looked uniformly dulled and worn down.

Bade took a last hard look at the map, then he and Runckel turned. Bade glanced at Veth, Landing Site Commander. "What's your impression of the way things are going?"

Veth scowled. "Well, we're still getting eight to ten sizable missile hits a day. Of course, there's no predicting when they'll come in. With the men working outside the ships, any single hit could vaporize large numbers of essential technical personnel. Until we get the underground shelters built, the only way around this is to have whole site damped out all the time." He shook his head. "This takes a lot of energy."

Bade nodded, and turned to Rast, Ground Forces Commander.

"So far," said Rast frowning, "our situation on paper looks not too bad. Morale is satisfactory. Our weapons are superior. We have strong forces in a reasonably large central area, and in theory we can shift rapidly from one front to the other, and be superior anywhere. But in practice, the enemy has so many missiles, of all types and sizes, that we can't take advantage of the position.

"Suppose, for instance, that I order XX and XXII Tank Armies from the eastern to the western front. They can't go under their own power, because of fuel expenditure, the wear on their tracks, and the resulting delay for repairs. They can't go by forceway network because there isn't any built yet. The only way to send them is by the natives' iron track roads. That would be fine, except that the iron track roads make beautiful targets for missile attacks. Thanks to the enemy, every bridge and junction either is, has been, or will be blown up and not once, either. The result is, we have to use slow filtration of troops from one front to the other, or we have to accept very heavy losses on route. In addition, we now know that the enemy has formidable natural defenses in the east and west, especially in the west. There's a range of hills there that surpasses anything I've ever seen or heard of. Not only is the difficulty of the terrain an obstacle, but as our men go higher, movement finally becomes practically impossible. I know this from personal experience. The result of it is, the enemy need only guard the passes and he has a natural barrier behind which he can mass for attack at any chosen point."

Bade frowned. "Don't the hills have the same harmful effect on the enemy?"

"No sir, they don't."

"Why not?"

"I don't know. But that and their missiles put us in a nasty spot."

Bade absorbed this, then turned to General Frotch, head of Atmospheric Flyer Command.

Frotch said briskly, "Sir, so far as the enemy air forces are concerned, we have the situation under control. And various foreign long-range reconnaissance aircraft that have been filtering in from distant native countries, have also been successfully batted out of the sky. However, as far as ... ah ... missiles ... are concerned, the situation is a little strained."

Bade snapped, "Go on."

"Well, sir," said Frotch, "the enemy has missiles that can be fired at the fastest atmospheric flyers, that can be made to blow up near them, that can be guided to them, and even that can be made to chase and catch them."

"What about our weapons?"

"They're fine, on a percentage basis. But the enemy has a lot more missiles than we have pilots."

"I see," said Bade. "Well—" He turned to speak to the Director of Intelligence, but Frotch went on:

"Moreover, sir, we are having atmospheric troubles."

"'Atmospheric troubles'? What's that?"

"For one thing, gigantic traveling electrical displays that disrupt plane-to-ground communications, and have to be avoided, or else the pilots either don't come out, or else come out fit for nothing but a rest cure. Then there are mass movements of air traveling from one part of the planet to another. Like land breezes and sea breezes at home. But here the breezes can be pretty forceful. The

effect is to put an unpredictable braking force on all our operations."

Bade nodded slowly. "Well, we'll have to make the best of it." He
turned to General Sozzle, who was Disseminator of Propaganda.

Sozzle cleared his throat. "I can make my report short and to
the point. Our propaganda is getting us nowhere. For one thing,
the enemy is apparently used to being ambushed daily by something called 'advertising,' which seems to consist of a series of
subtle propaganda traps. By comparison our approach is so crude
it throws them into hysterics."

Bade glanced at the Director of Intelligence, who said dully, "Sir,
it's too early to say for certain how our work will eventually turn
out. We've had some successes; but, so far, we've been handicapped
by translation difficulties."

Bade frowned. "For instance?"

"Take the single word, 'snow,'" said the Intelligence Director. "You
can't imagine the snarl my translators get into over that word. It
apparently means 'white solid which falls in crystals from the sky.'
Figure that out."

Bade squinted, then looked relieved. "Oh. It means, 'dust.'"

"That's the way the interpreters translated it. Now consider this
sentence from a schoolbook. 'When April comes, the dust all turns
to water and flows into the ground to fill the streams.'"

"That doesn't make any sense at all."

"No. But that's what happens if you accept 'dust' as the translation for 'snow.' There are other words such as 'winter,' 'blizzard,'
'tornado.' Ask a native for an explanation, and with a straight face
he'll give you a string of incomprehensible nonsense that will stand
you on your ear. Not that it's important in itself. But it seems to
show something about the native psychology that I can't quite figure
out. You can fight your enemy best when you can understand him.
Well, from this angle they're completely incomprehensible."

"Keep working on it," said Bade, after a short silence. He turned
to Runckel.

Runckel said, "The overall situation looks about the same from
my point of view. Namely, the natives are driven back, but by
no means defeated. What we have to remember is that we never
expected to have them defeated at this stage. True, our time schedule has been set back somewhat, but this was due not to enemy
action, but to purely accidental circumstances. That is, first the
atmosphere was so deficient in moisture that our ground vehicles
were temporarily out of order, and, second, we were disabled by

an unexpected disease. But these troubles are over with. My point is that we can now begin the decisive phase of operations."

"Good," said Bade. "But to do that we have to firmly hold the ground we have. I want to know if we can do this. On the surface, perhaps, it looks like it. But there are signs here I don't like. As the old saying goes, 'A shark shows you his fin, not his teeth. Take warning from the fin; when you see the teeth it's too late.'"

"Yes," said Frotch, turning excitedly to Rast, "that's the thought exactly. Now, will *you* mention it, or shall I?"

"Holy fangjaw," growled Rast, "maybe it doesn't really mean anything."

"The Supreme Commander," said Runckel angrily, "was trying to talk."

Bade said, "What is it, Rast? Speak up."

"Well—" Rast hesitated, glanced uneasily at Runckel, then thrust out his jaw, "Sir, it looks like the whole master plan of the invasion may have come unhinged."

Runckel angrily started to speak.

Bade glanced at Runckel, took out a long slender cigar, and sat down on the edge of the table to watch Runckel. He lit the cigar and put down the lighter. As far as Bade was concerned, his face was expressionless. Things seemed to have an unnatural clarity, however, as he looked at Runckel and waited for him to speak.

Runckel looked at Bade, swallowed hard and said nothing.

Bade glanced at Rast.

Rast burst out, "Sir, for the last ten days or so, we've been wondering how long the enemy could keep up his missile attacks. Flyer Command has blasted factories vital to missile manufacture, and destroyed all their known stockpiles. Well, grant we didn't get all their stockpiles. That's logical enough. Grant that they had tremendous stocks stored away. Even grant that before we got here they made missiles all the time for the sheer love of making them. Maybe every man, woman, and child in the country had a missile, like a pet. Still, there's got to be an end *somewhere*."

Bade nodded soberly.

"Well, sir," said Rast, "we get these missiles fired at us all the time, day after day after day, one missile after the other, like an army of men tramping past in an endless circle forever. It's inconceivable that they'd use their missiles like this unless their supply is inexhaustible. Frotch gets hit with them, I get hit with them, Veth gets hit with them. For every job there's a missile. We put our overall weapons superiority in one pan of the balance. They pour an endless heap of missiles in the other pan. *Where do all these missiles come from?*"

For an instant Rast was silent, then he went on. "At first we thought 'Underground factories.' Well, we did our best to find them and it was no use. And whenever we managed to spot moving missiles, they seemed to be coming from the coast.

"About this time, some of my officers were trying to convert a bunch of captives to our way of thinking. One of the officers noticed a peculiar thing. Whenever he clinched his argument by saying, 'Moreover, you are alone in the world; you cannot defeat us alone,' the captives would all look very serious. Most of them would be very still and attentive, but here and there among them, a few would choke, gag, make sputtering noises, and shake all over. The other soldiers would secretively kick these men, and jab them with their elbows until they were still and attentive. Now, however, the question arose, what did all this mean? The actions were described to Intelligence, who said they meant exactly what they seemed to mean, 'suppressed mirth.'

"In other words, whenever we said, 'You can't win, you're alone in the world,' they wanted to burst out laughing. My officers now varied the technique. They would say, for instance, 'The U.S.S.R. is our faithful ally.' Our captives would sputter, gasp, and almost strangle to death. Put this together with their inexhaustible supply of missiles and the thing takes on a sinister look."

"You think," said Bade, "that the U.S.S.R. and other countries are shipping missiles to the U.S. by sea?"

General Frotch cleared his throat apologetically, "Sir, excuse me. I have something new to add to this. I've set submerger planes down along all three of their coasts. Not only are the ports alive with shipping. But some of our men swam into the harbors at night and hid, and either they're the victims of mass-hypnosis or else those ships are unloading missiles like a fish unloads spawn."

Bade looked at Runckel.

Runckel said dully, "In that case, we have the whole planet to fight. That was what we had to avoid at any cost."

This comment produced a visible deterioration of morale. Before this attitude had a chance to set, Bade said forcefully and clearly, "I was never in favor of this attack. And this fortifies my original views. But from a strictly military point of view, I believe we can still win."

He went to the map, and speaking to each of the generals in turn, he explained his plan.

❧   ❧   ❧

In the three following days, each of the three remaining landing forces set down. The men of each landing force, as expected, became violently ill with the exploding sickness. With the usual course of the sickness known, it proved possible to care for this new horde of patients with nothing worse than extreme inconvenience for the invasion force as a whole.

The enemy, meanwhile, strengthened his grip around the occupied area, and at the same time cut troop movements within the area to a feeble trickle. Day after day, the enemy missiles fell in an increasingly heavy rain on the road and rail centers. During the height of this bombardment, Bade succeeded in gradually filtering all of Landing Force 3 back to the protection of the ships.

Rast now reported that the enemy attacks were mounting in force and violence, and requested permission to fall back and contract the defense perimeter.

Bade replied that help would soon come, and Rast must make only small local withdrawals.

Landing Forces 7, 8, and 9, cured of the exploding sickness, now took off. Immediately afterward, Landing Force 3 took off.

Landing Forces 3 and 7, under General Kottek, came down near the base of the Upper Peninsula of Michigan, and struck south and west to rip up communications in the rear of the main enemy forces attacking General Rast.

Landing Force 8 split, its southern section seizing the western curve of Cuba to cut the shipping lanes to the Gulf of Mexico. Its northern sections seized Long Island, to block shipping entering the port of New York, and to subject shipping in the ports of Boston, Philadelphia, Baltimore and Washington to heavy attack from the air.

Landing Force 9 remained aloft until the enemy's reaction to General Kottek's thrust from the rear became evident. This reaction proved to be a quickly improvised simultaneous attack from north and south, to pinch off the flow of supplies from Kottek's base to the point of his advance. Landing Force 9 now set down, broke the attack of the southern pincer, then struck southeastward to cut road and rail lines supplying the enemy's northern armies. The overall situation now resembled two large, roughly concentric circles, each very thick in the north, and very thin in the south. A large part of the outer circle, representing the enemy's forces, was now pressed between the inner circle and the inverted Y of Kottek's attack from the north.

A large percentage of the enemy missile-launching sites were now overrun, and Rast for the first time found it possible to switch his troops from place to place without excessive losses. The enemy opened violent attacks in both east and west to relieve the pressure on their trapped armies in the north, and Rast fell back slowly, drawing forces from both these fronts and putting them into the northern battle.

The outcome hung in a treacherous balance until the enemy's supplies gave out in the north. This powerful enemy force then collapsed, and Rast swung his weary troops to the south.

Three weeks after the offensive began, it ended with the fighting withdrawal of the enemy to the east and west. The enemy's long eastern and southern coasts were now sealed against all but a comparative trickle of supplies from overseas. General Kottek held the upper peninsula of Michigan in a powerful grip. From it he dominated huge enemy industrial regions, and threatened the flank of potential enemy counter-attacks from north or east.

Within the main occupied region itself, the forceway network and key-tools factories were being set up.

Runckel was only expressing the thought of nearly the whole invasion army when he walked into the operations room, heaved a sigh of relief and said to Bade, "Well, thank heaven *that's* over!"

Bade heard this and gave a noncommittal growl. He had felt this way himself some time before. During Runckel's absence, however, certain reports had come to Bade's desk and left him feeling like a man who goes down a flight of steps in the dark, steps off briskly, and finds there was one more step than he thought.

"Look at this," said Bade. Runckel leaned over his shoulder, and together they looked at a report headed, "Enemy Equipment." Bade passed over several pages of drawings and descriptions devoted to enemy knives, guns, grenades, helmets, canteens, mess equipment and digging tools, then paused at a section marked "Enemy clothing: 1) Normal enemy clothing consists of light two-piece underwear, an inner and an outer foot-covering, and either a light two-piece or light one-piece outer covering for the arms, chest, abdomen and legs. 2) However, capture of the enemy supply trains in the recent northern offensive uncovered the following fantastic variety: a) thick inner and outer hand coverings; b) heavy one-piece undergarment covering legs, arms and body; c) heavy upper outer garment; d) heavy lower outer garment; e) heavy inner foot covering;

f) massive outer foot covering; g) additional heavy outer garment; h) extraordinarily heavy outer garment designed to cover entire body with exception of head, hand, and lower legs. In addition, large extra quantities of the heavy cover normally issued to the troops for sleeping purposes were also found. The purpose of all this clothing is difficult to understand. Insofar as the activity of a soldier encased in all these garments would be cut to a minimum, it can only be assumed that all these coverings represent body-shielding against some abnormal condition. The presence of poisonous chemicals in large quantities seems a likely possibility. Yet with the exception of the massive outer foot-covering, these garments are not impermeable."

Bade looked at Runckel. "They do have war chemicals?"

"Of course," said Runckel, frowning. "But we have protective measures, and our own war chemicals, if trouble starts."

Bade nodded thoughtfully, slid the report aside, and picked up one headed, "Medical Report on Enemy Skin Condensation."

Runckel shook his head. "I can never understand those. We've had a flood of reports like that from various sources. At most, I just initial them and send them back."

"Well," said Bade, "read the summary, at least."

"I'll try," growled Runckel, and leaned over Bade's shoulder to read:

"To summarize these astonishing facts, enemy captives have been observed to form, on the outer layer of their skin, a heavy beading of moisture. This effect is similar to that observed with laboratory devices maintained at depressed temperatures—that is, at reduced degrees of heat. The theory was, therefore, formed that the enemy's skin is, similarly, maintained at a temperature lower than that of his surroundings. Complex temperature-determining apparatus were set up to test this theory. As a result, this theory was disproved, but an even more astonishing state of affairs was discovered: The enemy's internal temperature varied very little, regardless of considerable experimental variation of the temperature of his environment.

"The only possible conclusion was that the enemy's body contains some built-in mechanism that actually controls the degree of heat and maintains it at a constant level.

"Now, according to Poff's widely accepted Principle, no complex bodily mechanism can long maintain itself in the absence of need or exercise. And what is the need for a bodily mechanism that has the function of holding body temperature constant despite wide external fluctuation? What is the need for a defense against something unless the something exists?

"We are forced to the conclusion that the degree of heat on this planet is subject to variations sufficiently severe as to endanger life. A new examination of what has hitherto been considered to be the enemy's mythology indicates that, contrary to conditions on our own planet, this planet is subject to remarkable fluctuations of temperature, that alternately rise to a peak, then fall to an incredible low.

"According to this new theory, our invasion force arrived as the temperature was approaching its maximum. Since then, it has reached and passed its peak, and is now falling. All this has passed unnoticed by us, partly because the maximum here approached the ordinary condition on our home planet. The danger, of course, is that the minimum on this planet would prove insupportable to our form of life."

This was followed by a qualifying phrase that further tests would have to be made, and the conclusions could not be considered final.

Bade looked at Runckel. Runckel snapped, "What do you do with a report like that? I'd tear it up, but why waste strength? It's easier to throw them in the wastebasket and go on."

"Wait a minute," said Bade. "If this report just happens to be right, then where are we?"

"Frankly," said Runckel, "I don't know or care. 'Skin condensation.' These scientists should keep their minds on things that have some chance of being useful. It would help if they'd figure out how to cut down flareback on our subtron guns. Instead they talk about 'skin condensation.'"

Bade wrote on the report, "This may turn out to be important. List on no more than two sheets of paper possible defenses against reduced degree of heat. Get it to me as soon as possible. Bade."

Bade signaled to a clerk. "Snap a copy of this, send the original out, and bring me the copy."

"Yes, sir."

"Now," said Bade, "we have one more report."

"Well, I have to admit," said Runckel, "that I can't see that either of these reports were of any value."

"Well, read this one, then."

Runckel shook his head in disgust, and leaned over. His eyes widened. This paper was headed, "For the Supreme Commander only. Special Report of General Kottek."

The report began, "Sir: It is an officer's duty to state, plainly and without delay, any matter that requires the immediate attention of his superior. I, therefore, must report to you the following unpleasant but incontrovertible facts;

"1) Since their arrival in this region, my troops have on three recent occasions displayed a strikingly low level of performance. Two simulated night attacks revealed feeble command and exaggerated sluggishness on the part of the troops. A defense exercise carried out at dawn to repulse a simulated amphibious landing was a complete failure; troops and officers alike displayed insufficient energy and initiative to drive the attack home.

"2) On other occasions, troops and officers have maintained a high, sometimes strikingly high, level of energy and activity.

"3) No explanation of this variability of performance has been forthcoming from the medical and technical personnel attached to my command. Neither have I any assurance that these fluctuations will not take place in the future.

"4) It is, therefore, my duty to inform you that I cannot assure the successful performance of my mission. Should the enemy attack with his usual energy during a period of low activity on the part of my troops, the caliber of my resistance will be that of wax against steel. This is no exaggeration, but plain fact.

"5) This situation requires the immediate attention of the highest military and technical authorities. What is in operation here may be a disease, an enemy nerve gas, or some natural factor unknown to us. Whatever its nature, the effect is highly dangerous.

"6) A mobile, flexible defense in these circumstances is impossible. A rigid linear defense is worthless. A defense by linked fortifications requires depth. I am, therefore, constructing a deep fortified system in the western section of the region under my control. This is no cure, but a means of minimizing disaster.

"7) Enemy missile activity since the defeat of their northern armies has been somewhat less that forty per cent of that expected."

The report ended with Kottek's distinctive jagged signature. Bade glanced around.

Runckel's face was somber. "This is serious," he said. "When Kottek yells for help, we've got trouble. We'll have to put all our attention on this thing and get it out of the way as fast as we can."

Bade nodded, and reached out to take a message from a clerk. He glanced at it and scowled. The message was from Atmospheric Flyer Command. It read:

"Warning! Tornado sighted and approaching main base!"

Runckel leaned over to read the message. "What's this?" he said angrily. "'Tornado' is just a myth. Everybody knows that."

Bade snapped on the microphone to Aerial Reconnaissance. "What's this 'tornado' warning?" he demanded. "What's a 'tornado'?"

"Sir, a tornado is a whirling severe breeze of destructive character, conjoined with a dark cloud in the shape of a funnel, with the smaller end down."

Runckel gave an inarticulate snarl.

Bade squinted. "This thing is dangerous?"

"Yes, sir. The natives dig holes in the ground, and jump in when one comes along. A tornado will smash houses and ground-cars to bits, sir."

"Listen," snarled Runckel, "it's just *air*, isn't it?"

Bade snapped on Landing Site Command. "Get all the men back in the ships," he ordered. "Turn the dampers to full power."

"Holy fangjaw!" Runckel burst out. "Air can't hurt us. What's bad about a breeze, anyway?" He seized the Aerial Reconnaissance microphone and snarled. "Stand up, you! What have you been drinking?"

Bade took Runckel by the arm. "Look there!"

On the nearest wall screen, a wide black cloud warped across the sky, and stretched down a long arc to the ground. The whole thing grew steadily larger as they watched.

Bade seized the Landing Site Command microphone. "Can we lift ships?"

"No, sir. Not without tearing the power and damper networks to pieces."

"I see," said Bade. He looked up.

The cloud overspread the sky. The screen fell dark. There was a heavy clang, a thundering crash, the ship trembled, tilted, heeled, and slowly, painfully, settled back upright as Bade hung onto the desk and Runckel dove for cover. The sky began to lighten. Bade gripped the microphone and asked what had happened. He listened blank-faced as, after a moment, the first estimates of the damage came in.

One of the thousand-foot-long ships had been tipped off its base. In falling, it struck another ship, which also fell, striking a third. The third ship struck a fourth, which fell unhindered and split up the side like a bean pod. The mouth of the tornado's funnel then ran along the split, and the ship's inside looked as if it had been cleaned out with a vacuum hose. A few stunned survivors and scattered bits of equipment were clinging here and there. That was all.

The enemy chose this moment to land his heaviest missile strike in weeks.

It took the rest of the day, all night, and all the following day to get the damage moderately well cleaned up. Then a belated report came in that Forceway Station 1 had been subjected to a bombardment of desks, chairs, communications equipment, and odd bolts and nuts that had riddled the installation from one end to the other and set completion date back four weeks.

An intensive search now located most of the missing equipment and personnel—strewn over forty miles of territory.

"It was," said Runckel weakly, "only air, that's all."

"Yes," said Bade grimly. He looked up from a scientific report on the tornado. "A whirlpool is only water. Whirling water. Apparently this planet has traveling whirlpools of air."

Runckel groaned, then a sudden thought seemed to hit him. He reached into his wastebasket, fished around, and drew out a crumpled ball of paper. He smoothed it out, read for a while, then growled, "Scientific reports. Here's some kind of report that came in right in the middle of a battle. According to this thing, the native name for the place where we've set down is 'Cyclone Alley.' Is there some importance in knowing a thing like that?"

Bade felt severe prickling sensations across his back and neck. "'Cyclone,'" he said, "Where did I hear that before? Give me that paper."

Runckel shrugged and tossed it over. Bade smoothed it out and read:

"In this prevalent fairy tale, the 'cyclone'—corresponding to our 'sea serpent,' or 'Ogre of the Deep'—makes recurrent visits to communities in certain regions, frightening the inhabitants terribly and committing all sorts of prankish violence. On some occasions, it carries its chosen victims aloft, to set them down again far away. The cyclone is a frightening giant, tall and dark, who approaches in a whirling dance.

"An interesting aspect is the contrast of this legend with the equally prevalent legend of Santa Claus. Cyclone comes from the south, Santa from the north. Cyclone is prankish, frightening. Santa is benign, friendly, and even brings gifts. Cyclone favors 'springtime,' but may come nearly any time except 'winter.' Cyclone is secular. Santa reflects some of the holy aura of the religious festival, 'Christmas.'

"'Christmas comes but once a year. When it comes, it brings good cheer.' Though Cyclone visits but a few favored towns at a time, Santa visits at once all, everyone, even the lowliest dweller in his humble shack. The natives are immensely earnest about both of these legends. An amusing aspect is that our present main base is almost ideally located for visits by that local Ogre of the Sea, 'Cyclone.' We are, in fact, situated in a location known as 'Cyclone Alley.' Perhaps the Ogre will visit us."

At the bottom of the page was a footnote: "'Cyclone' is but one name for this popular Ogre. Another common name is 'Tornado.'"

Bade sat paralyzed for a moment staring at this paper. "Tornado Alley," he muttered. He grabbed the Flyer Command microphone to demand how the tornado warning system was coming. Then, groggily, he set the paper aside and turned his attention to the problem of General Kottek's special report. He looked up again as a nagging suspicion began to build up in him. He turned to Runckel. "How many of these 'myths' have we come across, anyway?"

Runckel looked as though a heavy burden were settling on him. He groped through his bulging wastebasket and fished out another crumpled ball of paper, then another. He located the one he wanted, smoothed it out, sucked in a deep breath, and read: "Cyclone, winter, spring, summer, hurricane, Easter bunny, autumn, blizzard, cold wave, Snow White and the Seven Dwarfs, lightning, Santa Claus, typhoon, mental telepathy, earthquake, levitation, volcano—" He looked up. "You want the full report on each of these things? I've got most of them here somewhere."

Bade looked warily at Runckel's overstuffed wastebasket. "No," he said. "But what about that report you're reading from? Isn't that an overall summary? Why didn't I get a copy of that?"

Runckel looked it over and growled, "Try to train them to send their reports to the right place. Yes, it's an overall summary. Here, want it?"

"Yes," said Bade. He took the report, then stopped to wonder, where was that report he had asked for on "reduced degree of heat?" He reached for a microphone, then remembered General

Kottek's special report. Bade first sent word to Kottek that he approved what Kottek was doing, and that the problem was getting close attention. Then he read the crumpled overall summary Runckel had given him, and ended up feeling he had been on a trip through fairyland. His memories of the details evaporated even as he tried to mentally review the paper. "Hallowe'en," he growled, "icebergs, typhoons—this planet must be a mass of mythology from one end to the other." He picked up a microphone to call his Intelligence Service.

A messenger hurried across the room to hand him a slip of paper. The paper was from Atmosphere Flyer Command. It read:

"Warning! Tornado sighted approaching main base!"

This time, the tornado roared past slightly to the west of the base. It hit, instead Forceway Station 1, and scattered sections of it all over the countryside.

For good measure, the enemy fired in an impressive concentration of rockets and missiles. The attack did only slight harm to the base, but it finished off Forceway Station 1.

An incoherent report now came in from the occupied western end of Cuba, to the effect that a "hurricane" had just gone through.

Bade fished through Runckel's wastebasket to find out exactly what a "hurricane" might be. He looked up at the end of this, pale and shaken, and sent out a strong force to put his Cuban garrison back on its feet.

Then he ordered Intelligence, and some of his technical and scientific departments to get together right away and break down the so-called "myths" into two groups: Harmful, and nonharmful. The nonharmful group was to be arranged in logical order, and each item accompanied by a brief, straightforward description.

As Bade sent out this order, General Kottek reported that, as a supplement to his fortified system, he was making sharp raids whenever conditions were favorable, in order to keep the enemy in his section off-balance. In one on these raids, his troops had captured an enemy document which had since been translated. The document was titled: "Characteristics of Unheatful-Blooded Animals." Kottek enclosed a copy:

"Unheatful-blooded animals have no built-in system for maintaining their bodily rate of molecular activity. If the surrounding temperature falls, so does theirs. This lowers their physical activity. They cannot move or react as fast as normally. Heatful-blooded animals, properly clothed, are not subject to this handicap.

"In practical reality, this means that as unheatful conditions set in, the Invader should always be attacked during the most unheatful period possible. Night attacks have much to recommend them. So do attacks at dusk or dawn. In general, avoid taking the offensive during heatful periods such as early afternoon.

"Forecasts indicate that winter will be late this year, but severe when it comes. Remember, there is no year on record when temperatures have not dropped severely in the depths of winter. In such conditions, it is expected that the Invader will be killed in large numbers by—untranslatable—of the blood.

"Our job is to make sure they are kept worn down until winter comes. Our job then will be to make sure none of them live through the winter."

Bade looked up feeling as if his digestive system were paralyzed. A messenger hurried across the room to hand him a thick report hastily put together by the Intelligence Service. It was titled:

"Harmful Myths and Definitions."

Bade spent the first part of the night reading this spine-tingling document. The second part of the night he spent in nightmares.

Toward morning, Bade had one vivid and comparatively pleasant dream. A native wearing a simple cloth about his waist looked at Bade intently and asked, "Does the shark live in the air? Does a man breathe underwater? Who will eat grass when he can have meat?"

Bade woke up feeling vaguely relieved. This sensation was swept away when he reached the operating room and saw the expression on Runckel's face. Runckel handed Bade a slip of paper:

"Hurricane Hannah approaching Long Island Base."

Intercepted enemy radio and television broadcasts spoke of Hurricane Hannah as "the worst in thirty years." As Bade and Runckel stood by helplessly, Hurricane Hannah methodically pounded Long Island Base to bits and pieces, then swept away the pieces. The hurricane moved on up the shoreline, treating every village and city along the way like a personal enemy. When Hurricane Hannah ended her career, and retired to sink ships further north, the Atlantic coast was a shambles from one end to the other.

Out of this shambles moved a powerful enemy force, which seized the bulk of what was left of Long Island Base. The remnant of survivors were trapped in the underground installations, and reported that the enemy was lowering a huge bomb down through the entrance.

In Cuba, the reinforced garrison was barely holding on.

A flood of recommendations now poured in on Bade:

1) Long Island Base needed a whole landing force to escape capture.

2) Cuba Base had to have at least another half landing force for reinforcements.

3) The Construction Corps required the ships of two full landing forces in order to power the forceway network. Otherwise, work on the key-tools factories would be delayed.

4) Landing Site Command would need the ships and dampers of three landing forces to barely protect the base if the power supply of two landing forces were diverted to the Construction Corps.

5) The present main base was now completed and should be put to efficient use at once.

6) The present main base was worthless, because Forceway Station 1 could not be repaired in time to link the base to the forceway network.

7) Every field commander except General Kottek urgently needed heavy reinforcements without delay.

8) Studies by the Staff showed the urgent need of building up the central reserve without delay, at the expense of the field commanders, if necessary.

Bade gave up Long Island Base, ordered Cuba Base to hold on with what it had, told the Landing Site Commander to select a suitable new main base near some southern forceway station free of tornadoes, and threw the rest of the recommendations into the wastebasket.

Runckel now came over with a rope smoldering stub jutting out of the corner of his mouth. "Listen," he said to Bade, "we're going to have a disciplinary problem on our hands. That Cuban garrison has been living on some kind of native paint-remover called 'rum.' The whole lot of them have a bad case of the staggering lurch from it; not even the hurricane sobered them up. Poff knew what was going on. But he and his staff covered it over. His troops are worthless. Molch and the reinforcements are doing all the fighting."

Bade said, "Poff is still in command?"

"I put Molch in charge."

"Good. We'll have to court-martial Poff and his staff. Can Molch hold the base?"

"He said he could. If we'd get Poff off his neck."

"Fine," said Bade. "Once he gets things in order, ship the regular garrison to a temporary camp somewhere. We don't want Molch's troops infected."

Runckel nodded. A clerk apologized and stepped past Runckel to hand Bade a message. It was from General Frotch, who reported that all his atmospheric flyers based on Long Island had been lost in Hurricane Hannah. Bade showed the message to Runckel, who shook his head wearily.

As Runckel strode away, another clerk put a scientific report on Bade's desk. Bade read it through, got Frotch on the line, and arranged for a special mission by Flyer Command. Then he located his report on "Harmful Myths and Definitions." Carefully, he read the definition of winter:

"To the best of our knowledge, 'winter' is a severe periodic disease of plants, the actual onset of which is preceded by the vegetation turning various colors. The tall vegetables known as 'trees' lose their foliage entirely, except for some few which are immune and are known as 'evergreens.' As the disease progresses, the juices of the plants are squeezed out and crystallize in white feathery forms known as 'frost.' Sufficient quantities of this squeezed-out dried juice is 'snow.' The mythology refers to 'snow falling from the sky.' A possible explanation of this is that the large trees also 'snow,' producing a fall of dried juice crystals. These crystals are clearly poisonous. 'Frostbite,' 'chilblains,' and even 'freezing to death' are mentioned in the enemy's communication media. Even the atmosphere filled with the resulting vapor, is said to be 'cold.' Totally unexplainable is the common reference to children rolling up balls of this poisonous dried plant juice and hurling them at each other. This can only be presumed to be some sort of toughening exercise. More research on this problem is needed."

Bade set this report down, reread the latest scientific report, then got up and slowly walked over to a big map of the globe. He gazed thoughtfully at various islands in the South Seas.

Late that day, the ships lifted and moved, to land again near Forceway Station 2. Power cables were run to the station across a sort of long narrow valley at the bottom of which ran a thin trickle of water. By early the morning of the next day, the forceway network was in operation. Men and materials flashed thousands of miles in a moment, and work on the key-tools factories accelerated sharply.

Bade immersed himself in intelligence summaries of the enemy

communications media. An item that especially interested him was
"Winter Late This Year."

By now there were three viewpoints on "winter." A diehard faction doggedly insisted that it was a myth, a mere quirk of the alien
mentality. A large and very authoritative body of opinion held the
plant juice theory, and bolstered its stand with reams of data sheets
and statistics. A small, vociferous group asserted the heretical water
crystal hypotheses, and ate alone at small tables for doing so.

General Frotch called Bade to say that the special Flyer Command mission was coming in to report.

General Kottek sent word that enemy attacks were becoming
more daring, that his troops' periods of inefficiency were more
frequent, and that the vegetation in his district was turning color.
He mentioned, for what it was worth, that troops within the fortifications seemed less affected than those outside. Troops far
underground, however, seemed to be slowed down automatically,
regardless of conditions on the surface, unless they were engaged
in heavy physical labor.

Bade scowled and set off inquiries to his scientific section. Then
he heard excited voices and looked up.

Four Flyer Command officers were coming slowly into the room,
bright metal poles across their shoulders. Slung from the poles was
a big plastic-wrapped bundle. The bundle was dripping steadily,
and leaving a trail of droplets that led back out the door into
the hall. The plastic was filmed over with a layer of tiny beads
of moisture.

Runckel came slowly to his feet.

The officers, breathing heavily, set the big bundle on the floor
near Bade's desk.

"Here it is, sir."

Bade's glance was fastened on the object.

"Unwrap it."

The officers bent over the bundle, and with clumsy fingers pulled
back the plastic layer. The plastic stood up stiffly, and bent only
with a hard pull. Underneath was something covered with several
of the enemy's thick dark sleeping covers. The officers rolled the
bundle back and forth and unwound the covers. An edge of some
milky substance came into view. The officers pulled back the covers
and a milky, semitransparent block sat there, white vapor rolling
out from it along the floor.

There was a concerted movement away from the block and the
officers.

Bade said, "Was the whole place like that?"

"No, sir, but there was an awful lot of this stuff. And there was a compacted powdery kind of substance, too. We didn't bring enough of it back and it all turned to water."

"Did you wear the protective clothes we captured?"

"Yes, sir, but they had to be slit and zippered up the legs, because the enemy's feet are so small. The arms were a poor fit and there had to be more material across the chest."

"How did they work?"

"They were a great help, sir, as long as we kept moving. As soon as we slowed down, we started to stiffen up. The hand and foot gear was improvised and hard to work in, though."

Bade looked thoughtfully at the smoldering block, then got up, stepped forward, and spread his hand close to the block. A numbness gradually dulled his hand and moved up his arm. Then Bade straightened up. He found he could move his hand only slowly and painfully. He motioned to Runckel. "I think this is what 'cold' is. Want to try it?" Runckel got up, held his hand to the block, then straightened, scowling.

Bade felt a tingling sensation and worked his hand cautiously as Runckel, his face intent, slowly spread and closed his fingers.

Bade thoughtfully congratulated the officers, then had the block carried off to the Testing Lab.

The report on defense against "reduced degree of heat" now came in. Bade read this carefully several times over. The most striking point, he noticed, was the heavy energy expenditure involved.

That afternoon, several ships took off, separated, and headed south.

The next few days saw the completion of the first key-tool factory, the receipt of reports from insect-bitten scouts in various regions far to the south, and a number of terse messages from General Kottek. Bade ordered plans drawn up for the immediate withdrawal of General Kottek's army, and for the possible withdrawal by stages of other forces in the north. He ordered preparations made for the first completed factories to produce anti-reduced-degree-of-heat devices. He read a number of reports on the swiftly changing state of the planet's atmosphere. Large quantities of rain were predicted.

Bade saw no reason to fear rain, and turned to a new problem: The enemy's missiles had produced a superabundance of atomic debris in the atmosphere. Testing Lab was concerned over this, and suggested various ways to get rid of it. Bade approved the projects and turned to the immediate problem of withdrawing the bulk of General Kottek's troops from their strong position without losing completely the advantages of it.

Bade was considering the idea of putting a forceway station somewhere in Kottek's underground defenses, so that he could be reinforced or withdrawn at will. This would involve complicated production difficulties; but then Kottek had said the slowing-down was minimized under cover, and it might be worthwhile to hold an option on his position. While weighing the various intangibles and unpredictables, Bade received a report from General Rast. Rast was now noticing the same effect Kottek had reported.

Word came in that two more key-tools factories were now completed.

Intelligence reports of enemy atmospheric data showed an enormous "cold air mass moving down through Canada."

General Frotch, personally supervising high-altitude tests, now somehow got involved in a rushing high-level air stream. Having the power of concentrating his attention completely upon whatever he was doing, Frotch got bound up in the work and never realized the speed of the air stream until he came down again—just behind the enemy lines.

When Bade heard of this, he immediately went over the list of officers, and found no one to replace Frotch. Bade studied the latest scientific reports and the disposition of his forces, then ordered an immediate switching of troops and aircraft through the forceway network toward the place where Frotch had vanished. A sharp thrust with local forces cut into the enemy defense system, was followed up by heavy reinforcements flowing through the forceway network, and developed an overpowering local superiority that swamped the enemy defenses.

Runckel studied the resulting dispositions and said grimly, "Heaven help us if they hit us hard in the right place just now."

"Yes," said Bade, "and heaven help us if we don't get Frotch back." He continued his rapid switching of forces, and ordered General Kottek to embark all his troops, and set down near the main base.

Flyer Command meanwhile began to show signs of headless disorientation, the ground commanders peremptorily ordering the air forces around as nothing more than close-support and flying artillery. The enemy behind-the-lines communications network continued to function.

Runckel now reported to Bade that no reply had been received from Kottek's headquarters. Runckel was sending a ship to investigate.

Anguished complaints poured in from the technical divisions that their work was held up by the troops flooding the forceway network.

The map now showed Bade's men driving forward in what looked like a full-scale battle to break the enemy's whole defensive arrangements and thrust clear through to the sea. Reports came in that, with the enemy's outer defense belt smashed, signs of unbelievable weakness were evident. The enemy seemed to have nothing but local reserves and only a few of them. The general commanding on the spot announced that he could end the war if given a free hand.

Bade now wondered, if the enemy's reserves weren't there, where were they? He repeated his original orders.

Runckel now came over with the look of a half-drowned swimmer and motioned Bade to look at the two nearest viewscreens.

One of the viewscreens showed a scene in shades of white. A layer of white covered the ground, towering ships were plastered on one side with white, obstacles were heaped over with white, the air was filled with horizontal streaks of white. Everything on the screen was white or turning white.

"Kottek's base," said Runckel dully.

The other screen gave a view of the long narrow valley just outside. This "valley" was now a rushing torrent of foaming water, sweeping along chunks of floating debris that bobbed a hand's breadth under the power cables from the ships to Forceway Station 2.

The only good news that day and the next was the recapture of General Frotch. In the midst of crumbling disorder, Flyer Command returned to normal.

Bade sent off a specially-equipped mission to try and find out what had happened to General Kottek. Then he looked up to see General Rast walking wearily into the room. Rast conferred with Runckel in low dreary tones, then the two of them started over toward Bade.

Bade returned his attention to a chart showing the location of the key-tools factories and the forceway network.

A sort of groan announced the arrival of Rast and Runckel. Bade looked up. Rast saluted. Bade returned the salute. Rast said stiffly, "Sir, I have been defeated. My army no longer exists."

Bade looked Rast over quickly, studying his expression and bearing.

"It's a plain fact," said Rast. "Sir, I should be relieved of command."

"What's happened?" said Bade. "I have no reports of any new enemy attack."

"No," said Rast, "there won't be any formal report. The whole northern front is anaesthetized from one end to the other."

"Snow?" said Bade.

"White death," said Rast.

A messenger stepped past the two generals to hand Bade a report. It was from General Frotch:

"1) Aerial reconnaissance shows heavy enemy forces moving south on a wide front through the snow-covered region. No response or resistance has been noted on the part of our troops.

"2) Aerial reconnaissance shows light enemy forces moving in to ring General Kottek's position. The enemy appears to be moving with extreme caution.

"3) It has so far proved impossible to get in touch with General Kottek.

"4) It must be reported that on several occasions our ground troops have, as individuals, attempted to seize from our flyer pilots and crews, their special protective anti-reduced-degree-of-heat garments. This problem is becoming serious."

Bade looked up at Rast. "You're Ground Forces Commander, not commander of a single front."

"That's so," said Rast. "I should be. But all I command now is a kind of mob. I've tried to keep the troops in order, but they know one thing after another is going wrong. Naturally, they put the blame on their leaders."

The room seemed to Bade to grow unnaturally light and clear. He said, "Have you had an actual case of mutiny, Rast?"

Rast stiffened. "No, sir. But it is possible for troops to be so laggardly and unwilling that the effect is the same. What I mean is that there is the steady growth of a cynical attitude everywhere. Not only in the troops but in the officers."

Bade looked off at the far corner of the room for a moment. He glanced at Runckel. "What's the state of the key-tools factories?"

"Almost all completed. But the northern ones are now in the reduced-degree-of-heat zone. Part of the forceway network is, too.

Using the key-tools plants remaining, it might be possible to patch together some kind of a makeshift. But the reduced-degree-of-heat zone is still moving south."

A pale clerk apologized, stepped around the generals and handed Bade two messages. The first was from Intelligence:

"Enemy propaganda broadcasts beamed at our troops announce General Kottek's unconditional surrender with all his forces. We have no independent information on Kottek's actual situation."

The second message was from the commander of Number 1 Shock Infantry Division. This report boiled down to a miserable confession that the commanding officer found himself unable to prevent:

1) Fraternization with the enemy.
2) The use of various liquid narcotics that rendered troops unfit for duty.
3) The unauthorized wearing of red, white, and blue buttons lettered, "Vote Republican."
4) An ugly game called "footbase," in which the troops separated into two long lines armed with bats, to hammer, pound, beat, and kick, a ball called "the officer," from one end of the field to the other.

Bade looked up at Rast. "How is it I only find out about this now?"

"Sir," said Rast, "each of the officers was ashamed to report it his superior."

Bade handed the report to Runckel, who read it through and looked up somberly. "If it's hit the shock troops, the rest must have it worse."

"Yet," said Bade, "the troops fought well when we recaptured Frotch."

"Yes," said Rast, "but it's the damned planet that's driving them crazy. The natives are remarkable propagandists. And the men can plainly see that even when they win a victory, some freak like the exploding sickness, or some kind of atmospheric jugglery, is likely to take it right away from them. They're in a bad mood and the only thing that might snap them out of it is decisive action. But if they go the other way we're finished."

"This," said Bade, "is no time for you to resign."

"Sir, it's a mess, and I'm responsible. I have to make the offer to resign."

"Well," said Bade, "I don't accept it. But we'll have to try to straighten out this mess." Bade pulled over several sheets of paper. On the first, he wrote:

"Official News Bureau: 1) Categorically deny the capture of General Kottek and his base. State that General Kottek is in full control of Base North, that the enemy has succeeded in infiltrating troops into the general region under cover of snow, but that he has been repulsed with heavy losses in all attacks on the base itself.

"2) State that the enemy announcement of victory in the area is a desperation measure, timed to coincide with their almost unopposed advance through the evacuated Northern Front.

"3) The larger part of the troops in the Northern Front were withdrawn prior to the attack and switched by forceway network to launch a heavy feinting attack against the enemy. State that the enemy, caught by surprise, appears to be rushing reserves from his northern armies to cover the areas threatened by the feint.

"4) Devoted troops who held the Northern Front to make the deception succeed have now been overrun by the enemy advance under cover of the snow. Their heroic sacrifice will not be forgotten.

"5) The enemy now faces the snow time alone. His usual preventive measures have been drastically slowed down. His intended decisive attack has failed of its object. The snow this year is unusually severe, and is already working heavy punishment on the enemy.

"6) Secret measures are now for the first time being brought into the open that will place our troops far beyond the reach of snow."

On the second sheet of paper, Bade wrote:

"Director of Protocol: Prepare immediately: 1) Supreme Commander's Citation for Extraordinary Bravery and Resourcefulness in Action: To be awarded General Kottek. 2) Supreme Commander's Citation for Extraordinary Devotion to Duty: To be awarded singly, to each soldier on duty during the enemy attack on the entire Northern Front. 3) These awards are both to be mentioned promptly in the Daily Notices."

Bade handed the papers to Runckel, "Send these out yourself." As Runckel started off, Bade looked at Rast, then was interrupted by a messenger who stepped past Rast, and handed Bade two slips of paper. With an effort of will, Bade extended his hand and took the papers. He read:

"Sir: Exploration Team South 3 has located ideal island base. Full details follow. Frotch."

"Sir: We have finally contacted General Kottek. He and his troops are dug into underground warrens of great complexity beneath his system of fortifications. Most of the ships above-ground are mere shells, all removable equipment having been stripped out and carried below for the comfort of the troops. Most of the ships' engines have also been disassembled one at a time, carried below, and set up to run the dampers—which are likewise below ground—and the 'heating units' devised by Kottek's technical personnel. His troops appear to be in good order and high spirits. Skath, Col., A.F.C., forwarded by Frotch."

Bade sucked in a deep breath and gave silent thanks. Then he handed the two reports to Rast. Bade snapped on a microphone and got in touch with Frotch. "Listen, can you get pictures of Kottek and his men?"

Frotch held up a handful of pictures, spread like playing cards. "The men took them for souvenirs and gave me copies. You can have all you want."

Bade immediately called his photoprint division and gave orders for the pictures to be duplicated by the thousands. The photoprint division slaved all night, and the excited troops had the pictures on their bulletin boards by the next morning.

The Official News Service meanwhile was dinning Bade's propaganda into the troops' ears at every opportunity. The appearance of the pictures now plainly caught the enemy propaganda out on a limb. Doubting one thing the enemy propaganda had said, the troops suddenly doubted all. A violent revulsion of feeling took place. Before anything else could happen, Bade ordered the troops embarked.

By this time, the apparently harmless rain had produced a severe flood, which repeatedly threatened the power cables supplying the forceway network. The troops had to use this network to get to the ships in time.

As Bade's military engineers blasted out alternate channels for the rising water, and a fervent headquarters group prayed for a drought, the troops poured through the still-operative forceway stations and marched into the ships with joyful shouts.

The enemy joined the celebration with a mammoth missile attack.

The embarkation, together with the disassembling of vital parts of the accessible key-tools factories, took several days. During this time, the enemy continued his steady methodical advance well behind the front of the cold air mass. The enemy however, made no sudden thrust on the ground to take advantage of the embarkation. Bade pondered this sign of tiredness, then sent up a ship to radio a query home. When the answer came, Bade sent a message to the enemy government. The message began:

"Sirs: This scouting expedition has now completed its mission. We are now withdrawing to winter quarters, which may be: a) an unspecified distant location; b) California; c) Florida. If you are prepared to accept certain temporary armistice conditions, we will choose a). Otherwise, you will understand we must choose b) or c). If you are prepared to consider these armistice conditions, you are strongly urged to send a plenipotentiary without delay. This plenipotentiary should be prepared to consider both the temporary armistice and the matters of mutual benefit to us."

Bade waited tensely for the reply. He had before him two papers, one of which read:

" ... the enemy-held peninsula of Florida has thus been found to be heavily infested with heartworms—parasites which live inside the heart, slow circulation, and lower vital activity sharply. While the enemy appears to be immune to infestation, our troops plainly are not. The four scouts who returned here have at last, we believe, been cured—but they have not as yet recovered their strength. The state of things in nearby Cuba is not yet known for certain. Possibly, the troops' enormous consumption of native 'rum' has interacted medicinally with our blood chemistry to retard infestation. If so, we have our choice of calamities. In any case, a landing in Florida would be ruinous."

As for California, the other report concluded:

" ... Statistical studies based on past experience lead us to believe that myth or no myth, immediately upon our landing in California, there will be a terrific earthquake."

Bade had no desire to go to Florida or California. He fervently hoped the enemy would not guess this.

At length the reply came, Bade read through ominous references to the growing might of the United States of the World, then came to the operative sentence:

" ... Our plenipotentiary will be authorized to treat only with regard to an armistice; he is authorized only to transmit other information to his government. He is not empowered to make any agreement whatever on matters other than an armistice."

The plenipotentiary was a tall thin native, who constantly sponged water off his neck and forehead, and who looked at Bade as if he would like cram a nuclear missile down his throat. Getting an agreement was hard work. The plenipotentiary finally accepted Bade's first condition—that General Kottek not be attacked for the duration of the armistice—but flatly refused the second condition allowing the continued occupation of western Cuba. After a lengthy verbal wrestling match, the plenipotentiary at last agreed to a temporary continuation of the western Cuban occupation, provided that the Gulf of Mexico blockade be lifted. Bade agreed to this and the plenipotentiary departed mopping his forehead.

Bade immediately lifted ships and headed south. His ships came down to seize sections of Sumatra, Java, and Borneo, with outposts on the Christmas and Cocoa islands and on small islands in the Indonesian archipelago.

Bade's personal headquarters were on a pleasant little island conveniently located in the Sunda Strait between Java and Sumatra. The name of the island was Krakatoa.

Bade was under no illusion that the inhabitants of the islands welcomed his arrival. Fortunately, however, the armament of his troops outclassed anything in the vicinity, with the possible exception of a bristly-looking place called Singapore. Bade's scouts, after studying Singapore carefully, concluded it was not mobile, and if they left it alone, it would leave them alone.

The enemy plenipotentiary now arrived in a large battleship, and was greeted in the islands with frenzied enthusiasm. Bade was too absorbed in reports of rapidly-improving morale, and highly-successful mass-swimming exercises to care about this welcome. Although an ominous document titled "War in the Islands: U.S.—Japan," sat among the translated volumes of history at Bade's elbow, and served as a constant reminder that this pleasant situation could not be expected to last forever, Bade intended to enjoy it while it did last.

Bade greeted the plenipotentiary in his pleasant headquarters on the leveled top of the tall picturesque cone-shaped hill that rose high above Krakatoa, then dropped off abruptly by the sea.

The plenipotentiary, on entering the headquarters, mopped his brow constantly, kept glancing furtively around, and was plainly ill at ease. The interpreters took their places, and the conversation opened.

"As you see," said Bade, "we are comfortably settled here for the winter."

The plenipotentiary looked around and gave a hollow laugh.

"We are," added Bade, "perfectly prepared to return next . . . a . . . 'summer' . . . and take up where we left off."

"By next summer," said the plenipotentiary, "the United States will be a solid mass of guns from one coast to the other."

Bade shrugged, and the plenipotentiary added grimly, "And *missiles*."

Despite himself, Bade winced.

One of Bade's clerks, carrying a message across the far end of the room, became distracted in his effort to be sure he heard everything. The clerk was busy watching Bade when he banged into the back of a tall filing case. The case tilted off-balance, then started to fall forward.

A second clerk sprang up to catch the side of the case. There was a low heavy rumble as all the drawers slid out.

The plenipotentiary sprang to his feet, and looked wildly around.

The filing case twisted out of the hands of the clerk and came down on the floor with a thundering crash.

The plenipotentiary snapped his eyes tightly shut, clenched his teeth, and stood perfectly still.

Bade and Runckel looked blankly at each other.

The plenipotentiary slowly opened his eyes, looked wonderingly around the room, jumped as the two clerks heaved the filing case upright, turned around to stare at the clerks and the case, turned back to look sharply at Bade, then clamped his jaw.

Bade, his own face as calm as he could make it, decided this might be as good a time as any to throw in a hard punch. He remarked, "You have two choices. You can make a mutually profitable agreement with us. Or you can force us to switch heavier forces and weapons to this planet and crush you. Which is it?"

"We," said the plenipotentiary coldly, "have the resources of the whole planet at our disposal. You have to bring everything from a distance. Moreover, we have captured a good deal of your equipment, which we may duplicate—"

"Lesser weapons," said Bade. "As if an enemy captured your rifles, duplicated them at great expense, and was then confronted with your nuclear bomb."

"This is our planet," said the plenipotentiary grimly, "and we will fight for it to the end."

"We don't want your planet."

The plenipotentiary's eyes widened. Then he burst into a string of invective that the translators couldn't follow. When he had finished, he took a deep breath and recapitulated the main point, "If you don't want it, what are you doing here?"

Bade said, "Your people are clearly warlike. After observing you for some time, a debate arose on our planet as to whether we should hit you or wait till you hit us. After a fierce debate, the first faction won."

"Wait a minute. How could *we* hit *you*? You come from another planet, don't you?"

"Yes, that's true. But it's also true that a baby shark is no great menace to anyone. Except that he will grow up into a big shark. That is how our first faction looked on earth."

The plenipotentiary scowled. "In other words, you'll kill the suspect before he has a chance to commit the crime. Then you justify it by saying the man would have committed a crime if he'd lived."

"We didn't intend to kill you—only to disarm you."

"How does all this square with your telling us you're just a scout party?"

"Are you under the impression," said Bade, "that this is the main invasion force? Would we attack without a full reconnaissance first? Do you think we would merely make one sizable landing, on *one* continent? How could we hope to conquer in that way?"

The plenipotentiary frowned, sucked in a deep breath, and mopped his forehead. "What's your offer?"

"Disarm yourselves voluntarily. All hostilities will end immediately."

The plenipotentiary gave a harsh laugh.

Bade said, "What's your answer?"

"What's your real offer?"

"As I remarked," said Bade, "there were two factions on our planet. One favored the attack, as self-preservation. The other faction opposed the attack, on moral and political grounds. The second faction at present holds that it is now impossible to remain aloof, as we had hoped to before the attack. One way or the other, we are now bound up with Earth. We either have to be enemies, or friends. As it happens, I am a member of the bloc that opposed the attack. The bloc that favored the attack has lost support owing to the results of our initial operations. Because of this political shift, I have practically a free hand at the moment." Bade paused as the plenipotentiary turned his head slightly and leaned forward with an intent look.

Bade said, "Your country has suffered by far the most from our attack. Obviously, it should profit the most. We have a number of scientific advances to offer as bargaining counters. Our essential condition is that we retain some overt standing—some foothold— some way of knowing by direct observation that this planet—or any nation of it—won't attack us."

The plenipotentiary scowled. "Every nation on Earth is pretty closely allied as a result of your attack. We're a world of united states—all practically one nation. And all the land on the globe belongs to one of us or the other. While there's bound to be considerable regional rivalry even when we have peace, that's all. Otherwise we're united. As a result, there's not going to be any peace as long as you've got your foot on land belonging to any of us. That includes Java, Sumatra, and even this . . . er . . . mountain we're on now." He looked around uneasily, and added, "We might let you have a little base, somewhere . . . maybe in Antarctica but I doubt it. We won't want any foreign planet sticking its nose in our business."

Bade said, "My proposal allows for that."

"I don't see how it could," said the plenipotentiary. "What is it?"

Bade told him.

The plenipotentiary sat as if he had been hit over the head with a rock. Then he let out a mighty burst of laughter, banged his hand on his knee and said, "You're serious?"

"Absolutely."

The plenipotentiary sprang to his feet. "I'll have to get in touch with my government. Who knows? Maybe— Who knows?" He strode out briskly.

About this time, a number of fast ships arrived from home. These ships were much in use during the next months. Delegations from both planets flew in both directions.

Runckel was highly uneasy. Incessantly he demanded, "Will it work? What if they flood our planet with a whole mob—"

"I have it on good authority," said Bade, "that our planet is every bit as uncomfortable for them as theirs is for us. We almost lost one of their delegates straight down through the mud on the last visit. They have to use dozens of towels for handkerchiefs every day, and that trace of ammonia in the atmosphere doesn't seem to agree with them. Some of them have even gotten fog-sick."

"Why should they go along with the idea, then?"

"It fits in with their nature. Besides, where else are they going to get another one? As one of their senators put it, 'Everything here on Earth is sewed up.' There's even a manifest destiny argument."

"Well, the idea has attractions, but—"

"Listen," said Bade, "I'm told not to prolong the war, because it's too costly and dangerous; not to leave behind a reservoir of fury to discharge on us in the future; not to surrender; not, in the present circumstances, to expect them to surrender. I am told to somehow keep a watch on them and bind their interests to ours; and not to forget the tie must be more than just on paper, it's got to be emotional as well as legal. On top of that, if possible, I'm supposed to open up commercial opportunities. Can you think of any other way?"

"Frankly, no," said Runckel.

There was a grumbling sound underneath them, and the room shivered slightly.

"What was that?" said Runckel.

Bade looked around, frowning. "I don't know."

A clerk came across the room and handed Runckel a message and Bade another message. Runckel looked up, scowling. "The sea water here is beginning to have an irritating effect on our men's skin."

"Never mind," said Bade, "their plenipotentiary is coming. We'll know one way or the other shortly."

Runckel looked worried, and began searching through his wastebasket.

The plenipotentiary came in grinning. "O.K.," he said, "the Russians are a little burned up, and I don't think Texas is any too happy, but nobody can think of a better way out. You're in."

He and Bade shook hands fervently. Photographers rushed in to snap pictures. Outside, Bade's band was playing "The Star-Spangled Banner."

"Another state," said the plenipotentiary, grinning expansively. "How's it feel to be a citizen?"

Runckel erupted from his wastebasket and bolted across the room.

"Krakatoa is a *volcano*!" he shouted. "And here's what a volcano is!"

There was a faint but distinct rumble underfoot.

The room emptied fast.

On the way home, they were discussing things.

Bade was saying, "I don't claim it's perfect, but then our two planets are so mutually uncomfortable there's bound to be little travel either way till we have a chance to get used to each other. Yet, we *can* go back and forth. Who has a better right than a citizen? And there's a good chance of trade and mutual profit. There's a good emotional tie." He frowned. "There's just one thing—"

"What's that?" said Runckel.

Bade opened a translated book to a page he had turned down. He read silently. He looked up perplexedly.

"Runckel," he said, "there are certain technicalities involved in being a citizen."

Runckel tensed. "What do you mean?"

"Oh— Well, like this." He looked back at the book for a moment.

"What is it?" demanded Runckel.

"Well," said Bade, "what do you suppose 'income tax' is?"

Runckel looked relieved. He shrugged.

"Don't worry about it," he said. "It's too fantastic. Probably it's just a myth."

Environment

by Chester S. Geier

The sun was rising above the towers and spires of the city to the west. It sent questing fingers of brightness through the maze of streets and avenues, wiping away the last, pale shadows of night. But in the ageless splendor of the dawn, the city dreamed on.

The ship came with the dawn, riding down out of the sky on wings of flame, proclaiming its arrival in a voice of muted thunder. It came out of the west, dropping lower and lower, to cruise finally in great, slow circles. It moved over the city like a vast, silver-gray hunting hawk, searching for prey. There was something of eagerness in the leashed thunder of its voice.

Still the city dreamed on. Nothing, it seemed, could disturb its dreaming. Nothing could. It was not a sentient dreaming. It was a part of the city itself, something woven into every flowing line and graceful curve. As long as the city endured, the dream would go on.

The voice of the ship had grown plaintive, filled with an aching disappointment. Its circling was aimless, dispirited. It rose high in the sky, hesitated, then glided down and down. It landed on an expanse of green in what had once been a large and beautiful park.

It rested now on the sward, a great, silver-gray ovoid that had a certain harsh, utilitarian beauty. There was a pause of motionlessness, then a circular lock door opened in its side. Jon Gaynor appeared in the lock and jumped to the ground. He gazed across

623

the park to where the nearest towers of the city leaped and soared, and his gray eyes were narrowed in a frown of mystification.

"Deserted!" he whispered. "Deserted— But why?"

Jon Gaynor turned as Wade Harlan emerged from the lock. The two glanced at each other, then, in mutual perplexity, their eyes turned to the dreaming city. After a long moment, Wade Harlan spoke.

"Jon, I was thinking— Perhaps this isn't the right planet. Perhaps . . . perhaps old Mark Gaynor and the Purists never landed here at all—"

Jon Gaynor shook his brown head slowly. He was a tall, lean figure in a tight-fitting, slate-gray overall. "I've considered that possibility, Wade. No—this is the place, all right. Everything checks against the data given in that old Bureau of Expeditions report. Seven planets in the system—this the second planet. And this world fits perfectly the description given in the report—almost a second Earth. Then there's the sun. Its type, density, rate of radiation, spectrum—all the rest—they check, too."

Gaynor shook his head again. "Granted there could exist another system of seven planets, with the second habitable. But it's too much to suppose that the description of that second planet, as well as the description of its sun, would exactly fit the expedition report. And the report mentioned a deserted city. We're standing in the middle of it now. The only thing that doesn't check is that it's still deserted."

Harlan gave a slight shrug. "That may not mean anything, Jon. How can you be certain that Mark Gaynor and the Purists came back here at all? The only clue you have is that old Bureau of Expeditions report, describing this city and planet, which you found among the personal effects Mark Gaynor left behind. It may not have meant anything."

"Perhaps— But I'm pretty sure it did. You see, old Mark and the Purists wanted to live far from all others, somewhere where there would be none to laugh at them for their faith in the ancient religious beliefs. The only habitable planets which answered their purposes were a tremendously remote few. Of them all, this was the only one possessing a city—and a deserted city at that."

"So you think they must have come here because of the benefits offered by the city?"

"That's one reason. The other . . . well, old Mark had a pile of Bureau of Expedition reports dating back for two hundred years. The report relating to this planetary system was marked in red, as being of special interest. It was the only report so marked—"

Harlan smiled in friendly derision. "Add that to a misplaced hero-worship for a crackpot ancestor—and the answer is that we've come on a goose chase. Lord, Jon, even with the Hyperspacial Drive to carry us back over the immense distance, it's going to be a terrific job getting back to Earth. You know what a time we had, finding this planet. The Hyperspacial Drive is a wonderful thing—but it has its drawbacks. You go in here, and you come out there—millions of miles away. If you're lucky, you're only within a few million miles or so of your destination. If not—and that's most of the time—you simply try again. And again—"

"That's a small worry," Gaynor replied. "And as for old Mark, he was hardly a crackpot. It took one hundred and twenty years for the world to realize that. His ideas on how people should live and think were fine—but they just didn't fit in with the general scheme of things. On a small group, they could have been applied beautifully. And such a group, living and thinking that way, might have risen to limitless heights of greatness. Hero-worship? No—I never had such feelings for my great-great-uncle, Mark Gaynor. I just had a feverish desire to see how far the Purists had risen—to see if their way of life had given them an advantage over others."

Harlan was sober. "Maybe we'll never learn what happened to them, Jon. The city is deserted. Either the Purists came here and left—or they never came here at all."

Gaynor straightened with purpose. "We'll learn which is the answer. I'm not leaving until we do. We'll—" Gaynor broke off, his eyes jerking toward the sky. High up and far away in the blue, something moved, a vast swarm of objects too tiny for identification. They soared and circled, dipped and swooped like birds. And as the two men from another planet watched, sounds drifted down to them—sweet, crystalline tinklings and chimings, so infinitely faint that they seemed to be sensed rather than heard.

"Life—" Harlan murmured. "There's life here of sorts, Jon."

Gaynor nodded thoughtfully. "And that may mean danger. We're going to examine the city—and I think we'd better be armed."

While Harlan watched the graceful, aimless maneuvers of the aerial creatures, Gaynor went back into the ship. In a moment, he returned with laden arms. He and Harlan strapped the antigravity flight units to their backs, buckled the positron blasters about their waists. Then they lifted into the air, soared with easy speed toward a cluster of glowing towers.

As they flew, a small cloud of the aerial creatures flashed past. The things seemed to be intelligent, for, as though catching sight of the two men, they suddenly changed course, circling with a clearly evident display of excited curiosity. The crystalline chimings and tinklings which they emitted held an elfin note of astonishment.

If astonishment it actually was, Gaynor and Harlan were equally amazed at close view of the creatures. For they were great, faceted crystals whose interiors flamed with glorious color—exquisite shades that pulsed and changed with the throb of life. Like a carillon of crystal bells, their chimings and tinklings rang out—so infinitely sweet and clear and plaintive that it was both a pain and a pleasure to hear.

"Crystalline life!" Harlan exclaimed. His voice became thoughtful. "Wonder if it's the only kind of life here."

Gaynor said nothing. He watched the circling crystal creatures with wary eyes, the positron blaster gripped in his hand. But the things gave no evidence of being inimical—or at least no evidence of being immediately so. With a last exquisite burst of chimings, they coalesced into a small cloud and soared away, glittering, flashing, with prismatic splendor in the sunlight.

On the invisible wings of their antigravity flight units, Gaynor and Harlan had approached quite close to the cluster of towers which was their goal. Gliding finally through the space between two, they found themselves within a snug, circular enclosure, about the circumference of which the towers were spaced. The floor of the enclosure was in effect a tiny park, for grass and trees grew here, and there were shaded walks built of the same palely glowing substance as the towers. In the exact center of the place was a fountain, wrought of some lustrous, silvery metal. Only a thin trickle of water came from it now.

Gaynor dipped down, landed gently beside the fountain. He bent, peering, then gestured excitedly to Harlan, who was hovering close.

"Wade—there's a bas-relief around this thing! Figures—"

Harlan touched ground, joined Gaynor in a tense scrutiny of the design. A procession of strange, lithe beings was pictured in bas-relief around the curving base of the fountain. Their forms were essentially humanoid, possessed of two arms, two legs, and large, well-formed head. Except for an exotic, fawnlike quality about the graceful, parading figures, Gaynor and Harlan might have been gazing at a depiction of garlanded, Terrestrial youths and maidens.

"The builders of the city," Gaynor said softly. "They looked a lot like us. Parallel evolution, maybe. This planet and sun are almost twins of ours. Wade—I wonder what happened to them?"

Harlan shook his shock of red hair slowly, saying nothing. His blue eyes were dark with somber speculation.

Gaynor's voice whispered on. "The city was already deserted when that government expedition discovered it some one hundred and thirty years ago. The city couldn't always have been that way. Once there were people on this planet—beings who thought and moved and dreamed, who built in material things an edifice symbolic of their dreaming. Why did they disappear? What could have been responsible? War, disease—or simply the dying out of a race?"

Harlan shrugged his great shoulders uncomfortably. His voice was gruff. "Maybe the answer is here somewhere. Maybe not. If it isn't, maybe we'll be better off, not knowing. When an entire race disappears for no apparent reason, as the people of this city seem to have done, the answer usually isn't a nice one."

The two men took to one of the paths radiating away from the fountain, followed it to a great, arching entranceway at the base of a tower-building. Slowly they entered—the sunlight dimmed and they moved through a soft gloom. Presently they found themselves in a vast foyer—if such it was. In the middle of the place was a circular dais, with steps leading to a small platform at the top.

They mounted the steps, gained the platform. Of a sudden, a faint whispering grew, and without any other warning, they began to rise slowly into the air. Harlan released a cry of surprise and shock. Gaynor ripped his positron blaster free, sought desperately to writhe from the influence of the force that had gripped him.

And then Gaynor quieted. His eyes were bright with a realization. "An elevator!" he gasped. "Wade—we stepped into some kind of elevating force."

They ceased struggling and were borne gently up and up. They passed through an opening in the ceiling of the foyer, found themselves within a circular shaft, the top of which was lost in the dimness above. Vertical handrails lined the shaft. It was only after passing two floors that they divined the purpose of these. Then, reaching the third floor, each gripped a handrail, and they stepped from the force.

They found themselves within a vast, well-lighted apartment. The source of illumination was not apparent, seeming to emanate from the very walls. Room opened after spacious room—and each was as utterly barren of furnishings as the last. Barren, that is, except for two things. The first was that the walls were covered with murals or paintings—life-sized, rich with glowing color, and almost photographic in detail. The second was that one wall of each room contained a tiny niche. Gaynor and Harlan investigated a niche in one room they entered. Within it was a solitary object—a large jewel, or at least what seemed to be a jewel.

"This is screwy," Harlan muttered. "It doesn't make sense. How could anyone have lived in a place like this?"

Gaynor's eyes were dark with thought. He answered slowly, "Don't make the mistake of judging things here according to our standard of culture. To the builders of this city, Wade, these rooms might have been thoroughly cozy and comfortable, containing every essential necessary to their daily lives."

"Maybe," Harlan grunted. "But I certainly don't see those essentials."

"This thing—" Gaynor lifted the jewel from its niche. "Maybe this thing holds an answer of some kind." Gaynor balanced the jewel in his palm, gazing down at it frowningly. His thoughts were wondering, speculative. Then the speculation faded—he found himself concentrating on the thing, as though by sheer force of will he could fathom its purpose.

And then it happened—the jewel grew cold in his hand—a faint, rose-colored glow surrounded it like an aura. A musical tinkling sounded. Harlan jumped, a yell bursting full-throated from his lungs. Gaynor spun about, surprised, uncomprehending.

"I . . . I saw things!" Harlan husked. "Objects, Jon— The room was full of them—angular ghosts!"

Gaynor stared at the other without speaking. His features were lax with a dawning awe.

Harlan said suddenly, "Try it again, Jon. Look at that thing. Maybe—"

Gaynor returned his gaze to the jewel. He forced his mind quiet, concentrated. Again the jewel grew cold, and again the tinkling sounded. Harlan was tense, rigid, his narrowed eyes probing the room. Within the room, outlines wavered mistily—outlines of things which might have been strange furniture, or queer, angular machines.

"Harder, Jon! Harder!" Harlan prompted.

Gaynor was sweating. He could feel the perspiration roll down his temples. His eyes seemed to be popping from their sockets.

Harlan strained with his peering. The outlines grew stronger, darkened—but only for a moment. The next they wavered mistily again, thinned, and were gone.

Gaynor drew a sobbing breath, straightened up. He asked, "Wade—what did you see?"

"I don't know for sure. Things—or the ghosts of things. Here—give me that. I'm going to see what I can do."

Gaynor relinquished the jewel. Holding it in his palm, Harlan gathered his thoughts, poised them, focused them. And, watching, Gaynor saw the ghostly outlines for the first time—misty suggestions of angles and curves, hints of forms whose purpose he could not guess. Alien ghosts of alien objects, summoned by will from some alien limbo.

Abruptly, the outlines faded and were gone. The tinkling of the jewel thinned and died.

Harlan drew a shuddering breath. "Jon—you saw them?"

"Yes. Dimly."

"We ... we haven't got the strength, Jon. We haven't got the power necessary to materialize the objects—whatever they are."

"Maybe that's the drawback. Or—maybe we've got the strength, but simply can't materialize things—objects—whose size, shape, and purpose we do not know and cannot guess."

"That might be it." Harlan's voice grew sharp. "But, great space, Jon, what possibly could be the idea behind it? Why did they—that other race—construct buildings in which the rooms were left unfurnished, or which could be furnished merely by concentrating on ... on these jewels? What could have been the reason behind it?"

Gaynor shook his head. "We'll never know that, perhaps. At least, we'll never know if we persist in thinking in terms of our own culture. The builders of this city were humanoid, Wade—but mentally they were alien. Don't forget that. These rooms may not have been living quarters at all. They may have been repositories for valuable things, of which the jewels were the means of materializing. Only those who knew how could materialize them. Thus, perhaps, those things were kept safe."

"That might be it," Harlan muttered. "It makes sense."

"These pictures"—Gaynor gestured at the paintings on the walls—"might contain the answer. If we knew how to read them, they might tell us the purpose of these empty rooms—why the furnishings or machines had to be materialized. I wonder, Wade ... I wonder if each of these pictures is complete in itself, or if each is part of a greater series. You know—like a book. You read one page, and it doesn't make sense. You read the whole thing—and it does."

"The beginning, Jon," Harlan whispered. "We'd have to start at the beginning."

"Yes—the beginning."

Harlan replaced the jewel in its niche, and on the invisible wings of their antigravity flight units, they glided back to the force shaft. Here they switched off their units, allowed the force to carry them up. But the apartments on the upper floors contained nothing new or illuminating. Like the first they had visited, these were empty, save for the wall paintings and the jewels in their niches. They returned to the shaft again, this time to meet a complication.

"Say—how do we get down?" Harlan puzzled. "This thing has been carrying us up all the time, and there doesn't seem to be another one for descending."

"Why, you simply *will* yourself to go down," Gaynor said. Then he looked blankly surprised.

Harlan nodded gravely. "Of course," he said. "That's the answer. I should have thought of it myself."

They descended. Outside, the sun was bright and warm. Under its light the city dreamed on.

Gaynor and Harlan soared through the warmth. The city was very bright and still. Far away and high in the blue, glittering swarms of the crystal creatures darted. Their tinkling and chiming drifted down to the two men.

Gaynor and Harlan descended several times to investigate tower buildings, but these were very much like the first they had visited. The spacious apartments seemed to echo in their strange emptiness, each one seemingly louder than the last. Twice they took turns, attempted to materialize the unguessable furnishings of the rooms. Each time they failed. And afterward they did not disturb the jewels in their niches. They merely gazed at the flaming wall paintings, and came away.

Again they glided through the air, though slowly and thoughtfully, now. They were silent. Beneath them, the city dreamed. Once a cloud of crystal creatures flashed past, sparkling, chiming, but the two did not seem to notice.

"Jon—?" Harlan's voice was hesitant.

"Yes?"

"I don't know how to put it into words, but—well, don't you feel that you are beginning to *know?*"

"Yes—there's the ghost of something in my mind. Those pictures, Wade—"

"Yes, Jon, the pictures."

Again they were silent. Gaynor broke the silence.

"Wade—all my life I've been reading primers. Someone just gave me a college textbook, and I glanced through several pages. Naturally, I did not understand, but here and there I found words familiar to me. They left a ghost in my mind—"

"You've got to go back to the beginning, Jon. You've got to read all the books which will help you to understand that college textbook."

"Yes, Wade, the beginning—"

They drifted on while the city dreamed beneath them. The sun was a swaddling blanket of brightness. Like memory-sounds, faint chimings and tinklings wafted on the air.

And then Gaynor was grasping Harlan's arm. "Wade—down there. Look!" He pointed tensely.

Harlan stiffened as he saw it. The ship was a tiny thing, almost lost amid the greenery of the park. Almost in unison, the two touched the controls of their antigravity flight units, arrowed down in a swift, gentle arc.

The ship was very big, like no ship they had ever seen before. It was a thing of harsh angles, built of some strange red metal or alloy that gleamed in the sunlight with the hue of blood. A square opening gaped in its side. Slowly, Gaynor and Harlan entered it.

It was as though they entered the gloom of another world. Little of what they saw was familiar to them, and they had to guess the purpose of the rest. There were passageways and corridors, and rooms opened from these. A few they were able to identify, but the rest, filled with queer, angular furniture and sprawling machines, escaped classification. They left the ship—and the sunlight felt good.

Gaynor's voice rustled dryly. "They were humanoid, Wade, the people who built that ship. If nothing else made sense, the things we saw showed that. But the people who made that ship were not of the city. They were spawned on some planet circling another sun."

"They came here," Harlan rasped. "They came—and they left that ship behind—Jon . . . they came . . . and they never left this world—"

"Wade—I'm thinking. There might have been other ships—"

Harlan touched the butt of his positron blaster, and his face was pale. "We've got to look, Jon. That's something we've got to know."

They lifted into the air. Circling and dipping, they searched. The sun was at zenith when they found the second ship. By mid-afternoon they had found a third and a fourth. The fourth was the *Ark*, the hyperspacial cruiser in which old Mark Gaynor and his band of Purists had left the Earth some one hundred and twenty years before.

The four ships which Gaynor and Harlan had found had two things in common. Each had been built by a different humanoid people, and each was completely deserted. Other than this, there was no basis of comparison between them. Each was separate and distinct, unique in its alienness. Even the *Ark*, long outmoded, seemed strange.

In the *Ark*, Gaynor and Harlan found nothing to indicate what had happened to its passengers. Everything was orderly and neat—more, even in the most excellent condition. Nothing written had been left behind, not the slightest scrap of rotting paper.

Gaynor whispered, "They *did* come here, then. And the same thing happened to them that happened to all the rest of the people who landed here. The same thing, I'm sure, that happened to the builders of the city. Why did they leave these ships behind? Where did they go? What *could* have happened to them?"

Harlan shook his red head somberly. "We'd better not know that. If we stay and try to find out, the same thing will happen to us. The government expedition which discovered this planet encountered the same mystery—but they didn't try to find out. They returned to Earth. Jon—we'd better get back to the *Paragon*. We'd better leave while we can."

"And in time more people would come to settle here. And there would be more empty ships." Gaynor's lips tightened to a stubborn line. "Wade—I'm not leaving until I crack the mystery of this place. I'm going to find what happened to old Mark and the Purists. We've been warned—we'll be on the alert."

Harlan met Gaynor's determined gaze, and then he looked away. He moistened his lips. After a long moment he gave a stiff nod. His voice was very low.

"Then we've got to start at the beginning, Jon. Those pictures—"

"Yes, Wade, the pictures. I'm sure they hold the answer to the whole thing. We've got to find that beginning. You've noticed how the city is strung out. At one end is the beginning, at the other—"

"The end!" Harlan said abruptly.

"No. Wade. The answer."

They returned first to the *Paragon*, to satisfy pangs of hunger too intense to be ignored any longer. Then, donning their antigravity flight units once more, they took to the air. They circled several times, set out finally for a point on the horizon where the city thinned out and finally terminated.

Their flight ended at a single, slender tower set in the midst of a parklike expanse. That they had reached the end of the city, they knew, for ahead of them no other building was in sight. They floated to the ground, stared silently at the tower. It glowed with a chaste whiteness in the late afternoon light—serene, somewhat aloof, lovely in its simplicity and solitariness.

Harlan spoke softly. "The beginning? Or—the end?"

"That's what we have to find out," Gaynor responded. "We're going in there, Wade."

The interior of the tower was dark and cool, filled with the solemn hush of a cathedral. It consisted solely of one great room, its ceiling lost in sheerness of height. And except for the ever-present wall paintings, it was empty—utterly bare.

Gaynor and Harlan gazed at the paintings, and then they looked at each other, and slowly they nodded. Silently they left.

"That . . . that wasn't the beginning," Harlan stated slowly.

"No, Wade. That was—the end. The beginning lies on the opposite side of the city. But we'll have to postpone our investigation until morning. We wouldn't reach the other end of the city until dark."

They returned to the *Paragon*. The sun was setting behind the towers of the city to the east, sinking into a glory of rose and gold. Slowly the paling fingers of its radiance withdrew from the city. Night came in all its starry splendor.

Gaynor and Harlan were up with the dawn. Eagerness to be back at their investigations fired them. They hurried impatiently through breakfast. Then, attaching kits of emergency ration concentrates to their belts and donning their antigravity flight units, they took to the air.

As they flew, Gaynor and Harlan had to remind themselves that this was the second day of their visit and not the first, so closely did the new day resemble the one preceding. Nothing had changed. The city beneath them still dreamed on. And far away and high in the blue, glittering clouds of the crystal creatures darted and danced, their chimings and tinklings sounding like echoes of melody from an elfin world.

The sun was bright and warm when Gaynor and Harlan reached the end of the city opposite the one which they had investigated the day before. Here they found no slender tower. There was nothing to show that this part of the city was in any way different from the rest. The general plan of tower-encircled courts was the same as everywhere else. The city merely terminated—or looking at it the other way, merely began.

Gaynor and Harlan glided down into one of the very first of the tower-encircled courts. They touched ground, switched off their flight units, stood gazing slowly about them.

Gaynor muttered, "The beginning? Or— Maybe we were wrong, Wade. Maybe there is no beginning."

"Those towers should tell us," Harlan said. "Let's have a look inside them, Jon."

They entered an arching doorway, strode into a great foyer. Within this they had their first indication that this part of the city actually was different from the rest. For within the foyer was no dais and force shaft as they had found previously. Instead, a broad stairway led to the floors above.

They mounted the stairs. The walls of the first apartment they investigated were covered with paintings, as everywhere else, but this time the spacious rooms were not empty. They were furnished. Gaynor and Harlan gazed upon softly gleaming objects which very clearly were tables and chairs, deep, luxurious couches, and cabinets of various sizes and shapes. At first everything seemed strange to them, and as they glanced about, they found themselves comparing the furniture to that which they had seen in homes on Earth. And after a while things no longer seemed strange at all.

Gaynor blinked his eyes rapidly several times. He frowned puzzledly. "Wade—either I'm crazy, or this room has changed."

Harlan was gazing at the wall paintings. His voice came as from far away. "Changed? Why, yes. Things are as they should be—now."

Gaynor gazed at the walls, and then he nodded. "That's right, Wade. Of course."

Gaynor walked over to a low cabinet. Somewhere before he had seen a cabinet like this one. He felt that he should know its purpose, yet it eluded him. He stared at it musingly. And then he remembered something—his eyes lifted to the paintings on the wall. No. The other wall? Yes.

Gaynor looked at the cabinet again—and now a slow murmur of melody arose within the room. Hauntingly familiar, poignantly sweet, yet formless. Gaynor looked at the walls again. The melody shaped itself, grew stronger, and the lilting strains of a spaceman's song flooded richly through the room.

> I'm blasting the far trails,
> Following the star trails,
> Taking the home trails,
> Back, dear, to you—

"The Star Trails Home to You," Gaynor whispered. Sudden nostalgia washed over him in a wave. Home. The Earth— His eyes lifted to the walls, and he was comforted.

Gaynor looked around for Harlan. He found the other standing before a second cabinet across the room. Gaynor approached him, noting as he did so that Harlan stood strangely rigid and still. In alarm, Gaynor ran the remaining distance. Harlan did not seem to notice. His face was rapt, trance-like.

Gaynor grasped Harlan's arm, shook him. "Wade! Wade—what is it? Snap out of it!"

Harlan stirred. Expression came back into his features—his eyes sharped upon Gaynor's face. "What . . . what— Oh, it's you, Jon. She . . . she had red hair, and . . . and her arms were around me, and—" Harlan broke off, flushing.

Investigation of the cabinets in the other rooms produced still more interesting results. One had a spigot projecting from its front, with a catchbasin below, much like a drinking fountain. Gaynor looked at the wall paintings, and then he looked at the spigot, and suddenly liquid jetted from it. He tasted it cautiously, nodded approvingly, not at all surprised.

"Scotch," he said. "I'll have it with soda."

"Hurry up, then," Harlan prompted impatiently.

There was another cabinet that they found particularly interesting. This one had a foot-square opening in its front, and after Gaynor and Harlan had gotten their proper instructions from the paintings, they moved on—each munching at a delicious leg of roast chicken.

Not all the cabinets produced things which were edible or audible, but all opened up new vistas of thought and experience. Gaynor and Harlan learned the purpose of each, and already in their minds they were devising new methods of test and application. The wall paintings were very extensive, and they were learning rapidly.

That was the beginning—

After the cabinets, which supplied every possible physical or mental want, came the machines. Simple things at first, for Gaynor and Harlan were still in the equivalent of kindergarten. But they were humanoid—and, therefore, inquisitive. The machines were delightful and of absorbing interest. Once their purpose and function became known, however, their novelty died, and Gaynor and Harlan quested on for new fields to conquer. Thus, in a very few days, they moved to the next unit.

Here was the same plan of tower-encircled court, but the cabinets and machines had become more complicated, more difficult of operation. But Gaynor and Harlan had become quite adept at reading the wall paintings which were their primers. They learned—

Instruction followed application, and in a very few days again, Gaynor and Harlan moved on. Thus they went, from unit to unit, and always the wall paintings pointed out the way.

The sun rose and the sun set, and the city dreamed on. And always, high in the sky, the crystal creatures circled and soared, tinkling and chiming. The days passed gently, mere wraiths of sunlight.

The machines grew larger, more intricate, ever more difficult of solution. Each was a new test upon the growing knowledge of Gaynor and Harlan. And each test was harder than the last, for the wall paintings no longer pointed out the way, but merely hinted now.

Gaynor and Harlan progressed more slowly, though none the less steadily. They were not impatient. They had no sense of restless striving toward a future goal. They lived for the present. They were submerged heart and soul in the never-ending fascinations of their environment to the exclusion of all else.

The machines continued to grow larger. At one point they were so huge, that a single machine filled an entire apartment. But that was the climax, for afterward the machines grew smaller, ever smaller, until at last they came to a unit the apartments of which were empty. Empty, that is, except for the wall paintings and the jewels in their niches.

Harlan peered about him, frowning. "I seem to remember this place."

"It is familiar," Gaynor said. His brows drew together, and after a time he nodded. "We were here before, I think. But that was many toree ago, when we were children."

"Yes—when we were children. I recall it, now." Harlan smiled reminiscently. "It is strange we knew so little as children that it should be so easily forgotten."

"Yes, we have grown. The memories of childhood are very dim. I can recall some things, but they are not very clear. There was a purpose that brought us to the city. A purpose— But what else could it have been than to learn? And there was a mystery. But there is nothing mysterious about the city, nothing strange at all. Mere imaginings of childhood perhaps—meaningless trifles at best. We will not let them concern us now. We have grown."

Harlan nodded gravely, and his blue eyes, deep with an ocean of new knowledge, lifted to the painting-covered walls. "Events of the past should no longer concern us. We have entered upon the Third Stage. The tasks of this alone should occupy our thoughts."

"Yes—the past has been left behind." Gaynor was looking at the walls. "The Third Stage. The tasks will be very difficult, Wade—but interesting. We'll be putting our knowledge into practice—actually creating. This means we'll have to deal directly with the powers of the various soldani and varoo. As these are extradimensional, control will be solely by cholthening at the six level, through means of the taadron. We'll have to be careful, though—any slightest relaxation of the sorran will have a garreling effect—"

"I guessed that. But there must be some way to minimize the garreling effect, if it should occur."

"A field of interwoven argroni of the eighth order should prevent it from becoming overpowering."

"We can try it. You're working on the woratis patterns?"

"Yes. I've managed to cholthen them into the fifth stage of development."

"Mine's the vandari patterns. I've found them more interesting than those of the woratis. Fourth stage of development. I'm starting at once. I'll use the next room."

Harlan left, and Gaynor took the jewel from its niche—the taadron, that is—and set his cholthening power at the sixth level. The thing flamed gloriously in his hand—light pulsed out in great, soft waves, washed over the wall paintings, made them glow with exquisite richness. Unearthly melody filled the room, tuneless, silver-sweet. Gaynor was creating. And as he did so, things began to take on form and substance within the room—things which might have been machines, but weren't machines, because they were intelligent and alive in a way no machine can ever be. Finally, Gaynor and his creations communicated. It was somewhat difficult at first, but he was well along now, and took the difficulty in his stride.

Gaynor learned things—just as, in the other room, Harlan was learning, too. And then he took up the taadron again and chol-thened. The things which he had created vanished. He began to develop the woratis patterns into the fifth stage—

Bright day blended into bright day, gently, unnoticeably. The city floated on the gentle, green swells of the planet, and float-ing, dreamed.

After a time, Gaynor and Harlan moved on to the next unit. Then the next—and the next. Soon it came to pass that they entered the Fourth Stage. This, they knew, was the last one, but what came afterward did not worry them. They had reached a level of mind which was beyond all worrying.

The Third Stage had changed them greatly, though they were not aware of it. They would not have been concerned even if they had. They no longer used their natural vocal apparatus, now, for they had come to think in terms which simply could not have been put into words. They had become telepathic, conversing in pure ideas of the highest order. And they no longer materialized their food from the atoms of the air. A simple rearrangement of their body cells—simple, when understood as they understood it—now enabled them to feed directly upon certain nourishing extradimensional subatomic energies. And the antigravity flight units, which they had reduced to the size of peas for convenience, were now discarded entirely. They had learned to fly without the aid of any device.

The Fourth Stage changed them still further. They created now—the word does not quite describe their activities—without the aid of the taadron, for they had learned to ennathen, which was as great an advancement over cholthening as telepathy is over speech. Thus is came about that Gaynor and Harlan—or the beings who once had been Gaynor and Harlan—found their bodies an annoying encumbrance. For arms and legs, heart and lungs, and the senses and nerves which use of these required, had become quite unnecessary to them. They had outgrown these impedimenta of their childhood.

They spoke of this now by a telepathic means that was not quite telepathy, and they wondered what to do. For though they had mastered well the wall paintings which were their college textbooks, there was no clear answer. Their discussion of the problem could not have been made understandable, however roughly it might have been put, but suffice it to say that at last they reached a decision.

They had progressed from one end of the city to the edge of the other. Not quite the edge, though—for there was one building in which they had not yet narleened. They had examined it before, of course, but that was when they had been children—in those dim, pale days when they did not understand.

They decided to vogelar to this very last building. Here, perhaps, every question would be answered.

It was dawn when they vogelared through the arching doorway. The first feeble rays of morning crept through the opening—the interior of the Temple was very dark and cool. All the dreaming of the city seemed to be concentrated here in one vast stillness.

The beings who once had been Gaynor and Harlan narleened the paintings on the walls of the Temple, gazed upon them with this new, all-embracing sense which went far beyond the limited realms of mere vision—so that almost the paintings spoke to them and they answered back. They narleened the paintings.

Their every question was answered—for all eternity.

And thus it came about, after a time, that two great, faceted crystals emerged from the doorway of the Temple, and lifted, pulsing with a vibrant new life, flashing in rainbow splendor, into the sky. Higher, they lifted, and higher, chiming and tinkling, soaring to join the others of their kind.

The sun shone brightly in the sky. High and far away in the blue, glittering clouds of crystal creatures darted and danced, sending wave after exquisite wave of crystalline melody upon the gentle shores of air. Among them now were two who had still to learn the intricacies of flight.

And the city dreamed on.

A perfect environment, the city. Ideal for the inquisitive humanoid.

~

AFTERWORD BY DAVID DRAKE

When I read "Environment" in Groff Conklin's *The Omnibus of Science Fiction* I didn't know who Chester S. Geier was. At the time I barely knew who Heinlein was, so that isn't surprising.

Geier wrote quite a lot of SF in the '40s, during the Golden Age—but not *of* the Golden Age, because he wrote mostly for the Ziff-Davis magazines, *Amazing* and *Fantastic Adventures*, which were then edited by Ray Palmer. These magazines were and are widely reviled as the worst kind of juvenile trash . . . but issue for issue, they outsold John W. Campbell's *Astounding* by more than three to one.

Geier did sell four stories to Campbell, though: this story and another to *Astounding*, and two more to *Unknown*, *Astounding*'s fantasy companion. "Environment" is the only one that stands out, but it stands very far out.

When I first read "Environment," I thought it was about a trap of the most subtle and effective kind, one which the victim can't resist even when he sees it clearly. And you know, maybe that *is* what the story's about: you start with human beings and at the end they've been destroyed.

But consider another way of describing the action: you start with animals, and at the end all their animal nature has been polished away.

When I reread "Environment," I remembered the time I looked into the back of a second-year Latin book before I'd started taking the language. "How could anyone make sense of this?" I thought. But a few years later I was sight-reading those passages from Caesar easily; and now I translate far more difficult Latin authors for the pleasure of keeping my mind supple.

"Environment" is a story about education.

Liane the Wayfarer

by Jack Vance

PREFACE BY ERIC FLINT

In his afterword, Dave Drake will have a lot more to say about this story. For my part, the moment we decided to do this anthology one of the things that was clear to me was that there *would* be a Jack Vance story in it. To think of such an anthology without one, assuming we could obtain the rights, would have been ...

Well, maybe not "unthinkable." But, for me at least, damn close.

We agreed that Dave would select the specific story, because the impact Vance had on me as a teenager was based mainly on his novels, not his short stories—I'm thinking especially of *The Dragon Masters, Big Planet*, and the first of the Demon Princes novels—and there was simply no room for a novel here, even a short one. But I can't imagine how science fiction would have ever looked to me without Jack Vance. That's because I've never had to. From almost as far back as I can remember, Vance and his unique style of storytelling has been one of the inseparable aspects of the genre's orchestral coloration.

As it is here, in "Liane the Wayfarer." Dave and I both strongly recommend this story. It's thirty-five hundred words long. You've got time to read thirty-five hundred words.

Through the dim forest came Liane the Wayfarer, passing along the shadowed glades with a prancing light-footed gait. He whistled, he caroled, he was plainly in high spirits. Around his finger he twirled a bit of wrought bronze—a circlet graved with angular crabbed characters, now stained black.

By excellent chance he had found it, banded around the root of an ancient yew. Hacking it free, he had seen the characters on the inner surface—rude forceful symbols, doubtless the cast of a powerful antique rune . . . Best take it to a magician and have it tested for sorcery.

Liane made a wry mouth. There were objections to the course. Sometimes it seemed as if all living creatures conspired to exasperate him. Only this morning, the spice merchant—what a tumult he had made dying! How carelessly he had spewed blood on Liane's cock comb sandals! Still, thought Liane, every unpleasantness carried with it compensation. While digging the grave he had found the bronze ring.

And Liane's spirits soared; he laughed in pure joy. He bounded, he leapt. His green cape flapped behind him, the red feather in his cap winked and blinked . . . But still—Liane slowed his step—he was no whit closer to the mystery of the magic, if magic the ring possessed.

Experiment, that was the word!

He stopped where the ruby sunlight slanted down without hindrance from the high foliage, examined the ring, traced the glyphs with his fingernail. He peered through. A faint film, a flicker? He held it at arm's length. It was clearly a coronet. He whipped off his cap, set the band on his brow, rolled his great golden eyes, preened himself . . . Odd. It slipped down on his ears. It tipped across his eyes. Darkness. Frantically Liane clawed it off . . . A bronze ring, a hand's-breadth in diameter. Queer.

He tried again. It slipped down over his head, his shoulders. His head was in the darkness of a strange separate space. Looking down, he saw the level of the outside light dropping as he dropped the ring.

Slowly down . . . Now it was around his ankles—and in sudden panic, Liane snatched the ring up over his body, emerged blinking into the maroon light of the forest.

He saw a blue-white, green-white flicker against the foliage. It was a Twk-man, mounted on a dragon-fly, and light glinted from the dragon-fly's wings.

Liane called sharply, "Here, sir! Here, sir!"

The Twk-man perched his mount on a twig. "Well, Liane, what do you wish?"

"Watch now, and remember what you see." Liane pulled the ring over his head, dropped it to his feet, lifted it back. He looked up to the Twk-man, who was chewing a leaf. "And what did you see?"

"I saw Liane vanish from mortal sight—except for the red curled toes of his sandals. All else was as air."

"Ha!" cried Liane. "Think of it! Have you ever seen the like?"

The Twk-man asked carelessly, "Do you have salt? I would have salt."

Liane cut his exultation short, eyed the Twk-man closely.

"What news do you bring me?"

"Three erbs killed Florejin the Dream-builder, and burst all his bubbles. The air above the manse was colored for many minutes with the flitting fragments."

"A gram."

"Lord Kandive the Golden has built a barge of carven mo-wood ten lengths high, and it floats on the River Scaum for the Regatta, full of treasure."

"Two grams."

"A golden witch named Lith has come to live on Thamber Meadow. She is quiet and very beautiful."

"Three grams."

"Enough," said the Twk-man, and leaned forward to watch while Liane weighed out the salt in a tiny balance. He packed it in small panniers hanging on each side of the ribbed thorax, then twitched the insect into the air and flicked off through the forest vaults.

Once more Liane tried the bronze ring, and this time brought it entirely past his feet, stepped out of it and brought the ring up into the darkness beside him. What a wonderful sanctuary! A hole whose opening could be hidden inside the hole itself! Down with the ring to his feet, step through, bring it up his slender frame and over his shoulders, out into the forest with a small bronze ring in his hand.

Ho! and off to Thamber Meadow to see the beautiful golden witch.

Her hut was a simple affair of woven reeds—a low dome with two round windows and a low door. He saw Lith at the pond bare-legged among the water shoots, catching frogs for her supper. A white kirtle was gathered up tight around her thighs; stock-still she stood and the dark water rippled rings away from her slender knees.

She was more beautiful than Liane could have imagined, as if one of Florejin's wasted bubbles had burst here on the water. Her skin was pale creamed stirred gold, her hair a denser, wetter gold. Her eyes were like Liane's own, great golden orbs, and hers were wide apart, tilted slightly.

Liane strode forward and planted himself on the bank. She looked up startled, her ripe mouth half-open.

"Behold, golden witch, here is Liane. He has come to welcome you to Thamber; and he offers you his friendship, his love..."

Lith bent, scooped a handful of slime from the bank and flung it into his face.

Shouting the most violent curses, Liane wiped his eyes free, but the door to the hut had slammed shut.

Liane strode to the door and pounded it with his fist.

"Open and show your witch's face, or I burn the hut!"

The door opened, and the girl looked forth, smiling. "What now?"

Liane entered the hut and lunged for the girl, but twenty thin shafts darted out, twenty points pricking his chest. He halted, eyebrows raised, mouth twitching.

"Down, steel," said Lith. The blades snapped from view. "So easily could I seek your vitality," said Lith, "had I willed."

Liane frowned and rubbed his chin as if pondering. "You understand," he said earnestly, "what a witless thing you do. Liane is feared by those who fear fear, loved by those who love love. And you—" his eyes swam the golden glory of her body—"you are ripe as a sweet fruit, you are eager, you glisten and tremble with love. You please Liane, and he will spend much warmness on you."

"No, no," said Lith, with a slow smile. "You are too hasty."

Liane looked at her in surprise. "Indeed?"

"I am Lith," said she. "I am what you say I am. I ferment, I burn, I seethe. Yet I may have no lover but him who has served me. He must be brave, swift, cunning."

"I am he," said Liane. He chewed his lip. "It is not usually thus. I detest this indecision." He took a step forward. "Come, let us—"

She backed away. "No, no. You forget. How have you served me, how have you gained the right to my love?"

"Absurdity!" stormed Liane. "Look at me! Note my perfect grace, the beauty of my form and feature, my great eyes, as golden as your own, my manifest will and power...It is you who should serve me. That is how I will have it." He sank upon a low divan. "Woman, give me wine."

She shook her head. "In my small domed hut I cannot be forced. Perhaps outside on Thamber Meadow—but in here, among my blue and red tassels, with twenty blades of steel at my call, you must obey me . . . So choose. Either arise and go, never to return, or else agree to serve me on one small mission, and then have me and all my ardor."

Liane sat straight and stiff. An odd creature, the golden witch. But, indeed, she was worth some exertion, and he would make her pay for her impudence.

"Very well, then," he said blandly. "I will serve you. What do you wish? Jewels? I can suffocate you in pearls, blind you with diamonds. I have two emeralds the size of your fist, and they are green oceans, where the gaze is trapped and wanders forever among vertical green prisms . . ."

"No, no jewels—"

"An enemy, perhaps. Ah, so simple. Liane will kill you ten men. Two steps forward, thrust—*thus!*" He lunged. "And souls go thrilling up like bubbles in a beaker of mead."

"No. I want no killing."

He sat back, frowning. "What, then?"

She stepped to the back of the room and pulled at a drape. It swung aside, displaying a golden tapestry. The scene was a valley bounded by two steep mountains, a broad valley where a placid river ran, past a quiet village and so into a grove of trees. Golden was the river, golden the mountains, golden the trees—golds so various, so rich, so subtle that the effect was like a many-colored landscape. But the tapestry had been rudely hacked in half.

Liane was entranced. "Exquisite, exquisite . . ."

Lith said, "It is the Magic Valley of Ariventa so depicted. The other half has been stolen from me, and its recovery is the service I wish of you."

"Where is the other half?" demanded Liane. "Who is the dastard?"

Now she watched him closely. "Have you ever heard of Chun? Chun the Unavoidable?"

Liane considered. "No."

"He stole the half to my tapestry, and hung it in a marble hall, and this hall is in the ruins to the north of Kaiin."

"Ha!" muttered Liane.

"The hall is by the Place of Whispers, and is marked by a leaning column with a black medallion of a phoenix and a two-headed lizard."

"I go," said Liane. He rose. "One day to Kaiin, one day to steal, one day to return. Three days."

Lith followed him to the door. "Beware of Chun the Unavoidable," she whispered.

And Liane strode away whistling, the red feather bobbing in his green cap. Lith watched him, then turned and slowly approached the golden tapestry. "Golden Ariventa," she whispered, "my heart cries and hurts with longing for you ..."

The Derna is a swifter, thinner river than the Scaum, its bosomy sister to the south. And where the Scaum wallows through a broad dale, purple with horse-blossom, pocked white and gray with crumbling castles, the Derna has sheered a steep canyon, overhung by forested bluffs.

An ancient flint road long ago followed the course of the Derna, but now the exaggeration of the meandering has cut into the pavement, so that Liane, treading the road to Kaiin, was occasionally forced to leave the road and make a detour through banks of thorn and the tube-grass which whistled in the breeze.

The red sun, drifting across the universe like an old man creeping to his death-bed, hung low to the horizon when Liane breasted Porphiron Scar, looked across white-walled Kaiin and the blue bay of Sanreale beyond.

Directly below was the market-place, a medley of stalls selling fruits, slabs of pale meat, mollusks from the slime banks, dull flagons of wine. And the quiet people of Kaiin moved among the stalls, buying their sustenance, carrying it loosely to their stone chambers.

Beyond the market-place rose a bank of ruined columns, like broken teeth—legs to the arena built two hundred feet from the ground by Mad King Shin; beyond, in a grove of bay trees, the glossy dome of the palace was visible, where Kandive the Golden ruled Kaiin and as much of Ascolais as one could see from a vantage on the Porphiron Scar.

The Derna, no longer a flow of clear water, poured through a network of dank canals and subterranean tubes, and finally seeped past rotting wharves into the Bay of Sanreale.

A bed for the night, thought Liane; then to his business in the morning.

He leapt down the zig-zag steps—back, forth, back, forth—and came out into the market-place. And now he put on a grave demeanor. Liane the Wayfarer was not unknown in Kaiin, and many were ill-minded enough to work him harm.

He moved sedately in the shade of the Pannone Wall, turned through a narrow cobbled street, bordered by old wooden houses glowing the rich brown of old stump-water in the rays of the setting sun, and so came to a small square and the high stone face of the Magician's Inn.

The host, a small fat man, sad of eye, with a small fat nose the identical shape of his body, was scraping ashes from the hearth. He straightened his back and hurried behind the counter of his little alcove.

Liane said, "A chamber, well-aired, and a supper of mushrooms, wine and oysters."

The innkeeper bowed humbly.

"Indeed, sir—and how will you pay?"

Liane flung down a leather sack, taken this very morning. The innkeeper raised his eyebrows in pleasure at the fragrance.

"The ground buds of the spase-bush, brought from a far land," said Liane.

"Excellent, excellent . . . Your chamber, sir, and your supper at once."

As Liane ate, several other guests of the house appeared and sat before the fire with wine, and the talk grew large, and dwelt on wizards of the past and the great days of magic.

"Great Phandaal knew a lore now forgot," said one old man with hair dyed orange. "He tied white and black strings to the legs of sparrows and sent them veering to his direction. And where they wove their magic woof, great trees appeared, laden with flowers, fruits, nuts, or bulbs of rare liqueurs. It is said that thus he wove Great Da Forest on the shores of Sanra Water."

"Ha," said a dour man in a garment of dark blue, brown and black, "this I can do." He brought forth a bit of string, flicked it, whirled it, spoke a quiet word, and the vitality of the pattern fused the string into a tongue of red and yellow fire, which danced, curled, darted back and forth along the table till the dour man killed it with a gesture.

"And this I can do," said a hooded figure in a black cape sprinkled with silver circles. He brought forth a small tray, laid it on the table and sprinkled therein a pinch of ashes from the hearth. He brought forth a whistle and blew a clear tone, and up from the tray came glittering motes, flashing the prismatic colors red, blue, green, yellow. They floated up a foot and burst in coruscations of brilliant colors, each a beautiful star-shaped pattern, and each burst sounded a tiny repetition of the original tone—the clearest, purest sound in the world. The motes became fewer, the magician blew a different tone, and again the motes floated up to burst in glorious ornamental spangles. Another time—another swarm of motes. At last the magician replaced his whistle, wiped off the tray, tucked it inside his cloak and lapsed back to silence.

Now the other wizards surged forward, and soon the air above the table swarmed with visions, quivered with spells. One showed the group nine new colors of ineffable charm and radiance; another caused a mouth to form on the landlord's forehead and revile the crowd, much to the landlord's discomfiture, since it was his own voice. Another displayed a green glass bottle from which the face of a demon peered and grimaced; another a ball of pure crystal which rolled back and forward to the command of the sorcerer who owned it, and who claimed it to be an earring of the fabled master Sankaferrin.

Liane had attentively watched all, crowing in delight at the bottled imp, and trying to cozen the obedient crystal from its owner, without success.

And Liane became pettish, complaining that the world was full of rock-hearted men, but the sorcerer with the crystal earring remained indifferent, and even when Liane spread out twelve packets of rare spice he refused to part with his toy.

Liane pleaded, "I wish only to please with witch Lith."

"Please her with the spice, then."

Liane said ingenuously, "Indeed, she has but one wish, a bit of tapestry which I must steal from Chun the Unavoidable."

And he looked from face to suddenly silent face.

"What causes such immediate sobriety? Ho, Landlord, more wine!"

The sorcerer with the earring said, "If the floor swam ankle-deep with wine—the rich red wine of Tanvilkat—the leaden print of that name would still ride the air."

"Ha," laughed Liane, "let only a taste of that wine pass your lips, and the fumes would erase all memory."

"See his eyes," came a whisper. "Great and golden."

"And quick to see," spoke Liane. "And these legs—quick to run, fleet as starlight on the waves. And this arm—quick to stab with steel. And my magic—which will set me to a refuge that is out of all cognizance." He gulped wine from a beaker. "Now behold. This is magic from antique days." He set the bronze band over his head, stepped through, brought it up inside the darkness. When he deemed that sufficient time had elapsed, he stepped through once more.

The fire glowed, the landlord stood in his alcove, Liane's wine was at hand. But of the assembled magicians, there was no trace.

Liane looked about in puzzlement. "And where are my wizardly friends?"

The landlord turned his head. "They took to their chambers; the name you spoke weighed on their souls."

And Liane drank his wine in frowning silence.

Next morning he left the inn and picked a roundabout way to the Old Town—a gray wilderness of tumbled pillars, weathered blocks of sandstone, slumped pediments with crumbled inscriptions, flagged terraces overgrown with rusty moss. Lizards, snakes, insects crawled the ruins; no other life did he see.

Threading a way through the rubble, he almost stumbled on a corpse—the body of a youth, one who stared at the sky with empty eye-sockets.

Liane felt a presence. He leapt back, rapier half-bared. A stooped old man stood watching him. He spoke in a feeble, quavering voice: "And what will you have in the Old Town?"

Liane replaced his rapier. "I seek the Place of Whispers. Perhaps you will direct me."

The old man made a croaking sound at the back of his throat. "Another? Another? When will it cease? . . ." He motioned to the corpse. "This one came yesterday seeking the Place of Whispers. He would steal from Chun the Unavoidable. See him now." He turned away. "Come with me." He disappeared over a tumble of rock.

Liane followed. The old man stood by another corpse with eye-sockets bereft and bloody. "This one came four days ago, and he met Chun the Unavoidable . . . And over there behind the arch is still, a great warrior in cloison armor. And there—and there—" he pointed, pointed. "And there—and there—like crushed flies."

He turned his watery blue gaze back to Liane. "Return, young man, return—lest your body lie here in its green cloak to rot on the flagstones."

Liane drew his rapier and flourished it. "I am Liane the Wayfarer; let them who offend me have fear. And where is the Place of Whispers?"

"If you must know," said the old man, "it is beyond that broken obelisk. But you go to your peril."

"I am Liane the Wayfarer. Peril goes with me."

The old man stood like a piece of weathered statuary as Liane strode off.

And Liane asked himself, suppose this old man were an agent of Chun, and at this minute were on his way to warn him? . . . Best to take all precautions. He leapt up on a high entablature and ran crouching back to where he had left the ancient.

Here he came, muttering to himself, leaning on his staff. Liane dropped a block of granite as large as his head. A thud, a croak, a gasp—and Liane went his way.

He strode past the broken obelisk, into a wide court—the Place of Whispers. Directly opposite was a long wide hall, marked by a leaning column with a big black medallion, the sign of a phoenix and a two-headed lizard.

Liane merged himself with the shadow of a wall, and stood watching like a wolf, alert for any flicker of motion.

All was quiet. The sunlight invested the ruins with dreary splendor. To all sides, as far as the eye could reach, was broken stone, a wasteland leached by a thousand rains, until now the sense of man had departed and the stone was one with the natural earth.

The sun moved across the dark-blue sky. Liane presently stole from his vantage-point and circled the hall. No sight nor sign did he see.

He approached the building from the rear and pressed his ear to the stone. It was dead, without vibration. Around the side—watching up, down, to all sides; a breach in the wall. Liane peered inside. At the back hung half a golden tapestry. Otherwise the hall was empty.

Liane looked up, down, this side, that. There was nothing in sight. He continued around the hall.

He came to another broken place. He looked within. To the rear hung the golden tapestry. Nothing else, to right or left, no sight or sound.

Liane continued to the front of the hall and sought into the eaves; dead as dust.

He had a clear view of the room. Bare, barren, except for the bit of golden tapestry.

Liane entered, striding with long soft steps. He halted in the middle of the floor. Light came to him from all sides except the rear wall. There were a dozen openings from which to flee and no sound except the dull thudding of his heart.

He took two steps forward. The tapestry was almost at his fingertips.

He stepped forward and swiftly jerked the tapestry down from the wall.

And behind was Chun the Unavoidable.

Liane screamed. He turned on paralyzed legs and they were leaden, like legs in a dream which refused to run.

Chun dropped out of the wall and advanced. Over his shiny black back he wore a robe of eyeballs threaded on silk.

Liane was running, fleetly now. He sprang, he soared. The tips of his toes scarcely touched the ground. Out the hall, across the square, into the wilderness of broken statues and fallen columns. And behind came Chun, running like a dog.

Liane sped along the crest of a wall and sprang a great gap to a shattered fountain. Behind came Chun.

Liane darted up a narrow alley, climbed over a pile of refuse, over a roof, down into a court. Behind came Chun.

Liane sped down a wide avenue lined with a few stunted old cypress trees, and he heard Chun close at his heels. He turned into an archway, pulled his bronze ring over his head, down to his feet. He stepped through, brought the ring up inside the darkness. Sanctuary. He was alone in a dark magic space, vanished from earthly gaze and knowledge. Brooding silence, dead space ...

He felt a stir behind him, a breath of air. At his elbow a voice said, "I am Chun the Unavoidable."

Lith sat on her couch near the candles, weaving a cap from frogskins. The door to her hut was barred, the windows shuttered. Outside, Thamber Meadow dwelled in darkness.

A scrape at her door, a creak as the lock was tested. Lith became rigid and stared at the door.

A voice said, "Tonight, O Lith, tonight it is two long bright threads for you. Two because the eyes were so great, so large, so golden ..."

Lith sat quiet. She waited an hour; then, creeping to the door, she listened. The sense of presence was absent. A frog croaked nearby.

She eased the door ajar, found the threads and closed the door. She ran to her golden tapestry and fitted the threads into the raveled warp.

And she stared at the golden valley, sick with longing for Ariventa, and tears blurred out the peaceful river, the quiet golden forest. "The cloth slowly grows wider ... One day it will be done, and I will come home ..."

Eric and I were both sure that there had to be a Jack Vance story in this anthology, but I'm the one whom Vance had most affected. I even wrote a paper on Vance in my 11th grade American Lit class. (He is, after all, an American who writes literature.)

The slight glitch was that *The Dragon Masters*, the piece that made me a fierce and lifelong Vance fan, was a short novel and too long for this use. We'd run into this before. Both Eric and Jim would've liked to use the novel *Have Spacesuit—Will Travel* for Heinlein; in its place we put a novelette of similar tone, written at about the same time as the novel.

For Vance I picked "Liane the Wayfarer" without a second thought. It contains all the traits that attract me to Vance, and it also tells a satisfying story in a brief compass.

Vance's prose is remarkably colorful and inventive. His plots are complex, he creates neologisms which must be understood from context, and he better than any other writer I'm familiar with makes figments of his imagination concrete on the page.

Also—and this is a big one for me—he writes with a flat affect. Neither the narrator nor the internal dialogue of characters in a Jack Vance story explains how the reader should feel about what's being described. Liane, the viewpoint character in this story, is a sociopath, but Vance to a greater or lesser extent uses the same technique in all his fiction.

I was drawn to that tendency in the first Vance story I read ("The Moon Moth"). I didn't copy Vance when I began to write: I *naturally* wrote in a similar fashion. And because of that, I know that some people believe that because a writer doesn't tell readers how to feel, the writer himself feels nothing about the horrors he describes. That's not true of me; I very much doubt it's true of Vance.

So "Liane the Wayfarer" was in many ways the perfect choice for this volume. It's one of the first half dozen stories of Vance's long and productive career; it appeared in his first book, *The Dying Earth*. And to a great degree, it's a paradigm for all his work.

The Dying Earth was published in a very small edition in

1950. "Liane the Wayfarer" itself had appeared in an even smaller magazine at about the same time and wasn't seen again till the 1962 republication of *The Dying Earth*. That's where I first read it, a few months after I'd read *The Dragon Masters*. Not even *Revolt in 2100* had the impact on me that *The Dragon Masters* paired with *The Dying Earth* did.

Spawn

by P. Schuyler Miller

PREFACE BY ERIC FLINT

I'd never read this story until Dave told me he wanted it for the anthology. After I did, I understood why. He'll explain his view of it in an afterword, but what I'll say about it for the moment is...

This story really, really, really shouldn't work. If there's any "rule of writing" that P. Schuyler Miller doesn't violate somewhere in the course of it, I don't know what it is. The plot is...

Absurd. The characters are...

Preposterous. The prose is...

"Purple" doesn't begin to capture the color.

So much for the rules of writing. In its own completely over-the-top style, this story is a masterpiece.

Okay, a madman's masterpiece, maybe, and certainly one of a kind. It still qualifies for the term because it fulfills the ultimate criterion for a great story—and, ultimately, the only criterion worth talking about.

It works. It really, really, really works.

Pedants spout glibly of probability, quibble and hedge, gulp at imagined gnats. Nothing is impossible to mathematics. Only improbable. Only *very* improbable.

Only impossibly improbable.

656   *The World Turned Upside Down*

Earth, for example, is improbable. Planets should not logically exist, nor on existing planets life. Balances of forces are too impossibly delicate; origins too complexly coincidental. But Earth does exist—and on Earth life.

We see Earth and we see life, or we see something, however improbable, and call it Earth and life. We forget probabilities and mathematics and live by our senses, by our common sense. Our common sense sees Earth and it sees life, and in a kind of darkened mirror it sees men—but men are utterly improbable!

Ooze to worms and worms to fishes. Fishes to frogs and frogs to lizards. Lizards to rats and rats to men, and men at last to bloated, futuristic Brains. Brains are improbable: brains and senses, and above all, common sense. Not impossible—because nothing is impossible—but so improbable that nowhere in all the improbable stars, nowhere in all the improbably empty space between the stars, is there room for other Earths and other rats and men.

Nowhere—life.

An improbable man is tight. A man with improbably carrot-colored hair, with an improbably enormous nose. With a cold in that nose. With a quart of potato rot-gut to encourage the utter improbability of that cold and that nose, and of the world in general. With a plane's rudder bar under his feet and a plane's stick between his knees, and the Chilean Andes improbably gigantic underneath.

A man is tight. And coincident with that tightness he is witness to the Improbable:

Friday, the 25ᵗʰ of July: James Arthur Donegan, thirty-odd, red-haired, American, has witnessed the Improbable.

A cliff, hard and quartz-white, softening—puddling—pulping away in a vast heaped monstrousness fat with thick ropes of gold. Raw gold—yellow in the Andean sunlight. Mother-gold—knotted in wadded worm-nests in the shining rock. Medusae of golden fascination. Gold burning in hemp-dream arabesques in the naked cliff-face, in the white quartz that is pulping, dripping, sloughing into monstrosity.

Jim Donegan tipped his bottle high and lifted his plane out of insanity. Jim Donegan's brain reeled with the raw white fire of potato whiskey and the raw yellow lustre of fat gold. And with the gold a quartz cliff melting, puddling—stone into pudding—sense into nonsense.

Jim Donegan tipped his bottle again and remembered to forget. Landed in Santiago. Disappeared.

❧   ❧   ❧

An improbable man is sober. A thousand improbable men and a thousand even less credible women, and of them all only a hundred drunk. Only another hundred tight, or boiled, or mildly blotto. And half a thousand improbable men and women, drunk and sober, see and hear and photograph the Improbable eating whales:

Wednesday, the 20th of August: Richard Chisholm, fifty, grizzled, British, has entered the Improbable in his log. Has stirred one wrinkled cerebrum, accustomed to the investigation of probabilities, in unaccustomed ways.

Zoologist Heinrich Wilhelm Sturm leaned with polished elbows on a polished rail and stared at a burnished sea. Daughter Marie Elsa Sturm leaned and stared beside him. Secretary Rudolf Walter Weltmann leaned and stared, but not at waves.

Waves lifted lazily along a great ship's flank. Waves swelled and fell unbroken with the listless, oily languor of old dreams. And caught in the warm web of the sun and the malachitic waxenness of the waves a score of whales basked, rolling and blowing, under the weary eyes of Zoologist Heinrich Sturm.

The molten, lucent fluid of the sea clotted and cooled. Color went swiftly out of it: greenstone to apple jade, jade into chrysoprase, prase into beryl spume. It folded in uneven glistening hillocks of illogical solidity, and Zoologist Heinrich Sturm choked on his German oaths as a score of drowsing whales fought suddenly with death!

Acres of empty sea became quivering pulp. Grey puffs of it pushed out of the waves and sank again. Horrible, avid ripples shuddered and smoothed across its sleekness. And twenty whales were caught: gigantic, blunted minnows wallowing in a pudding mould; titanic ebon microbes studding an agar bowl. Drowned by the grey-green stuff that oozed into their gullets and choked their valved blow-holes! Strangled and stifled by it.

Swallowed and eaten by it!

The sound of it was unreal—the whoosh of blown breath splattering jellied ooze—the soft, glutting gurgle of flowing pulp—the single soughing sob as giant flukes pulled loose to fling aloft and smash into the rippled greenness that was darkening with the shadow of the ship.

One last sucking sigh—the fling of one mighty glistening *upsilon* against the sky—the babble of half a thousand human beings gulping breath. And Zoologist Heinrich Sturm, staring through thick, dark lenses at the blob of grey-green jelly on his wrist, at the spatter of jelly on the deck at his feet, and swearing happily his guttural German oaths . . .

A dead man lay in state.
And I was there:
Friday, the 22ⁿᵈ of August: Nicholas Svadin lies for the third day in solemn state before the peoples of the world.

Nicholas Svadin, Dictator of Mittel-Europa, lay waxen white under the heaped callas, under the August sun of Budapest. Nicholas Svadin, son of a Slavic butcher, grandson of German fuhrers, lay with six soft-nosed bullets in his skull and breast. Nicholas Svadin—whose genius for government had won the loyalty instead of the hatred of nations, whose greedy hand fed on the conflict of languages and races, whose shadow had covered Europe from the Volga to the Rhine. Nicholas Svadin—who had held all Europe under his humane tyranny save for the bickering fringe of Latin states and the frozen, watchful silence of the Anglo-Scandinavian confederacy.

Nicholas Svadin—dead in the August sun, with all Europe trembling in metastable balance under the fast-unfolding wings of Chaos.

And four men were the world. And four men were afraid.

They stood as they had stood when Svadin's great rolling voice burst in a bloody cough and his great body, arms upflung in the compassionate gesture of the Cross, slumped like a greasy rag on the white steps of the Peace Hall. They stood with the world before them, and the world's dead master, and the vision of the morrow brooded in their eyes.

Four men were the world. Rasmussen, bearded, blond, steel-eyed premier of Anglo-Scandia. Nasuki at his elbow, little and cunning with the age-old subtlety of the East. Gonzales, sleek, olive-skinned heir of the Neo-latin dictator. Moorehead the American, lean and white-headed and oldest of the four. Two and two in the August sun with the sickly scent of the death-lilies cloying in their nostrils, and I with my camera marking Time's slow march.

I marked the four where they stood by the open bier. I marked the spilling lines of mourners that flowed in black runnels through the silent streets of Budapest. I marked the priests where they came, slow-treading with the stateliness of an elder civilization.

I marked the resurrection of the dead!

Nicholas Svadin rose on his white-banked bier and stared at the world of men. Nicholas Svadin rose with the white wax softening in his massive jowls and the round blue scar of a soft-nosed slug between his corpse's eyes. Nicholas Svadin swung his thick legs with an ugly stiffness from the bier and stood alone, alive, staring at mankind, and spoke four words—once, slowly, then again:

"I—am—Nicholas Svadin."

"I am Nicholas Svadin!"

And men had found a god.

Svadin had been a man, born of woman, father of men and women, the greatest Earth had known. His genius was for mankind, and he enfolded humanity in his kindly arms and was the father of a world. Svadin was a man, killed as men are killed, but on the third day he rose from his bed of death and cried his name aloud for the world to hear.

Svadin the man became Svadin the god.

I photographed the world-assembly at Leningrad when Svadin called together the scientists of the Earth and gave them the world to mould according to their liking. I marked the gathering in America's halls of Congress when the rulers of the world gave their nations into his bloodless hands and received them again, reborn into a new order of democracy. I watched, and my camera watched, as the world poured itself into these new-cut patterns of civilization and found them good. And then, because men are men and even a Golden Age will pall at last, I turned to other things:

A bathysphere torn from its cable in mid-deep.

Fishing fleets returning with empty holds after weeks and months at sea.

Eels gone from their ancient haunts, and salmon spawning in dozens where once streams had been choked with their lusting bodies.

Cattleships lost in mid-Atlantic, and then a freighter, and another, gone without a trace.

Two men and a girl whose names were on the rolls of every ship that crossed and recrossed the haunted waters of the North Atlantic.

And from the South vague rumors of a god:

Miami's sun-bathed beaches were black with human insects. Miami's tropic night throbbed with the beat of music and the sway and glide of dancers. Maria Elsa Sturm glided and swayed in the strong, young arms of Rudolf Weltmann and laughed with her night-blue eyes and poppy lips, but Heinrich Sturm stood alone in the star-strewn night and stared broodingly at the sleeping sea. Maria basked in the smoldering noonday sun, a slender golden flame beside the swarthy handsomeness of her companion, but the old masked eyes of Heinrich stared beyond her beauty at the sea.

Long waves swelled sleepily against the far blue of the Gulf
Stream and sank and swelled again and creamed in tepid foam
along the sands. Gay laughter rippled and prismatic color played
with kaleidoscopic lavishness under the golden sun. Wave after
wave of the sea, rising and falling and rising against the sky—and
a wave that did not fall!

It came as the others had come, slowly, blue-green and glistening in the sunlight. It rose and fell with the ceaseless surge of the
Atlantic at its back, and rose again along the white curve of the
beach. It was like a wall of water, miles in length, rushing shore-
ward with the speed of a running man. Men ran from it and were
caught. Spots of bright color spun in its sluggish eddies and went
down. Tongues of it licked out over the warm sands, leaving them
naked and bone-white, and flowed lazily back into the monstrous
thing that lay and gorged in the hot sun.

It was a sea-green tumulus, vast as all Ocean. It was a league-
long hillock of green ooze, apple-jade-green, chrysoprase-green,
grey-green of frosted flint. It was a thing of Famine—not out
of Bibles, not out of the histories of men—a thing that lay like
a pestilence of the sea upon the warm, white beaches of Miami,
black with humanity running, screaming, milling—a thing that
was greedy and that fed!

Tatters of bright rag swirled in its sluggish eddies, oozed from
its gelid depths; fragments of white bone, chalk-white and etched,
rose and were spewed on the white sands. Arms of it flowed like
hot wax, knowingly, hungrily. Veins in it, pale like clear ribbons
of white jade in green translucency, ran blossom-pink, ran rose,
ran crimson-red.

Maria Elsa Sturm lay in the white sand, in the warm sun, in the
strong arms of healthy Rudolf Weltmann, under the unseeing eyes
of Heinrich Sturm. Zoologist Heinrich Sturm woke to the world
with horror in his eyes, horror in his brain, shrieking horror come
stark into this life. Zoologist Heinrich Sturm saw tongues of the
green-sea-stuff licking over Miami's bone-white sands, supping up
morsels of kicking life, spewing out dead things that were not food.
Zoologist Heinrich Sturm saw the Incredible, mountain-high, suck
up the golden straw that was Maria Strum, suck up the brown,
strong straw that was Rudolf Weltmann, swell like a flooding
river against the sea-wall at his feet, purling and dimpling with
greedy inner currents—saw it ebb and lie drowsing, relishing its
prey—saw the bright, scarlet rag that had wrapped Maria Sturm
oozing up out of its green horridness, saw the black rag that had

clothed Rudolf, saw two white, naked skulls that dimpled its glistening surface before they were sloughed away among tide-rows of eaten bones.

League-long and hill-high the wave that was not a wave lay glutting on young flesh, supping up hot blood. League-long and hill-high, with the little insect myriads of mankind running and screaming, standing and dying—with the buzzing wings of mankind circling over it and men's little weapons peppering at its vast, full-fed imperturbability. Bombs fell like grain from a sower's fist, streaming shadows of them raining out of the bare blue sky. Vast sound shattered the ears of gaping men, crushing in windows, shaking down ceilings, thundering with boastful vengeance. Fountains of green jelly rose stringily; wounds like the pit of Kimberly opened and showed sea-green, shadowed depths, stirring as the sea stirs, closing as the sea closes, with no scar. Bricks crumbled in little streams from a broken cornice; glass tinkled from gaping windows; men wailed and babbled and stared in fascination at Death. And Zoologist Heinrich Sturm stood alone, a gray old rock against which the scrambling tide beat and broke, seeing only the golden body of Maria Elsa Sturm, the laughing upturned face of Maria Elsa Sturm, the night-blue eyes and poppy lips of Maria Elsa Sturm ...

Long waves swelled sleepily against the far blue of the Gulf Stream, and sank and swelled again, and creamed in soft foam against the bone-white sands. Wave after wave, rising and falling and rising higher with the flooding tide. Waves rising to lap the sea-green tumulus, to bathe its red-veined monstrousness whose crimson rills were fading to pink, to grey, to lucent white. Waves laving it, tickling its monstrous fancies, pleasing it mightily. Waves into which it subsided and left Miami's white beaches naked for a league save for the windrows of heaped bones and the moist, bright rags that had been men's condescension to the morality of men.

Cameras ground clickingly along that league-long battlefront while horror fed; microphones gathered the scream of the sight of Death from a thousand quavering lips—but not mine.

Men turned away, sickened, to turn and stare again with horrid fascination at the wet white windrows that were girls' bones and men's bones, and children's—but not I.

Other eyes saw that vision of the Incredible; other lips told me of it when I asked. I did not see Zoologist Heinrich Sturm when he turned his back on the drift of smiling skulls and went wearily with the human stream, when he paid with creased and hoarded notes the accounts of Maria Elsa Sturm, deceased, and of Rudolf Walter Weltmann, deceased, of Heinrich Wilhelm Sturm.

I did not see Zoologist Heinrich Sturm when he stepped out of the hotel with his battered suitcase, plastered with paper labels, his round black hat, his thick dark glasses, and disappeared.

No one who saw cared.

There was no one, now, to care . . .

Out of the South the rumor of a god!

Out of the Andes word of a God of Gold, stalking the mountain passes with Wrath and Vengeance smoking in his fists. A god wrathful in the presence of men and the works of men. A god vengeful of man's slavery of rock and soil and metal. Jealous of man's power over the inanimable. A god growing as the mountains grow, with bursting, jutting angularities shifting, fusing, moulding slowly into colossal harmonies of foam and function, with growing wisdom in his golden skull and growing power in his crystal fists. A god for the weak, contemptuous of the weak but pitiless to the strong—straddling adobe huts to trample the tin-roof huddle of shacks at the lip of some gaping wound in the ancient flesh of Earth.

A god with power tangible and cruel, alien to pewling Black-Robe doctrines of white men's love of men. A god speaking voicelessly out of the distances of things that awoke old memories, roused old grandeurs in the blood of small brown men and in other men in whose veins the blood of brown kings flowed.

A god of red justice. A god of Revolution!

A god to bring fear again to men!

In the South—Revolution. Little brown men swarming in the mountains, pouring into the valleys, hacking, clubbing, stabbing, burning. Revolution in small places without names. Revolution in mud villages with names older than America. Revolution flaming in towns named in the proud Castilian tongue—in cities where white women promenaded and white men ogled, and brown men were dust in the gutters. Revolution in Catamarca, in Tucuman, in Santiago del Estero. Revolution half a thousand miles away, in Potosi, in Cochabamba, in Quillacolla. Revolution sweeping the royal cities of the Andes—Santiago, La Paz, Lima, Quito, Bogotá! Revolution stalking up the up-thrusting spine of a continent like a pestilence, sucking in crazed brown warriors from the *montes*, from the *pampas*, from barren deserts and steaming jungles. Blood of brown ancestors rising beneath white skins, behind blue eyes.

Revolution like a flame sweeping through brown man and white and mostly-white and half-white and very-little-white and back to the brown blood of ancient, feathered kings! Guns against machetes. Bayonets against razor-whetted knives. Poison gas against poison darts.

And in their wake the tread of a God of Gold!

Revolution out of Chile, out of the Argentine, into Bolivia, into Peru of the Incas. Revolution out of the hot inland through the Amazon, rippling through Brazil, through the Guianas, into Ecuador, into Colombia, into Venezuela. Revolution choking the ditch of Panama, heaping the bigger ditch of Managua with bleeding corpses, seething through the dark forests of Honduras, Guatemala, Yucatan. A continent overwhelmed and nothing to show why. A continent threatened, and only the whispered rumor of a God of Gold!

Men like me went to see, to hear, to tell what they had seen and heard. Men like me crept into the desolate places where Revolution had passed, and found emptiness, found a continent trampled under the running, bleeding feet of a myriad of small brown men driven by a Fear greater than the fear of Death—crushed and broken under the relentless, marching hooves of the God of Gold.

A village, then a city—a nation, then a continent—and the armies of the white nations mobilizing along the border of Mexico, in the arid mountains of the American south-west, watching—waiting—fearing none knew what. A necklace of steel across the throat of the white man's civilization.

Repeated circumstance becomes phenomenon; repeated phenomena are law. I found a circumstance that repeated again and again, that became phenomenal, that became certainty. A man with red hair, with a bulbous nose, with a bird's knowledge of the air. An old man peering through thick glasses muttering in his beard. How they came together no man knew. Where they went man could only guess. The wings of their giant plane slid down out of the sunset, rose black against the sunrise, burned silver white in the blaze of noon . . . They went—they returned—and none questioned their coming or going.

War on the edge of America. War between white man and brown—and more than man behind the brown. Death rained from the sky on little brown men scattering in open deserts, on green jungles where brown men might be lurking, on rotten rock where brown men might have tunneled. Death poisoned the streams and the rock-hewn cenotes, death lay like a yellow fog in the arroyos and poured through gorges where brown men lay hidden behind rocks and in crannies of the rock. Flame swept over the face of Mexico and the brown hordes scattered and gave way in retreat, in flight, in utter rout. White fury blazed where brown hatred had smouldered. Brown bodies sprawled, flayed and gutted where white corpses had hung on wooden crosses, where white hearts had smoked in the noon sun and white men's blood had dribbled down over carved stone altars. Hell followed Hell.

Then from Tehuantepac a clarion challenge, checking the rout, checking the white wave of vengeance. The challenge of a god!

Planes droned in the bare blue sky over Oaxaca, riddling the mountains with death. Polite, trim generals sat and drank and talked in half a dozen languages wherever there was shade. The sun blazed down on the plaza of Oaxaca in the time of *siesta*, and the grumble of war sank to a lullaby. Then out of the mountains of the east, rolling and rocking through the naked hills, sounded the shouted challenge of the God of Gold!

I heard it like a low thunder in the east, and a German major at the next table muttered "Dunder!" I heard it again, growling against the silence, and the Frenchman beside him looked up a moment from his glass. It came a third time, roaring like the voice of Bashan in the sky, and all up and down the shaded plaza men were listening and wondering.

Far away, across the mountains in Tehuantepec, the guns began to thud and mutter, and in the radio shack behind us a telegraph key was clicking nervously. The Frenchman was listening, his lips moving. An English lieutenant strode in out of the sun, saluted, melted into the shadow of the colonnade.

Out of the East the challenge of a God!

I heard the triumphant, bull-bellied shout thundering across the ranges as the guns of Tehuantepec grumbled for the last time. I saw a light that should not be there—a mad, frantic light—gleaming in the eyes of an officer of Spanish name, from the Mexican province of Zacatecas. The German's eyes were on him, and the Frenchman's, and those of the English subaltern, following him as he stole away. The wireless operator came out and saluted, and handed a slip of yellow paper to the Frenchman. He passed it, shrugging, to the German. A Russian came and looked over his shoulder, an Italian, an American, a Japanese, and their heads turned slowly to listen for the chuck and patter of distant guns that they would never hear again. And then, again, that voice of the mountains bellowed its triumphant challenge, stirring a cold current of dread in my veins—in the veins of all men of Oaxaca—of all men who heard it.

The victorious God of Gold shouted his challenge to mankind, and in answer came the distant burring of a plane in the north.

It passed over us and circled for a landing outside the city. An army car raced away and returned. I knew two of the three men who climbed stiffly out of the tonneau. I saw tall, red-headed air-fiend Jim Donegan. I saw stooped, grey, boggling Zoologist Heinrich Sturm.

I saw Nicholas Svadin, once-dead master of the world.

Svadin against the God of Gold!

Again that bull-throated, brazen thunder rolled across the ranges and I saw Svadin's blunt, hairless skull cocked sidewise, listening. Old Heinrich Sturm was listening too, and Red Jim Donegan. But I saw only Nicholas Svadin.

It was five full years since that August day in Budapest. Wax was heavy in his blue-white jowls. Wax weighted down his heavy-lidded eyes. A puckered blue hole probed his sleek white brow. His great body was soft and bloated and his stubby fingers blue under their cropped nails. There was an acrid odor in the air, the odor that heaped callas had hidden in the sun of Budapest, that not even the stench of a thousand sweating men could hide under the sun of Mexico.

They talked together—Svadin, the generals, Sturm, Red Jim Donegan of Brooklyn. Donegan nodded, went to the waiting car, disappeared into the white noon-light. Soon his great silver plane droned overhead, heading into the north.

One day—two—three. We on the outside saw nothing of Svadin, but men of all nations were at work in the blazing sun and the velvet night, sawing, bolting, riveting, building a vast contrivance of wood and metal under the direction of Heinrich Sturm. Four days—five, and at last we stood at the edge of the man-made city of Oaxaca, staring at that monstrous apparatus and at the lone figure that stood beside it—Svadin. His puffed blue fingers went to the switch on its towering side, and out of that giant thing thundered the bellowed defiance of Mankind, hurled at the giant thing that walked the ranges, bull-baiting the God of Gold!

Its vast clamor shuddered in the packed earth underfoot. Its din penetrated the wadding in our ears and drummed relentlessly against our senses. It boomed and thundered its contempt, and in answer that other voice thundered beyond the blue-tipped mountains. Hour after hour—until madness seemed certain and madness was welcome—until the sun lay low in a red sky, painting the ranges—until only Svadin and grey old Heinrich Sturm remained, watching beside their vast, insulting, defiant Voice. Then in the east a flicker of light tipped the farthest ranges!

It was a creeping diamond of light above the purple horizon. It was a needle of white fire rising and falling above the mountains, striding over valleys, vaulting the naked ridges, growing and rising higher and vaster and mightier against the shadow of the coming night. It was a pillar of scintillant flame over Oaxaca.

It was the God of Gold!

Quartz is rock, and quartz is jelly, and quartz is a crystal gem. Gold is metal, and gold is color, and gold is the greed of men. Beauty and fear—awe and greed—the Thing over Oaxaca was a column of crystal fires, anthropomorphic, built out of painted needle-gems, with the crimson and blue and smoky wine-hues of colloidal gold staining its jeweled torso—with veins and nerves and ducts of the fat yellow gold of Earth—with a pudding of blue quartz flowing and swelling and flexing on its stony frame. It was a giant out of mythery—a jinn out of hashish madness—a monster born of the Earth, thewed with the stuff of Earth, savagely jealous of the parasitic biped mammals whose form it aped. Its spiked hooves clashed on the mountaintops with the clamor of avalanches. Its flail-arms swung like a flickering scourge, flaying the bare earth of all that was alive. Its skull was a crystal chalice wadded with matted gold, brain-naked, set with eyes like the blue sapphires of Burma, starred with inner light. It roared with the thunder of grinding, tearing, grating atoms, with the sullen voice of earthquakes. It was the spectre of Earth's last vengeance upon delving, burrowing, gutting little Man, the flea upon her flesh. It stood, a moment, straddling the horizon—and out of the north a plane was winging, midge-small against the watching stars. So high it was that though the sun had gone and the shadow of the Earth lay purple on the sky, its wings were a sliver of light, dwindling, climbing to that unimaginable height where the rays of the vanished sun still painted the shoulders of the God of Gold. A plane—and in its wake another, and another—a score of whispering dots against the tropic night.

Red Jim Donegan saw the monstrous, faceless visage upturned to watch his coming. He saw the white fires chill in its moon-great eyes, saw vast arm-things forming on its formless body, like swinging ropes of crystal maces. He saw the sinews of massive yellow gold that threaded its bulk, tensing and twisting with life, and the brain of knotted gold that lay in its cupped skull like worms in a bowl of gems. He saw that skull grow vaster as his plane rushed on—mountain-vast, filling the night—saw these star-backed eyes blazing—saw the evil arms sweeping upward—then was in empty air, sprawled over vacancy, his ship driving down into that monstrous face, between the staring sapphire eyes.

He swung from a silk umbrella and saw those kraken-arms paw at the crystal skull where a flower of green flame blossomed—saw the second plane diving with screaming wings—a third beyond it—and a fourth. The air was full of the white bubbles of parachutes, sinking into the edge of night. He saw the shadow of the world's edge creeping up over that giant shape, standing spread-legged among the barren hills, and green flame burning in its golden brain. A flame eating quartz as a spark eats tinder. A flame devouring gold, sloughing away crystalline immensity in a rain of burning tears, ever deeper, ever faster, as plane after plane burst with its deadly load against that crystal mass.

In blind, mad torture the God of Gold strode over Oaxaca. Green fire fell from it like blazing snow, pocking the naked rock. One dragging hoof furrowed the rocky earth, uprooting trees, crags, houses, crushing the man-made lure that had dared it to destruction. Fragments of eaten arms crashed like a meteor-fall and lay burning in the night. A moment it towered, dying, over ruined Oaxaca, where Nicholas Svadin stood dwarfed among the shambles of broken houses, the slight, stooped form of Heinrich Sturm beside him. Then in the sky that consuming flame blazed bright as some vital source was touched. A pillar of licking light wiped out the stars. It took one giant stride, another, and the world shook with the fall of the living mountain that crashed down out of the burning night. Among the eastern hills the fractured limbs of the colossus of the South lay strewn like snowy grain, and in the rocky flank of San Felipe a pit of cold green fire ate slowly toward the heart of Earth.

One who had been a man turned away from that holocaust and vanished in the darkness. Nicholas Svadin, his dead flesh clammy with dew, his gross bulk moving with the stealthy silence of a cat, with Heinrich Sturm trotting after him through the night.

Svadin, who had met the challenge of a God of Gold—and won!

A Thing of the Sea—a Thing of the Earth—a Thing of Men!
Three Things outrageous to Man's knowledge of himself and of his

world, improbable beyond calculation, impossible if impossibility could exist. Three Things raised from the dead, from the inanimate, from the inanimable, who lived and ate and walked properly, probably, possibly. Three Things that sought the sovereignty of Earth—a Thing of ravening hunger, a Thing with a hate of men, and a Thing that was god-hero of all men.

One of the Three lay destroyed beyond Oaxaca, and the brown men who had done its will were fugitives from vengeance. One still basked and fed in the tropic sea. And the third was Nicholas Svadin.

Rumors spread like ripples in a quiet pool. Even a god grows old. Svadin was a god whose word was law, whose wisdom was more than human, whose brain devised strange sciences, who brought the world comfort and contentment greater than it had ever known. In life he was a genius; dead, a martyr. He rose from the dead, wearing the mark of death, and men worshipped him as a god, saw in him a god's omnipotent wisdom. He remade a world, and the world was content. He slew the giant God of Gold and men followed him like sheep. But there were others who were not impressed by gods, or men like gods, and there were rumors, whisperings, wonderings.

It was my work to hear such rumors, listen to whisperings, tell men the truth about what they wondered.

Few men were close to Svadin, but of those who were, one told strange stories. A man who in other times had made his living on the fruits of such stories. Svadin—from whom the marks of death had never vanished, though he had risen from the dead—in whose forehead the puckered mark of a bullet still showed, whose face was white with the mortician's wax, whose fingers were puffed and blue, whose body was a bloated sack. Whose flesh reeked with the fluids which preserve corpses. Who fed privately on strange foods, quaffed liquids which reeked as those fluids reeked. Who showed strange vacancies of memory, absences of knowledge about common things, yet was a greater genius than in life-before-death. Whose only confidant was the mad zoologist, Heinrich Wilhelm Sturm.

I heard of the strange wicker and elastic form which was made by a craftsman in Vienna and worn under his heavy, padded clothes. I heard of a woman of impressive birth who offered herself as women have—and of the dull, uncomprehending stare which drove her shivering from his chamber. I heard of the rats that swarmed in his apartments, where no cat would stay, and of the curious devices he had erected around his bed—of the day when a vulture settled on his shoulder and others circled overhead, craning their wattled necks.

I saw Nils Svedberg, attaché of the Anglo-Scandian legation in Berlin, when he fired three Mauser bullets into the flabby paunch of the Master of the World—saw too what the crowd discarded when its fanatic vengeance was sated, and children scampered home with bloody souvenirs of what had been a man. I heard Svadin's thick voice as he thanked them.

Rumors—whisperings—questions without an answer. Svadin— to some a god, born into pseudo-human form, immortal and omnipotent. To some a man, unclean, with the awakening lusts and habits of a man. To some a Thing brought out of Hell to damn Mankind.

And a Thing of the sea, feeding in the Caribbean, in the turgid outpourings of the Amazon, along the populous coasts of Guiana and Brazil. Devil's Island a graveyard. And at last—Rio!

A plane with a red-haired, large-nosed American pilot cruised the coasts of South America. A worn, greyed, spectacled old man sat with him, peering down into the shallow, shadowed waters for darker shadows. They marked the slow progress of Death along the tropic coasts, and in Rio de Janeiro, Queen City of the South, the mightiest engineering masterpiece of Man was near completion.

Jim Donegan and Heinrich Sturm watched and carried word of what they saw, while Nicholas Svadin schemed and planned in Rio of the south.

Rio—rebuilt from the shell of Revolution. Rio fairer than ever, a white jewel against the green breast of Brazil. Rio with her mighty harbor strangely empty, her horseshoe beaches deserted, and across the sucking mouth of the Atlantic a wall, with one huge gateway.

Crowds on the mountainsides, waiting. Drugged carrion bobbing in the blue waters of the harbor—slaughtered cattle from the Argentine, from America, from Australia—fish floating white-bellied in the trough of the waves—dead dogs, dead cats, dead horses—all the dead of Rio and the South, larded with opiates, rocking in the chopped blue waters of the harbor of Rio de Janeiro. And at the Gateway to the sea a glistening greening of the waves, a slick mound flowing landward between the guarding walls—a grey-green horror scenting prey. A silver plane above it in the sky. A small black dot on the curved white beach.

Svadin—and the Thing of the Sea.

Food was offered, and it fed. It poured sluggishly into the great land-locked harbor of Rio. It supped at the meagre morsels floating in the sea and flowed on toward the deserted city and the undead man who stood watching it. And as its last glistening pseudopod oozed through the man-made gates, a sigh went up from the people on the mountainsides. Slowly and ponderously the barrier gate slid shut behind it, sealing the harbor from the sea. Great pumps began to throb, and columns of clear green brine of a river's thickness foamed into the unfillable Atlantic.

The plane had landed on the beach and Svadin climbed in. Now it was aloft, circling over the city and the harbor. The Thing was wary. It had learned, as all preying things learn, that each tiny insect has its sting. It sensed a subtle difference in the tang of the brine in which it lay—felt a motion of the water as Svadin's colossal pumps sucked at the harbor—detected a tension in the air. Its eddying lust for flesh quieted. It gathered itself together—swirled uneasily in the confines of the walled harbor—lapped questingly against the rampart that barred it from the Atlantic. Its glistening flanks heaved high out of the blue waters. It gathered itself into a great ball of cloudy jade that rose and fell in the surge of the quiet sea. It lay as a frightened beast lies—frozen—but without fear, biding its time.

Day after day after day. Day after day under the burning sun, while curious human mites dotted the Beira Mar, thronged on the white moon-rind beaches—while devout thousands crammed the Igreja de Penha, spared by Revolution, knelt on its winding stair, prayed and knelt in the many Houses of God of Rio of the South—while inch by inch and foot by foot the sparkling waters of Rio's mighty harbor sank and the grey-black ooze of the sea floor steamed and stank in the tropic sun, and the vast green Thing from the sea lay drugged amid the receding waters.

Atop hunched Corcovado the majestic Christ of Rio stared down on Mankind and the enemy of Mankind. Atop sky-stabbing Sugarloaf, poised between sea and land, Nicholas Svadin stood and stared, and with him Heinrich Sturm. Above the sinking waters of the bay, great ships of the air droned and circled, dropping the fine, insidious chemical rain that drugged the Thing with sleep. And in the jewel-city below, Ramon Gonzales, human link between the Latin blood of old Europe and new America, stood and stared with burning eyes. Leagues across the oily, sleeping sea, three other men stood or sat staring, grim-eyed, into nothing.

Moorehead the American. Nasuki the Asiatic. Blond Rasmussen of Anglo-Scandia.

Day after day after day, while the miasmic stench of Rio's draining harbor rose over the white avenues of Rio de Janeiro, while the darkening waters lapped lower and ever lower on the glistening jade-green mountain of jellied ooze that lay cooking in the sun. Day after day after day, while those who had crept back to the Beira Mar, to rock-rimmed Nictheroy, returned to the green, cool hills to watch and wait. A handful of sullen men in the Queen City of the South. Another handful on the naked cap of Sugarloaf and at the feet of the mighty Christ of Corcovado, miraculously untouched by the ravening of the God of Gold. And above it all the whine and drone of the circling planes and the far, dull mutter of the giant pumps.

Living things acquire a tolerance of drugs, demand more and more and more to sate their appetite. Drugged meat had lulled the Thing, and the rain of drugs from circling planes had kept it torpid, soothed by the slow lap of brine against its gelid flanks, dreaming of future feasts. Now as the waters sank and the sun beat down on its naked bulk, the vast Thing roused. Like a great green slug it crept over the white thread of the Beira Mar, into the city of jewels. Buildings crumpled under its weight, walls were burst by the pressure of its questing pseudopods. Into the pockets of the hills it crept, over the broken city, and behind it on the summit of Sugarloaf was frantic activity. Nicholas Svadin's puffed blue hand pointed, and where he gestured a ring of fire slashed across Rio's far-reaching avenues, barring the exit to the sea. Slowly the zone of flame crept inward, toward the empty harbor, and before its fierce heat the Sea-Thing retreated, grinding the city under its slimy mass. Little by little it roused—its ponderous motion became quicker, angrier. Little by little fear woke in it, where fear had never been—fear of the little gabbling human things that stung it with their puny weapons. It lay like a glassy blanket over the ruined streets of Rio—a knot of twisting serpent-forms craving the cool wet blackness of the deep sea. Before its awakened fury the wall across Rio's harbor would be like a twig across the path of an avalanche. Its fringe of lolloping tentacles dabbled in the salt-encrusted pool that was all the pumps had left of the Bay of Rio, and in minutes the rippling mirror was gone, sucked into the Sea-Things' avid mass.

And then Svadin struck.

I stood with my camera beneath the Christ of Corcovado. The

sun was setting, and as the shadow of the western summits crept over gutted Rio the Sea-Thing gathered itself for the assault that would carry it over Sugarloaf, over the wall that men had made, into the welcoming Atlantic. Then in the north, where the sun yet shone, came a flicker of metal gnats against the cloudless sky, the burr of their roaring engines speeding them through the advancing twilight. From Sugarloaf a single rocket rose and burst, a pale star over the sea, showering spangled flame, and the heavens were filled with the thunder of Man's aerial hosts—bombers, transports, planes of all sizes and all nations in a monster fleet whose shadow lay long on the curling sea like a streamer of darkness. Their first rank swung low over the hollow harbor and out of them rained a curtain of white missiles, minute against the immensity of Rio's circling hills. Like hail they fell, and after them a second shower, and a third as the fleet roared by above. And then the first bombs hit!

A ribbon of fire burst against the twilight. Fountains of golden flame vomited skyward, scores of feet over the naked surface of the Thing. Hundreds—thousands of bursting dots of fire, sweeping swaths of fiery rain, cascades of consuming flame—until the Sea-Thing blazed with one mighty skyward-reaching plume of golden glory that licked at the darkening heavens where the wings of Mankind's army of destruction still roared past, the rain of death still fell like a white curtain, painted by the leaping yellow flame of burning sodium.

I saw it then as old Heinrich Sturm had seen it months and years before, as Nicholas Svadin had seen it when he began his colossal plan to bait the Thing into the land-locked bay of Rio de Janeiro. Flame, killing and cleansing where no other weapon of man would serve. Green flame devouring the Earth-born God of Gold, corroding its crystal thews and consuming its golden brain. Yellow flame feeding on the sea-green pulp of the Sea-born Thing—changing the water that was its life into the caustic venom that slew it. As that colossal golden torch flared skyward over broken Rio I saw the mountainous bulk of the Sea-Thing shrivel and clot into a pulp of milky curds, crusted with burnt alkali. Water oozed from it like whey from pressed cheese, and tongues of the yellow flame licked along it, drinking it up. The black ooze of the harbor was drying and cracking under the fierce heat. Palms that still stood along the bare white beaches were curling, crisping, bursting into splinters of red flame, and even against the rising breeze the steaming stench of cooked flesh reeked in our nostrils.

The murmur of voices behind me stilled. I turned. The crowd had given way before the little knot of men who were coming toward me, driven from the crest of Sugarloaf by the fierce heat of the burning Thing. Flame-headed, red-nosed Donegan pushing a way for those who followed him. Grey-whiskered Heinrich Sturm pattering after him. Behind them, surrounded by men in braided uniforms, the fish-white, corpse-flesh shape of Nicholas Svadin.

I gave no ground to them. I stood at the Christ's feet and gave them stare for stare. I stared at Red Jim Donegan, at Zoologist Heinrich Sturm, and I stared at the gross, misshapen thing that was master of the world.

I had not seen him since that night in Oaxaca, three years before. He had been hideous then, but now the scent and shape of Death were on him as they were on Lazarus when he arose blank eyed from the grave. A grey cloak swirled from his shoulders and fell billowing over a body warped and bloated out of all human semblance. Rolls of polished flesh sagged from his face, his neck, his wrists. His fingers were yellow wads of sickening fat, stained with blue, and his feet were clumping pillars. Out of that pallid face his two bright eyes peered like raisins burnt glassy and stuck in sour dough. The reek of embalming fluids made the air nauseous within rods of where he stood. Nicholas Svadin! Living dead man—master of the world!

I knew Donegan from Oaxaca. He told me what I had guessed. Old Sturm's researches, made on bits of the jelly left by the Thing, on fragments hewed from it by volunteers, showed it to be built largely of linked molecules of colloidal water. Water—stuff of the Sea—bound by the life-force into a semblance of protoplasm—into a carnate pulp that fed on the Sea and took life from it even as it fed on living flesh for the needful elements that the water could not give it. Living water—mountain huge—destroyed by forces that no water could quench—by bombs of metallic sodium, tearing apart the complex colloidal structure of its aqueous flesh and riving it into flames of burning hydrogen and crusting, gelling alkali. Chemical fire, withering as it burnt.

I knew, too, Ramon Gonzales. I had seen him when he stood beside Svadin's bier in the sun of Budapest—when Svadin gave him the United Latin states of two continents to govern—when he stood ankle-deep in the green slime that the Sea-Thing had left coating the white walls of gutted Rio. I saw him now, his dark face ghastly in the yellow glare, screaming accusation at the immobile, pasty face of Nicholas Svadin. Those button eyes moved flickeringly to observe him; the shapeless bulk gathered its cloak closer about it and swiveled to consider him. Higher and higher Gonzales' hysterical voice raged—cursing Svadin for the doom he had brought on Rio, cursing him for the thing he had been as a man and for the thing he was now. No sign of understanding showed on that bloated face—no sign of human feeling. I felt a tension in the air, knew it was about to break. My camera over Jim Donegan's shoulder saw Ramon Gonzales as his sword lashed out, cutting through Svadin's upflung arm, biting deep into his side, sinking hilt-deep in his flesh. I saw its point standing out a foot behind that shrouded back, and the flare of Jim Donegan's gun licked across my film as he shot Gonzales down. I saw, too, the thick, pale fluid dripping slowly from the stump of Svadin's severed arm, and the puffed, five-fingered thing that twitched and scrabbled on the gravel at his feet.

Above us, lit by the dying yellow flame, the Christ of Corcovado looked down on the man who had risen from the dead to rule the world.

Four men were the world when Svadin rose from the dead in Budapest. Nasuki. Rasmussen. Gonzales. Moorehead. Gonzales was dead.

Two men had stood at Svadin's side when he slew the Thing of the Earth and the gelid Thing of the Sea. Donegan. Heinrich Sturm. Sturm alone remained.

I showed the pictures I had taken on Corcovado to drawn-faced Richard Moorehead in the White House at Washington. I showed them to Nasuki in Tokyo and to Nils Rasmussen in London. I told them other things that I had seen and heard, and gave them names of men who had talked and would talk again. I wore a small gold badge under my lapel—a badge in the shape of the crux ansata, the looped Egyptian cross of natural, holy life.

I went to find Jim Donegan before it should be too late. It was too late. Since the morning of the day when Nicholas Svadin's silver plane slipped to the ground at the airport of Budapest, and Svadin's closed black limousine swallowed him, and Donegan, and Heinrich Sturm, the tall, red-haired American had not been seen. Sturm was there, close to Svadin, with him day and night, but no one could speak with him. And gradually he too was seen less and less as Svadin hid himself in curtained rooms and sent his servants from the palace, drew a wall of steel around him through which only Zoologist Heinrich Sturm might pass.

Something was brewing behind that iron ring—something that had been boding since long before Svadin stood in Oaxaca and lured the God of Gold to its death—since long before he was first approached by the bearded, spectacled little German scientist who was now the only man who saw him or knew that he was alive. Yet Svadin's orders went out from the great, empty palace in Budapest, and the world grew sullen and afraid.

When he was newly risen from the bier, Nicholas Svadin had in him the understanding of a leader of Mankind and the genius of a god. Men took him for a god and were not betrayed. He thought with diamond clearness, saw diamond-keenly the needs and weaknesses of men and of men's world. He made of the world a place where men could live happily and securely, without want, without discomfort—and live as man.

As the months went by Svadin had changed. His genius grew keener, harder, his thinking clearer. Scientist—economist—dictator—he was all. The things he ordained, and which men throughout the world did at his command, were things dictated by reason for the good of the human race. But at the same time humanity had gone out of him.

Never, since that day when the heaped callas fell from his stiffly rising frame in the sun of Budapest, had he spoken his own name. He was Svadin, but Svadin was not the same. He was no longer a man. He was a machine.

Conceivably, a machine might weigh and balance all the facts governing the progress and condition of one man or of all humanity, and judge with absolute, mathematical fairness what course each should take in order that the welfare of all should be preserved. If it meant death or torment for one, was that the concern of the many? If a city or a nation must be crushed, as Rio had been crushed, to wipe out a monstrous Thing that was preying on Mankind, should not Rio rejoice at its chance to be the benefactor of the race? No man would say so. But Svadin was not a man. What he was—what he had become—it was the purpose of the League of the Golden Cross to discover.

No movement is greater than its leaders. Those who wore the looped cross of Life were led by the three men to whom the world looked, next to Svadin, for justice—to whom they looked, in spite of Svadin, for human justice. Before he rose from his bier, they had ruled the world. It was their intention to rule it again. No lesser men could have planned as they planned, without Svadin's knowledge, each last step of what must happen. That things went otherwise was not their fault—it was the fault of the knowledge that they had, or their interpretation of that knowledge. I had not yet found Jim Donegan. I had not seen Heinrich Sturm.

Through all the world the seeds of revolt were spreading, deeper and further than they had spread among the little brown-blooded men who were rallied by fear of the God of Gold. But throughout all the world those seeds fell on the fallow soil of fear—fear of a man who had risen from death—of a man who was himself a god, with a god's power and a god's unseeing eye, with a god's revenge. Men—little superstitious men in thousands and millions, feared Svadin more than they hated him. At his word they would slay brothers and cousins, fathers and lovers, friend and foe alike. Reason, justice meant nothing to them. There must be a greater fear to drive them—and it was my job to find that fear.

In every place where Svadin had his palaces, his steel-jacketed guards, I peered and pried, watching for the sight of a red head, an improbably bulbous nose. And not for a long, long time did I find it.

Svadin's grim castle loomed among weedy gardens, above Budapest. I found old men who had planned those gardens, others who had laid them out, who had built their drains and sunk the foundations of the palace in a day before Svadin was born. Where only rats had gone for a generation, I went. Where only rats' claws had scrabbled, my fingers tapped, pressed, dug in the fetid darkness. Ladders whose iron rungs had rusted to powder bore my weight on the crumbling stumps of those rungs. Leaves that had drifted for years over narrow gratings were cleared away from beneath, and light let in. The little Egyptian *ankh* became the symbol of a brotherhood of moles, delving under the foundations of Nicholas Svadin's mighty mausoleum. And one day my tapping fingers were answered!

Tap, tap, tap through the thick stone—listen and tap, tap, and listen. More men than Donegan had disappeared, and they crouched in their lightless cells and listened to our questions, answered when they could, guided the slow gnawing of our drills and shovels through the rock under Budapest. Closer—closer. They had their ways of speaking without words, but no word came from the red-headed, big-nosed American of whom their tapping told. Something prevented—something they could not explain. And still we dug, and tapped, and listened, following their meagre clues.

There came a time when we lost touch with the world outside. Three of us, in a world of our own, forgot that there was an outside, that there was anything but the one great purpose that drove us on through the dark and the damp. We had no word of the world, nor the world of us. Nasuki grew impatient, and the man who was in Gonzales' place. The work of the Golden Cross was progressing, its ring of Rebellion strengthening. To Rasmussen, to Moorehead, they cried for action. The brooding stillness that lay over Svadin's palace, the brutal coldness of the orders that issued through Heinrich Sturm's lips, shaping the civilization of a world as a sculptor would chisel granite, drove them to the edge of madness. Revolution flamed again—and this time brother was pitted against brother all across the face of the planet—fear against fury—Svadin against the Four.

I have seen pictures of the Svadin whom that flame of war drew to the balcony of his palace, to shout his thunderous command of death above the kneeling throng. The disease, if disease it was that changed him, was progressing swiftly. There was little resemblance to the man who lay dead a handful of years before, and on whom life fell out of an empty sky. He was huge, misshapen, monstrous, but so utter was their fear and awe that those groveling thousands questioned no word of his and cut down their kin as they would reap corn. The looped cross was an emblem of certain death. Men cast it from them, forswore its pledge, betrayed others who were faithful. At least one desperate, embattled horde stormed the grim castle above Budapest, while the sullen ring of the faithful closed in around them. Under their feet, ignorant of what was happening above us, we three dug and tapped, tapped and dug—*and found!*

I remember that moment when I knelt in the stuffy darkness of the tunnel, digging my fingers into the cracks on either side of that massive block. For hours, two sleeping while one worked we had chiseled at it, widening the crevices, carving a grip, loosening it from the bed in which it had been set a lifetime before. My numbed fingers seemed to become part of the cold stone. Dunard was tugging at me, begging me to give him his chance. Then the great block shifted in its bed, tilted and slid crushingly against me. Barely in time I slipped out from under it, then I was leaning over its slimy mass, Smirnoff's torch in my hand, peering into the black cavern beyond. The round beam of the torch wavered across mouldering straw—across dripping, fungus-feathered walls. It centered on a face, huge-nosed, topped with matted red hair.

It was Donegan!

We fed him while Dunard hacked at the gyves that held him spread-eagled against the wall. As he grew stronger he talked—answering my questions—telling of things that grew too horribly clear in the light of past happenings. At last we parted, Dunard and Smirnoff to carry word to the Brotherhood of the Cross—Donegan and I into the donjon-keep of Nicholas Svadin!

The guard at the cell door died as other guards have died before; we had no choice. I remembered those voices which were only fingers tap, tap, tapping through stone. I knew what those buried men would do if only they could—and gave them their chance. We were a little army in ourselves when we charged up the great central staircase of Svadin's castle against the grim line of faithful guards. At the landing they held us—and outside, battling in the gardens beyond the great doors, we could hear the gunfire of that last stand of our Brotherhood against ignorance and fear. We thought then that Dunard and Smirnoff had won through, had given their message to those who could light the flame of revolt. We did not know that they were cut down before they could reach our forces. But armed with what we could find or wrest from the men who opposed us, we charged up that broad staircase into the face of their fire, burst over them and beat them down as a peasant flails wheat, turned their machine gun on their fleeing backs and mowed them down in a long, heaped windrow strewn down the length of the corridor to Svadin's door.

We stood there at the head of the stairs, behind the gun, staring at that door—half-naked, filthy, caked with blood. There was a great, breathless silence broken only by the patter of gunfire in the courtyard outside, muffled by the walls. Then Donegan picked up the gun and stepped over the crumpled body of a guard. His bare feet slapped on the cold stone of the hall and behind him our footsteps echoed, in perfect time, drumming the death-roll of Nicholas Svadin. We came to the door—and it opened!

Heinrich Sturm stood there. Sturm—grown bent and little. Sturm with horror in his eyes, with horror twisting his face and blood streaming down his chest from a ripped-out throat. Sturm—babbling blood-choked German words, tottering, crumpling at our feet, who stood staring over him into the great, dark room beyond, at Svadin, red-mouthed, standing beside the great canopied bed, at the ten foul things that stood behind him!

Donegan's machine-gun sprayed death over the bleeding body of Zoologist Heinrich Wilhelm Sturm. Soft slugs ploughed into the soft body of Nicholas Svadin, into the bodies of the ten things at his feet. He shook at their impact, and the pallid flesh ripped visibly where they hit, but he only stood and laughed—laughed as the God of Gold had laughed, in a voice that meant death and doom to the human race!

Laughed and came striding at us across the room with his hell-pack trotting at his heels.

There are fears that can surpass all courage. That fear drenched us then. We ran—Donegan with his gun like a child in his arms, I with old Heinrich Sturm dragging like a wet sack behind me, the others like ragged, screaming ghosts. We stumbled over the windrows of dead in the corridor, down those sweeping stairs into the lower hall, through the open doors into the courtyard. We stood, trapped between death and death.

A hundred men remained of the Brotherhood of the Cross. They were huddled in a knot in the center of the court, surrounded by the host who were faithful to fear, and to Svadin. As we burst through the great doors of the castle, led by the naked, haggard, flaming-haired figure of Jim Donegan, every eye turned to us—every hand fell momentarily from its work of killing. Then miraculously old Heinrich Sturm was struggling up in my arms, was shouting in German, in his babbling, blood-choked voice, and in the throng other voices in other languages were taking up his cry, translating it—sending it winging on:

"He is no god! He is from Hell—a fiend from Hell! Vampire—eater of men! He—and his cursed spawn!"

They knew him, every one. They knew him for Svadin's intimate—the man who spoke with Svadin's voice and gave his orders to the world. They heard what he said—and in the doorway they saw Svadin himself.

He was naked, as he had stood when that door swung open and Sturm came stumbling through. He was corpse-white, blotched with the purple-yellow of decay, bloated with the gases of death. Svadin—undead—unhuman—and around his feet ten gibbering simulacra of himself—ten pulpy, fish-white monsters of his flesh, their slit-mouths red with the lapped blood of Heinrich Sturm!

He stood there, spread-legged, above the crowd. His glassy eyes stared down on the bloody, upturned faces, and the stump of his hacked arm pounded on his hairless breast where the line of bullet-marks showed like a purple ribbon. His vast voice thundered down at them, and it was like the bellowing of a lusting bull:

"I am Nicholas Svadin!"

And in hideous, mocking echo the ten dwarfed horrors piped
fter him:

"I am Nicholas Svadin!"

In my arms old Heinrich Sturm lay staring at the Thing whose
lave and more than slave he had been, and his old lips whis-
ered five words before his head sagged down in death. Red Jim
)onegan heard them and shouted them for the world to hear.
vadin heard, and if that dead-man's face could show expression,
:ar sloughed over it, and his thick red lips parted in a grin of
:rror over yellowed fangs.

"Burn him! Fire is clean!"

I caught up the body of Heinrich Sturm and ran with it, out of
ie path of the mob that surged up the castle steps, Jim Donegan
t their head. Svadin's splayed feet sounded across the floor of
ie great hall, his hell-brood pattering after him. Then the crowd
iught them and I heard the spat of clubbed fists on soft flesh,
nd a great roaring scream of fury went up over the yammer of
ie mob.

They tore the little fiends to shreds and still they lived. They
ound the Thing that had been Svadin and carried him, battered
id twisting, into the courtyard. They built a pyre in the streets
f Budapest, and when the flames licked high they cast him in, his
:ll-spawn with him, and watched with avid eyes as he writhed and
·isped, and listened to his screaming. The beast is in every man
hen hate and fear are roused. Far into the night, when Svadin
id his brood were ashes underfoot, the mad crowd surged and
ught through the streets, looting, burning, ravening.

When Svadin died, four men had ruled the world. Today four
.en rule a world that is better because Svadin rose from the dead
.at day in Budapest, that is free because of his inhuman tyranny.
:oorehead—Nasuki—Rasmussen—Corregio. Red Jim Donegan is a
:ro, and I and a hundred other living men, but none pays homage
dead old Heinrich Wilhelm Sturm. He was too long identified
ith Nicholas Svadin for men to love him now.

What we know of Svadin, and of other things, Sturm had learned,
tle by little, through the years. He told certain things to Donegan,
:fore Svadin grew suspicious and ordered the American's death.
was Heinrich Sturm's mercy that won Donegan a cell instead
' a bullet or the knife, or even worse. For somewhere during
s association with the perverted dregs of Europe's royal courts
e reborn Svadin had acquired, among other things, a taste for
iman blood and human flesh.

"All I know is what Sturm told me," Donegan says. "The old man was pretty shrewd, and what he didn't know he guessed—and I reckon he guessed close. It was curiosity made him stay on with Svadin—first off, anyway. Afterwards he knew too much to get away.

"There must have been spores of life, so Sturm said. There was a Swede by the name of Arrhenius—back years ago—who thought that life might travel from planet to planet in spores so small that light could push them through space. He said that a spore-dust from ferns and moss and fungus, and things like bacteria that were very small, could pass from world to world that way. And he figured there might be spores of pure life drifting around out there in space between the stars, and that whenever they fall on a planet, life would start there.

"That's what happened to us, according to the old man. There were three spores that fell here, all within a short time of each other. One fell in the sea, and it brought the Sea-Thing to life, made mostly of complex molecules of colloidal water and salts out of the sea-ooze where the spore fell. It could grow by sucking up water, but it needed those salts from decomposed, organic things too. That's why it attacked cities, where there was plenty of food for it.

"The second spore fell on quartz—maybe in some kind of colloidal gel, like they find sometimes in the hard stuff. There was gold there, and the Thing that came alive was what I saw, and what the Indians thought was one of their old gods come to life again—the god of gold and crystal. Svadin killed it with some radium compound that he invented.

"The third seed fell on Svadin and brought him to life. He wasn't a man, really, but he had all the organs and things that a man would have. He had the same memories in his brain, and the same traits of character, until other things rooted them out. He came to life—but to stay alive he had to be different from other men. He had embalming fluid instead of blood, and wax in his skin, and things like that, and he had to replace them the way we eat food to replace our tissues. When he changed, it was in ways a dead man would change, except that he used his brain better and more logically than any live man ever did. He had to learn how a man would act, and he had some willing enough teachers to show him the rotten along with the good.

"Those other things grew as they fed, and so did Svadin, but he was more complex than they were—more nearly like men. Where they grew, he reproduced, like the simplest kinds of living things, by budding off duplicates of himself, out of his own flesh. It was like a hydra—like a vegetable—like anything but a man. Maybe you noticed, too—a couple of those things that grew after he lost his arm in Rio, had only one arm too. They were him, in a way. They called his name when he did, there at the last . . ."

The sweat is standing out on his weather-beaten forehead as he remembers it. I see the vision that he does—those ten miniature Svadins growing, budding in their turn, peopling the Earth anew with a race of horrors made in mockery of man. He reaches for the bottle at his elbow:

"We've seen Nature—the Universe—spawning," he says. "Maybe it's happened on Earth before; maybe it'll happen again. Probably we, and all the other living things on Earth got started that way, millions of years ago. For a while, maybe, there were all kinds of abortive monsters roaming around the world, killing each other off the way Svadin killed the Sea-Thing and the God of Gold. They were new and simple—they reproduced by dividing, or budding, or crystallizing, and it was hard to kill them except with something like fire that would destroy the life-germs in them. After a while, when the seed of life in them would be pretty well diluted, it would be easier. Anyway, that's how I figure it.

"Svadin looked human, at first, but he wasn't—ever. What he was, no one knows. Not even old Sturm. It's pretty hard to imagine what kind of thoughts and feelings a living dead man would have. He had some hang-over memories from the time he was really Svadin, so he started in to fix over the world. Maybe he thought men were his own kind, at first—at least, they looked like him. He fixed it, all right—only, after a while there wasn't anything human left in him, and he began to plan things the way a machine would, to fit him and the race he was spawning. It's no more than we've done since Time began—killing animals and each other to get what we want, eating away the Earth to get at her metals, and oil, and so on. The God of Gold was kin to the Earth, in a way, and I guess he resented seeing her cut up by a lot of flesh and blood animals like us.

"I said he learned some of our perversions. Once someone had taught him a thing like that, and he liked it, it became part of the heritage that he passed down to future generations. Somehow he got the taste for flesh—raw flesh—humans were just like another animal to him. After Sturm stopped being useful to him, he attacked the old man too.

"You see—he had a human brain, and he could think like a man, and scheme and sense danger to his plans. Only—he didn't ever really understand human psychology. He was like an amoeba, or a polyp, and I don't guess they have emotions. He didn't understand religion, and the feeling people had that he was a kind of god. He used it—but when awe turned into hate, and people thought of him as a devil instead of a god, they treated him like one. They burned him the way their ancestors burned witches!"

He tosses down a shot of rye and wipes his lips. "Next time it happens," he says, "I'm going to be drunk. And this time I'll stay drunk!"

AFTERWORD BY DAVID DRAKE

P. Schuyler Miller was very important to the SF field in two ways. The generally known fashion is that he was the first regular reviewer in an SF magazine, holding that position at *Astounding*, later *Analog*, from the late '40s to his death in 1974. The less familiar aspect is that Tom Doherty, when he was a salesman for other publishers, would arrange his route so that he could have lunch with Miller in Pittsburgh. Tom put Miller's encyclopedic knowledge of the field to good use when he became publisher of Ace in 1977 and in 1981 founded Tor Books.

From 1930 through 1947 Miller also sold SF stories. He was never a major writer, though some of his stories were reprinted often enough to be easily found in old anthologies. "Spawn" (which *isn't* generally available) had a major impact on me, however, when I read Miller's single-author collection *The Titan* in the Clinton Public Library.

Since then I've read all or nearly all of Miller's published fiction, and I can say with certainty that he never wrote anything else even remotely like "Spawn." In form it's less a story than a prose poem or a drama in blank verse. It really is SF—Miller had a degree in chemistry, and if you read carefully you'll note underlying the lush color and imagery that there's a degree of scientific rigor very unusual for 1939—but it appeared in *Weird Tales* rather than in an SF magazine (generally *Astounding* by that point) as most of Miller's other published stories did. (Miller had several stories in Campbell's *Unknown*, but "Spawn" would've been even more out of place there than in *Astounding*.)

"Spawn" demonstrates highly unusual stylistic touches—tricks, I'd say, but that would imply they were conscious and that the author could repeat them. Miller never did, making me suspect that the process of creation here wasn't completely intellectual.

The reader views the action as though it were on a movie screen or he were looking through multiple layers of glass, insulating her from vivid, horrific events. The narrator tells his story as though you were face to face with him. He doesn't bother to give his name, nor often enough does he name other men the first time they appear. He doesn't describe events in sequence; they rise in momentary importance, then sink back like porpoises into the sea of narrative.

Like porpoises, or like whales. Oh, yes: "Spawn" is a horror story.

And everything is in place for the climax, including the fact that the story opens and closes not in Berlin or Vienna or Warsaw, but in Budapest.

In addition to leaving me numb with horror at the infinite possible, "Spawn" showed me that there is no proper form or technique for a story: there is the proper form and technique of *the* story before you at this moment. That's why I picked "Spawn" for this anthology.

St. Dragon and the George

by Gordon R. Dickson

PREFACE BY DAVID DRAKE

Shortly after my parents gave me a subscription to *The Magazine of Fantasy and Science Fiction* in October 1959, the magazine offered back issues at the rate of fifteen for three dollars or twenty-five for five dollars. I sent three dollars; among the delights I found when the magazines arrived was "St. Dragon and the George." (There were *many* delights. I immediately scraped up another five dollars and sent it off. Thirteen of the twenty-five additional magazines were duplicates, but I didn't complain.)

Gordy Dickson at his peak was one of the best writers in the field. For my money (literally, in this case), "St. Dragon and the George" is the best thing he ever wrote. It's both funny and witty, but if those were its only virtues, I wouldn't have picked it for this anthology. The humor and wit overlie a series of very profound ideas:

There is evil;

It is the duty of human beings to stand firm against evil, even if evil most likely will destroy them;

And human beings come in all shapes and sizes.

If more people took those ideas to heart, the world would be a better place. Because I read "St. Dragon and the George," the world is at least slightly better than it might be if I hadn't.

I

Atrifle diffidently, Jim Eckert rapped with his claw on the blue-painted door.

Silence.

He knocked again. There was the sound of a hasty step inside the small, oddly peak-roofed house and the door was snatched open. A thin-faced old man with a tall pointed cap and a long, rather dingy-looking white beard peered out, irritably.

"Sorry, not my day for dragons!" he snapped. "Come back next Tuesday." He slammed the door.

It was too much. It was the final straw. Jim Eckert sat down on his haunches with a dazed thump. The little forest clearing with its impossible little pool tinkling away like Chinese glass wind chimes in the background, its well-kept greensward with the white gravel path leading to the door before him, and the riotous flower beds of asters, tulips, zinnias, roses and lilies-of-the-valley all equally impossibly in bloom at the same time about the white finger-post labeled s. CAROLINUS and pointing at the house—it all whirled about him. It was more than flesh and blood could bear. At any minute now he would go completely insane and imagine he was a peanut or a cocker spaniel. Grottwold Hanson had wrecked them all. Dr. Howells would have to get another teaching assistant for his English Department. Angie ...

Angie!

Jim pounded on the door again. It was snatched open.

"Dragon!" cried S. Carolinus, furiously. "How would you like to be a beetle?"

"But I'm not a dragon," said Jim, desperately.

The magician stared at him for a long minute, then threw up his beard with both hands in a gesture of despair, caught some of it in his teeth as it fell down and began to chew on it fiercely.

"Now where," he demanded, "did a dragon acquire the brains to develop the imagination to entertain the illusion that he is *not* a dragon? Answer me, O Ye Powers!"

"The information is psychically, though not physiologically correct," replied a deep bass voice out of thin air beside them and some five feet off the ground. Jim, who had taken the question to be rhetorical, started convulsively.

"Is that so?" S. Carolinus peered at Jim with new interest. "Hmm." He spat out a hair or two. "Come in, Anomaly—or whatever you call yourself."

Jim squeezed in through the door and found himself in a large single room. It was a clutter of mismatched furniture and odd bits of alchemical equipment.

"Hmm," said S. Carolinus, closing the door and walking once around Jim, thoughtfully. "If you aren't a dragon, what are you?"

"Well, my real name's Jim Eckert," said Jim. "But I seem to be in the body of a dragon named Gorbash."

"And this disturbs you. So you've come to me. How nice," said the magician, bitterly. He winced, massaged his stomach and closed his eyes. "Do you know anything that's good for a perpetual stomach-ache? Of course not. Go on."

"Well, I want to get back to my real body. And take Angie with me. She's my fiancée and I can send her back but I can't send myself back at the same time. You see this Grottwold Hanson—well, maybe I better start from the beginning."

"Brilliant suggestion, Gorbash," said Carolinus. "Or whatever your name is," he added.

"Well," said Jim. Carolinus winced. Jim hurried on. "I teach at a place called Riveroak College in the United States—you've never heard of it—"

"Go on, go on," said Carolinus.

"That is, I'm a teaching assistant. Dr. Howells, who heads the English Department, promised me an instructorship over a year ago. But he's never come through with it; and Angie—Angie Gilman, my fiancée—"

"You mentioned her."

"Yes—well, we were having a little fight. That is, we were arguing about my going to ask Howells whether he was going to give me the instructor's rating for next year or not. I didn't think I should; and she didn't think we could get married—well, anyway, in came Grottwold Hanson."

"In *where* came *who?*"

"Into the Campus Bar and Grille. We were having a drink there. Hanson used to go with Angie. He's a graduate student in psychology. A long, thin geek that's just as crazy as he looks. He's always getting wound up in some new odd-ball organization or other—"

"Dictionary!" interrupted Carolinus, suddenly. He opened his eyes as an enormous volume appeared suddenly poised in the air before him. He massaged his stomach. "Ouch," he said. The pages of the volume began to flip rapidly back and forth before his eyes. "Don't mind me," he said to Jim. "Go on."

"—This time it was the Bridey Murphy craze. Hypnotism. Well—"

"Not so fast," said Carolinus. "*Bridey Murphy . . . Hypnotism . . .* yes . . ."

"Oh, he talked about the ego wandering, planes of reality, on and on like that. He offered to hypnotize one of us and show us how it worked. Angie was mad at me, so she said yes. I went off to the bar. I was mad. When I turned around, Angie was gone. Disappeared."

"Vanished?" said Carolinus.

"Vanished. I blew my top at Hanson. She must have wandered, he said, not merely the ego, but all of her. Bring her back, I said. I can't, he said. It seemed she wanted to go back to the time of St. George and the Dragon. When men were men and would speak up to their bosses about promotions. Hanson'd have to send someone else back to rehypnotize her and send her back home. Like an idiot I said I'd go. Ha! I might've known he'd goof. He couldn't do anything right if he was paid for it. I landed in the body of this dragon."

"And the maiden?"

"Oh, she landed here, too. Centuries off the mark. A place where there actually were such things as dragons—fantastic."

"Why?" said Carolinus.

"Well, I mean—anyway," said Jim, hurriedly. "The point is, they'd already got her—the dragons, I mean. A big brute named Anark had found her wandering around and put her in a cage. They were having a meeting in a cave about deciding what to do with her. Anark wanted to stake her out for a decoy, so they could capture a lot of the local people—only the dragons called people *georges*—"

"They're quite stupid, you know," said Carolinus, severely, looking up from the dictionary. "There's only room for one name in their head at a time. After the Saint made such an impression on them his name stuck."

"Anyway, they were all yelling at once. They've got tremendous voices."

"Yes, you have," said Carolinus, pointedly.

"Oh, sorry," said Jim. He lowered his voice. "I tried to argue that we ought to hold Angie for ransom—" He broke off suddenly. "Say," he said. "I never thought of that. Was I talking dragon, then? What am I talking now? Dragons don't talk English, do they?"

"Why not?" demanded Carolinus, grumpily. "If they're British dragons?"

"But I'm not a dragon—I mean—"

"But you *are* here!" snapped Carolinus. "You and this maiden of yours. Since all the rest of you was translated here, don't you suppose your ability to speak understandably was translated, too? Continue."

"There's not much more," said Jim gloomily. "I was losing the argument and then this very big, old dragon spoke up on my side. Hold Angie for ransom, he said. And they listened to him. It seems he swings a lot of weight among them. He's a great-uncle of me—of this Gorbash who's body I'm in—and I'm his only surviving relative. They penned Angie up in a cave and he sent me off to the Tinkling Water here, to find you and have you open negotiations for ransom. Actually, on the side he told me to tell you to make the terms easy on the georges—I mean humans; he wants the dragons to work toward good relations with them. He's afraid the dragons are in danger of being wiped out. I had a chance to double back and talk to Angie alone. We thought you might be able to send us both back."

He stopped rather out of breath, and looked hopefully at Carolinus. The magician was chewing thoughtfully on his beard.

"Smrgol," he muttered. "Now there's an exception to the rule. Very bright for a dragon. Also experienced. Hmm."

"Can you help us?" demanded Jim. "Look, I can show you—"

Carolinus sighed, closed his eyes, winced and opened them again.

"Let me see if I've got it straight," he said. "You had a dispute with this maiden to whom you're betrothed. To spite you, she turned to this third-rate practitioner, who mistakenly exorcized her from the United States (whenever in the cosmos that is) to here, further compounding his error by sending you back in spirit only to inhabit the body of Gorbash. The maiden is in the hands of the dragons and you have been sent to me by your great-uncle Smrgol."

"That's sort of it," said Jim dubiously, "only—"

"You wouldn't," said Carolinus, "care to change your story to something simpler and more reasonable—like being a prince changed into a dragon by some wicked fairy stepmother? Oh, my poor stomach! No?" He sighed. "All right, that'll be five hundred pounds of gold, or five pounds of rubies, in advance."

"B-but—" Jim goggled at him. "But I don't have any gold—or rubies."

"What? What kind of a dragon are you?" cried Carolinus, glaring at him. "Where's your hoard?"

"I suppose this Gorbash has one," stammered Jim, unhappily. "But I don't know anything about it."

"Another charity patient," muttered Carolinus, furiously. He shook his fist at empty space. "What's wrong with the auditing department? Well?"

"Sorry," said the invisible bass voice.

"That's the third in two weeks. See it doesn't happen again for another ten days." He turned to Jim. "No means of payment?"

"No. Wait—" said Jim. "This stomach-ache of yours. It might be an ulcer. Does it go away between meals?"

"As a matter of fact, it does. Ulcer?"

"High-strung people working under nervous tension get them back where I come from."

"People?" inquired Carolinus suspiciously. "Or dragons?"

"There aren't any dragons where I come from."

"All right, all right, I believe you," said Carolinus, testily. "You don't have to stretch the truth like that. How do you exorcise them?"

"Milk," said Jim. "A glass every hour for a month or two."

"Milk," said Carolinus. He held out his hand to the open air and received a small tankard of it. He drank it off, making a face. After a moment, the face relaxed into a smile.

"By the Powers!" he said. "By the Powers!" He turned to Jim, beaming. "Congratulations, Gorbash, I'm beginning to believe you about that college business after all. The bovine nature of the milk quite smothers the ulcer-demon. Consider me paid."

"Oh, fine. I'll go get Angie and you can hypnotize—"

"What?" cried Carolinus. "Teach your grandmother to suck eggs. Hypnotize! Ha! And what about the First Law of Magic, eh?"

"The what?" said Jim.

"The First Law—the First Law—didn't they teach you anything in that college? Forgotten it already, I see. Oh, this younger generation! The First Law: *for every use of the Art and Science, there is required a corresponding price.* Why do I live by my fees instead of by conjurations? Why does a magic potion have a bad taste? Why did this Hanson-amateur of yours get you all into so much trouble?"

"I don't know," said Jim. "Why?"

"No credit! No credit!" barked Carolinus, flinging his skinny arms wide. "Why, I wouldn't have tried what he did without ten years credit with the auditing department, and *I* am a Master of the Arts. As it was, he couldn't get anything more than your spirit back, after sending the maiden complete. And the fabric of Chance and History is all warped and ready to spring back and cause all kinds of trouble. We'll have to give a little, take a little—"

"GORBASH!" A loud thud outside competed with the dragon-bellow.

"And here we go," said Carolinus dourly. "It's already starting." He led the way outside. Sitting on the greensward just beyond the flower beds was an enormous old dragon Jim recognized as the great-uncle of the body he was in—Smrgol.

"Greetings, Mage!" boomed the old dragon, dropping his head to the ground in salute. "You may not remember me. Name's Smrgol—you remember the business about that ogre I fought at Gormely Keep? I see my grandnephew got to you all right."

"Ah, Smrgol—I remember," said Carolinus. "That was a good job you did."

"He had a habit of dropping his club head after a swing," said Smrgol. "I noticed it along about the fourth hour of battle and the next time he tried it, went in over his guard. Tore up the biceps of his right arm. Then—"

"I remember," Carolinus said. "So this is your nephew."

"Grandnephew," corrected Smrgol. "Little thick-headed and all that," he added apologetically, "but my own flesh and blood, you know."

"You may notice some slight improvement in him," said Carolinus, dryly.

"I hope so," said Smrgol, brightening. "Any change, a change for the better, you know. But I've bad news, Mage. You know that inchworm of an Anark?"

"The one that found the maiden in the first place?"

"That's right. Well, he's stolen her again and run off."

"*What?*" cried Jim.

He had forgotten the capabilities of a dragon's voice. Carolinus tottered, the flowers and grass lay flat, and even Smrgol winced.

"My boy," said the old dragon reproachfully. "How many times must I tell you not to shout. I said, Anark stole the george."

"He means Angie!" cried Jim desperately to Carolinus.

"I know," said Carolinus, with his hands over his ears.

"You're sneezing again," said Smrgol, proudly. He turned to Carolinus. "You wouldn't believe it. A dragon hasn't sneezed in a hundred and ninety years. This boy did it the first moment he set eyes on the george. The others couldn't believe it. Sign of brains, I said. Busy brains make the nose itch. Our side of the family—"

"*Angie!*"

"See there? All right now, boy, you've shown us you can do it. Let's get down to business. How much to locate Anark and the george, Mage?"

They dickered like rug-pedlars for several minutes, finally settling on a price of four pounds of gold, one of silver, and a flawed emerald. Carolinus got a small vial of water from the Tinkling Spring and searched among the grass until he found a small sandy open spot. He bent over it and the two dragons sat down to watch.

"Quiet now," he warned. "I'm going to try a watch-beetle. Don't alarm it."

Jim held his breath. Carolinus tilted the vial in his hand and the crystal water fell in three drops—*Tink! Tink!* And again—*Tink!* The sand darkened with the moisture and began to work as if something was digging from below. A hole widened, black insect legs busily in action flickered, and an odd-looking beetle popped itself halfway out of the hole. Its forelimbs waved in the air and a little squeaky voice, like a cracked phonograph record repeating itself far away over a bad telephone connection, came to Jim's ears.

"*Gone to the Loathly Tower! Gone to the Loathly Tower! Gone to the Loathly Tower!*"

It popped back out of sight. Carolinus straightened up and Jim breathed again.

"The Loathly Tower!" said Smrgol. "Isn't that that ruined tower to the west, in the fens, Mage? Why, that's the place that loosed the blight on the mere-dragons five hundred years ago."

"It's a place of old magic," said Carolinus, grimly. "These places are like ancient sores on the land, scabbed over for a while but always breaking out with new evil when—the twisting of the Fabric by these two must have done it. The evilness there has drawn the evil in Anark to it—lesser to greater, according to the laws of nature. I'll meet you two there. Now, I must go set other forces in motion."

He began to twirl about. His speed increased rapidly until he was nothing but a blur. Then suddenly, he faded away like smoke; and was gone, leaving Jim staring at the spot where he had been.

A poke in the side brought Jim back to the ordinary world.

"Wake up, boy. Don't dally!" the voice of Smrgol bellowed in his ear. "We got flying to do. Come on!"

II

The old dragon's spirit was considerably younger than this body. It turned out to be a four hour flight to the fens on the west seacoast. For the first hour or so Smrgol flew along energetically enough, meanwhile tracing out the genealogy of the mere-dragons and their relationship to himself and Gorbash; but gradually his steady flow of chatter dwindled and became intermittent. He tried to joke about his long-gone battle with the Ogre of Gormely Keep, but even this was too much and he fell silent with labored breath and straining wings. After a short but stubborn argument, Jim got him to admit that he would perhaps be better off taking a short breather and then coming on a little later. Smrgol let out a deep gasping sigh and dropped away from Jim in weary spirals. Jim saw him glide to an exhausted landing amongst the purple gorse of the moors below and lie there, sprawled out.

Jim continued on alone. A couple of hours later the moors dropped down a long land-slope to the green country of the fenland. Jim soared out over its spongy, grass-thick earth, broken into causeways and islands by the blue water, which in shallow bays and inlets was itself thick-choked with reeds and tall marsh grass. Flocks of water fowl rose here and there like eddying smoke from the glassy surface of one mere and drifted over to settle on another a few hundred yards away. Their cries came faintly to his dragon-sensitive ears and a line of heavy clouds was piling up against the sunset in the west.

He looked for some sign of the Loathly Tower, but the fenland stretched away to a faint blue line that was probably the sea, without showing sign of anything not built by nature. Jim was beginning to wonder uneasily if he had not gotten himself lost when his eye was suddenly caught by the sight of a dragon-shape nosing at something on one of the little islands amongst the meres.

Anark! he thought. And Angie!

He did not wait to see more. He nosed over and went into a dive like a jet fighter, sights locked on Target Dragon.

It was a good move. Unfortunately Gorbash-Jim, having about the weight and wingspread of a small flivver airplane, made a comparable amount of noise when he was in a dive, assuming the plane's motor to be shut off. Moreover, the dragon on the ground had evidently had experience with the meaning of such a sound; for, without even looking, he went tumbling head over tail out of the way just as Jim slammed into the spot where, a second before, he had been.

The other dragon rolled over onto his feet, sat up, took one look at Jim, and began to wail.

"It's not fair! It's not fair!" he cried in a (for a dragon) remarkably high-pitched voice. "Just because you're bigger than I am. And I'm all horned up. It's the first good one I've been able to kill in months and you don't need it, not at all. You're big and fat and I'm so weak and thin and hungry—"

Jim blinked and stared. What he had thought to be Angie, lying in the grass, now revealed itself to be an old and rather stringy-looking cow, badly bitten up and with a broken neck.

"It's just my luck!" the other dragon was weeping. He was less than three-quarters Jim's size and so emaciated he appeared on the verge of collapse. "Everytime I get something good, somebody takes it away. All I ever get to eat is fish—"

"Hold on," said Jim.

"Fish, fish, fish. Cold, nasty fi—"

"Hold on, I say! SHUT UP!" bellowed Jim, in Gorbash's best voice.

The other dragon stopped his wailing as suddenly as if his switch had been shut off.

"Yes, sir," he said, timidly.

"What's the matter? I'm not going to take this from you."

The other dragon tittered uncertainly.

"I'm not," said Jim. "It's your cow. All yours."

"He-he-he!" said the other dragon. "You certainly are a card, your honor."

"Blast it, I'm serious!" cried Jim. "What's your name, anyway?"

"Oh, well—" the other squirmed. "Oh well, you know—"

"*What's your name?*"

"Secoh, your worship!" yelped the dragon, frightenedly. "Just Secoh. Nobody important. Just a little, unimportant mere-dragon, your highness, that's all I am. Really!"

"All right, Secoh, dig in. All I want is some directions."

"Well—if your worship really doesn't . . ." Secoh had been sidling forward in fawning fashion. "If you'll excuse my table manners, sir. I'm just a mere-dragon—" and he tore into the meat before him in sudden, terrified, starving fashion.

Jim watched. Unexpectedly, his long tongue flickered out to lick his chops. His belly rumbled. He was astounded at himself. Raw meat? Off a dead animal—flesh, bones, hide and all? He took a firm grip on his appetites.

"Er, Secoh," he said. "I'm a stranger around these parts. I suppose you know the territory . . . Say, how does that cow taste, anyway?"

"Oh, terrubble—mumpf—" replied Secoh, with his mouth full. "Stringy—old. Good enough for a mere-dragon like myself, but not—"

"Well, about these directions—"

"Yes, your highness?"

"I think . . . you know it's your cow . . ."

"That's what your honor said," replied Secoh, cautiously.

"But I just wonder . . . you know I've never tasted a cow like that."

Secoh muttered something despairingly under his breath.

"What?" said Jim.

"I said," said Secoh, resignedly, "wouldn't your worship like to t-taste it—"

"Not if you're going to cry about it," said Jim.

"I bit my tongue."

"Well, in that case . . ." Jim walked up and sank his teeth in the shoulder of the carcass. Rich juices trickled enticingly over his tongue . . .

Some little time later he and Secoh sat back polishing bones with the rough uppers of their tongues which were as abrasive as steel files.

"Did you get enough to eat, Secoh?" asked Jim.

"More than enough, sir," replied the mere-dragon, staring at the white skeleton with a wild and famished eye. "Although, if your exaltedness doesn't mind, I've a weakness for marrow . . ." He picked up a thighbone and began to crunch it like a stick of candy.

"Now," said Jim. "About this Loathly Tower. Where is it?"

"The wh-what?" stammered Secoh, dropping the thighbone.

"The Loathly Tower. It's in the fens. You know of it, don't you?"

"Oh, sir! Yes, sir. But you wouldn't want to go there, sir! Not that I'm presuming to give your lordship advice—" cried Secoh, in a suddenly high and terrified voice.

"No, no," soothed Jim. "What are you so upset about?"

"Well—of course I'm only a timid little mere-dragon. But it's a terrible place, the Loathly Tower, your worship, sir."

"How? Terrible?"

"Well—well, it just is." Secoh cast an unhappy look around him. "It's what spoiled all of us, you know, five hundred years ago. We used to be like other dragons—oh, not so big and handsome as you are, sir. Then, after that, they say it was the Good got the upper hand and the Evil in the Tower was vanquished and the Tower itself ruined. But it didn't help us mere-dragons any, and I wouldn't go there if I was your worship, I really wouldn't."

"But what's so bad? What sort of thing is it?"

"Well, I wouldn't say there was any real *thing* there. Nothing your worship could put a claw on. It's just strange things go to it and strange things come out of it; and lately . . ."

"Lately what?"

"Nothing—nothing, really, your excellency!" cried Secoh. "You illustriousness shouldn't catch a worthless little mere-dragon up like that. I only meant, lately the Tower's seemed more fearful than ever. That's all."

"Probably your imagination," said Jim, shortly. "Anyway, where is it?"

"You have to go north about five miles." While they had eaten and talked, the sunset had died. It was almost dark now; and Jim had to strain his eyes through the gloom to see the mere-dragon's foreclaw, pointing away across the mere. "To the Great Causeway. It's a wide lane of solid ground running east and west through the fens. You follow it west to the Tower. The Tower stands on a rock overlooking the sea-edge."

"Five miles . . ." said Jim. He considered the soft grass on which he lay. His armored body seemed undisturbed by the temperature, whatever it was. "I might as well get some sleep. See you in the morning, Secoh." He obeyed a sudden, bird-like instinct and tucked his ferocious head and long neck back under one wing.

"Whatever your excellency desires . . ." the mere-dragon's muffled voice came distantly to his ear. "Your excellency has only to call and I'll be immediately available . . ."

The words faded out on Jim's ear, as he sank into sleep like a heavy stone into deep, dark waters.

When he opened his eyes, the sun was up. He sat up himself, yawned, and blinked.

Secoh was gone. So were the leftover bones.

"Blast!" said Jim. But the morning was too nice for annoyance. He smiled at his mental picture of Secoh carefully gathering the bones in fearful silence, and sneaking them away.

The smile did not last long. When he tried to take off in a northerly direction, as determined by reference to the rising sun, he found he had charley horses in both the huge wing-muscles that swelled out under the armor behind his shoulders. The result of course, of yesterday's heavy exercise. Grumbling, he was forced to proceed on foot; and four hours later, very hot, muddy and wet, he pulled his weary body up onto the broad east-and-west-stretching strip of land which must, of necessity, be the Great Causeway. It ran straight as a Roman road through the meres, several feet higher than the rest of the fenland, and was solid enough to support good-sized trees. Jim collapsed in the shade of one with a heartfelt sigh.

He awoke to the sound of someone singing. He blinked and lifted his head. Whatever the earlier verses of the song had been, Jim had missed them; but the approaching baritone voice now caroled the words of the chorus merrily and clearly to his ear:

> "A right good sword, a constant mind
> A trusty spear and true!
> The dragons of the mere shall find
> What Nevile-Smythe can do!"

The tune and words were vaguely familiar. Jim sat up for a better look and a knight in full armor rode into view on a large white horse through the trees. Then everything happened at once. The knight saw him, the visor of his armor came down with a clang, his long spear seemed to jump into his mailed hand and the horse under him leaped into a gallop, heading for Jim. Gorbash's reflexes took over. They hurled Jim straight up into the air, where his punished wing muscles cracked and faltered. He was just able to manage enough of a fluttering flop to throw himself into the upper branches of a small tree nearby.

The knight skidded his horse to a stop below and looked up through the spring-budded branches. He tilted his visor back to reveal a piercing pair of blue eyes, a rather hawk-like nose and a jutting generous chin, all assembled into a clean-shaven young man's face. He looked eagerly up at Jim.

"Come down," he said.

"No thanks," said Jim, hanging firmly to the tree. There was a slight pause as they both digested the situation.

"Dashed caitiff mere-dragon!" said the knight finally, with annoyance.

"I'm not a mere-dragon," said Jim.

"Oh, don't talk rot!" said the knight.

"I'm not," repeated Jim. He thought a minute. "I'll bet you can't guess who I really am."

The knight did not seem interested in guessing who Jim really was. He stood up in his stirrups and probed through the branches with his spear. The point did not quite reach Jim.

"Damn!" Disappointedly, he lowered the spear and became thoughtful. "I can climb the dashed tree," he muttered to himself. "But then what if he flies down and I have to fight him unhorsed, eh?"

"Look," called Jim, peering down—the knight looked up eagerly—"if you'll listen to what I've to say, first."

The knight considered.

"Fair enough," he said, finally. "No pleas for mercy, now!"

"No, no," said Jim.

"Because I shan't grant them, dammit! It's not in my vows. Widows and orphans and honorable enemies on the field of battle. But not dragons."

"No. I just want to convince you who I really am."

"I don't give a blasted farthing who you really are."

"You will," said Jim. "Because I'm not really a dragon at all. I've just been—uh—enchanted into a dragon."

The man on the ground looked skeptical.

"Really," said Jim, slipping a little in the tree. "You know S. Carolinus, the magician? I'm as human as you are."

"Heard of him," grunted the knight. "You'll say *he* put you under?"

"No, he's the one who's going to change me back—as soon as I can find the lady I'm—er—betrothed to. A real dragon ran off with her. I'm after him. Look at me. Do I look like one of these scrawny mere-dragons?"

"Hmm," said the knight. He rubbed his hooked nose thoughtfully.

"Carolinus found she's at the Loathly Tower. I'm on my way there."

The knight stared.

"The Loathly Tower?" he echoed.

"Exactly," said Jim, firmly. "And now you know, your honor as knight and gentleman demands you don't hamper my rescue efforts."

The knight continued to think it over for a long moment or two. He was evidently not the sort to be rushed into things.

"How do I know you're telling the truth?" he said at last.

"Hold your sword up. I'll swear on the cross of its hilt."

"But if you're a dragon, what's the good in that? Dragons don't have souls, dammit!"

"No," said Jim, "but a Christian gentleman has; and if I'm a Christian gentleman, I wouldn't dare forswear myself like that, would I?"

The knight struggled visibly with this logic for several seconds. Finally, he gave up.

"Oh, well..." He held up his sword by the point and let Jim swear on it. Then he put the sword back in its sheath as Jim descended. "Well," he said, still a little doubtfully, "I suppose, under the circumstances, we ought to introduce ourselves. You know my arms?"

Jim looked at the shield which the other swung around for his inspection. It showed a wide X of silver—like a cross lying over sideways—on a red background and above some sort of black animal in profile which seemed to be lying down between the X's bottom legs.

"The gules, a saltire argent, of course," went on the knight, "are the Nevile of Raby arms. My father, as a cadet of the house, differenced with a hart lodged sable—you see it there at the bottom. Naturally, as his heir, I carry the family arms."

"Nevile-Smythe," said Jim, remembering the name from the song.

"Sir Reginald, knight bachelor. And you, sir?"

"Why, uh..." Jim clutched frantically at what he knew of heraldry. "I bear—in my proper body, that is—"

"Quite."

"A... gules, a typewriter argent, on a desk sable. Eckert, Sir James—uh—knight bachelor. Baron of—er—Riveroak."

Nevile-Smythe was knitting his brows.

"Typewriter..." he was muttering, "typewriter..."

"A local beast, rather like a griffin," said Jim, hastily. "We have a lot of them in Riveroak—that's in America, a land over the sea to the west. You may not have heard of it."

"Can't say that I have. Was it there you were enchanted into this dragon-shape?"

"Well, yes and no. I was transported to this land by magic as was the—uh—lady Angela. When I woke here I was bedragoned."

"Were you?" Sir Reginald's blue eyes bulged a little in amazement. "Angela—fair name, that! Like to meet her. Perhaps after we get this muddle cleared up, we might have a bit of a set-to on behalf of our respective ladies."

Jim gulped slightly.

"Oh, you've got one, too?"

"Absolutely. And she's tremendous. The Lady Elinor—" The knight turned about in his saddle and began to fumble about his equipment. Jim, on reaching the ground, had at once started out along the causeway in the direction of the Tower, so that the knight happened to be pacing alongside him on horseback when he suddenly went into these evolutions. It seemed to bother his charger not at all. "Got her favor here someplace—half a moment—"

"Why don't you just tell me what it's like?" said Jim, sympathetically.

"Oh, well," said Nevile-Smythe, giving up his search, "it's a kerchief, you know. Monogrammed. E. d'C. She's a deChauncy. It's rather too bad, though. I'd have liked to show it to you since we're going to the Loathly Tower together."

"We are?" said Jim, startled. "But—I mean, it's my job. I didn't think you'd want—"

"Lord, yes," said Nevile-Smythe, looking somewhat startled himself. "A gentleman of coat-armor like myself—and an outrage like this taking place locally. I'm no knight-errant, dash it, but I *do* have a decent sense of responsibility."

"I mean—I just meant—" stumbled Jim. "What if something happened to you? What would the Lady Elinor say?"

"Why, what could she say?" replied Nevile-Smythe in plain astonishment. "No one but an utter rotter dodges his plain duty. Besides, there may be a chance here for me to gain a little worship. Elinor's keen on that. She wants me to come home safe."

Jim blinked.

"I don't get it," he said.

"Beg pardon?"

Jim explained his confusion.

"Why, how do you people do things, overseas?" said Nevile-Smythe. "After we're married and I have lands of my own, I'll be expected to raise a company and march out at my lord's call. If I've no name as a knight, I'll be able to raise nothing but bumpkins and clodpoles who'll desert at the first sight of steel. On the other hand, if I've a name, I'll have good men coming to serve under my banner; because, you see, they know I'll take good care of them; and by the same token they'll take good care of me—I say, isn't it getting dark rather suddenly?"

Jim glanced at the sky. It was indeed—almost the dimness of twilight although it could, by rights, be no more than early after-noon yet. Glancing ahead up the Causeway, he became aware of a further phenomenon. A line seemed to be cutting across the trees and grass and even extending out over the waters of the meres on both sides. Moreover, it seemed to be moving toward them as if some heavy, invisible fluid was slowly flooding out over the low country of the fenland.

"Why—" he began. A voice wailed suddenly from his left to interrupt him.

"No! No! Turn back, your worship. Turn back! It's death in there!"

They turned their heads sharply. Secoh, the mere-dragon, sat perched on a half-drowned tussock about forty feet out in the mere.

"Come here, Secoh!" called Jim.

"No! No!" The invisible line was almost to the tussock. Secoh lifted heavily into the air and flapped off, crying, "Now it's loose! It's broken loose again. And we're all lost . . . lost . . . lost . . ."

His voice wailed away and was lost in the distance. Jim and Nevile-Smythe looked at each other.

"Now, that's one of our local dragons for you!" said the knight disgustedly. "How can a gentleman of coat armor gain honor by slaying a beast like that? The worst of it is when someone from the Midlands compliments you on being a dragon-slayer and you have to explain—"

At that moment either they both stepped over the line, or the line moved past them—Jim was never sure which; and they both stopped, as by one common, instinctive impulse. Looking at Sir Reginald, Jim could see under the visor how the knight's face had gone pale.

"In manus tuas Domine," said Nevile-Smythe, crossing himself.

About and around them, the serest gray of winter light lay on the fens. The waters of the meres lay thick and oily, still between the shores of dull green grass. A small, cold breeze wandered through the tops of the reeds and they rattled together with a dry and distant sound like old bones cast out into a forgotten courtyard for the wind to play with. The trees stood helpless and still, their new, small leaves now pinched and faded like children aged before their time while all about and over all the heaviness of dead hope and bleak despair lay on all living things.

"Sir James," said the knight, in an odd tone and accents such as Jim had not heard him use before, "wot well that we have this day set our hands to no small task. Wherefore I pray thee that we should push forward, come what may for my heart faileth and I think me that it may well hap that I return not, ne no man know mine end."

Having said this, he immediately reverted to his usual cheerful self and swung down out of his saddle. "Clarivaux won't go another inch, dash it!" he said. "I shall have to lead him—by the bye, did you know that mere-dragon?"

Jim fell into step beside him and they went on again, but a little more slowly, for everything seemed an extra effort under this darkening sky.

"I talked to him yesterday," said Jim. "He's not a bad sort of dragon."

"Oh, I've nothing against the beasts, myself. But one slays them when one finds them, you know."

"An old dragon—in fact he's the granduncle of this body I'm in," said Jim, "thinks that dragons and humans really ought to get together. Be friends, you know."

"Extraordinary thought!" said Nevile-Smythe, staring at Jim in astonishment.

"Well, actually," said Jim, "why not?"

"Well, I don't know. It just seems like it wouldn't do."

"He says men and dragons might find common foes to fight together."

"Oh, that's where he's wrong, though. You couldn't trust dragons to stick by you in a bicker. And what if your enemy had dragons of his own? They wouldn't fight each other. No. No."

They fell silent. They had moved away from the grass onto flat sandy soil. There was a sterile, flinty hardness to it. It crunched under the hooves of Clarivaux, at once unyielding and treacherous.

"Getting darker, isn't it?" said Jim, finally.

The light was, in fact, now down to a grayish twilight through which it was impossible to see more than a dozen feet. And it was dwindling as they watched. They had halted and stood facing each other. The light fled steadily, and faster. The dimness became blacker, and blacker—until finally the last vestige of illumination was lost and blackness, total and complete, overwhelmed them. Jim felt a gauntleted hand touch one of his forelimbs.

"Let's hold together," said the voice of the knight. "Then whatever comes upon us, must come upon us all at once."

"Right," said Jim. But the word sounded cold and dead in his throat.

They stood, in silence and in lightlessness, waiting for they did not know what. And the blankness about them pressed further in on them, now that it had isolated them, nibbling at the very edges of their minds. Out of the nothingness came nothing material, but from within them crept up one by one, like blind white slugs from some bottomless pit, all their inner doubts and fears and unknown weaknesses, all the things of which they had been ashamed and which they had tucked away to forget, all the maggots of their souls.

Jim found himself slowly, stealthily beginning to withdraw his forelimb from under the knight's touch. He no longer trusted Nevile-Smythe—for the evil that must be in the man because of the evil he knew to be in himself. He would move away ... off into the darkness alone ...

"Look!" Nevile-Smythe's voice cried suddenly to him, distant and eerie, as if from someone already a long way off. "Look back the way we came."

Jim turned about. Far off in the darkness, there was a distant glimmer of light. It rolled toward them, growing as it came. They felt its power against the power of lightlessness that threatened to overwhelm them; and the horse Clarivaux stirred unseen beside them, stamped his hooves on the hard sand, and whinnied.

"This way!" called Jim.

"This way!" shouted Nevile-Smythe

The light shot up suddenly in height. Like a great rod it advanced toward them and the darkness was rolling back, graying, disappearing. They heard a sound of feet close, and a sound of breathing, and then—

It was daylight again.

And S. Carolinus stood before them in tall hat and robes figured with strange images and signs. In his hand upright before him—as if it was blade and buckler, spear and armor all in one—he held a tall carven staff of wood.

"By the Power!" he said. "I was in time. Look there!"

He lifted the staff and drove it point down into the soil. It went in and stood erect like some denuded tree. His long arm pointed past them and they turned around.

The darkness was gone. The fens lay revealed far and wide, stretching back a long way, and up ahead, meeting the thin dark line of the sea. The Causeway had risen until they now stood twenty feet above the mere-waters. Ahead to the west, the sky was ablaze with sunset. It lighted up all the fens and the end of the Causeway leading onto a long and bloody-looking hill, whereon—touched by that same dying light—there loomed above and over all, amongst great tumbled boulders, the ruined, dark and shattered shell of a Tower as black as jet.

III

"—why didn't you wake us earlier, then?" asked Jim.

It was the morning after. They had slept the night within the small circle of protection afforded by Carolinus' staff. They were sitting up now and rubbing their eyes in the light of a sun that had certainly been above the horizon a good two hours.

"Because," said Carolinus. He was sipping at some more milk and he stopped to make a face of distaste. "Because we had to wait for them to catch up with us."

"Who? Catch up?" asked Jim.

"If I knew *who*," snapped Carolinus, handing his empty milk tankard back to the emptier air, "I would have said *who*. All I know is that the present pattern of Chance and History implies that two more will join our party. The same pattern implied the presence of this knight and—oh, so that's who they are."

Jim turned around to follow the magician's gaze. To his surprise, two dragon shapes were emerging from a clump of brush behind them.

"Secoh!" cried Jim. "And—Smrgol! Why—" His voice wavered and died. The old dragon, he suddenly noticed, was limping and one wing hung a little loosely, half-drooping from its shoulder. Also, the eyelid on the same side as the loose wing and stiff leg was sagging more or less at half-mast. "Why, what happened?"

"Oh, a bit stiff from yesterday," huffed Smrgol, bluffly. "Probably pass off in a day or two."

"Stiff nothing!" said Jim, touched in spite of himself. "You've had a stroke."

"Stroke of bad luck, *I'd* say," replied Smrgol, cheerfully, trying to wink his bad eye and not succeeding very well. "No, boy, it's nothing. Look who I've brought along."

"I—I wasn't too keen on coming," said Secoh, shyly, to Jim. "But your granduncle can be pretty persuasive, your wo— you know."

"That's right!" boomed Smrgol. "Don't you go calling anybody your worship. Never heard of such stuff!" He turned to Jim. "And letting a george go in where he didn't dare go himself! Boy, I said to him, don't give me this *only a mere-dragon* and *just a mere-dragon*. Mere's got nothing to do with what kind of dragon you are. What kind of a world would it be if we were all like that?" Smrgol mimicked (as well as his dragon-basso would let him) someone talking in a high, simpering voice. "Oh, I'm just a plowland-and-pasture dragon—you'll have to excuse me I'm only a halfway-up-the-hill dragon—*Boy!*" bellowed Smrgol, "I said you're a *dragon!* Remember that. And a dragon acts like a dragon or he doesn't act at all!"

"Hear! Hear!" said Nevile-Smythe, carried away by enthusiasm.

"Hear that, boy? Even the george here knows that. Don't believe I've met you, george," he added, turning to the knight.

"Nevile-Smythe, Sir Reginald. Knight bachelor."

"Smrgol. Dragon."

"Smrgol? You aren't the—but you couldn't be. Over a hundred years ago."

"The dragon who slew the Ogre of Gormely Keep? That's who I am, boy—george, I mean."

"By Jove! Always thought it was a legend, only."

"Legend? Not on your honor, george! I'm old—even for a dragon, but there was a time—well, well, we won't go into that. I've something more important to talk to you about. I've been doing a lot of thinking the last decade or so about us dragons and you georges getting together. Actually, we're really a lot alike—"

"If you don't mind, Smrgol," cut in Carolinus, snappishly, "we aren't out here to hold a parlement. It'll be noon in—when will it be noon, you?"

"Four hours, thirty-seven minutes, twelve seconds at the sound of the gong," replied the invisible bass voice. There was a momentary pause, and then a single mellow, chimed note. "Chime, I mean," the voice corrected itself.

"Oh, go back to bed!" cried Carolinus, furiously.

"I've been up for hours," protested the voice, indignantly.

Carolinus ignored it, herding the party together and starting them off for the Tower. The knight fell in beside Smrgol.

"About this business of men and dragons getting together," said Nevile-Smythe. "Confess I wasn't much impressed until I heard your name. D'you think it's possible?"

"Got to make a start sometime, george." Smrgol rumbled on. Jim, who had moved up to the head of the column to walk beside Carolinus, spoke to the magician.

"What lives in the Tower?"

Carolinus jerked his fierce old bearded face around to look at him.

"What's *living* there?" he snapped. "I don't know. We'll find out soon enough. What *is* there—neither alive nor dead, just in existence at the spot—is the manifestation of pure evil."

"But how can we do anything against that?"

"We can't. We can only contain it. Just as you—if you're essentially a good person—contain the potentialities for evil in yourself, by killing its creatures, your evil impulses and actions."

"Oh?" said Jim.

"Certainly. And since evil opposes good in like manner, its creatures, the ones in the Tower, will try to destroy us."

Jim felt a cold lump in his throat. He swallowed.

"Destroy us?"

"Why no, they'll probably just invite us to tea—" The sarcasm in the old magician's voice broke off suddenly with the voice itself. They had just stepped through a low screen of bushes and instinctively checked to a halt.

Lying on the ground before them was what once had been a man in full armor. Jim heard the sucking intake of breath from Nevile-Smythe behind him.

"A most foul death," said the knight softly, "most foul . . ." He came forward and dropped clumsily to his armored knees, joining his gauntleted hands in prayer. The dragons were silent. Carolinus poked with his staff at a wide trail of slime that led around and over the body and back toward the Tower. It was the sort of trail a garden slug might have left—if this particular garden slug had been two or more feet wide where it touched the ground.

"A Worm," said Carolinus. "But Worms are mindless. No Worm killed him in such cruel fashion." He lifted his head to the old dragon.

"I didn't say it, Mage," rumbled Smrgol, uneasily.

"Best none of us say it until we know for certain. Come on." Carolinus took up the lead and led them forward again.

They had come up off the Causeway onto the barren plain that sloped up into a hill on which stood the Tower. They could see the wide fens and the tide flats coming to meet them in the arms of a small bay—and beyond that the sea, stretching misty to the horizon.

The sky above was blue and clear. No breeze stirred; but, as they looked at the Tower and the hill that held it, it seemed that the azure above had taken on a metallic cast. The air had a quivering unnaturalness like an atmosphere dancing to heat waves, though the day was chill; and there came on Jim's ears, from where he did not know, a high-pitched dizzy singing like that which accompanies delirium, or high fever.

The Tower itself was distorted by these things. So that although to Jim it seemed only the ancient, ruined shell of a building, yet, between one heartbeat and the next, it seemed to change. Almost, but not quite, he caught glimpses of it unbroken and alive and thronged about with fantastic, half-seen figures. His heart beat stronger with the delusion; and its beating shook the scene before him, all the hill and Tower, going in and out of focus, in and out, *in* and *out* . . . And there was Angie, in the Tower's doorway, calling him . . .

"*Stop!*" shouted Carolinus. His voice echoed like a clap of thunder in Jim's ears; and Jim awoke to his senses, to find himself straining against the barrier of Carolinus' staff, that barred his way to the Tower like a rod of iron. "By the Powers!" said the old magician, softly and fiercely. "Will you fall into the first trap set for you?"

"Trap?" echoed Jim, bewilderedly. But he had no time to go further, for at that moment there rose from among the giant boulders at the Tower's base the heavy, wicked head of a dragon as large as Smrgol.

The thunderous bellow of the old dragon beside Jim split the unnatural air.

"*Anark!* Traitor—thief—inchworm! Come down here!"

Booming dragon-laughter rolled back an answer.

"Tell us about Gormely Keep, old bag of bones. Ancient mud-puppy, fat lizard, scare us with words!"

Smrgol lurched forward; and again Carolinus' staff was extended to bar the way.

"Patience," said the magician. But with one wrenching effort, the old dragon had himself until control. He turned, panting, to Carolinus.

"What's hidden, Mage?" he demanded.

"We'll see." Grimly, Carolinus brought his staff, endwise, three times down upon the earth. With each blow the whole hill seemed to shake and shudder.

Up among the rocks, one particularly large boulder tottered and rolled aside. Jim caught his breath and Secoh cried out, suddenly.

In the gap that the boulder revealed, a thick, slug-like head was lifting from the ground. It reared, yellow-brown in the sunlight, its two sets of horns searching and revealing a light external shell, a platelet with a merest hint of spire. It lowered its head and slowly, inexorably, began to flow downhill toward them, leaving its glistening trail behind it.

"Now—" said the knight. But Carolinus shook his head. He struck the ground again.

"Come forth!" he cried, his thin, old voice piping on the quivering air. "By the Powers! Come forth!"

And then they saw it.

From behind the great barricade of boulders, slowly, there reared first a bald and glistening dome of hairless skin. Slowly this rose, revealing two perfectly round eyes below which they saw, as the whole came up, no proper nose, but two air-slits side by side as if the whole of the bare, enormous skull was covered with a simple sheet of thick skin. And rising still further, this unnatural head, as big around as a beach ball, showed itself to possess a wide and idiot-grinning mouth, entirely lipless and revealing two jagged, matching rows of yellow teeth.

Now, with a clumsy, studied motion, the whole creature rose to its feet and stood knee-deep in the boulders and towering above them. It was man-like in shape, but clearly nothing ever spawned by the human race. A good twelve feet high it stood, a rough patchwork kilt of untanned hides wrapped around its thick waist—but this was not the extent of its differences from the race of Man. It had, to begin with, no neck at all. That obscene beachball of a hairless, near-featureless head balanced like an apple on thick, square shoulders of gray, coarse-looking skin. Its torso was one straight trunk, from which its arms and legs sprouted with a disproportionate thickness and roundness, like sections of pipe. Its knees were hidden by its kilt and its further legs by the rocks; but the elbows of its oversize arms had unnatural hinges to them, almost as if they had been doubled, and the lower arms were almost as large as the upper and near-wristless, while the hands themselves were awkward, thick-fingered parodies of the human extremity, with only three digits, of which one was a single, opposed thumb.

The right hand held a club, bound with rusty metal, that surely not even such a monster should have been able to lift. Yet one grotesque hand carried it lightly, as lightly as Carolinus had carried his staff. The monster opened its mouth.

"He!" it went. "He! He!"

The sound was fantastic. It was a bass titter, if such a thing could be imagined. Though the tone of it was as low as the lowest note of a good operatic basso, it clearly came from the creature's upper throat and head. Nor was there any real humor in it. It was an utterance with a nervous, habitual air about it, like a man clearing his throat. Having sounded, it fell silent, watching the advance of the great slug with its round, light blue eyes.

Smrgol exhaled slowly.

"Yes," he rumbled, almost sadly, almost as if to himself. "What I was afraid of. An ogre."

In the silence that followed, Nevile-Smythe got down from his horse and began to tighten the girths of its saddle.

"So, so, Clarivaux," he crooned to the trembling horse. "So ho, boy."

The rest of them were looking all at Carolinus. The magician leaned on his staff, seeming very old indeed, with the deep lines carven in the ancient skin of his face. He had been watching the ogre, but now he turned back to Jim and the other two dragons.

"I had hoped all along," he said, "that it needn't come to this. However," he crackled sourly, and waved his hand at the approaching Worm, the silent Anark and the watching ogre, "as you see ... The world goes never the way we want it by itself, but must be haltered and led." He winced, produced his flask and cup, and took a drink of milk. Putting the utensils back, he looked over at Nevile-Smythe, who was now checking his weapons. "I'd suggest, Knight, that you take the Worm. It's a poor chance, but your best. I know you'd prefer that renegade dragon, but the Worm is the greater danger."

"Difficult to slay, I imagine?" queried the knight.

"Its vital organs are hidden deep inside it," said Carolinus, "and being mindless, it will fight on long after being mortally wounded. Cut off those eye-stalks and blind it first, if you can—"

"Wait!" cried Jim, suddenly. He had been listening bewilderedly. Now the word seemed to jump out of his mouth. "What're we going to do?"

"Do?" said Carolinus, looking at him. "Why, fight, of course."

"But," stammered Jim, "wouldn't it be better to go get some help? I mean—"

"Blast it, boy!" boomed Smrgol. "We can't wait for that! Who knows what'll happen if we take time for something like that? Hell's bells, Gorbash, lad, you got to fight your foes when you meet them, not the next day, or the day after that."

"Quite right, Smrgol," said Carolinus, dryly. "Gorbash, you don't understand this situation. Every time you retreat from something like this, it gains and you lose. The next time the odds would be even worse against us."

They were all looking at him. Jim felt the impact of their curious glances. He did not know what to say. He wanted to tell them that he was not a fighter, that he did not know the first thing to do in this sort of battle, that it was none of his business anyway and that he would not be here at all, if it were not for Angie. He was, in fact, quite humanly scared, and floundered desperately for some sort of strength to lean on.

"What—what am I supposed to do?" he said.

"Why, fight the ogre, boy! Fight the ogre!" thundered Smrgol—and the inhuman giant up on the slope, hearing him, shifted his gaze suddenly from the Worm to fasten it on Jim. "And I'll take on that louse of an Anark. The george here'll chop up the Worm, the Mage'll hold back the bad influences—and there we are."

"Fight the ogre . . ." If Jim had still been possessed of his ordinary two legs, they would have buckled underneath him. Luckily his dragon-body knew no such weakness. He looked at the overwhelming bulk of his expected opponent, contrasted the ogre with himself, the armored, ox-heavy body of the Worm with Nevile-Smythe, the deep-chested over-size Anark with the crippled old dragon beside him—and a cry of protest rose from the very depths of his being. "But we can't win!"

He turned furiously on Carolinus, who, however, looked at him calmly. In desperation he turned back to the only normal human he could find in the group.

"Nevile-Smythe," he said. "You don't need to do this."

"Lord, yes," replied the knight, busy with his equipment. "Worms, ogres—one fights them when one runs into them, you know." He considered his spear and put it aside. "Believe I'll face it on foot," he murmured to himself.

"Smrgol!" said Jim. "Don't you see—can't you understand? Anark is a lot younger than you. And you're not well—"

"Er . . ." said Secoh, hesitantly.

"Speak up, boy!" rumbled Smrgol.

"Well," stammered Secoh, "it's just . . . what I mean is, I couldn't bring myself to fight that Worm or that ogre—I really couldn't.

I just sort of go to pieces when I think of them getting close to me. But I *could*—well, fight another dragon. It wouldn't be quite so bad, if you know what I mean, if that dragon up there breaks my neck—" He broke down and stammered incoherently. "I know I sound awfully silly—"

"Nonsense! Good lad!" bellowed Smrgol. "Glad to have you. I—er—can't quite get into the air myself at the moment—still a bit stiff. But if you could fly over and work him down this way where I can get a grip on him, we'll stretch him out for the buzzards." And he dealt the mere-dragon a tremendous thwack with his tail by way of congratulation, almost knocking Secoh off his feet.

In desperation, Jim turned back to Carolinus.

"There is no retreat," said Carolinus, calmly, before Jim could speak. "This is a game of chess where if one piece withdraws, all fall. Hold back the creatures, and I will hold back the forces—for the creatures will finish me, if you go down, and the forces will finish you if they get me."

"Now, look here, Gorbash!" shouted Smrgol in Jim's ear. "That Worm's almost here. Let me tell you something about how to fight ogres, based on experience. You listening, boy?"

"Yes," said Jim, numbly.

"I know you've heard the other dragons calling me an old windbag when I wasn't around. But I *have* conquered an ogre—the only one in our race to do it in the last eight hundred years—and they haven't. So pay attention, if you want to win your own fight."

Jim gulped.

"All right," he said.

"Now, the first thing to know," boomed Smrgol, glancing at the Worm who was now less than fifty yards distant, "is about the bones in an ogre—"

"Never mind the details!" cried Jim. "What do I do?"

"In a minute," said Smrgol. "Don't get excited, boy. Now, about the bones in an ogre. The thing to remember is that they're big— matter of fact in the arms and legs, they're mainly bone. So there's no use trying to bite clear through, if you get a chance. What you try to do is get at the muscle—that's tough enough as it is—and hamstring. That's point one." He paused to look severely at Jim.

"Now, point two," he continued, "also connected with bones. Notice the elbows on that ogre. They aren't like a george's elbows. They're what you might call double-jointed. I mean, they have two joints where a george has just the one. Why? Simply because with the big bones they got to have and the muscle of them, they'd never be able to bend an arm more than halfway up before the bottom part'd bump the top if they had a george-type joint. Now, the point of all this is that when it swings that club, it can only swing in one way with that elbow. That's up and down. If it wants to swing it side to side, it's got to use its shoulder. Consequently if you can catch it with its club down and to one side of the body, you got an advantage; because it takes two motions to get it back up and in line again—instead of one, like a george."

"Yes, yes," said Jim, impatiently, watching the advance of the Worm.

"Don't get impatient, boy. Keep cool. Keep cool. Now, the knees don't have that kind of joint, so if you can knock it off its feet you got a real advantage. But don't try that, unless you're sure you can do it; because once it gets you pinned, you're a goner. The way to fight it is in-and-out—fast. Wait for a swing, dive in, tear him, get back out again. Got it?"

"Got it," said Jim, numbly.

"Good. Whatever you do, don't let it get a grip on you. Don't pay attention to what's happening to the rest of us, no matter what you hear or see. It's every one for himself. Concentrate on your own foe; and *keep your head*. Don't let your dragon instinct to get in there and slug run away with you. That's why the georges have been winning against us as they have. Just remember you're faster than that ogre and your brains'll win for you if you stay clear, keep your head and don't rush. I tell you, boy—"

He was interrupted by a sudden cry of joy from Nevile-Smythe, who had been rummaging around in Clarivaux's saddle.

"I say!" shouted Nevile-Smythe, running up to them with surprising lightness, considering his armor. "The most marvelous stroke of luck! Look what I found." He waved a wispy stretch of cloth at them.

"What?" demanded Jim, his heart going up in one sudden leap.

"Elinor's favor! And just in time, too. Be a good fellow, will you," went on Nevile-Smythe, turning to Carolinus, "and tie it about my vambrace here on the shield arm. Thank you, Mage."

Carolinus, looking grim, tucked his staff into the crook of his arm and quickly tied the kerchief around the armor of Nevile-Smythe's lower left arm. As he tightened the final knot and let his hands drop away, the knight caught up his shield into position and drew his sword with the other hand. The bright blade flashed like a sudden streak of lightning in the sun, he leaned forward to throw the weight of his armor before him, and with a shout of *"A Nevile-Smythe! Elinor! Elinor!"* he ran forward up the slope toward the approaching Worm.

Jim heard, but did not see, the clash of shell and steel that was their coming together. For just then everything began to happen at once. Up on the hill, Anark screamed suddenly in fury and launched himself down the slope in the air, wings spread like some great bomber gliding in for a crash landing. Behind Jim, there was the frenzied flapping of leathery wings as Secoh took to the air to meet him—but this was drowned by a sudden short, deep-chested cry, like a wordless shout; and, lifting his club, the ogre stirred and stepped clear of the boulders, coming forward and straight down the hill with huge, ground-covering strides.

"Good luck, boy," said Smrgol, in Jim's ear. "And Gorbash—" Something in the old dragon's voice made Jim turn his head to look at Smrgol. The ferocious red mouth-pit and enormous fangs were frighteningly open before him; but behind it Jim read a strange affection and concern in the dark dragon-eyes. "—remember," said the old dragon, almost softly, "that you are a descendant of Ortosh and Agtval, and Gleingul who slew the sea serpent on the tide-banks of the Gray Sands. And be therefore valiant. But remember too, that you are my only living kin and the last of our line . . . and be careful."

Then Smrgol's head was jerked away, as he swung about to face the coming together of Secoh and Anark in mid-air and bellowed out his own challenge. While Jim, turning back toward the Tower, had only time to take to the air before the rush of the ogre was upon him.

He had lifted on his wings without thinking—evidently this was dragon instinct when attacked. He was aware of the ogre suddenly before him, checking now, with its enormous hairy feet digging deep into the ground. The rust-bound club flashed before Jim's eyes and he felt a heavy blow high on his chest that swept him backward through the air.

He flailed with his wings to regain balance. The over-size idiot face was grinning only a couple of yards off from him. The club swept up for another blow. Panicked, Jim scrambled aside, and saw the ogre sway forward a step. Again the club lashed out—*quick!*—how could something so big and clumsy-looking be so quick with its hands? Jim felt himself smashed down to earth and a sudden lance of bright pain shot through his right shoulder. For a second a gray, thick-skinned forearm loomed over him and his teeth met in it without thought.

He was shaken like a rat by a rat terrier and flung clear. His wings beat for the safety of altitude, and he found himself about twenty feet off the ground, staring down at the ogre, which grunted a wordless sound and shifted the club to strike upwards. Jim cupped air with his wings, to fling himself backward and avoid the blow. The club whistled through the unfeeling air; and, sweeping forward, Jim ripped at one great blocky shoulder and beat clear. The ogre spun to face him, still grinning. But now blood welled and trickled down where Jim's teeth had gripped and torn, high on the shoulder.

—And suddenly, Jim realized something:

He was no longer afraid. He hung in the air, just out of the ogre's reach, poised to take advantage of any opening; and a hot sense of excitement was coursing through him. He was discovering the truth about fights—and about most similar things—that it is only the beginning that is bad. Once the chips are down, several million years of instinct take over and there is no time for thought for anything but confronting the enemy. So it was with Jim—and then the ogre moved in on him again; and that was his last specific intellectual thought of the fight, for everything else was drowned in his overwhelming drive to avoid being killed and, if possible, to kill, himself . . .

IV

It was a long, blurred time, about which later Jim had no clear memory. The sun marched up the long arc of the heavens and crossed the nooning point and headed down again. On the torn-up sandy soil of the plain he and the ogre turned and feinted, smashed and tore at each other. Sometimes he was in the air, sometimes on the ground. Once he had the ogre down on one knee, but could not press his advantage. At another time they had fought up the long slope of the hill almost to the Tower and the ogre had him pinned in the cleft between two huge boulders and had hefted its club back for the final blow that would smash Jim's skull. And then he had wriggled free between the monster's very legs and the battle was on again.

Now and then throughout the fight he would catch brief

kaleidoscopic glimpses of the combats being waged about him: Nevile-Smythe now wrapped about by the blind body of the Worm, its eye-stalks hacked away—and striving in silence to draw free his sword-arm, which was pinned to his side by the Worm's encircling body. Or there would roll briefly into Jim's vision a tangled roaring tumble of flailing leathery wings and serpentine bodies that was Secoh, Anark and old Smrgol. Once or twice he had a momentary view of Carolinus, still standing erect, his staff upright in his hand, his long white beard blowing forward over his blue gown with the cabalistic golden signs upon it, like some old seer in the hour of Armageddon. Then the gross body of the ogre would blot out his vision and he would forget all but the enemy before him.

The day faded. A dank mist came rolling in from the sea and fled in little wisps and tatters across the plain of battle. Jim's body ached and slowed, and his wings felt leaden. But the ever-grinning face and sweeping club of the ogre seemed neither to weaken nor to tire. Jim drew back for a moment to catch his breath; and in that second, he heard a voice cry out.

"Time is short!" it cried, in cracked tones. "We are running out of time. The day is nearly gone!"

It was the voice of Carolinus. Jim had never heard him raise it before with just such a desperate accent. And even as Jim identified the voice, he realized that it came clearly to his ears—and that for sometime now upon the battlefield, except for the ogre and himself, there had been silence.

He shook his head to clear it and risked a quick glance about him. He had been driven back almost to the neck of the Causeway itself, where it entered onto the plain. To one side of him, the snapped strands of Clarivaux's bridle dangled limply where the terrified horse had broken loose from the earth-thrust spear to which Nevile-Smythe had tethered it before advancing against the Worm on foot. A little off from it stood Carolinus, upheld now only by his staff, his old face shrunken and almost mummified in appearance, as if the life had been all but drained from it. There was nowhere else to retreat to; and Jim was alone.

He turned back his gaze to see the ogre almost upon him. The heavy club swung high, looking gray and enormous in the mist. Jim felt in his limbs and wings a weakness that would not let him dodge in time; and, with all his strength, he gathered himself, and sprang instead, up under the monster's guard and inside the grasp of those cannon-thick arms.

The club glanced off Jim's spine. He felt the arms go around him, the double triad of bone-thick fingers searching for his neck. He was caught, but his rush had knocked the ogre off his feet. Together they went over and rolled on the sandy earth, the ogre gnawing with his jagged teeth at Jim's chest and striving to break a spine or twist a neck, while Jim's tail lashed futilely about.

They rolled against the spear and snapped it in half. The ogre found its hold and Jim felt his neck begin to be slowly twisted, as if it were a chicken's neck being wrung in slow motion. A wild despair flooded through him. He had been warned by Smrgol never to let the ogre get him pinned. He had disregarded that advice and now he was lost, the battle was lost. *Stay away*, Smrgol had warned, *use your brains . . .*

The hope of a wild chance sprang suddenly to life in him. His head was twisted back over his shoulder. He could see only the gray mist above him, but he stopped fighting the ogre and groped about with both forelimbs. For a slow moment of eternity, he felt nothing, and then something hard nudged against his right foreclaw, a glint of bright metal flashed for a second before his eyes. He changed his grip on what he held, clamping down on it as firmly as his clumsy foreclaws would allow—

—and with every ounce of strength that was left to him, he drove the fore-part of the broken spear deep into the middle of the ogre that sprawled above him.

The great body bucked and shuddered. A wild scream burst from the idiot mouth alongside Jim's ear. The ogre let go, staggered back and up, tottering to its feet, looming like the Tower itself above him. Again, the ogre screamed, staggering about like a drunken man, fumbling at the shaft of the spear sticking from him. It jerked at the shaft, screamed again, and, lowering its unnatural head, bit at the wood like a wounded animal. The tough ash splintered between its teeth. It screamed once more and fell to its knees. Then slowly, like a bad actor in an old-fashioned movie, it went over on its side, and drew up its legs like a man with the cramp. A final scream was drowned in bubbling. Black blood trickled from its mouth and it lay still.

Jim crawled slowly to his feet and looked about him.

The mists were drawing back from the plain and the first thin light of late afternoon stretching long across the slope. In its rusty illumination, Jim made out what was to be seen there.

The Worm was dead, literally hacked in two. Nevile-Smythe, in bloody, dinted armor, leaned wearily on a twisted sword not more than a few feet off from Carolinus. A little farther off, Secoh raised a torn neck and head above the intertwined, locked-together bodies of Anark and Smrgol. He stared dazedly at Jim. Jim moved slowly, painfully over to the mere-dragon.

Jim came up and looked down at the two big dragons. Smrgol lay with his eyes closed and his jaws locked in Anark's throat. The neck of the younger dragon had been broken like the stem of a weed.

"Smrgol ..." croaked Jim.

"No—" gasped Secoh. "No good. He's gone ... I led the other one to him. He got his grip—and then he never let go ..." The mere-dragon choked and lowered his head.

"He fought well," creaked a strange harsh voice which Jim did not at first recognize. He turned and saw the Knight standing at his shoulder. Nevile-Smythe's face was white as sea-foam inside his helmet and the flesh of it seemed fallen in to the bones, like an old man's. He swayed as he stood.

"We have won," said Carolinus, solemnly, coming up with the aid of his staff. "Not again in our lifetimes will evil gather enough strength in this spot to break out." He looked at Jim. "And now," he said, "the balance of Chance and History inclines in your favor. It's time to send you back."

"Back?" said Nevile-Smythe.

"Back to his own land, Knight," replied the magician. "Fear not, the dragon left in this body of his will remember all that happened and be your friend."

"Fear!" said Nevile-Smythe, somehow digging up a final spark of energy to expend on hauteur. "I fear no dragon, dammit. Besides, in respect to the old boy here"—he nodded at the dead Smrgol—"I'm going to see what can be done about this dragon-alliance business."

"He was great!" burst out Secoh, suddenly, almost with a sob. "He—he made me strong again. Whatever he wanted, I'll do it." And the mere-dragon bowed his head.

"You come along with me then, to vouch for the dragon end of it," said Nevile-Smythe. "Well," he turned to Jim, "it's goodby, I suppose, Sir James."

"I suppose so," said Jim. "Goodby to you, too. I—" Suddenly he remembered.

"Angie!" he cried out, spinning around. "I've got to go get Angie out of that Tower!"

Carolinus put his staff out to halt Jim.

"Wait," he said. "Listen ..."

"Listen?" echoed Jim. But just at that moment, he heard it, a woman's voice calling, high and clear, from the mists that still hid the Tower.

"Jim! Jim, where are you?"

A slight figure emerged from the mist, running down the slope toward them.

"Here I am!" bellowed Jim. And for once he was glad of the capabilities of his dragon-voice. "Here I am, Angie—"

—but Carolinus was chanting in a strange, singing voice, words without meaning, but which seemed to shake the very air about them. The mist swirled, the world rocked and swung. Jim and Angie were caught up, were swirled about, were spun away and away down an echoing corridor of nothingness . . .

. . . and then they were back in the Grille, seated together on one side of the table in the booth. Hanson, across from them, was goggling like a bewildered accident victim.

"Where—where am I?" he stammered. His eyes suddenly focused on them across the table and he gave a startled croak. "Help!" he cried, huddling away from them. "Humans!"

"What did you expect?" snapped Jim. "Dragons?"

"No!" shrieked Hanson. "Watch-beetles—like me!" And, turning about, he tried desperately to burrow his way through the wood seat of the booth to safety.

V

It was the next day after that Jim and Angie stood in the third floor corridor of Chumley Hall, outside the door leading to the office of the English Department.

"Well, are you going in or aren't you?" demanded Angie.

"In a second, in a second," said Jim, adjusting his tie with nervous fingers. "Just don't rush me."

"Do you suppose he's heard about Grottwold?" Angie asked.

"I doubt it," said Jim. The Student Health Service says Hanson's already starting to come out of it—except that he'll probably always have a touch of amnesia about the whole afternoon. Angie!" said Jim, turning on her. "Do you suppose, all the time we were there, Hanson was actually being a watch-beetle underground?"

"I don't know, and it doesn't matter," interrupted Angie, firmly. "Honestly, Jim, now you've finally promised to get an answer out of Dr. Howells about a job, I'd think you'd want to get it over and done with, instead of hesitating like this. I just can't understand a man who can go about consorting with dragons and fighting ogres and then—"

"—still not want to put his boss on the spot for a yes-or-no answer," said Jim. "Hah! Let me tell you something." He waggled a finger in front of her nose. "Do you know what all this dragon-ogre business actually taught me? It wasn't not to be scared, either."

"All right," said Angie, with a sigh. "What was it then?"

"I'll tell you," said Jim. "What I found out . . ." He paused. "What I found out was not, not to be scared. It was that scared or not doesn't matter; because you just go ahead, anyway."

Angie blinked at him.

"And that," concluded Jim, "is why I agreed to have it out with Howells, after all. Now you know."

He yanked Angie to him, kissed her grimly upon her startled lips, and, letting go of her, turned about. Giving a final jerk to his tie, he turned the knob of the office door, opened it, and strode valiantly within.

AFTERWORD BY ERIC FLINT

I'm not sure when I first encountered the writings of Gordon R. Dickson, except that it was sometime during my teenage years, and he's always been one of the writers who are inseparable from what I think of as "science fiction." As was usually the case with me, however, I was more interested in novels than short stories—a preference that was reflected many years later when I started writing myself. So the Dickson I remembered was the Dickson who wrote such things as *The Genetic General* (aka *Dorsai!*), *The Alien Way, Naked to the Stars,* and the two marvelous Dilbian novels. Even the Hoka stories he wrote with Poul Anderson were things I first encountered in their later novelized form.

So, when the time came to select a Dickson story for this anthology, I was a little stumped. There was no room for a novel in such an anthology, obviously. The only thing I could suggest was "Call Him Lord," because that was the only shorter piece of fiction by Dickson I could remember having had much of an impact on me. When Dave proposed "St. Dragon and the George" as an alternative, I was a little astonished. I'd read the *novel* version of the story, of course—and it had always been one of my favorites since the first time I read it. But I'd had no idea that he'd written a shorter version of it first.

The minute Dave advanced the proposal, I agreed to it. To be sure, "Call Him Lord" would have made a fine alternative. It's no accident that it won the Nebula award for best novelette in 1967 and was a finalist for the Hugo in the same year. Still, I didn't hesitate. That's because every writer knows what every actor knows: comedy gets little respect, but it's a lot harder to do well than serious drama. Whether you read this shorter version of the story or the novel-length *The Dragon and the George,* I think you're reading comic fantasy at its very best. And, as Dave says in his preface, when comedy is good enough it's more than just funny. A lot more.

Thunder and Roses

by Theodore Sturgeon

PREFACE BY DAVID DRAKE

Because I lived through the 1950s, I find the concept of Fifties Nostalgia hard to fathom. It was a terrifying time for me, and I don't think I was that unusual.

People—perfectly ordinary people in Middle America—actively expected nuclear war to break out. I knew families in Clinton, Iowa, with bomb shelters in the back yard. We had air raid drills, huddling in the elementary school basement, and we were taught to duck and cover if we saw the flash of a nuclear weapon. Mass circulation magazines—*Collier's, Popular Science, The Saturday Evening Post*—ran stories on fallout and nuclear holocaust. *On the Beach* and *Alas, Babylon* were *New York Times* bestsellers.

If you were a kid who read SF, the feeling of dread was even more acute. It wasn't formless for us, you see: there were hundreds of stories to describe nuclear war and its aftermath of lingering death, deformity, and savagery in vivid detail. "Thunder and Roses," which I read in *The Astounding Science Fiction Anthology* when I was thirteen, is one of the earlier stories of the type. It's possibly the best, because Theodore Sturgeon at his peak was one of the best writers of SF ever.

For those of you who haven't read "Thunder and Roses" before: Welcome to the fifties, my friends.

When Pete Mawser learned about the show, he turned away from the GHQ bulletin board, touched his long chin, and determined to shave, in spite of the fact that the show would be video, and he would see it in his barracks. He had an hour and a half. It felt good to have a purpose again—even the small matter of shaving before eight o'clock. Eight o'clock Tuesday, just the way it used to be. Everyone used to say, Wednesday morning, "How about the way Starr sang *The Breeze and I* last night?"

That was a while ago, before the attack, before all those people were dead, before the country was dead. Starr Anthim—an institution, like Crosby, like Duse, like Jenny Lind, like the Statue of Liberty. (Liberty had been one of the first to get it, her bronze beauty volatilized, radio-activated, and even now being carried about in vagrant winds, spreading over the earth . . .)

Pete Mawser grunted and forced his thoughts away from the drifting, poisonous fragments of a blasted liberty. Hate was first. Hate was ubiquitous, like the increasing blue glow in the air at night, like the tension that hung over the base.

Gunfire crackled sporadically far to the right, swept nearer. Pete stepped out to the street and made for a parked truck. There was a Wac sitting on the short running-board.

At the corner a stocky figure backed into the intersection. The man carried a tommy-gun in his arms, and he was swinging it to and fro with the gentle, wavering motion of a weather-vane. He staggered toward them, his gun-muzzle hunting. Someone fired from a building and the man swiveled and blasted wildly at the sound.

"He's—blind," said Pete Mawser, and added, "he ought to be," looking at the tattered face.

A siren keened. An armored jeep slewed into the street. The full-throated roar of a brace of .50-caliber machine-guns put a swift and shocking end to the incident.

"Poor crazy kid," Pete said softly. "That's the fourth I've seen today." He looked down at the Wac. She was smiling. "Hey!"

"Hello, Sarge." She must have identified him before, because now she did not raise her eyes nor her voice. "What happened?"

"You know what happened. Some kid got tired of having nothing to fight and nowhere to run to. What's the matter with you?"

"No," she said. "I don't mean that." At last she looked up at him. "I mean all of this. I can't seem to remember."

"You—well, it's not easy to forget. We got hit. We got hit everywhere at once. All the big cities are gone. We got it from both sides. We got too much. The air is becoming radioactive. We'll all—" He checked himself. She didn't know. She'd forgotten. There was nowhere to escape to, and she'd escaped inside herself, right here. Why tell her about it? Why tell her that everyone was going to die? Why tell her that other, shameful thing: that we hadn't struck back?

But she wasn't listening. She was still looking at him. Her eyes were not quite straight. One held his, but the other was slightly shifted and seemed to be looking at his temple. She was smiling again. When his voice trailed off she didn't prompt him. Slowly, he moved away. She did not turn her head, but kept looking up at where he had been, smiling a little. He turned away, wanting to run, walking fast.

How long could a guy hold out? When you were in the army they tried to make you be like everybody else. What did you do when everybody else was cracking up?

He blanked out the mental picture of himself as the last one left sane. He'd followed that one through before. It always led to the conclusion that it would be better to be one of the first. He wasn't ready for that yet. Then he blanked that out, too. Every time he said to himself that he wasn't ready for that yet, something within him asked "Why not?" and he never seemed to have an answer ready.

How long could a guy hold out?

He climbed the steps of the QM Central and went inside. There was nobody at the reception switchboard. It didn't matter. Messages were carried by jeep, or on motor-cycles. The Base Command was not insisting that anybody stick to a sitting job these days. Ten desk-men could crack up for every one on a jeep, or on the soul-sweat squads. Pete made up his mind to put in a little stretch on a squad tomorrow. Do him good. He just hoped that this time the adjutant wouldn't burst into tears in the middle of the parade ground. You could keep your mind on the manual of arms just fine until something like that happened.

He bumped into Sonny Weisefreund in the barracks corridor. The Tech's round young face was as cheerful as ever. He was naked and glowing, and had a towel thrown over his shoulder.

"Hi, Sonny. Is there plenty of hot water?"

"Why not?" grinned Sonny. Pete grinned back, wondering if anybody could say anything about anything at all without one of these reminders. Of course, there was hot water. The QM barracks had hot water for three hundred men. There were three dozen left. Men dead, men gone to the hills, men locked up so they wouldn't—

"Starr Anthim's doing a show tonight."

"Yeah. Tuesday night. Not funny, Pete. Don't you know there's a war—"

"No kidding," Pete said swiftly. "She's here—right here on the base."

Sonny's face was joyful. "Gee." He pulled the towel off his shoulder and tied it around his waist. "Starr Anthim here! Where are they going to put on the show?"

"HQ, I imagine. Video only. You know about public gatherings."

"Yeah. And a good thing, too," said Sonny. "Somebody'd be sure to crack up. I wouldn't want her to see anything like that. How'd she happen to come here, Pete?"

"Drifted in on the last gasp of a busted-up Navy helicopter."

"Yeah, but why?"

"Search me. Get your head out of that gift-horse's mouth."

He went into the washroom, smiling and glad that he still could. He undressed and put his neatly folded clothes down on a bench. There were a soap-wrapper and an empty tooth-paste tube lying near the wall. He picked them up and put them in the catchall, took the mop that leaned against the partition and mopped the floor where Sonny had splashed after shaving. Someone had to keep things straight. He might have worried if it were anyone else but Sonny. But Sonny wasn't cracking up. Sonny always had been like that. Look there. Left his razor out again.

Pete started his shower, meticulously adjusting the valves until the pressure and temperature exactly suited him. He did nothing carelessly these days. There was so much to feel, and taste, and see now. The impact of water on his skin, the smell of soap, the consciousness of light and heat, the very pressure of standing on the soles of his feet ... he wondered vaguely how the slow increase of radioactivity in the air, as the nitrogen transmuted to Carbon Fourteen, would affect him if he kept carefully healthy in every way. What happens first? Blindness? Headaches? Perhaps a loss of appetite or slow fatigue?

Why not look it up?

On the other hand, why bother? Only a very small percentage of the men would die of radioactive poisoning. There were too many other things that killed more quickly, which was probably just as well. That razor, for example. It lay gleaming in a sunbeam, curved and clean in the yellow light. Sonny's father and grandfather had used it, or so he said, and it was his pride and joy.

Pete turned his back on it, and soaped under his arms, concentrating on the tiny kisses of bursting bubbles. In the midst of a recurrence of disgust at himself for thinking so often of death, a staggering truth struck him. He did not think of such things because he was morbid, after all! It was the very familiarity of things that brought death-thoughts. It was either "I shall never do this again" or "This is one of the last times I shall do this." You might devote yourself completely to doing things in different ways, he thought madly. You might crawl across the floor this time, and next time walk across on your hands. You might skip dinner tonight, and have a snack at two in the morning instead, and eat grass for breakfast.

But you had to breathe. Your heart had to beat. You'd sweat and you'd shiver, the same as always. You couldn't get away from that. When those things happened, they would remind you. Your heart wouldn't beat out its *wunklunk, wunklunk* any more. It would go *one-less, one-less* until it yelled and yammered in your ears and you had to make it stop.

Terrific polish on that razor.

And your breath would go on, same as before. You could sidle through this door, back through the next one and the one after, and figure out a totally new way to go through the one after that, but your breath would keep on sliding in and out of your nostrils like a razor going through whiskers, making a sound like a razor being stropped.

Sonny came in. Pete soaped his hair. Sonny picked up the razor and stood looking at it. Pete watched him, soap ran into his eyes, he swore, and Sonny jumped.

"What are you looking at, Sonny? Didn't you ever see it before?"

"Oh, sure. Sure. I just was—" He shut the razor, opened it, flashed light from its blade, shut it again. "I'm tired of using this, Pete. I'm going to get rid of it. Want it?"

Want it? In his foot-locker, maybe. Under his pillow. "Thanks, no, Sonny. Couldn't use it."

"I like safety razors," Sonny mumbled. "Electrics, even better. What are we going to do with it?"

"Throw it in the—no." Pete pictured the razor turning end over end in the air, half open, gleaming in the maw of the catchall. "Throw it out the—" No. Curving out into the long grass. He might want it. He might crawl around in the moonlight looking for it. He might find it.

"I guess maybe I'll break it up."

"No," Pete said. "The pieces—" Sharp little pieces. Hollow-ground fragments. "I'll think of something. Wait'll I get dressed."

He washed briskly, toweled, while Sonny stood looking at the razor. It was a blade now, and if it were broken it would be shards and glittering splinters, still razor sharp. If it were ground dull with an emery wheel, somebody could find it and put another edge on it because it was so obviously a razor, a fine steel razor, one that would slice so—

"I know. The laboratory. We'll get rid of it," Pete said confidently.

He stepped into his clothes, and together they went to the laboratory wing. It was very quiet there. Their voices echoed.

"One of the ovens," said Pete, reaching for the razor.

"Bake-ovens? You're crazy!"

Pete chuckled, "You don't know this place, do you? Like everything else on the base, there was a lot more went on here than most people knew about. They kept calling it the bakeshop. Well, it *was* research headquarters for new high-nutrient flours. But there's lots else here. We tested utensils and designed vegetable-peelers and all sorts of things like that. There's an electric furnace in there that—" He pushed open a door.

They crossed a long, quiet, cluttered room to the thermal equipment. "We can do everything here from annealing glass, through glazing ceramics, to finding the melting point of frying pans." He clicked a switch tentatively. A pilot light glowed. He swung open a small, heavy door and set the razor inside. "Kiss it goodbye. In twenty minutes it'll be a puddle."

"I want to see that," said Sonny. "Can I look around until it's cooked?"

"Why not?"

They walked through the laboratories. Beautifully equipped they were, and too quiet. Once they passed a major who was bent over a complex electronic hook-up on one of the benches. He was watching a little amber light flicker, and he did not return their salute. They tip-toed past him, feeling awed at his absorption, envying it. They saw the models of the automatic kneaders, the vitaminizers, the remote signal thermostats and timers and controls.

"What's in there?"

"I dunno. I'm over the edge of my territory. I don't think there's anybody left for this section. They were mostly mechanical and electronic theoreticians. Hey!"

Sonny followed the pointing hand. "What?"

"That wall-section. It's loose, or—well, what do you know!"

He pushed at the section of wall which was very slightly out of line. There was a dark space beyond.

"What's in there?"

"Nothing, or some semi-private hush-hush job. These guys used to get away with murder."

Sonny said, with an uncharacteristic flash of irony, "Isn't that the Army theoretician's business?"

Cautiously they peered in, then entered.

"Wh—*hey!* The door!"

It swung swiftly and quietly shut. The soft click of the latch was accompanied by a blaze of light.

The room was small and windowless. It contained machinery—a "trickle" charger, a bank of storage batteries, an electric-powered dynamo, two small self-starting gas-driven light plants and a diesel complete with sealed compressed-air starting cylinders. In the corner was a relay rack with its panel-bolts spot-welded. Protruding from it was a red-topped lever.

They looked at the equipment wordlessly for a time and then Sonny said, "Somebody wanted to make awful sure he had power for something."

"Now, I wonder what—" Pete walked over to the relay rack. He looked at the lever without touching it. It was wired up; behind the handle, on the wire, was a folded tag. He opened it cautiously. "To be used only on specific orders of the Commanding Officer."

"Give it a yank and see what happens."

Something clicked behind them. They whirled. "What was that?"

"Seemed to come from that rig beside the door."

They approached it cautiously. There was a spring-loaded solenoid attached to a bar which was hinged to drop across the inside of the secret door, where it would fit into steel gudgeons on the panel. It clicked again.

"A Geiger counter," said Pete disgustedly.

"Now why," mused Sonny, "would they design a door to stay locked unless the general radioactivity went beyond a certain point? That's what it is. See the relays? And the overload switch there? And this?"

"It has a manual lock, too," Pete pointed out. The counter clicked again. "Let's get out of here. I got one of those things built into my head these days."

The door opened easily. They went out, closing it behind them. The keyhole was cleverly concealed in the crack between two boards.

They were silent as they made their way back to the QM labs. The small thrill of violation was gone.

Back at the furnace, Pete glanced at the temperature dial, then kicked the latch control. The pilot winked out, and then the door swung open. They blinked and started back from the raging heat within. They bent and peered. The razor was gone. A pool of brilliance lay on the floor of the compartment.

"Ain't much left. Most of it oxidized away," Pete grunted.

They stood together for a time with their faces lit by the small shimmering ruin. Later, as they walked back to the barracks, Sonny broke his long silence with a sigh. "I'm glad we did that, Pete. I'm awful glad we did that."

At a quarter to eight they were waiting before the combination console in the barracks. All hands except Pete and Sonny and a wiry-haired, thick-set corporal named Bonze had elected to see the show on the big screen in the mess-hall. The reception was better there, of course, but, as Bonze put it, "You don't get close enough in a big place like that."

"I hope she's the same," said Sonny, half to himself.

Why should she be? thought Pete morosely as he turned on the set and watched the screen begin to glow. There were many more of the golden speckles that had killed reception for the past two weeks . . . Why should anything be the same, ever again?

He fought a sudden temptation to kick the set to pieces. It, and Starr Anthim, were part of something that was dead. The country was dead, a once real country—prosperous, sprawling, laughing, grabbing, growing, and changing, mostly healthy, leprous in spots with poverty and injustice, but systemically healthy enough to overcome any ill. He wondered how the murderers would like it. They were welcome to it, now. Nowhere to go. No one to fight. That was true for every soul on earth now.

"You hope she's the same," he muttered.

"The show, I mean," said Sonny mildly. "I'd like to just sit here and have it like—like—"

Oh, thought Pete mistily. Oh—that. Somewhere to go, that's what it is, for a few minutes . . . "I know," he said, all the harshness gone from his voice.

Noise receded from the audio as the carrier swept in. The light on the screen swirled and steadied into a diamond pattern. Pete adjusted the focus, chromic balance and intensity. "Turn out the lights, Bonze. I don't want to see anything but Starr Anthim."

It *was* the same, at first. Starr Anthim had never used the usual fanfares, fade-ins, color and clamor of her contemporaries. A black screen, then *click!* a blaze of gold. It was all there, in focus; tremendously intense, it did not change. Rather, the eye changed to take it in. She never moved for seconds after she came on; she was there, a portrait, a still face and a white throat. Her eyes were open and sleeping. Her face was alive and still.

Then, in the eyes which seemed green but were blue flecked with gold, an awareness seemed to gather, and they came awake. Only then was it noticeable that her lips were parted. Something in the eyes made the lips be seen, though nothing moved yet. Not until she bent her head slowly, so that some of the gold flecks seemed captured in the golden brows. The eyes were not, then, looking out at an audience. They were looking at me, and at *me*, and at ME.

"Hello—you," she said. She was a dream, with a kid sister's slightly irregular teeth.

Bonze shuddered. The cot on which he lay began to squeak rapidly. Sonny shifted in annoyance. Pete reached out in the dark and caught the leg of the cot. The squeaking subsided.

"May I sing a song?" Starr asked. There was music, very faint. "It's an old one, and one of the best. It's an easy song, a deep song, one that comes from the part of men and women that is mankind—the part that has in it no greed, no hate, no fear. This song is about joyousness and strength. It's—my favorite. Is it yours?"

The music swelled. Pete recognized the first two notes of the introduction and swore quietly. This was wrong. This song was not for—this song was part of—

Sonny rat raptly. Bonze lay still.

Starr Anthim began to sing. Her voice was deep and powerful, but soft, with the merest touch of vibrato at the ends of the phrases. The song flowed from her, without noticeable effort, seeming to come from her face, her long hair, her wide-set eyes. Her voice, like her face, was shadowed and clean, round, blue and green but mostly gold.

> When you gave me your heart, you gave me the world,

You gave me the night and the day,
And thunder, and roses, and sweet green grass,
The sea, and soft wet clay.

I drank the dawn from a golden cup,
From a silver one, the dark,
The steed I rode was the wild west wind,
My song was the brook and the lark.

The music spiraled, caroled, slid into a somber cry of muted hungry sixths and ninths; rose, blared, and cut, leaving her voice full and alone:

With thunder I smote the evil of earth,
With roses I won the right,
With the sea I washed, and with clay I built,
And the world was a place of light!

The last note left a face perfectly composed again, and there was no movement in it; it was sleeping and vital while the music curved off and away to the places where music rests when it is not heard.

Starr smiled.

"It's so easy," she said. "So simple. All that is fresh and clean and strong about mankind is in that song, and I think that's all that need concern us about mankind." She leaned forward. "Don't you see?"

The smile faded and was replaced with a gentle wonder. A tiny furrow appeared between her brows; she drew back quickly. "I can't seem to talk to you tonight," she said, her voice small. "You hate something."

Hate was shaped like a monstrous mushroom. Hate was the random speckling of a video plate.

"What has happened to us," said Starr abruptly, impersonally, "is simple too. It doesn't matter who did it—do you understand that? *It* doesn't matter. We were attacked. We were struck from the east and from the west. Most of the bombs were atomic—there were blast-bombs and there were dust-bombs. We were hit by about five hundred and thirty bombs altogether, and it has killed us."

She waited.

Sonny's fist smacked into his palm. Bonze lay with his eyes open, open, quiet. Pete's jaws hurt.

"We have more bombs than both of them put together. We *have* them. We are not going to use them. *Wait!*" She raised her hands suddenly, as if she could see into each man's face. They sank back, tense.

"So saturated is the atmosphere with Carbon Fourteen that all of us in this hemisphere are going to die. Don't be afraid to say it. Don't be afraid to think it. It is a truth, and it must be faced. As the transmutation effect spreads from the ruins of our cities, the air will become increasingly radioactive, and then we must die. In months, in a year or so, the effect will be strong overseas. Most of the people there will die too. None will escape completely. A worse thing will come to them than anything they have given us, because there will be a wave of horror and madness which is impossible to us. We are merely going to die. They will live and burn and sicken, and the children that will be born to them—" She shook her head, and her lower lip grew full. She visibly pulled herself together.

"Five hundred and thirty bombs...I don't think either of our attackers knew just how strong the other was. There has been so much secrecy." Her voice was sad. She shrugged slightly. "They have killed us, and they have ruined themselves. As for us—we are not blameless, either. Neither are we helpless to do anything—yet. But what we must do is hard. We must die—without striking back."

She gazed briefly at each man in turn, from the screen. "We must *not* strike back. Mankind is about to go through a hell of his own making. We can be vengeful—or merciful, if you like—and let go with the hundreds of bombs we have. That would steril-ize the planet so that not a microbe, not a blade of grass could escape, and nothing new could grow. We would reduce the earth to a bald thing, dead and deadly.

"No—it just won't do. We can't do it.

"Remember the song? *That* is humanity. That's in all humans. A disease made other humans our enemies for a time, but as the generations march past, enemies become friends and friends enemies. The enmity of those who have killed us is such a tiny, temporary thing in the long sweep of history!"

Her voice deepened. "Let us die with the knowledge that we have done the one noble thing left to us. The spark of humanity can still live and grow on this planet. It will be blown and drenched, shaken and all but extinguished, but it will live if that song is a true one. It will live if we are human enough to discount the fact that the spark is in the custody of our temporary enemy. Some—a few—of his children will live to merge with the new humanity that will gradually emerge from the jungles and the wilderness. Perhaps there will be ten thousand years of beastliness; perhaps man will be able to rebuild while he still has his ruins."

She raised her head, her voice tolling. "And even if this is the end of humankind, we dare not take away the chances some other life-form might have to succeed where we failed. If we retaliate, there will not be a dog, a deer, an ape, a bird or fish or lizard to carry the evolutionary torch. In the name of justice, if we must condemn and destroy ourselves, let us not condemn all other life along with us! Mankind is heavy enough with sins. If we must destroy, let us stop with destroying ourselves!"

There was a shimmering flicker of music. It seemed to stir her hair like a breath of wind. She smiled.

"That's all," she whispered. And to each man listening she said, "Good night . . ."

The screen went black. As the carrier cut off (there was no announcement) the ubiquitous speckles began to swarm across it.

Pete rose and switched on the lights. Bonze and Sonny were quite still. It must have been minutes later when Sonny sat up straight, shaking himself like a puppy. Something besides the silence seemed to tear with the movement.

He said, softly, "You're not allowed to fight anything, or to run away, or to live, and now you can't even hate any more, because Starr says no."

There was bitterness in the sound of it, and a bitter smell to the air.

Pete Mawser sniffed once, which had nothing to do with the smell. He sniffed again. "What's that smell, Son?"

Sonny tested it. "I don't— Something familiar. Vanilla— no . . . No."

"Almonds. Bitter—Bonze!"

Bonze lay still with his eyes open, grinning. His jaw muscles were knotted, and they could see almost all his teeth. He was soaking wet.

"Bonze!"

"It was just when she came on and said 'Hello—you,' remember?" whispered Pete. "Oh, the poor kid. That's why he wanted to catch the show here instead of in the mess-hall."

"Went out looking at her," said Sonny through pale lips. "I—can't say I blame him much. Wonder where he got the stuff."

"Never mind that!" Pete's voice was harsh. "Let's get out of here."

They left to call the ambulance. Bonze lay watching the console with his dead eyes and his smell of bitter almonds.

Pete did not realize where he was going, or exactly why, until he found himself on the dark street near GHQ and the communications shack, reflecting that it might be nice to be able to hear Starr, and see her, whenever he felt like it. Maybe there weren't any recordings; yet her musical background was recorded, and the signal corps might have recorded the show.

He stood uncertainly outside the GHQ building. There was a cluster of men outside the main entrance. Pete smiled briefly. Rain, nor snow, nor sleet, nor gloom of night could stay the stage-door Johnnie.

He went down the side street and up the delivery ramp in the back. Two doors along the platform was the rear exit of the communications section.

There was a light on in the communications shack. He had his hand out to the screen door when he noticed someone standing in the shadows beside it. The light played daintily on the golden margins of a head and face.

He stopped. "S—Starr Anthim!"

"Hello, soldier. Sergeant."

He blushed like an adolescent. "I—" His voice left him. He swallowed, reached up to whip off his hat. He had no hat. "I saw the show," he said. He felt clumsy. It was dark, and yet he was very conscious of the fact that his dress-shoes were indifferently shined.

She moved toward him into the light, and she was so beautiful that he had to close his eyes. "What's your name?"

"Mawser. Pete Mawser."

"Like the show?"

Not looking at her, he said stubbornly, "No."

"Oh?"

"I mean—I liked it some. The song."

"I—think I see."

"I wondered if I could maybe get a recording."

"I think so," she said. "What kind of reproducer have you got?"

"Audiovid."

"A disc. Yes; we dubbed off a few. Wait, I'll get you one."

She went inside, moving slowly. Pete watched her, spellbound. She was a silhouette, crowned and haloed; and then she was a framed picture, vivid and golden. He waited, watching the light hungrily. She returned with a large envelope, called good night to someone inside, and came out on the platform.

"Here you are, Pete Mawser."

"Thanks very—" he mumbled. He wet his lips. "It was very good of you."

"Not really. The more it circulates, the better." She laughed suddenly. "That isn't meant quite as it sounds. I'm not exactly looking for new publicity these days."

The stubbornness came back. "I don't know if you'd get it, if you put on that show in normal times."

Her eyebrows went up. "Well!" she smiled. "I seem to have made quite an impression."

"I'm sorry," he said warmly. "I shouldn't have taken that tack. Everything I think and say these days is exaggerated."

"I know what you mean." She looked around. "How is it here?"

"It's okay. I used to be bothered by the secrecy, and being buried miles away from civilization." He chuckled bitterly. "Turned out to be lucky after all."

"You sound like the first chapter of *One World or None*."

He looked up quickly. "What do you use for a reading list—the Government's own *Index Expurgatorius*?"

She laughed. "Come now, it isn't as bad as all that. The book was never banned. It was just—"

"Unfashionable," he filled in.

"Yes, more's the pity. If people had paid more attention to it in the 'forties, perhaps this wouldn't have happened."

He followed her gaze to the dimly pulsating sky. "How long are you going to be here?"

"Until—as long as—I'm not leaving."

"You're not?"

"I'm finished," she said simply. "I've covered all the ground I can. I've been everywhere that . . . anyone knows about."

"With this show?"

She nodded. "With this particular message."

He was quiet, thinking. She turned to the door, and he put out his hand, not touching her. "Please—"

"What is it?"

"I'd like to—I mean, if you don't mind, I don't often have a chance to talk to—maybe you'd like to walk around a little before you turn in."

"Thanks, no, Sergeant. I'm tired." She did sound tired. "I'll see you around."

He stared at her, a sudden fierce light in his brain. "I know where it is. It's got a red-topped lever and a tag referring to orders of the commanding officer. It's really camouflaged."

She was quiet so long that he thought she had not heard him. Then, "I'll take that walk."

They went down the ramp together and turned toward the dark parade ground.

"How did you know?" she asked quietly.

"Not too tough. "This 'message' of yours; the fact that you've been all over the country with it; most of all, the fact that somebody finds it necessary to persuade us not to strike back. Who are you working for?" he asked bluntly.

Surprisingly, she laughed.

"What's that for?"

"A moment ago you were blushing and shuffling your feet."

His voice was rough. "I wasn't talking to a human being. I was talking to a thousand songs I've heard, and a hundred thousand blonde pictures I've seen pinned up. You'd better tell me what this is all about."

She stopped. "Let's go up and see the colonel."

He took her elbow. "No. I'm just a sergeant, and he's high brass, and that doesn't make any difference at all now. You're a human being, and so am I, and I'm supposed to respect your rights as such. I don't. You'd better tell me about it."

"All right," she said, with a tired acquiescence that frightened something inside him. "You seem to have guessed right, though. It's true. There are master firing keys for the launching sites. We have located and dismantled all but two. It's very likely that one of the two was vaporized. The other one is—lost."

"Lost?"

"I don't have to tell you about the secrecy," she said. "You know how it developed between nation and nation. You must know that it existed between State and Union, between department and department, office and office. There were only three or four men who knew where all the keys were. Three of them were in the Pentagon when it went up. That was the third blast-bomb, you know. If there was another, it could only have been Senator Vanercook, and he died three weeks ago without talking."

"An automatic radio key, *hm*?"

"That's right. Sergeant, must we walk? I'm so tired."

"I'm sorry," he said impulsively. They crossed to the reviewing stand and sat on the lonely benches. "Launching racks all over, all hidden, and all armed?"

"Most of them are armed. There's a timing mechanism in them that will disarm them in a year or so. But in the meantime, they are armed—and aimed."

"Aimed where?"

"It doesn't matter."

"I think I see. What's the optimum number again?"

"About six hundred and forty; a few more or less. At least five hundred and thirty have been thrown so far. We don't know exactly."

"Who are *we*?" he asked furiously.

"Who? Who?" She laughed weakly. "I could say, 'The Government,' perhaps. If the President dies, the Vice-President takes over, and then the Secretary of State, and so on and on. How far can you go? Pete Mawser, don't you realize yet what's happened?"

"I don't know what you mean."

"How many people do you think are left in this country?"

"I don't know. Just a few million, I guess."

"How many are here?"

"About nine hundred."

"Then, as far as I know, this is the largest city left."

He leaped to his feet. "*No!*" The syllable roared away from him, hurled itself against the dark, empty buildings, came back to him in a series of lower-case echoes: nonono*no* . . . *no*-no.

Starr began to speak rapidly, quietly. "They're scattered all over the fields and the roads. They sit in the sun and die. They run in packs, they tear at each other. They pray and starve and kill themselves and die in the fires. The fires—everywhere, if anything stands, it's burning. Summer, and the leaves all down in the Berkshires, and the blue grass burnt brown; you can see the grass dying from the air, the death going out wider and wider from the bald-spots. Thunder and roses . . . I saw roses, new ones, creeping from the smashed pots of a greenhouse. Brown petals, alive and sick, and the thorns turned back on themselves, growing into the stems, killing. Feldman died tonight."

He let her be quiet for a time. Then:

"Who is Feldman?"

"My pilot." She was talking hollowly into her hands. "He's been dying for weeks. He's been on his nerve-ends. I don't think he had any blood left. He buzzed your GHQ and made for the landing strip. He came in with the motor dead, free rotors, giro. Smashed the landing gear. He was dead, too. He killed a man in Chicago so he could steal gas. The man didn't want the gas. There was a dead girl by the pump. He didn't want us to go near. I'm not going anywhere. I'm going to stay here. I'm tired."

At last she cried.

Pete left her alone, and walked out to the center of the parade ground, looking back at the faint huddled glimmer on the bleachers. His mind flickered over the show that evening, and the way she had sung before the merciless transmitter. "Hello, you." "If we must destroy, let us stop with destroying ourselves!"

The dimming spark of humankind ... what could it mean to her? How could it mean so much?

"*Thunder and roses.*" Twisted, sick, non-survival roses, killing themselves with their own thorns.

"*And the world was a place of light!*" Blue light, flickering in the contaminated air.

The enemy. The red-topped lever. Bonze. "They pray and starve and kill themselves and die in the fires."

What creatures were these, these corrupted, violent, murdering humans? What right had they to another chance? What was in them that was good?

Starr was good. Starr was crying. Only a human being could cry like that. Starr was a human being.

Had humanity anything of Starr Anthim in it?

Starr was a human being.

He looked down through the darkness for his hands. No planet, no universe, is greater to a man than his own ego, his own observing self. These hands were the hands of all history, and like the hands of all men, they could by their small acts make human history or end it. Whether this power of hands was that of a billion hands, or whether it came to a focus in these two—this was suddenly unimportant to the eternities which now enfolded him.

He put humanity's hands deep in his pockets and walked slowly back to the bleachers.

"Starr."

She responded with a sleepy-child, interrogative whimper.

"They'll get their chance, Starr. I won't touch the key."

She sat straight. She rose, and came to him, smiling. He could see her smile, because, very faintly in the air, her teeth fluoresced. She put her hands on his shoulders. "Pete."

He held her very close for a moment. Her knees buckled then, and he had to carry her.

There was no one in the Officers' Club, which was the nearest building. He stumbled in, moved clawing along the wall until he found a switch. The light hurt him. He carried her to a settee and put her down gently. She did not move. One side of her face was as pale as milk.

He stood looking stupidly at it, wiped it on the sides of his trousers, looking dully at Starr. There was blood on her shirt.

A doctor . . . but there was no doctor. Not since Anders had hanged himself. "Get somebody," he muttered. "*Do* something."

He dropped to his knees and gently unbuttoned her shirt. Between the sturdy unfeminine GI bra and the top of her slacks, there was blood on her side. He whipped out a clean handkerchief and began to wipe it away. There was no wound, no puncture. But abruptly there was blood again. He blotted it carefully. And again there was blood.

It was like trying to dry a piece of ice with a towel.

He ran to the water cooler, wrung out the bloody handkerchief and ran back to her. He bathed her face carefully, the pale right side, the flushed left side. The handkerchief reddened again, this time with cosmetics, and then her face was pale all over, with great blue shadows under the eyes. While he watched, blood appeared on her left cheek.

"There must be somebody—" He fled to the door.

"Pete!"

Running, turning at the sound of her voice, he hit the doorpost stunningly, caromed off, flailed for his balance, and then was back at her side. "Starr! Hang on, now! I'll get a doctor as quick as—"

Her hand strayed over her left cheek. "You found out. Nobody else knew, but Feldman. It got hard to cover properly." Her hand went up to her hair.

"Starr, I'll get a—"

"Pete, darling, promise me something?"

"Why, sure; certainly, Starr."

"Don't disturb my hair. It isn't—all mine, you see." She sounded like a seven-year-old, playing a game. "It all came out on this side. I don't want you to see me that way."

He was on his knees beside her again. "What is it? What happened to you?" he asked hoarsely.

"Philadelphia," she murmured. "Right at the beginning. The mushroom went up a half-mile away. The studio caved in. I came to the next day. I didn't know I was burned, then. It didn't show. My left side. It doesn't matter, Pete. It doesn't hurt at all, now."

He sprang to his feet again. "I'm going for a doctor."

"Don't go away. Please don't go away and leave me. Please don't." There were tears in her eyes. "Wait just a little while. Not very long, Pete."

He sank to his knees again. She gathered both his hands in hers and held them tightly. She smiled happily. "You're good, Pete. You're so good."

(She couldn't hear the blood in his ears, the roar of the whirlpool of hate and fear and anguish that spun inside of him.)

She talked to him in a low voice, and then in whispers. Sometimes he hated himself because he couldn't quite follow her. She talked about school, and her first audition. "I was so scared that I got a vibrato in my voice. I'd never had one before. I always let myself get a little scared when I sing now. It's easy." There was something about a window-box when she was four years old. "Two real live tulips and a pitcher-plant. I used to be sorry for the flies."

There was a long period of silence after that, during which his muscles throbbed with cramp and stiffness, and gradually became numb. He must have dozed; he awoke with a violent start, feeling her fingers on his face. She was propped up on one elbow. She said clearly, "I just wanted to tell you, darling. Let me go first, and get everything ready for you. It's going to be wonderful. I'll fix you a special tossed salad. I'll make you a steamed chocolate pudding and keep it hot for you."

Too muddled to understand what she was saying, he smiled and pressed her back on the settee. She took his hands again.

The next time he awoke it was broad daylight, and she was dead.

Sonny Weisefreund was sitting on his cot when he got back to the barracks. He handed over the recording he had picked up from the parade-ground on the way back. "Dew on it. Dry it off. Good boy," he croaked, and fell face downward on the cot Bonze had used.

Sonny stared at him. "Pete! Where you been? What happened? Are you all right?"

Pete shifted a little and grunted. Sonny shrugged and took the audiovid disc out of its wet envelope. Moisture would not harm it particularly, though it could not be played while wet. It was made of a fine spiral of plastic, insulated between laminations. Electrostatic pickups above and below the turntable would fluctuate with changes in the dielectric constant which had been impressed by the recording, and these changes were amplified for the scanners. The audio was a conventional hill-and-dale needle. Sonny began to wipe it down carefully.

Pete fought upward out of a vast, green-lit place full of flickering cold fires. Starr was calling him. Something was punching him, too. He fought it weakly, trying to hear what she was saying. But someone else was jabbering too loud for him to hear.

He opened his eyes. Sonny was shaking him, his round face pink with excitement. The Audiovid was running. Starr was talking. Sonny got up impatiently and turned down the volume. "Pete! Pete! Wake up, will you? I got to tell you something. Listen to me! Wake up, will yuh?"

"Huh?"

"That's better. Now listen. I've just been listening to Starr Anthim—"

"She's dead," said Pete.

Sonny didn't hear. He went on, explosively, "I've figured it out. Starr was sent out here, and all over, to *beg* someone not to fire any more atom bombs. If the government was sure they wouldn't strike back, they wouldn't've taken the trouble. Somewhere, Pete, there's some way to launch bombs at those murdering cowards—and I've got a pret-ty shrewd idea of how to do it."

Pete strained groggily toward the faint sound of Starr's voice. Sonny talked on. "Now, s'posing there was a master radio key—an automatic code device something like the alarm signal they have on ships, that rings a bell on any ship within radio range when the operator sends four long dashes. Suppose there's an automatic code machine to launch bombs, with repeaters, maybe, buried all over the country. What would it be? Just a little lever to pull; that's all. How would the thing be hidden? In the middle of a lot of other equipment, that's where; in some place where you'd expect to find crazy-looking secret stuff. Like an experiment station. Like right here. You beginning to get the idea?"

"Shut up, I can't hear her."

"The hell with her! You can listen to her some other time. You didn't hear a thing I said!"

"She's dead."

"Yeah. Well, I figure I'll pull that handle. What can I lose? It'll give those murderin'—*what?*"

"She's dead."

"Dead? Starr Anthim?" His young face twisted, Sonny sank down to the cot. "You're half asleep. You don't know what you're saying."

"She's dead," Pete said hoarsely. "She got burned by one of the first bombs. I was with her when she—she— Shut up now and get out of here and let me listen!" he bellowed hoarsely.

Sonny stood up slowly. "They killed her, too. They killed her! That does it. That just fixes it up." His face was white. He went out.

Pete got up. His legs weren't working right. He almost fell. He brought up against the console with a crash, his outflung arm sending the pickup skittering across the record. He put it on again and turned up the volume, then lay down to listen.

His head was all mixed up. Sonny talked too much. Bomb launchers, automatic code machines—

"*You gave me your heart,*" sand Starr. "*You gave me your heart. You gave me your heart. You . . .*"

Pete heaved himself up again and moved the pickup arm. Anger, not at himself, but at Sonny for causing him to cut the disc that way, welled up.

Starr was talking, stupidly, her face going through the same expression over and over again. "*Struck from the east and from the struck from the east and from the . . .*"

He got up again wearily and moved the pickup.

"*You gave me your heart you gave me . . .*"

Pete made an agonized sound that was not a word at all, bent, lifted, and sent the console crashing over. In the bludgeoning silence, he said, "I did, too."

Then, "Sonny." He waited.

"*Sonny!*"

His eyes went wide then, and he cursed and bolted for the corridor.

The panel was closed when he reached it. He kicked at it. It flew open, discovering darkness.

"Hey!" bellowed Sonny. "Shut it! You turned off the lights!"

Pete shut it behind them. The lights blazed.

"Pete! What's the matter?"

"Nothing's the matter, Son," croaked Pete.

"What are you looking at?" said Sonny uneasily.

"I'm sorry," said Pete as gently as he could. "I just wanted to find something out, is all. Did you tell anyone else about this?" He pointed to the lever.

"Why, no. I only just figured it out while you were sleeping, just now."

Pete looked around carefully, while Sonny shifted his weight. Pete moved toward a tool-rack. "Something you haven't noticed yet, Sonny," he said softly, and pointed. "Up there, on the wall behind you. High up. See?"

Sonny turned. In one fluid movement Pete plucked off a fourteen-inch box wrench and hit Sonny with it as hard as he could.

Afterward he went to work systematically on the power supplies. He pulled the plugs on the gas-engines and cracked their cylinders with a maul. He knocked off the tubing of the diesel starters—the tanks let go explosively—and he cut all the cables with bolt-cutters. Then he broke up the relay rack and its lever. When he was quite finished, he put away his tools and bent and stroked Sonny's tousled hair.

He went out and closed the partition carefully. It certainly was a wonderful piece of camouflage. He sat down heavily on a workbench nearby.

"You'll have your chance," he said into the far future. "And, by Heaven, you'd better make good."

After that he just waited.

AFTERWORD BY ERIC FLINT

When editors put together an anthology like this one, sooner or later they have to deal with what may be the thorniest problem of all:

Which story do you end with?

In this case, the decision . . . almost made itself. Not quite, I suppose. But in the course of the discussions the three of us had on the subject, "Thunder and Roses" came to the forefront with a certain kind of inevitability. Some of that, no doubt, is due to the factor that Dave discusses in his preface: all three of us were children of the Fifties, and we were shaped to some degree, one way or another, by that ever-looming fear of nuclear obliteration.

But there's more to it than that. "Thunder and Roses" is a horror story, but it's not *just* a horror story. It's also a story of transcendent courage, and, in the grimmest possible way, a very inspiring story.

I stated in my preface to the first story in the anthology, Arthur Clarke's "Rescue Party," that since I was a boy of thirteen I associated that story, perhaps more than any other, with the inspiring nature of science fiction, which has always been to me its single most important characteristic.

If it has a contender, though—perhaps even a superior—it's this story by Sturgeon. I knew that even as a boy, although I rarely let myself think about it.

Inspiration, like courage, comes in different forms. There's the sort of courage that Achilles exemplifies, which is inseparable from fame and glory and played out in front of a vast audience. And then there's what I think of as cellar courage—a quiet refusal to yield that goes unrecognized and is noted, if at all, only by the executioner. The courage of nameless heroes who die in the darkness.

I've never liked Achilles—and I wouldn't trust him any farther than I could throw him. Give me cellar courage. If the human race continues to survive, it will ultimately be due to that kind of heroism. Heroism which has none of the trappings of heroes, and is therefore all the more reliable.

We began this anthology with inspiration on a galactic scale, and we end it with a man sitting on a bench waiting to die. But not before he made the right decision, after wrestling with it like a quiet Titan.

It seems . . . a very good way to end. A cycle, if you will. The logic of the first story depends, in the end, on the logic of the last. Without the one, you will never reach the other. The road to the stars begins in a cellar. Or, as the poet William Butler Yeats put it:

Those masterful images because complete
Grew in pure mind but out of what began?
I must lie down where all the ladders start
In the foul rag and bone shop of the heart.